QUOTE THE DROW
NEVERMORE

QUOTE THE DROW NEVERMORE

GOTH DROW™ BOOK TWO

MARTHA CARR

MICHAEL ANDERLE

DISRUPTIVE IMAGINATION

Copyright © 2020 Martha Carr and Michael Anderle
Cover Art by Jake @ J Caleb Design
http://jcalebdesign.com / jcalebdesign@gmail.com
A Michael Anderle Production

LMBPN Publishing
PMB 196, 2540 South Maryland Pkwy
Las Vegas, NV 89109

First US Edition, April, 2020
Version 1.03, December 2020
eBook ISBN: 978-1-64202-868-3
Print ISBN: 978-1-64202-869-0

THE QUOTE THE DROW NEVERMORE TEAM

Thanks to the JIT Readers

If I've missed anyone, please let us know!

Angel LaVey
Daniel Weigert
Dave Hicks
Deb Mader
Debi Sateren
Diane L. Smith
Jackey Hankard-Brodie
Jeff Eaton
Jeff Goode
John Ashmore
Micky Cocker
Paul Westman
Peter Manis
Veronica Stephan-Miller

Editor
The Skyhunter Editing Team

DEDICATIONS

From Martha

To everyone who still believes in magic
and all the possibilities that holds.
To all the readers who make this
entire ride so much fun.
And to my son, Louie and so many wonderful friends who remind
me all the time of what
really matters and how wonderful
life can be in any given moment.

From Michael

To Family, Friends and
Those Who Love
To Read.
May We All Enjoy Grace
To Live The Life We Are
Called.

CHAPTER ONE

Sitting in a cheap metal folding chair on his side of the iron bars, L'zar Verdys studied his halfling daughter with a feral grin. "I suppose I owe it to you to give you the first shot at this. So. Is there anything you want to ask me?"

"Yeah. Why'd you just leave her that night without a word?" Cheyenne's anger burned even stronger inside her, racing up her spine and across her shoulders, fueling her. But she was already in her drow form—the purple-gray skin and bone-white hair, pointed ears and glowing golden eyes just like her father's—so there really was nothing to hold back.

L'zar let out a soft, low chuckle like a rumbling purr. "Going right for the throat, I see."

"Don't tell me you expected a bunch of polite small talk?"

"Honestly, I didn't expect much of anything." L'zar stretched his legs out in front of him, crossing one ankle over the other in his gray prison-issue sweatpants, and scratched the side of his chin. "So far, I've been nothing but pleasantly surprised."

"Are you gonna answer my question or not?" Cheyenne studied the drow prisoner's calculating gaze, the secret smile on his dark lips. *He looks real cozy behind those bars. Like he doesn't care where he is.*

"There's a short and long answer for everything," he said. "Right now, all you need to know is I left the way I did because I had to."

"Bullshit."

L'zar shrugged. "You can believe whatever you want, but you're getting your answers from the source now. I left without a word because I couldn't let your mother know who I really am. I also couldn't run the risk of *you* knowing until you were ready to find me. Which, apparently, you now are."

Cheyenne shook her head. "You escaped from Chateau D'rahl that night on your own. Why'd you come back to turn yourself in?"

"Because I had to. And so you could find me when you were ready."

"Are those gonna be your answers for everything?"

L'zar cocked his head. "Only for the questions you're asking right now. Anything else?"

He doesn't want to tell me anything. The halfling pressed her lips together and glared at the drow who'd given her all her power and left her to figure it out on her own.

"Well, while you think about it, I'll just keep the ball rolling." He tossed the loose strands of white hair out of his eyes. "How's school?"

She blinked. "It's a joke."

"That doesn't surprise me. I imagine there's very little your professors can teach you at this point, after everything you've managed on your own. The dark web feels like a remarkably fitting place for a dark elf to spend her time, even a halfling."

How the hell does he know about that?

Cheyenne shifted in the chair. "As the guy who knocked up Bianca Summerlin and abandoned her—*and* me—you seem to think you actually know who I am."

"I'm sure there's much more beneath the surface." L'zar chuckled again, his golden eyes flashing in the dim yellow lights bolted to the stone walls of the Dungeon. "I really am anxious to dig deeper. I know there's plenty you don't show the rest of the world."

"You don't know anything about me. Whatever drow spy trick you're trying to pull, I'm not buying it."

"I'm not asking you to buy into anything, Cheyenne." He rocked back in his chair like he was buckling down to really get comfortable. "Tell me about your friend in the hospital."

"What?"

"The one born Earthside who can't use what was passed down to her by blood. I hope she's recovering well."

He won't flat-out say what Ember is when Sir and the guard are listening. What kinda bullshit game is that?

"That's none of your business," she muttered. "And I didn't come here to talk about someone else."

"No, of course not." L'zar licked his lips, and the next smile he gave her almost looked gentle. "You came here to see your drow father with your own eyes. To size up the man who made you what you are, just to know if he fits into the same shape your imagination gave him. Well? Were you close?"

Her nostrils flared as he spread his arms and chuckled again. *This is just a game to him.*

"Don't you have any questions about *her*?"

L'zar shook his head. "Not really. You're far more interesting, Cheyenne. And you wouldn't tell me anything about your mother even if I wanted to know. Let's cut the bullshit, huh? You and I are the same that way. We don't do very well with pretenses."

Cheyenne scoffed. "Fine. Why did you leave her the box?"

"For you. Don't ask questions you already know the answer to. It's boring, and it's not who you are."

"Then tell me what it's for. How does it work?"

L'zar shook his head. "That's for you to discover on your own. And I am *so* looking forward to the day when you reach that point. I hope you'll come and tell me all about it."

A new flash of rage churned through her. *He has to give me something.*

"Okay. Since you think you know so much about my life and what I'm getting into, tell me about the bull's head."

For the first time, L'zar reacted to her words with something other than blasé amusement. His eyes widened, and he pulled his legs in toward the chair again before leaning forward. "What about it?"

Can't give too much away with our FRoE audience in the booth. "I've been seeing it around a lot lately on magicals who think they know something about me too. What does it mean?"

The drow on the other side of the bars sucked his teeth and hissed. "That's an issue that should have stayed in Ambar'ogúl where it belongs."

"Yeah, well, it didn't. And now it's my issue." Cheyenne leaned toward his face, so much like her own. "Now's your chance to make this little meeting worth my time. What does it mean?"

He shook his head. "We're not gonna talk about that."

"Then I've run out of things to say. Easter Bunny."

A high-pitched whine filled the Dungeon a second before those iron bars lit up with crackling green fell energy, buzzing and sparking between father and daughter. The low lights inset into the walls flashed from a dull yellow to an eerie red, and a blaring alarm cut through the cavern every five seconds. L'zar glanced quickly at the ceiling and the fell energy crackling down the iron bars of his visitation cage. In one swift movement, he stood from the chair and stepped away from the bars. His white teeth glinted in the red alarm lights when he grinned at her and offered her one slow nod.

Cheyenne stood from her chair and meant to push it aside. Instead, the thing went flying sideways across the cavern and clattered against the stone wall. Swift, urgent footsteps echoed behind her, then a warning arm settled on her elbow.

"Let's go," the guard said over the alarm.

The halfling jerked her elbow away and glared at L'zar. The drow prisoner threw his head back and laughed, the sound ringing out across the Dungeon between the blaring bursts of the alarm splitting Cheyenne's head.

"Come see me again when you've learned how to ask the questions that really matter," he said through his laughter. "Then these little talks will be a lot easier for both of us."

Forcing herself not to fling her magic at those bars and tear the whole cell apart to get to him, Cheyenne spun on her heels and stormed back toward the booth. Sir stood just beside the open door, his arms folded, his face showing no expression. L'zar's laughter followed her toward the booth, and she didn't bother turning around to see what would happen to him next.

Should've known the real L'zar would be a lot more disappointing than I imagined.

She didn't look at Sir as she stepped into the booth stretching across the cavern. He entered behind her with the prison guard close on their heels, then the door shut with a loud click and a metallic echo. The guard slammed his hand down on the control panel and the obnoxiously screaming alarm cut out entirely, at least inside the booth. The red lights still illuminated the Dungeon and L'zar's overlarge cell and the fell energy still fizzled along those thick iron bars, creating a muddy halo of green and red light around them.

"That was a lot shorter than I expected," Sir muttered.

"Why are *you* complaining?" Cheyenne spat. "Now you have plenty of time to make it back for lunch."

Sir didn't find that very funny and folded his arms again as she pushed the door on the other side of the booth.

She glanced back at the guard and spread her arms. "You gonna open this thing or what?"

The man raised his eyebrows and pressed another button on the control panel. When the door buzzed, Cheyenne shoved her hands against it and stormed out the other side of the booth. The alarm was probably supposed to be silent now, but her drow hearing picked it up from the other side of the booth just the same. And L'zar's laughter continued.

The elevator doors were closed when she reached them. *Where's the damn button?*

She searched the stone walls but couldn't find anything to call the stupid elevator back down.

"It's on its way," Sir said from behind her.

"Whatever." Cheyenne clenched her fists by her sides and stared at the closed doors set into the stone wall. *And I woke up early for this.*

CHAPTER TWO

As soon as Cheyenne and Sir stepped into the elevator, the blaring alarm cut out entirely. The lights inset in the walls stayed red, though, and the bars still hummed with green fell energy.

L'zar smoothed his white hair away from his face and pulled a deep breath in through his nose. Another chuckle escaped him. *That went well.*

Waiting for the prison guards to make their way down here with their magical cattle prods and their dampening cuffs and all the fell-powered firearms they could hold, the drow moved toward the back of the cell and lowered himself to the floor. He faced the back wall, crossing his legs beneath him, and centered his focus again. *Just to be sure. A little double-checking never hurt anyone.*

Hidden from the Dungeon's security cameras and the guard in that damn booth, his hands moved in one more complicated pattern, drawing the power toward him for his next little spell. It was not to fight what was coming for him or make things harder for the guards, although the thought was tempting. Right now, the distant past would give him more reassurance than anything.

When he finished casting the spell, a wavering silver light

bloomed in his hands and illuminated the stone wall of the cell in front of him. The shimmering, opalescent forms took shape quickly, and L'zar watched the conjured image of himself from so many centuries ago.

There he sat in the Oracle's lair in Ambar'ogúl, the dark walls much lighter in his memory. There was a lot less blood on those walls too, but the surroundings weren't important, just the conversation.

The wizened, shriveled Oracle with black lines all over her wrinkled face opened her eyes. They'd been a dark storm-gray before he'd asked her for the prophecy of his lineage. Now they were a swirling, misty white.

"The Cu'ón is doomed to lose his bloodline time and again." The voice was a raspy croak, rattling like death from an ancient mouth perpetually stained red. "The endless search for an heir will bring each one of them to death's door. Only the scion never pursued will rise to their destiny. When the shackles of the old laws crumble, their purpose will be fulfilled."

In this vision of L'zar's memory, he heard his own voice—so steady, so sure of itself. So goddamn foolish. "Explain this, Oracle."

The prophetic whiteness filtered away from the Oracle's eyes, and a wrinkled, gnarled hand reached into a bowl of blood sitting beside her. Fingers dipped into all that red, and she drew a line of it down her face from forehead to beneath her chin. "Every child you sire is doomed to the same fate, Cu'ón. You will go to them to mold each one into the shape of your heir, but you will fail. Death rides on the heels of your eagerness. Every child will fall beneath your guiding hand, and you will pursue them over and over to the same end."

The L'zar from centuries ago, wavering in the silver light of the memory spell, folded his arms and lifted his chin. "Will any of them survive?"

"No. Not while you try so hard to bring them to their destiny. And you will keep trying, drow. You will never stop." The crone snickered and pressed a blood-covered finger against L'zar's chest.

"Your greed and your pride make you unstoppable." Then she bent over her aged lap and fell into a fit of wheezing, paper-thin cackles.

Sitting in the cell in the Dungeon, L'zar swiped his hand through the glistening light of his memory, and the vision disappeared. His knuckles cracked as he clenched his fists. *I was such a cocksure idiot then. That prophecy proved itself, all right. Not this time. This time, my pride sits behind bars with me. We'll wait together for as long as it takes.*

CHAPTER THREE

S ir didn't ask Cheyenne to put the stupid black bag over her head again when they got back into his orange Kia Rio. Maybe he'd forgotten the route to Chateau D'rahl was supposed to be a secret. Maybe he knew if he told her to put it on, she'd send a blast of drow magic into his stupid mustache.

Cheyenne didn't care what he thought, and she wasn't paying attention to the roads he drove them down anyway. *L'zar can laugh all he wants. He's the one spending the rest of his life in a damn cage.*

After ten minutes of strained silence, Sir cleared his throat. "I'm guessing that didn't go the way you were hoping."

"No shit."

"The guy's been nothing but a pain in the ass since we put him behind bars." Sir shrugged and gripped the steering wheel with both hands. "Don't take it personally, halfling. It's not just you."

She had nothing to say.

"Hey, at least he didn't try to throw you around the giant cavern or anything. Or try to phase you through the bars to hold you hostage. He's a real piece of shit. You can count yourself lucky—"

"We're not having a heart-to-heart right now," Cheyenne muttered. "Just stick to being an asshole. You're a lot better at that."

A choking sound came from Sir's mouth—he might have tried to hold back a laugh. Instead, he readjusted his aviator sunglasses and cleared his throat again. "Yeah, I know."

Trees and cars and highway signs whizzed past them as he took her back toward the business park where she'd left her car. Cheyenne ran a hand through her hair and rolled her eyes. "So, what has to happen before I get another escort to Chateau D'rahl?"

Sir did a double-take. "You wanna see him again?"

"Probably not. Just give me my options."

"All right, halfling. I'd say our deal's still on the table if you're willing to keep sitting at it. You keep the phone on you and your schedule open. Stay chummy with Rhynehart for whatever ops we think could benefit from you stickin' around. That will earn you more points to turn in for another fun get-together with Daddy."

Cheyenne snorted. "Didn't think we were working on a point system."

"Like a goddamn arcade, right? You win the tickets, you get a prize." He shook his head. "We'll say, three ride-alongs with my men equals one ride on the Chateau D'rahl Express. The thought of going back there to see the drow's ugly mug and listen to you two talk over each other doesn't make me jump for joy, but I'll take you again after the three more jobs."

"Don't call it a job if you're not paying me anything." She turned her head just enough to shoot him a sideways glance. "I thought Bianca drilled that into you hard enough."

Sir grunted but ignored the jibe about how quickly and easily her mom had buried him in legalities on the back veranda of her estate. "I'm paying you in visitations, halfling. You can't buy your way into Chateau D'rahl. Plenty of people have tried."

"Plenty of magicals break out of there, too. Or was that just an extra special night for everyone?"

The morning sunlight glinted across Sir's face as it passed like a strobe light through the trees lining the highway. She caught a glimpse of his eyes darting toward her beneath the dark sunglasses before returning to the road. "That was a first. I'm not surprised it hasn't happened again."

"Good to know you have so much faith in your security over there." The halfling thumped her head back against the headrest.

"Those men know what they're doing, and the prison's security has gone through more updates than the iPhone I don't have. I'll tell you what, though. If the bastard really wanted out right now, he'd be out. He already did it once."

She didn't say anything to that. Sir had heard her entire conversation with L'zar and already knew the answer the drow inmate had given for that one.

"I wanna know why he's still playing prisoner," Sir continued. "Find out for me the next time you cash in your FRoE points for another visit, and you'll have unrestricted access to the guy. Then I can quit spending my Sundays being a goddamn halfling chauffeur."

Cheyenne turned to look at him full-on. *He's serious.* "Game on."

Sir nodded and gave another little grunt. "Smart move, halfling."

"Hey, while we're stuck in your car together, anything *you* can tell me about those bull's-head pendants?"

The man's head rocked back in confusion, and he shot her a quick glance. Whatever she might have been able to see in his eyes was hidden by the tinted lenses. "I don't have a goddamn clue what you're spoutin' off about. Didn't even understand half the shit you two were talking about in there. If you want answers to useless questions, don't ask the guy who doesn't do useless."

Right, like Sir's been useful for much of anything.

"Didn't expect you to have an answer."

"Oh, sure. Just wanna keep up the small talk, huh? You suck at that, just like I suck at emotions."

Cheyenne took a deep breath. *He sounds a lot more desperate, the longer I'm with him.* She glanced at the sign for the next exit coming up—just two more before they'd turn off into the business park. *Time to shut down drow mode. Think of the woods.*

The heat of her drow magic fizzled out in a second, drawing itself back inside her to wait for the next time she needed it. Her purple-gray skin faded back to its unnatural human paleness, the bone-white hair returning to High Voltage Raven Black. She lifted a hand absently to her ears to feel their rounded tops and dropped her forearm back onto the armrest. *I can't wait to get out of this car.*

When Sir turned into the huge, empty parking lot, the buckle of Cheyenne's seatbelt clicked against the side of the car before they'd come to a complete stop. She jerked open the passenger-side door as Sir shifted into park, and he snorted as she leaped out. "You and me both, halfling. Keep the phone—"

The door slammed shut, and Cheyenne walked briskly to the driver's side of her matte-gray Ford Focus with its chipped and peeling paint. "Yeah, yeah. I know. It's still on me."

Sir sped away in his screaming-orange Kia Rio, and the halfling slipped quickly behind the wheel of her car. She took a deep breath to calm herself even further. As soon as she started the car, her personal phone let out a little chirp from inside her jacket pocket. Another text from Ember.

Hey, if you're awake and not too busy, can you run by my place and pick up more of my things? Since it looks like I'll be staying here a little longer after all.

Cheyenne smirked and texted back.

No problem. What do you need?

Clothes. Don't forget the underwear this time. Bathroom stuff. It's all pretty much in a bag on the counter. A couple of books. Literally, anything stacked on my desk that isn't for classes. This place has shitty cable, and I'm not about to buy an issue of Good Housekeeping just to have something to read.

Very specific. I'll try not to screw it up.

Ember sent crazy-face emojis and a heart, followed by, **You're the best. See you soon.**

Cheyenne just sent her a thumbs-up and stuck her phone back into her pocket. Then she strapped herself in and got the hell out of the business park.

It took her about twenty minutes to get back to the north side of Jackson Ward and Ember's apartment. There weren't that many people out and about yet, at least in the apartment complex. She walked through the hallway on the ground floor, which was open to the air, and stopped at the last apartment on the left. After squatting to lift the corner of the doormat, she pulled the spare key out from underneath and unlocked the door. *First floor. That'll make things easier when they let her out.*

Ember's apartment was almost the exact opposite of Cheyenne's because the fae grad student had furniture in her living room, with brightly colored throw pillows and everything. It smelled like lavender hand soap and the Nag Champa incense beside the small pot of bamboo on a table by the window.

The halfling went straight back to the bedroom and rummaged through her friend's drawers, tossing everything that might work onto the blue bedspread covered in gray stars. When she found the underwear drawer, she paused. *I should bring her some handmade troll lingerie.*

She burst out laughing, grabbed a handful of underwear from the drawer, and tossed that on the bed too. A quick search through the closet netted her another tote bag, and Cheyenne stuffed everything into it. Without bothering to look at the titles, she grabbed the top three books stacked on the desk beside the bed, then headed into the bathroom. *Damn, she keeps things clean in here.*

There wasn't even a toothbrush on the counter by the sink, and she had to search through the medicine cabinet up top and the one below before she found the toiletries bag. She opened it to make sure it had what Ember needed, then shrugged and tossed the small zipped bag into the tote with everything else. As she slung the bag over her shoulder and stepped into the hall to leave, her drow hearing picked up heavy footsteps from the open hallway outside.

She didn't think anything of it until the footsteps came all the way down the row of apartments and stopped outside the last door on the left. Ember's.

Cheyenne slowly lowered the bag off her shoulder. The doorknob turned. She dropped the tote.

By the time the front door to Ember's apartment burst open, the halfling had already let the heat of her drow magic race up her spine and take over—just in time for a tall, gangly troll to storm inside. There was a disturbingly yellow tint around the edges of his purple eyes and lips, which he licked nervously. A bright-orange skaxen with long, greasy red hair falling over his shoulders stepped in behind the troll.

Now, that looks like a rat.

The door slammed behind them, and it took the intruders a moment to see the drow halfling standing in the hallway to the bedroom. Cheyenne summoned a crackling black orb of energy with bright purple churning at the core and cocked her head. "Bet you were expecting someone else, huh?"

The troll let out a high-pitched giggle. "Just you, *mór úcare.*"

CHAPTER FOUR

A spark of neon-yellow light burst from his fingertips and streaked across the living room. Cheyenne's enhanced speed kicked in, and she stepped sideways to avoid the attack of sickly electric magic. When time sped up again, she stood two feet from where the troll's spell cracked against the back of the hallway. A burst of drywall puffed out into the living room. The halfling shrugged. "Your aim sucks."

Then she launched her black sphere at the troll's chest. He dove out of the way just before her magic blasted the edge of a cabinet above the stove, splintering the wood and ripping the door off the hinges.

"You think sneaking Earthside is gonna hide you from us?" The skaxen leered at her, his words whistling through the many gaps between his razor-sharp teeth. "The O'gúl Eye searches across more than one world, *mór úcare*. And the head follows."

With surprising speed, the skaxen leaped onto the kitchen counter, knocking down a jar of loose change and hissing like a rat. The thick silver chain lurched out from beneath his shirt, another bull's-head pendant dangling off it.

"Lemme guess, you're talking about cattle." Purple sparks flared at the tips of Cheyenne's fingers, but she waited a little longer. *Whatever the hell he just said, he thinks I know what it means.*

The skaxen whipped something that looked like an AA battery out of his jacket pocket and raised it like he meant to throw the thing. A dark shimmer erupted from his hand and trembled there before slowly growing. He shrieked in excitement, spit flying from his bright-orange lips.

"Looks like your spells are stalling on you, asshole." The halfling went to toss sparks at the idiot, just to see what he'd do after his totally unnecessary jump onto the counter, but the troll had pushed himself back to his feet and summoned another piss-yellow bolt of energy. The light it gave off was the same color as the yellowing skin around his mouth.

Cheyenne let him get closer before she whipped her hand out toward him. Black tendrils of magic shot from her fingertips and writhed across the living room. The first one coiled around his wrist and jerked it aside. His spell hurtled into the beige couch, sending orange throw pillows and puffs of feathers in every direction. Then she balled her fist and yanked the troll off his feet, the black tendrils coiled around both his ankles and the other shoulder.

He screamed as she hurled him across the living room toward the wall beside the TV stand. First he crashed into the wall, then he dropped and almost knocked the flat-screen TV to the floor. She thought about trying to save her friend's furniture, but then the skaxen leaped from the counter and screeched. More spit flew from his mouth.

Mostly to avoid the stench and whatever messed-up diseases the ratlike skaxen carried in his mouth, Cheyenne slipped into her enhanced speed mode again and stepped aside. The slavering orange magical sailed through the air, his beady eyes focused on where she'd just been standing. He still clenched that weird battery in his clawed hand, and the growing circle of black light expanded faster than it should have with its caster suspended. *What is that?*

Cheyenne shot her black tendrils toward the flying skaxen and coiled them around his middle. The rest of the world sped back up as she jerked him down out of the air and smashed him into the carpeted floor. The skaxen screamed when she launched him back up and maybe broke his back against the apartment's ceiling. More drywall and plaster came down with him as she bashed the magical one more time into the floor. The battery-thing sailed from his hand toward the window and vanished, drawing the black circle of light into it with a little pop.

After withdrawing her writhing whips of drow magic, the halfling stopped and allowed herself a moment to survey the damage. *Gotta quit fighting these assholes in other people's apartments.*

The skaxen wheezed and coughed out a spray of spit and what looked a lot like orange blood, but he lay still after that and didn't look like he'd be getting back up anytime soon. The troll lying in a heap beside the TV stand tried to growl at her, but it came out more like a groan.

Cheyenne stormed across the living room toward him, summoning another sparking black orb to keep his attention. The troll's red-black eyes—the whites now taking on the same yellow tinge—rolled as he clung to consciousness. When she saw the glint of another thick chain beneath the guy's t-shirt, she bent and yanked the rest of the chain out so she could see it. She shook the bull pendant and snarled, "Wanna tell me what the hell this is?"

After a quick, surprised blink, the troll burst into more high-pitched cackling with a little rasping at the end. "More of us hear the call every day, *mór úcare*. Now that she has your scent, the rest will be coming for you. And trust me, there are way more of us now than there were before the crossing."

She tossed the pendant against his chest and straightened. "Now that who has my scent?"

Another creepy giggle burst from the troll. "You're as stupid as you look."

"Yeah, you too." The halfling closed her fist around the sizzling orb of black energy and smashed it into the troll's skull. He thumped against the TV stand, causing the flatscreen, which had already come precariously close to falling off, to wobble again.

Cheyenne's hand clamped on the corner of the TV, and she swiveled it back into place. Then she stepped away from her unconscious attacker and shot the skaxen another glance. *That was easy.*

She stepped back into the hallway to pick up the tote of Ember's things and slung it across her shoulder. An automatic grimace passed over her face, but when she realized the black-magic holes in her shoulder were as healed as they'd been in the Dungeon, she snorted. *That was the only good thing to come out of that little visit. And I can't waste my time with these idiots.*

When she didn't hear any other footsteps coming down the walkway outside, she reached into the other pocket of her jacket and pulled open the FRoE burner phone. There were only two numbers on there, which made it a lot easier to know which belonged to whom. Cheyenne hesitated for a second, then shrugged and called the second number. "They owe me, and they know it."

Rhynehart picked up on the third ring. "I don't have to tell you how weird it is to see this number pop up on my phone."

"This isn't my favorite call to make, either."

"What do you want, rookie?"

"You people have *got* to start some kinda cleanup crew."

A wry laugh came over the line. "I'll send the suggestion up to my superiors. You get yourself in some magical-on-magical trouble?"

"More like they tried to bring the trouble to me. And failed."

"How stupid of them." There was another long pause, then Rhynehart chuckled. "All right, rookie. Text me the address, and I'll send someone over. Just hang out until my guys show up."

"Better not take all day."

"You're welcome." He hung up, and Cheyenne just rolled her eyes.

But she texted him Ember's address and shoved the phone back into her jacket pocket. *Great. Now I get to babysit.*

Forty minutes later, the front door opened again. Two FRoE operatives in black fatigues stepped into Ember's apartment, to find the drow halfling slumped on the beige couch in the living room, one arm thrown over the back. There was a huge charred hole in the fabric and feathers everywhere. Two goblins this time, and one of them was the abnormally tall, muscular one with the yellow braid down the center of his head and the giant bullring in his nose. The shorter goblin shut the door behind them and let out a low whistle. "Stepped into the wrong apartment, huh?"

The female voice coming from the shorter goblin surprised Cheyenne. This one's head was shaved bald, showing the scars on her scalp. Only when she turned to look at the halfling did Cheyenne see the eyepatch over the goblin's right eye.

"Something like that."

The tall goblin with the bull-ring chuckled and nodded for his partner to start what they'd come here to do with two unconscious thugs on the floor. Then he made his way toward Cheyenne on the couch and stuck out his hand. "If Rhynehart had told me we'd find *you* here, I probably wouldn't have bitched so much about being put on maid duty."

The halfling stood. She didn't think she'd actually shake the goblin's hand until she did. "I'm guessing you guys know more about how to take out the trash than I do."

"Probably, yeah."

The sound of the troll's body thumping onto the floor made them both turn. The female goblin had pulled the unconscious magical away from the stand and now knelt beside him as she unfastened a pair of dampening cuffs from the loop at her belt. She paused, looked up at Cheyenne and Bullring, and muttered, "What are you losers staring at?"

Cheyenne snorted. "I like her."

"Yeah, Payton's been a real dick since that imp's dagger took out her eye."

Payton rolled her good eye and didn't even try to be gentle while jerking the unconscious troll's arms behind his back. "I was a real standup goblin before that."

The halfling smirked. "Oh, yeah?"

"No." The one-eyed operative clamped the dampening cuffs together with a metallic click and pushed to her feet to head toward the skaxen.

"We'll take care of these idiots," Bull-ring said before taking another sweeping glance of Ember's apartment. "Not sure we can do anything about the walls, though. Or the couch."

"Don't worry about it. I didn't think FRoE Special Forces were trained in redecorating, anyway."

The tall goblin let out a gruff laugh and folded his arms. "You know, I wasn't sure about you 'til I saw the way you blasted through those bastards at the church the other night. These two were probably a walk in the park compared to that, but I'm still impressed."

"Yeah, thanks." *My newest FRoE fan, huh? Yeah, this isn't weird.*

"I'm Yurik." He nodded at her, and Cheyenne nodded back, not quite ready to give him her name just yet, whether or not Sir and Rhynehart had already shared it. Yurik tried to wipe the smirk off his lips. "You got a phone on you?"

She frowned. "How else do you think I called for backup?"

"Lemme see it." The goblin gestured for her to cough it up, and Cheyenne gladly pulled the burner phone from her jacket pocket before dropping it into Yurik's outstretched turquoise hand. He flipped it open and started typing, thankfully without any comments about the crappy flip phone. When he was done, he snapped the phone shut again and handed it back. "All right. Now you have my number, just in case you make another mess and need to call in a crew."

Cheyenne pocketed the phone with a crooked smile. "Is 'Maid' your new official title?"

"Nice try. It's the least I can do, given the way you helped round up those kid-killers and their black-magic bullshit. I don't offer that service to just anybody."

"Right. Well, I appreciate it."

"Looks like we're on the same page, then." Yurik chuckled again, his yellow eyes glinting at her.

"Hey, pretty boy," Payton called from where she stooped over the knocked-out skaxen. The dampening cuffs clamped down around those bright-orange wrists, and the goblin grunted. "Unless you wanna cough up your MREs for the next week, cut it out with the chatting and do your job."

Yurik scoffed and turned a crooked smile on his partner. "You need help cuffing two idiots who can't even move?"

"You need me to beat your ass? Again?"

"I better get outta here." Cheyenne grabbed the tote full of Ember's things off the couch and nodded at Yurik as she made her way across the living room. "Thanks for the cleanup."

"No problem."

She couldn't help herself when she passed the one-eyed goblin on her way to the door. "Nice to meet you, Payton."

The goblin sent a half-assed kick into the skaxen's ribs and muttered, "Fuck off."

With a snort, Cheyenne opened the door and stepped out into the open-air hallway of the apartment building. Before she forgot, she locked the door from the inside and left it cracked a little before returning the spare key to its place under the mat.

The halfling slipped back into human Goth grad student just as Ember's neighbor across the hall opened his front door. The guy froze, then shut his eyes and tried to shake off what he'd just seen. "Did you just…"

Cheyenne lifted her chin and gave him a tight smile. "Nice morning, huh?"

She didn't wait for a response before heading back down the hall toward the parking lot. For having been attacked by a couple of crazies who clearly thought she was someone else, Cheyenne felt pretty good—even if she was apparently digging herself deeper and deeper into the FRoE when she wanted the exact opposite. *Whatever makes it easier to squeeze what I want out of L'zar. Because I will.*

CHAPTER FIVE

Ember pushed herself up a little straighter in the hospital bed when Cheyenne stepped through the door of Room 317. The fae shot her friend a wide grin. "I was starting to think you'd gone back to sleep or something."

"Nope. Just got a little hung up." The halfling slipped the tote off her shoulder, and Ember patted the bed beside her.

When she reached into the bag, she looked like a kid opening presents on Christmas morning, all grinning and wide-eyed. Until she pulled out the books. "Cheyenne."

"Yeah."

"What the hell is this?"

"You said any of the books on your desk, so I grabbed the ones on top and stuck 'em in."

Ember pulled out the first and turned it so her friend could see the cover. "*The Grapes of Wrath*? Seriously?"

"How was I supposed to know you weren't in the mood for Steinbeck? It's better than *Good Housekeeping*." The halfling pulled the uncomfortable armchair up beside the bed and lifted herself into it, crossing her legs beneath her.

"I'm in the hospital, and I can't walk. Reading's supposed to help me escape, not make me even more depressed."

Cheyenne couldn't hold back a little laugh. "It's not that depressing. I like that kinda stuff. When I feel like reading."

Ember puffed out a sigh through loose lips and took in the sight of her friend—black shirt, black pants, heavy black eye makeup, chains around her wrists, and all the piercings. "Yeah, you would. I didn't know you liked reading much of anything."

"I don't. I'll go back later and get you something about rainbows and unicorns if you want."

"Ha." The fae rolled her eyes and shoved the book back into her bag. "It's fine. Thanks for picking all this up for me."

"Nothing I couldn't handle." *Not a lie.* "So, question."

"Go."

"Who else knows about you being a third-generation Earthside fae with no magic?"

Ember shot her friend a curious frown. "You mean, besides my whole family, who wishes I didn't exist just to shame the bloodline? You. And then, well, Trevor and his other halfling friends."

Who left you to bleed out without a second thought. Cheyenne cleared her throat. "Anyone else?"

"It's not the best conversation starter." The fae shot her friend a sidelong glance. "And it's not like I have anything to hide. Not like you."

"Hey, what's that supposed to mean?"

"I just mean the whole trying-not-to-let-the-pointy-ears-stick-out-of-all-that-hair thing." Shaking her head, Ember let out a small laugh and scooted the tote of her things up the bed so she could throw her arm over it. "You know what I mean. Why? Who brought it up?"

"No one brought it up, exactly." The halfling scratched the back of her head. "I ran into a little trouble at your apartment. Just wondering if anyone else knew what you were and thought they'd come to find you or something."

"What kinda trouble?"

"I took care of it. It's fine."

"Cheyenne." Ember folded her arms and shot her friend a stern look. "Remember when I told you you're a really bad liar?"

"Okay, fine. A couple of scumbags showed up at your place, looking for a fight." The halfling chuckled. "And I gave it to them."

"They did what now?"

"Well, I'm pretty sure they were just trying to get me if no one else knows about you. I guess they wouldn't have been spouting all that weird shit about eyes following me and some lady who apparently 'found my scent.'" Cheyenne shrugged and picked at a black-painted nail.

"You're kidding."

"Nope. I have no idea what those guys were goin' on about, but they seemed pretty sure I was someone else." The halfling tapped her chest. "And they had these weird pendants in the shape of a bull's head. I've been seeing them on a lot of messed-up magicals running around. Any idea what they mean?"

Ember sighed and brushed her hair away from her face. "No clue. Sounds like a bunch of crazy to me."

"Yeah, that's what I thought. But L'zar said it was an issue that should've stayed in Ambar'ogúl—"

"Wait, wait, wait! Back up. *L'zar?*"

Cheyenne looked up from her nails and broke into a crooked smile. "Oh, yeah. Maybe I should've started with that."

"Ya think? Did you go see him?"

"This morning."

Ember smacked her hands together and bounced a little in the hospital bed. "How is that *not* the first thing you tell me when you walk in the door? Come on!"

"Sorry." Cheyenne laughed. "I know it's not even noon, but it's already been a weird day."

"No shit. Tell me everything."

The halfling took in her friend's surprising eagerness and debated saying anything, but only for a second. *At least someone cares.* "It, uh, well, it definitely didn't go the way I expected."

Ember snorted. "What *did* you expect?"

"I don't know. An apology, maybe. More of an explanation for why he just left my mom instead of some bullshit excuse."

"Which was…"

Cheyenne rolled her eyes and did her best impression of L'zar's low, apathetic voice. "'Because I had to.'"

"Oh, come on."

"I know. And that's how the whole conversation went. I mean, it wasn't even a real conversation, just a bunch of vague answers and him laughing at me. The worst part is, he didn't even ask about my mom. Like, not a single thing, and then he said he didn't want to hear about her because I was more interesting."

Ember's jaw dropped, and she blinked. "What a dick."

Cheyenne shrugged. "Yeah, that's pretty much the conclusion I came to. So, I…" Another short laugh escaped her.

"What?" Ember leaned toward her, eyes wide with curiosity.

"I said this safe word that turned on the alarm and put him under lockdown. Red lights, siren, turned the bars of his cell into a giant bug zapper for magicals."

"Good." The fae barked a laugh. "Bet *that* pissed him off."

"No. He just laughed like the whole thing was just one big game, and he just wanted to see what I'd do."

"Woah." Leaning back against the propped-up bed and all the pillows behind her, Ember let out a long sigh. "You gonna go see him again?"

"No clue. I'm not sure I even wanna think about that right now. I have other things going on that feel more important."

"Oh, yeah? Like what?"

Cheyenne pressed her lips together and tried not to laugh. "Well, for starters, I'm gonna have to find the time to go back to your place and…clean up the little mess I made."

"'Little' mess?"

Squinting, the halfling slowly met her friend's blue-eyed gaze. "Medium-small, maybe. Hey, I saved the TV, so there's that."

"Lovely." Ember plastered on a tight smile. "Please tell me the bamboo survived."

"I promise, no plants were harmed in the ass-kicking of the magical intruders." Cheyenne drew a cross over her heart, and they both laughed. "Dunno if your couch survived. Maybe if you get it reupholstered…"

"Nah. I wanted a new one, anyway."

"Cool. I'll buy you new pillows, too."

Ember barked out a laugh. "How did my *pillows* get pulled into a fight?"

"We don't have to go into details." With another chuckle, Cheyenne shook her head and thought about Yurik and Payton in her friend's apartment. "But all the evidence got taken care of. Oh, and I almost forgot the most important thing."

The fae threw her arms in the air and let them drop back into her lap with a thump. "It better not be worse than blowing up my living room with drow magic."

"No, no. It's way better." Licking her lips, Cheyenne leaned toward the bed and took a deep breath. "Guess who I found on the—"

A light knock came at the door, then Dr. Andrews stepped into Ember's hospital room and paused. "Oh. You're back."

"Hey, Doc." The halfling shot him a sarcastic salute. *This guy has the worst timing.*

"Just coming in to check on my favorite patient in Room 317." The doctor closed the door behind him and walked slowly toward the bed, his tablet cradled in the crook of his arm. "While you're here, though, how's the shoulder?"

"Oh, yeah. It's feeling great, actually. Good work." Nodding quickly, Cheyenne slid out of the armchair and pushed it back into place against the wall beside the window.

Ember shot her a confused look. "It's feeling great?"

The halfling leaned in to wrap Ember in a quick hug and whispered in her friend's ear, "L'zar. I'll tell you about it later." She pulled back and gave the fae's shoulders a squeeze. "Now that you have your personal effects, I gotta get goin'. Happy reading, right?"

She shot Ember a wink, and her friend rolled her eyes. "Oh, jeez."

"See ya later, Doc. Keep up the good work with my friend. She deserves it." Nodding at the confused doctor, Cheyenne patted the foot of the bed as she stepped around it and headed for the door.

"You know, if you want me to take another look at your shoulder, I'm happy to—"

"No, thanks. I'm good. Enjoy your Sunday." She slipped out the door and headed quickly down the hall. *That guy gets nosier every time I see him. And I have more work to do.*

She wished she could have at least told Ember she was finally about to bash in the front door of the orc scumbag who shot her, but the look on her friend's face when Cheyenne gave her the news afterward would be just as satisfying.

CHAPTER SIX

Glen finished booting up in Cheyenne's tiny living room just as the microwave beeped. She went to grab the steaming tray of now-unfrozen enchiladas from the convenience store down the street. The silverware drawer was empty, all the forks either in the sink or tossed haphazardly in the dishwasher. She pulled open the junk drawer in the kitchen, rummaged around, and snatched a plastic fork wrapped in more plastic with salt and pepper packets. *No downside to takeout.*

She brought it all back to her computer setup, dropped into her chair, and set the enchiladas down to cool off just a little. Getting her VPN and the torrent fired up to hop onto the dark web took her no time at all, and then she was right back in the Borderlands forum to search for a few more things before her long-awaited reunion with Durg. *This time, I'm going in prepared.*

She skimmed through the newest topics, looking for anything about the area of Jackson Ward just on the other side of the skatepark. One of the topics titled, *Bombs Underground Gets Freaky on East Clay* caught her eye, only because that street was just blocks from the skatepark. But apparently, Bombs Underground was actually a heavy-metal band with all magical members that was set to play at some tiny little venue a block down from Gnarly's Pub. She wrinkled her nose and went ahead with leaving a comment, just to see what might stick.

Shyhand71: Sounds like fun. Hey, has anybody put together a magicals-only list of where people are? You know, like for networking or something?

The minute she posted it, she let out a grunt of disgust. *I sound like such a noob.*

The other users on the Borderlands forum were just as quick to jump to the same conclusion.

holdmyGrog911: @Shyhand71 You trying to get us all together in one spot so we can hold hands and make a big-ass target for the F-force? Looks like somebody's trip Earthside fried all their brain cells.

2Magic2Quit: @Shyhand71 I call narc right here.

Fists4Daze: @Shyhand71 We went through the Reservations, dumbass. Why would we want more eyes on us when they already have us in the goddamn system? What the hell's wrong with you?

CrownUndone21: Okay, everybody throwing their insecurities at a new commenter (and I'm pretty sure @Shyhand71's new around here) needs to back the hell up and calm down. It was an innocent question. I'm pretty sure there are running lists somewhere. Maybe not by area where people live now, but I think I saw something maybe a year ago that had groups by trade, either back home or Earthside. Can't remember. @Shyhand71, I'll take a look around and hit you up here if I find anything.

CantCuffThis: I second everything @CrownUndone21 just said to all the haters. By the Crown, y'all hopped on this comment quickly. I thought we came Earthside to avoid the bloodshed, not to sit behind computer screens and try to draw more of it. @Shyhand71's right to ask, especially if they're new. Not everyone who made the crossing logs onto the fucking dark web to come watch you assholes make a circus of the Border- lands. Lay off.

Fists4Daze: @CrownUndone21 @CantCuffThis You trying to be peacekeepers now? I sure as shit could've used some backup two months ago when my shop got raided. Oh, yeah. That's right. Everyone's a damn hero when all they have to do is sit down at a keyboard and play around.

"Woah." Cheyenne lifted her hands from her keyboard and watched the comments roll in one right after the other. "Hit a sore spot, huh?"

With a shrug, she leaned back over the keys and left one more comment. Otherwise, she really would look like just another troll trying to stir up shit where it wasn't needed.

Shyhand71: @CrownUndone21 @CantCuffThis Thanks. I'll keep looking. Feel free to DM me if you find something that might help. We can leave the peanut gallery out of it.

CantCuffThis: @Shyhand71 Yeah, just ignore those guys. They're probably still shaking off the smell of whatever rez they just got themselves booted out of. You brought up a good point. It's good to keep an eye open for ways we can help each other.

Nodding, Cheyenne clicked out of that particular topic thread, not wanting to waste her time reading through whatever other angry comments anyone else left her. She ran a search on the forum for anything about Jackson Ward, but before she could sort through the results, a private chat box popped up in the top corner of her monitor.

She'd expected something else from gu@rdi@n104, who she now knew was the Nightstalker Corian, mainly because the guy always seemed to be on the Borderlands forum when she was and generally hit her with a message. But this new chat box had come directly from the user handle CrownDown4What.

"Who the heck is that?" The halfling hadn't seen the handle before on any of the open topics or in comment threads, though of course, she hadn't been through all of them. The message, though, was even more confusing.

CrownDown4What: Just saw your comment about lists of

people in certain areas. I might be able to help if you tell me why you're looking.

"Huh." Cheyenne cocked her head, frowned, then scooted a little closer to the desk and started typing again.

Shyhand71: Just thought it might be helpful. I'm sure other people would appreciate knowing what kind of neighborhood they're stepping into. Where to find friends. Who to stay away from.

CrownDown4What: Well, you're definitely not the first to come up with the idea. You stepping into a new neighborhood or something?

Shyhand71: Kind of. I just want to make sure I'm not about to put all my eggs in one basket before somebody steps on it.

CrownDown4What: I hear ya. What neighborhood?

Shyhand71: Jackson Ward. North side, mostly.

Her new friend took over a minute to reply. Cheyenne managed to sit patiently through the wait, hoping whoever it was had enough balls to tell her to scram if they didn't want to dig any deeper into this with her. Then a new message popped up at the bottom of the chat.

CrownDown4What: Maybe this'll help. It's a section of a longer list I have access to, and that's just one list of a lot more. If you have any other questions, I'm here.

Cheyenne rolled her eyes. Why can't people just put it in the chat instead of making me do all the work?

She fired up the Bunker again because she had no idea who this CrownDown4What was and was too smart not to cover her bases. A link was a link, sure, but on the dark web, it could literally be anything else, too.

Once her custom program had fully opened, she clicked on the link and downloaded CrownDown4What's little present through a bit torrent and right in. Five seconds later, the new file had been tested and scrubbed of nothing; it was as clean as the file gu@rdi@n104 had sent her on Durg, and it was just as small.

A list of names and races identified by "class" took up three-quarters of a page. Some of them had addresses, and several had professions listed after that. There were apparently only twenty or so other magicals listed in Jackson Ward altogether, not just the north side. She scanned the list again and clicked back into the chat.

Shyhand71: Definitely helpful. How long ago was this list updated?

CrownDown4What: About twenty seconds ago. My system's pretty thorough.

Shyhand71: Nice. Any tips for how a noob can get access to a system like that?

CrownDown4What: You don't have to pretend like you don't know what you're doing. The way you've been answering my questions proves enough. Wish I could help with more than sending over a list now and then. Built the system myself, though. Not looking to bring in partners.

"No kidding." The halfling couldn't help being a little impressed by that, if CrownDown4What was telling the truth. *Looks like I'm not the only one who knows their way around serious coding.*

Shyhand71: Makes sense. I appreciate the file anyway.

CrownDown4What: No worries. Let me know if you're stepping into any other neighborhoods and want the same kind of info. You'll eventually get the hang of working this stuff out on your own. When you've been Earthside as long as I have, you get real good at keeping a bird's-eye view.

Shyhand71: Just for fun, how long have you been here?

CrownDown4What: Longer than the Accord. Not safe to say much more than that.

Shyhand71: Right. I'll keep in touch.

CrownDown4What: Sounds good.

Cheyenne sat back in her office chair and read over their conversation one more time. *Longer than the Accord, huh? So, before I was born, and before the FRoE started making their own lists. Who is this guy?*

It made her curious, but it wasn't the most important thing right now. She had the information she wanted about Durg's neighborhood, and she had some time to kill, thanks to her new friend from the Borderlands forum. *And no stupid scavenger hunts first. I like this guy.*

It took her another fifteen minutes to cross-reference the addresses on that list with the area of Jackson Ward where Durg lived. There were other orcs living in the area, and all of them were at least four blocks away from her new target's house. Those with listed jobs mostly worked on the other side of Richmond. If she wanted to make certain most of them were out of the way, she would wait until tomorrow, skip class, and go for the bastard in the middle of the day.

Cheyenne rubbed her forehead and glanced at her backpack on the floor by the kitchen counter's half-wall. *Can't keep skipping. And most people are home on a Sunday night anyway.*

Especially the orc she was bent on paying back for what he'd done to Ember.

CHAPTER SEVEN

No matter how badly she was itching to head to Durg's place—which would have only taken her about twenty-five minutes to walk and maybe two minutes to run at full drow speed—Cheyenne did the smart thing and waited it out. She glanced at the clock on her computer—5:47 p.m. "Might as well warm up."

She shut off the monitor and powered Glen down all the way before stepping into the tiny space between her desk and her kitchen. After a second's thought, she let the heat of her drow magic flare at the base of her spine and wash over her. Then she conjured up the purple sparks shooting off the tips of her fingers and stared at them. *How about something I haven't mastered yet?*

The sparks went out, and she closed her eyes to take herself back to her final "test" with Rhynehart the day before. *Black fire on my skin. How the hell does that work?*

The halfling tried to bring up the protective rage she'd felt fighting Rhynehart's mountain of an ogre operative. Jamal's face pulled up quickly in her memory—his sneer, the mottled gray flesh covering his lumpy head, the way he'd dropped to one knee in the middle of their fight and given up.

'Cause it was a lie.

She clenched her fists and opened her eyes, hoping to see the black flames flickering across her black shirt and the purple-gray skin of her forearms showing beneath her three-quarter-length sleeves. Nothing.

One and done, then. What about the shield?

The chains on her wrists clinked when she shook out her hands, then she shot out her arm and threw her hand toward the window at the far end of her tiny living room. "Takes more than intention, huh?"

With a sigh, Cheyenne focused harder on what a shield was supposed to be—protection and a last-minute defense. She sucked in a breath and spun, raising both hands toward the closet just inside the front door. The doorknob might have rattled a little, but that was it.

Then a muted golden glow sputtered inside her backpack on the floor, and the halfling pointed at it. "Uh-uh. I'm not dealing with that tonight."

There was a knock on her front door, and she started. The knock was repeated. "Yeah, I'm coming. Hold on."

When she passed her backpack, she wanted to send a swift kick into the thing to get the copper puzzle box to quit flashing light. *Nobody else needs to see that.* But her laptop was in there too, so she just gave the thing a less-than-gentle nudge with the side of her foot and smirked when the golden light winked out.

Then she slipped out of her drow form and slowly opened the door. It didn't surprise her all that much to find one of her troll neighbors on the other side of it.

"Cheyenne." R'mahr grinned at her, his deep-scarlet eyes lighting up because she'd answered. "I hope this is a good time. Yadje's almost finished with the cooking, and we would love to invite you into our home now to join us."

"Right now?"

The troll cocked his head, his grin fading into a confused smile. "Yes. It's Sunday. I mentioned this the other day. And you...well, I thought…"

I never said no.

Cheyenne nodded and shot him as much of a reassuring smile as she could manage. "Uh, yeah. Okay. You guys already started cooking and everything?"

R'mahr nodded vigorously. "As close to the food back home as we could get. I don't know how Yadje does it with what little we can find at the bazaar, but she makes it work. You'll be very happy with it."

"Yeah, I bet."

They stood there awkwardly on either side of her door, then R'mahr's gaze drifted to her right toward the basket of all that brightly colored underwear they'd made her. "You still have our gift…"

"Yep." Cheyenne followed his gaze and had to keep herself from laughing. "I can't get rid of a present like that, can I?"

The troll's grin returned with full force, and he let out a satisfied little chuckle. "Yadje will be so glad to hear you've found a use for them—"

"Okay, let's head on over to your place, huh?" Not wanting to be rude, the halfling opened the door all the way before slipping into her black Vans that were tossed against the closet, then she hurried quickly out of her apartment and shut the door. "After you."

"Yes. Well, it's not very far." The troll shot her an amused glance and chuckled again, shaking his head at the worn, stained carpet lining the hallway of the second floor. "I told Yadje you would be very pleased to walk inside and have this meal already prepared. She wasn't convinced you were coming, you know."

"Good thing I cleared my schedule, then." Yadje had a better grip on how to make plans. Still plenty of time before dark.

The troll's head bobbed up and down, his long scarlet hair bouncing against his back. They passed the two other apartments between them, and he stopped at his front door to shoot the drow halfling another wide grin full of clean but crooked teeth. "We're honored to have you here with us."

"No problem. I'm, uh, honored to be invited." *Can't break the guy's heart over this.*

R'mahr sucked in a sharp breath, his eyes growing even wider as he whispered, "Thank you."

Then he opened the door and gestured for her to step inside first.

A thick wave of pungent spices almost knocked her over when Cheyenne stepped into the troll family's home. The air was filled with the sizzle of something frying on the stove beside a thick something else boiling in a huge pot.

R'mahr ushered her in even farther and closed the door. He clapped his hands and almost scampered toward the kitchen. "Our guest is here, Yadje. She's here. How much longer for the meal?"

"You can't hurry perfection," Yadje snapped from the kitchen, completely hidden by the wall jutting out from the entryway. "I'll finish it when I finish it, and you'll just have to keep your greedy little hands *out*—" A sharp smack was followed by R'mahr's exclamation of surprise and his wife laughing. Then Yadje poked her head around the corner and settled her scarlet gaze on the halfling standing just inside the door. "Make yourself at home, *phér móre*. We won't be much longer."

"Sure." The halfling nodded, but the woman's head had already disappeared back into the kitchen. Raising her eyebrows, Cheyenne took in the family's living room, which looked more or less like it had the first time she'd stepped inside under much more urgent circumstances.

R'mahr and his family had made quick work of patching up the place. The planter hanging from the ceiling had been put back together with an insane amount of duct tape coating the bottom, the plant returned to its place after having been blasted by drow magic. The leaves drooped sadly over the mended plastic sides of the planter. More duct tape had been applied liberally to the broken leg of the armchair, as well as added for extra hold around two different pieces of thin plywood already nailed to the walls.

Cheyenne still felt a little draft from the covered hole in the wall beside the door. *If they're happy with it, guess it works.*

"Hi."

The halfling glanced quickly across the room and found Bryl sitting on the floor in front of the sunken couch, an open book laid across her lap. "Hey. Your parents really went all out with the duct tape, huh?"

The young troll glanced around the room and sighed. "It's one of their favorite new things on this side."

"Yeah, well, it's good for a lot of things. Glad they figured that out, at least." Holding back a laugh, Cheyenne moved across the living room and stopped beside the girl, dipping her head to take a look at the book. "What're you reading?"

Bryl shrugged. "*Harry Potter.*"

"Oh, yeah," the halfling said as she wrinkled her nose and let out a little chuckle. "It's a good story."

"But they didn't get any of the magic parts right."

Cheyenne laughed and covered it with a hand, rubbing her mouth. "Well, it's made up. Kinda fun to think about things in a different way."

"I guess…"

"Bryl, put that thing away and come help me set the table." Yadje waved her daughter into the kitchen. With a small, knowing smile, the kid looked up at Cheyenne and tossed her book aside before going to help her parents.

Turning toward the kitchen, Cheyenne spread her arms and figured she might as well be a part of this while she was here. "I can help too."

"Oh, no." Yadje shook her head and pulled her daughter into the kitchen.

"Absolutely not." R'mahr rounded the corner, waving his hands furiously like he was trying to flag somebody down on the highway. "No. The *phér móre* won't lift a finger in our home."

"You can just call me Cheyenne. Really."

"The *phér móre* Cheyenne was not invited here to help. You've done that and more already." R'mahr hurried toward her and settled his hands on her shoulders before steering her toward the wooden table with legs so thin, it didn't look like it would be able to hold much of anything. He pulled out a chair and pointed. "*You* will sit right here."

She didn't try to fight him on that one and slowly lowered herself into the chair. It creaked and wobbled a little under her weight, and the halfling forced herself not to take up her usual position and lean all the way back with her feet stretched out in front of her under the table. *I already broke too much of their stuff.*

"We'll take care of everything else." R'mahr gave her a firm nod and hurried back into the kitchen.

A moment later, his wife stepped out into their makeshift dining room with a huge clay bowl piled high with something which looked like rice and noodles scrambled together, steam wafting off the top. She grinned and set the bowl in the center of the table, then disappeared again. Bryl brought out the next plate of what was maybe pita bread, only with purple streaks running down the sides of the still-warm pastry. The bowl R'mahr brought out next had vegetables Cheyenne recognized—bok choy and carrots and broccoli piled around something blue that couldn't have possibly been grown in this world. The dishes seemed never-ending as the troll family brought out one after another. The halfling rubbed the side of her face and gave up on trying to give each of them a genuine smile when they came toward her from the kitchen.

Finally, when the wobbly table was sufficiently loaded with more food than they could possibly eat in one sitting, all three trolls moved quickly toward the other chairs around the table and slipped into them. Silence fell over the dining room. R'mahr and Yadje beamed at Cheyenne with pride. Bryl glanced at her parents and their guest, biting her purple lower lip to keep from laughing.

"Now." Yadje took a deep breath and pulled herself up straighter in the chair. "Our *phér móre* first—"

"Cheyenne. Really."

"Take whatever you like, and we'll begin." The troll woman gestured toward the overloaded table.

"Uh…" The halfling gazed at all the steaming dishes and lifted her shoulder in a hesitant shrug. "Was I supposed to bring the plates and silverware?"

R'mahr and Yadje burst out laughing, and Cheyenne couldn't tell if it was forced amusement or if they genuinely thought she was making a joke. *Apparently, my ignorance is showing.*

A small, warm finger tapped her forearm on the table, and Bryl mimed scooping up the food. "With your hands."

"Oh." The halfling eyed the bowl of cooked vegetables and reached across the table to pull a carrot out of the pile. She stuck it in her mouth and almost choked on the heavy spices, but she managed to nod through her chewing as R'mahr and Yadje watched her like their lives depended on it. "Yeah, that's good."

Yadje smacked her husband's arm with the back of her hand. "I *told* you she'd like it. You worry too much about everything and nothing."

Laughing, R'mahr bobbed his head, picked up one of the pita-bread-looking things, then passed the plate of them toward his wife. Then all the hands were dipping into all the bowls, and Cheyenne tried not to frown. *They think I know how this works.*

"Look." Bryl picked up a piece of bread and used it like a glove made of food. "Just do what I do."

The halfling was more than happy to follow the lead of a six-year-old troll.

CHAPTER EIGHT

"Cheyenne, have some more *borsni*." Yadje gestured toward the bowl of vegetables and the piles of blue something the halfling had avoided.

"No, thanks. I think I saw it glowing."

"That's where all the flavor is." Bryl grabbed one of the blue veggies that looked like a bioluminescent turnip and took a huge bite. A bright light flashed in her mouth, and Cheyenne shook her head.

"You were talking about your town, though." The halfling nodded at the troll couple and tore off another piece of bread that tasted a little like strawberries. "I wanna hear more about it."

"It was a fine place," R'mahr replied, nodding quickly. "Such a beautiful place in the Oronti Valley. So many *radan* with their bright coats. That's how we used to get so much of the color for our houses, you know. Soak the *radan* pelts in river water, and you have the color to put on whatever you want. Here, I think you just buy it in cans."

"Paint?"

"Yes. That's it."

"We were very happy there," Yadje added. "The best place to raise a family."

Cheyenne scooped up another handful of the rice-noodle stuff—the trolls had had to assure her three times there was nothing alive in there when the noodles started moving on their own—and popped it all into her mouth. "So why did you leave?"

R'mahr paused with his hand halfway to his mouth, then jammed his next bite between his lips and avoided the question by chewing.

Yadje shared a glance with her husband and dipped her head. "It was no longer safe."

"What happened?"

R'mahr swallowed thickly and sighed. "You know the Crown has different ideas of the places under their rule, Cheyenne. I doubt a single one of them ever made it out to Opéle to see our home for themselves, but they wanted it for the reaping all the same."

"Sorry." The halfling licked heavily spiced sauce off her lips. "I don't know what that is."

"Then you're a very lucky *phér móre*." Yadje gave her a stern look, then reached for more food. "We left before things became too difficult. I'm not sure many of the others were as prepared to do what was necessary."

"You mean, crossing the Border." Cheyenne looked back and forth between R'mahr and Yadje, neither of whom would look up at her as they kept chewing. *That's a definite yes.*

"I thought it was fun." Bryl brushed the shorter scarlet hairs away from her forehead, but they kept falling back into place. "An adventure. Just like Dahi said."

"You were an excellent adventurer, Bryl." R'mahr winked at his daughter, but the smile was just for show.

"We walked for days through the woods to get to the portal." Bryl rested both elbows on the table and looked up at Cheyenne with wide scarlet eyes. "Built shelters every night. There wasn't always water close by, but when we found the river, there was plenty to drink."

"Really?" The halfling raised her eyebrows, waiting to hear more.

"Yeah, and that was the easy part." The kid grinned and lifted both hands to animate her story. "The Border is like its own world. We had to say the spell on one side. I messed up, but Dahi reminded me. Then when you pass through, everything's all dark everywhere you look. And there are these *things* that come out of the—"

"That's enough, Bryl." Yadje shot her daughter a warning look.

"But that's the best part, Maji!"

"Your mother said enough, *nin mel*." Now R'mahr shot the young girl the same look, and a bloom of dark purple spread across Bryl's cheeks. "Cheyenne doesn't want to hear about our journey through."

His dark-red eyes flickered toward the halfling before he had to look away.

Rhynehart had said the crossing was rough. And they had done it with their kid.

Bryl bowed her head and dropped her hands into her lap, biting her lip to keep from saying anything else. There was a tense, awkward silence again, but this one wasn't in anticipation of starting the meal.

Yadje took a sharp breath. "What did you think of the *aesdur*, Cheyenne?"

"Uh, which one was that?"

R'mahr let out a little chuckle as his wife pointed to a smaller dish of what looked like soup. The halfling had already figured out that when she touched the stuff, it hardened and drew itself into little round balls that tasted like chicken covered in chocolate.

"Right. Yeah, it was different."

"I know." The troll woman sighed and offered a shrug. "I always try to find the best ingredients to make the same meals from home. Peridosh has so many wonderful things, but they're more focused on bringing in grog and fellwine and ingredients for spells than fresh O'gúleesh foods."

Cheyenne couldn't hold back a snort. "Did you say fellwine?"

R'mahr's hand came down on the table, making the whole thing wobble dangerously on its thin legs. He got a silent reminder to watch himself from his wife's quick glance. He ignored her. "You haven't had fellwine?"

"Nope. Can't say that I have."

"Yadje, do you hear that? She's never had fellwine!"

"I heard her say it the first time." Yadje looked at the halfling and rolled her eyes.

"We can't let her go any longer without tasting it." The troll shook his head and puffed up his chest. "I told you we should have bought a flagon at Peridosh."

"You say that every time, and we have more important things to spend our money on. You're brain-addled enough as it is."

R'mahr barked a laugh and clapped. "We'll have to change that, Cheyenne."

The halfling shrugged and couldn't help but smile. "Sounds like fun."

"Not for you or anyone around you the next morning," Yadje added. "Have you been to Peridosh?"

"No. *They must think I live in a box.* "Didn't even know it existed."

"Richmond's very own O'gúl market." Yadje licked the sauce from her fingers. "We try to make it out there once a week."

"A magicals-only type of place." R'mahr wiggled his eyebrows. "One of the only places we can get to these days where we don't have to hide everything about who we are. It's all out in the open at Peridosh, just like back home."

Suddenly feeling a lot fuller than she'd thought, Cheyenne leaned slowly back in the chair and folded her arms. "That's good to have around. How do they keep the place hidden?"

"Ha!" R'mahr gestured toward the halfling across the table and grinned at his wife. "She doesn't know."

"That settles it, then." Yadje nodded at Cheyenne and grinned. "You should come with us the next time we go."

"Wednesday!" R'mahr blinked, then turned toward his wife and leaned in. "That's it, isn't it?"

"Yes, R'mahr. We go on Wednesdays."

"Wednesday!" The troll grabbed a heaping handful of the

remaining blue *borsni* and shoveled it into his mouth, chewing with overexcited enthusiasm. "You'll come with us, Cheyenne, and we'll show you the best Peridosh has to offer."

Yadje eyed the glowing bits of blue vegetable spilling from her husband's mouth and shook her head. "He left his manners back in Ambar'ogúl with everything else."

Cheyenne laughed as R'mahr waved off the insult.

"I'll show you the potions tent," Bryl exclaimed, gripping the edge of the table in her excitement. "You'll love it. They have everything you can think of. Like, what you threw on that asshole orc last time you were—"

"Bryl!" Her mother snapped, then added, "Watch your tongue."

"What? The potionmaster says it all the time!"

"You're not the potionmaster, are you?" R'mahr raised an eyebrow, and her daughter made a face before dropping her gaze to the table again.

"I'll show you when we go," Bryl muttered, shooting Cheyenne a sideways glance.

"Can't wait." The halfling's smile was tight as she tried not to alarm her odd magical hosts. *Potions and kids haven't been a good mix lately.*

"Yes, yes." R'mahr just kept nodding, oblivious to his daughter's precocious cursing. "We'll show you everything. You'll be cooking O'gúleesh meals in no time."

His wife snorted. "That's not a promise, Cheyenne. He's been going with me every week and still can't figure out how to cook a *damahs-dur.*"

"Well, that's because I have you," R'mahr said, grinning at his wife. He leaned toward her again. "And you do it so very well."

She brushed him off and rolled her eyes, although her small smile broke through with the playful banter.

Cheyenne glanced over her shoulder into the kitchen at the clock above the stove. *After nine already? I guess I did enjoy myself.*

"Well, thanks for dinner." She grabbed the table to push herself up, but thought better of it when it wobbled. She scooted her chair back instead. "It was filling."

"Yes, it sticks with you, eh?" Chuckling, R'mahr rose from the table and nodded. "Let me walk you to the door."

The halfling raised her hand toward Bryl for a high-five, and the girl didn't hesitate to smack her palm with a loud slap.

Yadje gasped. "Bryl!"

"Oh, no. It's okay." Cheyenne mimed another high-five with herself this time. "It's just a high-five. A good thing here."

The troll woman pressed her lips together and hummed in response, then she forced a smile aimed at their guest. "Thank you for coming tonight, Cheyenne. Our door is always open to you."

"Thanks. You guys already figured out you can knock on mine any time."

"Yes, yes." R'mahr rounded the table and gestured across the living room. "I'll walk you back to the door right now."

"Uh, you don't have to. I'm just down the hall."

"I didn't leave *all* my manners on the other side of the Border, Cheyenne. Even though my wife thinks otherwise." He shot Yadje another wink and laughed when she tossed the last piece of bread at him. Then he opened the door and gestured for the halfling to step out into the hall.

"Don't forget about Wednesday," Bryl called after them.

"Not a chance."

R'mahr walked beside her past the two apartments between them, patting his belly beneath another of his oversized t-shirts. "We are very glad you came to share a meal with us, Cheyenne. It means more than you can imagine, having a *phér móre* in our home. A friend."

"Yeah, I enjoyed it." She stopped beside her door and paused when she grabbed the handle. Then she turned back toward R'mahr and took a deep breath. "So, I wouldn't feel right about it if I didn't say something."

The troll's eyes widened in concern. "What happened? You really didn't like the *borsni*, did you?"

"No, no. The *borsni* was good. It's about the Peridosh market."

"Oh. Yes?"

Cheyenne dropped her hand from the doorknob. Was there a way to say this without freaking him out?

"Bryl mentioned a potions tent."

"She does love potions. Takes after my father, ancestors watch over him."

"Right." She licked her lips. "You guys should be careful in that place. There's been a lot of nasty stuff floating around Richmond. All of Virginia, really, and some other states."

R'mahr's scarlet eyebrows drew together. "Nasty?"

"Potions. Charms. Black magic." When she swallowed, it stuck in her throat for a second, and she pushed it down with the image of the dead kid in the damn ritual robes. "The guy who was making it got taken care of, but a lot of what he made is still out there. Most of it is targeted at kids."

The troll's mouth popped open. "To…"

"Yeah. I don't think you guys have anything to worry about. Your kid's a lot younger than the ones who got caught up in that stuff. Just keep an eye on her. Make sure she's not picking anything up you wouldn't touch yourself, okay?"

"Oh. Yes, of course." Blinking furiously and blushing deep purple just like his daughter, R'mahr brought a fist up to his chest and held Cheyenne's gaze with a surprising intensity. "Thank you, *phér móre.* You still do so much for us."

She ignored his refusal to just use her name. "I'd do this for everybody, but I've actually met your daughter, and I like you guys. She's a good kid. I don't want to see her get hurt. Or you and Yadje."

The troll thumped his chest again, closed his eyes, and nodded. Cheyenne stood there waiting for him to move again so she wouldn't feel like an ass just leaving him there like that in the hallway. When he finally opened his eyes, they held a determination she hadn't seen there before. "Forever grateful, Cheyenne."

"You're welcome."

Then he broke out into a grin and pointed at her. "I look forward to Wednesday. You'll see how impressive it is, what Yadje can do with the leftovers those vendors call fresh O'gúl crops."

With a chuckle, Cheyenne opened the door to her apartment and gave him a little wave. "Can't wait. Have a good night."

"And you." R'mahr bowed and fortunately turned away to hurry down the hall again before Cheyenne proved once again that she didn't really know how to respond.

She slipped inside her apartment and closed the door behind her before kicking off her Vans again. Then she leaned against the door and closed her eyes with a sigh. *That was harder than I thought, but worth it if it keeps one more kid from dying.*

After she pulled herself back together, she headed for her desk and the slip of scrap paper on which she'd written Durg's address. She took her phone out of her pocket just long enough to type the address into her GPS, then she grabbed her jacket off the floor and shrugged it on. *There's one more asshole who needs to pay.*

CHAPTER NINE

She chose to walk from her apartment on the southeast end of the VCU campus. It was more than enough time to get herself all amped up for kicking some orc ass, and the crisp night air of late September helped her focus her energy. *A lot harder to find me later if no one sees me get out of my car.*

East Clay Street was crowded as usual, even on a Sunday night. The bars were full, the music playing so loud she heard five different songs at once, and no one paid much attention to the Goth chick on a mission stalking through Jackson Ward. Then she found herself on the same route Ember had taken from the bar two weeks ago to the skatepark. A new swell of rage burned through her when she walked down the street beside the park and caught a glimpse of the skatepark at the other end. The city had repaired the shredded chain-link fence she'd ripped apart with her magic after her first round of going full drow berserker in front of everyone.

Wonder if they got the blood out yet.

Cheyenne walked around the park, heading toward the northwest side tonight instead. Durg's house was close to the park.

Ten minutes later, she found herself on Durg's street, just where she was supposed to be. The streetlights were on, casting halos of dim light across the asphalt and the sidewalks around them. Dim enough not to put a drow halfling in the spotlight, at least.

She pulled out her phone and double-checked where she was on the GPS. The house she wanted was another block down. The halfling headed that way, forcing her drow power down until she was really ready to use it. *No accidental magic tonight. No failures.*

When she stopped in front of the house just beside Durg's, she almost laughed. Not that she'd expected a rotting, crumbling shack like Q'orr's, but this just looked like every other two-story family home on the street, except for where the trees had been planted and the length of the grass in each lawn. Durg's house was pale-blue, almost green in the glow of the streetlamps.

With a final glance up and down the street, Cheyenne let her drow magic take over. It bloomed at the base of her spine and traveled up, filling her from head to toe as she made the transformation in a second. Then she stalked down the sidewalk past just one more house and moved quietly up the steps. *This is it. Cover your bases.*

Cheyenne pressed her hand against the pale-blue siding beside the front door and closed her eyes. The image of Durg's house shimmered in her mind's eye—the hallway, kitchen, staircase in the back, three bedrooms upstairs. And there in the front living room was the glowing green outline of an orcish shape sitting on the damn couch with his feet propped up on a low table.

Removing her hand, the halfling forced herself not to punch through the door when she knocked. A loud grunt rose from inside, followed by the lumbering footsteps of a magical who had no idea what was coming for him. The lock turned in the doorknob, then a deadbolt slid aside and the door opened.

"What the—"

She slammed her fist against the door, sending it swinging back against the wall with a bang. Purple sparks flared at her fingertips, and she tossed them at Durg's shoulder to make it clear she meant business.

The door's frame splintered when she slammed it closed behind her. The orc staggered backward, clutching his fried shoulder, and snarled, "You!"

"Well, at least you recognize me." A black orb of crackling energy churned in the palm of her hand, and she stalked across the hallway toward him. "What about the girl you shot and left for dead? You remember her too?"

"What are you, nuts?" Spit flew from Durg's mouth as he stumbled sideways out of the hallway and into the living room. "This is my fucking house! You can't just walk in and—"

"Hey, you answered the door. Now you're gonna answer my questions." Cheyenne launched the energy ball over his shoulder, missing him on purpose. Her magic crashed against the far wall of the living room, taking down a shelf filled with metal knickknacks and books. *I'm gonna make this good.*

Durg ducked anyway and whirled to see the damage before scrambling back into the living room. "What do you *want?*"

"I already told you," she spat. "I'm talking about Ember. In the group of halflings you and your lowlife friends met at the skatepark two weeks ago. You shot her and ran away the minute things got bumpy. *Do you remember?*"

"Yeah, I fucking remember. The goddamn human running around with halflings. Blonde hair. I remember!" He tripped over the edge of the rug beneath his coffee table and managed not to fall on it. "Why do you care so much about that Earthside piece of—"

"She's not a human, Durg. And even if she was, you need to be stopped."

The orc's glowing yellow eyes grew wide, then he lunged for the side table next to the couch. His fingers fumbled at the drawer before he pulled out a handgun and leveled it at her.

With a roar, Cheyenne launched black tendrils of magic from her fingertips and slapped the gun out of his thick, meaty green hands. It clattered to the floor out of his reach, and Durg stepped back against the couch. "What the hell are you doing with a gun? Trying to make up for shooting magical blanks?"

Durg snarled again and summoned a ball of green magic in his hand. "At least I can hit what I'm aiming for at close range."

"Oh, no, I was aiming for your bookshelf." She conjured another black sphere as Durg launched his spell across the living room. The halfling stepped aside and the green spell slowed mid-air, sailing across the room inches at a time. She stormed across the living room until she stood right in front of the orc's outstretched hand, his eyes wide above a snarling grimace and his tongue poking out from between two stained tusks. Batting his arm aside, she pulled her fist back and sent a killer right hook into his beefy jaw.

The world sped up again as she dropped out of drow speed. Green fire hurtled through the house. Durg flew backward over the arm of the couch with a bellow. Beneath his cry of pain and surprise, Cheyenne heard the crunch of his shoulder, dislocated by her little nudge at hyperspeed.

The orc collected himself enough to scramble back across the couch, his left arm dangling at his side before he cradled it against his stomach with another roar. "You weren't even part of it," he growled. "I don't know who you are, and I wasn't gonna try to find out after that night, but now I'm gonna hunt you down like a fucking animal."

Cheyenne grimaced and headed after him as he pushed himself off the couch, spit flying from between his giant tusks. "You just don't have your head on straight, Durg. I beat you to it."

With a last-ditch effort to fight her off, the orc raised his other hand and lit the living room with crackling shards of dark-orange light. The halfling lashed out with her black tendrils from both hands. Half of them pinned Durg's arms to his sides, making him howl in pain when the tendrils jerked his dislocated shoulder. The other half whipped across his face before coiling around his thick neck and tightening. It took everything she had not to clench her fist, draw the whips of her magic even tighter, and break his neck.

Durg let out a strangled croak, his dark-gray tongue darting out from between his huge lips and those nasty-looking tusks.

"See, from what I hear, you're just another thug running around trying to scare the shit out of innocent magicals who made the trip out here. Rough 'em up for 'protection money.' Isn't that what you called it?"

The orc's mouth opened and closed, but only choking gurgles came out.

"Because the ones who *want* to make a life for themselves Earthside are traitors. Right? They gave up on Ambar'ogúl, and you figured you'd follow them out here and make them pay for it. Not too bad if you line your pockets a little or put some halflings in the hospital, huh?"

His eyes bulged, and he managed to croak out one word. "Stop…"

"I'm just getting started." She took a step toward him, taking in every bit of his terrified face as her tendrils tightened around his neck. "You almost killed her, asshole, but you didn't. Right now would be a really good time to pray to whatever O'gúl gods you want that you're half as lucky."

"I…I can't…" The croak that came out of Durg's gaping mouth this time sounded a lot quieter and weaker.

Cheyenne stepped toward him and drew back her fist again, ready for another swing. Before she could follow through, the orc crumpled at her feet, jerking her toward him by the black tendrils connecting her other hand to his neck. The halfling stumbled forward with a grunt and released him from her magic. The tendrils withdrew, and she stepped away from the pile of knocked-out orc lying between the coffee table and the couch. A hiss of disappointment escaped her, and she shook out her hand, her fingers aching from the tight fist she'd made and hadn't gotten the chance to use. The clink of the chains knocking against her wrists was the only sound in the living room above the low hum of *Cops* playing on the TV.

"Shouldn't have squeezed so hard," she muttered, then nudged the orc with the toe of her shoe. "Shit."

Turning away from Durg, the halfling tried to calm her

breathing and decide what she was going to do next. *That was too easy. And not enough.*

She scanned the living room, her drow magic humming through her with every heartbeat. The back of the orc's brown leather couch was covered in woven blankets that looked a lot like what she'd seen being sold at the magical market in Rez 38's Q3. Instead of framed pictures on the wall, the guy had hung long, draping tapestries in dark reds and blues and black. When she caught sight of the tapestry on the wall just above the TV, she froze.

On a blood-red background striped with dirty white was the shape of a bull's head in black. The eyes were red, all the other lines marking the features of the animal's face done in shimmering silver thread. But the shape was unmistakable, even with the three jagged daggers stuck through the center of the bull's head and the slashes at the corners of the tapestry.

Looks like somebody else has a problem with whatever the bull represents. At least he didn't put it on a damn chain around his neck.

She stepped toward the opposite wall and the tapestry over the TV to get a better look at those daggers. The blades were curved in undulating lines, all the more painful when they were ripped out of whatever poor sucker found one buried in his flesh. Cheyenne leaned closer to be sure it was real blood dried like a smear of dirt on one of the blades. *Not just decorative.*

"Huh." Turning around again, she eyed the unconscious Durg and felt a little better when she saw his chest rising and falling slowly. *Okay, I kicked his ass. Now I have something even better.*

CHAPTER TEN

The first thing Durg Br'athol saw when he came to were those glowing golden eyes looming over him. He couldn't see the face they belonged to, because the hissing, sparking ball of black and purple magic drowned it out, but he knew.

He coughed and tried to claw his neck with his left hand, but moving it made him grunt in pain. And that made him cough all over again.

Cheyenne sat back on the couch and lowered her magic toward the cushion so he could see her face. "Have a nice nap?"

"You're fucking crazy." Spit flew from his mouth as he hacked and wheezed and drew in raw, gasping breaths. "Why are you still here?"

"You're alive, aren't you?"

The orc's eyes widened, and he tried to scramble away from her across the floor. The halfling sent a burst of purple sparks into the floor beside his hand as a warning and Durg froze.

"On purpose, okay? Relax."

"Yeah, right."

"Don't get me wrong, Durg. The thought ran through my head and hung out for a while. I don't like you." Cheyenne snuffed out the black energy sizzling in her palm, and the air went still around them. "But I think you might be a lot more useful to me if you're not zipped up in a body bag. Trust me. I know people who do that for a living. They're very good."

"Yeah? I have friends too, drow."

She sucked a breath through her teeth. "Not like mine. My friends have a record of putting your friends in cages, which is where you belong right now." *I just called the FRoE my friends. Ignore the semantics.*

"Then where's my damn cage?" Durg growled.

"We're not there yet. If you tell me what I wanna know, you might be able to stay home a little longer. Nice place, by the way." The halfling took a quick glance around the room. "Minus the spell-burns."

"Fine. I'll tell you whatever you want as long as you keep those damn whips away from my neck."

"We'll see. Tell me about the bull's head."

"What the hell do you—"

Cheyenne's hand darted toward the other side of the living room. Purple sparks burst from her fingertips and struck all three of the daggers buried in the tapestry and the wall behind it. Her magic crackled along the steel handles and the blades before fizzling out. "*That* bull's head. And don't tell me it's nothing. Nobody uses an O'gúl symbol for a dartboard unless there's a lot of bottled-up hostility behind it."

The wounded orc stared up at her from the floor, his eyes wide as he caught his breath and sized up the dark-skinned drow with the wild bone-white hair making herself comfortable on his couch. "For someone who doesn't know what it is, you sure use a lot of phrases from back home."

"I'm a quick learner. Talk."

The orc sneered at her and pushed himself up enough to sit on the floor and snarl at the pain in his dislocated shoulder. "You know how much shit I could bring down on my head just by talking about this?"

"You're already swimming in shit, Durg."

"You couldn't stand up to those assholes even if you knew who they were. I swore I was done with it when I—"

Cheyenne blasted him with another few purple sparks, this time in his good shoulder just to even it out. Then she pulled up another sphere of black magic and shoved it toward his face. "Quit stalling! I'll use this if you don't spit it out already."

"Okay, okay. You're crazy!" The orc leaned away from her crackling magic, his yellow eyes wide again as he let out a nervous hiss. "That fell-damned bull is the insignia for the O'gúl head."

"The what?"

"Guardians of the Crown. Shit, will you take that thing out of my face?"

The halfling withdrew her hand, but she kept the black energy churning in her palm, just in case. "You're gonna have to break it down even further."

He glanced up at her and let out a snorting laugh of surprise. "You been living under a damn rock, drow? The royal guards. That insignia was branded into every shield and weapon and sewn into every patch on their fell-damn—" Durg tried to lift his arm and grunted, freshly reminded of his dislocated shoulder. He lifted his other hand to the same shoulder and tapped it again. "They wore it here. Took their orders directly from the Crown."

Cheyenne frowned. "What are a bunch of royal guards doing Earthside?"

"That's not—" The orc rolled his eyes. "That was me dumbing it down for you, drow. They're not guards, not these days. But their loyalty to the Crown's made them even crazier than they were when the Rís needed real guards. Now they're just screwed-up henchmen. Again, dumbing it down."

When the halfling moved her sphere of black energy slowly closer to his face, Durg hissed. "So, what are they doing *Earthside*?"

"Spreading the Crown's fucking crusade. They've been trying to bring the same shit to this world that's been rotting the heart of Ambar'ogúl for centuries."

"What does that mean?"

"Exactly what I said." Durg licked his spit-covered lips and glanced quickly from her to her threatening black spell and back. "I came over here to get away from all that, just like everyone else. Don't bring me into it."

I'm not gonna get anything else outta this scumbag. Snuffing out her black orb one more time, Cheyenne leaned away from him and pressed her hands into her thighs. "No. I won't bring you into it. But I'll be watching you from here on out, Durg Br'athol. I know you made your crossing in March. That you came off Rez 7. That you apparently didn't start making trouble until you thought all eyes were finally off you and focused somewhere else."

The orc just stared at her, breathing heavily.

She pushed to her feet and loomed over him. "If I want any more information out of you, you'd be even more of an idiot not to give it to me when I ask. 'Cause I know where you live now, too."

Durg just growled at her as she turned away from him, fully intending to step right back through his front door and leave him there to deal with the mess. Then the doorknob turned with a squeak, and the front door swung open.

Before the halfling could turn around and ask if the asshole was expecting friends tonight, a girl stepped through the door. She couldn't have been older than seventeen and was dressed in all black, with more than one ring on each of her fingers. Half of her head was shaved, the hair on the other half falling just below her chin, and if Cheyenne didn't know better, she would've said she was staring at a fifteen-year-old version of herself. The girl closed the door behind her, her pale face with too much makeup lit up by the glow of her cell phone screen. "Uncle Durg. I'm home."

She shoved her phone into the back pocket of her skintight black leather pants, then pulled a ring off her thumb. The air shimmered around her, and the Goth teenager standing in the front hallway was now a green-skinned orc teenager, and the Goth part was extra. "Uncle Durg?"

Cheyenne cocked her head when the girl finally looked into the living room, pocketing the ring as well. The young orc froze, taking in the smashed bookshelf, her rattled uncle on the floor, and the scowling drow standing in her living room. "Uh, what's going on?"

"Hey." The halfling smiled and spread her arms. "Your uncle and I were just having a little chat. Trying to clear up a misunderstanding from a couple of weeks ago."

Durg huffed behind her but didn't argue.

Cheyenne turned again and pointed at him. "You better start behaving, my friend. No more shakedowns, got it?"

He glared at her, his yellow eyes burning.

"Trust me, Durg, I'll know if you try to slide anything by without me noticing. See ya soon." With that, the drow halfling stalked across the living room and raised her eyebrows at the Goth orc who was shooting back the same deadpan stare. The girl stepped aside to give Cheyenne plenty of room to get to the door. Cheyenne swept her gaze over the teenager and nodded. "Looks good on you."

"Uh-huh."

The halfling's gaze landed on the massive metal skull painted black and silver; it dangled at the end of a black satin ribbon tied around the orc's neck. "Nice skull."

"Nice jacket."

Cheyenne jerked her chin at the girl, then opened the door and stepped back out into the crisp September night. The door closed behind her as she reached the bottom of the stairs leading up to the porch. She couldn't help but smirk as she headed back down the dark street with an extra bounce in her step.

"Everything comes with a price." Bianca Summerlin had drilled it into her daughter from the very beginning, and the saying kept popping up in Cheyenne's mind.

Guess the price this time was an epic fight with revenge at the end. Worth it.

She hadn't expected to feel this good about letting Durg off as easily as she had. Maybe that was part of what Bianca had meant. Even revenge had a price, and if she'd paid it, she never would've figured out what those damn bull's-head pendants meant.

CHAPTER ELEVEN

Cheyenne checked her phone as she walked down the hall toward her apartment. *Only ten-thirty. Productive night.* She pulled her keyring from the pocket of her black canvas jacket and stuck the key in the lock. When she opened the door, she almost leaped back out into the hall again.

The copper drow puzzle box had freed itself from her backpack and lay right on the carpet in front of her. *Not where I left you.*

She shut the door quickly, then nudged the box across the floor with her foot. It rolled a little on its edges and came to a stop beside her backpack again. *Corian wants me to haul this thing back across town. Not with a bunch of O'gúleesh loyalists hunting me.*

Rolling her eyes, she kicked off her black Vans and headed back into the hall. Raising both arms high above her head, she gave a massive yawn and shuffled into her bedroom. "Like a Nightstalker knows anything about drow legacies."

The halfling scratched her right shoulder and stopped. With a snort, she pulled the shirt away from her shoulder and ripped off the gauze bandage she'd been wearing all day like an idiot. The gauze and extra tape fluttered to the floor, then she stripped down and climbed into bed with her cell phone, set her alarm, and stuck it on the bedside table. She took one more look at her shoulder, rubbing the smooth, healed skin with a smile. *Best thing that drow bastard ever did for me. Probably won't be able to top it.*

Pushing aside her thoughts of L'zar Verdys, Cheyenne climbed under the sheets and her comforter with the giant skull sprawling across the center and snuggled down. *Finally, a good night's sleep.* She yawned again and buried her head in the pillow.

Another crazy dream filled her head that night, and Cheyenne knew from the beginning it was just a dream. That didn't make it any less vivid or any less terrifying.

She was walking down a cold, dark corridor of black stone. This wasn't anything like the damp walls of the Dungeon at Chateau D'rahl. The stone had been cut and laid with skill and was worn by time. The hallway seemed to stretch on forever until she was suddenly at the end of it, looking into a huge circular room of the same black stone with high, vaulted ceilings. It was even colder.

Blood splattered the black walls everywhere she looked. Every few feet, long, thin, frayed banners spilled down the walls toward the floor. They fluttered in the freezing draft kicking up from all directions. Then the halfling noticed the floor.

It was littered with bodies of all different sizes strewn in the positions they'd been standing in when they'd been struck down. She didn't recognize the clothing—loose, flowing things frayed like the banners and soaked with blood, only the blood on their clothes glistened in the light of the torches blazing around the room. Everybody lying on the floor had the dark, purple-gray skin and the bone-white hair of the drow.

In the center of the bodies knelt a huddled shape draped in black robes. Another drow, judging by the stark white hair falling around the bowed head and the dark ears poking through. When the drow lifted his head and met her gaze, Cheyenne's throat tightened. *L'zar.*

His golden eyes glowed in the darkness, far brighter than the torches sending shadows flicking across the black stone. But the careless half-smile was gone, replaced by a creased brow and a grimace of anguish that didn't look right on her father's face. L'zar stared at her through the curtain of his white hair, a silent cry not yet released from his open mouth.

"I thought I could stop it." His voice echoed around the huge stone room, the torches flickering with each resounding word. "But I wasn't strong enough. Now it's your turn."

Cheyenne jolted out of sleep with a gasp, only to scramble across her bed until her back thumped against the wall. The copper puzzle box hovered near her, emitting rays of golden light. The thing clicked and whirled, each piece of the spastic Rubik's cube spinning wildly in front of her.

The halfling reacted without thinking. Heat bloomed at the base of her spine, and her now-purple-gray hand reached out to snatch the box out of the air. "Leave me alone!"

An orb of black energy flared to life in her other hand, and she clamped it around the puzzle box that was vibrating madly in her palm. The golden light filling her bedroom was muted by a flash of black and purple between her hands, then the legacy box fell still.

Breathing heavily, Cheyenne snarled and dropped the box onto the bed. It rolled a little, stopped, and then one row of those shifting runes etched into the metal slowly turned. The thing let out a soft click, and the outer layer of symbols that had turned flashed one last dim light.

"What the hell?" The halfling pulled her gaze away from the copper box to stare at her drow-dark hands. *Did my magic just turn that thing?*

Her eyes widened, and she lunged across the bed to grab the box and try again. She did everything the same—black spheres of her magic with purple sparks bursting into her hands before she smothered the box again with the spell. There was a dull thump, and purple sparks flew through her fingers across the room, but that was it.

"Fine." Cheyenne tossed the box back onto her comforter. *We both have a limit.* Then she grabbed her phone off the bedside table just as her alarm went off. She snorted. "Right on time."

Once she'd showered, blow-dried her now-black hair, and donned her whole outfit of black on black on black, putting a little more black around her eyes, Cheyenne headed out to the living room. She stopped in the doorway to her bedroom, feeling another little prickle at the back of her neck, and scowled over her shoulder at the drow puzzle box resting on her bed. *Don't move.*

The shower had woken her up, but she still yawned when she stooped beside the kitchen's half-wall to snatch up her backpack and sling it over her shoulder. *More crazy dreams. No wonder L'zar got locked up.*

The image of her drow father kneeling in the center of those drow bodies was pretty hard to shake out of her head. *Might have some truth to it. Like the raug Oracle said, everyone who touched that box is dead. Not this halfling.*

She slipped into her Vans and hesitated before grabbing the doorknob, but nothing from her dream flashed out at her this time, and she was only too happy to get the hell out of her apartment and away from the box. Before she closed the door, she paused to take another sweeping glance across her apartment, then shook her head. *Forget it.*

Cheyenne sat through her classes, and one more time fought not to rip her hair out and claw her eyes with boredom. Just like every Monday. Just like every day of the week. Apparently, showing up on time to every class spared her from the snide remarks and dubious glances from her professors, and the first conversation she had with anyone wasn't until after her last class as she walked across the quad toward the Computer Sciences building.

She shot a skeptical glance at the student message board and the bench halfway across the lawn, where a group of other college students was gathered to check out the new fliers posted there. A guy in a button-down shirt with a messenger bag slung over his shoulder and brown hair hanging over his eyes caught her looking and thought she was interested.

"Hey." He headed toward her, even as she sped up. "We're looking for more people to join the chess club. You interested?"

The halfling glanced at the flyer he waved at her and stopped. Squinting at him, she gestured toward her black clothes and the silver zippers and safety pins studding her shirt, then spread her arms. "Really?"

The guy tossed his shaggy hair out of his eyes and gave her a crooked smile. "Hey, don't judge a book by its cover, right?"

"Probably a good idea with this book." Cheyenne took off down the walkway again, and Mr. Chess Club laughed behind her.

"Okay. The flyers are up if you change your mind. Have a great day!"

This was a normal college. She should've stuck with online classes between chasing down magical scum.

She reached the Computer Sciences building without any more interruptions and found Mattie Bergman's office door wide-open as usual. With a quick knock, Cheyenne stepped into her professor's office and shrugged. "Happy Monday?"

Mattie looked up from the work on her desk and chuckled. "You're saying one thing, but your face says the complete opposite."

"Good to know I'm an open book." The halfling cocked her head. "Second time I've been compared to a book today."

"Well, get ready for one more. A book, I mean. Actually," the professor said, chuckling, "not so much a book as a giant stack of papers. I made copies. I hope you weren't expecting anything fancy."

The woman pulled open the bottom drawer of her desk and

withdrew a huge stack of paper, thumping it down on the edge of her desk. "Just like I promised."

"Woah." Slipping her backpack off, Cheyenne stepped toward the desk and eyed the words printed on the top sheet. "Cheyenne S., huh? Way to keep it top-secret."

"You know what? That's the only way I'd remember what the hell I'm supposed to do with a monster stack like this. Otherwise, I'd have a heart attack, thinking it was a bunch of papers I forgot to grade, and I'd probably end up throwing it in the trash." Mattie looked up at her student and smirked. "It's better than *Collection of Spells and Healing Magic*."

"Fair enough." The halfling slid the papers off the desk and cradled them in one arm while she quickly flipped through. These were spells all right, most of them labeled in a language she didn't know, but they all had drawings of hands doing different things with different fingers. "You brought this across with you from the other side?"

Mattie chuckled and shook her head. "Definitely not. Trust me, the books over there are a *lot* harder to read and even more impossible to pin down without someone holding your hand every step of the way. Maybe literally. I simplified it."

"Oh, yeah. This looks real simple." Cheyenne sighed and shook her head. "You could've pulled out a whole bunch and then tied all this together with a piece of string, at least."

"Please, Cheyenne. You can write me into a box with your programming skills, and you expect me to believe you don't know how to keep a bunch of loose paper together?"

Ignoring the jab, the halfling set the stack on the desk again and flipped through it again for a better look. "Seriously, how is this simplified? All these drawings and diagrams, plus, what? Like, a hundred spells?"

"More. And the recipes for all those healing salves and whatever are in the back."

With a laugh, Cheyenne looked at the copied pages, just now

registering how they'd gotten on the paper. "Did you write all this yourself? And the drawings?"

"I sure did, halfling. Took me damn near a year to get down even that much, and that's just the beginner's guide." Mattie sat back in her office chair and tucked her wavy black hair behind her ear. "That's why you get copies only."

"How much more is there?"

"The advanced stuff? Oh, three or four times as much." The woman laughed when Cheyenne looked at her with wide eyes. "I'll say this much, kid. I had a *lot* of time on my hands when I first came over. And in some weird, naïve burst of inspiration, I thought it would be a good idea to get all this down. Thought I'd find myself some kind of apprentice and make a living that way. Worked out pretty well, huh?"

"You know enough about computer programming to make a living this way, too." Cheyenne picked her backpack up off the floor and propped it on her knee before unzipping the main pocket. "I can't believe you crossed the Border with a bunch of training-with-magic books just so you could rewrite them."

"What? That would've been crazy!" Mattie said with raised eyebrows. She looked more than a little overwhelmed at the thought. "I never would've made it if I'd done that. I copied it all down from up here."

When Cheyenne looked up again, she found the woman tapping her temple with a knowing smile. "Huh. Remind me never to try getting into your head."

"That's not something you can do, is it?" The anxiety in the question made the halfling pause. "No mind-reading on that list of surprise magic you mentioned?"

"Not that I know of." *That's a thing?*

"Right. Good. You know me. Just had to ask." Mattie shrugged and tried to laugh it off, but the fact that she'd asked hung between them.

"Well, if that ever shows up, I'll make sure to tell you before I use it on you."

The professor almost choked and brought a fist to her mouth to clear her throat. "I wouldn't expect anything like that, Cheyenne. There were a very small number of magicals who could work their way into someone else's head before I came here, and I don't think they've been working on cultivating that particular skill since I left."

"Why not?"

"Let's just say it's a lot harder than it sounds. For both parties."

The halfling nodded, staring at the Nightstalker under her human disguise. Then she grabbed the stack of spells again and stuffed it into her backpack as neatly as she could. "Stay away from mind-reading. Got it."

She felt Professor Bergmann's gaze wandering all over her even before the woman opened her mouth.

"Cheyenne." Mattie squinted when the halfling looked at her. "Something's different about you."

It could be anything from the last twenty-four hours. "Like what?"

"I don't know." The woman tipped her head back and frowned. "Just different. What did you get into over the weekend?"

Cheyenne smirked. "We both know you don't want me to answer that."

"No. You're right. Keeping my mouth shut." Mattie mimed zipping her lips and nodded. "Whatever it is, it looks good on you, halfling."

"Thanks. I guess."

The tense silence of ending a conversation they never started returned, then Mattie clapped and plastered on a polite grin. "Well, I guess you're on your own now, learning those spells. That should be enough to get you started, but come back if you have any questions."

"I always do." *Even when she won't answer half of them.* The halfling slung her backpack over her shoulder again but paused before heading across the office. "Actually, I have some questions right now if you still have time for your one and only drow halfling in training."

Sitting back in her chair, Mattie folded her arms. "You know it depends on the questions."

"Yeah, I know, but they are just about magic. I promise."

"Then fire away. Not literally."

With a playful roll of her eyes, Cheyenne readjusted the strap of her backpack and shifted her weight to the other hip. "Based on what little you know about drow in general and drow halflings specifically—"

"Ha, ha."

"How much do drow magic and Nightstalker magic have in common?"

Mattie's lips opened in surprise, and she blinked. "In regards to those spells I gave you? They're accessible to everyone."

"No, I mean inherent abilities. You know, like my purple sparks or something stronger."

"Oh, yeah. The cute ones."

Cheyenne snorted. "Very funny. I mean, if you knew more about all the abilities I have, which may or may not still be on the surprise-magic list, would you say they're like what you can do?"

"Huh. Well, your magic isn't like what an orc or a troll can dish out. Maybe even a faery—"

"A faery?"

Mattie shook her head and gave a dismissive wave. "If there are any of them left. Probably not. But I honestly don't know enough about drow magic to be able to say it's much like anything but drow magic."

Very helpful. The halfling took a deep breath. "Can you move super-fast? Or aim lightning bolts across the ground?"

Her professor raised an eyebrow and eyed her sideways. "What gave you that idea?"

"Just pulling it out of my head. This is all hypothetical."

"Uh-huh." The woman chewed the inside of her bottom lip for a second, still frowning at her student. "For a Nightstalker, and that's all I can speak to when we're talking inherent abilities, that kind of power comes from a lifetime of intense training and honing one's skills. Most of my race don't get that far before they give up and settle for what they can already do."

"Which group do you fall into?"

"That's another question to stick on the 'don't ask again' list, Cheyenne."

The halfling raised her hands in surrender and stepped back. "I get it. Not trying to push. But say you *were* at that level with your magic."

"Uh-huh."

"Would you know enough to train someone else to get to the same place?"

"If I were working with another Nightstalker, kid, I'd only be able to say maybe. There's a lot more to the equation than the level of my powers. Seeing as we're talking about one very specific drow halfling, *hypothetically*, I still don't know."

"Right." Cheyenne sniffed and hiked the strap of her backpack up on her shoulder. *Still no idea if Corian can deliver on his promise.* "Okay. Thanks for not running away from me this time."

Mattie burst out laughing and brought a hand to her forehead. "Is that the first thing that goes through your head every time you come to my office now?"

"Kinda, yeah." With a snicker, the halfling started to turn toward the door again and stopped one more time. *Now that I caught her in a good mood...* "Hey, just for fun. You ever run into any magicals wearing a bull's-head pendant around their—"

"Stop." All the humor had drained from Mattie's face, and she lifted a warning finger without quite pointing it at her student. "*Don't* go down that road, Cheyenne."

"So you know what it is."

"Not trying to push. You tried to get me all loosened up before you brought out your secret weapon of a question, didn't you?" A quick light flashed behind Mattie's glittering green eyes. "Real sly, halfling."

"I'm trying to fit the pieces together—"

"I can't imagine a single scenario where all the different pieces you bring up in my office belong to the same puzzle. Look, I told you to stay away from the FRoE, and you clearly had your own ideas about listening to me, but this is a serious warning. Whatever you think you can find out from whoever you saw wearing those pendants, don't. It's not worth it. And I'm not exaggerating when I say that if I had to choose between the bull's head and the FRoE, I'd pick the FRoE any day of the week."

Cheyenne pressed her lips together and watched Mattie's raised finger tremble almost imperceptibly before the woman dropped her hand. *She's serious.* "Okay."

"Just 'okay?' You're not gonna chase me down and try to pry it out of me?"

The halfling shook her head. "No. I believe you. I was just curious, and now I'll back off."

The professor shook her head. "I'd say I was relieved to hear that if I thought you meant it."

"You can think whatever you want." Cheyenne shrugged and finally headed toward the door. "Don't worry about me, though. Seriously. I'm not trying to hunt those people down or anything." *It's the other way around.*

"You know what? If you keep coming by my office every day, I'll believe you."

"Okay. Thanks for the copy of your book." She shot the woman a thumbs-up as she stepped out of the open doorway, and Mattie returned the gesture with not even half as much enthusiasm. The halfling felt her mentor's eyes on her as she stepped out of view and headed down the hall.

CHAPTER TWELVE

Cheyenne didn't waste any time getting back to her apartment after the strange Monday meeting with Professor Bergmann. As soon as she closed the door behind her, she dropped her backpack by the half-wall and crouched to take out the huge stack of copied spells. She brought the whole thing to her desk, dropped it, then paused and went to take a quick peek through her open bedroom door. The puzzle box was where she'd left it on her bed, no lights, no buzzing, no spinning like a possessed toy. *Don't get paranoid.*

When she returned to her desk, the halfling dropped into her chair and scooted forward to start flipping through the pages one at a time. *An illusion spell would be great. So would a table of contents.*

Sighing, she skimmed the names of the spells at the top of each page, which were fortunately written in English below the language she didn't understand. Cheyenne's hand slammed down on the next page, and she barked out a laugh. "Here it is."

Personal Illusion Charm

Whether the caster intends to bind the illusion to a physical totem or to cast the spell directly with each use, the first working of a personal illusion charm must be branded by ritual with the following items: dridnet hair, bundled darkfire twigs, and a chicken's egg laid two days before.

Cheyenne pulled away from the page and groaned. Maybe R'mahr and Yadje would bump their weekly shopping to Monday.

Shaking her head, she flipped quickly through the other pages, scanning the first paragraphs for the list of ingredients. She'd gone through the first half of Mattie's spell collection before she found just one which didn't need some weird magical ingredient she couldn't even pronounce. Her eyes widened as she looked back at the title of the spell.

Phasing? How does that not need something?

The ability to move one's corporeal form through objects on the physical plane requires a working knowledge of spells typically possessed by the advanced beginner.'

Cheyenne snorted. "Yeah, I'll try this one."

Taking out the sheet of paper with the phasing spell, she stood and walked into the hall outside her bedroom. She closed the door and stared down at the instructions in her hand, clarified by convenient diagrams of bodiless hands and bent fingers making a series of shapes one right after the other. *With arrows and everything.*

Cheyenne copied the first few gestures with her right hand, then grunted in frustration when she realized this was a two-handed spell. Dropping to her knees, she laid the paper on the carpet in front of her and started over. *Got moves one and two. Are those both the left hand?* She squinted at the diagram, shook her head, and kept going. When she finished the final gesture in the epic game of finger-Twister, a spark of pale silver light bloomed around her hands. The halfling tried to sound out the foreign words of the spell that had to be O'gúleesh, stumbling a little over a ridiculously long word in the middle. The silver light flared again around her hands, and she brought both palms slowly toward the door.

Time to phase through shit.

A short tingle flared through her hands when she pressed them against her bedroom door, and then she applied more pressure.

When nothing happened, she closed her eyes and tried to focus. *Just lean into it...*

She felt something give, then a loud snap sounded in the hallway. Cheyenne opened her eyes and sat back on her heels, dropping both hands to her thighs. "I wanted to go *through* the door, not..." The halfling tossed a hand at the massive splinters jutting out of the crack that ran almost all the way to the ceiling. "Not *through* it."

The sheet with directions for a useless phasing spell crumpled in her hand when she snatched it off the carpet. She stopped halfway back to her desk and tried to smooth out the paper with a sigh. *Maybe not advanced beginner. I'll find something else.*

Two hours later, the drow halfling had gone through all the spells she could find in Mattie's starter collection that didn't require magical ingredients. She dropped into her office chair and slapped the last sheet of paper down on her desk. "She should've named these spells *Charred Carpet, Stink Bomb,* and *Pissed-Off Drow.*"

That made her laugh, but only for a second as she took inventory of the damage to her apartment from so many backfired spells. With a sigh, she shoved all the pages together in something like their original order and dropped them into the bottom drawer of her desk. The drawer slammed shut with a bang, and the drow halfling shook her head vigorously. The chains dangling around her wrists jingled when she shook her hands out. *Maybe I'm just not a spell-casting halfling. Maybe I need to figure out my magic first.*

She drew her hands down both sides of her face and let out a little groan. Then she hopped out of her chair and headed for her bedroom again. The door stuck a little in its frame, and she had to shove it open. Once she'd reassured herself the splintered wood wasn't going to fall apart right in front of her, she went to the foot of her bed and scowled at the copper legacy box lying on her comforter.

"This was what you wanted all along, wasn't it?"

The metal trinket didn't offer a reply.

"Fine. We'll try it your way." Cheyenne snatched the puzzle box off the bed and turned it over in her hands. The metal stayed innocuously cool, and no light burst out through the hair-thin runes etched into the sides. Rolling her eyes, the halfling stormed back out of her bedroom and stopped to drop the legacy box into her backpack.

Corian better know as much as he thought he did.

The drow halfling pulled her battered Ford Focus to the curb in front of the address Corian had given her before they'd met in person. Unbuckling her seatbelt, she shut off the engine and grabbed her backpack from the passenger seat. *This thing better not start a disco light show before I get to the basement.*

She locked up and took a quick glance up and down the street. Nothing moved in the darkness punctured by the dim yellow street-lamps, and the two rental houses only had one or two lights on inside. Frowning up at the top floors, Cheyenne headed toward the far-left side of Corian's building, waiting to hear a dozen tires rolling over the asphalt before more idiots wearing bull's-head pendants stepped out of their cars for round two. That sound never came.

The cement stairs were just as dank and creepy as they had been two nights ago, but she moved swiftly down them anyway and stopped to knock on the metal door with the giant D at the top in peeling black paint. The door opened almost immediately, with Corian behind it.

"Not bothering with illusions this time, huh?"

The Nightstalker's catlike, almond-shaped eyes narrowed, the silver pupils flashing in the muted light. "Just like lounging around in my underwear after a long day at the office."

Cheyenne snorted and stepped inside when he moved out of the way to let her enter. "That's an image I don't need."

Corian shrugged, then nodded at her backpack. "Did you bring it?"

"Yeah, I brought it. Not sure how I feel about having that thing on me while I drive all the way across Richmond."

"Not a lot of options unless you've figured out how to teleport inanimate objects."

She blinked at him.

"That was a joke, Cheyenne."

"Uh-huh. Very funny."

"All right. Let's see it, then."

The halfling watched him from the corner of her eye as she went to the cheap folding card table and the two chairs in the unfinished basement. Her backpack went down on the vinyl tabletop with a thump, then she unzipped it and pulled out the puzzle box. "Please tell me this is what you meant. 'Cause it's the only one I have."

The Nightstalker sucked in a breath, the flattened bridge of his feline nose wrinkling. "That's it. Let's get to work."

Corian went to the long metal shelving unit against the back wall and rummaged through the piles of junk on the shelves. Cheyenne stood by the table and set the puzzle box down beside her backpack while she waited. *I'm not touching it more than I have to.*

Items toppled from the shelves and onto the floor as the Nightstalker swept things aside to find whatever he was looking for. He ignored the mess, moving like they were on a deadline. Finally, he turned with a small cardboard box nestled under one arm and brought it to the center of the basement's single large room.

"So…" Cheyenne folded her arms and watched Corian pull out one small white tea candle after another, setting them on the cement floor to form a large circle. "You know any other Night-stalkers on this side of the Border, or are you all pretty solitary?"

"I've had a run-in with one or two. Didn't cross over to make friends with my own kind." Corian finished the circle of white candles and tossed the cardboard box across the floor.

"Ever heard the name Maleshi?"

The Nightstalker jerked his head up and fixed her with those flashing silver eyes. "Where'd you hear that name?"

She shrugged and wrinkled her nose. "Heard it in passing. Slipped out of someone's mouth."

"Fine. Don't tell me." Corian stepped out of the circle of unlit candles and studied his work. "Just don't expect me to buy into that lame excuse. That's not the kind of name that just 'slips out.'"

"You know her, don't you?"

He looked at her sharply again but quickly lowered his gaze toward the candles. "You need to drop all that until you can handle the truth, Cheyenne. Then maybe we'll talk about it."

What I can't handle is people not answering my damn questions. The halfling watched him with a little frown until Corian dusted off his hands and vigorously scratched the back of his head. "And when are you gonna tell me I *can* handle it?"

One pointed ear covered in a tuft of light-brown fur twitched as the Nightstalker rubbed his jaw. "That starts with the *Cuil Ani*. When you've figured it out and finished what you started, I'd say you're ready."

"I didn't start anything—"

"Right. And I'm just wearing a cat suit. Now pick that thing up and come stand over here." Corian pointed to the floor beside him.

With a sigh, Cheyenne snatched the puzzle box off the table and brought it with her to take her place. "Now what?"

"No talking for the next minute. You think you can do that?"

First time I've been told I talk too much. The halfling stared at him and waited for Corian to see her sarcastic glare, but his focus was somewhere else.

The Nightstalker stretched out his arms, then pushed up his sleeves to reveal a thin coat of light fur running down his forearms. Exhaling, Corian twisted one hand in a quick series of precise gestures, each flowing into the next. Every candle in the circle burst to life, and he rolled his shoulders back to get ready for something else.

A spell that doesn't have a whole grocery list.

When Corian closed his eyes and slowed his breathing, an electric current rippled through the air away from his body. Cheyenne felt it prickle her skin and whisper into her ears. Then she picked up the faint sound of rushing water from across the room. The Nightstalker lifted both hands, palms facing the floor, and slowly curled his fingers into tight fists. A sphere of dark light bloomed in the air at the center of the circle of candles, steadily expanding as the air inside the circle shimmered.

In seconds, the dark sphere had grown and elongated into a huge oval stretching almost all the way to the ceiling. The halfling blinked and leaned forward. Inside the oval, she saw an open field of moonlit grass, plus pine trees scattered among yellow poplar and black cherry trees. "Is that…"

"You're nowhere close to conjuring portals, kid. After you." The Nightstalker nodded toward the oval doorway leading who knew where and waited for Cheyenne to do what she was told. "Make sure you step *over* the candles. I don't wanna have to clean up the mess before we even get a chance to start."

"Right." She clutched the copper puzzle box in both hands and took a slow step over the closest flickering candle into the circle. Another burst of charged energy flowed through her, and her black hair fluttered around her face in the sudden cool breeze. *Just like that. Right through an actual portal.*

Gritting her teeth, she took one more step toward the dark, shimmering light of the oval doorway and forced herself not to look back at Corian before she walked through to the other side.

CHAPTER THIRTEEN

The burning zap of the passage lasted a fraction of a second before Cheyenne was all the way through. With a sharp breath, she gasped at the star-studded sky and took in the scent of fresh earth and crushed leaves and a body of water not too far away. *Smells like home.*

A bright flash rose behind her, casting her shadow across the damp grass of the clearing before it winked out again. The halfling turned and found Corian staring up at the sky too. His nose twitched. "I always knew this place would be good for something."

"Uh, where's the portal?"

"Don't worry about it. We're anchored to the other side, or at least I am. Don't run off through the woods unless you wanna take the long way back."

"I don't even know where we are."

Corian waved her off and stepped farther out into the meadow. "Doesn't matter. The important thing is that we're here. And it's safe, which is a lot more than I can say about the basement."

Moving silently across the grass after him, Cheyenne swept her gaze across the clearing and searched for anything moving through the trees, just in case. When she glanced back over her shoulder, the portal was still closed. *He better teach me that trick, too.*

"All right. Bring it over here and set it down." The Nightstalker waved her forward, nodding absently at the grass in front of him.

"There something special about this place?" She raised an eyebrow and moved slowly toward him. "'Cause I just met you, and it's a little weird that you took me out to the middle of nowhere at night without an explanation."

"Right. I saved your ass on the front lawn two nights ago just so I could kidnap you tonight and steal a drow *Cuil Aní* I couldn't use if I jumped into a spawning pool."

The halfling gave him a blank stare.

"We need a lot of open space for this, Cheyenne. Without witnesses. Or casualties."

"What?"

He pointed at the grass again and winced when she tossed the legacy box onto the ground.

"It's been through worse."

Shaking his head, the Nightstalker ran a fur-covered hand over what looked more like a mane than hair and sighed heavily. "Here's the deal. As a drow, even a halfling, you have certain abilities inherent to your race. Some of them you've figured out pretty well on your own."

The halfling folded her arms. "Yeah, relatively."

"But that's just the surface, kid. There is more power running through your veins than you can imagine right now. The rest of it has to be unlocked, bit by bit, like making it to the next level in a videogame. You've played plenty of videogames, right?"

"Not really."

He shot her a sideways glance and pursed his lips. "Yeah, but you get the point. With enough focus and enough time spent training with each new ability, you will eventually master one and move on to the next. Then, when you get through every part of your magic that needs to be understood and controlled, the metal box you just tossed aside will know. All the different layers will slide into play one by one, and when you've fully embraced everything you were meant to do, it'll open. *That's* your true legacy."

Licking her lips, Cheyenne glanced down at the copper artifact in the grass and frowned. "What's in the box?"

Corian sighed. "You wouldn't be able to handle it now. Just focus on the present, yeah? It's the only way to get where you need to be."

"That's awfully Zen of you."

"Nothing wrong with a little Zen. You might wanna try it if you want to get through the trials and solve the puzzle box."

The halfling tilted her head. "Trials?"

"Don't get ahead of yourself. So, tell me. You pull out any new types of magic lately without being able to control it?"

She almost burst out laughing. "You could say that. I had a bunch of black flames burst out of my skin the other day. And a shitload of power I didn't get to use."

"That's something we should hold off on unless it's the only thing you've noticed." Corian wrinkled his nose. "Then we might be in trouble. Anything else?"

"A shield." Cheyenne shrugged. "Black energy forcefield or something."

"Go on."

Sighing, she went back across the grass and shook out her hands, the coiled chains around her wrists clanking. "That's basically it. I've conjured it a handful of times. You know, to *save* people."

"Yes, Cheyenne. I know what a shield is."

She shot him a sarcastic glare. "But it's a knee-jerk reaction, I guess. I can't bring it up on command. Believe me, I've tried."

"Well, it's a start, I guess." Cocking his head, the Nightstalker looked down at the thick silver ring on his thumb, which had a thick raised circle welded to the band. "Good thing you found me before you killed yourself trying to use the black flames if you ever managed to conjure them again."

"You can't kill yourself with your own magic." The halfling blinked. "Can you?"

"The list of what one can do with their magic is long. Maybe even endless, once you've mastered the abilities you were born to manifest. But trying to use a certain power without being fully prepared for it, without knowing what it might do or how much it might take out of you? Don't tell me you've never pushed your magic too hard and worn yourself out."

"Once or twice." *At drow speed.*

"Well, then. Take that experience and multiply it by a thousand. Chances are the answer to the equation is death. Most of the time." Corian pressed down on the top of the metal circle in his ring, and a thin lid flipped open to reveal a ridiculously tiny compartment. He removed something just as tiny, closed the silver lid again, and offered it to the halfling in his open palm. "Here."

Cheyenne stared at the glowing purple bead, which was a little bigger than a grain of rice. "What is it?"

"A seed from the Nimlothar." When she gave him another blank look, he frowned and stared down at the seed. "I keep forgetting you don't know anything."

"Okay, wait a minute—"

"About *this*, Cheyenne. Correct me if I'm wrong, but I believe I'm the first and only person so far, magical or otherwise, to give you anywhere near this much information about your drow heritage or your legacy or *who you are*. Right?"

The halfling nodded once. "Pretty much."

"So, don't take it personally when I say you don't know anything. Anyone who's insulted by the truth isn't ready for it. The Nimlothar is an O'gúleesh tree that used to grow…oh, just about everywhere, as I remember it." Corian blinked down at the seed, sounding sentimental beneath his curt instruction. "The life energy of the Nimlothar is more directly linked to drow magic than any other. Don't ask me why. That's just the way it's always been."

"And they don't grow there anymore." When the Nightstalker just closed his eyes, Cheyenne had to keep pressing. "What happened?"

"They were cut down. Plenty of drow in Ambar'ogúl still going through their legacy trials and using a Nimlothar seed, but it's regulated now."

She snorted. "I have a hard time picturing anyone who'd want to regulate a bunch of drow mastering their magic while they try not to blow everything up."

Corian's lips twitched, but he didn't quite smile. "Yes, I'm sure it's hard to imagine much of anything from that world when you've never stepped foot across the Border and only just discovered its name."

"Hey, at least I'm trying." The halfling folded her arms, and Corian closed his fist around the glowing purple seed before dropping his hand back down by his side.

"The order to raze whole forests of Nimlothar came straight from the O'gúl Crown a few hundred years ago. *That's* who'd want to regulate and oversee the drow legacy trials. They still happen, of course, but I've heard the drow in Ambar'ogúl have a much harder time controlling their magic with the Crown breathing down their neck. There's very little room for inherent mastery when a monarch tells you when and how to do what can only be commanded from here." He knocked his closed fist against his chest right over his heart. "The only remaining Nimlothar I know of grows in the courtyard at the center of the O'gúl Crown's great hall. Not the kind of place you wanna find yourself in these days."

"And you just waltzed in there to take a seed from the last drow tree?" Cheyenne cocked her head. "For me?"

"What? I've only crossed the Border once, Cheyenne, and I don't know when or if I'll be going back. I took this seed with me when I left. And yes, I've been saving it for you this whole time."

She studied the Nightstalker's impassive expression, then dropped her gaze to his fist. *He came Earthside before I was born.* "That doesn't make sense."

"I'm here to help you with *your* magic, not to talk about my personal timeline. Maybe another day."

"Okay..."

Corian stretched his fist toward her again, opened his hand, and nodded at the seed. "Go ahead."

A little zap of tingling energy shot through the halfling's fingers when she plucked the glowing Nimlothar seed from his palm. *Like my fingers fell asleep.*

The Nightstalker's flashing silver eyes moved from the seed to Cheyenne's face and back again. "Down the hatch."

She snorted. "Sorry. I thought I just heard you tell me to swallow this thing."

"We both know there's nothing wrong with your hearing."

Blinking around the meadow in disbelief, the halfling let out a dry, sharp laugh. "I'm not about to eat some magical seed from the other side of the Border just because you say so. If that's even what this is. And you can't be sure it'll do what it's supposed to do on *this* side."

"This is how it's done in Ambar'ogúl, kid, and a drow legacy doesn't care what world you're on. Obviously, it found you here. Eat the seed."

Scowling at the tiny glowing thing between her fingers, the halfling mumbled, "If I get some kinda O'gúleesh food poisoning—"

"I brought us through a portal, Cheyenne. Not into a time loop. Don't waste it."

She gazed at the stars in the black sky and slowly opened her mouth. The seed didn't taste like anything, warm from her hand before she dry-swallowed it with a grimace. The next second, a much stronger tingle bloomed in her stomach. She swallowed again and hunched forward, her eyes watering. *Don't puke.*

The tingling energy bloomed through her, shooting down her limbs and through her chest and all the way to the tips of her ears. Cheyenne lifted her hand to try rubbing the odd sensation out of one ear and felt the sharp, cartilage-hardened point beneath her fingers. She jerked her hand down and saw purple-gray flesh instead of pale skin glowing in the moonlight. "What the…"

"I'm pretty sure that's supposed to happen."

"*Pretty* sure?" She stared at Corian with wide eyes. "I thought this was supposed to help me *control* my magic, not shove me aside so a stupid seed can take the wheel."

"I've never seen a halfling go through the trials, and obviously, the drow I *have* seen don't have a second form to take." The Night-stalker spread his arms. "But with a boost from an ancient Nimlothar tied directly to the power flowing through your veins, kid, why are you this surprised?"

Sucking in a deep breath, Cheyenne closed her eyes and reached out with her awareness toward the woods encircling the meadow. *Better than a memory. This better work.*

When she opened her eyes, she let out a relieved sigh and turned her human-white hand back and forth, just to be sure. Then she let the heat of her drow magic take over again and slipped into her drow form. She thought she'd gotten a handle on it before, but it was a hell of a lot easier this time. With a nod at Corian, the halfling shook out her hands one more time and bounced on her toes. "Okay. Let's do this."

CHAPTER FOURTEEN

"Any more tests you wanna run before we get started?" Corian's feline face wrinkled in disapproval. His silver eyes glinted in the moonlight as he looked the drow halfling up and down.

"No, I'm good."

"Great. Close your eyes again."

She did, letting a slow breath hiss through her tight lips as the tingling from the seed in her stomach grew stronger again.

"We'll start with the shield. See it in your mind's eye. Remember what you felt right before you summoned it. If you can, remember what you felt when you saw its shape appearing right where you wanted it to be. Then hold onto that and focus on lifting the shield around yourself first."

"You're not gonna start attacking me, are you?" she muttered through a tiny smirk.

"Just pull up the shield, Cheyenne."

With another deep breath, the half-drow tried to ignore the tingle in her belly that was quickly growing into full-on indigestion. *Forget the seed. You need a shield.*

Her fingertips tingled again, sharp pieces of it shooting up her arms like an electrical current. The burn rose from her stomach to her throat this time, searing its way up and out of her in a giant belch that rolled across the meadow. Cheyenne's eyes flew open just in time to see the purple, glittering light bursting from her gaping mouth. Her hands only made it halfway to her lips before the light and the belch disappeared, and she froze.

Corian stepped back and covered his laugh with a quick cough. "Haven't seen that before."

"You're not helping."

"And you're not trying. You ate something from another world, only half of you is equipped to handle it, and then you burped." The Nightstalker cleared his throat, his fur-tipped ears twitching as he wiped the smile off his lips with his hand. Then he folded his arms. "Back to the shield."

She glared at him, then closed her eyes and started all over again. Her body still hummed with all the extra energy from the Nimlothar seed, but it had settled down into something much more manageable. *Maybe Peridosh has some magical Pepto-Bismol...*

"Remember how it felt to use it, kid. Remember how you felt to see it done. Bring that into this right now."

Corian's words were suddenly the only thing she could hear as her mind flew through the memories of only two, maybe three times she'd conjured the black, shimmering shield of drow magic. *I don't need to be hypnotized.*

She only noticed there had been a small, gentle breeze rolling across the meadow and ruffling her bone-white hair when it suddenly stopped. Cheyenne slowly opened her eyes and found herself staring at the Nightstalker's distorted outline, his features, the meadow, and woods around them muted by a dark light shimmering in front of her. Blinking, the halfling leaned back and flicked the wall of black energy she'd conjured right in front of her face. A dull, metallic ping echoed off the drow shield. "I did it."

"There's a first for everything." With his arms still folded, Corian took a step back and nodded. "Now get rid of it."

"Ha!" She slapped the shield one more time, and it gave a much louder, thicker clang. *Yeah, that's real.* "All right. Level one accessed."

When she tossed her hand like she was brushing crumbs off a table, the shield disappeared like a thin wisp of black smoke.

Corian grunted. "Looks like dropping your spells is the easiest part for you, huh?"

"I've had a lifetime of trying to shove it all back down where no one can see. So, yeah. That part feels pretty natural."

"People usually don't pay much attention to that side of the coin. They're a lot more focused on how to make an impression with all kinds of flashy abilities." The Nightstalker stroked his chin and gave her another appraising look from head to toe.

"You can make an impression by doing the exact opposite, too." *Another of Mom's lessons.*

"Indeed. How confident are you with using the magic you think you've *already* mastered?" Slowly, Corian moved without a sound across the grass in a wide circle around the drow halfling. "In a fight, I mean. When you're caught up in the heat of battle and have to think on your feet."

"Pretty confident." Cheyenne followed him with her eyes until he'd circled out of her view. But she felt him behind her, moving slowly around toward her other side. *And I can hear those footsteps.* When they stopped, the halfling summoned an orb of crackling black energy and held it there at her side.

The Nightstalker started walking again, and then he reappeared in her peripheral vision, his hands clasped behind his back. "Good to hear. I think it's to your advantage that the ability you're working on now is what it is. Defensive magic is just as important."

"Not if I'm faster than the other guy."

"You might have been so far." Corian just kept walking in the slow circle, staring at the grass as he passed in front of her one more time. "But it won't always be the case."

"Okay, show me *one*—"

The Nightstalker's hand shot out so quickly, she didn't see him move—just the silver streak of light hurtling toward her before it crashed into her shoulder and spun her sideways.

"Hey! I just got that healed."

"That shouldn't be a problem." He shot another bolt of lightning-like magic toward her chest this time.

Cheyenne activated her drow speed and stepped to the side as the Nightstalker's spell crackled past her, reaching out with wavering branches of light pretty much just like lightning. Then she dropped back into normal speed and spread her arms. Shadows danced behind her as Corian's attack flew across the meadow into the darkness on the other side. "I thought you said you weren't gonna start attacking me?"

"No, I told you to focus on your shield," he snarled. "You need to *listen*."

Two more bolts of silver light pierced the air between them.

The halfling moved with enhanced speed one more time to avoid them both, and Corian laughed. She whipped her head toward him as his magical attack moved in slow motion past her.

He just spread his arms and shot her a crooked smile, his elongated teeth flashing like fangs in the moonlight. "See? You're not always faster than the other guy."

Shit.

CHAPTER FIFTEEN

The Nightstalker's next crackling silver attack hurtled toward Cheyenne before the last two he'd thrown had fully passed her in their suspended motion. She tried to duck out of the way and hurl her sphere of black energy at Corian's face, but she wasn't fast enough. The lightning bolt caught her in the left shoulder this time and sent her spinning. The halfling shouted in pain and frustration as her knees hit the cold, damp grass. It knocked her out of her drow speed, the two silver attacks she'd dodged whizzed behind her into the woods, and the Nightstalker's low laughter rang out again.

She jerked her head up to glare at him and rubbed her burning shoulder. Corian's sharp teeth glinted in the moonlight as he prowled back and forth in front of her, chuckling. With his head ducked low like that and his fur-tufted ears twitching above silver eyes, he looked a lot less like a man and way more like a wild animal. *Like he wants to eat me.*

With a grunt, Cheyenne pushed to her feet. "That's not fair."

"Who's gonna fight fair, Cheyenne?" His voice burst across the meadow as he spread his hands. "This is how you learn. This is how you seize your—"

She hurled another black sphere of churning magic at his head, followed by a second. The Nightstalker jerked his head to the side and avoided the first completely. The second he caught in his outstretched hand with his magic. Purple and black light lit up his face, the fur on his cheeks and temples ruffling in the breeze. Then he pressed his other hand against her spell and shrank the black-and-purple orb until it disappeared between his clasped palms.

"You're not listening, and you're not staying on task." He tossed a small object toward her, which glinted under the stars before she snatched it out of the air.

Cheyenne scowled at the four-pointed metal star, then chucked it into the grass. *Nightstalker trick. Not just Mattie's.*

"I told you to focus on your shield. Bring it up when you run out of options, or I'll end up dragging deep-fried drow halfling back through the portal when we're finished."

Cheyenne snarled and dropped into a defensive crouch, clenching her fists. "Fine."

"Fine." Corian grinned and threw another silver bolt right at her.

She burst into drow speed to leap out of the way and was ready for him to join her there. The black tendrils shot from her outstretched hand and lashed out at the Nightstalker's face before coiling around his wrist and forearm. She didn't have the chance to jerk his hand aside. He beat her to it and spun away from her, yanking on her drow whips with his forearm and ripping her off her feet through the plane of enhanced speed.

As she lurched through the air, Cheyenne threw out her hand. *Pull up the damn shield!* Nothing happened, and one more Night-stalker lightning bolt burst across her right hip and the freshly healed bullet wound. Her scream cut off as she crashed and slid across the grass, but she twisted around and summoned another black sphere of magic to toss at Corian's head. He jerked her toward him again, with her lashing black tendrils still coiled around his forearm. The halfling's spell went wild, arcing up toward the night sky instead, and before she could lift her hand again, another silver streak slammed into her chest.

It knocked the air out of her lungs. The black tendrils wilted and dropped from around the Nightstalker's arm before withdrawing into her fingertips. Her next breath seared into her lungs, and she coughed, gasping for another.

"Get up," Corian growled. "Walk it off."

Easy for him to say.

With a growl of her own, Cheyenne pushed to her feet, her chest heaving. They circled each other on the dew-studded grass, silver eyes locked onto gold. This time, when Corian unleashed another bolt of silver, she raised her hand fast enough and locked onto something—another sharp burst of heat beneath her skin, a tightness in the air. Shimmering black light bloomed in front of her. Only half-formed, the shield was large enough to deflect the silver lightning crashing against it and rang like a gong struck over a radio full of static.

Then the ground lit up beneath her feet, and Cheyenne's eyes widened.

Silver light snaked toward her faster than she could react. In less than a second, the Nightstalker's magic crackling across the ground struck her feet and shot up her calves, blasting her backward across the air. *A shield!*

The halfling's back slammed into the ground. She skidded across the grass with a groan, then pushed herself up and tried to shake off the electric jolt. "Okay…"

Doubling over, she lifted a hand toward her new Nightstalker mentor and shook her head.

"Okay, I just need a second."

"That's not gonna work on the battlefield." Corian stalked toward her. "Not with the scent of death in the air and your blood boiling inside you."

"Come on, just let me—"

He struck her with another silver bolt just below the collarbone.

"Ow! Damnit, Corian. Give me two—" She staggered backward, but his next attack hit her in the upper thigh. She stumbled and managed to regain her balance as she flung out a hand, trying to find the pressure in the air again for a goddamn shield.

The Nightstalker relentlessly pressed on, and Cheyenne got maybe two inches of a shield up before he sent another blinding silver attack toward her shoulder again.

The drow halfling roared and turned back to face him again head-on. "*I said, stop!*"

The ground erupted in front of her, spraying clumps of grass and soil as thick shards of rocky pillars burst through the surface at an upward angle, all of them pointed at Corian. A spiderweb of thick cracks shattered across the trembling earth, scattering away from Cheyenne in every direction. The Nightstalker stumbled backward and was knocked off his feet when a second and then a third wave of stone shoved up from below the surface. Trees groaned and snapped behind her, felling each other like dominoes where the splintered earth had already uprooted them and done most of the work.

Cheyenne dropped her hands against her thighs, panting, and stared at the destruction her newest drow ability had caused. The rumbling chaos below the surface faded away, trees rustled against each other with the occasional snap, and then everything fell still again.

Surprise magic. Holy shit.

Corian cleared his throat and pushed himself to his knees, brushing the dirt and grass off his clothes. He took one more quick assessment of what she'd just done and scowled. "We have a lot of work to do."

She gestured at the upturned earth. "Looks like an improvement to me."

"Not when you were supposed to be summoning a shield."

Behind him, the copper puzzle box lifted slowly into the air, the golden light shining through all the etched runes. Then the different pieces spun wildly in every direction, letting out a low whir and hum. Corian turned to eye the legacy box.

Cheyenne stuck her hands on her hips. "Yeah, that's been happening a lot."

With a sigh, the Nightstalker turned away from her and stormed across the grass toward the floating copper box. "You should've started training for this when you could use any of your magic."

The halfling started after him. "When I was *eight?*"

"Gotta start sometime, right?" Corian stopped beside the floating box and cocked his head. "You're not focusing enough on *why* you want to master your magic, Cheyenne."

"Right, like you have any idea what I want."

"I don't need to know *what* you want. Just that you haven't figured out what it is yet, and that's why your magic is still all over the place this late in the game." He raised an eyebrow at her and pointed at the box. "That's what this means."

The half-drow rubbed her aching, lightning-struck shoulder and stopped on the other side of her floating legacy, the golden glow lighting up her dark elf features. "I know what I want."

"Oh, sure. The halfling who didn't have a clue about what this was and who'd never heard of a Nimlothar suddenly knows more than the ancient magic running through her veins and the trials every drow has mastered for more centuries than you can imagine." The Nightstalker shot her a sarcastic grimace. "That makes perfect—"

A sharp crack echoed across the darkened meadow behind them, halfway between the closest line of trees and where they stood beside the floating box. Both magicals turned to see a dark, shimmering circle of black light open in mid-air.

"You open another portal?"

Corian licked his lips. "That's not mine."

"If you know whose it is, now's a good time to share."

"Get the box." The Nightstalker pointed at her floating legacy and stepped back across the grass, away from the new portal, which was growing larger by the second. "We're calling it a night, kid. And I need time to put up better wards."

"Okay, see, this is the part where I *know* you're not telling me something important."

"Grab the damn box, Cheyenne!" More trees snapped and

groaned behind the new portal, bending toward the darkness spreading in mid-air.

She had to push herself up on her tiptoes before she could snatch the spinning box from the air. The glow went out, and the different sections stopped spinning. "What's going on?"

"Quiet. I need to focus." Closing his eyes, Corian took a deep breath and lifted his hands as if he held a basketball between them.

A harsh, hissing whisper floated out of the opening portal, chanting in a language Cheyenne didn't understand. It made the hair on the back of her neck stand on end, and her entire body erupted with a sharp, buzzing tingle. *Someone else is watching me this time.*

She glanced at the Nightstalker, who hadn't done anything but stand there with his hands raised. "Can't you center your chi some other time?"

"Shut up," he hissed through his teeth, then his fingers moved quickly in a long series of gestures with sharp, short pauses between.

An angry gust of wind picked up, blasting at them out of the portal as the whispered chanting grew louder. Purple light crackled and danced at the dark edges of the air, which was now half the size of a regular door. "You might wanna—ah!"

The halfling's head erupted with agonizing, stabbing pain. A face flashed before her and drowned out everything else—endlessly wrinkled, sallow skin studded with dots and lines of fading black ink; white, all-seeing eyes; a mouth with its few teeth and everything else inside it stained a dark, blood-red.

"The endless search for an heir will bring each one of them to death's door."

The crone's face disappeared, replaced by the image of L'zar Verdys kneeling in the cold black room surrounded by more than a dozen drow bodies.

"Now it's your turn."

The portal flashed black light again. Cheyenne didn't know she'd fallen to her knees until Corian grabbed her arm and pulled her roughly to her feet. Somehow, she held onto the legacy box.

"Time to move!" The Nightstalker jerked her away from the flashing portal and the chanting whispers, which had now become a constant roar.

The halfling stumbled behind him toward the new portal he'd opened. *My head's gonna split open.*

She recognized the cement floor of the basement in apartment D just before Corian yanked her through. Behind them, the ground trembled, half the trees behind the freaky black portal snapped in half or were ripped from the ground by the roots, and a low, demonic laugh echoed through the meadow.

CHAPTER SIXTEEN

The cement floor was a lot harder than grass when Cheyenne fell to her knees again. Corian's portal disappeared with a little pop, cutting off the insane laughter pounding through her head. The puzzle box bounced and skittered across the floor with a metallic ping.

"What the hell was that?" She braced herself on all fours, blinking away the pain until she saw two of her purple-gray hands again instead of four.

"A close call. That's what it was. Too close." The Nightstalker stooped beside the circle of white candles, the flames already snuffed out, and swept them all aside toward the empty cardboard box and the metal shelves.

"Yeah, I picked up on that part." Slowly, the halfling pushed herself up onto her knees and sat back on her heels. "I'm talking about the other portal. And the voice."

"I thought we had more time." Corian leaped to his feet and returned to the shelves, rummaging around in all the piled junk again while everything he didn't want clattered to the floor.

"Who tried to open the portal?" She watched him moving

quickly down the shelves. "The voice was inside my head. What did they want?"

The Nightstalker lifted a shiny black lump of charred wood and shrugged.

"Corian!"

He spun toward her, silver eyes flashing. "There are certain forces that *don't* want you to succeed with this, Cheyenne. Now that you've started the trial, those forces will find it a lot easier to hunt you down. We have to be careful."

Dropping to the floor again, the Nightstalker started scribbling a bunch of symbols with the charred wood, his hand moving in large circles.

"Hunt me down? Are you serious?"

Corian hissed in frustration, focusing on his drawing. "It wouldn't be this way if your father were around to help, so we just have to make do with what we've got."

"My father?" The halfling let out a sharp, bitter laugh. "I met L'zar, and he's not a very helpful guy."

The charred wood clattered to the floor, and the Nightstalker jerked his head up to stare at her, his tufted ears twitching. "You've spoken to him?"

"In person. It was seriously underwhelming."

He looked her over, and a small smile twitched at the corner of his mouth. "Can you get back in there again?"

"Yeah." Cheyenne grimaced. "But I still haven't decided if I want to—"

"You want to, kid. Trust me." Corian surveyed his work on the floor, then stood and brushed off his hands. "Get another visit with L'zar and tell him we've started. He'll be able to give you pointers on how to fast-track the trial so you can open the box as soon as possible."

"He didn't answer any of my questions the first time." Cheyenne pushed to her feet and swayed a little. "I don't think much has changed for him since yesterday morning."

"But it's changed for you, Cheyenne, and that means things have changed for L'zar."

She snorted. "The guy's locked up in a cage."

"By choice." Corian walked quickly across the basement and picked the copper legacy box up off the floor. Then he held it out to her and nodded. "Your father wants you to master the trial and claim your legacy as much as you do. Maybe even more."

"Right."

"L'zar doesn't give anything away for free, Cheyenne. But if you tell him we've already started and we need to speed up the process, he'll tell you what you need to know."

The halfling's nostrils flared as she stared at the Nightstalker. "Because there's something in it for him."

"Yes. At this point, kid, what's good for one of you is good for both of you. Set up another meeting. I'll make sure we're more prepared on this end next time."

Great. Everyone's giving me secret missions with L'zar.

She snatched the box from Corian's hand and went back to the card table to jam the thing back into her backpack. Then she slung the thing over her shoulder and grimaced. "You really beat me up out there, you know?"

The Nightstalker smirked. "Everybody gets their ass kicked sometimes, kid. That's how we learn."

"Oh, yeah? When was the last time someone kicked *your* ass?"

"Been a long time."

"Yeah, I bet." She looked him over from head to toe and slipped her other arm through the second backpack strap. "Don't worry. That'll change."

Corian chuckled as she headed toward the door, shaking his head as he knelt by his charcoal drawing on the floor and got back to work.

The halfling paused by the metal door out of the basement and turned back over her shoulder. "Did you know you'd give the Nimlothar seed to me the whole time you kept it in the ring?"

He looked slowly back up at her. The small smile looked a lot less predatory on his feline face. "No. Just that I'd be forcing it down some young drow's throat to help them with their trials. But I'm glad it's you."

"Yeah, me too. Thanks for being there to kick my ass."

Corian dipped his head. "Any time."

Cheyenne turned quickly around and jerked open the metal door. It shut behind her with a bang, and then her black Vans were crunching over the dried leaves in the stairwell and up the damp cement steps. She sighed, then she slipped quickly out of her drow form as she reached the top of the stairs. "Everybody wants something," she said aloud.

A pile of leaves rustled in the grass beside her, then a head the size of a navel orange, covered in a bright shock of ruby-red hair, burst from the top of the pile. "That's when you know you've got more bargaining chips."

The three-foot-tall man—he was orange—sitting under all the leaves lifted his hand and brought a huge pinecone to his mouth before taking a quick, crunching bite out of it like it was an apple.

The halfling narrowed her eyes at him. "Weren't you at the landfill?"

"What? Me? No way. My palate's way more refined than that." The pinecone crunched around in his mouth, sharp crumbs spilling back into the pile of leaves around him. "I'm into *compostable* trash."

She fought back a laugh. "I wouldn't call pinecones trash."

"Yeah, tell it to the trees." The man raised a grubby finger and pointed behind him at the row of pine trees between the rental houses.

Wrinkling her nose, Cheyenne nodded at the little guy and almost laughed again. "You got a name?"

The guy shrugged, closed his beady eyes, popped the last bit of pinecone into his mouth, and buried himself in the pile of leaves again.

Can't keep calling them trash-eaters. With a snort, she headed for her car parked at the curb, searching the empty street just in case. *He's right, though. Bargaining chips with both sides now. Sir and Corian.*

When I find some kinda leverage with L'zar, I'll really have the upper hand.

When she slid behind the wheel of her Focus and dropped her backpack on the passenger seat, a huge yawn broke free. Cheyenne shook her head quickly, wiped the one tear squeezing out of her eye, and started the car. *Can't sleep yet.*

She buckled up and turned on the radio. The beginning of Metallica's *Enter Sandman* filled the car, and she turned the volume up as loud as it would go before heading back to her apartment.

Her black Vans thumped against the hall closet by the front door, and Cheyenne shuffled through her apartment. Her keyring hit the counter on the half-wall with a clink, and her backpack slid off her shoulder onto the floor. Rolling her neck from side to side, the halfling grimaced and rubbed her chest just below her collarbone. *Man, he really got me.*

She unzipped her jacket and paused when a muffled buzz came from one of the outside pockets. Rolling her eyes, she jammed her hand in there and pulled out the FRoE burner phone. "There better be a good reason you're calling me after midnight on a Monday."

"Well, I didn't call just to shoot the shit, halfling." Sir cleared his throat on the other line. "How you doin'?"

"Peachy. Best day of my life."

"Okay, don't break into song or anything. Heads-up about our next op. Tomorrow."

"Sure. I'm free after lunch."

"Nope. You'll be meeting up with a team at oh-eight-hundred. Time-sensitive thing, kid. I know you're trying to have a life and everything, but this needs to happen ASAP, and ASAP means whenever I say we're ready to go."

Cheyenne took a deep breath and forced her fingers to loosen up around the flip phone. "I can't keep missing class—"

"Yeah, you can. Leave a paper trail that says you showed up.

That'll be a cakewalk for you. What we're doing is way more important. We're going after the second distribution center for the black-magic crap still spreading through the state like goddamn wildfire."

With a sigh, the halfling closed her eyes. "Fine. I'll be there. I assume you'll text me another address."

"Look at that—you're learning how to play the game. Listen, this op is gonna make the magical cult in the church look like kindergarten story time. After you help us bag these assholes, I'll let you cash it in for another visit with L'zar."

"I already said I'll do it."

"Good. Just wanna make sure you know what you're getting out of it. Get some sleep. You sound like my grandma when she's off her meds."

Cheyenne snapped the phone shut and glared at it. *Someone has to tell him about those analogies.*

She jammed the phone back into her pocket and stripped off the black canvas jacket. It thumped to the carpet with a little jingle of all the extra silver buttons, and the halfling shuffled through her apartment toward the bedroom. The splintered door made her roll her eyes before she nudged it open, shrugging out of her clothes on her way to the bed. The drow halfling set her cell phone on the nightstand and crawled under the sheets.

She lay there on her side, staring at the sliding door of her closet. *They're just dreams. Suck it up.* Cheyenne shut her eyes and willed herself to sleep.

CHAPTER SEVENTEEN

She gave herself enough time the next morning to stop by the gas station down the street for a quick pick-me-up and something like breakfast. When she set the twenty-ounce energy drink and the floppy croissant breakfast sandwich down on the counter, she tried to smile.

"Woah. Why so *serious*?" Katie laughed and rang up the halfling's breakfast. "Just kidding. Joker's got nothing on you. Rough night?"

"Kinda." Cheyenne tapped her fingers on the counter and shifted her weight. "I'll get over it. How've *you* been?"

"Still no guns pointed at my face, so I can't complain too much."

"Hey, anything's better than being robbed at gunpoint, right?"

The clerk shrugged and swiped her hair away from her face before pointing at the card reader. "Still having weird dreams about it, though."

"Oh, yeah? Must be something goin' 'round then." *And I caught the worst strain of weird dream there is.* Cheyenne pulled out her debit card and shoved it into the card reader.

"It's crazy. You'd think I'd stop dreaming about that night by now, right? It's been, like, two weeks."

"Sometimes things hang on a little longer." She punched in her pin and waited for the annoying beep. "You'll get through it."

"I hope so. My sister's really into dream interpretation, right?" Katie sniffed and opened a small plastic bag for her customer's things. "I told her about mine, and she's totally stumped."

The halfling chuckled. "Not that hard to figure out why you're dreaming about a robbery. Seeing as you were literally almost robbed."

"Not that part." The clerk playfully rolled her eyes. "I know I'm reliving the whole thing, except in my dreams, there's this scary-looking chick with white hair and really dark skin. I mean, like, almost purple. And weird..." Katie gestured toward her own ears, "pointy ears."

"What?" Cheyenne forced out a laugh.

"Right? It's *so* freakin' strange. I don't even know where my brain came up with that."

"Not like it could be anything you saw, though, right? I mean, besides the obvious." The halfling shrugged. "And didn't you kinda pass out anyway?"

Katie paused for just a second before sliding the bag across the counter. "How did you know I passed out?"

Shit. Cheyenne grabbed the handles of the plastic bag. "I think the asshole who works the nightshift now said something about it. Dude really likes to run his mouth."

"Oh, man. *Yeah*, he does." Katie rolled her eyes and let out a long sigh. "Whatever. I'm just glad I got switched to working mornings. It just feels safer. Wish I could figure out what the dream's about, though."

"Tell her to look up 'Keebler Elf' or something." The clerk burst out laughing as Cheyenne turned away from the register.

"Want your receipt?"

"Nope. Thanks."

"Okay, see ya later."

The halfling pressed her hip against the door, making the little electric bell chime over the checkout counter. Cheyenne stormed back toward her car and dropped the plastic bag on the seat. *Almost screwed myself on that one. I thought she didn't see me that night.*

With a grimace, she shook her head and pulled out the breakfast sandwich. The Focus coughed to life when she started it, then she was heading downtown with the floppy, soggy croissant spilling gas-station egg all over her lap.

Halfway to the address Sir had texted her, she glanced down at the GPS on her phone again and frowned. *Borderlands said the other warehouse was in South Richmond, not the West End.* Lifting her knee against the bottom of the steering wheel, she reached for the energy drink and opened it with a sharp crack. Then her other hand clamped down on the steering wheel, and she watched the road with her head turned to take long gulps.

I'll figure it out.

The address took her to a closed-down strip mall, half the windows boarded up and a huge sign at the front of the parking lot that said, Closed for Renovation.

The only other car in the parking lot was the black Jeep, and Rhynehart was leaning against the hood. She parked her car and downed the rest of the energy drink before getting out. "Does Sir ever show up to these things, or does he not wanna break a nail or something?"

The FRoE agent looked her up and down over his folded arms. "He's got his job, and we've got ours. Who pulled you into a food fight?"

Cheyenne glanced down and brushed the clumpy bits of over-cooked egg and the soggy croissant crumbs off her black t-shirt and black pants. "Me, I guess."

"Huh. Maybe leave your eating problems at home."

She shot him a warning glance. "Not funny."

Rhynehart chuckled and stepped around the front of the Jeep to jump in. Cheyenne slipped into the passenger seat, and he took off across the parking lot before she could buckle her seatbelt.

"I thought this was a bigger deal than the church."

"Oh, yeah. A lot bigger."

She frowned at him. "So why are you the only FRoE agent I'm looking at right now?"

"Aw, come on, rookie. Don't you believe in me?"

"Not when you sent me into Q'orr's house because you couldn't take care of him yourself."

He glanced at her for a second and shook his head. "Relax. I have backup."

"I don't count...woah!" Her hand shot up to grab the oh-shit handle above the door as the Jeep took a sharp right turn around the end of the strip mall. "Hey, man. I chugged a huge energy drink on the way here, and I still managed to drive like a sane person."

"Boy, somebody's uptight this morning, huh?" With another chuckle, Rhynehart steered around toward the back and slowed down. "And don't flatter yourself, rookie. *That's* the backup."

"Woah."

Five black Humvees were parked in a half-circle behind the strip mall. Almost two dozen FRoE operatives in black fatigues leaned against the vehicles, talking to each other, checking their weapons, slipping on dampening vests. They all looked up and straightened a little when the black Jeep slowed to a stop just in front of them.

The halfling blinked at the operatives and cocked her head. "If anyone had told me about the tailgating party, I would've brought something."

"Yeah, well, it's over now. Come on." He jumped out of the Jeep and gave the hood a quick thump as he headed toward the rest of his team.

Cheyenne closed the door and followed him.

"Look who decided to show up?" One of the agents reinserted whatever kind of magazine was necessary for a fell rifle and nodded at her.

"Hey, I got here on time."

Low laughter rumbled through the team. Jamal stepped around the last vehicle in line, his huge gray mouth open in a smile. "You're only on time if you're early."

The halfling scowled at him. The ogre ignored her warning look completely before nudging his meaty fist into her shoulder as he walked past.

"Yeah, and showin' up on time means you're late." A woman with a black bandana tied around her head jerked the straps of her dampening vest tighter with a little chuckle.

Cheyenne swept her gaze over the agents. "What happens if you're late, then?"

"You're dead," another agent shouted, followed by one more round of laughter.

"We've been here for twenty minutes." The troll woman Cheyenne recognized from her first messed-up visit to the common room in the FRoE compound slipped a fell pistol back into the holster at her hip and spread her arms. "What gives?"

The halfling clenched her jaw and shot Rhynehart a sidelong glance. "He told me to be here at eight."

"And you got here at seven fifty-five." Rhynehart smacked her arm with the back of his hand, then stopped when she stepped away and glared at him. "No touching. Right. Sorry. Look, these peons talk a lotta shit, rookie. Don't worry about it."

"Says the messenger boy for HQ." Yurik shut the back door of the closest Humvee and turned toward Rhynehart with a smirk. Then the muscular goblin's gaze settled on Cheyenne, and he frowned. "You look really familiar."

The drow halfling shot an irritated look at Rhynehart, who just shrugged. She summoned up the heat of her magic at the base of her spine and slipped into drow form. "Ring any bells?"

"Oh, *yeah*." Yurik grinned, the huge metal ring through his nose flashing in the morning sun. "Thought I was seeing things. Hey, Payton!"

"What the hell do you want?" The shorter goblin hefted a massive fell cannon into the back of the closest vehicle before slamming the door. Her one good eye squinted at them beside the eyepatch.

"Look who it is."

Payton's eye widened, then she stormed toward the drow

halfling and thrust a stubby turquoise finger into Cheyenne's face. "I don't wanna hear a fell-damn thing about the other day, got it?"

The halfling stared at the warning finger but stayed where she was. "If you're not gonna pick my nose for me, get your hand out of my face."

Yurik barked a laugh and folded his arms. Payton snarled but lowered her hand, sneering at the drow halfling with crooked teeth. "Don't expect me to clean up after you on this one."

"Yeah, okay."

Payton stalked off with a grunt.

"Just ignore her, rookie." Rhynehart smirked after the grumpy goblin. "She's always like that."

"That's what I heard."

"If she's talking to you at all, it means she likes you." Rhynehart rubbed his chin, then stuck two fingers in his mouth for a loud whistle, which made Cheyenne lean away from him. "All right. Let's roll out."

Muttered replies came from the other agents as they picked up the pace and got into their prospective FRoE vehicles. Yurik jerked his chin up at the drow halfling, then pointed at her as he turned toward the closest Humvee. "Feel free to pull out your tricks, huh? I've told these guys what you can do, but the stupid ones still think I'm full of shit."

She snorted and nodded back. "They'll figure it out."

"Yeah." With another laugh, the tall goblin shook his head and opened the passenger-side door. Payton was already there behind the wheel, starting up the engine just like the others around them. The parking lot behind the strip mall echoed with the growl of revving motors.

Cheyenne leaned toward Rhynehart and muttered, "You guys let her drive with that eyepatch?"

"Well, she hasn't run anyone over yet. All right, come on, rookie." Rhynehart jerked his head toward the Jeep and took off.

She followed him and hopped back into the passenger seat, this time buckling up her seatbelt before he had a chance to start driving. The FRoE vehicles pulled slowly one right after the other in a wide circle around the mall's back parking lot before heading out again. Rhynehart brought the Jeep around as the last vehicle in line. Four minutes later, the caravan turned onto the highway headed northwest and really stepped on the gas.

"So, where are we *actually* going?"

"'Bout half an hour outside Richmond. Those scumbags dealing Q'orr's supplies thought they were being smart. One setup inside the city…"

"The church."

"Yeah." Rhynehart nodded at the highway and the line of black vehicles stretching out in front of them. "And this second one a little farther away. We think this is where they're holding most of it."

"I thought they had more in Richmond." Cheyenne folded her arms, blinking against the bright sunlight flashing through the window. "Like, another distribution center in South Richmond or something."

He shot her a quick frown. "Oh, yeah? Where'd you hear that?"

On the Borderlands forum he doesn't know about. "Just spit-balling."

"Well, maybe they had something else on the other side of town, but we're not too worried about any more popup shops like the church. Whoever's still in charge of this whole screwed-up operation must've gotten wind of our raid on the church. These guys have eyes and ears everywhere, apparently." Rhynehart shrugged and flashed Cheyenne a wide grin. "We have more."

"So, they moved all that crap out where we're going after they heard about the church."

"Bingo. We got a tip last night. Wherever they were holding the black-magic contraband before, they packed up and shipped out. We're trying to get on it now before they figure out we're onto them."

"If you got a tip last night, why wait 'til this morning?"

"Hey, we know what we're doing, rookie." Rhynehart shook his head. "Gave 'em just enough time to settle in and think they made it outta the line of fire. Even if they somehow figured out we're comin' for 'em now, there's no way they have enough time to pack everything up again from an even bigger warehouse and find some other location."

"I keep hearing about how *big* it is." The halfling ran her hand through her white hair. "Do you know how much of Q'orr's stuff they have?"

Rhynehart's chuckle was low and a little maniacal. "Why do you think we have five vehicles loaded down? Trust me, we're prepared. Wait 'til you see what we've got in the back of those Humvees."

CHAPTER EIGHTEEN

Less than half an hour later, they pulled up in a construction zone outside Richmond a few miles away from the closest country clubs. The FRoE vehicles rumbled down the dirt drive to the site, which was enclosed by a ring of trees without any other side streets cutting through.

Rhynehart parked at the end of the line facing the half-built business complex and reached into the back seat.

"Just a little weird that no one's working on that place, don't you think?"

"Nope. Work stalled 'cause of some funding problem, I guess. And these scumbags figured it was a good place to squat. Here. I know you don't do the gloves or a helmet, but you should put this on."

A heavy black dampening vest thumped into her lap, and Cheyenne just stared at it.

"Do it, rookie. It saved you from getting holes burned through your chest instead of just your shoulder—"

"We're not talking about my shoulder."

He studied her as if trying to get a good view of her nonexistent wound beneath her t-shirt. *He has to know what L'zar did.*

"Right. We don't have to talk about it. Just put it on."

He got out of the Jeep and left the door open. With a sigh, the halfling got out after him and paused long enough to slip the vest over her head. She thumped it with a fist, the silver chains jingling around her wrist, then walked off toward the quick, urgent activity around all the other vehicles.

The FRoE agents had this down, slipping silently out of the cars and pulling dampening gloves and helmets and fell weapons out of trunks. Their gear let off muffled clicks as pistols were holstered and rifle straps were slung over shoulders. Cheyenne caught three different sizes of fell rifles, all heavy and bulky and deadly-looking.

With a stifled grunt, Jamal hefted a massive fell cannon up onto one shoulder. Yurik lifted a second one and settled it on the ogre's other shoulder before slapping Jamal's back with a gloved hand and tugging on his black helmet.

"Why does *he* get to be Rambo?" the halfling muttered.

"Don't hold a grudge, rookie. Jamal was doing his job, just like the rest of us." Rhynehart snorted. "Plus, O'Malley had a little trouble with the last fell cannon. Remember? The one that didn't go off before you got shot in the hip?"

"Is he gonna be able to use those things, holding 'em like that?"

"He's good. That's all you need to know. Pays to have an ogre on our side. Come on."

The FRoE team moved quickly across the upturned dirt, heading silently toward the open construction site. Rhynehart jammed his helmet down over his head, and now the drow halfling was the only one among them with her face exposed for anyone to see. *Won't recognize me half the time anyway.*

They paused at a thick drape of plastic sheet nailed over the unfinished entrance. The agent at the front pulled it aside and gestured with a gloved hand. The operatives split up into two groups, one heading inside to the left, the other to the right. Cheyenne glanced back at their parked vehicles and all the open doors, then she saw a blue and red zip-up jacket tossed onto a pile of dirt just outside the building's frame. *Weird thing to leave behind.*

The split lines of FRoE agents filtered inside, and then Rhynehart was moving again right in front of her, and she followed. When he went right, so did she. Both teams moved swiftly over the unsanded plywood and the two-by-fours laid out to frame the different rooms. Cheyenne glanced across what was supposed to be the hallway and saw the other half of the team moving just as quickly, their black shapes flitting between the exposed beams and pieces of coated wiring dangling from the second floor.

A silver keychain flashed in the sunlight, and the halfling paused to squint across the unfinished building. *Who brings a backpack to work?*

She kept moving behind Rhynehart and the others, looking around to check for movement. Another plastic sheet rippled in the breeze, and that was about it. *It's too quiet.*

The frames of what eventually would be offices opened into a much larger room at the center of the building. The FRoE team poured into it and surrounded the open area, rifles and pistols sweeping in every direction as they searched for the magical criminals who should've been here.

"What the hell?" One agent jammed his pistol back into its holster and ripped off his helmet. "There's no one here."

"Someone's jerking you around, Rhynehart."

Pulling off his helmet too, Rhynehart scowled at the open rooms and the tables lining the perimeter. "Hey, our sources are solid, okay? No, they were here. They brought in those tables and all these boxes. Shit."

He spun around and surveyed the area.

"Looks like they forgot some things." Yurik set his helmet down on one of the tables and peered into an open box. "All kinds of creepy shit in here."

"Why would they just leave it all?" another agent asked, holstering her weapon.

"Hell if I know." Rhynehart scratched the back of his head. "Problem's not on our end. We timed this right."

Jamal grunted and lowered into a squat before lowering both heavy fell cannons onto the partially constructed floor.

"Hey." An agent pointed at the ogre and cocked his head. "Careful with those, Sasquatch."

"Piss off."

"At least aim 'em away from the rest of us, huh?"

Yurik moved down the line of tables, peering into each of the open boxes. He hissed in disgust and stepped back. "There's way too much shit in here. Pretty easy to just pick up the boxes and carry 'em out if they smelled us coming."

Rhynehart joined the tall goblin and peered into the first box before stepping away again, scratching his chin. "Yeah, they wouldn't leave all this here for us to find. Not with their supplier behind bars."

Cheyenne scanned the open room around them, sunlight filtering in through the wooden frames and casting flickering shadows across the plywood floors. A soft, warning buzz crawled across her shoulders. "Something's wrong."

"No shit, Sherlock." The troll who'd helped keep her captive her first day at the FRoE compound tossed a hand toward the drow halfling and turned toward Rhynehart. "She'd better be more useful than that."

"She's not the problem, Bhandi," Rhynehart said, running a gloved hand over his head. "Not when we're *all* standing here with our dicks in our hands."

"I mean, something else." Cheyenne turned in a slow circle, scanning the floor and the boxes on the tables and the open frames of the rooms above them on the second floor. "Something's still here."

"Yeah, a fat load of zero assholes we were supposed to bring in."

The halfling ignored the other agent's irritated quip, biting her lower lip against the buzz along her shoulders quickly growing into a painful itch. Then she spotted a pile of brightly colored clothes on the far side of the open room and took off toward it. "Wait a minute."

"Unless you found a trapdoor into a bunch of tunnels, rookie, I don't think there's anything worth our time in here."

She turned back over her shoulder and pointed at the pile of clothes. "I'd say it's worth our time to find out why whoever was in here last stripped off all their clothes and dumped them over here."

"What?"

"Yeah, look at this." When she reached the pile, it was a lot bigger than it looked from the other side of the room. *What the hell happened?*

There were tons of clothes—pants, t-shirts, sweatshirts, jackets. Socks were tossed around the outside of the pile, and then she spotted all the shoes. Sneakers, boots, a pair of dark-brown UGGs. Cheyenne glanced down at her black Vans. *About the same size. But I have small feet.*

A bright-green backpack strap peeked out from the bottom of the pile, and she reached down to pull it out. When she turned the backpack around, she found herself staring at the Incredible Hulk bringing a fist down on a squashed car. "This isn't right."

"Does somebody need to tell our friend we didn't come here to window-shop?" another agent shouted.

"Come on, rookie."

"Just wait a second." Cheyenne turned and held out the backpack for the team to see. "Anybody else think it's weird that these guys dealing black magic are running around with cartoon backpacks?"

Jamal shrugged. "I like the Hulk."

"It's a damn backpack," Rhynehart shouted across the room. "We kinda have bigger problems right now?"

Rolling her eyes, the halfling dropped the backpack and swallowed. She rubbed her lips and stared at the pile. *What am I not seeing?*

She took a step around the pile, and something hard crunched between the plywood and the bottom of her shoe. Picking up her foot, she looked down and felt her stomach drop. *No!*

Some of the black and silver paint had chipped away, but the huge metal skull was exactly the same. So was the black satin ribbon strung through the top of the pendant.

"Shit. Rhynehart!"

"I'm not helping you with a new wardrobe, rookie." The man pointed toward a stack of wooden crates across the open room from the row of tables. "Payton. Zynd'r. Go check out what's in there. The lids look bolted down. Might be something we can work with."

Cheyenne whirled around to face him, clenching her fists. "They didn't care about the potions or any of this other crap. They took the kids!"

Rhynehart turned slowly toward her and frowned. "I know you didn't skip breakfast this morning, rookie. What the hell are you talking about?"

Payton and Zynd'r bent over the first crate, struggling to pry open the lid.

"Like the troll kid in the church. They're being used for some kind of—"

"Hey, ogre face!" Zynd'r turned over his shoulder with a hand on his knee and waved Jamal toward him. "You're good for more than aiming those cannons, right?"

Rolling his eyes, Jamal cracked his knuckles and headed toward them.

The burning itch across Cheyenne's shoulders crept up into her neck now. *I'm still missing something...*

"I'm serious, Rhynehart. This is a pile of kids' clothes. Backpacks, shoes. I saw a girl wearing this necklace two nights ago. They took the kids."

"Yeah." One of the other agents gestured toward Cheyenne and the pile, then folded his arms. "A bunch of black-magic-dealing thugs walked out of here with a shitload of naked magical kids, and nobody noticed."

Rhynehart's eyes widened. "No. The troll kid at the church was in a black robe."

"What kid?"

The team leader shot his agent a dismissive glance and took off toward Cheyenne. "The dead one."

Jamal grunted as he tried to open the first crate with brute strength. He let out a roar and finally released the wood, snarling at the whole thing.

"Hey, look." Payton bent down and picked up a crowbar lying beside the stacks. "Here you go, big guy."

"Stupid box." The ogre snatched up the crowbar and tried again.

Rhynehart reached Cheyenne beside the pile of clothes, and his eyes widened. Drawing a gloved hand down the side of his face, he clenched his teeth and muttered, "Those pieces of shit. This is all kid stuff."

"That's what I'm saying—"

The wooden crate creaked again, nails squealing out of the wood as Jamal pressed down on the crowbar.

Cheyenne spun around and glared at the ogre trying way too hard to open something that just didn't matter.

Zynd'r chuckled. "Don't hurt yourself, Bigfoot."

Through the thick wood of the crate, Cheyenne saw two round shapes glowing brighter with golden light. None of the agents noticed, even when the light grew so bright, it should've been streaming through the slatted wood. *That's not good.*

"Hey, hold on." The halfling moved across the room, pointing at the crate and the round glowing shapes inside it. "Are you guys seeing this?"

"What, you mean a giant ogre who can't outsmart a box?" Payton slapped Jamal on the back, eliciting a low growl from her fellow agent.

"No. Inside the crate."

"That's what they're trying to figure out." Bhandi folded her arms, her scarlet eyes flashing beneath a frown. "No one calls you Einstein, do they?"

"I'm serious. Jamal, stop for a second." The halfling picked up the pace because now the glowing shapes were solidifying into much more detail. *Shit. That's a bomb.*

CHAPTER NINETEEN

Cheyenne reached toward the ogre with the crowbar. "Hey, don't open the fucking crate—"

The last few nails gave way with a screech. The lid didn't peel open so much as it exploded off the top of the crate, sending splintered wood and loose nails and a spray of black, shimmering sludge in every direction. The crowbar clattered to the floor as Jamal staggered back with a bellow. The other agents beside him screamed, and then the sound was cut off by the next massive explosion a second later.

All three of the agents around the crate were tossed backward across the open room. The other agents burst into action, shouting and lifting their weapons at the ready again, sweeping them across the room. Some went to help their fallen, screaming comrades as thick, green-black smoke billowed from the fractured crate. A low hum rose from two metal spheres on the ground, both of them sparking and spewing out more of the dark, glistening sludge while black light strobed from the orbs.

Cheyenne reached out with both hands and shot her black tendrils of magic toward what remained of the wooden crate. A breeze kicked up and filtered the green-black smoke through the

118

room. It burned her nose and eyes, but she snatched up both of the metal orbs with her lashing whips of magic and jerked her arms toward the outer wall of the building. The orbs sailed through the air toward the trees around the site and detonated with two deafening cracks. Sludge and smoke and strobing lights sprayed across the side of the construction site. Metal shards peppered the wooden support beams and the building's frame.

"What the hell?" Rhynehart yelled as he ran toward her, coughing and choking on the dark-green smoke swirling around in the wind. "Goddamnit. Everybody move your asses!"

Another explosion made the rough flooring beneath them tremble. Cheyenne glanced up at the source of it on the second floor and watched with widening eyes as one magical bomb after another detonated in a chain every few feet around the room right above them.

"Shit!" Rhynehart waved everyone out of the room. "Get out—"

A final blast erupted one more floor up, and the top of the unfinished building crumbled. Plywood and nails, rebar, wiring—all of it came down from the top floor and dropped straight toward them.

Cheyenne skidded to a stop and shot both hands up toward the falling wreckage with a roar of effort. The shimmering black wall of her drow shield bloomed five feet above her and arced out over the open room. Splinters and metal shards rained down on the dome she'd created, followed by larger chunks of snapped two-by-fours and thick beams. They pounded onto her shield and scattered off, filling the site with one loud rush like golf-ball-sized hail hitting a metal roof.

"Holy shit…" Yurik stared up at the partially translucent underside of her spell, then launched back into action.

"Okay, everybody out!" Rhynehart waved his team back through the building, glancing up occasionally to double-check the shield.

The drow halfling's arms shook with the force of holding up such a massive spell, watching the other side of the room as one FRoE operative in black after another raced back the way they'd come. One of them tried to dart through the side of the building but pulled up short when a huge beam crashed to the dirt outside the frame, more debris raining down.

"Move!" Cheyenne screamed, gritting her teeth against the force of her magic, battling a lot of gravity and a lot of weight.

Two agents stopped to slip their arms around Payton's and Zynd'r's chests before dragging their wounded back out through the building. It took three more to lift Jamal from the floor and hurry him out. The halfling caught sight of the ogre's face, half of it bubbled and mutilated by the explosion of black magic.

Then the pressure forced her down. One knee slammed into the rough floor, and she let out another roar through her clenched teeth. Her shoulders burned. Everything burned. More green-black smoke filtered through the open room on the breeze and made her eyes water so much, she couldn't see.

"Okay, we're good." Rhynehart doubled back and helped her to her feet. "On the count of three. One, two—"

More of the exterior framing of the third and second floors crashed down on her shield, and a straggling explosion shuddered through the site.

"Three!" Rhynehart grabbed her wrist and half-pulled, half-dragged her toward the other side of the room. The shield held long enough to protect them until they got to the framework of the hall. Then it dropped, and everything else rained down on them.

The building in front of them caved in, the upper levels dropping toward them with a splintering crunch. Cheyenne jerked her hand out of Rhynehart's grip.

"What are you—"

She slipped into her drow speed and ran toward him. Crouching, she lifted the suspended FRoE agent up and over her shoulder like a sack of laundry and just kept moving. *That's gonna hurt. Sorry.*

The halfling ran as fast as she could through the crumbling building falling in slow motion. The opening on the other end sank lower and lower by the second, like a giant, shattered mouth closing down on its next meal.

She reached the end and had to duck beneath the first beam

dropping slowly to the ground. Then her drow speed failed her. The halfling stumbled over her own feet, and Rhynehart went flying off her shoulder across the dirt. The other agents shouted in surprise when their superior skidded toward them and a drow halfling appeared out of nowhere.

"How the hell did she do that?"

"Grab Rhynehart!"

"Keep moving!"

"Somebody get the—"

Another explosion erupted in the crumbling building, muted by all the debris. The blast of dust and compressed air hit Cheyenne in the back, and she staggered forward on her feet. She caught sight of someone helping Rhynehart up, the man doubled over with an arm wrapped around his ribs.

The drow halfling's body wouldn't do what she wanted anymore. She finally dropped to her knees in the dirt, catching herself with both hands. *I pushed too hard.* With a grunt, she tried to stand and only lurched forward about a foot before dropping again. *Worth it.*

"Hey." A blue-green hand shot out toward her. "I thought I told you not to wear yourself out?"

Cheyenne looked up to see Yurik smirking at her. "You're welcome. I'll just let the building bury you next time."

Her arm shook when she lifted it to grasp his hand. The muscular goblin with the ring through his nose pulled her to her feet with a chuckle. "Yeah, there's always a price, huh?"

"You have no idea how many times I've heard that." Her voice sounded muted and watery to her own ears. When she took her next step toward the black vehicles and the FRoE agents helping the wounded into the seats, her legs wobbled. *Not now.*

"Whoa. You got it?"

"Yeah." She swallowed, trying to blink away the wave of dizziness and the line of way more than five black vehicles dancing back and forth in front of her. "You have any more of those gross energy bars?"

"Probably. In one of the Humvees." Yurik dipped his head toward her with a concerned frown. "Maybe we should get you a portable IV instead. You don't look so good."

"I'm fine. I just need a little—" Cheyenne took two more steps. *Push through it.*

"Watch it."

Her hand clamped down on Yurik's arm and slipped off again as she watched the ground rise to meet her face. *I can't feel anything...*

"Aw, shit." The goblin knelt beside her to help her back to her feet, but her eyes fluttered closed, and even her drow hearing didn't catch the guy telling her to hang in there.

CHAPTER TWENTY

When she woke up, the first thing she saw were bright white lights shining right into her face. *Not again.*

She lurched up, her magic flaring from the base of her spine and purple sparks erupting from the fingertips of both hands.

Blinking heavily, she shut down the spells and raised a hand to her throbbing head. *Did I hit this somewhere?*

Then she realized her wrists weren't chained to the bed this time. Cheyenne jerked her foot across the hospital bed, and it moved freely too. A glance at her shirt showed nothing but her regular black-on-black clothes, coated in sawdust and brown dirt. *How considerate.*

She looked around the room. The only difference between the first time and now was the lack of dampening cuffs and monitors beside the bed. Groaning, the halfling swung her legs onto the floor and pushed herself slowly to her feet. Her arms shot out to her sides when she wobbled. "Woah. Pull it together."

Her head settled down a little more with every step toward the door on the other side of the room. The only thing on the low stainless-steel table against the wall was another one of those energy bars for magicals in the silver cellophane wrapper. Cheyenne snatched it off the table, then jerked open the door and stepped out into the hall.

The wrapper split apart between her teeth, then she bit off a huge chunk and grimaced.

A short, squat goblin woman with thick yellow hair spilling out from beneath a black baseball hat pushed a silver cart down the hall toward her. "Tastes like shit, huh?"

"Yeah." Cheyenne kept chewing.

"End of the medical wing's back that way."

"Thanks."

The cart's wheels squeaked as the goblin kept pushing it down the hall. The halfling turned left and made her way past a bunch of rooms identical to hers. Her black Vans moved quickly and quietly across the linoleum floors, and she looked both ways at the next corner before turning left again. *Yeah, now it's coming back to me.*

It was hard enough to swallow the gross, overly chewy energy bar that made her jaw ache. She rolled her shoulders back and walked a little steadier, picking up the pace and biting off another chunk. The more she ate, the faster she walked.

She finally reached the short hallway that opened into the common room and paused. Two of the round tables had been pushed together, and at least a dozen FRoE operatives sat around them, speaking in low tones. Except for Sir.

"I don't give a flying rat's ass what they're saying. The intel went bad before I took my morning shit, and I wanna know why."

Cheyenne stepped slowly into the common room, which was empty except for the meeting taking place right out in the open. The wrapper crunched in her hand as she popped the last bite of energy bar into her mouth. The conversation stopped, and everyone at the tables looked up or turned to see the drow halfling munching away with a grimace of disgust.

"Sorry." She swallowed and stuffed the wrapper into her front pocket. "Someone really needs to fix the flavor of these things. It's almost bad enough not to want one."

"There she is." Sir slapped the table and pushed himself out of his chair. "Back on her feet in no time."

The other operatives around the table broke out into applause. Someone whistled. A few stood, nodding and clapping and shooting her small, approving smiles.

Cheyenne slowly looked back over her shoulder. *Nope. That's for me.*

"Get your ass over here, halfling." Sir waved her forward, and an orc she hadn't met got out of his chair and gestured toward it before leaning against the back of the couch and folding his arms.

Frowning, Cheyenne headed slowly toward the table. The applause died down, but Bhandi nodded at her with a tiny smile. "Good work."

"Uh, thanks."

"That's how we look after our own." A man sitting beside the open chair with hair so blond it was almost white shook a fist at her.

Across the double table, Yurik crossed his arms and leaned back in his chair. "I knew I should've started a betting pool before we shipped out. Would've split it fifty-fifty with you, too."

"For real?" Cheyenne lowered herself into the chair and scooted toward the table. "You think starting a betting pool and me saving your ass are on the same level?"

Surprised laughs rose around the tables, and Yurik just smirked.

"All right, people." Sir sat back down and scooted toward the table. "We all agree, if we even gave out goddamn medals for this kinda crap, the halfling would get a whole damn box of them."

"Medals?" Beside Sir, an orc with a crack running the length of one tusk leaned away from his superior and snorted. "We don't need no stinkin' medals."

Someone else thumped the table.

The corner of Sir's mouth twitched, and he glanced around the table while waving his hand in front of his face. "Jesus, Bozni. Anyone got a breath mint? No? Then the party's over."

On the other side of him, Rhynehart caught Cheyenne's gaze and gave her a short nod. She just raised her eyebrows at him and sat back in the chair. *Someone better tell me what's going on.*

Sir thumped his elbow down on the table and pointed at her. "The halfling did us all a goddamn service this morning. All of you jerkoffs on the op know what I'm talking about. And thanks to this one, Jamal, Payton, and Zynd'r are all gonna say the same thing when they wake up."

Cheyenne leaned forward. "Where are they?"

"Medical ward." Rhynehart's eyebrows flickered together.

"That bad, huh?"

Sir dipped his head with a half-assed shrug. "They got hit worse than you did on Rez 38, halfling."

His mention of her shoulder wound made her clench her fists in her lap, but Sir didn't seem to notice. Rhynehart's eyes widened, and he dropped his gaze to the table.

"Those lucky bastards are healing as much as they can under Dr. Minkert's nurturing hand," Sir continued. Someone else at the table snorted. "And when they're conscious, yeah, they might have to look a little extra hard in the mirror to recognize their reflection. In Jamal's case, it might be an improvement. But they're still breathing, and that's what matters."

"And that everyone else got outta the building alive," someone else added.

"Well, the halfling's the only person who gets a damn cookie for that one." Sir pointed at Cheyenne again, to another round of wry laughter. "Now that we've all put on our shoes and socks like functioning goddamn adults, let's get back to the point. How did we screw this up?"

The ogre leaning against the back of the couch grunted. "Might've been a bad tip."

"It wasn't a bad tip." Rhynehart shook his head, staring at the table with his arms folded.

"You sure about that?"

The team leader glanced briefly at Sir. "One-hundred percent.

They loaded up the building with contraband, and they were in there for long enough to get comfortable."

"How comfortable?"

Bhandi leaned toward Sir across the table. "Comfortable enough to plant a bomb on a tripwire in one of those crates, plus at least a dozen others around the building."

"Then someone better fucking enlighten me." Sir folded his hands on the table with forced civility and just kept shouting. "'Cause I can't figure out why the hell you people went all the way out there just to blow up their sloppy seconds and get pulled out of the fire by a halfling as green as Bozni."

The orc beside him rolled his eyes.

"I'm waiting for a goddamn answer. Pull it out of your ass for all I care. But somebody better start talking."

"Does our informant have any buddies? Maybe someone's taking a piece of both pies?"

"If somebody squealed, it's an inside job on their end. Not our job to smoke out *their* rats."

"No, our job is to get that black-magic shit off the streets and away from any more kids."

"Bet your parents never locked you out of their medicine cabinet, huh, Franklin?"

The conversation faded into the background as the operatives tossed insults back and forth between quickfire brainstorming. Cheyenne tuned it all out and stared at Rhynehart, who wouldn't look up from the table and hadn't moved since he'd folded his arms. *He knows. Why won't he say it?*

"They're stealing kids now."

The common room fell silent as everyone looked at Cheyenne. Sir snorted. "Right. They have plenty of time and energy to round up a bunch of magical tweens and take 'em all out on a field trip. Keep trying, halfling."

"I'm serious." Cheyenne widened her eyes at Rhynehart, but he wasn't helping. "The group we took down in the church had a kid in there too. Dressed him up in a robe and sacrificed him for a ritual."

Sir blinked at her. "Someone's been watching too much Netflix."

"I don't watch Netflix. Or TV."

"And I don't do very well with dumbass ideas."

The halfling snatched the empty plastic water cup in front of the agent beside her and chucked it at Rhynehart. "Tell them!"

Sir leaned away from the agent and scowled at Cheyenne. "Hey, who shit in your Frosted Flakes?"

"Rhynehart saw it too. The huge pile of clothes at the back of the building. *Kids'* clothes. Shoes. Backpacks." She started to rise from the table, but Sir snapped his fingers and pointed at her.

"Sit *down—*"

She leaped up from her chair and pulled up a burst of purple sparks in one hand. No one at the table moved. "I'm not a dog you can train with hand gestures."

"Looks like I can't train you at all."

Ignoring him, the halfling shook her head and snuffed out her reactionary magic. "Rhynehart. Did you tell them anything?"

The operative took a deep breath and let it out slowly through his nose. Then he finally looked up at her. "I had the same thought when we were there, rookie, but we haven't heard anything about missing kids. We don't have any proof that what you and I saw didn't come from some imp who raided a teenager's trashcan and wanted to go through it all in private."

Is that what they're called? She shook the thought away. "There was a necklace in the pile. I saw an orc Sunday night who was wearing the exact same one. She was still in high school, and I'm willing to bet the necklace was taken right off of her and tossed into that pile with everything else."

"One orc kid, halfling." Sir spread his arms. "That doesn't mean a whole bunch of kids was snatched up to be turned into sacrifices. For all you know, the kid could've dumped her crap there and took off."

"Not half an hour away from where she lives."

"Not a strong enough case, rookie." Rhynehart shrugged. "Until we're a hundred percent on this, it's just a theory."

"Those kids could be *dead* before you're a hundred percent on anything!" Cheyenne slammed her palm on the table.

"Not your call to make," Sir shouted back. "Our priority is figuring out where those assholes went with the *rest* of the crap before they hawk it all and split. Then we'll have all the proof in the world and a lot more dead kids. Now get lost before I take back those medals I never gave you."

It was a stupid threat, but he waved her off, scowling beneath his bushy graying eyebrows.

Cheyenne removed her hands off the table and glared right back at him. "You guys have your priorities seriously mixed up."

"Well, a dark elf with daddy issues is the *last* person who's gonna screw my head on straight. Get lost."

Gritting her teeth, the halfling stayed where she was. "What about cashing in my points?"

"Uh-uh. I said *after* we brought those thugs down, halfling. You haven't even taken down one."

"*What?*"

"That was the deal. Don't worry, he's not going anywhere."

She snarled at him and stormed away from the table, feeling all those agents' eyes prickling her skin as she went. *He's too scared to say L'zar's name where they can hear it. I can be scary too.*

CHAPTER TWENTY-ONE

Cheyenne leaned against the wall, her arms folded, and listened to Sir's little meeting for the next five minutes. Nobody asked her opinion or even looked at her until Sir stood and thumped his fist on the table.

"We all have work to do, people. Get to it. And don't make me come after you for results." The man spun sharply and stormed out of the common room, his thick boots clomping across the floors.

The table burst into multiple conversations at once, agents groaning and rolling their eyes, nodding and heading off to their own tasks, leaning toward each other and muttering. Some looked at Cheyenne with nods of approval or a quick, apologetic shrug.

The halfling stayed where she was, glaring at Rhynehart as he moved around the awkward shape of two round tables pushed together. He headed toward her.

"Just the way things have to be done around here, rookie."

"You made me sound like an idiot."

"Hey, no one thinks you're an idiot. Pretty much the opposite. You really stepped up your game at the site this morning." He gestured behind him toward the other FRoE agents, slowly clearing out of the common room. "You didn't have to, but you proved yourself to my guys. They trust you now. That's a big deal."

"And what about who *I* can trust?"

Rhynehart just frowned at her.

"How am I supposed to keep going out there with you to take these assholes down if you won't back me up?"

"Hey, I've backed you up plenty."

"No. You just bring a gun with you and hope you won't have to use it while I'm around." Cheyenne shook her head. "First you have a healer stick a *tracking device* in my—"

"Those were my orders, rookie."

"Sure. Just like you had your orders to make me think we were bursting into some goblin woman's house to take her out for selling love potions. You had orders to lie to me then too. Just for one last *test*, right?"

His eyes narrowed. "Right. A test you passed with flying colors, so I don't know why you're whining about it."

"Nobody ordered you to sit at the table next to your master and tear down everything I said. That was all on you."

"We don't have *proof*—"

"Bullshit. You *saw* that pile of clothes. You agreed with me at the site before your ogre with oatmeal for brains opened the crate. I know the people we're looking for took those kids, Rhynehart, and you know it too."

"Okay." The agent lifted a hand toward her and turned halfway around to look at the agents still in the common room. Some of them were watching the tense conversation. Most of them clearly tried not to. "Keep it down, huh?"

"If being loud saves those kids from whatever they did to the kid in the church, I'll scream all damn day."

"Come on, rookie. Look. I can't tell you your theory is just plain wrong—"

She snorted. "It's not a theory."

"Fine. What I'm trying to say is I don't think you're wrong. I agree with you. That pile of stuff wasn't just dumped there by some random person for fun. And sure, maybe a whole bunch of kids got lured onto the construction site and…I don't know. Magicked into tossing all their clothes away. Whatever. But we don't have any leads, kid. Not a single piece of evidence that ties any kids to the magicals trying to sell them that crap, so we can't follow it."

Cheyenne pressed her lips together and let out a slow, furious breath through her nose. *Breathing fire would be some nice surprise magic right now.* "What if we *did* have proof?"

Rhynehart blinked and leaned toward her. "You have something you didn't share at the table?"

"No. Not yet. But what if I brought you guys something that proves those kids are missing? Kidnapped. What then?"

"Then we follow it down the rabbit hole. For now, we have to go with what we've got." He ran a hand through his hair and sighed. "Tracking down those dealers is the priority right now. If you can find proof about the kids, great. And if you're right, we'll find the kids when we find the scumbag dealers, won't we?"

The halfling looked away from him, forcing her rage back down just enough to keep from socking him in the face. "It better be fast. I have a bad feeling about this."

"Yeah, me too, rookie. Me too." Looking her up and down, Rhynehart shook his head and stepped hesitantly away. "Go get some rest or something. Let off a little steam. Whatever you gotta do to pull yourself together. Who knows? Maybe you'll find what we can't."

Averting his gaze, he nodded and headed for the other side of the common room. The halfling glared after him until he turned the corner toward the side of the compound where they kept the padded training room and whatever else went on in this place.

I will. Just wait.

"Hey, halfling!"

Cheyenne slowly turned her head to see Yurik, Bhandi, and another troll with black and dark-blue tattoos swirling up both sides of his neck. The agents moved quickly toward her, taking their chance now that Sir and Rhynehart were both out of the picture.

"Don't let the higher-ups ruffle your feathers, yeah?" The metal ring through Yurik's nose wobbled a little when he nodded. "Sir only knows how to give orders. He sucks at taking suggestions."

"I noticed."

"We're with you, though," Bhandi added, her dark-purple lips pressed together in determination. "There's definitely something going on with those kids. We just gotta find out what it is."

"Yeah. Well, thanks." The halfling nodded, feeling her rage settle even more. *They just won't say it in front of Sir.*

"Oh, hey. This is Tate." Yurik thumped the tattooed troll across the chest.

"What's up?"

Cheyenne gave him a little smile. "Nice to meet you."

Yurik clapped his hands and rubbed them together. "You got any plans for the rest of the day?"

"It's still Tuesday, right?"

The agents laughed, and the muscular goblin just nodded. "Yeah, halfling. It's still Tuesday. Listen, we're heading down to Union Hill in about ten minutes. Gotta go change first. Figured we'd stop by the pub, have some drinks. Pretend to forget about what happened this morning. You interested?"

"Drinking with you guys?" Cheyenne squinted at them, her smile growing wider. "You don't care about bringing a civilian with you?"

"No one gives a shit about that," Tate replied. "You're half-drow, man. And at this point, you might as well be one of us anyway. That's the only thing that matters."

Bhandi snorted. "So, you in, or what?"

Taking a deep breath, the halfling shrugged. "Why the hell not?"

"That's right." Yurik pointed at her. "There literally isn't a good answer to that question. Hang out here. We'll be back in a jiff."

The troll woman turned toward him and raised an eyebrow. "In a jiff?"

"That's what I said."

Tate turned with his fellow agents. "Nobody actually says that."

"Well, *I* just did. Maybe I'm bringing it back. You ever think of that, you inked-up grape?"

Cheyenne watched them walk away, and she couldn't help a little smile. *Drinking with magical FRoE operatives. Yeah, why the hell not?*

When the trio came back almost exactly ten minutes later, they'd all changed out of their black fatigues and into civilian clothing. Bhandi wore a pair of maroon corduroys almost the same color as the scarlet braids falling down her back. The t-shirt and gray blazer made her look a lot more friendly. Tate came out in a white t-shirt and jeans, and Yurik apparently thought mustard-yellow pants and a sweater with jagged stripes in brown and bright-orange were a good look for bar hopping.

Cheyenne choked back a laugh. "Where'd you find *that* getup?"

"What?" The muscular troll glanced down at his clothes, the yellow braid running down the center of his otherwise bald blue-green head swinging behind his neck. "It's fall, right? I'm autumnal."

"Yeah, okay."

Tate let out a low laugh. "Come on. Better get outta here before somebody decides we look like we could use more paperwork."

They headed across the common room, which was still fairly empty except for two ogres sitting on the couch watching a basketball game on the huge flatscreen mounted above the fireplace. One of them thumped the other in the chest. "They call it a slam-dunk. Ha. I could get the ball in a net twice as high."

"Yeah, right. You can't even get your trash in the right can."

Biting back another laugh, Cheyenne followed her new maybe-friends through the much shorter hallway leading out toward the lobby of the FRoE compound. Nobody sat at the little cubicles lining the back of the room, but apparently, these guys didn't need to check out of anywhere.

"How often do you guys get to leave like this?"

"About twice a month, usually." Yurik turned and walked backward toward the front door, spreading his arms. "Unless we get into some really hairy shit like this morning. Then we get the rest of the day off to do whatever we want."

"If we're not laid up with Minkert, anyway." Tate snorted and rubbed his shaved purple head. There were swirling designs tattooed on his scalp, too.

"Man, Payton's gonna be so pissed when she finds out we went without her." Bhandi shot Yurik a warning look.

"So what? She's always pissed." Yurik held the door open for everyone, letting it swing shut again after Cheyenne stepped outside into the early evening light. "We'll take her out again when Minkert's done with her."

"Yeah, whenever it is." Tate pointed at the troll. "You gonna try sneaking her out for an extra night off base?"

"Not like I haven't done it before."

The agents laughed and walked quickly across the parking lot, almost bouncing in their excitement to get the hell out of there. Cheyenne stuck her hands into the pockets of her black canvas jacket, ignoring the weight of the FRoE burner phone against her left hand. *This is gonna be an interesting night.*

The line of black FRoE vehicles looked exactly the same as the last time she'd walked down it. *Better not get any needles in my back this time.*

Yurik stopped at one of the black Range Rovers and pulled open the driver-side door. "Okay, it's in here somewhere. Oh. Yep!"

He pulled a keyless fob out from under the floormat and turned toward the others, dangling it with a grin. "Ta-da."

"Nope. Uh-uh." Bhandi lurched toward him and snatched the key fob out of his hand. "You drove the last two times, and I could've downed two pitchers of grog in the time you wasted getting us there."

"Hey, at least I got us there." Yurik spread his arms and tipped forward in a little bow.

Tate snorted. "But you drive like my grandma."

"Like *Sir's* grandma," Bhandi added. "Off her meds."

Cheyenne laughed. "He's used that one on you too, huh?"

"Pretty sure everyone's heard about Sir's grandma." Shaking his head, Yurik stepped around the front of the Range Rover and opened the passenger-side door.

Tate opened the door behind Bhandi and gestured inside. "Hop in, halfling."

Cheyenne didn't have to be told twice. She climbed into the back seat behind Yurik as Bhandi started the car. Tate jumped in beside her and slammed the door.

"Better buckle up," Yurik muttered.

"Oh, come on." Bhandi laughed and shifted into drive. "I'm a good driver."

"Yeah, on a racetrack, maybe—woah!"

The Range Rover squealed across the asphalt as they lurched forward in a fast, tight turn. Cheyenne grabbed the oh-shit handle again, nearly sliding across the seat into Tate, who'd braced himself against the door. The troll behind the wheel let out a maniacal laugh.

"Told you." Yurik grunted, and all three passengers quickly strapped on their seatbelts the minute Bhandi straightened out the car.

They headed quickly toward the end of the parking lot and the two security booths on either side. "Where are we going?"

"What?" Yurik turned to look at her. "We say we're going out to Union Hill, and you have no idea what we're talking about?"

The halfling raised her eyebrows. "Correct."

Tate whistled. "Where the hell did Rhynehart dig *you* up?"

"Nobody dug me up. I *showed* up."

"Uh-huh. But you don't know what's in Union Hill." Yurik turned back around, shaking his head.

"So, anyone gonna spill the beans, or are you guys gonna stick with keeping me in the dark too?"

"Attitude," Bhandi called out from the front. "I like it. Sir's tight-lipped policy's making you a little itchy, huh?"

Tate barked out a laugh. "Yeah, jock itch."

"Shut up."

"We're going to Peridosh, halfling," Yurik finally said. "Ever heard of *that?*"

"What, you mean the underground bazaar?"

"Ha! It's bizarre, all right." The goblin up front slapped his knee, ignoring Bhandi's eye roll and Tate shaking his head before looking out the window. "But that's the way we like it, huh? Good to know you've heard of that, at least."

"Yeah, but I've never been there."

"Well, hold onto your pointy little ears, halfling." Bhandi chuckled and slowed the car to a stop beside the gate booth on the right. "You're in for a treat."

Cheyenne frowned at the troll behind the wheel.

Tate leaned toward her and muttered, "They're not that little. Don't take it personally. She just likes to fuck with people."

Pointing to her ears, the drow halfling shot him a sarcastic grin. "Trust me, I'm not overly sensitive about ear jokes." *Just don't call my sparks "cute."*

The vehicle fell silent, then Bhandi huffed and turned a wide-eyed stare toward Yurik.

"What? You wanted the wheel. Go ahead and take charge."

"Right. You can slide over and take my seat while I'm grabbing us all masks? I don't think so. Out."

"Jeez. You're taking this way too seriously, you know that?" Yurik unbuckled his seatbelt and jerked open the door. His jaunty whistle followed him out of the car and into the unmanned booth.

Tate chuckled and rubbed the top of his bald head. Cheyenne glanced at him and whispered, "Masks?"

"Oh, yeah. You don't have to worry about that one, do ya? We'll get goin' in a minute."

Yurik kept whistling all the way until he slid back into the passenger seat. Then the door thumped close, and he held out his open hand toward Bhandi. "One for you."

"Thanks."

"Here you go, Grapeface." Yurik shoved his hand into the back seat and dropped a black metal ring into Tate's open palm.

"All this time, and that's the best name you can come up with?" Tate closed his hand around the ring, slipping it on just as Bhandi and Yurik did the same with theirs.

"The other option was Eggplant, buddy. You decide."

Cheyenne leaned toward the door beside her when the air shimmered around the other FRoE agents in the car. Then what had been two trolls and a goblin in the Range Rover with her were now three more humans. At least human-looking. "Woah. Masks."

"Yeah, that's a name we've been throwing around for a while." Yurik flipped over his tanned hands, studying them. "We get to borrow these when we go out on our rec time. Turn 'em in when we roll back. I heard the guys before us had to drink nasty potions before they went off base."

Cheyenne raised an eyebrow. "Couldn't be worse than those energy bars you keep throwing at me."

The FRoE operatives burst out laughing. Yurik turned again to look at her and nodded. "You're all right off duty too, you know that? Now let's ride!"

Bhandi looked up in the mirror on the sun visor, rearranging her auburn hair, which now ran in one braid down the back of her head instead of countless smaller ones. "Can't wait to slip these damn things back off again."

"Then *go*." Yurik laughed and gestured toward the road ahead of them. "Come on. I could've put down at least half a pitcher of grog in the time it took you to ogle yourself."

"Bite me, Blueface."

"Not anymore." Yurik patted his human-looking cheeks and lurched against the passenger seat when Bhandi floored the gas pedal. "Jesus. You got a demon buzzing around inside you or something?"

Bhandi gripped the steering wheel tighter with both hands and wiggled her head. "Probably."

Cheyenne's face hurt from trying not to smile too much. *Friends are good, I guess.*

The Range Rover sped down the narrow road away from the FRoE compound, filled with Bhandi and Yurik's nonstop banter while Tate just shook his head in the back seat.

The halfling kept a careful eye on where they were going, cementing the route in her memory. *No sedatives or black bags this time. I won't say anything if they don't.*

CHAPTER TWENTY-TWO

Half an hour later, they pulled into a public parking lot in Union Hill. Four doors opened and shut, letting out four human-looking magicals. Tate nudged Cheyenne's arm and jerked his chin up. "Must be pretty nice to just slip in and out of that look whenever you want."

The halfling spread her arms and looked down at her clothes. "The Goth thing?"

"Ha, ha. Very funny."

She smirked and followed the off-duty FRoE agents toward the parking meter in the lot. Bhandi punched in the license plate, then hissed out a sigh. "Shit. Anybody have a dollar?"

"You're so worried about driving fast, you forgot to bring cash." Yurik folded his arms. "I'm gonna end up paying for all your drinks too, aren't I?"

The troll woman—temporarily a brunette with hazel eyes and freckles—shot him a cheesy grin and batted her lashes. "That would be, like, *so* incredible."

One side of Yurik's face wrinkled, lifting the same side of his upper lip in wary distaste. "Okay, now you're taking it too far."

"Here, just use my card." Cheyenne slipped her hand into the pocket of her jacket.

"Nope. You're gettin' everything on us, tonight, halfling." Tate nudged her again and pulled a brown leather wallet from the back pocket of his jeans. It looked totally normal in the human hands of the guy with dirty-blond hair who was almost exactly Cheyenne's height. He whipped out a debit card and passed it to Bhandi. "And I mean *everything*."

"You guys don't have to do that—"

"*Oh*, yes, we do." Bhandi paid for their parking, slapped the card back into Tate's hand, and took off toward the row of shops ahead of them. "Don't try pulling the humility card tonight. Oh, shit." The troll in a brunette mask turned over her shoulder to frown at Cheyenne. "What's your name, anyway?"

The halfling swallowed under their gazes. *Guess I couldn't keep this up forever.* "Cheyenne."

"Cheyenne." Yurik grinned, bobbing his head while they took off across the street again. "I was thinking something more like Beatrix. Or Rowena."

Bhandi and Cheyenne burst out laughing. The other woman shoved him away, shaking her head. "You're an idiot, Yurik. What kinda names are those?"

"Hey, I can't help what pops into my head."

Tate frowned at the halfling. "Like the city in Wyoming?"

She rolled her eyes. "Same spelling and everything. And no, I was born and raised in Virginia."

The troll with sandy-blond hair and blue human eyes sniggered. "Sounds like you've had a lot of practice with that answer."

"You have no idea."

They stopped in front of a Fro-Yo shop, which had an Open sign in the window and patrons at the tables. Tate opened the door and held it for everyone. The agents filed in and Cheyenne followed, and then she stared at the inside of the shop. "This isn't what I expected."

Bhandi shot the halfling a wide grin and wiggled her eyebrows. "This ain't nothin', Cheyenne. Just wait."

They moved back toward the counter, where a middle-aged man in a brown tweed suit jacket nodded at them.

"What's up, Tony?" Yurik called. "Havin' a good night?"

"If you call standing here playing guard dog for twelve hours six days a week a good night, then sure. I'm having loads of fun."

"Whoa, sorry I asked." Yurik raised both hands in surrender and walked past the counter toward the back of the store.

Tate rapped his knuckles on the counter. "Want us to bring you anything, big guy?"

"Yeah, get me a raise, will ya?"

The blond troll shot Tony the guns with both hands and winked. "I'll keep my eyes open."

"I bet you will."

Bhandi reached the door at the back of the shop first, jerking it open with a flourish. She held it for the others, waving for them to hurry up. The piece of paper taped to the wooden door had the words "Employees only. Keep out" written in huge bright-red letters.

Cheyenne glanced back at Tate and pointed toward the door. "Guess it doesn't apply to us, huh?"

"Even if it did, would you wanna be the one to tell Bhandi she can't walk in there?"

"Good point."

It looked like a door to a storage room or maybe an office, but it wasn't either of those. Cheyenne stepped into the tiny room with the FRoE agents, and the door clicked shut behind them. Then two metal doors the same brushed silver as the floor and walls closed in front of them and met in the middle. The halfling opened her mouth and paused before blurting, "Did we just walk into an elevator?"

Yurik stuck out his lower lip and nodded. "Yeah. I'd say that pretty much sums it up."

"This isn't just any elevator." Bhandi patted the metal wall as the box around them jolted and moved down. "Cheyenne, this is the elevator to the best damn bazaar this side of the Border."

"Oh, right." Yurik scoffed. "Like you can have anything to compare it to."

"Hey, I've heard the stories. And I'm not the first person to give it the same kinda high praise."

"You spend too much time listening to those ancient farmers talking a big game about 'back in their day.'" Yurik pulled a face, and Tate leaned back against the elevator wall, smirking.

"You think they have pigs on the other side? Really?" Bhandi looked at the muscular goblin dressed like a 1970s remake and shook her head. "Shut your mouth before I rip the stupid leash right out of your face."

Yurik shot her a wounded look of fake insult, his eyes wide, and lifted a human-looking hand to the much smaller ring through his human-looking septum. "It's not a leash."

"Not yet." Pressing her lips together to hold back a laugh, Bhandi twisted the black ring on her index finger before yanking it off. The air shimmered in front of her, and then she was all violet skin and scarlet braids again. She rolled her shoulders back and tipped her head from side to side. "Oh, man. Much better."

"Please." Yurik grunted and struggled to take off his ring as Tate slipped his neatly off his pinky and stuffed it into his front pocket. "You can't feel an illusion spell."

"But I can *feel* better knowing I *look* better." Bhandi pocketed her ring too. "You might get it if you bothered to buy yourself some new clothes. Like from this century."

The black ring finally popped off Yurik's thumb, and then his dark hair lightened and turned into the racing stripe of yellow braid down his blue-green head. The ring through his nose more than tripled in size, and he pocketed his ring too. "I am perfectly happy with my choice of clothes, thank you very much. And since when did you give a shit about fashion?"

Bhandi shrugged. "I don't. I give a shit about busting your balls, though."

Cheyenne glanced up at the ceiling of the elevator, scanning the top of all four walls without seeing a single button or one of those little screens which counted which floor they were on. "How far down are we going?"

Tate clicked his tongue. "Far enough. Plus, this thing is really slow."

"Has to be with all the wards, yeah?" Yurik sighed and laced his fingers together, pushing them out to crack his knuckles. "Feels like we haven't been down here in weeks."

Bhandi folded her arms. "Huh. Maybe it's 'cause we haven't been down here in weeks."

"Hey." Tate nudged Cheyenne with the back of his hand again. "You don't have a mask to take off, but you should…you know."

The troll gestured to his face and shrugged.

"Yeah, better go drow for this, Cheyenne," Bhandi added. "Not sure anyone down here's gonna know what to do with a human-looking chick. Even a Goth chick."

Yurik leaned toward the halfling. "Especially 'cause halflings are supposed to be, well…"

"A myth?" Cheyenne cocked her head.

"Listen to her." Yurik pointed at her, nodding. "You do know *some* stuff. I'll give you that."

"Well, I wasn't born yesterday."

Tate laughed and bobbed his head. "Compared to us, halfling, yeah, you kinda were."

Ignoring the jab, Cheyenne took a breath and let the heat of her drow magic flare from the base of her spine. Her skin darkened, hair faded to bone-white, and she stood with the other magicals—FRoE agents, but still magicals—looking like a full drow.

"Yeah, that's more like it." Yurik grinned.

Bhandi stared at the halfling's hair and slowly shook her head. "Love those ears, man."

Cheyenne snorted. "Wouldn't say they're my best feature, but okay. Thanks."

"What's your best feature, then?" Tate asked. "In your personal opinion."

She stared at him and conjured a sphere of her black, crackling magic, purple light sparking at its center. The elevator filled with the loud buzz of the spell in such an enclosed space. The agents cracked up laughing, then the elevator shook with a squealing groan and stopped moving.

"Okay, put that shit away." Bhandi waved off the halfling's spell and chuckled again. "We all know you're a badass."

Tate spread his arms. "Hey, it's her best feature."

The elevator doors opened slowly, letting in the startlingly loud rumble of hundreds of voices talking all at once.

How did I not hear this first?

Cheyenne leaned back before the doors opened all the way, her nostrils flaring. "Whew. Smells like my neighbors' apartment times a million."

"You got magical neighbors, huh?" Bhandi shrugged. "Bet they got what you're smelling right here."

"They did, yeah. Every Wednesday."

The off-duty agents chuckled again and stepped quickly out of the elevator. Tate nudged Cheyenne's shoulder again before walking past her. "You're gonna love this."

Bhandi spun around and spread her arms, walking backward into the long, crowded walkway with a grin. "Welcome to Peridosh, halfling."

CHAPTER TWENTY-THREE

Like Q3's marketplace on steroids. Cheyenne gazed at all the brightly colored banners and pendants streaming across the wide underground room, dipping in the center just out of reach if the halfling jumped with an outstretched hand. Vendors had set up their carts, forgoing tents in a place closed off from the elements. Everywhere she looked, magicals bartered, laughed, bought and sold, ate, drank, and clapped each other on the back.

"Hey, watch yourself, greenskin," a short, squat goblin woman barked at the orc who'd stepped back into her cart. "Or you can pay me for the whole fell-damned bushel."

"Piss off, Heesha. Everyone knows you're trying to sell us last week's leftovers."

The magicals who'd heard the jab laughed and Cheyenne kept walking after her new FRoE friends. *There's always someone trying to make trouble.*

The sound of at least four drums beating a fast-paced rhythm echoed toward them from up ahead. Yurik did a weird little jig and spun to grin at her. "What do you think?"

"It's big."

"Ha. Big and loud and noisy and smelly. Best way to blow off steam." The beefed-up goblin rubbed his hands together and glanced at a cart with some kind of produce, bubblegum-pink with a bunch of dangling roots like floppy carrots sprouting from the sides. "Woah. No, thanks."

More vendors shouted out into the fray, trying to draw in new customers. One storefront had a table set up just outside the front door, laid out with plates, cups, vases, and shields, all of it made of one metal or another. Tate caught Cheyenne staring and pointed at the table. "Those are supposed to have been made on the other side. You know, across the Border. Protective talismans or something."

The halfling frowned and peered at the items spread out on the bright purple-and-red-striped table runner. "Are those *lamps?*"

"Oh, probably. I wouldn't rub any of *those*, though. Good luck trying to deal with a genie down here."

"Don't tell me there are genies in there?"

The troll laughed. "I seriously doubt it."

Brightly woven rugs, tapestries, and clothing hung from the fronts of the next few shops on either side of the wide avenue, and the group navigated their way through the thick crowd of magicals in every shape, size, and color. Two skaxens snarled and hissed at each other as the orc trying to buy a curved sword from them stood by and waited for the orange guys to figure it out.

When they passed the stall, Cheyenne stopped short and pulled her head away, blinking quickly. "Woah."

Yurik turned back toward her with the same grin, but it faded when he saw her. "You okay?"

"Yeah."

"Not gonna pass out on me again, are ya?" He laughed when she shot him a glare in response.

"Just a lot of…smells."

"Tell me about it. Drow are supposed to have super-noses. Better than the rest of us. That true?"

The halfling closed one eye and wrinkled her nose. "No one else looks like they're about to get a headache."

"Aw, you'll get used to it. We're almost to the pub anyway. Here, it's right down—"

"Hey! What's the holdup?" Bhandi spread her arms in front of a building, the wooden sign over the door reading in thick black letters The Empty Barrel. "We doin' this or what?"

Tate had almost reached her, and he turned to spread his arms too and shoot Cheyenne and Yurik an exaggerated imitation of Bhandi's irritation.

"Come on." Yurik stuck his hands in the pockets of those ridiculous yellow pants and nodded at the others. "This is the best part."

"If you say so." The halfling blinked quickly again, surprised to find no tears squeezing out of her eyes from the thick spices blasting through the air, then rubbed her nose. *Probably won't get used to this.*

She followed Yurik toward the front door of the Empty Barrel, glancing at the smaller storefront beside it. A wiry, wrinkled orc whose skin was more brown than green stood inside the shop. Thick gray hair covered the sides of his face without meeting at his chin like a beard, and his yellow eyes stared at her. Cheyenne's skin prickled, and she pulled her gaze away from the old orc to see all kinds of dried herbs and plants hanging upside down from the ceiling. A row of bottles and vials of both clear and brown glass filled the back wall behind the orc. *Potions. I'll check that out later.*

"Christ, you look like a lost puppy, Cheyenne." Bhandi laughed and waved the halfling forward as she held open the door. "We wanna get a seat, at least. This place fills up faster than you can imagine."

"Hey, I'm just trying to soak it all in." Cheyenne shrugged and couldn't help but smile as she stepped through the door.

Bhandi tossed an arm around her shoulders and nudged her. "Oh, you'll take it all in, all right. The Empty Barrel has the best grog for getting plastered quickly. Not the best taste, though, but who gives a shit, right?"

The halfling's smile tightened, and she shrugged out from beneath the troll woman's arm. "Sure."

"Woah. Sorry." Bhandi lifted her hands and stepped away as they headed toward the bar along the right wall. "Didn't know you were so hands-off."

"Not the hugging type."

"Yeah, I'm pickin' up on that." Bhandi tossed scarlet braids back over her shoulder and shot a hand up in the air. "Hey, Ogsa!"

A huge orc woman with giant golden hoops strung one after the other up both ears nodded at Bhandi as she wiped the rim of a copper cup with a stained rag. "What do you want, Bhandi?"

"The usual. For four this time. Wait." The troll turned quickly back toward Cheyenne and leaned in close. The halfling fought not to pull away. "You ever had fellwine?"

"Nope."

Bhandi looked her up and down, then nodded. "Yeah, this is your lucky night. Ogsa! Add two cups of fellwine. It's on Yurik's tab."

Grinning, Bhandi almost skipped down the bar toward where the other agents leaned against the chipped and sticky wood. Yurik groaned. "Are you kidding me right now? I swear, if you don't buy the drinks next time, I'll—"

"What?" Bhandi leaned against the bar beside him and laughed.

"You'll quit coming down here? Come on. I'm your best drinking buddy, and you know it."

"Not if I'm paying for you every single goddamn time."

Cheyenne leaned against the bar beside Bhandi, though she left a lot more space between her and the troll than Bhandi seemed to leave anybody when she was this worked up. She looked up at the shelf on the wall behind the bar while Yurik and Bhandi kept up their back-and-forth payment dispute, looking for alcohol she recognized. There wasn't any. Instead of liquor bottles or a tap or even a fridge, the wide shelf was stacked with wooden barrels with spigots and unmarked brown bottles nearly as wide as they were tall. Something like a metal urn sat at the far end, and there was only one of those.

The orc bartender stepped into view, the apron around her waist damp with spilled drinks. "Not every day we see a drow in here."

The halfling looked up at the orc's glowing yellow eyes and the intricate gold wiring around the tips of both tusks. "How many come through here?"

The bartender raised the thick ridge of her eyebrows. "You're the first."

"Come on, Ogsa." Bhandi drummed her hands on the bar. "We've been waiting all day for this. Don't make us wait any longer."

The orc eyed Cheyenne again before turning toward the off-duty agents and sticking a hand on her hip. "Do I need to cut you off already, troll?"

The buzzing energy making Bhandi pretty damn annoying petered out in seconds. She blinked and slumped her shoulders, her forearms propped on the bar. But she held the orc woman's gaze. "No."

"Great. Then I'll make you wait as long as I damn well please. And then you'll pay me for it."

"Naw, Yurik's gonna pay you for it." Tate laughed and nudged the huge goblin's muscular shoulder beneath the zig-zagging sweater. Yurik rolled his eyes but didn't try to argue.

Ogsa turned and pulled two massive metal pitchers from a shelf beneath the wooden casks. Bhandi bounced a little where she leaned against the bar, watching the orc's movements with eager anticipation.

Yurik shot her a frown. "You need to take a piss?"

"Fuck off."

A minute later, Ogsa set the metal pitchers down on the bar in front of the off-duty agents. Brown-red foam spilled over the sides, and Bhandi licked her lips.

"Woah, woah, woah." Yurik stuck an arm between the troll and the closest pitcher. "At least wait for a cup, will ya?"

The orc stared at them with a deadpan expression as she grabbed two metal tankards in each hand and thumped them down on the bar.

"*Yes.*" Bhandi didn't waste any time pouring grog into the closest tankard, which went immediately to her lips. Cheyenne could hear her swallowing like she hadn't had a thing to drink in days. The troll's fellow agents stared at Bhandi with mixed expressions of amusement and concern.

"Not sure if I wanna pour you two cups of fellwine *now*," Ogsa grumbled.

Bhandi lowered the cup with a loud sigh. She wiped the foam off her mouth with her forearm and shot Cheyenne a quick glance. "Oh, yeah. Pour the fellwine. *She* definitely needs one. I don't care who gets the other. I got my grog, and I am happy."

The tankard tilted back again as the troll guzzled more down.

"For fuck's sake, Bhandi." Tate leaned over the bar to peer around Yurik. "Wanna wait 'til we get to the table?"

"Oh, come on. He wants me to wait for a cup. You want me to wait for a table. Can't a troll drink her goddamn grog in peace?"

Tate let out a low whistle and met Cheyenne's gaze with a helpless shrug.

The halfling just shook her head and turned back toward Ogsa to watch the bartender pour the fellwine. *I'd drink like that if I was FRoE too.*

The fellwine came from the metal urn at the end of the shelf, as it turned out. Ogsa's broad back blocked Cheyenne's view of the process, and then the orc woman turned and brought back two copper cups. When she set them on the bar, Yurik leaned sideways to glance at the drinks and quickly pulled away. "Whew. You couldn't pay me to drink tonight. Not after last month."

"I'll take it." Tate reached across his buddy and slid one nearly overflowing copper cup across the bar.

"Running tab?" Ogsa asked, wiping her hands on her stained apron.

Yurik let out a long sigh. "Guess so. Hey, and none of you assholes orders anything else without me knowing about it. You hear me?"

"Blah, blah, blah." Bhandi grabbed her tankard in one hand and a pitcher in the other before turning away from the bar. "Thanks, Ogsa."

"Uh-huh."

"What?" Yurik growled and picked up the three empty tankards while Tate grabbed the other pitcher and a copper cup. "She should be thanking *me*."

Smirking, Cheyenne stared into the cup of fellwine in front of her and frowned. *Green wine, huh? Should've known.*

"Enjoy it, drow." Ogsa nodded at the halfling, a smirk rippling around the giant tusks.

Cheyenne lifted the cup and nodded. "Thanks."

She turned to follow the agents as a skaxen wearing a green suit as bright as his orange skin slammed his clawed hands down on the counter. "Ogsa! I'm dyin' over here."

"You shut your rat-faced trap, Rork! You're not the only one breathing down my neck."

The halfling moved as quickly as she could across the tavern toward a metal table in the back corner. The off-duty agents had already taken the chairs facing the rest of the room, and she set down her copper cup with a sigh. "So, I get the chair with my back turned to the whole damn bar, huh?"

Yurik shrugged with a little smirk as he poured brown-red

foaming grog into the other three tankards. "We pulled rank. And you're the new guy. You can handle it."

Cheyenne pulled out the chair and slowly lowered herself into it, staring at Bhandi beside her. "Maybe *she* should've sat here instead. Doesn't look like she's paying attention to anything but the tankard."

The troll woman leaned back in her chair, tipping the tankard until her head almost hit the wall behind her. Then she slammed the thing down onto the table with a clang, wiped her mouth again, and let out a massive belch.

"Woah," Cheyenne muttered with a hushed laugh.

"Jesus." Yurik shook his head.

All the other conversations from the tavern's patrons died down, then someone shouted from across the room, "Goin' for a fell-damn record over there, Bhandi?"

"I will for twenty bucks." The troll woman pumped her fist in the air without turning to see who'd yelled at her, then the drone of many voices picked back up again. Bhandi looked up at everyone else around the table and smacked her lips. "What were you guys saying about me?"

"Oh, just that you might need to find some kinda twelve-step program," Yurik replied. Tate snorted into his tankard.

"Yeah? Like Magicals Anonymous? Shit, Yurik, if that's it, we're *living* a goddamn twelve-step program."

Tate held up three fingers and gulped his grog.

"What's that, Tate?" Yurik cupped a blue-green hand around his ear. "Didn't hear you."

The troll lowered his tankard with a hissing sigh and thumped his elbow down on the table, his fingers still raised. "Three-step program. Don't let them see you, don't be late—"

"And don't fucking die," the three agents shouted, lifting their tankards to crack them together at the center of the table. Dark grog sloshed over the sides, and they drank.

Cheyenne laughed, her hand wrapped around the untouched copper cup. "That's all that matters, huh?"

"When you do what we do for long enough, Cheyenne, yeah." Yurik took another long drink. "That's all that matters."

Bhandi grabbed a pitcher to fill her tankard again. "And grog. Everything and everyone else can kiss my purple ass."

Tate barked a laugh and smacked the table. "Could've gone another fifty years without that image."

"Yeah, you'd like that, wouldn't you?"

On the other side of Cheyenne, Yurik nodded. "You tryin' to hatch an egg or something?"

"What?"

Bhandi waved at the halfling like she'd shove the cup up to Cheyenne's lips if she had to. "Drink, Goth drow. Come on!"

Laughing, Cheyenne grabbed the copper handle and stared down at the swirling bright-green fellwine. "This stuff any good?"

"Good *for* you, yeah. *That'll* put hair on your chest." Tate thumped his chest and drank more grog.

"Man, half the shit you say doesn't even make sense." Bhandi leaned back in her chair and scowled at the other troll, shaking her head.

"It's a figure of speech. Come on. I don't think any of us wanna see Cheyenne with a hairy chest."

"Okay, quit talking about my chest." The halfling tilted her head at him in warning. "You're digging the hole even deeper for yourself."

Bhandi threw her head back and cackled. Smirking, Yurik glanced from the copper cup to Cheyenne and leaned forward. "Drink. I gotta see this."

"Reassuring. Thanks."

"Yeah, just take a big ol' swig." Tate mimed knocking back the drink. "Goes down smoother that way."

"Yeah, okay." She lifted the cup to her lips and didn't have to sniff to catch the fumes rising from the fellwine. "Shit. What *is* this?"

"Go!" Bhandi shouted.

With a disbelieving laugh, Cheyenne cocked her head and lifted the cup even higher. "Fuck it."

She took a huge gulp of the overly sweet fellwine and almost dropped the copper cup into her lap. Green liquid sloshed over the sides when she set it sharply on the table, and she doubled over with wide eyes. "Holy shit!"

The off-duty agents burst out laughing. Bhandi slapped the halfling's back. "*There* you go! Now you're in."

"She did it." Tate's low chuckle filled their little corner. "The damn drow actually did it."

Cheyenne pounded on her chest and gasped for breath. "Jesus, how much worse is it if you drink it slowly?"

"It isn't." Tate lifted his cup and took a much smaller drink. Bhandi and Yurik snickered and the troll lowered the cup again, smacking his lips. "Fellwine's for sipping."

"Shit!" Sniffing back the burn in her nose, Cheyenne wiped the stinging tears from the corners of her eyes and let out a little chuckle. "I think I get step three now."

"*Yeah*, you do." Yurik lifted his tankard in another toast for the drow halfling. "If you survive tonight, Cheyenne, you're, well..." He laughed and shook his head. "You're gonna wish you were dead in the morning."

Cheyenne grinned and toasted him right back with her copper cup. "You're on."

"Here." Bhandi filled the last empty tankard with grog and slammed it on the table in front of the halfling. "Have a chaser."

CHAPTER TWENTY-FOUR

"Wait, a minute. Wait." Cheyenne stuck her hand out and leaned over the table. "*None* of you made the Border crossing?"

Tate puffed out a breath through loose lips. "Are you kidding? That'd be like, I dunno. Driving down the wrong side of the street."

Bhandi grunted into her tankard and quickly lowered it. "That's the stupidest analogy I've ever heard. Wait. Not including Sir's."

"But you're all, you know..." Cheyenne took another long drink of foamy grog to cover her cluelessness. *Is there even a word for it?*

"Purebloods?" Yurik's head wobbled in an imitated of superiority. "Genuine G-class?"

Tate snorted. "You're the only goblin at this table, man."

"Right. Not human." Cheyenne nodded, the room jerking up and down. She widened her eyes and put a hand on the table to steady herself in the chair.

"You think every single magical Earthside crossed over the Border? Shit." Bhandi slung her arm over the back of her chair and pointed at the halfling, her finger swinging from side to side. "Don't tell me you've never met a magical who was born in this world?"

"No, I have. A friend of mine is a...fourth-generation fae over here. No, wait. Third-generation." She shook her head, then glanced over her shoulder at the bar. "They serve water here?"

"Did you just say 'fae?'" Yurik's yellow eyes bulged in his blue-green face. "For real?"

"Uh, yeah." *Don't talk so much. Leave Ember out of it.*

"Woah." Tate rubbed the top of his tattooed head. "Didn't know there were any left."

"Except for ones who made it Earthside and kept having little fae babies." Bhandi shivered and wrinkled her nose.

"You should hook us up, Cheyenne." Yurik nodded and wagged his finger at her. "Having a fae on the team might be useful."

"Not gonna happen." The halfling leaned toward him and held him in a steady gaze. *Yeah, that sobered me right up.* "No."

"Okay, okay. Found the drow's weak spot. Sorry." Yurik leaned back in his chair, chuckling.

"We don't bring in magicals from the other side," Tate added. "I mean, we bring in magicals all the time."

"Yeah, in cuffs." Bhandi snorted and took another long drink.

"Just not on the team. You know?" Tate gave the halfling a conspiratorial nod.

"Is that word off-limits in here too?" Cheyenne asked, looking from one of the off-duty agents to the next.

"Not unless we wanna fight our way outta here." Bhandi swung her tankard to the side, sloshing more grog onto the table. "Same kinda hush-hush as you walking around looking like that instead of the H-word."

Cheyenne frowned. "human?"

"No. The other one."

"Oh. Right."

"The magicals coming in from the other side bring their expectations with them when they pop across the Border," Yurik added. "I heard the higher-ups tried to take some off the rez and put guns in their hands, but it apparently caused problems."

Tate nodded. "So now they pull from the pool of us who've never stepped foot off this Earthen realm."

"What are you, an Oracle now?" Bhandi laughed and leaned over the table. "Who says that? 'Earthen realm.'"

"That's what it is," Tate shot back. "And you wouldn't know an Oracle if it narrated your little escapade last month down to every nitty, gritty detail."

"Hey." Bhandi slammed her elbow on the table and flipped the other troll the middle finger. "Unspoken pact, man. What happens in Peridosh *stays* in Peridosh."

"Huh." Tate spun and glanced at the bar and the rest of the tables, which had filled up in the last hour. "Are we somewhere else?"

Cheyenne took a small sip of fellwine and felt a tingle spread across her shoulders. *Yeah, I think I'm done with that.* She grabbed the tankard of grog instead. "What happened last month?"

Yurik burst out laughing, leaning so far back, the front legs of his chair left the ground. He flung himself forward again and reached for the table. "Shit."

"No." Bhandi flipped middle fingers at both other agents this time. "No one says a goddamn word."

Tate winked at Cheyenne. "We'll tell you later."

"You little—" Bhandi lunged across the table and sent a ball of churning red magic at the other troll's head. She missed by at least a foot, and the spell smashed into the wall at the back of the tavern.

"Hey!" Ogsa pounded a fist on the bar, then pointed at their group. "We had a deal, Bhandi. Don't make me throw you out. I do *not* want a repeat of last month."

"We're good!" Bhandi tossed both hands up beside her head and sat back in her chair. "No problem over here, Ogsa."

"I'm watching you, Bare-Ass Bhandi."

Yurik and Tate lost it and erupted into howling laughter. Bhandi thumped against the back of her chair and folded her arms. One scarlet eye twitched as she glared at them. "It's not even a little funny."

Cheyenne tried to wipe a grin off her face. "Did you really—"

"That's enough outta you too." Bhandi pointed at her and shot her a sidelong, warning glance. "I like you, Goth drow. But not that much."

With a shrug, Cheyenne just returned to drinking her grog, the fellwine left safely half-full in the abandoned copper cup. While the other agents pulled themselves back under control, the halfling felt another prickling tingle race across her shoulders. She glanced into the tankard. *Didn't think I drank that much.*

"Hey." Tate's laughing smile faded, and he nodded toward the other side of the tavern. "Don't look now, but I think somebody's got a problem."

Bhandi immediately swiveled to the side in her chair and made a quick sweep of the other patrons.

"Goddammit, Bhandi, I said, *don't* look."

"Nah." She waved off the rest of the bar and turned back to drop her elbow on the table. "You're seeing things."

The tingle grew stronger across Cheyenne's shoulders, crawling back and forth. *That's what I'm feeling.*

"I don't think anyone cares about *you*, Bhandi." Yurik glanced covertly over the halfling's shoulder before tipping his face into his tankard. "They're mean-mugging Cheyenne."

"What?" Bhandi stared at the halfling now and nudged their new friend's shoulder. "impressive. You didn't even do anything."

"You piss anyone off lately?" Tate asked.

Cheyenne glanced at him, loosening her grip on the tankard's handle. "Are you serious?"

The tattooed troll nodded.

"Yeah, the list is pretty long. But I haven't been here before, so I don't know why." *Not the first time magicals have tracked me down, though.*

"Why what?" Bhandi waved a hand in front of the halfling's face. "Earth to Cheyenne. You can't not finish *that* sentence."

The halfling looked at the off-duty agents and shrugged. "Doesn't matter."

"It might, though, if those guys decide to step it up a notch."

Yurik dipped his chin and stared right back at whoever it was. "So far, it's just the death stare."

"Yeah, well, it never actually killed anyone." Cheyenne glanced at her grog and let go of the handle completely. *Totally sober now. I think.*

"It might if one of them was a raug."

Cheyenne choked in surprise. "What?"

"Oh, yeah." Tate had joined Yurik in the mean-eyed staring contest too. "A raug can strike you down just by looking at you the right way."

The halfling muttered, "That would've been good to know."

"What, before you went and had dinner with a raug, huh?" Bhandi chuckled. "Good one."

"No, I didn't have dinner with him. But he ate a bunch of… sticks?" Wrinkling her nose, Cheyenne shook her head and tried to shake the warning buzzing tingle off the back of her shoulders.

"For real?" Bhandi leaned toward her, the grog fumes pouring off her now almost as strong as they'd lifted from the fellwine. "You hung out with a raug?"

"Yeah, who just happened to be an Oracle." Cheyenne stared at the table. *Great. The tingle gets stronger, and I get a loose tongue.*

"No shit? Hey." Bhandi slapped the table. "Are you guys hearing this?"

"Not now, Bhandi." Tate narrowed his eyes, his voice dropping into a warning growl.

"A damn *raug*. And you two boneheads don't think that's—"

"Shut up," Yurik hissed.

"Okay, what the hell crawled into your—" The troll woman turned to look behind Cheyenne and sighed. "Shit."

A shadow fell across Cheyenne and most of the table. The halfling didn't turn around, but her fists clenched in her lap.

"Fancy seeing you here, *mór úcare*."

Don't know the voice. Definitely heard that name, though.

"Private table, asshole." Tate glared at whatever magical stood behind Cheyenne, his fist curling tighter around the handle of his tankard.

"I wasn't talking to you." It came out as a slow, rumbling growl. "I'm here for the drow."

"Not tonight, you aren't." Yurik pointed toward the other side of the bar, his yellow eyes flashing in the overhead lights. "Go on back to your buddies and finish off the night making good choices. Hell, have another round on me, and we'll call it good."

The looming magical behind Cheyenne leaned close enough for her to feel his breath on the back of her neck. "I'm talking to you, *mór úcare*. Show some manners at least, huh?"

She stared at the wall between Tate and Yurik. "Maybe if you brush your teeth first. Guess nobody told you that's kind of a priority Earthside. Even when you're breathing down someone's neck."

"You talk a lotta shit for someone who won't turn around and face me."

Slowly, the drow halfling lifted her hands and settled them on the table. Yurik cocked his head at her while the other off-duty agents stared at the asshole behind her. "You good?"

"I just chugged fellwine, man. I'm good."

CHAPTER TWENTY-FIVE

Cheyenne's chair scooted back as she stood. The agents shifted in their seats, but she shook her head at them. "I'll handle this."

The magical behind her stepped back, his shadow clearing from the table, and the drow halfling turned to face him. Her gaze landed on the center of the guy's chest, and she looked up slowly to see an ogre even taller and beefier than Jamal looming over her. *It had to be an ogre.*

The hulking magical sneered at her, his thick gray lower lip glistening with spit and maybe a little grog. "Yeah, that's what I thought."

"You got somethin' to say to me?" Cheyenne's fists clenched by her sides again, but she waited. *Keep the berserker down until you need it.*

"Oh, I got plenty to say." The ogre pressed one fist into his palm, his knuckles cracking like giant rocks smashing against each other. "Not the kinda conversation for mixed company, though."

"Naw. Whatever you gotta say to me, you can say in front of my friends here." She jerked her head back toward the table. "They're cool."

"*We're* not, *mór úcare*. You see *my* friends over there? They're not cool with you, either."

Four other magicals stood from a table halfway across the bar. The halfling had to peer around the giant dude's frame, which was at least twice as wide as her body.

"Goblin, orc, *skaxen*, troll. Huh." She craned her neck back at the guy hunching over her. "Looks like you brought the whole rainbow with you tonight."

"Almost." One side of the ogre's mouth lifted in another twitching sneer, revealing black-stained teeth. "We just need a little drow blackberry to add to the mix."

Cheyenne snorted. "Are you talking about *me*? 'Cause honestly, I don't know if it was supposed to be an insult or some kinda pet name."

"We've been looking for you, *mór úcare*. Ever since we got the calling."

"What calling?"

A low chuckle escaped the mountainous magical, then his arm swung toward her like a fallen tree. Cheyenne slipped into her enhanced speed and sidestepped the guy's clumsy punch. She tried to reach up and grab his head to slam into her knee at hyper-speed. Standing on her tiptoes, she could only reach the tops of his shoulders. A frustrated sigh escaped her. "Fine."

The halfling stepped back and sent a high kick into the center of the ogre's chest. Time sped up again, and the ogre flew into the wall just beside Bhandi with an ear-splitting crack.

"Oh, shit!"

"What the hell was that?"

The other patrons in the tavern backed away in surprise as the ogre dropped to the floor. The magicals at the table on the other side of him scrambled out of their chairs, snatching up their half-full tankards and pitchers.

Cheyenne looked at the four other dirtbags who'd stood when the ogre was still able to make threats, then pointed at the fallen mountain of gray meat. "You guys gonna come help your friend, or what?"

All four of the other thugs rushed toward her, snarling and conjuring flaring lights of different-colored magic in their hands. The troll let off a burst of icy-white shards. Cheyenne ducked, and the spell crashed against the back wall of the cavern.

She straightened again and rolled her eyes. "That's not what I meant!"

The skaxen launched a shimmering vortex of silver and green like a miniature tornado. Cheyenne grabbed the closest thing at hand—the mostly empty first pitcher of grog from her table—and batted his spell aside. A green crackle raced up her arm, making her drop the tankard again. It toppled onto the table and spilled the last of the grog.

"Hey," Bhandi shouted. "I was drinking that."

I really need to master that shield.

The orc conjured a burst of green fire in his palm as the skaxen leaped up onto the vacated table with a hiss, clawed hands at the ready. The halfling hurled a crackling black sphere of energy at the orc, which caught him in the shoulder of his raised arm and sent his green fire hurtling into the floor. He roared and slapped his shoulder as the skaxen leaped from the table.

What is it with those guys and all the jumping?

"Watch—"

Cheyenne slipped into her enhanced speed and shot black, whipping tendrils from her fingertips. They curled around the skaxen's chest and neck, and she jerked him back into the wall. Everything sped up again, the orange ratface crashed and bounced off the still-stunned ogre as Yurik finished his warning.

"—out!"

She turned toward him with a sarcastic nod. "Yeah, thanks. But I got—"

The orc rushing her made contact and bowled her over, lifting her partially up over his shoulder before slamming her into the back wall of the tavern. It knocked the wind out of her, and a collective groan rose from the tavern's patrons.

The halfling slammed her elbow down once, twice, three times into the back of the orc's neck before he finally pulled away from her. She ducked the huge green fist flying toward her face, and it crashed into the wall behind her instead. He stumbled backward, shaking out his hand and looking down at the floor to find his target. Cheyenne slipped between him and the wall and finally got to crack someone's nose against her knee.

The orc roared when she released his sweaty, hairless head. Then she saw the troll stomping toward her. Yurik jumped up from his chair to get in the troll thug's way, pulling his fist back for a swing. The troll's attention turned toward the body-building goblin with the huge ring in his nose and yellow sparks in his hand.

Cheyenne sent her black tendrils flying from both hands. Half of them coiled around the troll's neck and yanked him backward with a startled choke. The other half slapped against Yurik's cocked-back arm.

"Ow! Fuck!" He shook out his arm as the drow halfling cracked her knee against the side of the orc's face, spraying nearly-black blood and spit everywhere before he dropped. "Well, the hell was that for?"

She stormed toward the table and grabbed his shoulder, jamming him firmly back down in the chair again. Yurik landed with a thud, his eyes popping open even wider as he stared at her. "I said, I got this."

The ogre roared and managed to pull back up to his feet. His skaxen friend scrambled off him with a little yelp before they both turned to face the drow halfling. "You can't fight all of us off, *mór úcare*," the orange ratface hissed. "Might as well make it easier for us."

"This *is* easy." She blasted his pointy, sharp-toothed face with a barrage of crackling purple sparks like automatic bullets and hurled another crackling black energy ball at the ogre. The skaxen shricked, batting at his face, and the ogre just looked dumbly down at where her much more powerful spell had fizzled out across his chest. The halfling's shoulders sagged. "Oh, yeah. That's right."

The ogre lumbered toward her and swung his fist again. She slipped into her enhanced speed to avoid the punch, but her head jerked back, with agonizing pain ripping across the back of her skull. With a scream of pain, she tried to whirl toward his other suspended fist and got a face full of bone-white hair.

"What the...are you *kidding* me?" Cheyenne slapped the back of her head and the giant magical's fist right behind her. "Motherfucker grabbed my hair. What kind of—"

With another shout of frustration, she twisted enough to clamp both hands around the ogre's clenched fists. His fingers wouldn't budge, even in her drow speed, so she squeezed as hard as she could and summoned the churning spheres of black fire in both hands. *This'll be nothing like the puzzle box.*

In less than a second, she felt his hand opening beneath hers, then she ripped the rest of her hair free and dropped the hyperspeed.

The ogre's fist exploded, sending gray flesh and muscle and bits of bone flying in every direction. A yellow-nailed thumb thumped onto the table behind her, and the off-duty FRoE agents leaped out of their chairs. "Oh, *come* on!"

The ogre bellowed and Cheyenne moved away from him, clamping her hands over her ears and seeing two orange skaxen staring at the mangled, shredded stump of the ogre's detached wrist.

The troll came up behind her and sent his purple fist into her kidney. Cheyenne screamed and stumbled forward, barely avoiding the bellowing, lurching ogre as he gripped his mangled arm and waved it around like a lunatic. The drow halfling spun around to face the troll, staggering sideways because of the pain still echoing through her lower back. Another blast of icy shards erupted from his palm. She threw a hand up in front of her face, and the shards pinged off the tiny black shield she'd somehow managed to cast.

"Huh." She glanced at her hand, the shield dropped, and the troll launched another attack at her as the skaxen leaped at her from the other side. Her tendrils lashed out to wrap around the orange ratface, catching him in mid-air and jerking him in front of her toward the troll. The shards peppered his face over the slashes left by her purple sparks. The skaxen's scream broke off when he crashed into the troll and sent them both tumbling across the floor.

"My fucking *hand!*" Spit flew from the ogre's mouth, his eyes bulging as he stared at the bleeding stump. He just kept flailing it around.

"Hey, *you* brought dirty fighting into this." With a grunt, Cheyenne stalked toward him and cocked back her arm.

When he caught sight of her, he threw his arms open wide like he meant to end this fight by crushing her spine in a giant hug. Blood sprayed from his mangled stump, hitting her friends' table just after Bhandi snatched up her tankard and jerked it safely out of the way.

Slipping into drow speed, the halfling ran between his open arms and cracked the palm of her hand against the underside of his chin. A shudder of agony jolted down through her forearm, and she pulled it back with a hiss.

Time sped up again, the tavern filled with noise, clicks, crunches, and thumps, and for all her drow strength and speed and the ogre's gargantuan mass, his feet only lifted about an inch as his head whipped back. Shattered teeth sprayed from between his lips, and this time when he crashed against the wall, he didn't move.

"Okay, who's next, huh?" The drow halfling whirled to face the skaxen and the troll.

They'd untangled themselves and gotten back to their feet, but they swayed a little, hunched over and panting.

"Aw, come on." Cheyenne shrugged. "You wanted a party, right? Let's party."

When she stormed toward them, the troll hesitated before drawing up a hissing, flashing rod of yellow and green light between his hands. He yanked it tight with a snap, then lashed out at her with the crackling whip of his spell.

"Hey, that's cute."

"You're done, *drow*." The way the troll spat the word sounded a lot more hateful than whatever they kept calling her. "If we don't take you in, someone else will."

"See, I think you got that backward." She opened her hand, just to see what the last two thugs would do.

They both flinched, but the troll recovered quickly and drew his arm back to snap the yellow-green whip sparking in his hand. Before he could bring it down, the drow halfling shot her whipping black tendrils toward him. They coiled around the whip and jerked his spell toward his throat. The yellow magic fizzled, and her other hand sent more tendrils coiling around the troll's arms, torso, and neck. She yanked him toward her, released her whips with one hand, and landed a mean right hook to his jaw.

The troll's bright-red eyes rolled back in his head. Behind him, the skaxen snarled and leaped, not toward Cheyenne but past her, jumping across the tables lining the tavern and sending tankards and metal plates flying onto the floor behind him.

The halfling released the troll, who dropped like a purple bowling ball and turned after the skaxen. All she saw was a bunch of magical patrons at the Empty Barrel, staring at her with wide eyes and gaping mouths.

CHAPTER TWENTY-SIX

"Anyone know that guy or where he's headed?" Cheyenne pointed toward the tavern's door as it swung shut again behind the skaxen's desperate escape. "No? Okay."

With a shrug, she turned back around and eyed the bloody, nearly toothless ogre against the wall, the troll in a heap at her feet, and the bloody orc lying face-down in a pool of his own blood and spit. No one moved.

The drow halfling sighed and moved quickly toward the off-duty FRoE agents. All three of them stared at her with wide eyes. Bhandi cradled her tankard against her chest. Tate's scarlet eyebrows went up even farther, and Yurik's open mouth let out a dry click when he swallowed.

Cheyenne reached across the table and pointed at the copper mug in Tate's hand. He gave it up immediately. The halfling took one glance inside, blinked, then knocked back half a cup of fellwine and slammed the cup back onto the table with a clang. She sucked a sharp breath through her teeth. "Pretty sure I know why they made this stuff now."

Bhandi pointed to her head and stared at Cheyenne's. "You got a little…"

"What?" The halfling picked at her hair, finding a spray of someone's blood on her hand before a yellow fingernail and teeth tumbled onto the table. "Gross."

"That was…" Yurik blinked. "I'm not sure what I just watched."

She pointed at him. "Yeah, well next time, when I say I got it, that means don't—"

A loud clang rose behind her. Cheyenne turned slowly around just as an old, skinny goblin with dull-green hair sprouting from his ears slammed his tankard on the table again. And again. The magicals around him picked up the banging, crashing tankards, cups, pitchers, and fists on the metal tables filling the tavern. They all banged together, faster and faster until everyone but Cheyenne and her FRoE friends were doing it. The halfling's head vibrated with the noise. *What the hell does that* mean?

"Come on." Tate stepped out from behind the table and clapped Yurik on the shoulder. "I think it's time to go."

"It's…what?" Yurik blinked, then shook himself out of it and moved again. "Yep."

Bhandi downed the last of her grog before dropping the tankard onto the table. She brushed pieces of ogre fist off the front of her shirt with a grimace of disgust, then joined the others on their way out.

Cheyenne stepped over the troll's body and saw a glint of silver beneath his shirt. She dropped into a crouch and yanked on the chain to pull the whole thing out. *Of course, it's another bull's head.*

With a snort, she tossed the pendant back down and stood. The patrons stared at her, drumming metal wildly on metal. As the FRoE agents headed toward the door, she moved closer to the bar and nodded at Ogsa. "Want me to send someone in for cleanup, or…"

The orc woman stared at Cheyenne, thumping an empty tankard on the bar over and over with the rest of them. Her upper lip lifted in a twitching smile, and she leaned toward the drow halfling.

"Uh, did you hear me? Sorry about the mess."

The bartender grunted and smiled even wider, forcing the halfling with the zeroing-in stare to keep moving.

"Okay."

"Hey!" Tate waved her toward the front door, glancing at all the other magicals, who were still pounding on metal tables with fists and heavy metal tankards. "Time to move."

"Yep." Cheyenne turned away from the bar and headed toward the door. "Creepy."

Every single patron was staring at her, following her with their gazes. She nodded, but the feeling of so many eyes on her made her shiver, and she picked up the pace.

Bhandi and Yurik were already out the door, and Tate settled a hand on the halfling's back to usher her out onto the main avenue before the door swung shut behind them. The rhythmic, metallic clanging kept up briefly, then someone inside let out an earsplitting roar, and the rest of the Empty Barrel erupted with the same.

"Jesus." Tate flinched and eyed the tavern over his shoulder. "You'd think *they* were the ones who just took those guys out."

"Sounds like a goddamn battle cry to me," Yurik added, rubbing his shaved head beside the yellow braid.

"I've seen it before," Cheyenne muttered, shooting the tavern one more glance as the off-duty agents led her back toward the far side of Peridosh's wide avenue.

"Seriously?" Bhandi swiped at a stain on her gray jacket and let out a little grunt of irritation. "I've never seen it, and I *know* I've been around a lot longer than you."

"What happened the last time?" Tate asked.

"I, uh, took out a lunatic goblin at Rez 38. Everyone did the same thing there, too."

Yurik puffed out a sigh. "Did they seem as happy about it as that bunch of drunks smashing in those tables?"

"Yeah, actually." The halfling rolled her shoulders back and tilted her head from side to side. "This was a little weirder, though."

"Weird isn't the half of it, Cheyenne." Tate shoved his hands into the pockets of his jeans and swerved around two goblin women carrying woven baskets of what looked like animal skins. When they caught sight of the drow halfling, they gave her matching stares of curiosity and approval.

Cheyenne stared right back until she passed them.

"What you did back there was…insane, honestly." The troll looked at her over his shoulder. "That wasn't even you going full-out, was it?"

"Not really." When the halfling looked across the avenue, she found an orc couple, his arm around her shoulders, staring at her with the same intensity. She licked her lips and focused her attention on Tate's back. "We're getting outta here, right?"

"Hell yeah, we are." Bhandi let out a sharp laugh, but she'd sobered up enough so it just sounded flat. "Christ, I thought *I* was the crazy one."

"I'm not crazy."

"Nah. Sure you're not." Bhandi just waved her off. "I mean the whole damn situation. Where'd you learn that little arm-exploding trick?"

Cheyenne shrugged. "It just came to me." *When I tried to blow up my legacy.*

"I'll tell you what, though, Cheyenne." Yurik let out a surprised laugh and sniffed, rubbing his hand under the huge ring dangling from his nose. "Now we know the best way to take out an ogre. I mean, you saw the size of that fucker, right?"

The other operatives burst into tense chuckles.

"Would've loved to have you with us in the field two months ago. Took out a whole family of ogres up in Jersey trying to reenact *The Godfather* in real life." Tate nudged her in the shoulder again, and the halfling stepped sideways, not bothering to resist the pressure this time. "Took us damn near half an hour and four fell cannons to whip all the fight out of them."

"Hey, man. She doesn't like to be touched." Bhandi nodded at Cheyenne and raised her eyebrows. "Or hugged."

"Well, I wasn't planning on huggin' her *before* anyway." The tattooed goblin laughed. "Now I'm definitely not."

They reached the end of the underground magical bazaar and

stopped in front of the elevator doors that didn't have a call button down here. The doors opened, and the group filtered inside before they were closed back in and started moving up.

"Is this the only way down?" Cheyenne frowned at the metal walls again and shoved her hands into the pockets of her black canvas jacket.

"No, I think there are two other entrances. Maybe three."

Bhandi snorted. "Ma'kdo told me last week he found one through the sewers."

"What the hell was he doing in the sewers?"

"Beats me."

Yurik nodded. "Yeah, there are probably more ways into Peridosh than that. We only just saw…what? Not even a quarter of it?"

"If that." Tate shrugged.

"Crazy place to keep underground," Cheyenne muttered.

"Where else were they supposed to put it, under the train tracks at Triple Crossing?" With a chuckle, Yurik just shook his head. "First step, Cheyenne: don't let them see you."

"Yeah, that was always my—" She stopped and cleared her throat. *Not a good time to bring up my mom.* "That's been my first rule for a long time too."

"And it's a good one to have. Especially for a halfling, right?"

"Right." Cheyenne leaned against the wall of the elevator as it made the slow, wobbly climb to the Fro-Yo shop. *And no one chasing me seems to know.* The elevator fell silent. Bhandi swayed on her feet a little and quickly shook her head. "Hey, you guys ever seen a silver pendant shaped like a bull's head?"

Tate snorted. "No, but I bet *someone's* made that shape before."

"No, I mean other magicals wearing them. Like the guys we've been dragging in."

"Not that I remember." Yurik folded his arms and nodded at her. "Does the bull's head mean something?"

"Not sure. I've just seen it around." The halfling shrugged. "Thought you might have an idea about what it is."

"We couldn't tell you the first thing about fashion from the other side, Cheyenne." Bhandi pointed at Yurik and narrowed her eyes. "Except that their tastes are worse than his."

Tate snorted.

"Uh-huh. You think you're pushing my buttons, don't you?" Yurik smoothed down the front of his loud zig-zagging sweater, then slapped his chest with both hands. "But under this muscular physique is a—"

"Flabby Blueface?"

"Bunch of tasteless gristle?"

The goblin looked at his troll friends and cocked his head. "I was gonna say 'goblin with a thick skin,' but don't hold back. Tell me how you really feel."

The trolls chuckled and swayed with the elevator's bumpy ride to the surface.

Cheyenne couldn't help a little smile, and when Yurik saw it, he nodded at her again. "Cheyenne knows what I'm talkin' about."

"Uh, I can't speak for a thick-skinned goblin."

"Or a thick-skulled idiot," Bhandi muttered.

"But you *can* speak to having thick skin, right?" Yurik gestured toward her, then shoved his hand into the front pocket of his yellow pants. "Forget the Goth part. You're a halfling. When people see what you are, I bet they've got more to say about it than Bhandi's dumbass imagination can say about my clothes."

The halfling gave him a little frown. "More people comment on the Goth thing, actually."

The elevator jerked to a stop, sending the half-drunk magicals and the wasted Bhandi staggering against the walls. The troll woman tried to cram her hand into her pocket, grunting with the effort.

"You need some help with that?" Tate asked, chuckling and slipping his black illusion ring onto his pinkie.

"*Oh*, no. Those mitts aren't goin' anywhere near my..." Bhandi grunted again and finally whipped out her ring. "Shit."

The black band flew from her fingers, and Cheyenne leaned

forward to snatch it out of the air. Then she offered it to the troll with a knowing smile. "Probably wanna hold onto this."

Bhandi's scarlet eyes moved lazily across the halfling's face, then she snatched the ring and jammed it onto her finger. "Thanks. Showoff."

The elevator doors screeched open, revealing the back of the fake Employees Only entrance. Yurik laughed. "Someone sounds a little jealous."

"What? I don't do jealous." Bhandi grabbed the handle and jerked inward on the door until Tate pushed it out. The troll woman stumbled forward, now looking like a human with auburn hair and blue eyes. "Stupid. I swear this thing opened the other way."

"From the outside, yeah." Chuckling, Yurik and Tate stepped out of the elevator, and Cheyenne followed.

The guy running the shop that fronted one of Peridosh's entrances stared at the group as they passed him toward the front door. "What the hell are you jokers doing back up here?"

Bhandi snorted and spread her arms. "What? You disappointed to see we made it out alive? Again?"

Tony's mouth twisted in an amused grin. "Well, there's that too. But you people are usually down there a lot longer than two hours."

"What time *is* it?" Yurik asked.

He turned and eyed the clock on the wall behind his desk. "Just after eight."

"Jesus." Yurik shook his head and walked toward the front of the shop.

Tate lifted a fist at Tony, and Bhandi clapped her hands together. "Fast and hard, Tony. That's how we roll."

"Yeah, don't forget shitfaced." The man chuckled until he saw Cheyenne, and the laughter cut off as his eyes widened.

Oh, right. She slipped out of her drow form, returning to the black-haired, pale-skinned Goth chick, and shot the man a smirk. "Have a nice night."

"Uh-huh." Tony rubbed his chin and watched the group pass through his store.

Yurik shoved the door open and laughed. "See that, Bhandi? I'm pretty sure most places make you push to get *out*."

"Don't make me push *you*."

"So, Cheyenne." Tate reached out to nudge her again, then thought better of it and shot her a thumbs-up. "Minus the whole barfight you wouldn't let the rest of us enjoy, what do you think of Peridosh?"

"Uh…" A laugh escaped her. "I think I could handle it about as often as you guys get to leave the compound."

"Ha." Yurik turned back toward her as they crossed the street toward the parking lot. "'Cause it got crazy in there, huh? Yeah, this wasn't a normal night. It's usually more chill."

"Yeah, and Bhandi's usually the one making trouble when we go out," Tate added.

"Hey, I didn't start a single one of those fights." Bhandi rolled her shoulders back and stumbled before stepping up onto the sidewalk. "But I sure as hell finish 'em."

"Not like Cheyenne, you don't." Tate leaned toward the halfling and muttered, "Most of her fights end with the other guy giving up or Bhandi passed out on the floor."

"Gotta get the job done somehow."

Cheyenne barked a laugh. "Please don't tell me 'Bare-ass Bhandi' is your fighting name."

Yurik and Tate exploded with laughter, turning around to give the halfling approving looks before pointing at Bhandi and falling all over each other. Bhandi shot the half-drow a withering glare that cut off when she stumbled over her own feet and almost ate asphalt. Cheyenne snatched the troll woman's arm and jerked her upright, grinning.

"Cheyenne, Cheyenne," Bhandi sighed through loose lips and shook her head. "You make it really hard not to like you."

"I'll take it."

They got back to the Range Rover, and Bhandi jammed her hand into her back pocket to fish around for the key fob. She leaned on the driver's side door and bent her knees, leaning back way too far to get her hand in.

Tate snorted. "You look like Ma'kdo trying to take a piss."

"Yeah? Piss on this." Bhandi yanked the fob out with a grin, and the thing flew out of her hand onto the asphalt. The troll looked down at it, blinked, then turned toward Cheyenne. "Couldn't you catch that one too?"

"Hey, I'm not your maid."

The guys cracked up again, and Yurik stooped to pick up the fob before pointing at Cheyenne. "Cheyenne's nobody's maid. Damn straight. Hell, she called us to come clean up a mess she made the other day. Nothing like what Ogsa's gonna have to scrub out of the floor after tonight, but if anyone's a maid, it's me and Payton."

His chuckle died, then he blinked at the key fob in his hand and rolled his eyes. "Shit."

"There it is." Tate thumped the goblin with brown human hair on the back. "You good to drive, Grandma?"

"Yeah. I'm good."

"I call shotgun," Bhandi announced, stumbling around the front of the car.

Tate went around the back to climb in behind the troll woman, and Yurik glanced at Cheyenne with a little frown. "Like I said, you can pretend to forget about what happens. That's what blowin' off steam's for, right?"

"Right." Cheyenne opened the door behind the driver's seat, then paused. "Hey, it wasn't you who put Payton in a hospital bed. You know that, right?"

The goblin sighed. "Course I know that. It doesn't change us being a team. The whole damn unit. I tell you what, though. Next time you come with us in the field, I don't give a shit about what my orders are. I'm listening to you first."

"That's...probably not a good idea. For you."

"Hey, if we'd listened to you and Jamal hadn't opened the goddamn crate, he wouldn't be lyin' in a bed, either. Or Payton. You knew what was gonna happen." Yurik leaned toward her and cocked his head. "How'd you know?"

Cheyenne shrugged. "It's a drow thing, I guess."

"Drow thing. Yeah." He opened the driver's side door and paused again. "Yeah, that's why I'm listening to *you* from here on out."

They climbed inside and shut the doors behind them. Yurik started the car, everyone buckled up, and then they pulled slowly out of the parking lot. Tate let out a massive belch in the back seat. "Whoa. That would've been grog if Bhandi was behind the wheel."

"Hey." Bhandi slumped against the passenger door and dropped her head against the window. "The night's not over yet."

CHAPTER TWENTY-SEVEN

"Hey, Yurik." Cheyenne grabbed the back of the driver's seat and leaned forward. "Can you drop me off at the strip mall from this morning?"

"The one under construction?"

"Yeah. That's where my car is."

"Come on, Cheyenne." Bhandi waved a drunken hand. "We get back to base, and I'm pullin' out the cards. Got a winning streak against Kinzuro, and I plan to take everything the little shit has."

Tate snorted. "What'd the guy do to you, huh?"

"Nothin'. He just keeps losing and comin' back for more. Hey, Cheyenne. You any good at poker?"

"I don't know."

"*What*? Goth drow blows up an ogre's hand, but she doesn't play poker?" Bhandi didn't lift her head from against the window, but her voice got louder. "You sure you were born Earthside?"

"Not everyone on this side plays poker." The halfling sat back in her seat and stared out the window.

"Well, for someone who's never played, you've got one hell of a poker face." Tate chuckled.

"So, you in or what?" Bhandi asked.

"No. Thanks, but I'm gonna call it a night."

"Before eight-thirty?"

Yurik slapped Bhandi's arm with the back of a hand. "Give it a rest, huh?"

"What, you gonna get back on base and go hug your pillow too?"

"Maybe. Sounds better than sitting around watching you sober up."

"Not gonna happen, Yurik. I drank enough grog to last me all night."

Tate snorted. "You drank enough to last you all *week*."

Bhandi sighed but didn't say anything else, and the car fell back into silence.

Ten minutes later, Yurik pulled the Range Rover into the parking lot of the strip mall under renovation and parked several spaces from Cheyenne's Ford Focus.

"That's your car?" Bhandi asked.

"Yep." The halfling unbuckled her seatbelt.

The troll woman laughed. "Anyone notice that people tend to look like their cars?"

"That's *dogs*, grog-brain." Tate shook his head.

Cheyenne snorted and grabbed the handle of the back passenger door. "How do I look like my car?"

"Rough around the edges, Goth drow." With a grunt, Bhandi peeled herself away from the passenger window and twisted around with effort to grin at the halfling. "But you get the damn job done, don't you?"

"Guess so. You're not gonna try to hug me, are you?"

The agents laughed, and Bhandi slumped in her seat again. "*So* hard not to like you."

"Thanks for the ride." Cheyenne thumped the back of Yurik's seat. "And the fellwine. I needed that."

"Ha. Yeah, that's on me anytime."

"Oh, sure, *she* gets a free pass."

"Bhandi, if you had free drinks for life, I don't know what would happen first—you drinking every single ounce of the stuff on this side of the Border, or you dropping dead from trying."

"Hey, why pick one? If I achieved a goal like that, I'd die happy."

Shaking her head and hiding a small smile, Cheyenne pushed the door open and stepped out of the Range Rover. "Have a good night, guys."

"Drive safe, Cheyenne." Tate lifted his hand in farewell. "See ya."

"Yep." She closed the door and headed for her car as the black FRoE vehicle pulled away across the parking lot. When she slipped into the driver's seat and stuck her keys in the ignition, she dropped her head back against the headrest. "Crazy."

Then she shook it off and headed back to her apartment. A quick glance at the clock on the dash made her sigh. *Only eight-thirty. Plenty of time to get some real work done.*

The pizza box from Mellow Mushroom in her hand made her mouth water, and her stomach growled in response as she walked down the hall toward her apartment. Her keys jingled in her hand before she unlocked the front door, then she stepped inside and froze. "Not again."

The puzzle box had worked its way out of her backpack one more time and floated mid-air in front of her. Cheyenne kicked the door shut behind her and dropped her keys and the pizza on the counter beside the basket of troll-crafted underwear. Her shoes thumped against the door as she kicked them off, then she opened the pizza and pulled out the first huge, greasy slice. "Now, *this* is how to end a day like—ow!"

The pizza dropped from her hand, and she spun to face the glowing, floating puzzle box. It vibrated in the air, the low hum growing louder and louder. She squinted at it, then bent her arm behind her back to rub the fading sting there. *Probably just leftovers from the fight.*

She shook her head and started to turn around again, but the drow legacy box shot another dart of golden magic—at her shoulder this time. The halfling jerked away and hissed. "Seriously?"

The box started spinning, all the sections but the one she'd locked into place whirling, shifting in every direction. When it shot two more tiny magical attacks at her, Cheyenne's body erupted with the heat of her drow magic and she ducked aside. The golden darts left charred holes in the counter.

She backed into the living room, and the hovering box followed. "This is *not* my idea of a—"

Another golden burst shot toward her, and Cheyenne tossed her hand up. The black shield appeared just before the legacy box's attack sparked off it with a metallic ping. She cocked her head and smirked. *That's getting easier.*

Then a volley of golden sparks sprayed from the whirling, humming copper box. The halfling ducked and ran, circling her tiny living room as the attacks peppered the back wall of the hallway and the bathroom like a machine.

"Cut it out!" She brought up another shield the length of her body in front of her, and the golden attacks ricocheted off the translucent black spell. Charred holes appeared in the matted carpet, walls, and ceiling. The halfling tossed another shield in front of Glen, then growled at the legacy box and raised both hands. "I said, stop!"

The black light of one more shield burst into existence around the box, filling her apartment with bright sparks and muted golden light as it whirred and sprayed magical darts at the shield around it. The attacks bounced back, and the thing gave up. The box hovered inside her shield, motionless. Then the shield disappeared, and one more layer of etched runes slid slowly into place with a series of soft clicks before locking into place beside the first. The two locked levels lit up from within, then the puzzle box dropped to the floor with a thud.

Cheyenne eyed the thing and stepped slowly across the carpet. "You done?"

The box replied by sitting there on the floor like…a box.

Waving down her shield and the one she'd cast to keep Glen safe, the halfling picked it up. The metal was cool and dull in her hands. She flipped it over and grinned. *Looks like I'm getting the hang of these stupid drow trials after all.*

She took the box with her to the counter and set it inside the basket of brightly colored troll gifts before snatching up her pizza again. The first bite made her close her eyes and sigh as she chewed. *Fellwine, fistfights, and fast food. I think I just found the trifecta.*

Standing at the kitchen's half-wall counter, Cheyenne wolfed down the first slice, picked up the second, and grabbed a bottle of water from the fridge and her last clean plate before heading toward her office chair. She powered Glen up and turned the monitor on, chugging half the water while she waited.

Once she logged into the dark web and navigated into the Borderlands forum, she felt almost as good as if she'd eaten another barf-worthy energy bar. The halfling scooted her chair toward the desk and sucked in a sharp breath. "Ow."

She rubbed the ache in her lower back, which was much more painful than the bruised ribs she probably had. *All that magic, and it's being crushed by an orc and punched by a troll that hurt the worst.* Her hand moved toward the bottom drawer of her desk, but she paused and shook her head. *Mattie's healing recipes can wait.*

When she looked up again at the Borderlands forum and the top five posts showing on her monitor, her eyes widened. *Woah. The Borderlands just exploded.*

CHAPTER TWENTY-EIGHT

The first topic at the top was actually a pinned announcement created a little over an hour ago: *'Posted Names, Class, Age, and Time.'* There were already about sixty comments on this one, but what really caught the halfling's attention were the other most recently created topics below.

I'm Looking for My Son.
My 16-Year-Old Daughter Hasn't Come Home.
Trying to Get hold of Kalyss.
Troll Brothers Missing ages 8 and 11.

The first slice of pizza curdled in Cheyenne's stomach, and she grimaced at the second on her desk before sliding the plate away from her keyboard. Then she scrolled through the newest topics and found at least two dozen others having to do with missing kids. All of them were made after 5:00 p.m. *Sir and Rhynehart wanted their proof. Here it is.*

She went back up to the pinned announcement and clicked on it.

Topic #215,637 by OP holdmyGrog911; pinned by gu@rdi@n104: Opened 8:16 p.m. EST

holdmyGrog911: I tried to make a running list, guys, but the new threads are coming in so quickly, I can't keep up. If you're

trying to post information about a kid missing from the Richmond or greater Richmond area, please put it here in a comment so we can have all the info in one place. I've got someone helping me put together a better list so we can run it for pattern recognition. If we can find anything else these kids have in common besides the obvious, it might help us figure out what the hell happened.

We're working on it, and we all want to help. As far as any of us knows, this is a first for this kind of thing Earthside. New territory here, but we're all in this together. That's why we came, right? O'gúleesh blood is thicker than the Border and stronger than anything we left behind. Don't forget it.

Also, if anyone has any information they think might help and is not posting about a missing kid, send me a DM. I'm trying to follow every lead I get, but it's not helping anyone to throw a bunch of conjecture out there just to stir the pot. This isn't the time for that kind of shit.

Amendment at 8:21 p.m. EST by gu@rdi@n104: Anyone who tries stirring up shit on this thread or any of the previous Missing Kids topics before we find these kids WILL be banned from the forum for life. First and only warning. No excuses.

Cheyenne pushed herself back into the office chair, wincing at the ache in her back, and sighed. *At least Corian hasn't given up moderating.*

She couldn't help but scroll through the pinned announcement to skim through the comments. Two-thirds of them had the name, race, and age of one missing kid after another. Most of them had extra commentary on what the parents or guardians had already tried, but some of them were just left up there with the necessary details and nothing else.

The halfling hissed another breath as her eyes and nose stung. The comments blurred together, and she shook her head. *Good thing I'm not a helpless bystander.*

She took screenshot after screenshot, scrolling to capture every name and age and race and exactly how many kids had up and disappeared, according to the adults caring for them, within the last four hours. Then she slapped at the outer pockets of her jacket and pulled out the burner phone. *Oh, come on. They really need to upgrade this thing.*

Pulling up a text to Rhynehart's number, she shook her head and got to work.

Got proof. Send me an email address and you'll have it.

Cheyenne dropped the phone onto the desk and slouched in her office chair, staring at the useless piece of technology. It felt like she sat there for an hour waiting for a reply, then she pushed herself away from her desk and stood. *I'm not waiting all night for this.*

The phone buzzed. She snatched it up and almost ripped it in half when she flipped open the top.

Just text it to me.

"*What?*" Growling, Cheyenne loosened her grip on the phone and forced herself to take a deep breath.

You gave me a piece of crap phone without email, camera, or storage. No basics. Give me an email address, or I'll go take care of this myself.

Rhynehart's reply was instantaneous this time.

L.Rhynehart@froe.gov

Cheyenne dropped back into her chair and pulled up her VCU email account to send it from there. *Not giving the FRoE any personal info they don't already have.*

She pulled up a new email, attached ten screenshots of the Borderlands forum's missing-kids announcement, and filled in the address and typed, *Proof* in the subject line. Then she sent the email and slapped a hand on her desk.

Groaning, the halfling spun in her chair and ran her hands down the sides of her face. "I should be out there right now finding them, not playing secret messenger."

More rage and drow magic burst through her, and she launched out of the chair to stalk back and forth across the small strip of living room between the kitchen and Glen. From the apartment beside her, she heard whoever lived there tapping out a jerky, lazy rhythm on the table. The sound made her eye twitch as she paced.

Pull yourself together. Just wait.

The burner phone buzzed on her desk again, then kept buzzing as she raced around Glen to snatch it back up. She jerked it open and slapped it against her ear. "We have to go right now."

"Woah, rookie. That's not—"

"You said you needed proof. I just gave you a whole load of it. Now it's time for *you* to follow through."

"I don't even know what you sent me."

"Are you *blind?*" she shouted and picked up the pacing again, yelling into the phone. "There are dozens of kids reported missing. All since five o'clock, and nobody knows where they are."

"That's not enough to go on, Cheyenne."

She ignored his use of her name. "Why not?"

"First of all, if the guys selling black magic *did* round up a bunch of kids, it happened before eight o'clock this morning. There's a nineteen-hour gap here."

"Are you kidding me? These kids are all school-aged, Rhynehart, and it's a Tuesday. And what damn time do most people get off work to come home to their kids, even if they're magicals?"

"Huh." There was silence on the other end of the line.

"Yeah, genius. I'm telling you, these are the same kids."

"Okay, maybe. Maybe. But what you sent me doesn't have anything in it about where they went or who took them."

Cheyenne rolled her eyes and spun to keep pacing. "That's why we have to go *find* them. Now."

"Hey, do I really need to spell this out for you? Where the hell are you gonna start looking, huh? I've been in Richmond for seven years, rookie, and lemme tell ya, I'm *still* finding places I didn't know existed. Unless that drow nose of yours can turn you into a bloodhound, *we have no starting point.*"

The halfling forced a long sigh between her teeth, her chest heaving. *Cool it. Come on.* "Well, then have *you* found anything about where they are?"

"No. We're still looking."

"Oh, yeah? Where do *you* start?"

"Look, kid. We've got informants and friends keeping eyes on different areas of town. I'll make some calls and get more eyes on this thing, but I can't send out a team if I don't know where we're going or what we're up against. And...shit. And you know I have to run this through the chain of command first anyway, okay?"

"Well, you better make it convincing."

"I'll do what I can." Rhynehart sighed over the phone. "Just sit tight and don't go rushing into this without backup, yeah? Which I'm pretty sure is gonna come from my end."

"Whatever."

"Hey, where'd you find this stuff, anyway? Might be a good resource for us in the future."

Cheyenne swallowed and settled her gaze on Glen. "You wouldn't know what to do with it if I told you."

"Okay. Whatever it means, good work. We'll find them, Cheyenne. That's what we do."

Except the FRoE couldn't find me until I literally ran into them. "Call me when you have something."

She slapped the flip phone shut and almost chucked it across the room, but she shoved it into her jacket pocket instead and kept pacing. Her next-door neighbor had started humming a little tune with the drumming rhythm on the table, way out of key. Cheyenne's back ached and it didn't go away, even when the flaring heat of her drow blood rose up her spine. She shoved it back down and stormed toward the kitchen to snatch up her keys. *I gotta get outta here.*

Smashing her feet into her black Vans, she jerked open the front door and stopped. The halfling gritted her teeth and leaped back to grab the copper legacy box and tuck it under her arm.

CHAPTER TWENTY-NINE

She pulled up in front of the house-turned-into-rental-units and turned off the engine. The copper box glinted in the light of the streetlamp, and Cheyenne glared at it in the passenger seat. It was cold and lightless when she scooped it up and got out of the car. The slamming door echoed down the empty street, and the halfling stomped across the grass around the side of the house toward the steps leading down to the basement door of Apartment D.

Puffing out a sigh, she knocked once, and a blast of orange light flared between her knuckles and the metal door. A fiery jolt raced up her arm, and her drow form took over before her back hit the far wall of the bottom stairwell. "What the hell?"

The door shimmered with orange light again and jerked open. Corian's wide silver eyes stared at her from the foot-wide opening. "Cheyenne," he hissed. "What are you doing here?"

She lifted the legacy box in her hand and scowled at him. "What are you trying to do to *me*?"

"What?"

"Your door's a giant electrical socket."

The Nightstalker rolled his eyes. "I'm beefing up security around here, okay? Told you I had to put up some wards."

"Then you need to beef it up even more." The halfling shook out her hand. "That hurt, but I'm pretty sure I could have knocked the door off its hinges if I'd really wanted to."

"Yeah, well, the wards aren't for you." Corian leaned through the door to peer up at the top of the stairwell. "And if you'd told me you were coming, I would've taken them down until you got here."

"Oh, sorry. Did I need to schedule an appointment with your secretary?"

He met her gaze again, his tufted ears twitching where they poked up out of his messy brown hair. "You're pricklier than normal. What's going on?"

"Messed-up day, and it only got worse when I checked the forum about forty-five minutes ago."

Sucking his lower lip, the Nightstalker wrinkled his nose and stepped away from the door. "At least come inside before you start talking about it. Come on. Hurry up."

Cheyenne slipped through the door, careful not to brush the metal, and stood in the unfinished basement while Corian shut it again. He cast a spell in a few quick gestures with both hands, and the orange light rippled across the door again. Then he turned, looked her up and down, and walked past her toward his laptop on the cheap card table. "Heard about the kids, huh?"

"Yeah. Before anyone else. Probably even before their parents."

"What?" He stopped with his hand on the back of the chair and cocked his head. "You know something about this?"

"Those kids were taken this morning by the same assholes selling all that black-magic crap. To kids."

Scratching behind his ear, Corian gestured toward the other chair at the table. "Have a seat and tell me what you know."

Slowly, the halfling walked past him to pull out the other chair.

The Nightstalker sniffed the air and frowned at her. "You smell like blood, fellwine, and..."

"Spices? Yeah, I know." She sat and thumped the puzzle box onto the table. "Long story."

"Okay." He raised an eyebrow and clasped his hands in his lap. "I'm listening."

"I went out with some people this morning."

"I know you've been playing special ops with the FRoE, Cheyenne. You don't have to talk around it."

The halfling blinked and had to try twice before she could swallow. "And you're not freaking out about it?"

He snorted. "Please. Those people think they know what they're doing. Sometimes they get lucky, and it looks to everyone else like they know what they're doing too. But they've only been around for two or three decades, and that's nothing compared to how long some of us have been laying low Earthside."

"Like you."

"Yes, Cheyenne. Like me."

"It's not gonna be an issue if I'm working with those guys?"

Corian shrugged. "I couldn't care less, honestly. The only thing that matters is if it's an issue for you. Seeing as the FRoE has L'zar, and that's how you got into Chateau D'rahl to see him, I'm guessing they're still useful to you."

"Maybe."

"Look, my advice would be to keep using that connection until they don't have anything else to offer you. Then drop 'em."

"That was kind of the plan." Cheyenne leaned back in the chair and stretched her legs out under the table, careful to move them aside so she wouldn't touch the flimsy table legs or the Nightstalker's shoes. "Right now, they're pretty useless."

"You're talking about the kids."

"Yeah." She took a deep breath and closed her eyes. "We went out this morning to go after the magicals selling that crap. The FRoE had a tip about where to find them, but when we got there, the place was empty except for crates of supplies those assholes apparently didn't need and a—" She forced back the tears threatening to build up behind them. "A pile of clothes."

"Clothes."

"Kid's clothes, Corian. Backpacks. Shoes. All their stuff. And I saw a goblin kid the other day dressed in some stupid black robes. He was already gone by the time we got there, but I'm pretty sure there was some kinda sacrifice or something." Cheyenne rubbed her forehead. "I know it sounds crazy—"

"No." The Nightstalker's gaze was as steady as his voice when she looked back up at him. "It's not crazy at all. It's been a long, *long* time, but I've seen something like this before."

"With *kids?*"

The Nightstalker dipped his head. "Ambar'ogúl is rife with black magic, Cheyenne. It's always been there, sure, but the last century or so, things really started to get out of hand."

"You've been here longer than that, though."

"That doesn't mean I haven't heard stories. And you know the Border crossings aren't one-way trips."

"Are you trying to tell me everyone on that side practices black magic?"

"Not everyone, no. Not yet, anyway." Corian pressed his lips together in a grimace. "Why do you think so many O'gúleesh are making the crossing, now more than ever?"

"To get away from it."

He nodded. "And now it looks like someone's trying to push it Earthside, too. Or maybe some displaced and bitter magicals gave up on trying to make things work the way they were supposed to after they got here. Who knows? It's easy to turn to black magic if you think you've run out of options with everything else."

"That's no excuse." The halfling folded her arms.

"I agree with you there, Cheyenne." The Nightstalker closed his eyes, then crossed one leg over the other. "It wasn't supposed to take this long."

"What wasn't?"

He stood abruptly from the table and scanned the metal shelves against the wall. "You're not ready for that."

"That's also not an excuse." Cheyenne nudged the copper puzzle box across the table. "And I'm more ready now than the last time I was here."

"Yeah? How's that?"

"Solved another line of the legacy box."

The Nightstalker stiffened before slowly turning back toward her. His gaze traveled slowly from the box to Cheyenne's face. Then his hand lashed out toward her, and a crackling bolt of silver magic streamed toward her. The halfling leaped out of her chair, sending it to the cement floor, and raised a shield. Corian's spell crackled across the surface of the translucent black field, then fizzled out before the shield disappeared.

"Hmm." Corian cocked his head. "You've been practicing."

"Yeah, bar fights are good for that."

"That's good. One more ability mastered, and you're closer to solving that *Cuil Ani*." He turned back toward the shelf and started rummaging through the piles of junk there. "But it's not good enough."

"You know, I'm really getting tired of people telling me I'm not ready, or it's not good enough, or I need to wait and just do what I'm told."

"Whatever anyone else has told you, Cheyenne, trust me. You're not ready to face this until you've completed the drow trial and come into your own. You're not the only one affected by this."

"Really?" The halfling folded her arms. "It's supposed to be *my* legacy. What do you get out of it?"

Corian sighed and kept digging through his things. "It's not just about me either, but I get out of it what the rest of the Earthside magicals will get out of it, and if everything works out the way it's supposed to, you'll be changing things for O'gúleesh across the border, too."

"What are you talking about?"

"That doesn't matter. What matters is you mastered another ability and locked another section of the box into place. You're getting loud and bright now, kid. Like a comet."

The guy's lost his mind.

"Please tell me something that makes sense. I'm sick of riddles and analogies everyone thinks I'm supposed to understand."

"You'll understand eventually. When you're—"

"Ready. Yeah, I get it. Look, I've had a seriously messed-up day, and I thought I'd come over here to try *not* getting my ass kicked again so we can speed this thing up. Are we gonna go through another portal to train some more, or what?"

"Not tonight. Ah." Corian removed a small tin box from beneath a pile of unfolded clothes and set it to the side on the shelf. Then he jiggled the lid until it came free with a metallic squeal and pulled out a long, thin silver chain with a round pendant dangling from the end. "But this will help."

"You said it was your job to train me," Cheyenne muttered.

"I did, and that's true. But I have other things to take care of. One of those is trying to maintain a speck of sanity in this town with all those missing kids." The Nightstalker whispered something unintelligible, gestured with one hand while the chain dangled from his other fist, then lifted the pendant to blow on it. Then he flicked the pendant with his finger, and a burst of silver light flared in a bright circle around the necklace before quickly fading. "If you saw what's happening on the forum, kid, you know how precarious things are. If magicals over here start freaking out about their children or trying to go find them? Well, that's a whole new can of worms, isn't it?"

The halfling stared at the pendant dangling from the chain as Corian brought it back to her at the table. "I don't need any more jewelry."

"No. You need protection."

"The kind that fires off spells for me? 'Cause I wouldn't mind taking a *little* break from having to fight off all those idiots wearing bull's-head pendants."

Corian stopped and swung the pendant just out of reach with a frown. "Were you attacked again?"

"I mean, technically, yeah. It wasn't that big a deal." The halfling rubbed her lower back and grimaced. "Just left bruises."

"Well, this should help with that, too. The attacks. Not the bruises." He finally handed her the necklace.

Cheyenne took it from him and studied the round charm, which was the size of a quarter. The black gem set in the tarnished silver setting flashed in the yellow light of the bulb hanging from the ceiling. Glimmering specks caught the light here and there, with streaks of silver barely visible through the center. "What kind of stone is this?"

"It's called the Heart of Midnight. Used for a lot of drow spells in Ambar'ogúl. Powerful magic needs a binding agent to focus it. The stone was rare before I came Earthside. I don't know if there's any left now."

"Just like the Nimlothar trees, huh?"

"Unfortunately, yes."

"Sounds like somebody got pretty greedy over there."

The Nightstalker grunted. "You have no idea."

"Does this thing come with instructions, or…"

"Just wear it, Cheyenne. When you do, you should start having a lot less trouble with those idiots wearing the bull's head."

"How's that?" She unclasped the necklace and reached up to settle the chain around her neck. A wave of cool energy bloomed across her chest and filtered into her limbs. With it, her drow form melted, and she stood there in the basement looking like her regular human self. "An illusion charm?"

"Not quite. I told you that you were getting bright and loud. The stone is a…sound-proof booth, if you will. Almost like you never started the trials in the first place."

"So, those magicals wearing the bull's head are coming after me because I started solving the puzzle box?"

"That's part of it. I'd say to wear it as much as you can. The minute it's off, those trying to find you will pick right back up on the scent."

The halfling blinked up at him. "What did you say?"

"About what?"

"My *scent*. Is that some kinda weird euphemism from the other side, or what?"

Corian shook his head. "I don't..."

"You know what? Never mind. I can handle being a scentless drow for a little while." She peered down at the stone and shrugged. "At least it's my color, right?"

"Yes, Cheyenne. That's the most important part."

She smirked and wagged a finger at him before tucking the copper puzzle box beneath her arm again. "See, I can tell you're being sarcastic there."

"Oh, good. I was worried you'd take me seriously." He went back to his chair and sat down, tapping his mouse to wake up his laptop again. "I have a lot of things to take care of tonight, but assume we're good for another training session tomorrow unless I tell you otherwise."

"Or unless I'm out getting those kids back."

Corian turned to look at her and raised an eyebrow. "That's the only priority that tops your trials for the short-term. And don't forget about the second visit with L'zar, if you can swing it. I know a lot about how this works, but not nearly as much as he does."

"Trust me, I haven't forgotten. I'll see you tomorrow. Maybe."

"Mmhmm." The Nightstalker had stopped paying attention and was furiously typing on his keyboard.

Cheyenne reached out to open the door, and another electric burst of orange light flared at her fingertips and up her arm.

"Oh, *come* on." She shook out her hand and shot a glare at the back of Corian's head, gesturing toward the door. "Is there a secret password or something?"

He snapped his fingers without turning around, and the orange light fizzled across the door one more time.

Oh, sure. Just a snap. Good to know.

She opened the door and turned back to ask, "Is there anything else I should know about this necklace?"

"Just wear it, Cheyenne." He gave her a dismissive wave before lowering his hand to the keyboard again. "And try to stay out of trouble."

"What sage advice," she whispered, stepping through the door with a wry chuckle. It closed behind her, and the halfling headed back up the stairs toward her car. *I'll stay out of trouble once we find those kids.*

CHAPTER THIRTY

When she got back to her apartment, all her pent-up energy was gone. Cheyenne closed the door behind her, stepped out of her shoes, and dropped the legacy box on the counter. She braced her hands against her lower back and looked up at the ceiling with a grimace. *Of course, the end of the night is when everything really starts to hurt.*

In her bedroom, she pulled out her personal cell phone and stuck it on the nightstand, then peeled off her jacket and dropped it by the closet. A line of discarded clothes followed her from her bedroom to the bathroom; she was naked by the time she stood in front of the mirror. "Oh, boy."

Her ribs had started to bruise from the orc trying to turn her into a drow sandwich against the tavern wall. Wrinkling her nose, she turned and studied her lower back, but the troll she'd fought hadn't left much of a mark. *Guess I won't know 'til something stops working.*

With a sigh that somehow turned into a yawn, the halfling turned on the shower and waited thirty seconds until the water was nice and scalding, then stepped into the tub to wash off the day and loosen her tight muscles.

The first rinse through her hair made a pool of dark red-brown water at her feet, but by the time she'd gone through two rounds of shampoo, the water was clear. *Note to self: pull up your hair before a bar fight.* She prodded the back of her scalp and winced at the soreness, but at least her hair was still attached.

When she'd toweled off and brushed her hair enough times to be sure it wouldn't fall out, she slipped into an oversized black t-shirt and crawled into bed. Cheyenne sniffed, wrinkled her nose, and pressed a handful of hair to her face. *I need stronger shampoo.* Her alarm was set, the lights were off, and she rolled over before yanking at the chain and the black stone pendant around her neck. *I'm gonna choke myself sleeping in this thing.*

The halfling's tired fingers fumbled with the clasp, then she dropped the whole necklace onto the bedside table beside her phone and rubbed her neck with a sigh. Dropping off to sleep wasn't nearly as hard after that.

Cheyenne dreamt about the meadow where she'd trained with Corian. The same creepy portal was there, whispering in some other language and pulling all the trees in the forest behind it. Only this time, her dreams had started melting together. The meadow was studded with fallen drow bodies in a messy circle around another figure crouching in the center. The whispering grew louder as the portal sparked and crackled with electric purple energy.

The ground trembled, and the portal grew to twice the size she remembered it.

When the figure in the black cloak kneeling in the center of all those bodies lifted its head, she recognized the bone-white hair and the purple-gray skin beneath the hood. But it wasn't L'zar's face when the hood slid back.

It was hers.

Her burning golden eyes shone like beacons in the darkened meadow. "Now it's my turn."

Just as the words boomed across the meadow of the halfling's dream, a dark figure snaked through the portal. It wore the same black, shimmering cloak as the Cheyenne in her dream, and pitch-black fingers reached up to pull back the hood. There was no face beneath it—only a hollow darkness that hissed out the growing whispers. Then the language shifted, and the faceless figure made of nothing turned to face the real Cheyenne.

"If he found you, so will I."

The figure screamed and lurched toward Cheyenne, dark, glistening claws flashing as they came down across her face.

Cheyenne jolted upright in her bed, gasping for breath. She wiped the sweat from her forehead and stripped off the soaked oversized t-shirt before chucking it to the floor. "This is ridiculous."

Her hand slapped down on her cell phone, and she groaned. *Why am I up at five-thirty?*

She dropped back down on her back and winced, then rolled over and pressed a gentle hand to the back of her head. She clenched her eyes shut and just lay there, but then her eyes flew open again. *Yeah, I'm awake now.*

She pushed herself out of bed, and her gaze fell on the protection pendant beside her phone. Snatching it up, she clasped it around her neck again and looked down at the glimmering black stone. *Maybe choking in my sleep is worth it if this thing can keep out the bad dreams.*

The dresser drawers were almost completely empty, so she grabbed a pair of pants from the bottom of her pants drawer that she hadn't worn since freshman year—black with shiny vertical silver stripes. Her nose wrinkled when she buttoned them, but she shrugged and went to the closet. There weren't a lot of options there, either. Cheyenne snorted and jerked a black turtleneck off the hanger before tugging it on. She pulled the protective pendant out from beneath the turtleneck and shook her head. Then she went around the bedroom and piled all the dirty clothes she had left on the floor into her arms before taking them to the stacked washer and dryer just beside the bathroom.

After putting on a little more eyeliner and brushing her teeth—scowling the whole time at the memory of the ogre's nasty breath blasting into her face—the halfling went back out to her desk, scooted toward it in the chair, and clicked on the monitor.

Her university email had automatically signed her out, which didn't matter anyway before she closed the internet window. Then she was staring at the Borderlands forum and the pinned announcement still pulled up on her screen. With a massive sigh, Cheyenne sagged against the edge of her desk. *Great. Now I'm making stupid noob mistakes.*

She backed out of the dark web too and left her VPN up while she ran a diagnostic test of her server and her processing system. The results popped up with nothing to show for the oversight, and she powered Glen down before backing away from her desk again. "Got lucky this time."

Shaking her head, the halfling stuck both cell phones in the front pocket of her backpack, then grabbed a black corduroy jacket with rows of silver buttons down both sides out of the front closet. After she'd shrugged it on, she slung her backpack over her shoulder, grabbed her keys, and was out of her apartment half an hour before she normally left for school.

On her drive to the VCU campus, the halfling blinked at the sign for the Starbucks coming up on her right and rolled her eyes. *What the hell?*

She pulled off into the parking lot and drove around to the drive-thru window to sit and wait behind a sky-blue Prius, where a woman with short brown hair leaned halfway out the window to make her order. Even with her window rolled up, Cheyenne heard every bit of the woman's ridiculously long coffee order for a Wednesday morning. *This is why I don't do Starbucks. Should've just grabbed something at the gas station.*

Then the woman's car pulled through for what would be an even longer wait, and Cheyenne rolled her Ford Focus up to the speaker before the window came down.

"Welcome to Starbucks. Go ahead and order when you're ready." The weirdly chipper voice made Cheyenne pull away a little from the window and blink quickly.

"Yeah, just a… I don't know. Large coffee."

"A venti? Okay? What roast did you want this morning?"

"Um, caffeinated."

A muffled laugh came over the speaker. "Not a regular, are you?"

"What gave it away?"

"Okay, I personally am a fan of the Colombia roast. We have cold-pressed, too, if you want."

"Yeah, just go with the first thing, please."

"Got it. That'll be two fifty-eight. I'll see you at the window."

"Thanks." Cheyenne slowly rolled her car all of six feet forward before she stopped again behind the Prius and rubbed her cheeks, blinking heavily. Drumming her fingers on the steering wheel, she slowly rolled her head on her sore neck and looked out the passenger-side window. That was when she saw the walking pile of trash. "What…"

Old, crinkled wrappers and an empty paper soda cup flew off the top of the trash pile, followed by a half-eaten apple and a long pink ribbon. The pile of trash walked past Cheyenne's car, then slumped to the ground and revealed a two-foot man with bright-red skin who sifted through the armload of garbage with a grin and wide yellow eyes. This one's neon-orange hair was gelled into seven thick mohawk spikes.

Cheyenne glanced around the parking lot. *Why is no one seeing this guy?*

When she looked back at the little red dude sitting on the grass between the Starbuck's parking lot and the next lot over, the guy shrugged out of a backpack and propped it up beside him while he rifled through the trash. For the second time in twenty-four hours, Cheyenne found herself looking at a lime-green backpack with a print of the Incredible Hulk smashing cars on the front. *Oh, hell, no.*

She leaped out of the car and stalked across the parking lot toward the mohawked magical, her fists clenched at her sides. "Hey."

The little dude jerked his head up at her with wide eyes, then glanced around the parking lot and pointed at his chest.

"Yeah, I'm talking to you. Where'd you get that backpack?"

"You can see me."

"Yeah, and I asked you a question." When she reached him, she snatched the backpack from beside the guy and forced away the memory of all those other clothes piled in a heap before they were buried in construction rubble.

"Hey, lady. What I pull out of the trash is none of your business."

"This isn't trash. It's stolen."

"Yeah, by *you*." The bright-red man leaned forward to grab at the backpack, but the halfling lifted it out of his reach and glared at him.

"Where did you get this?"

"Some demolished building, okay? And I'll have you know, the goblin *told* me to go ahead and take whatever I wanted. Wouldn't give up the hat, though. Nice black hat, and thirty-eight's my lucky number! Turquoise bastard. Now hand it back. I gotta have something to put my best finds in, and you're making it pretty hard." The guy snatched up a wrinkled newspaper out of his lap, scanned the front, then tossed it over his shoulder before picking up the next item—a huge metal skull painted black and silver and dangling from the end of a black satin ribbon.

"No." Cheyenne yanked it out of his hand too. She couldn't look at it too long, or she'd lose her shit right here in front of the Starbucks at the start of rush-hour traffic. "What else did you take from that building?"

"Hey, if you wanted to keep this stuff so badly, you shouldn't have thrown it out. Jeez." He rolled his yellow eyes and rummaged through more junk, tossing aside loose papers and a string of fake pearls. "Nobody wants it until they see someone else does."

"Did you hear me?"

"*Nothing.* Got it? Those were the only two things worth my time in that heap, so give 'em back."

Cheyenne swallowed and shook the backpack at him. "You hear about all the missing kids?"

The half-pint magical froze and cocked his head. "Man, how the heck does a human know about any of that stuff?"

"'Cause I'm not a human." The halfling lifted a hand and got ready to slip into drow mode for a second to prove her point, but nothing happened. *What?* She glanced down at her empty hand, still human-looking and even paler against her black-painted nails. "I…" She clenched her fist and tried again, but the flaring heat at the base of her spine didn't even spark.

The little orange trash-collector let out a shrieking cackle and gripped himself around the middle, rocking so far back he almost tumbled over into the grass. "Oh, *wow!* You hit your head one too many times in a mosh pit or what? Not human." He guffawed, his yellow eyes wide as he leaned back toward her and pointed. "Or you're a dud. Give me a break."

What's going on with my magic? Staring at her hand, Cheyenne blinked again and took a quick step toward the cackling magical. He stopped instantly and stared at her, licking his lips. "This stuff belongs to those kids. Not for you. Stick to raiding dumps, got it?"

"Says the not-human human. Can't tell *this* imp what to do." His voice broke a little as she stared him down.

"I can do a lot more than that. Don't let me find you with any more stuff from that building."

He scoffed and went rifling back through the junk in his lap again. "Whatever."

With wide eyes, Cheyenne headed back toward her car, the backpack and satin ribbon of the necklace clenched tightly in her hand. She reached the Focus just as the woman's Prius pulled away from the window, and the halfling slid behind the wheel. She set the backpack and necklace gently down in the back seat, then glanced in the side mirror and rear-view mirror one more time. The annoying little imp was gone, empty wrappers and the rest of the newspaper fluttering in the breeze on the grass. *At least I know what they are now.*

She rolled up to the window and gave the barista a weak smile.

"Got your coffee right here. You didn't want cream or sugar?"

"No. Thanks." Cheyenne stuck her hand in her jacket pocket and groaned. *Other jacket.* "Sorry. Hold on."

Reaching into the front pocket of her backpack, she felt around for some change just as one of the phones in there started buzzing. *Whoever it is can wait.* She pulled out a wad of bills, fumbled through it for a five, and handed it to her.

"One of those mornings, huh?" The barista smiled and took the halfling's money.

"Yeah. That's why I need coffee."

The girl handed down a huge paper cup and shot Cheyenne an even bigger smile. "Let me get your change."

"Just keep it." Without waiting for a reply, the halfling shifted into drive and took off out of the parking lot before she got held up by fifty cars on the road instead of by a woman ordering fifty coffee drinks. She sipped the coffee as she headed toward the VCU campus and smacked her lips. *Okay, fine. Better than the gas station.*

She set it in the cupholder to strap on her seatbelt again, then glanced back at the stuff she'd seized from the imp, which shouldn't have been left anywhere. *What am I gonna do with those?*

CHAPTER THIRTY-ONE

Cheyenne made it to the Computer Sciences building for her first Wednesday graduate class at quarter past eight in the morning. *Plenty of time for a pit stop.*

The minute she stepped into the one-person bathroom down the hall, she hung her backpack up on the door hook and turned to face the mirror. "What happened?"

With a deep breath, she closed her eyes and pulled up all the images she could of guns and firing weapons. Nothing.

"Come on!" She slapped her lower back, waiting for the flare to kick into gear. Then she looked up at her reflection, her nostrils flaring, and thought of Ember falling onto the cement in the skatepark. The halfling gritted her teeth and pulled up everything she felt from the night two weeks ago until her face reddened and she saw a vein popping out on her forehead. Her breath burst out of her, and she slammed her hands on the edge of the sink. *There's no way that troll punched the drow right out of my kidney. Right?*

Breathing heavily, she gave herself one more solid stare in the mirror, then gave up. Cheyenne unzipped the front pocket of her backpack and pulled out both phones. Her personal cell phone didn't have any missed notifications, and she rolled her eyes before slipping it back into the open pocket and flipping open the burner phone. Just one unread text from Rhynehart's number.

Meeting at the diner at 15:00. We need your brain on this.

The next line had the address for the diner, and Cheyenne sent a text which only said, **Fine**. Then she shut the phone, dropped it into the pocket, and grabbed her backpack to head to class. *I can do three o'clock. I can't keep missing classes.*

Her Advanced Social Network Analysis and Security professor didn't seem to notice that Cheyenne had made it to two consecutive classes in a row this week. He went on and on about all the different viruses and malware one could use to hack into someone else's social media accounts, followed by a list of known scams used over the last decade to lure unsuspecting users into giving up their private information. The halfling's eyes drooped as she sank lower in her chair by the minute, and no one seemed to notice that, either.

Her other two classes for the day weren't any different. The only notable difference was the short, mousy girl even smaller than Cheyenne staring at her necklace during her Theory of Programming Languages class like she'd never seen jewelry before. Cheyenne stared right back at her, waiting for those wide, blinking eyes to look up and see that the halfling noticed. But they didn't. *Everyone's busy staring, and it's not even at the Goth thing.*

The last class let out at one-thirty in the afternoon with Professor Dawley finished shouting out some assignment Cheyenne didn't hear. The rustling and shuffling of ten students gathering their things jolted her out of her half-conscious stupor, and she grimaced at the tightness in her back. Her bruised ribs cried out when she bumped the edge of the long desk before standing up, but she just gritted her teeth against the pain with a long, slow sigh.

Professor Dawley blinked at her and nodded. "See you on Friday."

Cheyenne lifted a hand in a half-assed wave and slung her backpack over her shoulder. "Yep."

Great. Now she'll notice if I don't show up.

She moved quickly down the hall, glancing at all the other

students filtering through the building and heading to and from their other classes. A chill raced across her back, but it wasn't the magical kind. *That's a serious problem.*

Mattie Bergmann's office door was open as usual when Cheyenne showed up just before 2:00 p.m. The halfling walked in, shut the door behind her, and went straight to the desk.

"You forgot your usual knock," Mattie said, looking the halfling up and down. "And you look awful."

"Rough night. Bad dreams. Weird morning. And then I sat through all my classes, so that didn't help." Cheyenne dropped her backpack on the floor and smoothed her hair back from her face with both hands. "I have a problem."

Mattie leaned back in her chair and folded her arms. "I don't think I could pin it down if you gave me *ten* guesses. Unless it's those pants."

"No, I'm serious. Is there..." The halfling closed her eyes. "Is there any way to *lose* your magic?"

The professor let out a chuckle and looked confused, her green eyes scanning Cheyenne's face. "Not unless you were cursed or poisoned. Or almost killed."

"What about punched?"

Mattie barked out a laugh, then clamped a hand over her mouth and took a deep breath. "What did you do to get punched?"

"I didn't *do* anything. At first." When Mattie just raised an eyebrow, the halfling relented. "I might've gotten into a bar fight last night."

"Uh-huh. And you think it just took your magic right out of you?"

"A bar fight in Peridosh."

The professor's eyes widened, and the corners of her mouth twitched into a smile she tried hard to contain. "So, you're branching out and getting to know Richmond's magical underground, huh?"

"Something like that. But that's what I want to know. Some troll got in a good hit somewhere around my kidney, and yeah, it hurts, but that's also where everything starts when I—"

"Whoa, whoa. Okay. Slow down for a minute." Mattie licked her lips. "You should keep an eye on that kidney, first of all. You know, if you start seeing blood in the toilet—"

"Yeah, I know how that part works."

"Okay." Lifting both hands in surrender, Mattie nodded. "Listen. I'm one-hundred-percent positive a troll did not punch you hard enough to knock the drow out of you. Okay?"

"Then why can't I do anything? No magic at all. No changing forms. Not even sparks. It's kinda freakin' me out."

"Yes, I can see that." The professor folded her arms again and glanced away from Cheyenne's face. "Why don't you tell me about the necklace?"

"What?" Cheyenne glanced down at the pendant resting against the front of her turtleneck and frowned. "That might be one of the things you don't wanna hear about."

"Cheyenne, I know you didn't get it from the FRoE. They wouldn't know Heart of Midnight if it smacked them in the face."

The halfling glanced quickly at her professor and her mouth popped open. "You know what this is?"

"I know what the stone is and a little about how it's used. My gut's telling me you don't. Where'd you get it?"

"From a friend." Her smile didn't feel convincing.

"I see." Mattie leaned forward. "Did this friend tell you what it does?"

"Uh…" *Walkin' a thin line, here.* "We had a conversation about my magic getting too bright and loud. This thing is supposed to dampen it."

The professor just widened her eyes and pressed her lips together.

"Oh. Seriously?" Cheyenne jerked the pendant back and forth across the chain, wishing it would loosen up. "He said dampen, not completely turn off."

"Looks like you found your answer."

"Okay." The halfling unclasped the chain from around her neck and coiled the whole thing into one hand, then slipped into drow form the instant she thought about it. She nodded at her purple-gray hand, then slipped back into her eerily pale skin again. *Corian better have a good reason for not explaining this.* With a sigh, she wrapped the necklace around the collar of her turtleneck and fastened it again. "So, I officially feel like an idiot now."

"Oh, that's not the most embarrassing thing to happen in this office, kid. Trust me." Mattie chuckled and gazed at the pendant one more time. "Plus, it's almost impossible to know the exact effects of any charm if you're not the one who casts it. Especially using a stone like that. Boy, I haven't seen one of those in a long time. Your new friend doesn't happen to be a drow, does he?"

"No." Cheyenne picked up her backpack again and stared at her professor's desk as she slung it over her shoulder. "Just friends with one, apparently."

"Ah. That's where he got it, I'm sure." The professor squinted at the necklace. "It's an interesting thing to carry across the Border."

"Yeah, well, he's an interesting guy." *And infuriating.* "Oh, hey. What time is it?"

Mattie glanced up at her computer. "Two-fifteen. Did you get the chance to look at any of those spells yet?"

"Kind of." Cheyenne shrugged. "I'll keep you updated. I gotta get going, but thanks for…talking me down."

"No problem." The professor winked at her. "Try not to get in any more fights, huh? And go see a doctor if something doesn't feel right."

"I'm fine. Really." Opening the door, the halfling gave her professor a final nod before slipping out into the hall. *So many things don't feel right. A doctor won't fix any of them.*

CHAPTER THIRTY-TWO

Cheyenne pulled into the parking lot of the retro red diner just off the highway and glanced at the clock on her dashboard. *Ten minutes early. Guess this counts as being on time.*

There were only a few cars in the parking lot, so she had no problem picking out Rhynehart's black Jeep or Sir's stupid orange Kia Rio. Slipping her hands into the shallow pockets of her jacket, the halfling stalked across the parking lot toward the diner's front door.

The little bell jingled as she stepped inside, filling her nose with the scent of fried onions and grease and pancakes. Shaking her head, she glanced over the rows of red vinyl booths and saw Rhynehart immediately. He looked at her and raised his eyebrows but didn't say a word.

Sir sat across from his second in command, and next to Rhynehart was a tall, broad-shouldered woman with tan skin and a short blonde bob. Cheyenne gritted her teeth as she approached the table.

When she stopped at the edge, all three FRoE members looked up at her, and none of them smiled. Sir blinked, his mustache twitching as he eyed the drow halfling. "Well, look who's right on time? Don't tell me you dressed up just for this meeting."

"Had a problem with the laundry," Cheyenne muttered, watching Sir's gaze settle on the Heart of Midnight pendant resting below her turtleneck collar.

"I don't care if you wear the same damn thing every time I see you. Hell, maybe you do. I can't tell." Sir slid over to sit across from the massive woman, who stared impassively at Cheyenne with her hands in her lap. "Cop a squat, halfling."

Cheyenne tried to hide her grimace as she lowered herself into the booth, and she sat as close to the edge as possible.

Sir watched her lean away from him, then snorted and shook his head. "Interesting stuff you sent in email last night. Care to tell us where you found it?"

She stared at Rhynehart, who just leaned back and folded his arms. *At least he didn't keep the list a secret.* "Did I get invited to an interrogation?"

Sir reached out for his diner mug of black coffee and took a long, slurping sip. "Don't flatter yourself, kid. We already know everything we want or need to know about you. We're sitting here in this glorious craphole with the best damn coffee I've ever tossed down to talk about those kids, not you."

"Good. Someone finally started listening to me."

"So, where'd you find the list?"

Cheyenne looked at the huge blonde woman beside Rhynehart, then turned just enough to shoot Sir a sidelong glance. "That's not something I can tell you."

"Why the hell not?"

"Because it's not just something *I* found, and the list doesn't belong to me. It's borrowed."

Sniffing quickly, Sir shrugged and looked across the table. "Doesn't matter. Fact is, we're looking at those names and have confirmation now that every single one of them belongs to a kid who hasn't been seen since before oh-eight-hundred hours yesterday. Sheila here double-checked each of them personally."

The blonde woman dipped her head at Cheyenne, then lifted her forearms onto the diner table. Rhynehart glanced down at Sheila's elbow poking into his personal space but said nothing. There was a thick black ring around the middle finger of Sheila's right hand.

Another FRoE magical. Must be huge without the ring, too.

Silence fell over the table, and when no one else spoke up, Cheyenne shrugged. "You could've just texted me."

"Oh, sure." Sir slid his coffee mug closer. "But I hate texting. And phones, really. Kinda hard to have the conversation we're having now when we're all plugged into a screen like a bunch of moody teenagers without any friends."

"Yeah, I'd really hate to miss this." The halfling folded her hands on the table and stared at Sir with wide eyes.

He ignored her sarcasm and cocked his head at his mug. "Here's the thing. We have the kids' names and ages. We know they're missing. We've got eyes on the magical families who reported some tween snatched up at some point yesterday, and...well, I'm just gonna put it bluntly."

Cheyenne blinked. *This'll be interesting.*

"We have no leads and no theories and no goddamn clue how to find those sons of bitches playing Pied Piper with registered Border immigrants." As if he couldn't believe he'd just said it out loud, the man lifted his mug quickly to his lips and took a long, steaming drink. When he almost slammed the mug back down again, thick drops of coffee fell from his mustache and disappeared into his lap.

"Huh." The halfling stared at the last tiny glittering drop above his lip. "*That's* why you 'wanted my brain.'"

"Well, don't get all cocky about it," Sir muttered quickly. "Just give us some damn ideas."

She let that sink in for a minute. *They think I know something.* Cheyenne glanced at Rhynehart again, who'd opted for meeting her gaze. Sir was now diligently staring at the table. Sheila raised an eyebrow. "I want that visit. Now."

Rhynehart sucked his teeth and rubbed the back of his neck. Sir choked on his next sip of coffee, sending spray up out of the mug and into his face. He wiped it away quickly with a hand. "What?"

"And then I'll help you find the kidnappers and take the whole thing down." The halfling widened her eyes at Sir and waited for him to meet her gaze. *So he knows I'm serious. Tables have turned, asshole.*

"Hey, don't get me wrong. You've got serious balls making a request like that—"

"It's not a request. Take me to see L'zar, then I'll tell you everything I know."

Sir's beady eyes narrowed. "You know I'm the one giving orders around here. Rhynehart, she *knows* that, right? 'Cause I'm pretty goddamn sure I made it perfectly clear from the beginning."

"Sure." The halfling nodded slowly. "When you have all the cards in your hand. But you brought me here because you don't have a choice. And we all know that."

The man's nostrils flared, then he wiped the last glistening bit of coffee from his mouth.

"Look, I'm pretty sure every single agent at the construction site would've come back in body bags instead of just the three lying in the medical ward on base." The silver chains around her wrists clinked when Cheyenne folded her arms. "I'm not handing out any more favors, but after yesterday, I'd say you owe me one."

All three FRoE members at the table stared at the drow halfling. Then Sheila opened her mouth and let out a low, growling chuckle. "I like her."

"Yeah, well, you can keep your opinion to yourself, you big pile of—" Sir caught Sheila's warning glare and her raised eyebrow and stopped. "I'm not inclined to agree with it."

Cheyenne shrugged. "Clock's ticking, Sir. I wanna find those kids as much as you do, but I can't do it if I don't cash in those extra tickets you were talking about."

Sir growled into his coffee cup but lowered it again without drinking this time. "You want to visit the splinter in my asscheek to ask *him* about those kids?"

"And some other things, but yeah."

"Jesus, Bugs Bunny, and Marilyn Monroe."

While Sir buried his face in his hand, Cheyenne looked at Rhynehart again. The man shrugged and shook his head.

"If you give a drow a plate, she's gonna want the whole enchilada. All right. Guess you're callin' the shots on this one, halfling."

Cheyenne's mouth twitched into a victorious smirk. "Just so we're clear, that's a yes, right?"

"It's whatever you want it to be. Don't make me spell it out for you. I know you can read." Sir pushed his mug away from him, sloshing a little more over the sides. "And now you ruined my damn coffee."

"I'm sure they'll make you a fresh pot later." Slapping her hands on the table, the halfling slid over the one inch left at the end of the booth and stood. "Let's go."

Sir pointed at Rhynehart and grunted. "She's riding with you. I'm already seeing damn drow closing in on me from every side."

"Sure." Rhynehart nodded at Sheila. "Get ready for whatever we send your way, huh?"

The huge, human-looking magical folded her arms. "I'm always ready."

"Hey, Sheila." Cheyenne nodded at the woman and let her smile widen. "Nice mask."

Sheila snorted. Rhynehart and Sir gave each other confused looks.

Then the halfling turned and headed back toward the diner's entrance. Once the FRoE agents could no longer see her, she let herself break into a wide grin. *Pretty sure we're playing* my *game now.*

CHAPTER THIRTY-THREE

Cheyenne closed the passenger door of Rhynehart's black Jeep, buckled her seatbelt, and waited for him to say something. With a sigh, the man started the car, then reached across Cheyenne's lap and opened the glove box. A black satin sleeping mask dropped into her lap, then the glovebox thumped shut again.

The halfling stared at her lap. "What, no black bag over my face this time?"

"Just put it on. And if I see you peeking, I have more of those nifty little syringes stored in here." Rhynehart strapped himself in and pulled out of the diner's parking lot behind Sir's Kia.

"I'm afraid to ask why you have *this* in your car." She picked up the mask and stretched the elastic band.

"And I might be afraid to ask what you got up to with three of my agents last night."

"Fair enough." Slipping the elastic band around her head, Cheyenne settled the mask over her eyes and thumped her head back against the headrest. They drove in silence until she just had to ask. "What did they tell you?"

"Enough to know I don't wanna know. Everybody's gotta blow

off steam sometimes, rookie. As long as you don't let it affect the way you do your job, I don't care."

She snorted. "How many times do I have to say this isn't my job?"

"If you have a better word for it, I'm all ears."

The halfling shrugged, all the light blocked out by the sleeping mask. "It's more of a hobby."

Rhynehart snorted. "Yeah, a hobby none of us can afford for you to drop. Including you."

They drove for another twenty-five minutes at least, and Cheyenne found herself jolted out of a light doze when the black Jeep finally stopped and the engine cut off.

"We're here."

She ripped the sleeping mask off her face and stared at it. *These things actually work.* Tossing it on the dash, she unbuckled her seatbelt and slipped out of the car after Rhynehart, who'd already started walking toward the cement entrance and the rolling chain-link gates in front of Chateau D'rahl. They were still open.

Sir stormed toward the front door with a cell phone pressed against his ear. "Don't talk to *me* about paperwork. I don't care how many pencils you need to push, Johnson. Get it done. You have about twenty minutes."

He jerked the phone away from his ear and jammed it into the back pocket of his jeans. The armed guards standing in front of the prison entrance nodded at the man as he stalked toward them without slowing. Cheyenne hurried to catch up to Rhynehart, who didn't look at her as they passed the guards and kept moving. No one said a word.

Sir grunted at the glass front door, peered inside, then yanked open the door. "Can't handle a goddamn change in schedule. We're paying out the ass to keep this place running."

Rhynehart caught the door before it closed and held it for the halfling. A guard hurried toward them from the other side of the front room and stopped short when he saw Sir's scowl. "A little late for that now, don't you think?" Sir grumbled. "Back the hell up, man. I'm not in the mood."

The guard quickly stepped back, then Cheyenne was following the FRoE's head honcho and his right-hand man toward the huge, broad metal detector. The other guards stationed there stared at the halfling, and one of them grabbed the radio at his shoulder to mutter, "They just stepped inside."

Pockets were emptied into plastic trays and jackets shrugged off. Sir and Rhynehart walked through the metal detector first, and the alarm and blinking lights again went off when Cheyenne went next. The same guard who'd asked her about concealed weapons the last time spent a lot longer than necessary staring at the halfling's facial piercings, but he didn't try to take out the wand this time to run it over her.

"Finally." Sir nodded at the guard. "Somebody's using their goddamn head to get us through here quickly. Now, who the hell's taking us down?"

"They're not quite ready, Sir."

"No shit. I'm not standing here all day while my hair falls out. Where's Donahue?"

The guard glanced at Cheyenne and Rhynehart, but only for a second. "Beta block, Sir."

"Buzz me in. And radio it in when these two get back from the Dungeon."

"Sir." The guard nodded and said into his radio, "Open Door 2."

The door just behind him on the left let out a loud warning buzz, and Sir yanked it open before disappearing inside without another word.

Cheyenne glanced at Rhynehart, who frowned at Door 2 as it closed again with a loud click. Then he turned away from her to wait for their escort. "You been down there before?" the halfling asked.

He shot her a sidelong glance, his jaw working as he clenched his teeth. "You have one over me, rookie. Don't push it."

She fought hard to keep from smiling. *Yeah, he's in for a nice surprise.*

The next ten minutes felt like an hour as they waited on the other side of the metal detector. The guards in the room just stared at them—mostly Cheyenne—without loosening up enough to talk amongst themselves. Then another breathless guard rounded the corner, his eyes wide and his hand pressed against his belt, where the large ring of keys jangled with every step. "This way."

Cheyenne and Rhynehart followed closely behind, then they stepped into the single elevator at the end of the hall and headed down however far the thing took them into the bowels of Chateau D'rahl. Their escort bounced on his heels, staring up at the top of the elevator doors like there was a floor-counter up there.

"You okay?" the halfling asked.

The guard stiffened, then turned his head but didn't quite manage to look at her over his shoulder. "Busy day."

With a pissed-off Sir storming through the front doors? Yeah, I bet.

When they finally reached the bottom level, the elevator creaked open, and the guard shoved the metal grate back against one side before gesturing for them to get out. The minute Cheyenne and Rhynehart stood in the first corridor of the Dungeon, the metal grate clanged back and the guard took the elevator back up.

Even through the reinforced seal between the booth and the stone walls, Cheyenne heard the echoing bang of more doors shutting in the main chamber of the prison's visitation cell. Muffled curses rang out, followed by a low chuckle. *Or maybe it's just for L'zar.*

The halfling glanced at Rhynehart and raised an eyebrow. "Don't look so terrified, man. It's not like you're going in there with me."

"I'm not—" He gave an aggravated sigh and shook his head. "You're gonna keep rubbing it in, aren't you?"

"Until it stops bothering you, yeah." Cheyenne took off down the damp stone corridor. The guard stationed in the booth stared at her through the wall of windows. When she reached the door, she thought for a few seconds the guy wouldn't let her in. He finally slapped a hand on the controls, but the halfling had to open the door herself. She stepped into the booth and moved aside in the cramped space to make room for Rhynehart. "I'm back."

"Good for you." The guard's eyebrows lifted and dropped, then he nodded at Rhynehart. "Finally let you take the plunge, huh?"

The FRoE agent shrugged. "First time for everything, I guess."

"Yeah. Lotta firsts goin' on around here." Once Rhynehart closed the door, the guard shuffled toward the other side of the booth and nodded out the other wall of windows. "He's all yours. Word this week is Batman."

"Really?"

"Hey, safe words are above my paygrade. I just hand 'em out and wait to hear it shouted. Or not. Both of you headin' in this time?"

"No." Rhynehart and the halfling blurted it at the same time, and Rhynehart shuffled backward as far as he could in the narrow booth, rubbing his mouth.

"Yeah, I'd probably stick by that choice too."

Cheyenne scanned the countless buttons covering the control console. "Can you turn the sound off in here?"

The guard snorted. "Not for you. It takes special clearance. You ready?"

She nodded and stared out into the darkness of the Dungeon. *That might come in handy.*

When the guard pressed another button and the door buzzed open with a little click, the drow halfling didn't hesitate. She pushed open the door this time and stepped into the main cavern. Her nose filled with the scent of damp stone and a stronger metallic odor and the same undertone of freshly baked bread.

The booth's door banged shut behind her, and she didn't turn around this time before stalking across the open space toward the thick iron bars running floor to ceiling and the huge half-circle of prison cell on the other side.

L'zar was waiting for her, his arms folded and his body turned sideways toward the bars as she approached. Bright white teeth flashed at her from behind his slate-gray lips, and his bone-white hair was pulled back behind his head a little tighter this time. "I wait twenty-one years, and now it's twice in four days. Just can't stay away, can you?"

"I tried." Cheyenne stopped near the bars, echoing her drow father's posture and folding her arms too. She didn't grab the chair this time. "But I didn't come back just for me."

"That's a sweet gesture, kid, but I'm doin' okay. Got the luxury suite and everything." L'zar spread his arms and gazed around the cell with another low chuckle.

"Not here for you either, but there might be something we can both get out of this." The halfling lifted her chin and waited for him to settle his attention on her again.

His gaze fell to the pendant against her turtleneck and the Heart of Midnight stone at its center. L'zar's eyebrows lifted, and he stepped toward the iron bars before leaning sideways against them. "That's a nice little bauble."

The halfling studied her father's face and took a deep breath. *They can hear everything in the booth. Careful.* "You've seen it before, haven't you? And you know who gave it to me."

L'zar's lips parted in the same feral grin. The image of her dream flashed without warning through Cheyenne's mind—this drow looking at her, not with self-satisfaction and a secret knowing, but with fear and pain contorting his face. She shook it away and stood her ground in front of the bars.

"I should." The drow's eyes lingered on the stone, then slowly traveled up to his daughter's face. "I gave it to *him.*"

"Right. Well, you should know we've started."

"You have?" L'zar's smile and wide golden eyes went from feral to crazed, maybe even starving. "That's very good to hear."

What's good for me is good for him, right? The halfling nodded and stepped toward the bars, lowering her voice. "I heard you can tell me how to speed things up."

"Look at you. *Now* you're asking the right questions." Another chuckle escaped the prisoner, ending in a low growl. Then he took one lunging step toward the bars and wrapped those long, slender fingers of purple-gray around them. "I would *love* to, Cheyenne."

She took a quick, small step back, leaning away from the mad glow of those eyes between the bars.

He chuckled again. "How have your dreams been lately?"

Pressing her lips together, the halfling took a deep breath and stood her ground. *He's talking in riddles. Talk back.* "Only the scion never pursued will rise to their destiny."

L'zar's eyes widened before narrowing into glowing slits, and he tilted his head. "Does that part stand out for you above all the others, then?"

"I've heard it before. Yes."

"Mm. So have I." The drow pressed the side of his head against the closest iron bar and blinked slowly. "Try meditating on it. I hear meditation has a long list of benefits."

"That's your advice?" Cheyenne's fists clenched against her folded arms. *It means something. Just keep going.*

"That's my advice. How does it speed things up for you? You won't find out until you try. But *do* try, yeah?" His gaze traveled up and down the bars closest to his face. "I'm anxious to hear what happens when you do. And tell our mutual friend to show you the Don'adurr Thread. It's an effective spell, and a little extra support never hurt anyone."

"I'll tell him. Thank you."

L'zar's next slow, lazy chuckle was quieter. "Don't thank me just yet, Cheyenne. There's much between the end of the beginning and the beginning of the end. Just like this conversation, hmm?"

The halfling swallowed. *That one went over my head.* "Maybe."

"Now, what else did you come here to ask?"

Cheyenne's skin crawled with the anger that question brought up. She automatically drew herself back together to push down the inevitably rising heat of her drow magic, but it wasn't there. The pendant suddenly felt incredibly heavy hanging around her neck. "A bunch of kids went missing yesterday."

"Right." L'zar pulled back away from the bars, and his maniacal interest died out. Purple-gray nostrils flared a little. "I heard about that. Somebody's overstepping their bounds."

"Do you know who it is?"

With a deep breath through his nose, the drow glanced past Cheyenne at the security booth spanning around the narrow hall behind her. "Before we get into that, satisfy one small, niggling bit of curiosity for me."

She shrugged. "Okay."

"Did Carson step into the observation booth with you today?"

Cheyenne shook her head. "I don't know who you're talking about."

L'zar tsked and nodded, leaning farther to the side to get a better view of the booth. "You know, I'd forgotten about the little games *he* likes to play. Frustrating, isn't it? How are you supposed to trust a man who won't give you his name?"

The halfling's eyes widened. *He's talking about Sir.* "No, he's somewhere else."

"Why am I not surprised?" With another deep sigh, L'zar met his daughter's gaze again and cocked his head. "The people you're looking for are the same people who've been looking for you, Cheyenne. I suppose it's time for you to find each other, isn't it?"

CHAPTER THIRTY-FOUR

A jolt of excitement shot through the halfling. *Keep going. Carefully.* "How do I find them?"

"Well, I'm assuming you've already seen them once or twice. That's why you're so upset by this whole thing, isn't it? You *know* you have the answer, but it keeps slipping away, doesn't it?" L'zar asked, wiggling his long fingers between the bars.

How do I already know? I have no idea where to start. Cheyenne forced herself not to look away from the drow prisoner, growing more irritated by the second. "I have a feeling you're about to tell me how to catch it."

Chuckling, L'zar sniffed the air, then stepped away from the bars and clasped his hands behind his back. "You know, it's incredibly hard to completely wash out the smell of ogre blood and fellwine."

"Yeah, I noticed."

"I bet you've noticed other things, haven't you? Things those humans in helmets couldn't possibly understand. Maybe even the other magicals they use to run their little errands for them."

Cheyenne wrinkled her nose. *Those are clues. Read between the lines, just like Mom taught you.* "All of them?"

"Listen to you, searching through so many dark, narrow places. I like it." L'zar winked, and a chill ran up the halfling's spine. "Yes, Cheyenne. I'd go so far as to say all of them are unaware of the things you see, the strangeness. Many things have been brought together at certain points between this world and the other I no longer call home, like you. Even then, it's inevitable the key points get lost in translation."

Cheyenne shoved her hands into the pockets of her jacket and stalked along the outside of the bars. L'zar watched her intently, his small smile returning. *Everything he just said means something. He knows I was at that tavern in Peridosh, or at least a tavern. That's one of those places where both worlds meet, just like the reservations.*

She spun to pace back along the bars and looked at her father. L'zar tilted his head toward the other shoulder and narrowed his eyes. "Keep going. You're almost there."

"Can you read my mind?"

He snickered. "Not at all. I can *see* it." The drow bit down on the end of his dark tongue and grinned again before the smile faded.

"*That's* not helping." She stared at the stone again and kept moving across the floor. *What did I notice?*

"Do most people know who you are, Cheyenne? I don't mean who your parents are, I mean *you*."

"Not most people, no." She kept pacing.

"Why not? Don't you think they'd approve?"

The halfling jerked and froze. "Say that again."

"There it is." L'zar's golden eyes burned from behind the bars, and he leaned toward her like he was about to pounce. "I see it right there before it comes crawling out. So close you could almost..."

The drow's fist came down on the closest iron bar, which filled the chamber with a loud, metallic echo. Cheyenne's eyes darted toward that bar of the cell, and L'zar hit it again. He kept pounding at it in a slow, steady rhythm, the sound of fist on metal ringing through the wide chamber of the Dungeon until it drowned out the sound of the halfling's breath in her ears.

The drow prisoner raised his eyebrows and kept pounding with a tiny, knowing smile lifting the corners of his mouth.

Like the other magicals at that tavern. And at Rez 38. What did I notice?

"Someone's been lying to you, Cheyenne," L'zar shouted over the clang of his fist against the iron. "Would *they* approve?"

Then it clicked.

"Holy shit," she whispered and whirled to stalk back toward the booth at the other end of the Dungeon.

"And now she's back in the game," L'zar roared behind her. "Give 'em hell!"

The halfling sped up as she neared the booth, and she slapped a hand on the door. L'zar laughed behind her as he pounded the iron bar.

The door buzzed, and the guard pushed it open to let her inside. "No safe word this time, huh?"

"I didn't need it. Didn't really need it last time, either." Cheyenne reached the opposite door in two huge steps and tried to shove it open. "Hey, press the button already. We gotta go."

"What the hell was all that about, rookie?" Rhynehart stared at her, then glanced uncertainly through the window at the Dungeon and the crazed drow having some kind of mental breakdown.

"I know where to find those kids." The guard buzzed the door open, and Cheyenne slammed against it before stepping down into the narrow stone hallway.

Rhynehart quickly followed her, and the guard pulled the door closed again. "I call bullshit. The drow didn't say a damn thing about the kids or who took them. I heard the whole thing, kid. Just a bunch of crazy talk."

"Yeah. That's what it sounded like, huh?" The elevator doors opened just in time for her to shove the grate aside without stopping and storm inside. She didn't bother closing it behind Rhynehart before the elevator doors shut and they started moving.

"Then what kinda game are you playing, Cheyenne?"

She turned toward the FRoE agent and shook her head. "Not a game. I'm sure about this."

He folded his arms and leaned against the wall of the elevator. "Then you better spill it right now."

The halfling laughed and ran a hand through her dyed-black hair. "The FRoE's got a mole."

"A *what?*"

"Turncoat. Traitor. Double agent. Whatever."

"You're as crazy as L'zar."

"I'm not crazy!" With clenched fists, Cheyenne forced herself to breathe. *Would've gone full drow there without this pendant.* "Who was in the gate tower on Rez 38 the day you took me there? The goblin."

"Hell, rookie, I don't know every operative's goddamn name."

"Well, you should. 'Cause that's the guy we need to find to find those kids."

"That's real funny." Rhynehart scowled at her. "I'm not going on a manhunt in my own organization just because you pulled a name out of a hat. Or a face. Whatever."

"Rhynehart, it's him."

"Nope. Sorry. I can't take your word for it without any proof. And from where I'm standing, it looks like you're grasping at straws."

"No, that's what *you're* doing." The halfling stared at the elevator ceiling and shook off the urgent frustration crawling across her back. "Okay, I'll try to map it out for you. The FRoE only enlists magicals who were born Earthside, right?"

He frowned. "Yeah. As long as I've been doin' this, yeah."

"There's a big difference between the people born here and the people who made the crossing. Sure, they're all magicals, same races, same basic understanding of how the Border and the reservations work. But there's a *lot* of stuff brought across the Border the magicals who were born here don't even know about."

"Oh, yeah? Like what?"

"Do *you* know what it meant when they all started banging on stuff at Rez 38?"

Rhynehart lifted his chin and frowned down at her like he was actually insulted. "No. And neither do you."

"Yeah, I don't have to know what it means. I just have to know the difference between the magicals from the other side and ones your people hire to be FRoE agents."

"Okay, you've lost me completely."

"The goblin in the gate tower, Rhynehart! He's one of yours, or at least he's pretending to be. I went out with Yurik and the others last night, and the same thing happened there. A bunch of magicals started pounding on metal crap, and none of those agents knew what the hell it was about. But the goblin on Rez 38? He sure as hell did."

The elevator came to a stop, and Cheyenne would've blasted through the slowly opening doors if it weren't for the pendant. Then they were finally open, and she stormed across the linoleum floors toward the metal detector.

"Okay, how the hell is that supposed to prove this is our guy? Maybe he's spent too long on the rez, huh? Maybe he's heard the stories and thought he'd try playing old-school from the other side."

"Well, that's the other part." Cheyenne stopped in front of the metal detector when the closest guard held up a hand.

He bent toward the radio at his shoulder. "Donahue, they just came back up. *Yeah*, I'm sure. They're standing in front of me."

Rhynehart stared at her and shoved his hands into his pockets with a shrug. "I'm still waiting for the other part."

The halfling rubbed her forehead. *One thing to know something. Now I have to put it into small, easy words for the guy.* "Who else knows about the construction site we blew up yesterday?"

"Just those of us who went in. And Sir." The man chewed his bottom lip. "No one else needed to know."

"Right, and did you send anyone back there after we took off?"

"No. Even if I did, there's nothing left for anyone to find."

"Almost nothing. But I—"

Door 4 buzzed and burst open with a clang, letting out a fuming Sir. "I brought you all the way out here so you could have another sit-down with that goddamn drow, halfling, and you're down there for what? Twenty minutes? Don't tell me you got L'zar to sing like a bird in twenty minutes."

"He didn't sing anything," Rhynehart muttered.

"Just *listen* to me!" The halfling glared at both men, and even with the pendant dampening her ability to slip into drow mode, Sir and Rhynehart shut their mouths and paid attention. "I saw an imp yesterday with stuff from the site—the backpack and a necklace. Not the kind you see everywhere."

"Oh, now you're asking imps for help, huh?" Sir spread his arms. "How stupid do you think we are?"

"Pretty damn stupid if you don't hear me out on this. The imp said he got the stuff from a demolished building. He said a goblin told him he could have whatever he wanted from the wreckage."

"Lotta goblins in Virginia, rookie."

Cheyenne leaned toward him and raised her eyebrows. "Not wearing black hats with a thirty-eight on the front."

Rhynehart's eyes widened as a flush climbed up his neck. "Son of a bitch."

He whirled away from the halfling and stomped back through the metal detector. Cheyenne took off after him, and Sir tossed his hands in the air. "Bunch of goddamn chickens runnin' around this place. Who else hasn't gotten their head cut off yet?"

Stepping up to the intake window of tempered glass, Rhynehart tapped on the counter and nodded at the officer on the other side. "Can you reach the duty logs from in here?"

"Yeah. What do you need?"

"Can't remember the guy's name. goblin agent working the gate tower for Rez 38 on…"

The blood rushing through Cheyenne's ears drowned out pretty much everything as Rhynehart went to go double-check what she'd just told him. *He'll find out I'm right. I know I'm right.*

Sir stepped up beside her and muttered, "You better hope you know what you're doing."

"Well, that makes two of us, doesn't it? Carson."

Sir's eyes twitched when she said his name, then he stepped sideways to face Rhynehart at the counter and clasped his hands behind his back. "That's Major Carson, Cheyenne. Don't make me tell you again."

CHAPTER THIRTY-FIVE

"You sure about that?" Rhynehart leaned toward the guard on the other side of the tempered glass, his eyes wide.

"Yeah, it's right here. Didn't show up for his post this morning. It's a real bitch, too, 'cause he was scheduled for a two-week shift on the rez. They found someone else, but it threw a wrench in his stacked vacation time."

"All right, thanks. Shit." Rhynehart turned back toward Cheyenne and Major Carson, then pointed at the halfling. "I don't know how you put all that together, rookie, but I think you're right."

"About what?" The major jerked his chin at his operative, his nostrils flaring as if he'd just walked past an open sewer.

"Guard named Ranzig didn't show up for duty at Rez 38's gate tower. It makes sense if he was poking around the construction site instead. Wait." Rhynehart stepped back toward the counter and knocked on it again. "Pull up the guy's address, huh?"

"Sure thing. Hold on." The guard typed away at his keyboard and froze. "What the hell?"

"You better explain that one right now," Rhynehart muttered.

"It's, uh, not pulling anything up."

"Well, check again."

The guard nodded quickly and typed away, clicking around before more typing. "Sorry, sir. There's nothing in here for Ranzig Ca'admar."

"Who the hell's been shittin' in the goddamn pool?" Sir shouted. "Somebody better have a good explanation!"

"He's not an agent." Cheyenne stared at the men around her. *Are they seriously not getting this?* "Bet you'll find his name *and* an address if you look in your other system."

Rhynehart turned back to the guard. "Can you pull up the B.I.T.CH from here too?"

"We're the highest-security prison for magicals on this side of the border, sir."

"Yeah, I know."

"Why the hell are we poking the B.I.T.CH for this kerfuckle?" Sir bellowed.

Rhynehart nodded at the guard behind the counter. "Just run the name!"

Cheyenne snorted. "Someone really needs to tell me what this B.I.T.CH is."

The FRoE operative shot her a quick, dismissive glance. "The Borderlands Immigration Tracking Channel. Cute, I know."

The guard typed and typed, his eyes scanning what was obviously way more information popping up on his screen. "Got it. Ranzig Ca'admar. Pure G-class. Came over May seventh at Rez Twenty-one. Last registered address—"

"Yeah, yeah. I know the drill." Rhynehart slammed his elbows on the counter and rubbed his forehead. "When did Ca'admar get his first post at Rez 38?"

The guard blinked. "You want me to go back into the duty log?"

"That's how you'd find it, isn't it? Wait. Print out the writeup on Ca'admar, *then* go check the logs. Gives you one less reason to wanna shoot me."

"Rhynehart." Sir had folded his arms and now stared at the agent with more quivering rage than Cheyenne had ever seen in the man.

"Just give it a minute."

Trying not to roll his eyes, the guard switched gears. It took a little longer to find what he was looking for this time. "Okay, yeah." He snatched the printout with Ranzig's info on it and slid it through the slot beneath the tempered glass. "Ca'admar started the second week of June."

"Motherfucker." Rhynehart slammed his fist on the counter, crumpled the printed sheet in one hand, and hightailed it for the front doors of Chateau D'rahl. Cheyenne took off after him, and Major Sir Carson growled again before bringing up the rear.

"You better start flappin' those lips, Rhynehart."

"Ca'admar took the goddamn post a week before Q'orr's shit got smuggled off the rez."

The doors shut behind them, and Cheyenne paused for two seconds as Sir barreled after Rhynehart with a sharp, "Fuck!"

I knew it. She hustled to catch up with Rhynehart in the parking lot in the middle of nowhere, waiting for their next move. *Now we're gonna get those kids.*

"I'm gonna go drown myself in my office before I have to see any more of this goddamn mess," Sir shouted, breaking off toward his orange car. "Rhynehart, take whoever you need. However many you need. Bring the fucking armada."

"Sir."

The major turned to point at Cheyenne. "Now we're even."

"Sir."

"Not another goddamn word." The man jumped behind the wheel and slammed his door shut. The Rio peeled out of the parking lot before the halfling had reached the passenger side door of the Jeep. She and Rhynehart both hopped in, and the FRoE agent turned to look at her as he started the engine.

"Whatever kind of secret language you and L'zar Verdys just pulled out of thin air in the damn cave?" He sighed and slapped both hands on the wheel. "Keep it up, rookie. This is all on you, and now we have something to show for it."

Cheyenne strapped herself in and studied him as the agent

pulled the Jeep out of the parking lot. "I think 'rookie' has lost its charm at this point."

"Yeah, I know. I'll let you know when something catchy comes to me." He snorted, then nodded at the black sleeping mask on the dash. "Put that back on."

"Are you serious right now?"

"Rules are rules. But I'll put in a good word after this and see what we can do about changing them."

It's a start, at least. The halfling snatched up the mask and pulled it over her head. Then she had to listen to Rhynehart calling whoever at the FRoE compound to bring in the big guns and send a whole team to Ranzig Ca'admar's address. "We'll be there in twenty. No, I seriously doubt the sonofabitch is keeping over two dozen kids in his damn house, but whoever gets there first goes in first. Bag the fucker if he's home. If not, turn the place upside-down and find us what we're looking for. Yeah, that's right."

He dropped his cell phone into his lap and let out a long, slow breath as the Jeep took them away from Chateau D'rahl on a route Cheyenne couldn't see.

"I know this is the guy," the halfling muttered. "We'll find those kids through him."

"Yeah, I agree. And I'd bet my left nut he's the same magical smuggling all Q'orr's shit off Rez 38." The agent slapped a hand down on the steering wheel again while the half-drow sat beside him, straight-backed and blinded by the sleeping mask. "You know what I just can't get over?"

"No idea." Cheyenne shrugged. "It could be anything."

"I'm serious. How the *hell* did the little chat with L'zar help you figure all that out? That wasn't a real conversation."

It didn't have to be. The halfling folded her arms and leaned back. "It's a drow thing."

"Yeah, that's a top-notch answer."

"It's the only answer you're gonna get."

Fifteen minutes later, Rhynehart's phone sliced through the silence in the Jeep. Cheyenne heard the man jump in his seat before his hand found the cell phone and he brought it to his ear. "What do you have? Uh-huh. Shit. Good work, Presley. Yeah, we'll be there. Hey, no one goes in until I'm on-site, you got it? Asses in seats and everything. Damn right, she'll be there."

The phone dropped back into his lap, then the Jeep took a star-tlingly tight left turn. Cheyenne braced herself against the passen-ger-side door and hissed, "Who taught you to drive?"

"You can take the mask off, rookie. Change of plans."

The halfling didn't miss a beat. She jerked the mask off her head, blinking against the evening sunlight. It was just before sunset.

"My guys went by the goblin's house. Didn't find him, but they found some pretty incriminating emails, the way Presley told it. New address, new objective."

"Oh, yeah?"

"Yeah." Rhynehart shot her a quick glance and nodded. "We're goin' in to get those kids. Right now."

When they pulled up at a huge three-story house, Cheyenne's jaw almost dropped. Seven FRoE vehicles had parked in a line down the street, and every single agent had followed their orders.

"Yeah, asses in seats. Good." Rhynehart reached into the back seat and picked up another dampening vest before dropping it into the halfling's lap. "You know the drill."

"Yep." Cheyenne slipped it on and waited for Rhynehart to get out of the Jeep before she followed.

He moved quickly to the back and pulled out his dampening vest, gloves, and helmet, then closed it and moved up the line of black vehicles toward what was almost a mansion. Rhynehart thumped the door of each vehicle he passed, and the agents inside got out quickly and quietly, already geared up in their dampening armor and with weapons at the ready. They opened the trunks to pull out one giant fell rifle after another, and then nearly thirty

FRoE agents were storming up toward the house as a single swift, deadly unit.

Cheyenne caught sight of Yurik as he fastened a utility belt around his waist, loaded with the same round devices Rhynehart had used to pepper the drow halfling in the padded training room. She stopped and waited for him to step onto the sidewalk before he jammed his helmet onto his head and fell in line with the others. "No cannons today?"

"Working on a new commission, I guess." Yurik shrugged. "Jamal had the last two."

"Great."

"Don't sweat it, Cheyenne." Bhandi pulled her helmet out from under her arm and nodded at the halfling before pulling the thing over her head. "Fell cannons aren't the only things that can take down an ogre anymore, are they?"

She and Yurik chuckled, then they unholstered the fell pistols from their hips, and Yurik handed the troll woman fell grenades from his belt.

The beefy goblin nudged Cheyenne in the shoulder. "Better gear up too, huh?"

"What?'

Bhandi smacked a hand against her helmet. "We need a drow. She better show up before we get inside."

As they stormed toward the house, the first agents in line running up the steps to the front door, Cheyenne tried to pull up her drow form. Then she glanced down at the pendant hanging from the chain and grunted. *Gotta pick my poison. This has to go.* She reached back to unclasp the chain just as the first few FRoE agents knocked down the front door. Shouts and brilliant flashes of green and purple light rose from inside, and her fingers just wouldn't do their job.

Snarling, the halfling yanked on the chain and pulled it free. The purple-gray skin and bone-white hair of her drow form took over before she stuffed the Heart of Midnight pendant into her jacket pocket, and then she was running up the front steps beside two

FRoE agents she knew a lot better after last night. *I trust them. Time to nail those shitheads.*

Corian sat in the basement apartment, scrolling through the newest topic threads posted by desperate parents on the Borderlands forum. With a sigh, the Nightstalker scrubbed a hand over his face and shook his head. *How the hell am I supposed to keep this under wraps as long as I need to? I should be looking for those blood-traitors.*

He started to type out another response to the latest panicked inquiry, then a bright silver flash erupted from his finger. Corian froze. "No. She wouldn't!"

The chair scooted back across the cement with a hollow screech when he leaped to his feet, then the Nightstalker stormed across the basement toward the metal shelves full of pretty much everything he needed. The metal box was right there where he'd left it, and he jiggled off the lid again to peer inside. His eyes widened, and he hissed in anger before slamming the lid onto the box again. "Damnit, Cheyenne!"

The laptop shut with a click beneath his hand, then he pulled down the wards protecting the metal door and stepped out into the crisp autumn evening. *I don't care whose kid she is. This better be the last time I have to save her halfling ass.*

CHAPTER THIRTY-SIX

"Hands up, asshole!"

A burst of green light hurtled toward the FRoE agent standing just inside the doorway. Whoever it was fired fell darts, then Cheyenne Summerlin burst through the door into the chaos of another FRoE raid—this time on purpose.

A column of violet fire streaked toward her head, and the drow halfling ducked before sending a missile of crackling black energy toward the sneering goblin who'd attacked her. His blue-green grin disappeared when her spell hit him in the face a second before the fire crashed into the wall behind her. Something heavy and metal toppled to the ground with a clang.

Cheyenne spun around to see the helmet rolling away from the rest of a fallen suit of armor before she returned to the fight.

"Jesus, what a place, huh?" Beside her, Yurik fired his fell pistol. The skaxen he'd aimed at dodged the first and caught the rest of the weapons fire in the gut, screaming as he hit the floor.

"Shitbags in a mansion are still shitbags," Bhandi said, ducking a flashing attack of red magic spinning toward her like a throwing star. Her fell pistol caught the attacking troll in the hip and then the knee, and she growled when he went down.

The FRoE spread out across the huge foyer and into the multiple rooms on the first floor, magic and fell darts flying everywhere and obliterating the expensive décor.

Cheyenne's lashing black tendrils shot from her hands and wrapped around an orc with his meaty fist clamped down around an agent's arm. The tendrils whipped around the orc's wrist and jerked his arm back. The FRoE agent was tossed aside, but the orc was a lot more focused now on the thick coils of drow magic crushing his windpipe.

The halfling let the orc drop and raised a black, shimmering shield of magic between Yurik and the bullet some asshole had tried to put in his helmet. The bullet pinged off Cheyenne's shield and the huge, muscular goblin turned toward her, his grin barely visible through the mask of his helmet. "Yeah, I'm stickin' with you."

"I don't care what you do as long as we find those kids," Cheyenne snarled. She let off one crackling burst of black energy after another at the screaming, sneering magicals poorly defending their new hiding place. "That's why we're here."

She moved through the chaos and the multi-colored spells crossing the foyer against fell darts and larger fell explosives. Glass shattered somewhere behind her, and Bhandi nudged Cheyenne forward from behind just before a massive pane of stained glass crashed to the floor where the halfling had stood.

"We got your back, drow." The troll woman nodded toward the rest of the battle and the agents destroying the well-kept mansion. "Let's go."

Cheyenne flung attacking magicals aside with her lashing tendrils, ducking under flying spells and weaving around the black-magic targets and FRoE agents alike. Bhandi and Yurik flanked her without a word, picking off their own targets as they moved through the house.

On the other side of the foyer, a huge, winding staircase led up to the second floor. Five FRoE agents were spread out along the first few steps, exchanging fire with a giant ogre crashing down the staircase toward them. Cheyenne glanced up at the second-floor landing and the balcony overlooking the fight below. Off the top of the stairs was a set of double doors guarded by another ogre and a scrawny orange skaxen. Both of them hurled attack spells into the fray, but they didn't move from their post beside the door.

"There! Second floor," Cheyenne shouted.

Bhandi and Yurik glanced up at the balcony and nodded.

The ogre on the staircase let out a mighty bellow and swung a huge fist at the agents in front of him. Most of them leaped aside, firing before one poor bastard took an ogre fist to the side of the helmet. The agent staggered sideways into the staircase banister, and the ogre lifted his fist to bring it down on the stunned operative's head.

Cheyenne threw a shield up over the agent's helmet. The ogre's fist struck it like a giant gong, and he reeled backward, roaring.

"Let's go."

She led her new FRoE friends past all the fighting, dodging flying spells and throwing up shields to keep whatever agents she could from getting a face or a belly or a back full of criminal magic. *Yeah, I think I'm getting the hang of this.*

They reached the bottom of the staircase as the stunned agent against the banister gained his footing. The other four trained their fell weapons on the bellowing ogre. Yurik detached one of the round black grenades from his belt and shouted, "Fellfire in the hole!"

The agents nearly skidded down the last few steps before the muscular goblin launched the fell grenade. It struck the ogre in the chest and stuck there, flashing green light before it erupted.

The mansion trembled, and dust and bits of chipped plaster rained down on everyone. The ogre bellowed and crashed against the wall following the staircase.

"Dammit," Yurik spat. "They just don't go down."

The ogre pushed himself back up to his feet, shaking his head. Plaster and drywall spilled off his hulking shoulders. A magical screamed in the foyer before something else exploded, and Cheyenne headed up the stairs. "He will."

The agents flanked her as she made her way toward the ogre, who glared at her with heavily lidded eyes. She threw crackling black energy balls and struck the asshole in the hip, belly, and chest. One huge foot crashed down another step toward her, and a dagger of orange magic materialized in his scarred gray palm.

The halfling sighed. "Ogres and magical weapons, huh?"

"Looks like it." Bhandi trained her pistol on the ogre's hand and fired. The fell shots glanced off the ogre's wrist before he threw the orange dagger toward the troll woman.

Cheyenne raised another shield, deflecting the tossed weapon-spell, and advanced up the stairs again. High-pitched laughter came from more than one magical behind her on the first floor, but she ignored it. *I've got backup. I better.*

The ogre moved faster than she expected, flinging orange daggers left and right with both hands. The halfling managed to raise a shield in front of each intended target—mostly herself—but couldn't get enough downtime to attack. Then the skaxen and the other ogre guarding the door upstairs started flinging spells at the FRoE agents and the drow halfling. A shrill, maddened cackle escaped the skaxen's gaping orange mouth.

Bhandi aimed her weapon at the balcony and squeezed off a quick round. The banister exploded in shards of green light and wood, then the magicals upstairs were fully engaged too.

"We'll keep 'em busy," another agent shouted.

Cheyenne dodged another orange dagger from the ogre's huge fist and used that moment to lash out with her black tendrils. They curled around the hulking gray magical's wrists, tightening instantly. For a moment, the half-drow and the ogre struggled against each other, their strength nearly matched. Then the ogre quit trying to spread his arms and jerked them up instead.

That yanked Cheyenne up the stairs. Grunting, she caught herself on the next step just before the ogre reared sideways and threw his wrists in a sweeping arc over his head and up the stairs toward the second floor. The halfling flew too, barely avoiding the bursts of purple and red magic shooting through the mansion. She crashed against the wall at the top of the stairs, grimacing while the ogre chuckled and headed toward her.

Her black tendrils drew back, and she kicked off against the wall to enter drow speed.

With a crack, time in the entire mansion slowed, and Cheyenne darted down the stairs again. The ogre's foot was lifted halfway in his attempt to climb the stairs. She let off half a dozen black spheres, peppering his body from knee to head, then sent black tendrils to coil around his standing leg. When she jerked sideways, the ogre's foot barely moved. So, she slipped behind him on the stairs and clamped both hands down around the backs of his knees. "More than one way to take you down, asshole."

Her black energy spheres crackled in her hands, their light bursting around the ogre's legs before something splintered beneath her fingers. Then she shoved with all her strength and sent the huge magical crashing toward the railing.

A wave of dizziness passed through her, and time sped up again. The mansion erupted with shouts and growls and hissing magic crashing into bodies and walls. The ogre added his bellowing scream to the din as he crashed through the balcony and dropped like a boulder on the unsuspecting goblins below.

Blinking off the dizziness, Cheyenne pushed off the wall and started climbing the steps.

"Oh, shit!" Bhandi peered through the splintered banister. "Did you just blast off his legs?"

A spiraling yellow bolt cracked against the next shield the half-drow lifted in front of the troll agent, and Cheyenne turned her attention to the second ogre and the skaxen trying to defend that door.

The other agents rushed up the stairs, firing fell rounds at the magicals. The halfling had to steady herself with a hand against the wall again, and Yurik stopped beside her with his weapon raised. "You okay?"

"Yeah. Just get them away from the door, huh? I think the kids are in there, but I gotta check first, and I need a moment to do that."

"No repeat of that bomb in a crate." Yurik nodded. "We'll cover you." Then he darted off down the second-floor hallway toward the ogre and the skaxen, added his own fell shots to the melee.

Cheyenne shook out her hands and headed after him toward the door.

The second ogre didn't go down beneath the fellfire either. Roaring, he swept his huge arms left and right, fending off the agents who didn't have enough firepower to do much more than distract him.

The skaxen leaped onto the balcony and ran across it on all fours like a giant orange rat. Someone shot at him as he scrambled forward, but the fell darts went wild, then the skaxen leaped toward Cheyenne. She unleashed another crackling black sphere and hit the snarling orange magical in the thigh before he crashed into her and knocked them both against the wall, then fell to the floor in a heap.

Snarling, the halfling batted the skaxen's sharp claws away from her face as he scrambled to get a good hold on her. He somehow managed to get a grip on the collar of her jacket and lifted her off the ground before slamming her head back down.

"All you have to do is swear fealty, *mór úcare*," the orange guy hissed, spit flying from between his razor-sharp teeth. "That's all she wants. This'll all be over if you just give yourself to the Crown and let her handle the rest."

"No fucking way!" Cheyenne brought her elbow down on the side of the skaxen's head. It knocked him off her just enough for her to roll out from under him. His claws raked through her jacket and into the flesh beneath as she grabbed him by his thin black shirt and threw him off her.

The rat-like magical screamed as he soared over the balcony. Leaping to her feet, the halfling launched two more crackling black orbs at his chest, both of which hit him before he slammed into the floor beside the bloody stumps of the fallen ogre's legs.

I don't know who these assholes think I am, but I'm not swearing shit to anyone.

With a deep breath, she turned back toward the seven FRoE agents trying to bring down a snarling, raving ogre on their own.

CHAPTER THIRTY-SEVEN

Cheyenne darted around the agents, who were firing round after round of fell shots into the ogre's gray flesh. It was enough of a distraction for the halfling to get to those guarded double doors unseen. *Just a few seconds to make sure.*

She pressed her palm against the door and closed her eyes, bringing up her drow sight. A hot blast of green fire erupted by her hand, and she leaped aside before glancing over the balcony. Two orcs pulled up more fire to launch at her, and she scattered them with handfuls of hissing black energy.

"I need cover!"

Yurik ducked under the ogre's sweeping arm and turned on one knee to level his pistol at the orcs. They dodged his first few shots, and Cheyenne turned back to the door.

Make it quick. She closed her eyes and pulled up her drow sight again, pouring all her focus into that one ability because that was the only way. Another crackling dart of magic whizzed past her head, and she hissed out a frustrated breath. *Come on!*

A faint blue outline appeared in her mind's eye, huddled on the ground just beyond the door. Then another blast of magic struck the wooden floor beside her feet, and the halfling jerked back. *That's good enough for me.*

"They're in here!" she shouted and reached for the door handle. But there wasn't one. *Of course not.*

Cheyenne stepped back and blasted the door with a black sphere. An orange and red light flared around the door, and that was it. "Shit. Wards too?"

The FRoE agents repeated the shout of getting upstairs to break down those doors. The operatives fighting the ogre were busy enough as it was, and the others downstairs were sweeping through the mansion, trying to gather at the stairs and getting cut off by the kidnappers.

Bhandi let out a battle cry and tossed two fell grenades at the ogre. The other agents hit the deck before the black disks detonated. The blast sent Cheyenne reeling away from the door as more spells flew up from the foyer and hit the wall beside her head. The ogre roared and slapped a meaty gray hand to his eye, blood spewing everywhere.

Then Yurik was at Cheyenne's side, studying the double doors from top to bottom. "Didn't think a drow needed to use doorknobs."

"Wards." She pointed at the door and threw up a shield in front of three more agents running up the stairs. The purple shards of some goblin's attack ricocheted off the black light of the shield, and the agents kept running. They skirted past the ogre, who still roared and stumbled around, blinded by shrapnel.

"You know anything about wards?" Yurik asked.

"That door would be open if I did."

"Right." He stepped back and fired fell shots into the door, which only brought up the orange and red glow of protective wards without doing any damage. Turning back toward the fighting, the goblin roared, "Anyone got a blaster?"

A massive explosion made the floor tremble beneath their feet. Cheyenne staggered as a blast of smoke and debris hurtled into the foyer from another room downstairs. FRoE agents ran away from the blast, ducking debris and throwing spells and firing their fell rifles where they could.

A raging scream below made Cheyenne peer over the balcony. Three skaxen stood in a half-circle, their arms outstretched in front of a black circle opening in mid-air. "What the hell is that?" Yurik shouted.

"A portal," the halfling snarled and stormed toward the balcony. "Get that door open." *Or we're screwed.*

She launched black energy spheres over the balcony, hitting two of the skaxens' legs. They screamed and jumped around. The growing portal downstairs shivered but held steady. Cheyenne reached out with her flailing black tendrils, but she was too far away. The drow whips smacked one skaxen's sweaty orange face, but that was it. Then a troll spewed a column of dripping blue magic up at her. The halfling retracted her tendrils to throw up a shield around herself, the blue spell splashing against it like thick magical mud.

Someone fired more shots at the doors behind her, and the orange and red wards flashed even brighter.

Cheyenne glanced quickly from the skaxens' growing portal to the agents locked in battle at the foot of the stairs. More of them climbed the stairs, occasionally turning back to fire their weapons and keep the pursuing magicals at bay. The ogre kept fighting, swinging blindly but still not going down. *We bit off more than we could chew this time.*

A bright flash of silver light burst through the open door downstairs, and the entire fight changed.

The three skaxens summoning a portal were first. Two of them clutched their necks, blood spraying all over the third before he screamed and crashed into the wall. The portal fizzled out with a pop. The silver streak blurred across the foyer again. Fights between FRoE agents and magicals were broken up in an instant, the silver bursts of light striking the black-magic enemies. Some went flying through the air, while agents staggered back in surprise. Some magicals lost limbs or dropped where they stood, choking and gasping before falling over.

The silver lightning darted back and forth across the foyer, leaving the agents untouched and everything else destroyed in its wake. In a flash, it raced past the agents being pushed down the stairs again by the enraged and blinded ogre. Blinding silver light ripped his gray flesh from navel to chin, and the ogre dropped.

"What the hell?"

"Who's doing that?

"Just gutted the bastard like a fish!"

The silver streak moved in a blur that was impossible to see, heading for Cheyenne and Yurik beside the double doors. The orange and red wards erupted in a flash of light, the doors burst open, and then the silver flash darted away.

Cheyenne changed into drow speed, surrounded by FRoE operatives frozen in shock and bewilderment. She ran down the hall toward the staircase and leaped down two at a time. "Corian!"

The Nightstalker moved quickly down the stairs but didn't bother to look at her.

"Hey! I know you hear me."

When she'd made it halfway down the stairs, he whirled to face her and hissed, his silver eyes flashing in the super-speed stasis around them, "I didn't give you that pendant so you could take it off to play drow superhero, kid."

"What?" The halfling moved the rest of the way down the staircase toward him. "You know what? *You're* the one who didn't tell me what it does. And I asked!"

"Me telling you to do something should be enough. I'm not risking my neck to help you if you keep insisting on being a moron."

"Look, asshole, it's a good thing I figured out what that pendant does, or I would've walked in here without magic." Cheyenne glanced at the carnage in the foyer and pointed to the ogre with his legs blown off. "And I'd end up like one of those guys. I came here to find those kids, and I'm not about to turn my magic off just to make *you* feel safer."

"I *am* safe, Cheyenne!" Baring his teeth, Corian stormed toward her, his fists clenched at his sides. "I've *been* safe for hundreds of years on this side, and the only thing that's coming even remotely close to blowing my cover and bringing it all crashing down around me is *you*. I have my orders, and I'm following them. Suck it the hell up and do the same."

"I don't take orders, Nightstalker. That's not what this is about."

"Everyone in this house knew you were here. Who do you think that skaxen portal was for, huh? You charged in here like an idiot without any protection, and you need to get it through your thick drow head that the game has changed."

Cheyenne shook her head. "What are you talking about?"

The Nightstalker's silver eyes darted around the destroyed foyer littered with criminal bodies. "This is the last time I pull your head out of your ass for you, got it? Put the fucking pendant back on."

He turned without another word and stalked back out of the house. As he stepped through the doorway, Cheyenne's enhanced speed fell away.

"Holy shit," Yurik muttered, staring through the open double doors on the second floor before reaching out to nudge the halfling he still thought stood beside him. "You were right about— What?" He turned quickly and found her standing at the bottom of the stairs. "What the hell are you doing down there? We got the kids. Hey!" The goblin agent waved for the rest of the team to join him in front of the double doors.

Beside the debris spilling out of the room next to the foyer, Rhynehart ripped off his helmet and stared at the halfling. "What the hell was that?"

Cheyenne turned toward him and grimaced. "Those kids are a lot more important right now, don't you think?"

She ignored his irritated mumbling as she stalked back up the stairs with the other FRoE agents to join Yurik by the door. Some still gazed around in amazement, taking their helmets off to get a better view of the destruction.

"Hey, kids," one of the agents said gently from just outside the door. He set his helmet on the floor, holstered his weapon, and waved for the terrified kidnapping victims to come out of the warded dungeon they'd been crammed into for at least a day. "Everything's okay. We're gonna get you all outta here and take you home."

Cheyenne's enhanced hearing picked up heavy frightened breathing from the beings inside that room. Some of the magical kids started crying. A goblin boy about twelve or thirteen was the first to step through the door. He gazed around the mansion with wide eyes, taking in the dead bodies, the bloodstained floors, and the walls riddled with charred holes and cracks and missing huge chunks. Then he turned toward the agent who'd spoken to the kids and stuck out his hand. "Thank you."

The agent looked startled, then he gripped the goblin boy's hand and gave it a firm shake. "Doin' our job, kid. If you wanna thank somebody, go shake the drow's hand."

The kid's eyes grew wide when he saw Cheyenne standing at the top of the stairs.

The image of the goblin boy dressed up in robes and lying dead in that church came uninvited to Cheyenne's mind. She blinked at him, swallowed, and muttered, "Just help everyone else get outta there. You guys'll be fine."

Then the drow halfling brushed past the other FRoE agents. Rhynehart stared at her as she stormed through the foyer. She had to swerve to avoid the bodies scattered all over the place, and she felt his gaze on her even when she stepped outside into the early evening. *We only made it out of this because of Corian. Maybe he was right.*

Cheyenne jammed her hand into the outside pocket of her jacket and took out the Heart of Midnight pendant. The gem glittered at her in the orange and pink light of sunset, and she begrudgingly put it back on, tying a little knot in the thing's silver chain because she'd broken the clasp.

Her drow magic and the heat of her rage disappeared, squashed back down inside her by the protective spell of Corian's stupid necklace. Her bone-white hair darkened into her regular High Voltage Raven Black, the purple-gray of her drow skin lightening to her human paleness. The pointed tips of her ears disappeared beneath her hair again. Clenching her fists, she took off toward the line of FRoE vehicles parked at the curb just beyond the mansion. *I just need a minute to cool off. Then I'll come back to help those kids get to their parents.*

CHAPTER THIRTY-EIGHT

When the last wide-eyed and shell-shocked magical kid was loaded into the last black FRoE van called in for transport, Cheyenne nodded at the agent who shut the door. That agent got behind the wheel, her partner in the passenger seat beside her, and the van took off after all the other vehicles.

Rhynehart tossed his helmet, vest, and dampening gloves into the back of his Jeep and whistled. "Let's go."

It took a lot of willpower to pull her gaze away from that last retreating van, but she finally managed it and turned to head for the passenger-side door of the Jeep. Once she closed the door behind her, Rhynehart started the engine with a jerking twist and slowly left the neighborhood.

"Let me guess," Cheyenne muttered. "The cleaning crew comes later."

"Different department." His hands tightened on the steering wheel. "Let's focus on ours, huh? Now that the most important job's out of the way and the kids are heading back to base, this is the part where you tell me who the hell our lightning-bolt hero was."

The halfling turned to frown at the agent, who was so focused on playing hardball with her that he squinted against the sunset, his sunglasses forgotten.

"I can't tell you anything about that, Rhynehart." *Not if he doesn't already know we had our asses saved by a Nightstalker. Especially Corian.*

"You're getting really good at mimicry, you know that?" Rhynehart shot her a quick glance, blinked furiously against the sun, and jerked down the visor. It didn't do anything to block the glare. When he grunted in irritation, Cheyenne leaned forward and grabbed his sunglasses from the cubby beneath the dashboard.

"Here."

"Yeah." He snatched them from her, put them on with one hand, and shook his head. "Don't expect me to believe for one second that you don't know shit about what happened in there. One minute you're up there trying to knock down that door. The next minute, there's a goddamn silver tornado taking down every single one of our targets, and who's suddenly standing right there in front of me at the bottom of the stairs again?"

The halfling stared out the windshield, pressing her lips together.

"Not a rhetorical question, Cheyenne. I'm talking about you and the look on your face when our anonymous friend booked it back out that door. If you don't know who it was, you know *something*. Spill it."

"There's nothing to spill, man. Sorry." She couldn't look at him. *I can't trust him either, and I'm not about to throw Corian under the bus, even if he called me a moron.*

"You're not sorry at all." Rhynehart cleared his throat and turned onto the freeway to head toward Richmond.

Half an hour later, they pulled up in front of the red diner where Cheyenne had negotiated herself into another meeting with L'zar just hours ago.

Cheyenne glanced around the mostly empty parking lot and

licked her lips in frustration. "I'm still not hungry. Just take me back to the compound with you so we can finish this thing with those kids."

"Nice try, halfling." Rhynehart shifted into park and whipped his sunglasses off before fixing her with an angry scowl. "Wherever you're going tonight, it's not back to base. You have priorities to work out."

"Thanks for the pep talk." She snorted. "Right now, my top priority is helping those kids get back to their families."

"Cross it off the list. And don't even try to sneak back to the compound after you get out of my car. Yeah, I heard all about your fun little night out with my agents last night. There's no point in blindfolding you anymore on the drive over, but if I have to, I'll put out an order to keep you off the base for as long as it takes."

Cheyenne blinked furiously. "You can't just tell me to screw off—"

"That's exactly what I'm doin', kid. Get out."

"Hey, I'm the one who *found* those kids in the first place, asshole!" It threw her off more than she'd expected when the usual heat of her drow magic didn't show up at all with her anger. "They'd still be locked up in that psychotic ritual den if I hadn't found the connection to Ranzig Ca'admar."

"Yeah, you get full credit for that one. Go get yourself a cookie." Rhynehart nodded toward the driver's side door, his eyes narrowing. "*My* guys are the ones who get to deal with those kids now. You're off the hook. Unless you wanna spill this second what you're trying not to tell me."

I can't believe this. "There's nothing to tell."

"Then get the hell out of my Jeep and call me when you're ready to talk about what happened back there. We're done."

Biting down hard on her lower lip, Cheyenne let out a little growl and jerked open the passenger side door. Rhynehart took off in the Jeep the same second she slammed the door shut behind her. She was left standing in front of her scuffed, chipped, matte-gray Ford Focus in the diner's parking lot.

When she jammed her hand back into the pocket of her jacket to grab her keys, she hissed and glanced down at her forearm. The jacket sleeves had been ripped almost to shreds by that crazed skaxen spouting crazier demands about "swearing fealty," and her forearms burned now.

She unlocked her car, opened the door, and gingerly shrugged out of the jacket. It thumped onto the passenger seat, then the halfling studied the long red gouges in her skin, some of them a quarter of an inch deep. "Skaxen asshole."

Should've stocked up on healing ingredients at Peridosh last night.

Cheyenne bent and dropped into the driver's seat, slammed the door shut behind her, and started the engine. For a few minutes, she just sat there, debating whether Rhynehart's warning was worth listening to tonight. Then she shook her head and buckled up. "I already played my leverage card to get into Chateau D'rahl. Nobody likes a drow showing up uninvited and making more demands."

The gray Ford Focus pulled out of the parking lot, and the halfling headed onto the highway toward downtown Richmond.

With bags of takeout swinging from her hands, Cheyenne stalked down the corridor of the inpatient recovery ward of the VCU Medical Center. She didn't look up from the linoleum floor in front of her, even when she felt the nurses and care staff staring at the Goth chick. *This stupid necklace might block off my magic, but I'm still pissed enough to be one scary human.*

When she reached Room 317, she did a little shuffle with the takeout bags before knocking quickly on the door.

"Come in." Ember sounded cheery enough, and she looked happy to see Cheyenne when the halfling pushed open the door. Then her smile faded. "What happened to you?"

"Weird day." Cheyenne shut the door behind her and headed across the hospital room toward her friend's bed.

"That's an understatement. You look like shit."

The halfling stopped halfway across the room and looked at Ember in surprise. The magicless fae in the hospital bed smirked, and Cheyenne laughed. "Okay, fine. Weird and seriously messed-up day, with a side order of what-the-fuck."

Ember laughed. *"That's* more like it."

When she reached the other side of the bed, Cheyenne dropped the takeout bags on the rolling table, then turned to pull the ridiculously uncomfortable armchair as close as she could to her friend. "Hope you're in the mood for burgers."

"Come on, Cheyenne. I'm *always* in the mood for burgers." Ember started unpacking the food, slowing a little when she noticed the nasty gouges in the half-drow's forearms. "I'm also in the mood for hearing the wild story of how your arms met Freddy Krueger and why you have chunks of wall in your hair. That *is* just wall, right?"

"What?" The halfling leaned over the side of the armchair and ruffled her hair. The chains around her wrists clinked as drywall and plaster chunks dropped onto the floor. "Oh, yeah. That. Just another day in halfling paradise, right?"

"Uh-huh." Ember pulled one of the burgers into her lap and slowly unwrapped it. "I'm listening."

With a sigh, Cheyenne ran her hand through her hair again and looked at the ceiling for a good neck stretch. "We found those kids."

"The kids?" Eyes trained on the halfling, Ember took a huge bite of her burger, barbeque sauce and a piece of onion ring landed on the paper wrapper with a splat.

"I didn't tell you about that?" Cheyenne shrugged. "Damn. I guess it's only been two days. Feels like two weeks."

When she looked at Ember, the fae girl just stared at her and shoved more burger into her mouth, silently waiting for the halfling to keep going.

"Okay, this is gonna sound nuts."

Ember laughed and managed not to spray her mouthful of greasy dinner all over her lap and the hospital blankets. "Compared to *what?* All your stories are crazy, Cheyenne. It's the best part of my day when I get to hear 'em."

"You're just itching for your next fix of halfling drama, huh?"

"Believe it or not, the entertainment's pretty lacking around here." Ember leaned toward her friend and whispered, "I think the nurses are going out of their way to make sure I'm as bored as possible."

"Good thing we're friends." For the first time since finding out those magical kids had been kidnapped yesterday morning, Cheyenne Summerlin had a reason to smile. "Okay. You eat, and I'll talk."

Ember took another huge bite and wiggled her eyebrows.

CHAPTER THIRTY-NINE

Ember finished her burger and the side of sweet potato fries halfway through Cheyenne's story—the bomb at the construction site, all the kids' clothes in a pile, the halfling's second stay in the FRoE's medical wing. The fae sucked down the raspberry iced tea like she hadn't had anything to drink in days when Cheyenne got to the part about visiting L'zar a second time at Chateau D'rahl.

"Sounds like he lost his mind in that place."

The halfling shook her head. "I'm pretty sure he was like that before they locked him up. Still not convinced he's sane."

"But he knew about that goblin pretending to be a FRoE agent, right?" Ember wiped her hands on a napkin and tossed it into the plastic takeout bag, shaking her head. "I can't believe that sentence just came out of my mouth."

Cheyenne chuckled and shrugged. "Pretty weird to hear about all this insider FRoE crap when you've been trying to stay away from them your whole life, huh? Maybe that's how I got into this mess. I had no idea who they were."

"Maybe. Or you're just a badass who can handle anybody."

"Yeah, right." Rolling her eyes, the halfling finished off the last of her burger and turned to her side of fries. "And L'zar didn't know who the traitor was."

"Really? How do you figure that?"

"How *would* he know? He's been locked up in there for decades. Okay, minus the three-day vacation when he met my mom."

Ember snorted.

"I think it's more like L'zar knew that *I* knew, and he was just trying to dig up the pieces so I could see it all clearly and ignore everything else. Which is totally weird when I think about it like that."

"No kidding. Estranged prisoner dad knowing your head better than you do? Yeah, Cheyenne, I bet that's pretty creepy."

The halfling munched on more fries. "But it worked. And we found the assholes who took those kids. Got 'em all out of there safely, and they'll be back home by the end of the night." *They better be.*

"There's one thing I don't get, though," Ember said, then drained the last of her tea.

"What, I didn't give you enough of a detailed play-by-play?" Cheyenne smirked.

"No, that part was great. Super efficient. But the half-drow I know wouldn't walk away from a bunch of terrified kids freshly pulled out of a kidnapper mansion." The fae frowned with a small, confused smile. "Why the hell did you come to see me instead of going with those kids?"

With a groan, Cheyenne slumped against the back of the armchair, grimacing at the dull ache in her forearms. "We had a little help in that house. From a Nightstalker friend."

"For real?"

"Who's apparently really pissed that I took off this stupid neck-lace to save all those kids. And nobody knows about him."

"Huh."

"Yeah, so my options were to give up the one person I know who knows L'zar Verdys or be on my merry way. I've been kicked out of the FRoE compound for now."

Ember snorted. "Their loss."

"Yeah. And Corian's pissed at me. I'm not going over to his place tonight after his little lecture on not being a halfling idiot. I thought about checking out the Borderland forums and at least letting the families know their kids are safe, but the guy's one of the admins on there too. Guess I'm just not feeling the whole, 'Let's pretend he didn't call me an idiot so we can act like nothing happened' part."

"He'll cool off." Ember ran a hand through her hair and shrugged. "You need him. He knows it. And it sounds like he's got a lot invested in your drow trials, or whatever."

"Don't remind me." Cheyenne laughed. "It's still weird. I have a Nightstalker professor showing me the ropes of not going apeshit whenever I'm pissed, and now I have a Nightstalker mentor who knows more about these stupid trials than I do. Because he knows L'zar."

"And he *found* you at that mansion." Ember wrinkled her nose. "That's creepy. Really puts the stalker in Nightstalker."

"I'm pretty sure he's been watching me for a long time. Waiting for me to be ready. Jesus, I'm so tired of people telling me I have to wait 'til I'm ready."

With a small laugh, Ember sat back against the elevated hospital bed and fluffed the limp pillow behind her back. "You're the only person who gets to decide when you're ready, Cheyenne. And everybody knows it."

The halfling studied the long gashes in her arms and let out another heavy sigh. "And yet, everybody's trying to hold the halfling back."

"Trying and failing. They'll get it through their thick heads eventually."

The fae's grin was infectious, and Cheyenne found herself laughing with her friend. "Thanks, Em. I'm glad I'm not the only person who gets it."

"That's what I'm here for, right? Your sidekick holed up in a—"

A knock came at the door, and without waiting for a reply, Dr. Andrews stepped into the room with a stack of papers in his hand.

He paused when he caught sight of the Goth chick looking like she'd just been dragged through a demolition site, then closed the door behind him. "I see your mysterious friend's come back for another visit."

"Hey, Doc." Cheyenne gave him a tight smile. "How's it goin'?"

"Well, I can say with complete confidence that my night's been a lot less exciting than yours."

The halfling shrugged and shared a knowing glance with her friend. "If you say so."

"But I do have some exciting news for *you*, Ms. Gaderow. Should I assume you'd like your friend here with you to hear it?"

"That's a pretty safe assumption, yeah." Ember grinned as Dr. Andrews approached the foot of her hospital bed, her eyes trained on the paperwork in his hands.

"Okay, then. We've got everything set up to get you discharged and out of here tomorrow, Ember. At this point, there's not much more we can do for you here at the hospital, so you get to go home. If you're ready for it, I've got a referral to get you started with physical therapy on Monday."

"Seriously?" Ember's face lit up, and she turned toward Cheyenne to flash her friend a goofy, open-mouthed expression of surprise. "I'm getting *out!*"

"Tomorrow, yes." Dr. Andrews glanced at the friends and readjusted his glasses. "You'll need someone to help you get home and settled into a slightly different routine."

Cheyenne snorted. "I've met doctors with zero bedside manner. You're not one of them."

"If that's a compliment, thank you."

"You're welcome."

"These are your discharge instructions." Dr. Andrews stepped around the other side of the bed to hand the papers to Ember. "You'll sign everything else tomorrow, and then you're on to the next step."

"Awesome." Ember scanned the papers, flipping through them quickly and shaking her head in disbelief. "Thought this was gonna take a lot longer. Hey, Cheyenne, I know you have a lot going on right now, but—"

"I gotcha." With a wry laugh, the halfling patted her friend's leg and nodded. "Whatever you need, Em, I'm here. All the other *stuff* I've got going on can wait."

Ember tried to bring her grin back under control and failed. "I'm one seriously lucky chick in a hospital bed."

"That's one way of putting it."

"Then make sure you two go over the discharge instructions together," Dr. Andrews added. "There's a lot of information in there, and there'll be a lot more when you start your PT, Ember."

"Yeah, no problem." The magicless fae went back to scanning the ten different documents he'd given her.

Then the doctor's gaze settled on the halfling's forearm. "Got yourself more battle wounds, I see."

Don't laugh. He has no idea. "Yeah, I'm prone to accidents, I guess."

"Yes, I remember you mentioning that last time. What happened there?"

"Uh…" Cheyenne studied the gashes in her arm. "Rat problem."

Ember turned toward the bedside table and reached for her empty tea so Dr. Andrews wouldn't see her shoot the halfling a warning look.

The doctor frowned. "That's one big rat."

"Growth hormones in the food or something, right?" Cheyenne lowered her hand into her lap again and shrugged. "I know it's against the rules and all to even ask—"

"You don't have to." Dr. Andrews raised an eyebrow at the halfling and shook his head. "I'll be right back with some antibacterial ointment and bandages. Unless you need someone to pull another piece of sci-fi tech out of those wounds."

Ember barked a laugh and clapped her hands over her mouth.

"Naw, Doc. Nothing to pull out this time." The halfling hunched forward a little as she fought back her laugh.

"Okay. You don't ask, I won't ask, and we'll leave it at that. Give me a few minutes."

"Thank you."

"And it goes without saying, but I have to say it anyway. Ms. Gaderow's recovery will be a lot smoother and faster without flying shrapnel and rat problems. We can all agree it's best to keep those out of the equation?"

"Absolutely." Cheyenne raised one hand in a silent oath.

Ember shrugged. "And I hate rats, so…"

"Uh-huh." Dr. Andrews gave the chuckling women another dubious glance, then hesitantly turned back toward the door before slipping out into the hall.

Ember's laughter finally exploded out of her with full force. "'Sci-fi tech?'"

The halfling wiggled her head and lowered her voice to mimic the doctor's attempt at seriousness. "That's one big rat."

They burst out laughing again, and Cheyenne almost forgot about her stinging arms.

CHAPTER FORTY

With both forearms professionally doctored and wrapped in fresh bandages, Cheyenne pulled up in the parking lot of her apartment complex south of Jackson Ward. She grabbed her backpack and shredded jacket from the passenger seat, then glanced behind her. She stared at the Incredible Hulk backpack on the back seat and shrugged. "Yeah, okay. Who knows what that imp would do to try to steal these back?"

She grabbed the backpack—with the metal skull necklace she knew belonged to Durg's orc niece—and got out of her car. The autumn air was chilly through what was left of her tattered turtleneck. The halfling eyed her bandaged forearms just beneath where Dr. Andrews had cut the shredded sleeves away and dipped her head in acknowledgment. "Clean, wrapped, *and* warm. The doc does good work."

The hallway on the third floor was empty and silent. Cheyenne let out a little sigh of relief when she passed her troll neighbors' front door without it opening. *Not in the mood for a troll family tonight, as nice as they are. And weird.*

After she unlocked her apartment door, the halfling grimaced and slowly opened it. But everything was just as she left it, including the copper drow legacy box lying on the floor. "Good. I'm done with surprises today."

She set the Incredible Hulk backpack down on the half-wall of the kitchen counter right next to the basket of troll-crafted underwear. All the bright colors next to each other made her snort, and she shook her head before kicking off her shoes and dropping her keys on the counter. A huge yawn escaped her, and she shook her head as she dropped her backpack against the half wall and tossed her shredded jacket against the front closet door.

Shuffling sleepily across the tiny living room, Cheyenne spared a considering glance at Glen. "Mm...nope. All that can wait for—" Another yawn interrupted her, and she blinked the tears out of her eyes before moving into the hall. "Tomorrow. It better just be a normal day."

The splintered door to her bedroom creaked open as she entered, and the halfling didn't bother undressing before she fell into bed. For a second, she considered taking off the damn necklace again to keep it from cutting into her chest while she slept, but Corian's furious feline face kept darting through her mind.

Fine. Until I figure out a better way, I'll keep the damn thing on.

Her alarm woke her the next morning at 6:30, but when she slapped a hand down on her nightstand, she hit only bare wood. "What?"

Pushing herself groggily up off the mattress, Cheyenne blinked and realized she'd left her phone in the front pocket of her backpack. She groaned and slid out of bed. Crumbs of plaster fell off the sheets, and she swiped them quickly under the bed.

By the time she reached her backpack and the irritating alarm on her phone, she was fully awake and considered kicking her phone just to stop the noise. But she pulled it out instead, shut off the alarm, and found a text from Ember.

2:00. I'm breakin' outta here!

With a chuckle, Cheyenne texted back that she'd be there, then headed to the shower to wash off the crust of mansion plaster and sweat and probably a little blood. *I took an ogre out by the kneecaps, after all.*

No calls on the FRoE burner phone interrupted her while she got ready for another interminably boring day of sitting through her two graduate classes on a Thursday morning. No one tried to get in touch with her or send her messages as she pulled clean clothes out of the dryer and tugged them on. Then she dried her hair, brushed it out, and applied the pasty-white foundation and thick black lines smudged up into dark-gray eyeshadow. The halfling studied her reflection in the mirror and found herself glaring at the dark, glittering Heart of Midnight resting beneath her throat.

"Okay. I'd be totally happy with just one normal day. If nothing else goes right, I have to be there for Em, so don't stir up any shit."

Cheyenne nodded at herself, brushed her hair over her shoulders, and stepped back through her apartment to gather her stuff. She kicked aside the shredded black jacket and opened the closet door. Wrinkling her nose, she shoved the last few jackets aside and settled instead on a baggy black zip-up sweater with a hand throwing devil horns printed on the back. Shrugging it on, she smirked and zipped it up all the way. *Mom was cool with the Goth thing, but she hated this hoodie. Comfier than I remember.*

She grabbed her keys, slung her backpack over her shoulder, and scanned her small apartment one more time. *Everything's normal. Just let it go.*

Then she shoved on her black Vans and headed out the door to start her day. When she closed the apartment door behind her, though, the feeling of something being not quite right was justified.

"What the hell?"

Under the apartment number tacked to her front door was a blood-red symbol that hadn't been there before. It looked like a four-pointed star, the points stretched long into sharp ends. A thick drop of paint had collected at the bottom point, though it had crusted around the edges and wasn't running down the wood anymore.

Grimacing, Cheyenne leaned closer and sniffed. *Not paint. That's blood.*

"Shit." She glanced down the hall and paused, her drow hearing ready to pick up any sound of someone running away. Or toward her. The hall was empty and silent. "The last thing I need is some crazy marking my door for...whatever."

She studied the four-pointed star painted in blood and shook her head. *I'd love to know what the hell this symbol means.*

The door three apartments down squeaked when the doorknob turned, then the sound of her neighbors R'mahr and Yadje arguing about something spilled out into the hall. Cheyenne didn't even think about it before swiping the sleeve of her hoody across the bloody symbol and hissed when it smeared across the door. The brick-red smudge on her black sleeve wasn't any better, and she stopped herself from wiping it on her black cargo pants before dropping into a crouch and trying to wipe it off on the stained carpet of the hallway.

That's one benefit of not updating this crappy place since the '80s.

"Cheyenne!"

The halfling leaped to her feet and turned, quickly slipping her hand through the strap of her backpack to hide the smudge of blood soaking into the sleeve. "Morning."

"She's here," R'mahr said, turning back to shoot his wife an I-told-you-so glance.

"She *lives* here, R'mahr." Yadje jostled her husband aside before poking her head out into the hall. Long scarlet braids fell over her shoulder and dangled beside the troll woman's violet cheeks. "We were a little worried about you."

Cheyenne forced herself to smile and headed down the hall. "Worried about *me*? I appreciate it, but everything's fine."

"Well, we missed you yesterday." R'mahr smiled in a poor attempt to hide his disappointment. "You know, we were hoping you'd come to Peridosh with us last night."

"Oh, right." The halfling paused in front of their door. *I knew I'd forgotten something.* "I'm sorry, guys. I got held up. Maybe next time, huh?"

"Yes. Next time. We go every Wednesday, don't forget." R'mahr bobbed his head up and down, grinning at her now as she passed their front door.

"We might make another trip sooner than that," Yadje added, then glanced over her shoulder when a loud, metallic rattle filled the apartment behind her. "Bryl, I told you to keep an eye on that pot. It's boiling over."

"I'll get it," their daughter shouted.

The troll woman shook her head with a forced smile and looked back up at Cheyenne with deep scarlet eyes. "Apparently, Bryl forgot to grab the most important ingredient from the potion-master last night. I'm not sure I can go another week listening to that child whine about not having had enough time last night to find it. If we end up going later this week, Cheyenne, would you like to come?"

The halfling paused again just past the troll family's front door now and turned halfway around. "Yeah, maybe. Just let me know when, and we'll figure it out."

"Excellent, yes." R'mahr's grin widened even more, and he stepped out into the hall. "Oh, and if you—"

"Sorry, I really do have to get going. Lots of stuff to do today. We can talk about it later."

"Okay, uh…"

"Bye, Cheyenne!" Yadje said through the door before tugging her husband back inside their apartment.

The halfling chuckled a little as she pushed open the door to the stairwell. *Now I'm gonna have to make up for bailing on my biggest fans.*

The morning air was a little crisp but not nearly as cold as the night before. Taking a deep breath, Cheyenne hurried outside across the parking lot. *I know the morning's not gonna go by quickly, but that doesn't stop me from hoping.*

"Hey!" she shouted. "Not your car, buddy!"

The guy crouching beside the rear door of her Focus jolted and spun on his heel.

"What the hell are you doing?"

A shrieking giggle burst from the guy's mouth before he scampered across the parking lot, his sneakers pounding on the asphalt. Cheyenne took off after him and reached him quickly enough, even without her drow speed. She grabbed him by the back of the jacket and jerked him sideways as he ran onto the open grass outside the apartment complex. The guy spilled across the grass with a thump, and the halfling leaped after him.

Her knees skidded across the grass, and she seized the front of his shirt with both hands, shaking him a little to get his attention. Another insane giggle escaped him as his head whipped back and forth.

"You picked the wrong car to break into," she seethed. Then she saw the bull's head pendant dangling around his neck. *Shit. More loyalists. And this one's wearing a human mask.*

The guy saw her staring at his pendant and guffawed in her face.

She grimaced and turned briefly away. "Dude, ever heard of mouthwash?"

"Nothing else matters." The guy's eyes were wide and glassy, spit flying from his lips as he grinned like a madman at the drow halfling.

"Trust me, your bad breath matters." Cheyenne shook him again. "What the hell do you people want from me, huh? Did you leave that crappy symbol on my door, too?"

The guy hyperventilated, still grinning as he studied the half-drow who was close to punching him unconscious. "You don't belong here, *mór úcare*," he muttered. "She's calling you back, you know. We can all feel it. Stop fighting, huh? Blood bonds with blood."

"Okay, quit the cryptic bullshit and tell me something I can use." Cheyenne pulled her hand back and meant to slip into drow mode, but of course, nothing happened. *This pendant's really cramping my style.* When the crazy human-looking magical shrieked with laughter again, the halfling shook him so hard that he fell backward, and she almost went over right on top of him. "Start talking, asshole. If I don't belong here, tell me why!"

A massive explosion ripped through the air behind her. Cheyenne whirled around, forgetting the cackling madman on the ground, and saw a pillar of flame, thick smoke, and twisted metal where her beat-up Focus had been. Three car alarms went off at the same time, and the rear door from the driver's side clattered to the asphalt.

"She's got your scent!" the guy shrieked, slipping away from the halfling and scrambling to his feet. "Blood's the only tie you have now, *mór úcare*. And when she finds you—" He cackled again and took off across the grass on wobbly legs.

Cheyenne looked over her shoulder to see him disappear around the corner of another apartment complex and clenched her eyes shut. *Literally let him slip through my fingers. Those guys are relentless.*

Pushing to her feet, she walked slowly off the grass until the heat of her flaming car made her stop in her tracks. She chewed her lower lip and slid her backpack off one shoulder to pull her cell phone from the front pocket. People stepped slowly out of the apartment complex to see what all the noise was about, and Cheyenne lifted her chin as she made the call.

"9-1-1. What's your emergency?"

"Uh, my car just exploded."

CHAPTER FORTY-ONE

The halfling's Ford Focus had settled into smoldering remains by the time the Richmond PD arrived. The dispatcher sent two squad cars, and Cheyenne quirked her lips in irritation when all four officers stepped out of their cars.

"Is this your car, ma'am?"

"Yeah." The halfling glanced from one officer to the next. "I'll start by saying I didn't blow up my own car, and I don't know who did, so you can cut those questions out."

The officer standing beside her looked up as the firetruck rolled into the parking lot. "What's your name?"

"Cheyenne."

"Do you have any ID on you, Cheyenne?"

She slipped her backpack off her shoulders again and lowered it to the ground. "My wallet's in my backpack."

"Go ahead and grab it."

As she rummaged through the front pocket, a firefighter headed toward her car with a portable fire extinguisher and unleashed what looked like the whole thing onto what few flames remained. The white foamed sprayed with a loud rush, and the other officers chuckled.

Cheyenne finally found her wallet and stood, slipping her ID out of the clear plastic slot. She handed it over with a deadpan stare and waited for the officer's reaction. *Yep. There it is. Wide eyes. Confusion. Better believe you're staring at Bianca Summerlin's daughter, Mr. Policeman.*

"Well, Ms. Summerlin—"

"Cheyenne. Ms. Summerlin's my mom." She tried not to smirk when the officer sputtered a little and cleared his throat.

"Right." He turned around again to eye the foam-splattered wreckage that was kind of shaped like a Ford Focus. "Any idea how this happened?"

"Your guess is as good as mine."

"Hey, Higgins." The tall, skinny officer crouched on their side of the ruined car and pointed at the rear wheel well. "What does that look like to you?"

The female officer beside him cocked her head. "Somebody got really cute with a homemade bomb is what it looks like."

"Dammit. Okay, I'll call it in to forensics."

"Do you know anyone who would want to hurt you by planting an explosive device under your car?"

A bunch of crazy magical assholes from a world you've never heard of. "Not really."

"You get on anyone's bad side lately?"

It took all her willpower not to start laughing. "I'm not on anyone's side, Officer. Good or bad. I came out to my car to head to class." Cheyenne nudged her backpack with her shoe. "Saw a guy running out of the parking lot toward that building, then boom."

"Did you get a good look at this person's face?"

Like they're ever gonna find it. "Nope. Just his back."

"All right. Wait here, Miss—Cheyenne. I'll be right back." The officer hooked his thumbs through his belt loops and headed back toward his squad car. His partner and the other officers joined him, and the halfling didn't even have to look their way to hear the conversation.

"Cheyenne Summerlin."

"What? Like the politician Summerlin?"

"I think so, yeah."

"Someone's got a serious death wish if they're screwin' around with that woman's daughter."

"Says she doesn't know anything."

"Probably doesn't. I didn't even know the woman *had* a kid."

"I'll run her driver's license. Then we'll know more." The officer with her ID slipped into his squad car as the other three turned together to eye Cheyenne.

She just raised her eyebrows and gave them a curt nod. No one said a thing until the officer stepped out of his car again and lifted her ID toward the others. Apparently, his wide eyes and cocked head meant that yes, the Goth chick was who she said she was.

He cleared his throat when he approached her. "I'm sorry this is the way your day started, Miss Summerlin. You have insurance?"

Cheyenne took her ID when he returned it to her and shoved it into her pocket with her wallet. "Yeah."

"I'd file a claim with them. You'll have to call a towing company to get that thing out of the parking lot if you want it inspected for..."

They both glanced slowly at the foam-covered skeleton. The officer cleared his throat.

"Probably the junkyard," Cheyenne muttered. "If they'll take it."

"Yeah. That's probably best. Take some pictures of the damage for when you file a claim. And you'll have to fill out an incident report." He took a business card out of his back pocket and handed it to her. "Feel free to call if you need any help with that."

"Right. Thanks."

"Okay. Have a nice day." The man stepped jerkily away from her, turning around to shoot her one more glance before nodding at his partner to return to the squad car.

It took ten minutes for the gawking police and the firetruck to get the hell out of that parking lot. Then Cheyenne crumpled the business card and dropped it into the pocket of her backpack before slinging that over her shoulder again.

File a claim. Yeah, right. She snorted and pulled out her phone again to call a cab. "Time for a new car anyway."

That afternoon, Cheyenne pulled into the VCU Medical Center parking lot in her new ride. *System of a Down* blasted through the sound system, and the shiny black Porsche Panamera rolled to a stop in the closest parking spot to the front doors that didn't have a handicap parking sign. The woman pushing her toddler in a stroller up to the automatic double doors of the hospital shot the Goth chick a wide-eyed, judgmental stare.

Cheyenne met the woman's gaze, her head bobbing to the music, and lifted her hand to wiggle her fingers in a cheerful wave. The woman shook her head and scurried into the hospital lobby while her toddler laughed and clapped along to the music.

"This'll be fun."

She turned off the engine and stepped out of the car. The fancy chirp when she pressed the lock button on the key fob made her smirk again. *Oh, yeah.*

When she stepped inside the automatic sliding doors, Ember was in the lobby—dressed, hair brushed, her paperwork and her personal bags in her lap where the discharge nurse had parked her wheelchair. The magicless fae grinned when Cheyenne approached. "You're early."

"Trust me, it wasn't intentional." The halfling smiled back and stopped in front of the wheelchair, giving it an appraising once-over. "Nice wheels."

Ember barked a laugh. "Yeah, you too. Did I really just watch you pull up in a Panamera?"

"Hey, if that's what you saw, I'm not gonna try to change your mind."

"Just felt like getting an upgrade, huh?" Ember peered around her friend to glance through the glass automatic doors at the shiny black car with the temporary taped in the back window. "*That* is not what I expected."

"Yeah, it's funny now." The halfling leaned toward her friend to mutter, "Wait 'til I tell you what happened."

"I'm on the edge of my seat."

Cheyenne stepped back and glanced at the wheelchair again. "Ready?"

"Almost." Ember wiggled her eyebrows and nodded toward the front doors. "Let's blow this joint, huh?"

A surprised laugh escaped the half-drow. When Cheyenne caught her friend's questioning frown, she just said, "You'll get why that's funny in a few minutes. You ready to go?"

"Yep. Got my release papers and everything." Ember winked, and Cheyenne figured out how to unlock the wheels before taking them both out into the sunshine and crisp autumn air.

The car chirped again before they approached, making Ember laugh again. "This is real."

"Oh, yeah. Perfect timing, really."

"You're not just borrowing the car for a 'Welcome home, Ember' joyride?"

Cheyenne opened the passenger door and draped her arm over the top of it before shooting her friend a satisfied smile. "Cute."

"Just checking."

Once they got Ember situated in the front seat and her wheelchair folded up and stowed in the trunk, the halfling slipped behind the wheel again and started the engine. Heavy metal blasted through the speakers, and Ember lurched forward to turn the volume down to half. "Holy shit."

Cheyenne buckled up, chuckling. "I'm having fun with it, okay? Low volume, no problem. Just don't change the station."

"Look at you." Ember buckled up too and gazed around the brand-new car. "Buying us both a new set of wheels on the same day."

"What?" The halfling tried to look surprised, maybe even a little confused.

"Uh-huh. You can cut the shit, Cheyenne. I know hospitals don't send their patients home with top-of-the-line wheelchairs as a starter kit. Trust me. I saw this old guy with a cast on his leg being wheeled around this morning. *Not* the same gear."

"Huh." Fighting off a smile, the Goth chick turned her attention to pulling out of the parking lot and getting them the hell away from the hospital. She felt Ember staring at her but pretended not to.

"Thank you, Cheyenne."

The halfling shot her friend a quick wink before she turned onto the street. "Guess it's a lucky day for both of us."

CHAPTER FORTY-TWO

"Wait a minute. Just back up." Ember laughed when the Panamera chirped again in the parking lot of her apartment complex. "The guy wearing that bull's head pendant looked *human?*"

Smirking, Cheyenne pushed her friend's wheelchair down the outdoor hallway of the apartment on the ground floor. "Yeah. Probably some kind of illusion spell."

Looking over her shoulder at her friend, the fae girl raised a joking eyebrow. "Listen to *you*. Girl doesn't know shit about magicals and borders and spells before I got shot, and now she's wheeling me to my front door talking about illusion spells and O'gúl loyalists."

They stopped at the last door on the left, and Cheyenne bent to pull the spare key out from under her friend's welcome mat. "What can I say, Em? It's been an illuminating three weeks."

"Yeah, no shit."

The halfling unlocked the door, shoved it open, then stepped behind the chair again to wheel Ember inside. "For both of us, I bet. But look. Now you're back home, and I'll be here to help you get back on your feet. Yes, I mean that both ways—"

Cheyenne stopped when she looked up from wheeling her friend, and they both stared at Ember's destroyed living room. The magicless fae laughed, then cut it short.

"Oh. Yeah." The halfling stepped away from the chair to take in the smashed dishes and broken cupboard, the charred holes in the wall, the ripped-up couch still covered in loose feathers from throw pillows used as target practice. "Shit, Em. I totally forgot about the mess in here."

"Yeah, me too."

When she turned around to look at her friend with a grimace, Cheyenne only found an amused grin on Ember's face. "I'm sorry."

"Don't be."

"I should've cleaned all this up. Some kinda welcome home, huh? You don't need to deal with this—"

"Cheyenne."

The halfling stopped. *If she tells me to get out and leave her alone, that's fair.*

"First of all," Ember said with a little chuckle, "quit apologizing. It's just a crappy apartment. Okay, admittedly not as crappy as yours." She chuckled, and Cheyenne laughed. "But seriously, I really don't care. My lease is almost up anyway, and this place needed some serious renovations." The fae girl glanced around the living room and shrugged. "You just gave them a head start."

The halfling hissed a laugh. "At least I saved your TV."

"What?"

Cheyenne pointed to the TV stand and Ember's flatscreen. "Asshole orc almost took it down with him."

"Well, thank you for saving the most valuable thing in my living room. I think. What happened to the guys who broke in here and started redecorating?"

"I, uh, I called in a cleaning crew." The halfling snickered.

"I had no idea that was a thing."

"It wasn't. Until I made a call and got my own personal FRoE-agent body-removal team."

Ember's eyes widened. "There were FRoE agents in my *apartment?*"

Cheyenne wrinkled her nose and spread her arms. "Sorry?"

Laughing again, Ember glanced down at the wheels of her chair before reaching out to grab them and push herself forward. "Oh. Carpet's gonna be a little hard to move on around here."

"Hey, if your lease is almost up, it's the perfect time to find a new apartment, right? One with no carpet."

"Cheyenne, I can't move into a new place with hardwood floors everywhere." Ember raised her eyebrows and waved her hand at the living room. "I'm barely scraping by with this one."

"Scratch 'barely scraping by' off the list, Em." The halfling stepped behind the wheelchair again and pushed Ember toward the couch. Then she dropped onto it and nodded. "I wasn't just being polite when I said I'd help you with everything after the hospital."

The fae girl snorted. "You don't do 'just being polite.'"

"You really know me."

They shared another laugh, then Ember shook her head. "I can't piggy-back off you forever, Cheyenne. I appreciate all the help, but you have a bunch of other stuff going on, and I don't want to drag you down—"

"Shut up."

"What?"

Cheyenne grinned. "I just told you to shut up. Want me to say it again?"

Ember cocked her head and took a deep breath. She didn't say anything, but her disbelieving smile made it clear that she was about to give in.

"Look, Em. Part of the reason you were in the hospital in the first place is because of me. Because I didn't stand up when you asked me to."

The fae girl snorted. "You're not getting all mushy on me now, are you?"

"Not this time. But I'm serious. I'm the reason your apartment's blown to pieces, too, and beyond that, you're my best friend. I kinda need you around." The halfling slapped the couch cushion beneath her and nodded. "So, if you start feeling like you don't deserve my help or like you're dragging me down, just remember I told you to shut up about it, and we're good."

Ember dipped her head and stared at her friend. "You're really not gonna let me off the hook with this one, are you?"

"Not even a little. I'll take care of it, Em. Like I said." Cheyenne glanced around the living room one more time. "You should start looking for a place, huh? I'll help you with the move too. Make sure it has hardwood floors."

"That's too much." Ember shook her head.

"No, it's not. Some asshole loyalist blew up my car this morning, and I bought a new Panamera for cash. Might as well start dipping into my inheritance, right? Didn't even make a dent."

"I'm pretty sure your inheritance wasn't intended to buy your newly disabled friend an updated apartment."

"Em, I can use it for whatever I want. And this is what I wanna do. There's nothing you can do to stop me."

Ember tried to make her laugh sound irritated, but it didn't quite work. "Oh, I know. But I had to at least try."

"Okay. You tried and failed. Now get over it." Cheyenne's lips twitched into another smirk. "Besides, I'm not sure it's safe for you to live here anymore. Whoever came after me saw me here at your place. They might come back."

"And they know where *you* live now too, don't they?"

That made the halfling pause, and she narrowed her eyes at the fae girl sitting in front of her. "Yeah. That's a minor issue."

"You know, if you're gonna be helping me all the time with my PT and getting me back on my feet, hopefully literally, it wouldn't be a bad idea if we were roommates for a while." Ember shrugged. "Just until I get the hang of this chair and doing everything on my own again."

Cheyenne studied her friend's hopeful eyes. *She's embarrassed about that part, too.* "You really don't want me to get you a brand-new apartment, do you?"

Laughing, Ember swept her hair away from her face with both hands. "Okay, I'm coming up with another excuse. So what? It makes sense, though. You won't be driving all over the place to come help me. I'll be right down the hall. I won't feel weird about it if there's something in it for you too—"

"There'll be something in it for me anyway, Em."

"This is the part where you shut up and let me finish." Grinning, Ember pointed at her friend, and the halfling lifted both hands in surrender. "Good. The final point of my argument is you not living in the same place where some freak drew a symbol on your door in blood before blowing up your car with a bomb instead of magic. Which is a little confusing but doesn't change the fact that I don't think it's safe for you to keep living in your dumpy apartment, either."

Cheyenne opened her mouth to protest, then cocked her head. "You make an excellent argument."

"I know."

"And I can't see any downsides, so okay."

"Okay?"

The halfling pursed her lips and nodded. "Yeah. Okay, as in let's start looking for a new place that has everything a drow halfling and her temporarily wheelchair-bound best friend might need to make this work. Stepping up in the world."

"Ha. Get a new place to match that shiny new drowmobile you got parked outside."

Cheyenne let herself laugh without holding back at that. "I really fucking love that car."

"I can tell." Ember dropped the overnight tote out of her lap and onto the floor, then rummaged around in her purse and pulled out her phone. "I'll start looking. It's what, not even three o'clock. If we find a good place fast enough, we can head out, go talk to the office, get something set up—"

Settling into the cushions, the halfling lifted her arm over the back of the couch and snorted.

Her friend looked at her with a self-conscious smile. "What?"

"I'm really into your enthusiasm, Em, but maybe we should hold off on running around Richmond for a new apartment until at least tomorrow, huh?"

"Why the hell would we do that?"

"Oh, I don't know. Maybe because you just got released after weeks in the hospital after, you know, coming kinda close to not making it back out again."

Ember lowered her phone into her lap and shot her friend a knowing smile. "But I did. And I blame you for that one-hundred-percent."

"Yeah, okay. I'll take the blame for saving your life."

The girl snorted and sat there in the destroyed living room, letting the entire conversation sink in. Then Ember lifted her phone and wiggled it. "So, I start looking for apartments *now*, or…"

"You can look for whatever you want." Cheyenne slapped her thighs, the chains around her wrists clinking, and pushed herself to her feet. "I'm gonna clean this place up as much as I can because I should've done that already. You don't need to get those wheels stuck on a chunk of drywall or something."

Ember laughed. "Okay. If I'm in your way, feel free to wheel me around the room. I'm not going anywhere, and I'll be focused on finding the perfect apartment."

"I don't think that exists, Em."

"Trust me, it does. And I'll find it." Ember pressed her lips together and eyed her friend as Cheyenne walked into the kitchen to start picking up huge chunks of splintered cabinet. "You might be ridiculously skilled with computers, Cheyenne, but that doesn't mean the rest of us don't have any tricks up our sleeves."

The halfling stepped on the lever to open the trashcan and dumped a handful of wood and broken ceramic into the mostly empty trash bag. "Listen to you now. Pullin' out all the surprise skills."

Smirking, Ember just stared at her phone, her fingers flying across the screen as she typed. "At least one of us learned something in undergrad."

CHAPTER FORTY-THREE

Cheyenne stayed at Ember's apartment until a little after 9:30. They'd had a pizza delivered, then the halfling helped her friend get ready for bed and made sure the fae girl had everything she needed before she took off.

"Text me if anything comes up." She stood in the doorway of Ember's bedroom. *Should I really be leaving her on her own? She doesn't even know how to work that wheelchair.*

Already curled up beneath the covers with her back facing the halfling, Ember stuck a hand out of the blankets and shot Cheyenne a thumbs-up without turning around. "I'm good. Nothing's gonna happen while I'm sleeping."

"You want me to come by in the morning before I head to class?"

"I'll text you about that too," Ember muttered. "Right now, I can't tell if I'm still awake...or..."

Asleep. Got it.

Cheyenne turned off all the lights except for the standing lamp on the far side of the living room. The place still looked awful, but at least it wasn't cluttered with broken pieces of wall and cabinet or feathers anymore. *She's a big girl. She'll be fine. And if she's not, I'll be the first to know about it.*

The halfling slipped quietly out the front door and locked it behind her. Ember's spare key went into the front pocket of her black cargo pants, then she headed back out to her new car in the parking lot.

By the time she got home, Cheyenne was itching to drop in on the Borderlands forum. *I don't care what Rhynehart says. If those kids haven't gotten back to their parents yet, I'm storming the compound.*

Glen fired up, then the halfling pulled up her VPN and dove into the dark web. The Borderlands forum came up, and she didn't notice how hard she'd been squeezing her mouse until she sighed in relief and loosened up a little.

There we go. Things are looking up.

The four newest topic threads were from magical parents letting their little dark-web community of friends know their kids had been brought home. The pinned topic serving as a single place for all the missing kid reports was still at the top, but a new announcement had been stuck at the top of the page.

Kids Are Coming Home – Check here for updates.

Cheyenne scrolled through the comments and smiled. Dozens of posts from relieved parents and supportive friends—as friendly as anyone could get on the dark web—filled the topic thread.

Looks like the FRoE still knows how to keep their word. At least with the important stuff.

She rapped her knuckles on the surface of her huge desk, then pulled up a private message to gu@rdi@n104. She wished Corian would change his avatar or give her another avenue for contacting him.

Shyhand71: This is me asking ahead of time. Trials tonight?

The reply came immediately.

gu@rdi@n104: Oh, so now you're ready to listen?

Gritting her teeth, Cheyenne sat all the way back in her office chair and thought about the best response. *Can't blame him for being pissed.*

Shyhand71: You know what? Neither one of us was wrong yesterday, but you made your point. I put the thing back on.

gu@rdi@n104: Good. If you can keep your head screwed on straight, I'm here.

Shyhand71: Be there in 20.

She closed out of the chat, got off the dark web, and shut down her VPN. Glen, though, stayed powered on. "Gotta keep you warmed up. When I get back, I'm checking to make sure every single kid is back where they belong."

The halfling grabbed her backpack and stuffed the copper legacy box inside. It didn't flash or grow warm or give her any indication that it had anything planned for her tonight. *Not yet, anyway.*

Before she left her apartment, she stripped the last paper towel off the roll on the counter, soaked it, and took it with her. The mostly smeared blood on the outside of her front door had dried to a dark-brown stain, which made it that much harder to scrub off. When it looked like all the other crummy, unmentionable stains on her apartment walls and in the hallway, Cheyenne shrugged and called it good. *I just keep learning how to blend in, don't I?*

With everything locked up, she hurried down the hall toward the staircase. The thought of getting behind the wheel of her Panamera again made her smile.

The Panamera rolled silently down the street toward the house. For the first time since she'd tracked Corian down after his ridiculous scavenger hunt, there was someone standing out on the lawn in front of the house. "Who the hell just stands out—oh. Great."

Her bright, clear headlights flashed over Corian standing on the grass, his human illusion back up and his human-looking arms folded. The halfling turned off the radio, but her chest still buzzed from the deep bass she'd adjusted in the souped-up sound system. She sat there longer than she had to, waiting to see if the Nightstalker would act on his anger before she had a chance to do or say anything. He didn't move.

"This'll be fun. Not." She turned off the car before grabbing her backpack. Then she stepped out and quietly shut the door. *Even the doors are in stealth mode. Love it.*

Slinging her backpack over her shoulder, she locked the car with the keyless fob, grinning again at the expensive-sounding chirp as she slipped the fob into her back pocket.

Corian tilted his head. "If you're trying to keep a low profile, kid, your new ride's not helping."

"Hey, I gave myself a well-deserved bonus, okay? I needed a new car, and this one happened to be right in front of me." *After I stormed through the showroom at the dealership. Call it destiny.*

"What happened to your old car?"

Cheyenne blinked at him as she stepped up onto the sidewalk. "Totaled."

Corian raised an eyebrow and turned his head toward her, though his eyes remained on the shiny black Panamera. "Please tell me you didn't do something stupid like run a red light or try to drag race in a beat-up Focus."

She snorted. "Thanks for the vote of confidence, *Mom*." The Nightstalker finally spared her a cynical glance from the corner of his eye. "I'm a great driver. Never been in an accident. Including today."

"Congratulations."

Cheyenne shot him a deadpan stare. "If I told you that another of those O'gúl loyalists wearing that stupid bull's head—*and* looking like a human—blew up my old car with a non-magical bomb, would it get you to cheer up a little and quit holding a grudge?"

Corian's eyes widened when he turned to face her, and his gaze darted up and down the street. "We should be having this conversation inside."

"By all means. Lead the way." The halfling gave him a mocking little bow and gestured toward the side of the house and the stairwell leading down to Apartment D.

With one more glance around the dark, quiet, empty row of rental units, the Nightstalker headed across the grass toward the stairs. Cheyenne followed, and they didn't say another word until Corian had removed the wards from the metal front door and they were both safely inside his empty, unfinished single room.

After he closed the door behind the half-drow, Corian's fingers moved in quick, precise gestures, and the orange light flared up around the inside of his door again. "What did he look like?"

"A human who just broke out of a mental hospital."

Clearing his throat, the Nightstalker smoothed down the front of his charcoal-gray sweater and headed across the room toward another circle of candles arranged in the center of the floor. "And the bomb didn't have any magic involved?"

"Not that I could tell. Just a good old-fashioned homemade." Cheyenne chewed the inside of her bottom lip, waiting for her newest mentor to say something else. Corian just stared at the circle of candles. "He told me I don't belong here. That *she's* calling me back, whatever that means."

She didn't think it was possible for the Nightstalker's back to stiffen any more, but it did.

"Did he say anything else?" The words came out as a low, warning growl.

The halfling shrugged. "Something about blood."

"Blood bonds with blood."

"So, you *do* know why these assholes are coming after me." Her fingers tightened around the straps of her backpack. "Now would be a great time to let me in on the secret everyone knows but me."

"I already told you, Cheyenne. When you're ready to know the truth of things, you will." The Nightstalker's fingers moved quickly at his side, and he dropped his illusion spell. It gave him a few more inches in height, the sweater hugged him tighter, and the pointy, catlike ears emerged from beneath his short, mussed hair. "Until then, it's too dangerous to go down that road."

"Dangerous for who?"

Corian turned around and fixed her with those glowing silver eyes in his feline face. "Everyone. Mostly you."

"Really? 'Cause at that mansion yesterday, it sounded like you were a hell of a lot more worried about saving your own skin." Cheyenne gritted her teeth when the usual flare of her drow magic didn't appear with the heat of her anger. *Still weird.*

"If you just came here to point fingers and get all defensive again, I'm more than happy to take down those wards. You can show yourself out." One of the Nightstalker's ears twitched, but his face remained emotionless.

Taking a deep breath, Cheyenne forced herself to let it out slowly through her nose. *Suck it up and make some progress.* "You know that's not what I want."

"Then act like it and tell me you're ready to table this for later so we can train. *That's* why you're here."

The halfling held his gaze for a little longer, then slid her backpack off her shoulders and set it down against the wall by the door. She pulled out the copper legacy box, a little surprised when it still didn't react to her touch, and took it with her to join Corian beside the circle of unlit candles. "Consider it tabled."

"Excellent." Corian cast another spell, his hands working quickly as he whispered words in O'gúleesh. Flames winked to life on every candle, and the air above the center of the circle shimmered with dark light. The orb of his portal grew in seconds, revealing a shadowy doorway looking out onto a sloping grassy hill. "Let's not waste any more time, huh?"

Cheyenne was stepping over the closest candles when he gestured toward the portal. She passed through the large, dark oval in the air.

The smell of saltwater and fish hit her instantly, followed by cold, slightly damp air that didn't belong to Richmond at the end of September. The moonlight sparkled across a black expanse of water, joined by the reflection of thousands of tiny, glittering lights behind her. The halfling turned around to watch Corian step through the portal before the dark opening disappeared with a soft pop. "Where'd you take us this— What the hell is that?"

Corian smirked and faced the steep incline of the hill behind them and the wide, sweeping expanse of the stone building that would have been white in the daylight. Now, it was light gray, the tower of the lighthouse rising into the starry sky. "You ever been to the Rock?"

"My first thought is a resounding no." The halfling stepped to the side, trying to peer around the massive building in front of them. In the distance, she saw more land jutting out into the water and all the sparkling lights from the city.

"Nowhere to go but here, kid. Being on an island and all."

"Yeah, I'm starting to figure that out." Cheyenne gestured toward the walls of the huge building above them. "The Golden Gate Bridge is right on the other side, isn't it?"

"As far as I know."

I really wanna punch that smirk off his face. "Why the hell did you bring me to Alcatraz?"

"Well, it's not so I can lock you in an empty jail cell. As fun as it would be." He snorted. "For me."

"What happened to the field in the woods?" Cheyenne turned around again and stared at the glittering Pacific Ocean stretching out in front of her. "Or at least an ocean with *warm* water?"

"Riker's Island is still an active prison so that one's off the table."

"I'm serious." She spun around again and found him chuckling. "There's a whole city of people over there who are gonna want to know why Alcatraz is lighting up like the Fourth of July in September."

"Huh. I didn't think about that."

"Are you serious?"

"No." Corian flicked his hand out toward the ocean. A shimmering dome of orange-tinted light appeared, stretching from the edge of the island and arcing over them toward the other side. "I don't rush blindly into a new plan, Cheyenne. That's another thing to put on your to-be-learned list."

The orange dome disappeared, and the halfling shook her head. "You don't have to rub it in, man. I get it. Still not sure why your portal had to take us all the way to California."

"Got something against the Golden State?"

"Yeah. Too much sun." When the Nightstalker snorted, the corner of Cheyenne's mouth quirked into what was almost a smile. "I'm a fan of the woods."

"That particular location was compromised, kid. I'm trying to keep our trail clean."

She headed toward him, just to fall under the shadow of the prison building again. *It still feels like people can see us.* "We got out of there before the other portal opened."

"Yeah, but they found where we were first." Corian blinked in surprise and let out a wry chuckle. "Look at that. I'm talking to somebody who'll understand this on the same level."

"Not quite."

He shook his head. "Opening a portal leaves a trace. Think of it like diving into the dark web, Cheyenne. No official VPN for a portal, but we have time to do what we came here to do tonight before I have to find another safe place for us to work the next time. Once you take off that pendant, I can only keep you hidden for so long. By the time they find this place and whatever markers we left here that I can't cover up, we'll be somewhere else."

"They?"

"The people who almost crashed our last training session. I'm sure you and I are on the same page when it comes to not wanting them to succeed."

"Yeah, we are." The halfling grabbed the thin silver chain around her neck and lifted the pendant out from beneath her hoody. "So, can I get rid of this thing now?"

"Temporarily." The Nightstalker took a deep breath of the salty ocean air and cocked his head. "You hear that?"

A low honk drifted over the constant rush of waves breaking on the ocean and crashing up against the sharp drop off the Rock. Another echoed it, followed by more.

Cheyenne blinked and shot her mentor a disbelieving stare. "Does your magical island bubble keep out seals, too?"

Corian shrugged. "Guess we'll find out. Ready to start?"

Rolling her eyes, the halfling spun the chain around on her neck so she could untie the knot she'd put there yesterday. "Give me a second."

"We don't have all night, kid. Hurry up so we can make the most of it."

Finally, she loosened up the broken ends of the chain and jerked off the pendant before stuffing it into one of the many pockets lining her cargo pants. It surprised them both that she didn't automatically slip into drow mode, but Cheyenne only had to think about it to make it happen.

The drow halfling faced the cat-like Nightstalker and spread her arms. "Let's do this."

CHAPTER FORTY-FOUR

"Do you have any progress to report before we get started?" Corian stepped toward the sharp incline of the earthen walls cut into the island. "Seemed like you had plenty of practice at that giant house yesterday."

"I did, actually." Cheyenne turned the drow legacy box over in her hands, then bent and set it on the dry grass growing in patches across the dirt. "Got one more piece of that thing locked in place, and I'm pretty sure I mastered the shield."

"Mastered is a strong word. For now, you *understand* how and when to use it."

The halfling snorted. "I *understood* enough to use it perfectly when we were going after those kids."

"Good to hear." The Nightstalker cleared his throat. "While we're on the subject, who found them?"

"The kids?"

He widened his eyes and lifted his chin, waiting for her to continue.

"I did."

"*You* found them?"

Cheyenne laughed without any amusement. "You know, for

someone who's supposed to be teaching me how to be better, you don't sound all that confident."

"It's not a lack of confidence, Cheyenne. Just surprise." He scratched his tufted ear, his silver gaze darting around the thin grass and the dry shrubs. "And I might be rethinking my abilities if you found something on the dark web that I didn't."

"That's not what happened, so don't worry. No black mark on your reputation or anything."

The Nightstalker met her gaze again and frowned. "Not on the net?"

"I tried, but no. I negotiated my way into another visit with L'zar."

Corian's silver eyes narrowed. "L'zar Verdys knows a lot of things, kid. Hard to believe the location of a bunch of kidnapped magicals he had nothing to do with is one of them."

"He didn't tell me where they were." Cheyenne glanced at the stars and took another deep breath. *He doesn't believe anything he can't see with his own eyes, does he?* "It was more like he helped me figure it out."

"Still sounds off."

"Tell me about it. It was one of the weirder conversations I've had recently."

Folding his arms again, Corian studied her. "Well, I suppose all those kids and their parents have both of you to thank for that."

"I don't think either of us is waiting for a thank you. The FRoE only came to me about it because they were out of options, and I did what I had to do."

"How did he jog your memory?"

The halfling rolled her eyes. "Mostly, it was a lot of banging on iron bars. Like a drow monkey at the zoo."

That made the Nightstalker chuckle. "Did you at least remember to tell him we'd started your trials?"

Cheyenne pressed her lips together and stared her mentor down. "Yeah, I remembered. He got pretty excited about it, and that was probably the only reason he helped me put the pieces together about those kids. You were right about that, at least. The guy's looking out for number one."

"Which includes looking out for you too, Cheyenne. Even if it's from behind bars."

"You know, if he ever gets out of Chateau D'rahl and comes to help me with a new problem, I might believe that. He did give me a spell for speeding this whole trial thing up, though. Don'adurr Thread, I think?"

"The Don'adurr Thread?"

"That's what I said."

Corian's amusement disappeared, and he rubbed a fur-covered hand over his mouth before shaking his head. "That wily sonofabitch."

"Not gonna argue with you about that one."

"He gave you more than a simple spell, Cheyenne." Frowning, Corian rubbed his hands together, shook them out in preparation for another spell, then cocked his head. "Not what I would've given you to start with, but if L'zar thinks you're ready for it, it's not my place to say he's wrong."

Bad news when a Nightstalker starts looking uncomfortable. "What is it?"

"I can set it up for you, but you have to do the work on your own."

"Let me guess." Cheyenne folded her arms. "Because I'm not ready."

"More like because I can't do anything else. It's a drow ritual, kid. I don't have what it takes to show you the ropes on this one." Shaking his head again as if that would get rid of his astonishment, the Nightstalker muttered a spell and opened a new portal directly in front of him. This one was a lot smaller, and he ducked through the opening into his basement to reach for something in the junk on the metal shelves lining the walls.

"And this *ritual* will make my trials go faster?"

"That's for the two of you to figure out. I'm just the messenger at this point. Supplier. Alchemist. Damn babysitter."

"Someone's getting grumpy." The halfling stepped around the portal to watch him grab random items from the shelves, which he tossed behind him into the dirt on Alcatraz Island. *Not sure I like where this is headed.*

"I've spent hundreds of years waiting to guide L'zar's halfling kid through the drow trials." Corian uncovered an ornately decorated silver box with the engraving of a tree on the lid and tucked it under his arm. "Never thought I'd be whipping up a Don'adurr Thread, but that's on me."

When he stepped back, the small portal disappeared with another soft pop, and Corian lowered himself to the ground with all the things he'd pulled from his basement on the other side of the country.

Stepping toward him, Cheyenne studied the small corked vials and dried herbs scattered on the sparse grass. "I'd appreciate a little more of an explanation before diving into this. Seriously."

"Just give me a minute." He stacked the dried herbs in a pile and wrinkled his nose. "This is the last of my riverwort, by the way. We'd be in a different situation if I'd used any of this sooner, but lucky for you, drow potions are low on my list of go-to options."

"Oh, yeah. I'm feelin' real lucky."

The Nightstalker looked at her with a raised eyebrow and said, "Sit. And be quiet so I can focus."

Digging deeper and deeper into a hole I can't see. This better be worth it. Forcing herself not to spit out any other smart remarks, the drow halfling sat on the ground and crossed her legs, watching her mentor get to work.

She didn't recognize any of the ingredients, but Corian moved so quickly, it wouldn't have mattered anyway. He crushed dried herbs in an alarmingly stained mortar, then dumped tiny vials of purple and clear liquid into the mix and stirred it. When he slid aside the lid of the fancy silver box with the tree rising in gnarled lines from the center, a soft golden glow illuminated his catlike features.

"What's—"

"Shh!" Corian reached into the box and pulled out another vial. It was long and slender, with an intricate wrapping of copper coils. Whatever it held was the source of the golden light. He uncorked it carefully and slowly tipped the lip into the mortar. Two drops, that was it. Then he closed the vial again and put it back inside the silver box. He tried to hide it, but Cheyenne's hearing picked up his tiny sigh of relief once the golden light faded.

With the pestle, he stirred the whole weird, glowing mixture again, then dropped the stone tool into the dirt.

"Okay. That's for you."

The halfling stared at the swirling concoction in the mortar, which flashed with gold and purple light a few times before it settled. "To do what?"

"To drink. That's the Don'adurr."

"I'm not drinking that." She shook her head and leaned away, scowling in distaste. "Not until you tell me what's in it and what it's supposed to do. That stuff smells like grapefruit."

"You don't like grapefruit?"

"Not without actual grapefruit."

"This is how it's done. You say his name and drink it, then I tell you good luck, and we wait for the Don'adurr to run its course."

Cheyenne eyed the mystery potion a little longer. "I should've asked that crazy drow for a Plan B."

"Hey." When she looked at him, Corian leaned toward her and raised his eyebrows. "Do you trust me?"

"I thought I did."

"Cut the smartass remarks. I'm serious."

"So far, yeah."

"Good. And I trust that crazy drow, however hard it is for you to believe." He pointed at the mortar. "Drink it. It won't hurt if that's what you're wondering about. Not that I've heard about, at least."

"See, comments like that are earning you negative points on the trust scale." Despite everything, Cheyenne reached for the mortar with both hands and lifted it into her lap. "How much of this is going down the hatch?"

"It'll be more effective with all of it, but as much as you can."

"Okay." With a hesitant nod at the stone bowl in her hands, she lifted it to her mouth and muttered, "L'zar Verdys."

The mortar was cold against her lips, but the potion inside it felt like melted ice. She chugged down as much as she could before the overwhelming, fruity bitterness almost made her choke. She put the bowl back down on the dry grass, and Corian leaned sideways to peer at what was left. "Good enough. Good luck."

With the potion still trailing an icy line down her throat and into her stomach, Cheyenne looked at her Nightstalker mentor with wide eyes. "What now?"

One of his ears twitched again, sending ripples of fur floating away from his face and dancing across the air. She giggled. *I don't giggle. What the hell?*

The grass grew in front of her eyes when she looked down, then shrank back to its normal size again. A wave broke somewhere off the island, echoing a hundred times before Cheyenne turned to look out across the ocean. Heavy dizziness made her sway when she turned her head. The starlight pulsed in her vision, brighter and brighter, and the next thing she knew, she sank down onto her back to lie in the dirt on Alcatraz Island.

Great. He just made me dark-elf LSD. Not that I have anything to compare it to, but I am tripping right now.

"Whoops!" The word escaped her in a high-pitched squeak, and the halfling giggled again. *Keep it together. Don't go all... Who put those faces in the sky?*

Her eyelids felt incredibly heavy when she closed them, her head spinning faster by the second. Then the dizziness and the feeling of floating out of her body and even the sound of the crashing waves stopped. Cheyenne couldn't even hear the muted rush of cars and pedestrians enjoying just a regular Thursday night in San Francisco. There was nothing.

When the halfling opened her eyes again, she found herself sitting on the stone floor of a small dark room. The steel door on her right wasn't a door at all but a wall of iron bars. Through the bars, she saw metal staircases and walkways, more rows of iron bars stretching across the far wall, and glowing red light shining down on all of it from somewhere up high. Then her gaze settled on the thin cot on the other side of the tiny room.

"What the hell?"

L'zar Verdys' eyes flew open and locked onto her with that unnerving golden glow. "Cheyenne," he whispered. Then his stoic face split into another one of those crazed grins, and he pushed himself up and gripped the edge of the thin mattress. "This is a nice surprise."

CHAPTER FORTY-FIVE

The halfling glanced around her drow father's cell at Chateau D'rahl and gritted her teeth. "What *is* this?"

"The Don'adurr Thread. I can only assume Corian made it for you," said L'zar, his loosely tied white hair coming undone and falling around his shoulders. "That was fast. I'll give you that."

"You're telling me crap I already know." Cheyenne tried to get up off the floor, but apparently, she couldn't move as much as she wanted. "You need to tell me how the hell I got into your *prison cell.* And why I can't move."

The grinning drow chuckled. "The Don'adurr allows us to speak a little more freely to each other. You know, without a moron in a booth listening in on every word. This is how I prefer it."

When he winked at her, a burst of purple sparks exploded in the halfling's hands. They both looked down at her spell, which wavered in and out of existence. Cheyenne frowned and lifted her hand toward her face until the sparks petered out—not because she'd cut off her magic, but because it didn't come through as clearly as she did. She turned her hand over and could see the cracks in the stone floor through her palm.

I know I'm pale in human form, but this is taking it a little too far.

"Corian made me drink that stuff for some kind of...drow astral projection?"

"If that's the best way for you to wrap your head around it, sure." L'zar sat up and propped his forearms on his thighs over the gray prison-issue sweatpants. "It's an old trick, but it never fails. I'm glad to see your drow blood runs as true on the inside as it does on the outside."

"Blood bonds with blood and all that, huh?"

The drow prisoner's grin disappeared, and he blinked once before plastering the mad smile on his face again. "That's something we can return to another time. Right now, I believe you want to ask me again how to speed up your trials. That's why you're here tonight." His low chuckle echoed a little in the cramped cell. "Well, in a manner of speaking."

"Sure. Let's go with that." *This is the last thing I expected, but it's a way in, I guess.* Cheyenne took a deep breath and stared at her incarcerated father until she realized he was waiting for her to move this weird-ass conversation forward. "Okay. How do I speed things up?"

"How many layers of the *Cuil Aníl* have you unlocked already?"

"Two."

L'zar cocked his head with a little frown. "So few, huh? Yes. Good thing you came to ask for help."

Cheyenne pressed her clenched fists into her thighs.

"That's all right, Cheyenne. Everyone starts somewhere. So, you've got two under your belt, and there are five. For most of us, at any rate. What other abilities have popped up out of nowhere?"

If he didn't know about the drow trials, I'd swear he's been stalking me. From a magical prison. The halfling licked her lips and forced herself to focus on the conversation and the answers she might finally receive. "Ripping up the ground, for starters."

"Oh." L'zar's thin white eyebrows rose. "A connection with the earth is a lot more subtle than most are willing to believe. No control with that one, I'm guessing."

"Clearly."

"Hmm." His smile was tight-lipped and grim now.

Good. Finally struck a nerve.

"Any others?"

Cheyenne lifted her chin and said, "I threw some goblins into the ceiling without casting a spell."

"Useful."

"And I almost knocked an ogre's head off his shoulders when my fist burst into black flames. Didn't get to use that one."

L'zar's eyes widened in tandem with that creepy grin again. "*There* it is. That! Now, *that* is something I would very much like to see."

"Then tell me how to speed it up." Cheyenne shot him a sideways glance. "And stop looking at me like I'm a sixteen-ounce steak."

He chuckled and shook his head, dipping it to his shoulder to run a hand over the top of his white hair. "Better save that one for later."

"You have no idea how sick I am of hearing that. Why save that one for later? You're obviously looking forward to it."

The drow lifted his head to peer at her from beneath those thin eyebrows. "When you get there, Cheyenne, you'll know why. Any other latent powers creeping up on you before we move on to the father-daughter advice *schtick*?" He spat the last word through his teeth.

He's insane. Excited and pissed off at the same time. Cheyenne closed her eyes and forced herself not to give away her thoughts. *Okay, admittedly, that applies to me too.*

"I see those wheels turning again. Something you'd like to get off your chest?" L'zar leaned closer, his golden eyes sweeping across her face, taking in every detail.

"I already covered the part about you not *looking* at me like that, didn't I?" Normally she would've stormed out at that point and left him to his messed-up thoughts, but she stayed right where she was with her legs crossed. *Drow ritual, my ass. Might as well be locked up in this prison right next to him.* The ghost of a shiver trickled down her spine.

"I've spent twenty-one years waiting to look at you, Cheyenne."

L'zar's smile remained, but his voice was low and threatening. "If I want to spend a few minutes taking in the sight of my daughter, that's exactly what I'll do." He pulled back a little as if he'd just ripped himself out of whatever rage had been building beneath that tight smile. "Besides, I'm an excellent multi-tasker."

"Then multi-task and tell me how to speed things up." The halfling swallowed. *He doesn't like being told what to do any more than I do.* "Please."

"Ah, yes. That was a good start." Leaning back, the drow prisoner propped his hands behind him on the mattress and crossed one long leg over the opposite knee. "Start with either the telekinesis or the earth-ripping, whichever comes easiest. And when you're working on those, focus on the Nimlothar seed. I'm sure Corian told you what that is already."

"Yeah. The tree tied to drow magic."

"Very simplistic. I suppose there's a time and a place for that too." L'zar tilted his head from side to side as he studied her. "Draw on the seed for an extra boost, yeah? When you learn to tap into the Nimlothar, you're unlocking a lot more than just the trials. Centuries of magic and knowledge grow on those trees, Cheyenne. Same as in the blood you and I share."

"That's it?" The halfling studied her father's apathetic expression. "Focus on a seed I swallowed while I'm trying to focus on training with new abilities?"

"Well, there's a certain art to it, but it becomes second nature. Eventually."

"Any tips on how to do *that?*"

He chuckled. "I heard meditating helps."

Cheyenne snorted and closed her eyes. *This was a waste of time. Maybe it doesn't have to be.*

"I'm serious about that, Cheyenne. A little meditation and centering go a long way."

"Yeah, I'm taking notes. Thanks." When she opened her eyes again, he laughed at her, his leg bouncing up and down where it crossed over his other knee. "So, since we're speaking more freely, maybe you can answer another question for me."

"Ooh. We're opening up, are we?"

Don't push it. "What's with the bull's head?"

L'zar's leg stopped bouncing. "You'll have to be more specific. Earth's a relatively big realm. Lotta bulls."

She gritted her teeth and forced herself to keep going. "Specifically, the ones worn by more assholes than I can count hunting me down and trying to open a bunch of portals around me. Ring a bell?"

For the first time, the drow prisoner looked like he didn't want her there. L'zar swallowed and pressed his lips together, but his smile lost all trace of amusement. "Portals."

"Yeah. And nobody will tell me what the hell those people want from me. They're everywhere. One of them blew up my car this morning, and I'm pretty sure he was the same moron who drew a bloody symbol on my front door. Same thing with the pieces of shit who kidnapped all those kids for whatever sick ritual they were planning. I can keep going if you need the full list."

"So, you found those kids after all."

"Yeah, by following a guy pretending to be— You know what? That's more stuff I already know. I asked you what the bull's head is and why those nutjobs are telling me to just give up already and swear fealty so some chick can finally get her way, or whatever." Cheyenne took a deep breath and brushed her hair away from her face. "I know it has something to do with the drow trials, too. Even Corian said someone doesn't want me to finish them—"

"Yeah, well, someone can go fuck themselves!" L'zar lurched forward again, his eyes blazing.

The inmate on the other side of L'zar's cell pounded a huge fist into the wall they shared. "Keep it the fuck down, Verdys. I'm tired of your shit."

The drow looked slowly over his shoulder to glare at the wall and pulled himself back together with a deep breath.

Cheyenne stared at the wall too. *They can all hear him talking to himself.*

Slowly, he turned back around and blinked quickly, like the interruption was sand grains in his eye. "None of that is for you to worry about, Cheyenne. That's not why I made the crossing as many times as I did, and it will *not* stop you from being who you were meant to become. Nothing will."

"It's something for me to worry about when those people know where I *live.*"

"Then move. I can't imagine you don't have the means to do that, at the very least."

The halfling barely felt her fingernails digging into her palms. Either she'd lost feeling already, or sensation wasn't as strong on the astral-drow plane. "I need something more than that. Please."

"You'll have plenty more than that in time." L'zar's sneer wasn't meant for her, but it made his daughter's stomach clench just the same. "Not now. Just keep the pendant on until I say otherwise."

She scoffed. "Should I be expecting a phone call?"

"Cute." His nostrils flared even as he smiled at her. "This connection can be used any time you like, by the way, to reach out to me again. I'll be—"

Footsteps pounded across the metal grate of the catwalks stretching across Alpha Block. Unintelligible shouts followed.

L'zar pushed himself back onto the bed and grimaced at the barred door of his cell. "They've got a knack for poor timing, I'll give them that. Gotta love a random cell search, am I right?"

"What?"

"Our time's up tonight, Cheyenne. The best time to reach me is after ten at night. Unless some asshole decides he wants to wake everyone up just to keep us on our toes," the drow said, "nobody comes around after lights out. I'll be here when you're ready to come back."

The red light outside his cell winked out just before the room beyond filled with bright light. The muffled sound of the other inmates groaning in protest followed, and L'zar shot the drow halfling another wink before kicking his legs up onto the cot again and lying back with his hands laced behind his head.

The prison cell inside Chateau D'rahl and L'zar Verdys vanished, and Cheyenne was pulled back into her body without another word being said.

CHAPTER FORTY-SIX

Cheyenne jerked awake again with a gasp, her wide eyes fixed on all the stars dotted across the black sky. "Oh, sure. After ten. I'll just call his assistant and have it put down on his schedule."

Corian looked at her from where he'd been sitting, his legs crossed beneath him. "What was that?"

"The last word I didn't have a chance to say." Grunting, the halfling rolled over onto her side and pushed herself up. She crossed her legs again and gave herself a minute to recover. "That was nuts."

"But it worked."

She turned toward the Nightstalker and cocked her head. "You couldn't have just said I'd be projecting myself into the prison to have a one-on-one with the guy? I mean, how hard is it to give me a warning?"

Corian shot her a crooked smile. "If I'd told you that, would you still have done it?"

Cheyenne blinked. "Okay, fair point. But you could've at least given me something more than 'good luck.'"

He laughed as he gathered the leftover ingredients and set everything aside in a neat pile. "I'm equipped to guide you through the trials, kid. Even to throw spells at you and hope you figure out how to use your magic to get the job done. And I can make the Don'adurr. But that's where my knowledge of it stops."

"Yeah, if I knew how to make it, I'd probably use someone else as a guinea pig too."

The Nightstalker shrugged and stood. "It's a drow thing, Cheyenne. Trust me, I know just as much drow magic as L'zar. That's helpful most of the time, but I can only use about a third of it."

He stepped toward her and offered her a hand up. The halfling rolled her eyes but took his hand. Then she brushed the dirt and dry grass off her clothes, metal wrist-chains clinking. "Not something I'm interested in doing again."

"But you can. If you want to. That's what matters."

"Well, right now, I'm focused on...training with you, I guess. We still have time for that, right?"

Corian's amused little smirk made her want to attack him. "Plenty of time for that, yeah."

"Okay." Cheyenne rolled her shoulders back and stretched her neck. *Time to switch gears from hardcore magical drugs to sparring with a Nightstalker. No big deal.* "We don't have to go through another round of 'eat the seed, Cheyenne,' do we?"

"The Nimlothar seed? No." Corian's feline nose wrinkled as he stepped backward, chuckling. "The trials start with one seed and end when that copper box over there is open and you've earned your legacy."

The halfling pursed her lips. "Once you pop, the fun don't stop, right?"

"Yes. A can of Pringles and your drow trials are exactly the same thing. Excellent parallel."

Despite her frustration with all the secrets and vague answers and L'zar Verdys cutting off their unexpected astral conversation, Cheyenne couldn't help but laugh. "Guess I'm just good at those."

"I hope you're better at sparring."

She grinned. "Don't act like you haven't seen me in action before."

"Oh, I've seen it." Corian dropped into a crouch like a huge panther on two legs about to jump into a tree. "I might even be impressed if I hadn't had to run into that house and take care of every last magical for you."

"For the record, I didn't ask you to do that."

"You didn't have to."

Stretching out her fingers, the halfling took a deep breath. "Also, for the record, thanks for showing up when you did."

"There, you see? A little appreciation goes a long way, kid."

She laughed and watched him pace in front of her, those glowing silver eyes locked onto hers. "I'll appreciate it a lot more when these trials are over and people quit telling me to wait until I'm ready."

The Nightstalker's long canines flashed in the starlight when he grinned back. "You ready now?"

"Yeah. No, wait."

Corian stood from his crouch and let out a quick burst of surprised laughter. "Wow."

"Just hold on a second, okay?" Fighting back a smile, Cheyenne shook out her hands again and closed her eyes. "The conversation was super weird, but he gave me a tip for tapping into new abilities, I think."

"Really? What was that?"

She did laugh then. "You wouldn't understand, Corian. It's a drow thing." *Yeah, okay. It feels good to say to someone else.*

The Nightstalker started pacing again. She could hear his footsteps on the coarse, dry grass and the dirt, even with her eyes closed. "Take your time, kid. Just don't take all night."

Ignoring him, Cheyenne took a deep breath. *Focus on the Nimlothar seed, huh? If I only need one, I'm guessing it hits the stomach and stays there.*

She focused on the memory of the glowing purple seed and the tingling magic spreading out from her core after she'd swallowed it. The image pulsed with violet light in her mind's eye, and the sensation returned. The halfling let out a slow, controlled breath when the tingling, buzzing heat resonated through her one more time. It reached out from her belly and chest, down through her limbs, and up into her head until she felt like she'd pressed her cheek against a humming motor. *This'll help. That crazy drow might be right.*

Corian watched her, chuckling silently as L'zar Verdys' daughter experimented with the first of many things she'd learn to do with her drow magic. *Just because she started late with the trials, it doesn't mean she's a slow learner. I'll give her that.* He licked his lips and waited for her to find whatever she was looking for.

When the halfling opened her eyes, he froze. A thin, quick glimmer of purple light flashed across her glowing gold eyes. *Now we're talkin'.*

"Okay, halfling," he called, jerking his chin at her in challenge. "Hit me."

Cheyenne sent a crackling black sphere of energy at him before he'd finished talking. Corian darted out of the way and responded with a bolt of blazing silver light. It pinged off the dark shield she raised and shot toward the sky before fizzling out against the dome of his wards.

She wasn't kidding about the shields.

"Which one are you focusing on now, kid?" he shouted, circling toward her as silver light flared in his hand.

"Not this time, Nightstalker. That'd make it too easy for you." Cheyenne darted into drow speed as Corian started to laugh. She thought she'd gain on him before he had a chance to react.

She got three feet away before he stepped into her hyper-speed, grinning. "Almost had me there."

He jerked his fist toward the ground, and the silver light exploded between them. The halfling threw up another shield in time to cut off the streaking lightning in its path, but the force of Corian's magic hitting the shimmering wall in enhanced speed let off more energy than either of them had expected. A metallic clang echoed off the rock and stone walls of Alcatraz prison, and the drow halfling and the Nightstalker were thrown away from each other by the shockwave.

Cheyenne grunted as she skidded across the dirt, blinking at the sky again. The sound of Corian's ringing laughter was fuel enough to get her to push to her feet again.

"Now things are getting interesting!" Silver lightning crackled in both of his hands as he spread them wide. "Looks like L'zar's little trick worked, huh?"

"Dunno. Haven't tried it yet." *Let's go with earth-splitting.*

The halfling reached out with both hands, her body humming with the extra boost of the Nimlothar seed, and wavering light flared around her fingertips. But that was it.

"Seriously?"

Corian shook his head and paced in front of her again. "Maybe I spoke too soon."

The ground in front of him erupted in a spray of loose earth and stone. He reeled away with a surprised shout, clawing the dirt out of his face.

Smirking, Cheyenne reached out again and tried to repeat the burst of fractured earth. A pulsing zing of extra power shot through her arm, and the air around her outstretched fingers shimmered again. *I could keep him running around in circles all night with this.*

The ground trembled, and a snake of upturned earth darted away from where the halfling stood. It zigzagged across the ground toward Corian, not as quickly as his lightning attack, but close. Another spray of rock hit him even as he tried to dodge it.

"No, I think I got this!" she shouted.

The earth shook again, and it sent them both staggering sideways. Then a massive crack rent the air, and the halfling gaped at the huge crevice splitting its way through the earthen walls around the abandoned prison. Bushes fell, taking large chunks of dirt with them. The crevice raced toward the base of the prison until it split the wall of white stone. Chunks of it crumbled, and the jagged crack kept climbing as the abandoned building groaned and shivered.

Corian finally escaped the spewing dirt and turned with wide eyes to look up at the unintended destruction.

"Shit!" Without thinking about how or why Cheyenne reached

toward her little drow-magic mistake. Unseen resistance met her fingers, but she closed them into a fist anyway and jerked back.

The island stopped trembling, and the split that had climbed halfway up the stone wall stopped. More crumbling bits of rock fell into the dirt, bouncing end over end on their way down the sharp drop outside the building.

The halfling dropped her hand. *Gotta pay attention with that one.*

The air popped beside her with a rush of wind just before Corian attacked. She wasn't fast enough to conjure a shield before his hissing streak of silver lightning glanced off her shoulder and sent her spinning sideways.

Gritting her teeth, Cheyenne clamped a hand on her throbbing shoulder and tried to walk it off. "Cheap shot, don't you think?"

"The lessons here aren't mutually exclusive, Cheyenne." The Nightstalker dropped into a crouch, his silver eyes widening with the thrill of battle, even when sparring with a halfling. "This lesson is about not letting yourself get distracted before you're sure your opponent is down for the count."

"What?" Rolling her shoulders back, she straightened and pointed at the huge split in the side of the prison. "You don't think magically vandalizing a historical monument is a good reason to tone it down a notch?"

Corian's gaze flickered toward the building, and he shrugged. "I can patch that up later."

"You're serious."

"Lotta tricks up my sleeve, kid. Better focus, or you'll walk out of here just as banged up as last time." He summoned two more orbs of blindingly bright light in his hands and grinned again. "Your call."

Without waiting for her answer, he shot the bolts of silver lightning toward her in quick succession. Cheyenne slipped into enhanced speed and stepped out of the way before launching her black tendrils toward him. They reached the Nightstalker as he joined her in the little bubble of hyper-speed and coiled around his wrist.

He tried to fling another spell at her, but she jerked his hand aside, and the crackling silver light went over her head. Corian's surprise made her chuckle. "At least you're dedicated."

With a snarl that somehow sounded like a laugh, Corian jerked his wrists down, yanking her forward, then grabbed the slack of her black tendrils in one hand. "You're getting cocky. Again."

The next lightning bolt he conjured wasn't aimed at her but at the lashing tendrils in her hands. The coiled whips tightened and sparked with silver light as his attack traveled all the way back to her hand.

"Wait—"

She tried to retract the lashing tendrils faster than the lightning flashed across them, but that made it even worse. Silver light erupted around her hands, and the halfling shouted in pain and surprise. She staggered out of her enhanced speed, shaking out her hands and hissing. "What the *hell?*"

"It was a good effort." Corian moved away from her in that stupid crouch. "Much better than last time. I still get the feeling you're holding back."

"Yeah, 'cause I'm not interested in destroying Alcatraz Island, thanks. Awful choice for a sparring ring, by the way."

"Don't use that as an excuse, Cheyenne. And quit holding back."

"You saw what happened." She shook her burning, tingling hands again, her chains jingling. "I can't do that again."

"Then use it as an incentive to hit what you're aiming for and quit whining about it like a little bitch."

"Dude, that's so not the right thing to—"

"Come *on!*" Snarling, Corian shot another streak of lightning at her head.

The halfling ducked, then whirled to watch the silver attack crash against the warded dome around the island. "You were *trying* to hit me in the face, weren't you?"

"No, I was trying to motivate you." The Nightstalker dropped into a squat and slapped both hands on the dirt. Dozens of snaking silver lines crackled across the ground toward the half-drow.

Cheyenne stepped back and shoved forward with both hands.

The ground erupted in front of the closest bolt, spraying dirt and dry grass and sending dart after dart of hissing silver light shooting into the air. She glanced briefly up at the deflected magic and grinned. *Okay...*

When she shoved again, the earth buckled away from her, rolling in a wave almost impossible to see before bursting beneath Corian's feet and flipping him through the air. A spray of dirt and clods of dry earth rained down around them. Once they settled, she found Corian squatting a few yards behind where she'd hit him, fingertips pressed to the ground while his splayed feet balanced his landing.

She rolled her eyes. "You're kidding."

"Cats land on their feet, right?" The Nightstalker cocked his head and stood, dusting off his hands. "That was good. Nothing like the first time in the meadow, but at least you hit your target."

Yeah, I bet he's got nine lives, too. "That happened because you pissed me off."

"Then get pissed, Cheyenne. We're not finished."

CHAPTER FORTY-SEVEN

With the wind knocked out of her, Cheyenne rolled onto her side and tried to ward her mentor off by raising a hand in surrender. "Okay, man. Okay. I think we're finished."

"I'm pretty sure the guy training you gets to decide that one." Chuckling, Corian stepped toward her and nodded. "But it looks to me like you might be done for the night."

"Yeah, good idea. Too bad *I* didn't think of that." When he leaned down and offered her his hand, the halfling snorted but took it. He pulled her to her feet, and she hissed in pain. "Ow. I honestly can't tell what hurts more."

"What are the options?"

"Everything." She tried to smirk but ending up grimacing again as she slowly brushed dirt and pebbles and dry grass off her clothes.

"That's a sign of improvement."

"Huh. Doesn't feel like it."

"It will. When you can feel anything but pain again." He laughed when she shot him a warning scowl. "That was good, kid. You worked hard. You focused. Still got a ways to go, but you're getting there."

"I have a feeling you're gonna keep telling me that, no matter how many times I end up on the ground."

"As many times as it takes." Folding his arms, Corian turned around to take in their impromptu sparring ring. Almost all the grass had been uprooted by spears of rock jutting up from below the surface or snaking lines of upturned earth. A huge sheet of the steep earthen wall beyond the prison building separated from the rest and dropped with a thump to the lower level. "I think we've just about used this place up."

Cheyenne snorted. "Ya think?"

The Nightstalker walked across the mess they'd made of Alcatraz Island and stooped to collect his potion ingredients and the intricate silver box off the ground. Pebbles and dust rained off the lid when he blew across it. "I'll come back and do a little cleanup later. You should get home and try to sleep off those bruises."

"Right. 'Cause they'll magically disappear if I get enough sleep."

Sticking the box under one arm, Corian cast the spell to open a portal back to his basement in Richmond and nodded for the halfling to join him. "You know, I used to look forward to a good stiff drink after sparring and then heading to bed. Might help if you're hurting too much to sleep."

"You didn't beat me up *that* much, cat man." Rubbing the sore shoulder she'd landed on too many times to count, Cheyenne snatched up the copper legacy box and moved toward him until they both faced the open portal hovering above Alcatraz Island. "And unless you have a bottle of something buried in your shelves somewhere, I'm gonna have to pass. If I walk into a store looking like this, people will *not* sell me alcohol."

Corian snorted and gestured for her to step through the portal. When she did, the salty, fishy tang of the ocean air was replaced by the smell of dust, cement, metal, and something a little like oranges. Then the Nightstalker joined her in his basement, and the portal shrank out of existence.

"I'm sure you'll figure out what works." He went to the metal shelves along the wall and carefully replaced the silver box before tossing everything else haphazardly onto different piles.

"Yeah, I'm getting pretty good at that."

Chuckling, he turned back around and folded his arms. "You're getting better. I'd be lying if I said I didn't see it. And you can take a hit."

"Or ten."

"We'll see if that number's any bigger next time." Corian peered at the metal door of his basement apartment and flicked his fingers at it. The orange light of his wards flashed and receded. "You're good to go. After you put the pendant back on."

With a nod, the halfling pulled the pendant out of her pocket and lifted it around her neck before tying another knot. She didn't have to think about slipping back into her human form; the Heart of Midnight did it for her. "I have one more question to ask before I head out."

The Nightstalker's nose twitched. "If it's about anything I've already said I can't answer, Cheyenne, I have to—"

"No, not any of that stuff. It's more like a favor, actually." She glanced at the metal door.

"A favor." Corian folded his arms and raised his eyebrows, leaning against the overstuffed shelf. "Go ahead, then."

What's the worst he could do? Say no again?

Cheyenne shrugged. "Any chance you could help me learn some spells? A friend of mine gave me this huge book of them, and I've already proven I have no idea what I'm doing with them."

"Spells, huh? How many?"

"All of them."

Corian snorted and dipped his chin to his chest in a failed attempt to hide his laughter. "You want me to teach you *all* the spells in someone else's spellbook."

"I like to think they were personally curated. Hopefully."

With a soft growl of indecision, the Nightstalker turned around again and took stock of the chaotically organized junk filling the shelves. "Spells come in handy, I'll give you that. Not for fighting, but for pretty much everything else."

"So, it's a plus for me to know a few."

"Yes, Cheyenne. It couldn't hurt." He clicked his tongue, then turned back toward her. "All right. If you want to add spells to this arrangement, that's fine. Under two conditions."

"Which are?"

"We hit the spellwork *after* your training. You should be focusing on the trials a lot more than learning fancy tricks with charms and wards. But if you think you have enough brainpower to do both, we'll give it a shot." He wrinkled his nose and turned back for one more sweeping glance at the overloaded shelving. "And you have to go get all the supplies. I'm almost out of everything remotely useful, and I try to stay out of Peridosh as much as possible."

"Done. Two conditions I can totally live with."

"Okay." Corian nodded curtly before turning away from her and stalking across the bare concrete floors toward his cheap folding card table.

That's my cue. "Okay." Cheyenne turned toward the door, then stopped again, clenching her eyes shut. "Hey, do you know any way to keep people from finding me?"

The Nightstalker's hand paused on the back of the metal chair. "Don't take off the pendant, Cheyenne."

"No, I mean people who already know where to find me. Like the guy who blew up my car this morning." When he turned around again to face her, she shrugged. "I don't like people showing up at my apartment without an invitation, and I'd *really* like to keep that Panamera in one piece."

"I'd say the best way out of that situation is to find a new apartment."

"That seems to be the only advice anyone has for me."

"Magic and spells are great, kid, but they don't solve all our problems. Sometimes they just make more."

Cheyenne pressed her lips together to fight back another biting remark and decided just to nod instead. "Helpful hint. Thanks."

She headed toward the door, stopping to drop the drow puzzle box into her backpack before slinging it over her shoulder.

"Once you find a new place, though," he called after her, "let me know. I can show you how to cast wards that will at least keep anyone else from finding you again. You can handle the rest of it yourself."

"That would be super helpful, yeah. Thanks."

"Get some rest." He pulled out the metal folding chair and sat, his attention switching from the drow halfling to the closed laptop on the table in front of him.

"See ya." Cheyenne opened the door and stepped out into the landing of the concrete stairwell. The metallic echo fell flat when she pulled the door shut behind her, and she slipped her other arm through the second strap of her backpack to redistribute the weight. *Guess I have to get used to my shoulders hurting all the time.*

She moved way too slowly up the stairs, grimacing when her knee popped every time she straightened it. *Or I could go with blazing through these trials and ending the fun little sparring sessions.*

With a snort, she stepped off the last stair and headed across the grass toward her car. The Panamera chirped when she unlocked it, headlights flashing twice. Her backpack went into the passenger seat, then she slipped behind the wheel, closed the door, and smiled. "Getting into a car like this almost makes the pain go away."

She brushed her fingers across the tight, glistening black leather of the steering wheel and started the engine. *Too bad I can't roll up to Peridosh in this thing. Nothin' like making a bigger statement than last time.*

CHAPTER FORTY-EIGHT

Cheyenne checked the Borderlands forum again when she got home, which confirmed the fairly good feeling she'd had about the rescued kids getting back to their families. Twenty more users had posted an update on another wayward minor coming back home, though none of them mentioned how they'd been found or who'd brought them back.

Even if they know, nobody wants to openly post about the FRoE playing the neighborhood hero.

She glanced at the time. "Almost one in the morning. Yeah, I bet every single one of those kids is accounted for here before I head off to class tomorrow. Oh, shit."

Wincing when she scooted her desk chair closer with just a little too much enthusiasm, the halfling logged onto her VCU student email address and checked for incoming emails. *Mattie won't care that I didn't show up today, but that's not gonna fly with everyone.*

The only email she had, though, came from Professor Mattie Bergmann, which made her pause before she forced herself to at least read the subject line.

Urgent: Academic Meeting with Cheyenne Summerlin.

"Oh, boy." The halfling clicked open the email and shut one eye. *This is where the other shoe drops. Just read it already.*

Dear Ms. Summerlin,

It has come to our attention that you seem to be experiencing difficulty in attending your graduate classes as scheduled this semester. As a result, the professors and staff taking part in your personal education have reached the conclusion that an alternative method for earning credits toward your graduate degree might be in the best interests of all parties involved, should you wish to continue. You are excused from attending all three of your scheduled classes this Friday in lieu of attending a meeting Saturday evening at 6:00 in the Computer Sciences building on campus, Conference Room A. We appreciate your cooperation and punctuality in this matter.

Sincerely,

Professor Mathilda Bergmann, Ph.D.

Professor of Computer Science

Virginia Commonwealth University'

Cheyenne hadn't realized she'd been grimacing through the whole email until her forehead and upper lip grew sore. "That doesn't sound good."

She scrolled back up to the top of the email, and her jaw dropped. "She CC-ed Hersh on this. And LePlant." The halfling clicked hastily through the added email addresses until she'd opened them all. "Every single one of my professors. A meeting with all of them."

With a grunt, she flung herself back into her desk chair and barely noticed the dull ache in the back of her shoulder. *Why?*

The email sent at 3:24 that afternoon had a second reply at the bottom. Cheyenne scrolled down slowly. *Wouldn't surprise me if Hersh thought this was the perfect time to hit reply all and rub it in some more.*

But the second email was from Mattie too, sent at 3:27 p.m. and addressed only to Cheyenne.

Don't miss this one!!!!

The halfling snorted. "Italics and four exclamation points. Something tells me she's serious."

Rolling her eyes, Cheyenne logged out of her university email and pushed out of the chair. Her knee popped again, and she glared at it. *Just had to be a Saturday. At least they're not kicking me out of the program. Yet. And I have a little more time to recover, I guess.*

After turning off her monitor, she grabbed her phone from the front pocket of her backpack and took it with her into the bedroom. A sliver of her fractured bedroom door fell onto the carpet when she brushed it. *I'll get Corian to show me how to fix that too. No problem.*

Slipping out of her clothes was a chore, but once she had them all tossed in a pile, she climbed into her bed and spread out under the covers. Three times, she had to readjust the pendant around her neck, slipping it away from her chest or out from under her pillow. "I'm gonna throw a party when I don't need this thing anymore."

Her eyelids drooped after she finally found a comfortable position. Everything ached, but beneath all of it, the buzzing presence of the Nimlothar seed she'd ignited on her own lulled her quickly to sleep.

The blaring alarm on her phone went off at 6:30 a.m., just like every weekday. Groaning, Cheyenne had to try more than once to lift her aching arm off the mattress. Then she smacked her hand down on her phone and dragged it off the nightstand and into bed with her.

Just snooze for like...two hours.

The minute she got the alarm to shut the hell up, her phone buzzed with a new text from Ember.

So, this is fun. I'm kinda knocking myself out with morning breath over here and realizing I left all the nurses at the hospital. Any chance you could pop by before class and help a girl out?

Cheyenne chuckled, then covered her mouth. "Not funny, halfling."

Blinking her eyes into focus, she sent an immediate reply.

Guess we didn't think this through all the way, huh? Don't worry. No class today, so I'm all yours. Can you hang in there another 30?

Ember sent her a thumbs-up emoji in response, and the halfling pushed herself off the mattress. She dropped the phone to rub her face, then slid out of bed and almost dropped to the floor right there.

"Whoa." Catching herself on the edge of the bed, Cheyenne took a few more seconds to wish her legs into working normally, then carefully stood. *Maybe I'm overdoing it with the training. I'm not doing Ember any favors if I can't walk, either.*

She limped toward her bedroom door and the bathroom on the other side of the short hall, then groaned and shook her head. *Not-walking comments are off the table too. This is real for her. She doesn't need a smartass friend making it worse.*

The sight of her reflection in the mirror made the half-drow pause again. She made a face at the darkening bruises covering her right shoulder and swallowing the left. Dark purple-red splotches peppered her torso. There were a few larger ones on her back, and most of her right thigh was one giant bruise.

Perpetually half in drow mode. That's the look I'm rockin' now. Frowning, Cheyenne grabbed her brush and got to work on her hair. *Add healing salves to the list of spell lessons too.*

A little over half an hour later, Cheyenne grinned through the pain of moving anything at all when her Panamera chirped behind her in the parking lot. She moved down the outdoor hallway of Ember's apartment complex, unlocked the last door on the left, and stepped inside. "Honey, I'm home."

"Very funny," Ember called from her bedroom. "This is probably as close as I'm ever gonna get to having a sugar daddy. And it's you, so that doesn't count."

Laughing, the halfling closed the door behind her and locked that too. Then she headed into the single bedroom and found her friend propped up in bed against the enormous pile of pillows they'd tossed to the foot of the bed the night before. "You look comfy."

"Much better than a hospital bed. I can say that for sure." Ember ran a hand through her hair and took a deep breath. "But I'm tired of beds, Cheyenne. *Please* tell me you're not gonna lock me up in my apartment and call it 'getting some rest.' I'm not a homebody."

"Yes, this I know." Cheyenne grabbed the wheelchair and brought it as close to the bed as she could. "One more thing to add to the list of why you and I being roomies for a while might work out."

"Might, huh?" Ember slung an arm around her friend's shoulders and hung on while the halfling half-dragged, half-lifted her into the chair. "I thought we already decided it was a perfect setup? *Ow!* I can still feel my upper back, you know."

"Sorry." Trying not to laugh, Cheyenne stuck her foot against the outside of one wheel to steady the chair and finally shifted the fae girl into place. "Note to self. Lock the wheels for this kinda thing."

Ember pushed up on the armrests to readjust herself in the chair, trying to hide a wince of discomfort the minute it crossed her face. "For a halfling who carried me from Jackson Ward to the hospital, you seem a little low on arm strength this morning."

"You don't."

"I'm chalking it up to all the rock-climbing." Ember waved the half-drow off and shrugged. "Good thing I picked *that* up when I did, am I right?"

Cheyenne watched her friend and bit her bottom lip. "I honestly can't tell if you're making jokes or being serious and trying to cover it with sarcasm."

Ember snorted. "Probably both. I'm testing the waters with self-deprecating humor. You of all people get that." She shot the halfling a sidelong glance with a little smirk, then grabbed both wheels and tried to push herself forward. The chair only moved a few inches before she gave up. "I hate carpet!"

"You got a little farther than the one attempt yesterday."

"It's not a new hatred, either, and now it's getting in the way of me being able to do *anything*." The fae dropped her hands in her lap with a thump and glared at the opposite wall of her bedroom.

Cheyenne let her have a moment. *We both knew this might get a little bumpy.* "Em?"

Ember closed her eyes and sighed. "Yeah."

"I'm not gonna ask if you're okay, 'cause there's not a simple answer for that one." The other girl snorted and shook her head, her eyes still closed. "But I *will* ask you if you're ready to get pushed into the bathroom, betting that your text this morning was a minor emergency."

A tiny, breathless laugh escaped Ember, and she nodded. "Everything's a minor emergency right now."

"Fair enough. I'm ready to tackle them one at a time when you are." The fae's lower lip started to tremble, so Cheyenne stepped toward the back of the wheelchair and gripped the handlebars. *She'll cry or she won't. Not gonna stand there waiting for a show.* "Just say when."

"When, Cheyenne." The other woman nodded and sniffed, then lifted a finger toward her open bedroom door. "Onward, halfling. For glory."

"Okay, I'll let that rallying cry slip into the passable category this time. Might be worth it to brush up on famous pre-battle speeches."

"I've only been home for a day, okay? Give a girl some time." Ember sniffed again, wiped her nose, and let out a little chuckle. "I've got some smiting to do in the bathroom."

"Oh, yeah?" Cheyenne rummaged through her friend's overnight tote on the floor beside the bed and pulled out Ember's toiletries bag. Out came the toothbrush and toothpaste, and the halfling handed them over with a smirk. "Can't smite anything without your weapons."

"Right." Ember nodded and pointed with her toothbrush toward the bedroom door. "Onward."

Chuckling, Cheyenne grabbed the wheelchair's handles again and pushed much faster than she had to across the room, out into the hallway, and into the bathroom on the other side. The magicless fae let out a whoop that was supposed to be a battle cry, and they burst out laughing as the wheelchair squeaked to a stop beside the sink. "We'll have to work on that one."

Ember opened the toothpaste and waved it at her friend. "Top of my list, halfling."

CHAPTER FORTY-NINE

Closing the driver's side door of her Panamera, Cheyenne turned toward Ember in the passenger seat and grinned. "I have a feeling all the hard work's out of the way, Em. Nothin' but fun today. All day."

Ember snorted. "I appreciate you playing hooky to go apartment-shopping with me, and I'm not gonna tell you to just drop me off somewhere so you can get to class." The fae buckled her seatbelt and gave the halfling a tight smile. "You sure missing classes today isn't screwing with your endgame?"

Cheyenne laughed. "I have an endgame, huh?"

"Yeah, you know, like a master's degree."

"Right. The endgame of all endgames." The halfling wiggled her eyebrows, her head wobbling in fake enthusiasm. "I want it for sure, but there are a lot more important things than getting a piece of paper with my name on it and VCU's stamp of approval. You're one of them."

"Well, that's awfully open-minded of you."

"Very funny." Gripping the steering wheel, Cheyenne pressed the start button, and the engine purred to life. "Win-win for both of us today. My classes were canceled."

"All of them?"

"Yep." Cheyenne backed out of the parking spot at the front of the apartment building and headed out of the lot toward the street. "If you think *that's* weird, try opening an email from your favorite professor with *all* your other professors CC-ed on it, saying they all had a little chat about your career in graduate education and decided they were gonna change things up to be 'in the best interest of all parties involved.'"

Ember laughed. "What the hell does that mean?"

"Right? They told me to forget about my classes today and join them for a meeting tomorrow night instead."

"On a Saturday."

"On a Saturday at six o'clock, Em."

They both laughed as Cheyenne drove them out toward the center of town.

Ember tucked her hair behind her ears and shook her head. "That's weird. Doesn't sound like they're trying to make you drop out, though. Hey, maybe they'll have you update all their systems. Or write new ones. A total overhaul of the university servers and they're just calling it learning so they don't have to pay you."

The Panamera rolled to a stop at the next red light, and Cheyenne turned slowly to shoot her friend a sidelong glance. Then they burst out laughing again. "You know what? If they want me to do glorified IT maintenance to earn my master's and they don't have to kick me out, I'll take 'em up on that. Get the whole thing done and out of the way in a week, and I'll have my degree before Christmas."

"And a happy New Year, huh?"

"Just like that."

A minivan pulled up beside them at the red light. The girl sitting in the passenger seat was probably still in high school, or maybe just out of it. She grinned at Cheyenne's new ride and pointed, saying something to the woman behind the wheel who looked like her mom.

Cheyenne threw devil horns at the girl and smirked. The girl's mom leaned forward to see who was driving the Panamera, and her eyes grew wide. She shook her head vehemently, talking way too fast and jerking her daughter by the arm to sit forward again and quit staring at the Goth chick behind the wheel of a fancy car.

"Can you believe that?" The halfling laughed as the light turned green and the minivan sped away. "Even when I'm rolling around in a Panamera, people *still* get turned off by the whole—" She turned to look at Ember, who'd been pulling at the corner of her mouth with one hand and dragging her cheek down to show the whites of her eyes with the other. Cheyenne burst out laughing. "*You're* the one who scared them off!"

"What?" Ember chuckled. "There's no way me making ugly faces is scarier than a Goth chick driving a Panamera."

"Yeah, no way." Cheyenne pulled through the intersection. Her stomach let out an obnoxious growl, and the girls shot the halfling's gut matching glances of surprise.

"Did we forget the most important meal of the day?" Ember's fingers drummed on the armrest.

"Not forgotten. Just delayed." The halfling glanced up the street and nodded. "Ready to fix that before we scour this city for the *perfect* apartment?"

"Ms. Summerlin!"

Cheyenne scowled and shook her head.

Ember fought not to laugh through her words. "I thought there was no such thing as the perfect apartment?"

"That was before I had a fae sitting in the front seat of my Panamera. Pretty sure there are exceptions to every rule."

"Then hell, yes. I can't wait to stuff my face with something I get to order myself that wasn't made in the hospital cafeteria."

The halfling nodded and stepped on the gas. "You got it."

By the time they'd battled the wheelchair to get out of the car, into the bagel shop downtown for fried eggs and bacon between everything-bagel buns and some of the best coffee Cheyenne had had in weeks, and back into the car again, Ember looked exhausted.

The halfling started the car and took a huge swig of the lavender-honey latte in a to-go cup. "Okay. Nine-thirty." She set the coffee down in the cup holder and strapped herself in. "I think we're making pretty good time."

Ember buckled her seatbelt again and thumped her head back against the headrest. "That's like half the morning gone already."

"Whoa, whoa, whoa." Cheyenne turned toward her friend and raised an eyebrow. "That also means we still have over seven hours to find our new digs. That's a whole damn day!"

"And we'll spend half of it getting that wheelchair in and out of the car and me in and out of the chair." The fae girl closed her eyes. "My arms are already sore."

The halfling smirked. "Not from wheeling yourself around, though."

Her friend let out a wry laugh. "No, Cheyenne. From propping myself up while you pretend to be a scrawny Goth human trying to lift her friend in and out of everything."

"Huh." Cheyenne turned off the engine, and Ember blinked before opening her eyes all the way again.

"What?"

Turning in the driver's seat to face her friend as directly as she could, the halfling raised her eyebrows and leaned forward a little. "You want to keep going?"

"Today?" Ember shrugged.

"I have no problem going out to find this apartment on my own." Smirking, Cheyenne tapped a finger on her lips and exaggerated a thoughtful stare. "I'm thinking something like a giant warehouse, right? Maybe a repurposed garage, like the kind they turn into cool new restaurants with the door all the way open in the summer. Except we'll have all the windows blacked out. I'm sure I could find a couple chandeliers from the 1800s. Complete with cobwebs. Fill 'em with black candles. We won't even need electricity."

Ember laughed and rolled her eyes.

"I'm serious. Maybe even purple velvet on the walls. I mean, don't get me wrong, black is totally my number one. Purple's a close second. But the floors, of course—all black, no carpet. Hell, we could find something *shiny* black and paint the wood floors. No rooms, though. Just one giant, open Goth box with a trapdoor to the toilet." The halfling cocked her head and frowned. "Might have to install some kind of access lift down into it, though."

"Okay, stop." Ember finally looked at Cheyenne. "That is the *worst* last-minute plan for an apartment I've ever heard."

"Hey, who said it was last-minute? I could've been planning this whole thing for *months*. You don't know."

"Cheyenne, you bought yourself a Panamera. We both know you have better taste than a Goth-box garage with chandeliers."

Lifting one shoulder in coy indecision, the halfling batted her lashes. "This car is Cheyenne on the outside. That awesome picture I just painted in your head of our new apartment, Em? That's Cheyenne on the *inside*."

"Just shut up already." Finally, Ember let herself smile.

Good. Pulled her back from the edge of that dark pit, at least.

Cheyenne couldn't swallow another burst of laughter. "All joking aside, we don't have to do this today if it's too much. I don't know what it's like to go through what you're going through, but I *might* know something about pushing myself too hard when I should've listened to my gut."

"No problems with my gut, Cheyenne. I think the issue is all in my head." Ember tapped a finger against her temple. "Way more than my legs right now, anyway."

"Fair enough. You wanna keep going, or just call it a fun morning out to breakfast?"

Ember squinted at her friend, then snatched the halfling's to-go cup and took a long drink of latte. With a satisfied grin, she lifted the cup toward the windshield and nodded. "We're finding that apartment today. No fucking way am I letting you grab us a Goth box."

"Excellent decision. I'm a little heartbroken, but I'll get over it."

Cheyenne started the car again and backed out of the restaurant parking lot. "If you change your mind, though…"

"Trust me, I won't. Not after *that* image in my head." Ember laughed and drank more of Cheyenne's coffee.

I don't even care.

"As you wish, O mighty smiter."

Ember rolled her eyes. "I think you've got us confused, halfling."

"Not today. We're gonna do this right, Em. Get us into a badass new place that's safe and has everything we need." *I owe her that much, at least.*

CHAPTER FIFTY

Five hours later, they pulled up in front of the Guest Center of the Pellerville Gables apartments on Libbie Mill East Boulevard. Cheyenne glanced at the tall buildings around them and shrugged. "Third time's a charm, right?"

Ember smirked and shook her head. "We've already been to three different apartment complexes. I think we missed the cutoff."

"What? No, in this situation, we're interpreting the saying as three duds in the apartment search equals a winner with number four."

"That doesn't even make sense."

The halfling chuckled and unbuckled her seatbelt. "Just let it percolate in your head. You'll catch up." With a wink, she popped the trunk and got out to grab the wheelchair one more time. *I'll be helping her for a while, so I better get used to it.*

She jerked the chair out of its folded position with an almost fluid motion and grinned. "Hey! I think I'm gettin' the hang of this."

Ember let out a mocking groan. "Awesome. You get the hang of *my* wheelchair. I'll wait."

"Whoa." Laughing, Cheyenne brought the chair around and locked the wheels. She stuck her hands on her hips and eyed her friend, still sitting in her car. "You're gonna have to go easy on me, Em. I'm on a learning curve here. Don't worry, I'll quit slowing you down in no time."

Ember snorted and steadied herself while Cheyenne bent down to help her transfer out of the car. It took the magicless fae only seconds this time to get herself adjusted in the chair, then Cheyenne wheeled her backward so Ember could shut the door. "We *are* getting pretty good at this."

"See?" The halfling pushed her friend toward the ramp onto the sidewalk as Ember pulled the keyless fob out of her jacket pocket and locked the car behind them. The little chirp made them both smile. "We make the best damn team in the world. Only makes sense that we're about to end up living together too."

"Okay, I might be misreading the signs, but you sound more excited about this setup with every awful apartment we say no to."

Cheyenne laughed as they headed up the walkway toward the front door of the Guest Center. "That's 'cause we're getting closer to that Goth-box garage."

"Maybe I should just say *this* is the one I want, no arguments, I'm putting my foot down *now*—" Ember froze in the chair and stared at the warped reflection of a girl in a wheelchair being pushed by a blurred black figure shaped like another girl. Then she laughed. "That's always metaphorical, isn't it? Putting one's foot down."

"Unless we're talking about toddler tantrums, yeah. Hey, look at this. Automatic doors with a handicap button." Cheyenne wheeled her friend up to the blue metal square on the outer wall of the building and nodded. "Would you like to do the honors?"

"That's the first one we've seen today, isn't it?" Ember leaned sideways and slammed her palm on the button. The door opened slowly to let them inside. "I like this place already."

"Okay, well, don't put your foot down just yet."

They made their way into the wide, sweeping lobby of the Pellerville Gables Apartments, everything in bold colors and sleek, clean lines.

Ember tipped her head all the way back to study the unusually high ceilings and the track lighting. "Does this place look like a hotel lobby to you?"

"Stole the words right outta my head. Not a lot of black, though."

The fae girl scoffed. "I'm pretty sure a good interior decorator can take care of that issue."

"*Oh.* Now we're talking about interior decorators, huh? When did we get so fancy?"

"Probably when you bought that super-fancy car outside and started throwing around the phrase 'inheritance.'" Ember looked over her shoulder to grin at the halfling. "Plus, I kinda have a weak spot for decorating."

"You know what? I'll buy that." Cheyenne found the receptionist's desk against the right-hand wall just past a half-circle of black leather armchairs around a curvy modern coffee table with no identifiable shape. *We need chairs like that.* "Even with all the broken cabinets and the holes in the wall, your apartment looks a lot nicer than mine."

"That's because I have furniture."

They laughed and pushed the sound level down into snickering as they approached the desk. The woman sitting there was only a few years older than they were, her platinum-blonde hair cut into a straight, severe bob. She readjusted the cat-eye frames of her lime-green glasses and smiled first at Ember. When she looked at Cheyenne, her smile faded a little, and her gaze moved to Ember again. "Hi. Can I help you?"

"That would be awesome," Cheyenne replied with a firm nod.

The woman blinked—the little plaque on her desk said "Caroline"—and kept smiling at Ember.

"I called earlier this morning and made an appointment for a showing," Ember said, her usual joking demeanor replaced by a perfectly polite bubbliness that matched Caroline's.

Cheyenne pressed her lips together to keep from laughing. *Like she was groomed by Bianca Summerlin.*

"All right." Caroline's smile widened, her blue eyes magnified behind the thick lenses. "What time was your appointment?"

"Two-thirty. If you took my name down, it would be under Ember Gaderow."

The receptionist clicked around and nodded. "Oh, yes. I have you right here. Right on time. That's excellent." Her gaze flickered across Ember's wheelchair. "Are you still wanting to look at the two-bedroom loft?"

"Definitely." Ember either didn't notice the woman's hesitation about her wheelchair or was really good at ignoring it.

At least she's got that part down already. Cheyenne stepped around the chair to stand beside her friend and stuck her hands in the pockets of her baggy black pants with small rips in the knees.

"Of course." Caroline clasped her hands together, glanced one more time at her computer, and smiled even wider. "I'll take you to one of our show units with the same layout. You can get a feel for what it might look like with all your things moved in."

"Sounds great."

"I'll just step into the back office to grab the keys, and we'll go take a look." Caroline patted her desk as she nodded at Ember, and her eyes flickered toward Cheyenne before she spun neatly around and headed through an unmarked door on the other side of her desk.

"This'll be fun," Cheyenne muttered.

Ember chuckled and folded her arms. "Something tells me you're not talking about going to check out another apartment."

"Well, yeah, that too. But I think she expected her two-thirty appointment to look a little different." The halfling turned to eye the closed door where Caroline had disappeared. "I think she's having a hard time deciding which of us to be more concerned about."

"What?" The fae pretended shock and pressed a hand to her chest. "You mean everyone can't already tell that we're both upstanding citizens looking to improve our current living arrangements?"

"Oh, man." Cheyenne hissed a laugh and shook her head. "I gotta take you to meet my mom sometime. She'd love you."

"I don't know if I'm quite her style."

"Ha. Maybe I just want to see the look on her face when you pull out the sarcasm."

Ember raised an eyebrow. "I'm sure she gets plenty of that from you."

Cheyenne slowly shook her head, her eyes wide as she fought to keep the image of Bianca Summerlin's reaction at bay. "Not for a long time. You might say she had a certain way of grooming it out of me. At least when I'm around her or any of her *peers*."

"Oh, I get it. You just want to make her squirm when she sees your best friend has the balls to act that way around her, and you don't."

The halfling pointed a warning finger at her friend and swallowed another laugh. "Low blow, but dead-on." Ember rolled her eyes. "No, for real, though, Em. It's a fun thought to entertain, but I know it won't happen. You're too adaptable."

"I can't tell if that's an insult or a compliment."

Cheyenne shrugged, laughing when the fae girl smacked her arm with the back of a hand. "Seriously, we'd have a good time. We'll wheel you out onto the veranda and open some wine. Eleanor makes a mean chicken cacciatore when the mood strikes."

Ember's eyes widened as she tried to process that mental image. "*Now* who's getting fancy?"

"Just sayin'. It's a whole new world out there in the middle of nowhere."

The unmarked door on the other side of the desk opened, and the receptionist stepped toward them, dangling a single key on a keyring. "Here we go. Can I offer either of you something to drink? We have wine, red or white. Mineral or flat water, if you prefer."

"No champagne?" Cheyenne asked with a deadpan stare.

"I'm sorry?"

"No, no. Don't apologize. It's fine." The halfling lifted a hand and dipped her head. *Wow, that even feels like Mom.*

"Of...of course." Caroline blinked furiously and turned her attention to Ember. "For you, Ms. Gaderow?"

Ember fought down another laugh and shook her head. "No, thank you. We're ready to go take a look at that loft."

"Absolutely. We'll just step outside the Guest Center and head to the first building on the right. This way." The woman nodded and brushed past them without looking at Cheyenne.

The halfling leaned down to whisper in her friend's ear, "I told you this would be fun."

"You're gonna make her pull her hair out," Ember muttered.

"Well, if we like this place and wanna seal the deal, just wait 'til we get to the paperwork-signing part."

"Oh, boy. Here we go."

They shared another quiet laugh that cut off abruptly when Caroline held the front door open for them. Then they were back outside on the pathway across the Guest Center's manicured lawn. The woman leading the way kept up a brisk pace to the first building on the right, and Cheyenne made it a point to stay several feet behind her at all times.

"Here we are." Caroline opened another entrance door, and in they went. "So tell me, Ms. Gaderow. What made you decide to visit Pellerville Gables Apartments this afternoon?"

Cheyenne wheeled her friend into the lobby of the apartment building, which was a smaller version of the Guest Center.

"Well, I checked out the website. The pictures looked really nice, and I saw two-bedroom lofts were still available, so I gave you a call."

"Excellent. And who referred you to us, if you don't mind my asking?" Caroline led them down the hallway in the back toward the two elevators.

"Um, Google."

The woman turned quickly to shoot Ember an incredulous glance and tried to cover her surprise. "I see."

She stabbed the elevator call button and stared up at the little upward-pointing triangle, now glowing with a soft white light.

Cheyenne drummed her fingers on the handles of the wheelchair and watched their apartment tour guide. *They don't get a lot of potential residents right off the street like this. She doesn't know what to do with herself.*

The elevator doors opened with a ding, and Caroline stepped back with a gesture for them to enter. "After you."

"Thank you." Ember dipped her head, and Cheyenne pushed the chair just roughly enough to wheel it over the metal strip without getting stuck. A small laugh of surprise burst from Ember's mouth as her head whipped back, then Cheyenne jerked the wheelchair to a stop before her friend's feet would have hit the back wall. "You're outdoing yourself, Cheyenne."

"Thank you."

The elevator doors closed behind them.

Caroline looked horrified.

CHAPTER FIFTY-ONE

The door to the show unit swung open without a sound, and Caroline stepped inside first. She opened her arm in a grand, sweeping gesture, the key dangling from her hand. "Here it is. The two-bedroom loft is one of our most popular units. Master bedroom and attached master bath to the right. Second bedroom on the left at the other end."

The woman's heels clicked across the hardwood floors with sharp, staccato echoes. "The entire north wall is windows, so there's more than enough natural light, but none of it direct. Insulated windows keep the unit remarkably energy efficient—no cold drafts in the winter or extra heat in the summer. And the door just there steps out onto the balcony. Plenty of room out there for chairs and a little bistro table. Open floor plan, all-new hardwood flooring throughout. Tile in the bathrooms. Stainless-steel appliances in the kitchen and granite countertops."

Caroline stepped toward the kitchen and flipped a switch on the side of the huge center island. "These lights up here are dimmable for ambiance. Every unit has a laundry room as well, with a side-by-side top-loading washer and dryer. That's down there in a separate room behind the second full bathroom."

Cheyenne wheeled Ember into the center of the loft, and they took a moment to stare at the phenomenal view of northern Richmond through the wall of windows. *I bet if I stared long enough, I could see DC from here.*

Ember said, "This is not like the other ones."

"You can say that again." The halfling turned around to take in the ceilings, high even for a loft, and ran her hand over the back of the gray suede couch in the center of the huge living area. "Do all these units come with that extra loft up there?"

Caroline followed her gaze and nodded at the wrought-iron staircase leading up to the raised platform above the second bathroom and hidden laundry room. "Most of them do, yes. A lot of people use that for an office, semi-private study, library, et cetera. I believe it can also fit a queen-sized bed and a short chest of drawers."

"Uh-huh." Cheyenne walked quickly toward the staircase and climbed it just enough to peer through the iron rail surrounding the miniature loft.

"Unfortunately, all of our two-bedroom units with this particular layout and the built-in loft are currently rented." Caroline fiddled with the single key in her hand. "Our available units with this floorplan don't have that specific feature, but it does open up the rest of the main room quite a bit."

With one more sweeping gaze around the loft, Cheyenne leaned over the staircase railing and grinned at the woman. "Not a problem."

Caroline started like she'd just been screamed at instead and turned toward Ember. "Can I answer any questions for you, Ms. Gaderow?"

Ember gazed through the wall of windows and took a deep breath. "Do the bedrooms have carpet?"

"Absolutely not. Hardwood flooring everywhere, though there's plenty of room for an area rug in the master. Would you like to see?"

Slowly, Ember spun the chair around on her own and pointed past the kitchen. "Right down there?"

"Yes."

With a nod, the fae wheeled herself toward the master bedroom, a little slowly at first, but she picked up speed soon enough and disappeared through the open doorway.

Cheyenne's black Vans clomped down the iron staircase, and she swung around the bottom stair, her hand squeaking on the end of the banister. "Definitely a nice setup."

"Yes. It is." Caroline's lips pressed tightly together.

Looks like she just bit into a lemon.

"It's good to hear there's no carpet in here." The halfling stopped beside their guide and folded her arms. "It's so outdated, don't you think?"

Caroline took a subtle step to the side to put more space between them, gazing out the windows. "We installed hardwood and tile flooring in all of our units in 2015. Everything's updated regularly. State of the art."

"Ms. Gaderow *really* hates carpet."

"I'm sure she'll be more than happy with one of these units. Your...employer seems like the kind of woman who knows what she wants."

There it is.

Blinking slowly, Cheyenne stared out at the incredible view. A slow, amused smile bloomed on her lips. "She certainly does."

I should tell her, but it's too much fun not to.

A little bump came from the master bedroom, followed by a light grunt of exasperation.

"Sorry." Ember wheeled back and forth a few times and managed to line the chair up again with the doorway. "Some doors are wider than others, huh?" She chuckled and glanced over her shoulder, then wheeled back out past the kitchen and into the main room. "Didn't leave a dent."

"I'm sure it's fine." Caroline grinned at her, relieved to not be left alone with the Goth girl in her fancy showroom. "What did you think of the master?"

"It's nice." Ember glanced up at Cheyenne and shrugged. "Jacuzzi bath."

"*Oh.*" The halfling widened her eyes and dipped her head. "Lovely."

Ember's eyebrows met as she frowned, then she glanced around the apartment one more time. "Definitely has a nice open feel to it."

"Almost like a garage, right?" Cheyenne pointed at the wall of windows. "If that whole thing could lift up and slide back across the ceiling."

With a muffled snort, Ember lowered her chin to her chest and said nothing.

"If you'll excuse me, Ms. Gaderow." Caroline pulled a cell phone out of the front pocket of her designer blazer and nodded. "I have to make a quick phone call, so I'll step outside and let you get a feel for the place on your own."

"Sure. Thank you."

The woman's heels clicked across the floor again, and she stepped out into the hallway, pulling the door closed behind her but leaving it cracked just a little. Her voice drifted into the loft as she made her call.

"Okay, Em. Thoughts on this one?" Cheyenne spread her arms and grinned.

"I really like it." Nodding, the fae glanced around the huge living room and wiggled her eyebrows. "Did you check out the other bedroom?"

"Pshh. A bedroom's a bedroom. They're all the same."

"Because what you're *really* into is that little private loft up there that I can't get to, huh?"

They shared a laugh, and Cheyenne smirked up at the private loft. "It'd be like giving Glen her own bedroom. I'm pretty sure my desk would fit up there too. Doesn't matter that it's up so high. The AC in this place would take care of the extra heat, no problem."

"If they had any more apartments left like this one."

"I'm not worried about it." Cheyenne stepped closer to her friend and leaned sideways to mutter, "She thinks I work for you."

"Are you serious?" Ember's mouth dropped open through her smile.

"She called you my employer."

"Oh, my God. And you didn't tell her that's not what's going on?"

The halfling pursed her lips, trying to keep another grin at bay. "Not yet."

"Jesus, Cheyenne. If anything, you're the one paying *me*."

"Ha. No. I'm renting *us* a new apartment. Don't expect an allowance or anything."

Ember threw her head back and cackled. The sound echoed jarringly through the apartment, and she covered her mouth with her hand. "This is crazy. You think we found the right one?"

"If you do."

"And you're sure that's... I mean, the rent on this place has to be six months of what I'm paying right now. That's cool?"

The halfling took a step back, folded her arms, and mocked the pinched, sour expression Caroline had given her. "I wasn't just throwing around the phrase 'inheritance' for no reason, Ms. Gaderow."

"You're right. I can't tell you what to do with it."

"Can't tell me what *not* to do with it, either." Cheyenne laughed. "This is the place we need. And *no* carpet. You rolled down to that master bedroom pretty damn fast, by the way. Spend a week in here, and you'll be faster than me."

Ember held up three fingers. "Three days, halfling. That's all I need to kick your ass into the—"

"Thank you for your patience, Ms. Gaderow." Caroline stepped through the open door, slipping her phone back into the pocket of her blazer. Her eyes were narrowed behind the green cat-eye frames. "Did you have a chance to think about the unit?"

"Yes, thank you." Ember grinned at the woman. "I really like it."

"Wonderful. Should we go take a look at the available units and schedule a convenient move-in date for you?"

"Absolutely." Ember lifted a finger into the air and wiggled it. "Come along, Cheyenne."

The halfling almost lost it right there, but she swallowed another laugh and grabbed the wheelchair's handles to push her friend toward the front door. *Okay, she caught on fast.*

Caroline waited for them to exit the apartment, then she closed the door behind her and locked it again. "I have no doubt we'll find the perfect unit for you, Ms. Gaderow."

"Oh, no doubt," Cheyenne replied in a lilting tone.

The woman ignored her and led them back down the hall toward the elevator. "As soon as we get back to the Guest Center, I'll pull up the available units so you can look at your options. The process is very quick and simple. You'll be moving into your new home in no time at all."

This time, when the elevator doors opened, Cheyenne turned the wheelchair around and pulled Ember backward. Ember clasped her hands in her lap and smiled sweetly up at their guide. "You had me sold at hardwood floors, Caroline."

CHAPTER FIFTY-TWO

Caroline left them in a private conference room in the Guest Center while she went to gather the paperwork for a new lease. Ember wheeled herself back from the table and scowled at it. "Didn't realize how high they made these things."

"We'll get you a lower table. Lower everything, if you want."

"That's a lot of work."

Cheyenne folded her arms, spinning back and forth in one of the black leather executive desk chairs around the table. "Not really. You just kind of point and click, and then someone else does the rest."

"Oh, yeah? You do a lot of online shopping?"

"Nope. But I'm sure I know someone who could take the lead on that one."

"Ha, ha." Ember shook her head, then froze. "Actually, we *would* still need somebody to handle all the moving and packing, right? And I'm not sticking a couch with a magically charred hole in it inside an apartment like that. Someone's gotta take care of making that place feel like we wanna live there, right?"

"Like you said, Em. I don't even have any furniture at my place. All this stuff is *way* over my head."

"Okay, I know what you're doing, and I appreciate it, but you can stop the whole clueless act." Ember laughed. "If you want me to do all that while you run around Richmond blowing up ogres and rescuing kidnapped kids, just say it."

Cheyenne spread her arms. "Doesn't matter what *I* want. If you're into it, I'm not gonna stop you."

"You're ridiculous."

"Thank you."

The conference room door opened swiftly, and in came Caroline with a thin stack of papers and two shiny, expensive-looking pens.

"Here we are, Ms. Gaderow. I'll need you to fill out all the information here. Your name, of course. Personal contact information, et cetera. Then you'll sign here and here, and this is where you provide your banking information. Account number and routing number. We use automatic withdrawal on the first of every month." After flipping through the paperwork, the woman sat on the other side of Ember and nodded. "We'll need the amount of two months' rent paid in full before you move in, plus an additional security deposit equal to half the monthly rental fee. Does that work for you?"

Ember placed her hand on the thin stack of papers and raised her eyebrows. "I guess so."

"Very good. Will you be paying by personal check, today, or... Oh! No, no. I'm sorry." Caroline's congenial cheeriness vanished when Ember slid the papers across the table toward Cheyenne. "Oh, I'm so sorry. I didn't think to ask if you needed assistance filling out the forms. I'll have to get us a new one, then, with room for an extra signature if you're not completing this paperwork yourself."

"No, this is fine." Cheyenne picked up one of the pens and started filling out the personal information on the front page.

"Excuse me, ma'am. I don't mean to be rude, but we do have a strict policy with our lease agreements. I'll just go get a different form, and we can start again. I'm sorry, Ms. Gaderow. I didn't even think—"

"Caroline?" Cheyenne looked slowly up from the papers and

shot the woman an understanding smile. "We don't need a different form. Does your system process debit cards?"

"Uh, yes, we do." The woman nervously licked her lips.

"Great. Then we'll go with that, and I'll be paying in cash today." The halfling turned her attention back to the paperwork and skimmed quickly over the contents.

Caroline slowly sank back down into the leather chair, her hands clasped in her lap as she stared at the Goth chick filling out the forms to become Pellerville Gables Apartments' newest resident. She glanced quickly from Cheyenne to Ember and back again, her lips moving without any sound.

Cheyenne filled out everything but left the signature lines blank. She tapped the pen on the conference table. "There's just one more detail, though, before we're finished." *Here we go. Now I'm channeling Bianca Summerlin.*

"I...we...yes?" Caroline stared at her like someone had pressed a gun against her back.

"I'd like to rent the unit you showed us today."

"Oh, I...we don't rent those, ma'am." The woman looked at Ember, but the fae girl just rolled her chair away from the table and smiled.

"Well, I'm sure we can make an exception, can't we?"

Caroline swallowed. "Not as far as I'm concerned."

"Okay." Cheyenne gave the woman a sharp, dismissive smile, her nose wrinkling, and set the pen down. "We'll try this another way, then."

When the halfling slid the completed paperwork back across the table toward Caroline, the woman pressed herself back in the executive chair, her eyes nearly popping out of her head.

Then Cheyenne stood and stepped toward the woman, tapping her pen on the top sheet of paper. "I know this is the apartment you've typed up, but I would really like to get into the one you showed us today. I have grown attached to that particular view."

Caroline cleared her throat, tried to speak, then cleared it again.

"I'm sorry, Ms...." The woman leaned stiffly forward over the papers to read Cheyenne's full name and almost choked. "Summerlin?"

"Cheyenne is fine."

The woman jumped up out of the chair and pressed a hand on the contract, her face flushing bright red as she blinked furiously. "Let me make some calls and see what I can do for you. If you don't mind waiting."

"I don't mind at all." Cheyenne grinned, and with another clearing of her throat, Caroline tried to nod before turning swiftly away and slipping right back out of the conference room again.

Ember slapped her hands down on the wheelchair's armrests. "What the hell was *that?*"

"That was me being a Summerlin."

The fae laughed and shook her head. "Lit a fire under her ass. Does that happen all the time?"

Cheyenne shrugged and dropped into the closest chair again. "Pretty much. Even when I'm not actively trying to use it for something, my name gets me the looks. It's super fun."

"I can't believe I've never seen you do that before."

"Actually, this is the first time I've pulled the Bianca's-daughter card like this. I don't need to use my last name as a crutch, but it *does* have its perks."

Ember let out a disbelieving snort and shook her head. "That's a serious understatement."

"But hey, she's *making calls.* That's gotta be worth something, right?"

"Not as much as throwing your name around, apparently. And she thought you *worked* for me!"

Ten minutes later, a tall, rail-thin man in a well-tailored business suit stepped into the conference room. "So sorry to keep you waiting, Ms. Summerlin."

Cheyenne stood to shake his outstretched hand, and the man

didn't flinch when she held his gaze and gave his fingers a squeeze with a little extra boost. *Like he's looking at Bianca instead of her Goth daughter. Here we go.* "Not a problem. Call me Cheyenne."

"Pleasure, Cheyenne. William Alban. Have a seat, please." He gestured toward the chair she'd been sitting in, then readjusted his suit jacket and took a seat. "It's not every day someone steps through those doors wanting to lease one of our show units."

"Well, it's not every day I find a show unit I like so much that I'll do what it takes to get it."

William chuckled and slid the paperwork toward him across the table, then removed a personal pen from the inside pocket of his suit jacket. "It's unit 301 in Building One you had your eye on, correct?"

"That's the one." As the man scratched out the unit number on the lease and initialed beside it, Cheyenne and Ember shared a knowing look.

"Very good. We shouldn't have a problem reallocating everything to a different unit to get you in as soon as possible. By Friday of next week, the place is yours." He looked at her with a small smile, like he'd been called in to handle something that should've been easy for Caroline to take care of. Which he had. "If you'll just initial beside where I've changed the unit number, you can sign the rest of this, and we'll get you that loft apartment."

Cheyenne sucked in a breath through her teeth and gave him an apologetic smile. "Friday's a little late for me."

"Oh. Well, when were you wanting to move in?"

"As soon as I sign this lease."

William laughed, but when Cheyenne didn't, he stopped immediately and cleared his throat. "Ms. Summerlin—"

"Cheyenne."

"Cheyenne, I'm sorry, but it's not possible to get that unit ready for you on such short notice. It's almost four o'clock on a Friday. At the earliest, we could have you in there Wednesday, maybe Tuesday."

The halfling took a deep breath and turned in the black-leather chair to face the man head-on. "Look, I'm not interested in waiting 'til next week, and I'm not interested in looking for any other apartment. That's the one I want. How much will it cost me to get that key in my hand right now?"

"Uh, well, I..." William scratched his temple and cleared his throat again. "I'm not sure we can get a moving crew in there to clear the place out on time—"

"So, it's the cost of replacing all the furniture and everything already in that apartment? That works for me." The halfling grinned, nodding slowly as the man processed what she was saying. *Come on, William. You'll get there.*

"Furnished? You want the unit as is?"

"Yes, I do."

"Well." He tugged his tie, then slapped a hand on the conference table and stood. "I'll go draw up an itemized bill, then. Should only take me about half an hour."

Cheyenne rose to her feet beside him and reached into the incredibly deep pocket of her baggy black pants to pull out her wallet. "Don't bother, William. I'll just give you my card, and you charge it for the total price you think is fair for everything in that apartment, plus the initial up-front cost as usual. Two months and a security deposit, right?" She pulled out the debit card linked to her inheritance and handed it to him.

The man blinked at it in surprise and swallowed thickly. "Ms. Summerlin, I don't know the exact cost of that furnished apartment off the top of my head."

They always forget my first name. "Don't worry about it. Use your best estimate. I trust you to come up with a number that's good for both of us."

She'd heard that line from her mother's mouth so many times, she knew exactly what it meant. So did William Alban. Not quite a threat and not quite a warning. *Don't even think about taking advantage of me. I know who you are, and you know who I am.*

"Of course, Ms. Summerlin." William dipped his head. "I'll be right back."

"Thank you."

The man turned and slipped out of the room just like Caroline had, and Cheyenne sighed. "I don't know how she does it."

"Are you kidding me? You just tore down the guy's defenses in less than five minutes." Ember wheeled around to stare at the door. "That was incredible."

"Yeah. Works like a charm." The halfling frowned. "A super-draining charm that takes a lot more mental energy than I realized until right now."

"Your mom taught you that."

"More like I watched and learned for eighteen years." Sitting back down again, Cheyenne dropped her forearms onto the chair's armrests and spun back and forth some more. "Always new meanings to the things she *did* tell me, though. Everything comes with a price."

"Kind of a big one for this apartment, huh?"

Cheyenne smirked. "I'm not even a little worried about the money, Em. That's not what she meant."

"Huh." Ember licked her lips and tried to put the pieces together. "So, you're talking about the price of being your mom for twenty minutes? Wearing you out like that, and almost giving Caroline and William Alban a heart attack."

"Sure, that counts." The halfling blinked at her friend and cocked her head. "That and by the end of next week, everyone who works here is gonna know Bianca Summerlin's daughter just moved in."

"Oh." Blinking slowly, Ember studied the edge of the conference table and let out a wry chuckle. "Well, you did say you were done hiding, right?"

"Yeah, thanks."

CHAPTER FIFTY-THREE

"I can't believe you did this." Ember wheeled herself farther into their new apartment and laughed. "For real."

"For real." Cheyenne jingled the two keys on individual keyrings and handed Ember one. "Don't lose that."

"Please."

"Okay." The halfling rubbed her hands together and looked at their new digs. "New car. New apartment. Change of lifestyle. This might be worth it."

"Yeah, now we just gotta keep those bull's-head idiots from breaking into the place and blowing up the Panamera, and we're golden."

Cheyenne laughed and spun around. "I'll handle that part, Em. You wanna call around and find some movers?"

"To move *what*? The only things I want out of my apartment are my clothes and my laptop. Probably that plant, too."

The halfling clicked her tongue and frowned in mock pity. "Can't leave the plant."

"Hey, at least it's alive. Seriously, most of my stuff is still packed in the bags you brought to the hospital. I don't think we need movers."

"Okay. Decorating, then. If you're up for it." Pulling out her wallet one more time, Cheyenne handed her debit card to her new roommate. "Seriously. Whatever you think is gonna look good in here. I trust you. Just no more of this white and silver and hardwood. Kinda makes it feel like we're standing in a glass box."

"I think that's the point."

"I think I prefer a Goth box."

They both laughed, and Ember stared at Cheyenne's debit card, shaking her head. "If you really want me to do this, I'll do it. But it'll be tasteful, got it? Don't expect me to go full Goth on this apartment."

"Ha, ha. I'll handle that part too. So. You think you'll be okay in this awesome new spot by yourself for a couple of hours?"

"Where are you racing off to now?"

"Just to go shove all my clothes into a trash bag and pack up Glen. My computer, Em. Server, tower, monitors, all that stuff?"

"I had no idea Glen was so multi-faceted."

Cheyenne pointed at her friend and grinned. "That's exactly what she is. All the different pieces working together to make magic. Which, actually, doesn't mix well with real magic. I found that out through personal experience."

Ember snorted and pushed herself closer to the wall of windows to get a better view. "Well, I've got a fully charged phone and the internet and Ms. Summerlin's debit card—"

"Ah! Everybody and the Ms. Summerlin spiel. *Et tu*, Brute?"

"So, if I need you for anything, which I probably won't since we already grabbed dinner, I guess you're off the hook for a few hours."

"Oh, *thank you*, Ms. Gaderow. You're so generous." Cheyenne spun around, spread her arms, and bent in a sweeping, exaggerated bow.

"Yeah, yeah. You can bow down before me when you get back." Ember waved the halfling off and chuckled as she started the process of making a fully furnished apartment feel more like they lived there.

"Seriously, call me about anything. Even if, I don't know, you need snacks or something."

"Oh, so only for emergencies. Got it. Bye." The fae wiggled her fingers, and Cheyenne spun back around with a snort before stepping out of their new apartment and into the hallway.

She locked the door behind her and paused. *That's a good habit to keep. Especially if she's in there by herself.*

Nodding, Cheyenne headed down the hall and smirked when she pressed the elevator call button. "So much better than stairs."

She got back to her old, crappy apartment half an hour later, chuckling to herself as she unlocked the front door. *This place was a dump even without comparing it to Pellerville Gables Apartments. Maybe now Mom will come down for a visit.*

That thought made her stop, and she blinked as the image of Bianca Summerlin heading into Richmond for the day entered her mind. "Not a chance." She laughed and shoved open the door.

Most of her clothes were still in the dryer, which made shoving them into a giant trash bag that much easier. Then she went through her closet and the bathroom, sweeping random things into the bag until it felt full enough. Cheyenne dropped the trash bag by the front door and got to work disassembling her desktop setup. *I didn't think I'd be moving again for a while, but at least I made it easy on myself.*

She found an empty shoebox in the front closet and stacked all the cords and cables into it, then broke Glen down as much as possible without compromising any of the larger tech pieces. She stood back and surveyed the scattered parts and shook her head. "Gonna take a few trips. Trash bag first."

Once she was sure the black plastic bag wouldn't rip open the way she'd slung it over her shoulder, Cheyenne stepped out into the hall again and walked toward the staircase. *I feel like Goth Santa right now.*

The door three apartments down from hers opened, and R'mahr stuck out his head. "Cheyenne! Hello! I was just about to come knock on your door and ask if you…" The troll's gaze fell on the huge black sack bouncing against the back of the halfling's legs, and his eyes widened in concern. "What's that?"

"Some things I'm taking…somewhere else." She smiled and watched the guy's excitement melt into confused sadness. *Oh, man. He's gonna take this personally no matter what I say.* "How you doin' today, R'mahr?"

"Are you…are you moving?"

"*What?*" Yadje stomped across their apartment before squeezing into the doorway beside her husband. "Why would you even suggest a fool thing like that, you—" When the troll woman caught sight of the halfling's black bag, her wide scarlet eyes took on the same level of deep hurt. "That's an awfully large bag."

"Yeah, I'm just taking a few things out to my car."

"You know, Cheyenne, if you're moving out of your apartment, you could have asked us for help." Yadje glanced over her shoulder at their young daughter curled up on the couch with another book. "Bryl is exceptionally talented at organizing. We would have helped you pack in a heartbeat."

"We would have?" R'mahr shot his wife a dumbfounded look.

"Oh, don't let your mouth hang open like that. You look like my Uncle Danriz." Clicking her tongue, Yadje stepped into the hallway and waved toward Cheyenne's trash bag. "We can help you *now*, at least. And then we'll be out of your hair when you're out of the building."

"Oh, no." Fighting back a laugh, the halfling dropped her bag onto the floor. "I'm not moving out, okay? I'll still be around."

"Then what's that?" R'mahr stared at the bag.

"Just a few things I'm taking with me. I found a new office on the other side of town. You know, like one of those co-working spaces." *Wow. Lies just rolling off the tongue.*

"You got an office job?" Yadje frowned. "That doesn't seem like you."

"No, it's…okay." Cheyenne scratched her head, her wrist chains clinking as they slid down her arm. "Space for me to do what I'm already doing, only not in my apartment."

The corners of R'mahr's mouth turned down in confusion. "Why would you do that?"

"I don't know. I read something about how unhealthy it is to stay in your house all the time, so I figured I'd try this out."

The troll man's laugh didn't sound convinced or amused. "Cheyenne, you're gone most of the time. We can see your car right outside our window."

"Oh, you can, huh?" *Trolls keeping an eye on me too. I know they mean well, but it's time to get out.* "Did you see it blow up yesterday?"

"That was *your* car?" Husband and wife gawked at her, then glanced at each other. "Who would want to blow up your car?"

"That's so far beyond me right now, R'mahr, I can't even pretend to come up with an answer."

"That's awful, Cheyenne." Yadje clasped her hands in front of her chest and slowly shook her head. "Are you okay?"

"Oh, yeah. I'm fine, thanks. Listen, I didn't mean to worry you guys. If I were actually moving out, of course I would've said something." *Not technically a lie.* "I'm just rearranging things and trying to keep everything running smoothly, you know?"

Yadje raised an eyebrow, her scarlet eyes narrowing as she lifted her chin toward the Drow halfling. "It's a good thing to strive for improvement."

Yeah, she's calling bullshit. "Right. That's what I'm doing, Yadje. Striving for improvement. Just had to make some changes."

"So, you'll be home even less than you are now?" R'mahr asked, barely noticing when his wife elbowed him in the ribs.

"Probably, yeah. But like I said, I'll still be around. You guys can't get rid of me that easily." Cheyenne pointed at the troll couple and chuckled, but they gave her thin, wan smiles in return. "Oh, by the way, I'm thinking about going to Peridosh tomorrow to grab whatever I missed last time. I know you normally head out there on Wednesdays, but do you wanna come with me tomorrow?"

Bryl's book thumped onto the floor, and the troll girl leaped off the couch to run toward her parents standing in the doorway. "Yes! Yes! Yes! Maji, can we go with her tomorrow? Please?"

The halfling fought back a laugh as the kid tugged on her mother's sleeve, a huge grin across her violet-colored cheeks.

Yadje deftly removed her daughter's fingers to hold Bryl's hand instead and shot her husband a sidelong glance. "What do you think, R'mahr?"

"Oh, *please?*" Bryl whined. "I *have* to have that calver fin to finish my Lightless Pike. And I want to go with Cheyenne. I can show her everything!"

"Hmm." R'mahr glanced slowly at Cheyenne and winked. "If your maji says she wants to go, we will go."

"Well, I can't possibly say no *now*, can I?" Yadje stared at her husband and raised a thin scarlet eyebrow.

He chuckled and shrugged. "I leave it entirely up to you."

The troll woman patted her daughter's hand, glanced at the ceiling, and couldn't keep a straight face any longer. "Yes, my love. If Cheyenne wants some company at Peridosh tomorrow, we'll go with her."

Bryl squeezed herself between her parents, her narrow shoulders bumping their hips. She didn't say a word but slowly raised clenched fists, her eyes wide and hopeful and bursting with excitement.

"Oh, kid, you're killing me." Cheyenne laughed. "Nobody could say no to a face like that."

"Yes! Yes! We're going, we're going, we're going!" Bryl jumped up and down in the doorway, knocking her parents against the doorframe and each other.

The troll couple laughed weakly and shared a look that made Cheyenne think the kid would be bouncing like this for the rest of the night. *Can't win 'em all, I guess.*

"There you have it then, Cheyenne." Yadje smiled and nodded once. "We'll join you tomorrow."

"Awesome. You guys know where the entrance is in Union Hill, right?" They nodded, and Cheyenne picked up her trash bag to sling it over her shoulder again. "Great. Meet you there at two?"

"An excellent time. Yes." R'mahr nodded vigorously, his usual enthusiasm back. "We'll see you there tomorrow."

"Okay. Cool. I'll be making trips back and forth to my car. In case it sounds a lot busier up here than usual, that's what's going on."

"Are you sure you don't want any help?"

The halfling nodded, smiling as she took off toward the stairwell again. "I'm sure. Thanks anyway. Looking forward to tomorrow."

"Yes, so are we!" R'mahr leaned out into the hall and pumped a fist in the air. Snorting, his wife grabbed his arm and pulled him back into their apartment before quickly shutting the door. Her muffled voice followed Cheyenne until she started down the stairs and the door to the stairwell closed behind her.

She focused on her footing with the relatively heavy bag bumping awkwardly against her back. *If they don't know where I am, that'll keep them safe too. A price for everything, huh?*

CHAPTER FIFTY-FOUR

On her sixth trip down to her car, Cheyenne finally had her clothes and all the pieces of Glen secured snugly in the trunk and the back seat of her Panamera. She dusted off her hands and turned to look up at the building she'd called home for the last few years. *I could break the lease if I wanted. Better to keep the place as a decoy. For now, at least.*

She got into the driver's seat, started the car, and flexed her fingers around the steering wheel. "I'm not gonna miss this place even a little."

Grinning, she pulled out of the parking lot and headed toward her fancy new apartment with an actual roommate, bringing everything she needed with her in the back of her fancy new car.

"Okay, I realize I already used the 'Honey, I'm home line,' so this time, I'll just go with—woah." Cheyenne turned around from closing the apartment door and found Ember sitting in her wheelchair in the center of the living room, surrounded by at least a dozen large boxes. "You went nuts on the online shopping, huh?"

"Did you know there are people out there who will pick your stuff up from any store in the area and bring it *to* you?" Ember grinned and swept an arm across the expanse of box-filled living room. "Like, it's their business."

"For anyone who wants it?"

"Yeah, I guess. I didn't think to ask." Ember laughed. "I mean, I'm not gonna make a bunch of phone calls like, 'Hi, I'm Ember. I'm in a wheelchair. Can you do this stuff for me?'"

Cheyenne bit her bottom lip and swerved around the closest stack of boxes. "Obviously, you don't have to."

"I know, right? Guess we have a lot of unpacking to do tomorrow anyway."

"Uh…" Cheyenne walked toward the kitchen island and showed her friend the pint of Ben & Jerry's she'd picked up before setting it down on the granite countertop. "About tomorrow."

"What happened now?" Ember wheeled herself down the aisle between boxes and went searching through the kitchen drawers.

"Nothing crazy. I told you about my troll-family neighbors, right? Well, ex-neighbors, I guess."

"Yeah, the underwear crafters." Ember snorted. "Holy shit. When they said fully furnished, they really meant fully." She closed the drawer and held up two spoons. "Silverware and everything."

"Look at that." The halfling stepped around the island to take the offered spoon, then opened the pint of ice cream and handed it over. "So, my troll friends have been trying to get me to go to Peridosh with them for a while, and I have to get over there soon anyway to pick up a bunch of ingredients I've never heard of for spells I don't entirely trust."

"Huh." Ember dug out a second huge spoonful of ice cream and passed the pint. "Sounds exciting."

"Yeah, maybe. I invited them to come with me tomorrow after lunch."

"Oh, *man*. You know, I've been in Richmond for, what? A little over four years? I've always wanted to go down there to see what it's like."

"So, come with us." Cheyenne shrugged and braved the chance of brain freeze with a giant bite of ice cream.

"You know, you're normally full of awesome ideas, Cheyenne." Ember snatched the pint out of her friend's hand. "But that's not one of them."

The halfling chuckled. "Why not?"

"First of all, I have zero magic." Ember took another bite, then shook her spoon at her friend and talked around the mouthful. "So, if we ran into any kind of trouble, I wouldn't be very useful. Forget the whole wheelchair thing."

"I was in a bar fight with five giant idiots the other night. By myself." Cheyenne folded her arms and leaned against the counter. "Not an issue if you don't have any magic to protect me."

"Okay, but I didn't start with the most important reason, did I?" The fae shoveled more ice cream into her mouth and handed back the pint. "I can't go because I look like a human, Cheyenne. Useful for keeping my magical-without-magic identity a secret, for sure. Not so great in a place where any human who steps inside *probably* isn't stepping back out again."

Cheyenne blinked. "Huh. I hadn't thought about that."

"Yeah, I know. You've been trying to keep your drow side a secret. Well, I've been trying to keep my magicless side a secret too. Which is every side. I can get by out in the open and call it an illusion spell. Plus, I've been told that fae have a pretty distinct smell, so I guess that's still going for me."

The halfling almost sprayed ice cream all over the counter when she laughed, then quickly handed the ice cream to her friend so she could focus. "A *smell?*"

"Yeah. A fae smell. I don't know."

"I never picked up on that. And the whole thing about drow having a seriously intense sense of smell is true."

Ember shrugged. "Maybe it's 'cause you didn't know I was fae 'til, like, last week. And you just thought it was me."

"We can stop talking about your fae scent any time now."

Laughing, Ember spread her arms. A glob of ice cream dripped off her spoon, but she didn't notice. "I'm just laying it out for you, Cheyenne. Unless there's a way for me to *look* fae, I can't go down there."

Cheyenne frowned with another bite of ice cream raised halfway to her mouth. "Maybe there is."

"I don't mean face paint, Goth girl."

"Very funny." The halfling stuck the spoon in her mouth. "I'm talking about illusion spells. It's not like they're human-illusion specific. I bet we could figure out how to cast a charm that makes you look as fae on the outside as you are on the inside."

"What you see is what you get, halfling."

"That's *my* line, by the way."

Ember laughed. "I'm pretty sure it belongs to everyone."

"Yeah, but I've been saying it a lot longer than you."

"You don't know."

With a snort, Cheyenne glanced into the almost empty pint in her friend's lap and turned to stick her spoon in the dishwasher. "Man. Nice kitchen, huh?"

"Yeah, I really picked a winner." Ember finished the rest of the ice cream, then rolled backward away from the island to search the rest of the kitchen. "So *that's* how you know it's just a demo apartment. No trashcan."

"Huh. You found the weak link."

"Didn't I just? All right. First empty box is our temporary trash can, I guess." The fae stuck the container on the counter, and Cheyenne took the spoon from her before the girl had a chance to wheel herself across the kitchen. "I can put a spoon in the dishwasher, Cheyenne."

"I know."

"Okay, so you'll be gone tomorrow on your awesome adventure at Peridosh with a family of trolls, and I'll just..." Licking her lips, Ember pulled something up on her phone and grinned. "How do you feel about me having someone come over to help put everything away?"

"Like who?" *Better not be Trevor or any of those other cowards.*

"There's a company that brings boxes from the store to our front door. If I had an extra hundred bucks, I'd bet you there's a company specifically for people who need help rolling out rugs and hanging curtains."

Cheyenne glanced at the huge wall of windows. "Please tell me you didn't order curtains for the entire wall."

"No, just my bedroom. I like curtains."

"Sure. Hire someone to help you with curtains."

"Oh, I will. And it'll be awesome."

"Whoa. Settle down, fae girl." With a short laugh, Cheyenne headed back across the apartment toward the door. "I'm gonna go bring up all our stuff from the car. Probably make a couple trips again. I'm really loving the elevator in this place, lemme tell ya."

"No problem. I'll be here." Ember nodded as the halfling stepped out of the apartment and closed the door behind her. Then she grinned and wheeled herself back into the living room to eye all the boxes of things she'd ordered in the last few hours. *Physical therapy's gonna be great. Dr. Andrews should've stuck retail therapy on the list too.*

The magicless fae and the drow halfling settled down in front of the coffee table an hour and a half later, with Netflix pulled up on Cheyenne's laptop. "And you're in the mood for…"

Ember shrugged and finished her third bottle of water. "Whatever. I don't even care that it's on your laptop. This is a million times better than the ridiculously awful selection of channels at the hospital."

"You'd think having more entertainment options would help people recover, huh?"

"Right? I guess they don't want their patients distracted from the hard work of lying there and getting better."

"Well, you're done with that. Roomie." Cheyenne snorted when her friend stared at the laptop screen and shook her head. "I'll grab your TV tomorrow if you want. Hook up the surround sound. It'll be very different in here."

"What about your desk?"

Both girls glanced at the narrow iron staircase up to the mini loft above the laundry room. "Yeah, I didn't think about trying to get that thing up those stairs."

"Even with super drow strength?"

"Sure, if I wanted to throw the whole desk up there and hope it landed perfectly without breaking anything."

Ember laughed so hard, she choked on nothing and had to cough. "I'd love to see that. *Not* in this apartment, but I'd still love to see it."

"Next time we find someone else's apartment where a desk needs to get upstairs like that, I'll make sure to let you know. I guess the showroom furniture already up there will have to be good enough for Glen. For now. She's like me, though—adaptable and nearly indestructible and can do what she does from just about anywhere."

"As long as there's an internet connection."

"Okay, that's only half-accurate."

"I get it. Just play something on the damn laptop already so I can turn my brain off and zone in on someone else's story for a minute."

CHAPTER FIFTY-FIVE

The next morning, Cheyenne went out to grab them breakfast sandwiches and lattes from some bakery trying to play off upscale chic two blocks away. By the time she got back to the apartment, three huge guys in matching shirts walked out her front door.

"Uh, can I help you?"

"We got it, but thanks." The tallest guy with both arms covered in tattoos gave her a friendly smile and a nod, then the guys headed down the hall toward the elevators. "Em?"

"Yeah!"

She found her fae friend leaning over an open box on the floor, pulling out the wrapping of whatever she'd bought. *She's gonna fall out of that chair.* Cheyenne turned around and grabbed the door.

"Oh, hey. Leave that open."

"Enlighten me as to why, exactly?"

Ember looked up and laughed. "I ordered more stuff. And I'm pretty sure I can get those guys to help me with the curtains when they bring up the next couple boxes."

"Em, it's not even nine-thirty in the morning."

"Yeah, I'm getting a head start."

Stepping over opened boxes and loose pieces of packaging,

Cheyenne made it safely to the coffee table to set down their breakfast and coffee. She almost fell on her face when her next step was jerked back by packing tape stuck to both the area rug and the bottom of her shoe. "I feel like I'm walking on a minefield."

"Sorry." Ember chuckled and wadded up the loose piece of packing paper. "You know what I need? One of those claws on a stick."

"A trash grabber?"

"Exactly! Trust me, I've already figured out how far I can bend down in this chair, and it's not all the way to the floor. I should order one."

Cheyenne stared at her friend, then she hooked her fingers into claws and roared, throwing her head back. "I've created a monster!"

Ember jumped in her chair, barked a laugh, and threw the balled-up paper at the halfling's face.

"It's destroying the apartment and taking my sanity with it!" Cheyenne stomped around, her voice bouncing off the wall of windows and the hardwood floors.

"I'll destroy *you*." Ember laughed when the halfling snarled in her face, shaking her head with her tongue hanging out. "Seriously, what the hell are you doing?"

"Ahh! Raaawwwrrrrrr—"

Someone cleared their throat in the doorway, and Cheyenne shut her mouth before slowly turning to see who was there.

"I hope I'm not interrupting." A tall man in his early thirties stood outside the open door, his hands thrust into the pockets of his jeans.

The halfling stayed in her crouch, hovering over Ember's chair with her monster claws. "Kinda."

"Shut up." Ember smacked her friend's arm, and Cheyenne chuckled before giving up the act. "Sorry. There've been a lot of people in and out of here already this morning. Remind me who you are?"

"Well, we haven't met yet, so don't feel bad if you don't remember me." With a lazy, crooked smile, the man ducked his head to peer around the apartment and raised his eyebrows. "I thought they used this apartment for showings?"

"Not anymore." Cheyenne spread her arms and crunched across a pile of bubble wrap toward the front door. "You have your eye on this place or something?"

"No." He glanced at her briefly, still smiling, and bent through the doorway to look up at the bottom of the mini loft. "I live across the hall. Seemed a little weird to have so many people stomping up and down, and the curiosity finally got me." The man pointed to the loft. "You know, I really wanted one of those."

Cheyenne snorted. "Yeah, me too."

"How'd you pull *that* off?"

"Oh, you know. Just negotiated a good deal."

Nodding, he straightened again and stayed put in the hall. "Well done."

"Thank you. I'd stick your name on the end of that, but you haven't given it yet."

The man blinked quickly and finally looked at her for the first time. Then he stuck out his hand. "Matthew Thomas."

"Hey, Matthew Thomas, neighbor across the hall." The halfling grabbed his hand with her usual firm grip, which made his smile grow wider. "Cheyenne."

"I'm assuming you have a last name."

"Yep." She raised her eyebrows and stepped aside to gesture toward Ember. "This is—oh, crap."

Ember had gotten the wheels of her chair tied up in loose strips of packing tape, and her struggle to push free had made it worse. Cheyenne jogged across the room and bent to rip off the tape before muttering, "You should've said something."

"Yeah?" Ember gritted her teeth and added in a harsh whisper, "I should've shouted across the room, 'Someone help me. I'm stuck in a wad of tape and can't free myself'?"

"Sorry." Cheyenne crumbled the tape into a tight ball and tossed it on the kitchen island. Then she straightened and nodded at Matthew Thomas standing in their doorway. "This is—"

"Ember. Hi." The fae wheeled back to chart a new course around the scattered boxes and packing trash. Cheyenne hurried in front of her to kick as much as she could out of the way.

"Hey, don't worry about braving the wreckage," Matthew said. "I helped my sister move recently. I totally get the chaos. Mind if I come in?"

"Enter at your own risk, but sure."

Ember shot Cheyenne a warning glance, and the halfling shrugged in reply. *What crawled in* her *lap?*

"Yeah, I don't envy anyone the—" Matthew grunted as he stepped over a stack of boxes, then side-stepped to avoid more piles of bubble wrap. "Dangers of unpacking." He finally reached Ember in the center of the living room and stuck out his hand. "Matthew."

The fae's eyes narrowed as she reached up to shake their neighbor's hand. "Nice to meet you."

"You too, Ember."

Cheyenne glanced at them and stuck her hands in her pockets. *That's a pretty long handshake.*

Matthew cleared his throat, their little moment ended, and he released her hand. Ember tucked her hair behind her ear and kept smiling, though a small frown creased her brow.

"Well." He chuckled. "I guess I should be welcoming you to the neighborhood, huh?"

"Thanks." Ember stuck her hands on the wheels again and rolled back a little. "Just got here yesterday, so everything's still...well, I guess it's obvious."

"Happens to the best of us."

Look at that grin-fest. I can't sit through this conversation. Cheyenne pulled her hands out of her pockets and clapped. Matthew and Ember both jumped and slowly turned toward her. "So, Matt. What do you do?"

"Matthew, actually. I'm a dabbler by trade."

Ember chuckled. "I didn't know dabbling *was* a trade."

"Well, if you're good at what you do, you can turn almost

anything into a business." He shot the fae girl a winning smile, his eyes crinkling at the corners.

"Sounds pretty exciting." She grinned right back.

Cheyenne blinked. *Not.*

"Sometimes, sure." Matthew-not-Matt shrugged and took a slow, lazy step closer to Ember's wheelchair. "Most of the time, I still feel like there's something missing, you know? Like it's right there in front of me, and I can't quite reach it."

Ember and Matthew kept staring at each other.

Oh, for Christ's sake. Cheyenne turned away and brought her fist to her mouth to fake a cough.

Their neighbor took a sharp breath and glanced around the apartment again. "So, I just keep looking. And dabbling, while I'm at it."

"Well, whatever it is, go get 'em." Cheyenne pumped her fist in front of her with a sharp nod.

"Yeah, okay. Thanks." Matthew chuckled a little and stepped back again, glancing at his newest neighbors. "What about you ladies? What do you do?"

Ember glanced up at Cheyenne and tilted her head. "Uh, we're grad students, actually."

"Really?"

"Yep. I'm on a little...hiatus, I guess. The university was pretty understanding about the whole thing and told me to take as long as I need. You know, recovery-wise." The fae swallowed thickly and plastered on a different kind of smile.

"I'm sorry." Matthew's eyebrows flicked together.

"Don't be. It's not your fault." Ember shrugged. "So, I'm just moving into a new apartment with Cheyenne and ordering a bunch of crap in boxes from a wheelchair. Hopefully, that doesn't last too long."

The man quickly gave a self-conscious smile. "I'll cross my fingers for you."

"How nice." Cheyenne grinned so wide, her cheeks hurt. *Watching this is a whole new level of torture.*

Ignoring her, Matthew nodded at Ember's wheelchair. "How long will you be...recovering?"

The halfling bit her bottom lip, and this time, the glance Ember shot her had the same thought written all over it. *This guy's pushing it with the questions.*

"I'm, uh, not sure." Ember blinked and stared at the wall behind him.

"Well, if you need any referrals, I know one of the best physical therapists in the state."

"She's got it covered, man. Thanks." Cheyenne nodded.

"Yeah, I appreciate it anyway." Ember drummed her fingers on the armrests of her wheelchair. "Starting PT on Monday, actually, so you can cross your fingers for that too."

"Oh, man." Matthew's airy chuckle was a lot more self-conscious. "I'm sorry. I didn't mean to overstep. That's none of my business."

Damn straight. Cheyenne glanced from the guy's sheepish smile to the open door behind him. *Take the hint, guy.*

"No, it's okay. I need to figure out how to have this conversation sometime, right?" Ember tucked her hair behind her ear again. "Still figuring out how all this works. This thing especially." She slapped her palms on the armrests and shrugged.

Matthew nodded and stepped toward the door. "I'll, uh, let you guys get back to it, then. Nice to meet you, Ember."

"You too."

He nodded at the halfling. "Cheyenne."

"Matthew."

He spun slowly on one foot, reached the open front door, and turned halfway back around again to catch Ember's gaze. "Just, for what it's worth, it looks like you've already figured out how it all works. At least from where I'm standing." He didn't quite wink at her, but his eye twitched as if he'd wanted to but realized it was a bad idea. Then their odd new dabbling neighbor stepped quickly across the hall.

Another door opened and closed in quick succession, and

Cheyenne walked swiftly to their front door to close it. "What a guy, huh?"

Ember burst out laughing and buried her face in her hands. Her voice came out high-pitched and muffled. "That was *awful*."

"Who gets up in people's personal business like that? I mean, seriously?"

"I think he was just trying to be nice, Cheyenne."

"I think he was just trying to get you hooked on that smile before he grabbed those handlebars and wheeled you right out of here."

"Oh, please. That's not what he was trying to do."

Cheyenne leaned back against the kitchen island, propping her forearms behind her on the granite countertop. "Oh, yes, it was. I stood right there and watched the whole thing. He's super into you."

"That doesn't make sense." Ember laughed again and smoothed her hair away from her forehead. "'It looks like I've already figured out how it all works?' Seriously?"

"At least from where *he's* standing. Don't forget that little nugget." The halfling stared at the door and shook her head.

"Like he was surprised that I haven't been in a wheelchair my whole life. *What?* I don't even know if I should be insulted or flattered by that." Ember glanced down at her lap and wrinkled her nose.

"Uh, maybe don't be anything?" When her friend looked at the closed door and started blushing, Cheyenne stepped away from the island toward her. "You okay?"

"I have no idea." The fae looked disbelieving. "That was the weirdest conversational Tetris I've ever had to play."

"That's a perfect analogy, Em."

"I mean, I can't just come out and say, 'Hey, I just got shot and lost the use of my legs a little over two weeks ago. Not looking to date someone right now, so kindly back off.'"

The apartment fell silent as Ember's words settled between them.

Don't laugh. Don't laugh.

Cheyenne snorted.

"It's not *funny*." Ember went through the motion of throwing something at her half-drow friend, but her hand was empty.

"It's kinda funny. Maybe you should've just said *that*."

"I can't say that out loud to someone!"

The halfling's mouth popped open, and she gasped. "Or *maybe* our new neighbor Matthew Thomas is just into chicks in wheelchairs."

"Stop."

"That might be it, Em. He *did* seem kind of disappointed when you said this whole thing was only temporary."

"Oh, my God." Ember buried her face in her hands again. "I can't tell if that's better or worse."

Cheyenne laughed and approached her friend. "Apparently, it doesn't matter. He's still into you hardcore."

"*Cheyenne.*"

"I don't have a drow's sixth sense for nothing."

A low, rhythmic buzz filled the apartment. The girls glanced around for the source of it, then the halfling's gaze fell on her backpack on the corner of the gray suede couch.

"Dammit. Right now?" She stalked toward the couch and jerked open the zipper on the front pocket.

"What's going on?" Ember chuckled again, her blush fading now. Her smile faded too when she saw the halfling's scowl.

"Fucking FRoE burner phone." Cheyenne lifted it toward her friend, her lower jaw jutting out in irritation. "Those guys have a perfect track record for shitty timing."

Ember stared at the clunky flip phone. "You gonna answer it?"

With a frustrated growl, Cheyenne cocked her head. "Well, now you get to watch me in action, huh?"

CHAPTER FIFTY-SIX

Cheyenne whipped open the burner phone and almost slammed it against her ear. "Yeah."

"Halfling." Major Sir Carson's voice was low, scratchy, and almost hesitant.

He's pissed about something and is calling me in as Plan B. Again.

She waited for him to start spouting commands at her as usual, and couldn't help herself when he didn't. "I'm assuming you called me for a reason. I'm waiting."

"You need to get your ass down to the compound stat. We got a problem."

"You don't say?"

Sir cleared his throat. "I can taste your sarcasm, kid. Not my favorite flavor."

Cheyenne frowned. "Yeah, well, I don't like the taste of you dragging out this call and not giving me a reason for dropping everything for you on a Saturday morning."

Muttered words were exchanged on the other end of the line, followed by a short, "Dammit." The line crackled, and Sir's voice came back loud and clear. "Sheila's got fifty-nine out of the sixty kidnapped chicklets back to their parents. The last one won't tell us a goddamn thing."

"You *still* have one of them with you?" The heat of the halfling's drow magic would have been tingling up her spine by now if she wasn't wearing that damn pendant.

"I don't want her here any more than you do. Since you're the kid-whisperer, get down here and help us put this last one back where she belongs. Right now, halfling."

Cheyenne hung up on him and flipped the phone shut. "What the hell are they doing?"

"I'm guessing that wasn't a congratulatory phone call with a side of thank you." Ember watched her friend with a concerned frown.

"I've only gotten one of those. Kinda." The halfling shook her head. "I have to go, Em. Apparently, all the gear and fancy fell weapons fall short of getting one last kid back to her family."

"The ones you rescued?" Ember wheeled across the living room, jerkily swerving around opened boxes and cluttered packing material.

"Yeah. Shit, if they'd just *listened* to me from the beginning, she'd be home right now with all the others." Cheyenne snatched up her black hoody and jerked it over her head. Then she grabbed both phones, her keyless fob, and her wallet and shoved them into various pants pockets. "Two days. *Two.* That kid has to be freaking out by now."

"Anything I can do?" Ember shot her a hesitant smile.

"Just hang tight, Em. Apparently, I'm the only one who can do anything about it." The halfling blinked and glanced around their apartment. "Sorry to have to skip outta here like this."

"Shut up. There's a kid locked up with a bunch of assholes in black and a magical family somewhere who's worried sick." The fae girl shrugged. "I can handle being by myself for a few hours."

"Okay. I have my phone, so if you need anything—"

"She's a kid, Cheyenne. I'm just in a wheelchair. I can hold down the fort."

With a wry chuckle, the halfling headed toward the door and

turned around to point at her roomie. "I know you can, Em. Even if Matthew Thomas comes knocking on the door again. You have all this figured out, right?"

"Don't make me push you out of here. With me in it, this chair packs a punch."

Laughing, Cheyenne opened the door and slipped out into the hall. "I won't be gone too long."

"'Kay, bye."

The door shut behind her, and Cheyenne jerked down the bottom of her hoody as she headed toward the elevator. *If Sir hasn't ripped Rhynehart a new one for leaving me behind, I am sure as hell about to.*

Her first drive out to the FRoE compound on her own was as easy as if she'd made it a hundred times. When Cheyenne turned onto the unmarked frontage road and saw the gate towers ahead, she smirked. "Drow sense of direction plus Bianca Summerlin's uncanny memory equals a halfling who never forgets. I'll have to thank her for that."

The Panamera rolled into the huge parking lot filled with FRoE utility vehicles, vans, and Rhynehart's Jeep, all of them black and glistening, just like Cheyenne's new ride. Spotting Sir's bright-orange Kia was easy enough.

A laugh escaped her when she recognized Sir's shitty parking job. The Rio sat diagonally behind Rhynehart's Jeep like the man had followed his second in command in a hurry and hadn't bothered to fall neatly in line with the rest of the vehicles. "It's like he set me up for this."

Cheyenne drove around the end of the lined-up vehicles and brought the Panamera in behind Rhynehart's Jeep. She stared at the shiny back bumper just outside the driver-side door, shifted into park, and turned off the engine.

Plenty of room for me to get out. She opened the door and slipped out into the chilly morning air. The Panamera chirped when she locked it, and she gave the top of her car a loving pat before flashing Rhynehart's Jeep the finger and stalking toward the building's entrance. *Let's see him try to slip out of that one.*

The unmarked door opened quickly when she jerked on the handle, then she stood in the secret organization's front lobby. *Empty again. Why is this room even here?*

The halfling made her way across the lobby and down the short hall toward the common room. Low conversation and sharp laughs drifted toward her before she stepped into the larger room, which was half-full of FRoE agents in black combat fatigues, black sparring uniforms, and civilian clothing.

Bhandi sat in the same chair at the same table as the day she'd threatened Cheyenne into captivity. The troll woman's scarlet braids were twisted up onto the top of her head, several stragglers hanging over the shoulders of the black t-shirt tucked into black combat pants. Her boots were crossed at the ankles, legs sticking out straight in front of her. "Well, look who it is."

Cheyenne stopped and couldn't help but return the agent's smirk. "In the flesh, right?"

Bhandi held up her phone and wiggled it at the halfling. "Saw you got yourself a new ride."

"What?" The halfling stepped forward to peer at the troll woman's phone. "Why do you have the security cameras in the parking lot synced to your phone?"

"Eh, it was a department-wide alert. The system sends it out whenever someone rolls through the gates. Every goddamn time."

"So, you like to spy on each other, huh?"

Bhandi shrugged. "I only pay attention when it's interesting. Had to do a double-take when I saw that shiny new Panamera roll up. Then I watched *you* get out, and hey! That was interesting."

Cheyenne snickered. *They all got a personal shot of me sending my love to Rhynehart. Yeah, I'm gonna hear about that one.* "I'm an interesting person."

"Uh-huh." The troll woman put her phone face-down on the

table and folded her arms. "Nice set of wheels you picked up. Only now you and your car don't match anymore, huh? Looks like Goth drow needs a makeover."

"Bite me, Bare-ass."

Someone barked a laugh on the other side of the common room, then a new round of low chuckling and jabs at Bhandi flew across the room.

"Yeah, hardy-har-har." Bhandi flipped them all the bird and glared, but the smirk remained on her dark-purple lips.

"'Bout time you let yourself have a little more fun, Cheyenne." At a table closer to the couches and the standing fireplace, Tate spread his arms and cocked his head. "I mean, I know we popped your Empty Barrel cherry, but you took it to a whole new level with that car."

"Don't expect me to be a chauffeur." The halfling pointed at the troll man sitting beside some other agents. Then she glanced at Bhandi again. "And no, you can't drive it."

"Pshh. If I got behind the wheel of *that* thing, none of you assholes would ever see me again."

Cheyenne glanced around the room and returned the other agents' nods. "Where's Yurik?"

"Who the fuck cares?" The goblin playing Texas Hold 'em with two beefy orcs chuckled and dealt another card.

"Probably scouring the internet for another of those sweaters just to make the rest of us puke when he wears it."

Another round of laughter rose at that, which only partially covered the sound of boots clomping quickly down the hall from the medical wing. Just as quickly, the laughter died again, and heads turned toward the hall beyond the standing fireplace.

Cheyenne caught on to the switch in attention a little late and found herself turning to follow the agents' stares with a grin. Her smile faded when she saw Rhynehart scowling at her with his arms folded. Someone cleared their throat. Another card flipped onto the table.

The halfling stared Rhynehart down. *I'm not walking over there with my tail between my legs. He can say it, or we can stand here all day.*

The little standoff lasted only a moment longer before Rhynehart tilted his head. "You gonna move it or what, kid?"

"Just waiting for you to ask nicely."

Another agent snorted, but that was as far as the laughter went.

Rhynehart unfolded his arms and gestured down the hallway behind him. "Yeah, pretty please with a fucking cherry. Let's go."

Cheyenne glanced at Bhandi, who widened her scarlet eyes and whispered, "Goth drow in the hole…"

Rolling her eyes, she jerked her chin at the troll woman and headed across the room. A few of the other agents spared her quick glances and apathetic smiles. *They all know I should've been here from the beginning, and no one's saying shit in front of Rhynehart.*

As she passed the chairs and couches in front of the fireplace, someone let out a massive fart, immediately followed by chuckles and groans of disgust. "Goddamn, Lunzi! What the hell are you eating?"

Cheyenne pressed her lips together and didn't drop Rhynehart's glare. When she reached him, he glanced briefly into the common room, then turned to usher her down the corridor.

"Trying to send me a message in the parking lot?" he muttered above the clomp of his boots.

"Looks like you got it." The halfling shot him a sideways glance, and the agent shook his head.

"I made a call, Cheyenne."

"Yeah, just one bad call after another, huh?"

Rhynehart looked aggravated. "You keeping secrets makes it pretty damn hard for me to do my job."

"*Me* keeping secrets?" Cheyenne snorted and stared at the end of the hallway up ahead. "You've been setting the bar since the very beginning. I'm just playing your game."

"None of this is a game, Cheyenne. You know that."

"Okay, you can cut it out with the whole 'big brother looking out for the drow halfling' act. You put a tracking device in my shoulder, staged a break-in to see if I'd kill an innocent person because you said so, shot me up with a drow tranquilizer, and didn't say a damn thing when I *knew* these kids were missing. That's the short list. Should I keep going?"

"Yeah. How about you tell me what the hell went down in that mansion?" They turned right at the end of the hall, moving down the rows of closed doors and the FRoE version of hospital rooms behind them.

"Not until I hear you tell me you were wrong."

"Secrets get good people killed in the field, Cheyenne."

She stopped dead in the middle of the hall, and when Rhynehart noticed, he stopped too. He sighed, but he didn't turn around.

"That's funny, Rhynehart. 'Cause the way I remember it, my secret saved your ass in that mansion. Did you hear a different version?"

The man stiffly turned just enough to glare at her from the corner of his eye. "And what happens when that secret decides to turn on us? Then we're caught with our fucking pants down and no way to pull 'em back up."

"You mean, like you turned on me."

"That's not—"

"That's *exactly* what happened." Cheyenne's fists clenched at her sides. *I'd really love to go full drow for this.* "You want to be able to trust me? Set a fucking example. That's what someone does when they're calling the shots."

"Look, kid, when I've got two options in front of me and one of them's following orders, it doesn't matter what the other one is."

"Yeah, that's your problem. You don't even *look* at the other option. That's how you ended up with an O'gúleesh meathead pretending to be FRoE." The halfling forced herself to walk toward him, hissing in frustration. "And you needed *me* to figure that one out for you too. If you don't wanna be caught with your pants down, man, maybe you shouldn't drop 'em in the first place."

Rhynehart's nostrils flared as he ran his tongue across his top teeth. He glared at the wall for a moment, then met her gaze head-on. "That's what I'm trying to do this time. And you're making that impossible."

"That's bullshit, and you know it. Your ignorance is *not* my fault, and I don't owe you a damn thing."

His jaw worked as he narrowed his eyes.

The halfling could smell his aftershave and the waffles he'd had for breakfast. *Yeah, he's feeling the sucker punch.*

"You know what? You take as long as you need to let that sink in." Cheyenne gestured down the hall. "I came here for that kid, not for you. We owe *her* the reassurance that she's getting back home in one piece. Which I'm sure she's starting to doubt after you've had her locked up in this place for two days. Trust me, I know the feeling."

The FRoE agent sniffed and turned back down the hall without a word. Shaking her head, the halfling followed him.

CHAPTER FIFTY-SEVEN

They went almost to the end of the medical wing before Rhynehart stopped at a door on the right and knocked twice. He didn't wait for an answer before opening it and gesturing for Cheyenne to step inside first. He followed her in and stood beside the door with his hands clasped behind his back.

What the hell is going on in here?

Sir stood beside two armchairs, his arms folded. In the chair closest to him sat a huge orc woman in black fatigues, her back perfectly straight, green palms lying flat on her thighs. In the other chair was Durg's teenage Goth orc niece. They all turned to look at the drow halfling in their midst, but Cheyenne could only focus on the girl's yellow eyes staring at her. "I have your necklace."

It was the only thing she could think to say, but the message hit home. The girl's eyes widened, and she dipped her head in silent acknowledgment.

"What the hell kinda fucked-up secret girl code is that?" Sir asked, glancing back and forth between them.

Cheyenne grimaced at the FRoE's head honcho. "That doesn't jog your memory, huh? Okay, let's try this, *Major*. Remember when I told you I recognized some of that stuff in the huge pile of clothes we found at the construction site?"

Sir grunted.

"That wasn't code either. Good thing I figured it out before anyone else."

Sir turned to shoot Rhynehart a questioning look. The agent blinked and dropped his gaze to the floor.

He's really stepping into his coward shoes, isn't he?

"So, what's her name?" Sir scowled at the halfling and gestured toward the teenage orc girl, who was still staring at Cheyenne. "Every single one of those kids gave it up within two minutes of Sheila sitting down with them for a little chat. This one hasn't said a goddamn word."

Cheyenne cocked her head. "Did you try saying please?"

"You're on thin ice, halfling."

"Yeah, walking across it to keep you from falling in." Cheyenne nodded at the massive orc woman in the other chair—Sheila without her human mask. "Anything you want to add?"

Sheila tilted her head. "I haven't been able to get through to her either. The way I see it, she's either still shell-shocked, or she doesn't want to go home."

"This one's a tougher nut to crack than you are, halfling." Sir glanced down at Durg's niece again and snorted. "If you have any bright ideas, I'm all ears."

The girl still hadn't taken her eyes off Cheyenne, but she finally took a deep breath and opened her mouth. "I'll talk to *you.*"

"Jesus Christ." Sir threw his head back to scowl at the ceiling. "That's it, huh? She says something about a goddamn necklace, and you two are best friends?"

Cheyenne ignored his outburst and nodded at the orc girl. Then she shot Sir an unamused glance. "Give us the room."

"Not gonna happen."

The halfling gritted her teeth and forced herself not to rip the Heart of Midnight pendant off her neck again just to blast Major Sir Carson across the room. "Look, if you're trying to make a point that doesn't include getting this girl back home, you shouldn't be here."

Sir stared at her, and the halfling joined him in a standoff she knew she would win. *Bring it.*

Sheila cleared her throat. "Sir."

"*What?*"

"I suggest we give the room to Cheyenne and the girl."

"Oh, you do, do ya?"

"First words in forty hours, Sir. Yes, I do."

With a growl of frustration, Sir rocked his bottom jaw back and forth, then broke away from the halfling's gaze. "Fine."

Cheyenne nodded at Sheila, who raised an eyebrow and stood from the armchair.

Sir stormed toward the open door and Rhynehart, who was standing beside it. "You have ten minutes, halfling."

"Twenty."

The man stiffened but didn't turn around.

The halfling gave the orc girl a small reassuring smile. "And if twenty minutes isn't enough for our conversation and I say we need more time, we'll get more time."

Sir grunted and stormed into the hallway. Sheila followed him without a word. Cheyenne felt Rhynehart's eyes on her even as he stepped out and closed the door behind him.

The room fell silent. Cheyenne studied the orc girl still sitting in the chair. *Normal heartbeat, clear as a bell. At least she's not scared of me.* "How're you doin'?"

The girl shrugged. "The dude with the mustache is only entertaining for so long. After that, I just want to punch him in the face."

Cheyenne snorted. "I know the feeling. Mind if I sit?"

"Not really."

The halfling lowered herself into the second armchair and folded her arms. "So. Now everyone knows you *can* talk. Why haven't you?"

The girl's eyes narrowed. "I know FRoE agents when I see them, and I don't trust any of them."

"Even when they got you and the other kids out of that mansion?"

"Yeah." Slowly, the girl leaned back in her chair and folded her arms. "Even then."

"They really do want to get you home."

"Trust me, I'd love to be home right now. My uncle's probably crapping his pants, wondering why I haven't turned up yet."

Cheyenne fought back a laugh. "Somehow, that isn't hard to imagine."

"Yeah. You met him. He talks a big game and likes to play warlord until somebody gives him a good shakedown. Then he's just…" The girl wrinkled her nose. "Annoying."

"I remember." Nodding, the halfling offered a little shrug. "I'm surprised you recognized *me*."

"Your face doesn't change with the rest of you." Smirking, the girl studied the half-drow's face and shrugged. "Kinda hard to forget when the only other thing you said to me was about that necklace."

"Fair enough."

"I'd really like to get that back, by the way. It was a custom-made thing. From a friend."

Cheyenne nodded slowly. "Yeah, I'm sure we could figure that out. Might be a little while, though. I don't have it with me."

"That's cool." The orc girl chuckled. "You know where I live."

"Yeah." Glancing at her lap, the half-drow couldn't help but smile. *This girl's got guts. I'll give her that.* "What's your name, kid?"

A frown creased the orc girl's thick brow, and she leaned away from the halfling before looking at the closed door. "I can't."

"Hmm. I'm just taking a wild guess here, but something tells me you're trying to protect your uncle."

The girl shrugged and kept staring at the door.

"Okay. They find your name in the system, it pulls up Durg Br'athol right next to it, and you're trying to help him keep his name clean." Cheyenne chuckled. "At least with the FRoE, right?"

No response.

"Listen, I'm gonna tell you a little secret, okay? Well, I guess it might not be much of a secret anymore, but it might help." The half-drow propped her forearms on her thighs. "I don't trust the FRoE either. Not completely. Sure, they're pretty reliable when it comes to busting the guys who need to be busted, and I know they've got *my* back when we're in the middle of it. At least some do. But beyond that? They're a pain in my ass."

The girl gave a little laugh, still unable to look at Cheyenne. "You're not FRoE."

"I am *not* FRoE. More like an independent contractor." *Getting paid in visits to Chateau D'rahl.*

Taking a deep breath, the orc girl slowly turned to the halfling with her yellow eyes. "My name's not even in the system."

"Really?" Cheyenne swallowed. "How'd you manage that?"

"Well, my Border crossing wasn't exactly legit."

Raising her eyebrows, the halfling leaned back in her chair again. "You were smuggled Earthside."

"A few months ago, yeah. My uncle sent word for me, and the guys back home did their jobs."

Durg was shaking down other magicals to pay for an unregistered crossing. I bet he just got too used to it to stop. This is getting complicated. Cheyenne clenched her eyes shut and took a deep breath. When she opened them again, the girl didn't look any more apologetic than she had before she'd spilled the beans. "Which reservation?"

The girl shook her head. "No rez."

"Huh. You're gonna have to explain that one, 'cause I'm pretty sure a Border portal doesn't exist without a reservation sitting right on top of it."

"Yeah, I know how it works. Most of the time." The orc girl glanced at the ceiling. "A new portal opened in the last...I don't know. Year? Eight months? The FRoE doesn't know about it. Most people don't know about it, but word gets around if you talk to the right people, I guess."

Cheyenne blinked. *No wonder she didn't talk. That opens up a whole new shitstorm for everybody.* "Where's the new portal?"

"I don't know. My uncle picked me up when I crossed and took me right back to his house. I'm just starting to get a handle on Richmond."

"So, it's not in Richmond."

"No. The drive was a couple hours, though." The girl shrugged and finally looked like she wished she could say more. "Two or three, I think."

"Well, that narrows it down, I guess. You think your uncle would remember where it is?"

"Maybe. Are you gonna go ask him?"

"I don't know." The halfling raised her eyebrows. "I'm not sure I *want* to know more details, you understand?"

"Between a drow and a FRoE place. I get it."

Cheyenne chuckled. "I knew you had it together the first time I met you."

"I knew you weren't really gonna kill my uncle. Guess we both have pretty good intuition."

"Yeah. Maybe we do." They exchanged smiles, then Cheyenne slapped her thighs and pushed to her feet. "Okay. Let's get you home, huh? It sucks to be cooped up in this place for longer than ten minutes."

The orc girl stood and smoothed down the front of the over-sized t-shirt some FRoE agent had given her to replace the creepy black robes her kidnappers had dressed her in. "My name's Aksu, by the way."

The halfling's smile widened, and she stuck out her hand. "Cheyenne."

They shook, and Aksu frowned. "That's not a very drow name, is it? Even for a halfling."

"Yeah, well, I got the short end of the drow-role-model stick."

"Sorry."

"Don't be." Cheyenne laughed again and headed toward the door. "I'm starting to think I'm better off the way things turned out."

CHAPTER FIFTY-EIGHT

When the door opened, Cheyenne found Rhynehart, Sheila, and Sir standing halfway down the hall. Sir scowled at her, and his eyes widened when Aksu stepped into the hall behind the halfling.

"What the hell do you think you're doing?"

"I'm taking her home."

"I don't remember giving you the go-ahead for that, halfling."

Cheyenne kept walking toward the major. She stopped about a foot away and narrowed her eyes. "I got the go-ahead when you called me to do what you can't. It took you two days to do that, and it took me about ten minutes to get her name and her story. Now I'm taking her home."

Sir's nostrils flared when he took a quick sniff, and he leaned down to meet the five-foot-six halfling's challenge. "I don't like the way you smell when you get cocky, Cheyenne."

"The feeling's mutual."

"And I don't like hearing that you know something we don't."

Cheyenne raised her eyebrows. "You can't call me in to fix something you broke and expect me to let you read my diary afterward. I can do things you can't, and I can know things you don't, and you'll just have to deal with it. Major."

The man's beady eyes locked on hers, his mustache bristling when his upper lip twitched. "If you keep cutting it close like this, you're gonna end up a lot bloodier than you expect."

The halfling grinned. "Are you threatening me, Sir?"

"Threats are for pencil-pushers and store clerks, Cheyenne. This is a professional courtesy. And don't forget our little arrangement, huh? If you can't figure out why that lunatic drow behind bars turned himself back in to keep playing prisoner just for fun, you'll have to go through me every time you want to have a little chat. And believe me, halfling, I don't like holding your short leash any more than you like being tied to it."

Cheyenne lifted her chin and took a small step forward so Sir was looking straight down at her. "You know what a mantis shrimp can do when it starts punching the water?"

"What the hell does a goddamn shrimp have to do with any of this?"

"Look it up. You can tell me about it the next time you call." With a curt nod, Cheyenne stepped around the major and brushed past him down the hall. She looked over her shoulder to nod at Aksu. "Come on."

Without a word, the orc girl followed the drow halfling down the hall. Before they stepped out into the common room, Aksu leaned toward Cheyenne and muttered, "He really doesn't like you."

"You don't have to like someone to need their help. I think it's one or the other with him, though."

The other agents sitting around at the tables in the common room looked up when Cheyenne and the last kidnapped magical minor entered. Someone started clapping, and a less than enthusiastic round of applause made its way toward them. The halfling smirked and kept walking. Aksu frowned at the agents, then looked at the halfling. "What did you do?"

"I didn't do anything. I'm pretty sure that's for you."

"What?" The orc girl stepped around Cheyenne to put the halfling between her and all the FRoE agents nodding at her and clapping like they'd just been forced to sit through the most boring speech of their lives. "I didn't do anything, either."

"You should give yourself more credit."

"Hey, Goth drow," Bhandi called. Aksu snorted at the nickname. "I'm free for a ride-along if you two want some company."

"You're not getting in my car, Bhandi."

"Oh, come on. *She* gets to sit in there. I'll just sit in the back and shut up. You won't even know I'm there."

Cheyenne shot the troll woman a little shrug before leading Aksu to the compound's empty front lobby.

Behind her, Bhandi thumped a hand on the table and growled, "I show a drow halfling a good time with fellwine, and she won't let me in her damn car."

"You and fellwine in the same sentence, Bhandi?" another agent shouted. "Nobody's having a good time but you."

Laughter spilled down the hall as Cheyenne pushed open the front door and held it for Aksu. The orc girl frowned over her shoulder but didn't stop. "Credit for what?"

"Huh?"

Aksu studied the parking lot and the line of black FRoE vehicles stretching from front to back. "You said I should give myself more credit. For what?"

Cheyenne shoved her hands into her pockets and smirked. "For being tough. I don't know how hard Major Sir tried to interrogate you, but I know that after two days of watching spit fly from under that mustache, I would've tried to rip it off."

The girl let out a low, surprisingly self-aware laugh.

The halfling studied her sidelong and smiled. "And because you kept it together after almost two days of being locked up with a bunch of other kids who didn't belong in that mansion, either."

"Like radan."

"Like what?"

Aksu stuck her hands in the pockets of the baggy sweatpants the FRoE had loaned her and shrugged. "Livestock back home."

"Oh, yeah. I thought I recognized the word. But the stories I heard were about a bunch of whatever those creatures are running around wild in some fields or something."

"They used to." Aksu swallowed. "Not so much anymore. Now it's just a bunch of Crown agents rounding them up into pens. The kind they don't come out of again."

"Got it." Cheyenne pulled the keyless fob out of her pocket and unlocked the Panamera. A quiet chirp greeted them, the headlights flashing in the mid-morning sun. She stopped right in front of her car and turned to meet the girl's yellow-eyed gaze. "Here's the thing, though. *You* came back out again. You're not a radan. You're a smart kid who's making the most of a pretty sticky situation on more than one level. Honestly, that should've gotten you a standing ovation when we walked through there, but I'm starting to get the feeling that outside active field operations, those agents are a bunch of slackers."

The orc girl snorted and shook her head, turning her attention to the half-drow's shiny new black car.

I saw those tears. She'll be okay.

Aksa looked at Rhynehart's Jeep just on the other side of the Panamera, then leaned sideways to peer past it at Sir's Kia Rio. "Who were *you* trying to piss off?'

Cheyenne laughed and slipped between the Jeep and her car to open the driver's side door. "You know, I don't have to try that hard anymore."

With another slow shake of her head, the orc girl opened her door and slid into the passenger seat. "Woah. I didn't know something like this even existed."

"It sure does. Hey, you've picked up on things pretty quickly for only being Earthside a short time."

Aksu shrugged. "Yeah, it was a lot easier than I thought it would be."

"Really? I have some troll friends who've been here for over a year, and their kid still had to remind them what a car is."

"Probably easier for the younger generations." The orc girl wrinkled her nose and hastily buckled her seatbelt once she saw Cheyenne doing the same.

"That makes sense, actually. It's like that over here too with technology, or so I've heard from the older generations." The halfling started the car, grinning when the engine purred and rumbled smoothly beneath her seat.

"Like smartphones and computers and stuff?"

Cheyenne snorted. "And stuff. Yeah. You got a handle on all that too?"

"That was like the first thing." Aksu peered briefly out the window as the Panamera pulled away from the FRoE compound. "You know, most of the O'gúleesh making the crossing come from way outside the capitol, right? Farmers and traders and...I don't know. Fishermen, I think. Not a lot of people leave the cities, even after everything—" The words stuck in the girl's throat.

The halfling spared her a quick glance, but the orc girl just shook her head again, still gazing out the window. *Something's happening over there, and nobody wants to talk about it.* "How come?"

Aksu said, "It's more convenient. I totally get wanting to leave a ranch or a village with a bunch of shacks to come Earthside and try to make things a little better. Nobody wants to give up city life and all the things that come with it to move backward by coming across the Border."

"Backward with what?"

The girl shot the halfling a sidelong glance and smirked. "Technology. And stuff."

"What?" Laughing, Cheyenne did a double-take as she drove down the frontage road toward the gate towers. "Technology over here is a step down?"

"More like jumping off a cliff."

"You're kidding."

"Nope." The girl scratched her arm and dropped her head back against the headrest. "I started school here. Junior year. It kind of feels like I walked back into the nursery, only everyone's, you know, my age."

Little Goth teen just called humans babies. Okay.

"Oddly enough, I know exactly what that's like." Cheyenne slowed the Panamera to a stop outside the gate towers and turned to look at her passenger. "Before we get outta here, I need you to promise me something."

Frowning, Aksu glanced at the booth in the gate tower with room enough for one person—despite being empty—then met the halfling's gaze. "Depends on what it is."

The halfling snorted. "You're startin' to sound a lot like someone I know." *She sounds like me.* "That's a good thing. And here's the deal. Normally, anybody coming on and off this base who isn't technically supposed to be here either takes a sleeping pill or gets a bag thrown over their face. Or a sleeping mask. They don't want people figuring out how to get back here, for obvious reasons."

"Yeah, super obvious. Trust me, I don't plan on ever coming back."

"I believe you, and I don't blame you. But I gotta tell you, okay?" Cheyenne glanced in her rearview mirror and saw nothing but a straight, empty stretch of road behind her. *Bet they're waiting to see if I remembered, too.* "I don't have any sleeping pills or face bags, so I'm not gonna try to blindfold you. You don't need it. I just need your word that you won't tell anyone where this place is."

Aksu studied the halfling's raised eyebrow, then pursed her lips. "You're putting a lot of trust in an orc girl whose uncle pissed you off enough to do whatever you did to him."

Cheyenne snorted. "Well, you've been a lot easier to talk to."

That made the girl laugh again, and she stared into her lap. "All right. How 'bout this? I won't tell anybody anything about this place if you don't tell anyone how I got Earthside."

"Huh." The halfling blinked and mulled over the deal. *Now I'm the one tightening the drawstring. Awesome.* "I can promise you I won't say anything about your uncle sending for you or the magicals who got you across under the FRoE's radar. But if things get dicey with that secret Border portal, I might have things to say to various people about *that* part."

Aksu shrugged. "As long as my name stays out of it, sounds like a pretty good deal to me."

Cheyenne dropped her hand off the steering wheel and held it out toward the girl whose uncle had put Ember in that wheelchair. *Everything still has a price.* "Deal."

The girl quickly took the half-drow's hand and gave it a firm squeeze and a single shake up and down.

"Let's get the hell out of here, huh?"

"Yeah, the faster, the better."

The halfling bit her lip and stepped on the gas. The Panamera's 4.8-liter V8 engine kicked into gear, and they sped down the rest of the long stretch of unnamed road that would take them back to civilization. Aksu gripped the armrest on the passenger-side door, but she was grinning.

"So, you know your way around technology on this side, then." Cheyenne took the wide left turn toward the highway at seventy-five miles an hour. "You bring any of that advanced O'gúleesh tech with you when you made the crossing?"

"I tried. Learned the hard way that that's the only thing that doesn't come with people over the Border."

"Seriously?"

"Yeah." The girl let out a wry chuckle. "People tried to tell me to leave it behind, but I figured nobody wanted humans to get their hands on the stuff. Turns out the Border takes it off you and does... whatever with it. Maybe it's gone, or maybe it showed up again on the other side. I don't know. Would've been really nice to have an O'gúl activator over here."

"What's that do?"

Aksu laughed. "Whatever I want it to."

"All right. Keep your little tech secrets. I see how it is." They both laughed a little, and Cheyenne readjusted her grip on the steering wheel. "So, the only things that make it through are magicals and magic, huh?"

"I guess. What else is there?"

That's what I wanna know, kid. It was obviously a rhetorical question, so Cheyenne didn't bother keeping up the conversation. *And I would* love *to get my hands on some O'gúleesh tech.*

CHAPTER FIFTY-NINE

Just after noon, the Panamera pulled up in front of Durg Br'athol's house on the north end of Jackson Ward. Cheyenne turned off the engine, and she and Aksu sat there in silence.

Then the halfling turned toward the teenage orc version of herself and nodded. "Ready?"

"Yeah." Aksu peered at her uncle's house. "I know you've already done a lot for me, but I kinda have one more favor to ask."

Cheyenne lowered her hands into her lap and shifted in her seat to turn toward the orc girl. *There's that racing heartbeat. Why's she only getting worked up now?* "Hey, don't worry about what I have or haven't done already. And you don't owe me anything, okay?"

Aksu turned toward the halfling and nodded. "Okay."

"So, what's the favor?"

"Can you come with me?"

The halfling blinked and tried not to laugh. "You want me to walk you to the front door?"

"Yeah." Aksu's eyes widened, then she rolled her eyes and slouched a little more in the passenger seat. "Okay, the thing is, I'm not a hundred-percent upfront with my uncle all the time."

"Oh, okay. Hey, I don't think there's a single teenager alive who hasn't lied to their parents about *something*. Or their uncle."

"Maybe. But it kinda put him in the habit of not believing anything I tell him if he's pissed off or worried about something. And the last time I snuck out overnight, he lost his shit a little."

Cheyenne nodded slowly and glanced through the passenger side window at the house. "You think me walking up there with you is gonna convince him that you're telling the truth?"

"Not really. If *you* told him, though, he can't ignore it. He tries to hide it, but he's terrified of you."

"Uh-huh." The halfling pressed her lips together and nodded again. *Can't laugh at that one either. Keep it together.* "All right. I'll help you 'cause I know the story. Still, it's probably a good idea to start working out your trust issues after this, yeah?"

"Already went through my mind."

"Okay. Let's go scare the crap out of your uncle again so he'll believe you."

Aksu snorted and unbuckled her seatbelt. They both got out of the car, and Cheyenne stepped onto the sidewalk with the orc teenager.

The girl stood there for a little too long, and the halfling pointed at the front door. "You're gonna have to take the lead on this one, kid. I'm just backup."

"Ugh. Fine." Aksu rolled her eyes and moved up the walkway toward the front porch. Her overly large sneakers thumped up the wooden stairs, and Cheyenne followed quietly behind her.

With a deep breath, the prodigal magical minor knocked on the door and folded her arms.

A muffled grunt came from inside, then Durg clomped toward the front door and jerked it open with a snarl. He wasn't expecting to see his niece in someone else's baggy clothes standing on the porch, and while his eyes widened in surprise, the snarl stayed. "Where the hell have you been?"

The girl glared defiantly up at him, but Cheyenne heard the little tremble in the young orc's breath.

"If you let us come inside, Durg, we'll tell you all about it."

The huge green orc started and blinked at the drow halfling, who looked human this time. "I don't know who you are, and I don't give a shit. Get off my porch."

The halfling folded her arms with a little shrug. "Or we could just go with me throwing you across the house again like last time. It worked pretty well once you regained consciousness."

A strangled wheeze escaped Durg's gaping mouth, his eyes almost popping out of his head as his jaw worked without any sound.

"But I'm not in the mood to break any more of your stuff, so, wanna let your niece into the house? I'll close the door behind me. Don't worry."

The huge orc tried to clear his throat and only got out a choking sound before he looked at Aksu again and stepped aside. "Get in here before someone sees you without an illusion." His eyes darted up and down the street, avoiding the halfling, and Aksu stormed past him. She headed into the living room where Cheyenne had conducted her Durg-Br'athol interrogation and plopped down on the couch.

The halfling stepped into the house next and nodded toward the living room. "Go ahead. I'm right behind you."

Durg sucked his teeth around the giant tusks poking up behind his lower lip, but he turned slowly and across the hall. It took everything Cheyenne had not to laugh or make any more smartass remarks when the orc kept glancing over his shoulder as he bumbled toward the couch and his grim-faced niece. She shut the front door and headed after them.

"You've got a lot to answer for, Aksu," the orc muttered when he stopped in front of the couch.

The girl bit her bottom lip and glared at the coffee table.

"She's been gone for over forty-eight hours, man."

Durg whipped his head up to stare at the halfling making her way toward him. He shuffled backward along the couch and stopped when she did.

"Were you even a little worried about her?"

The huge orc grunted, his eyes flicking between the half-drow in his living room and his niece on the couch. "Why should I be worried? She's a smart girl, and she decides to waste her time running around through Peridosh with a bunch of good-for-nothing blood traitors."

Aksu's silent laugh was laced with disgust. "You're such a hypocrite."

"Watch it." Durg breathed heavily through his nose and scowled down at his niece. "I put too much on the line to see you waste what you've got goin' for you on this side."

Fighting back tears, the orc girl kept glaring at the coffee table. "You weren't even happy to see me."

"No, I'm pissed that you think you can just stomp out of here and do whatever you want, then *lie* to me about it." The last few words growled out of him between clenched teeth.

"She hasn't even had a chance to tell you what's going on," Cheyenne added, watching the guy's growing anger with a raised eyebrow.

Durg jabbed a meaty green finger at her, but that was as far as he was willing to take it. "She doesn't need a damn drow in disguise to help her spit out another bullshit story. Why the hell are you even here?"

"Why don't you sit, and I'll tell you."

"Uh-uh. You can't just come into *my* house and—"

"Sit *down!*" Something rattled on a shelf in the living room. Cheyenne glared at the startled orc, who dropped sideways into the couch beside his niece and stared at the drow halfling speaking with magic.

Did I feel it flare up? The halfling's hand rose halfway to the Heart of Midnight at her throat, then stopped. *Or maybe it's just the commanding Summerlin voice.*

With both orcs' full attention, Cheyenne ignored her surprise. "There's obviously a good reason I showed up here today, now that you're finally listening. Aksu didn't run away, Durg. She was kidnapped Wednesday morning with fifty-nine other magical kids. By the same people wearing *that* damn thing around their necks." She pointed at the torn tapestry on the far wall, where Durg had used the bull's head symbol for knife-throwing practice.

The huge orc hissed.

"Yeah, I feel pretty much the same way about them." The halfling shook stray pieces of black hair out of her eyes. "I'm back with your niece because I'm one of the people who helped get Aksu and those fifty-nine other kids back. Got it?"

Durg blinked and turned his yellow eyes on his niece. The girl swallowed and lowered her gaze to her lap.

"I should probably clear the air right now and say that the only other person who knows about how your niece got Earthside is me. And that was by necessity, so I could get her back home. No one else is gonna hear about it. You both have my word on that."

The orc just raised his eyebrows, swimming in a spiral of disbelief.

"Aksu?" Cheyenne smiled when the orc girl looked at her. "Is there anything else we should put out in the open before I get outta here?"

"No."

"All right." Cheyenne pointed at Durg and cocked her head. "This isn't the last time I'll be stopping by, Durg. You and I are gonna sit down soon and have a chat about those loyalists and the bull's head. I'm giving you a heads-up now so you can figure out what's important for me to know, and don't even bother with whatever might waste my time. Got it?"

The orc grunted, scratching his cheek as he turned his gaze onto his niece.

"That's good enough for me. I think you guys have some catching up to do."

While Durg didn't look back up at the drow halfling hovering in his living room, Aksu slowly lifted her gaze and mouthed to Cheyenne, "Thank you."

Cheyenne couldn't quite bring herself to smile at the girl. There was too much relief and fear mixed together in Aksu's bright yellow eyes. Instead, the half-Drow dipped her head and shot the orc teenager a knowing wink. *She'll get it.*

Then Cheyenne turned and stalked out of Durg Br'athol's house. *And I'll be back. When I have the time.*

CHAPTER SIXTY

C heyenne opened the door to her new apartment and closed her eyes.

Sitting beside the stack of broken-down boxes, Ember laughed. "What are you doing?"

The halfling took a tentative step through the doorway.

"I'm almost afraid to look at what else you've crammed in here since I've been gone." Cheyenne opened her eyes and swept a glance across the living room. "Woah. How the hell did you get all this done in, what? Three hours?"

"I told you. There's a business for *everything*." Ember smirked and folded her arms to study her friend's reaction. "What do you think?"

"I'm..." Cheyenne burst out laughing. "You know, other than when I'm with you, I'm speechless by choice, but you've outdone yourself on this one, Em. I've been forced into speechlessness."

"You realize what an oxymoron that is, right? You just gave me a three-sentence response."

Stepping into the apartment, the halfling closed the door behind her. "Well, hanging out with you feels more like hanging out with myself, only more fun. So, I'm just thinking out loud at you."

"Ha. Whatever that's supposed to mean, I'll take it." Ember

wheeled around the boxes. "Go ahead and think out loud about the apartment, though."

"Well, for starters, I'm totally into these chairs." Cheyenne stepped around the couch and lowered herself into one of the black leather armchairs on the other side of the coffee table. "Holy crap, this is as comfy as it looks. Are these—"

"Yep. I saw you ogling those chairs in the Guest Center. You practically drooled."

Cheyenne snorted. "I don't drool."

"No, you *practically* drool. Didn't take me long to find them. Apparently Pellerville Gables Apartments source most of their furniture from this warehouse that's, like, ten minutes away." Ember grinned. "Still a few more things on the way, though. Custom stuff takes a little longer."

"*Custom* stuff?" The halfling slapped her hands on the armrests and stared at her friend. "Who are you, and what have you done with Ember?"

The fae laughed and wheeled herself between the couch and the armchairs, pulling up beside the coffee table. "Your worst decorator nightmare, Cheyenne. I'll release your friend when I'm finished."

"Oh, jeeze." Rolling her eyes, the halfling ran her hands over the soft leather on the armrests, nestling back into the perfectly supportive cushions. "You know, I know too many people who are either currently locked up or have been at some point in the recent past. That joke would've been funnier about three weeks ago."

"Shit. I didn't mean to bring up anything." Ember studied the halfling's face until Cheyenne's tiny smile morphed into a grin. "You're screwin' with me."

"Only a little. Don't worry, you're still funny."

Ember pulled an awful, sarcastic grimace, then wheeled back a little to look at the armchairs. "At least you like the chairs."

"This rug's not too bad, either." Cheyenne leaned down to brush the soft thread of the stark black area rug with thick silver horizontal stripes in front of her. "This is a gem."

"I know."

"What did you do with the other stuff that was here?"

Ember shot her friend a coy, secretive smile. "I'll tell you when the rest of this place looks like we live here."

"You…" Cheyenne pointed at her and shook her finger. "I think turning a wannabe-stylish show unit into the coolest not-Goth-box might just be *your* magic, Em."

The magicless fae tossed her hair out of her eyes and looked around. "Yeah, I'm pretty damn good, aren't I?"

"Resounding yes. Oh!" The halfling pulled her phone out of her pocket and wrinkled her nose. "Crap. I gotta get going."

She stood from the armchair, gave it a loving pat, then darted toward the wrought-iron staircase up to the mini loft.

"For your date with a family of trolls and all that, huh?"

"That's it." Cheyenne's shoes clanged up the metal stairs until she reached the top and the less impressive show-unit office where she'd set up Glen. She pointed at the computer tower beside the metal-and-glass desk. "It's just temporary, Glen."

Ember laughed. "I'm working on that too."

"What? For real?"

"Cheyenne, I'm sitting in this huge apartment by myself with nothing to do but decorate and charge everything to your card." Ember spread her arms with a sarcastic shake of her head. "You can't expect me not to think of everything."

"I don't even know what to expect from you anymore. Keep it up."

"Oh, I'm on a roll. Can't, don't, won't stop."

Chuckling, the halfling sifted through the boxes of extra cords and cables she hadn't gotten around to putting away yet and found the stack of loose papers that was Mattie Bergmann's hand-written spellbook. Then she took out her phone and snapped pictures of the ingredients lists for the things she wanted to try first. *Personal illusion charm and wards are priority one. Everything else is a bonus.*

"Okay." The halfling leaped to her feet and came back down the staircase. "You good in here?"

"Yep. Already ate lunch and scheduled a whole bunch of stuff.

You'll miss the party while you're gone, but I'll make sure everyone cleans up before they leave."

"Bummer." Cheyenne swung a fist in mock disappointment, then glanced back up at the mini-loft. "About the new desk…"

"Got it. Extra tips for anyone who *doesn't* touch Glen while they get it up there."

"You're suddenly thinking like a girl with a bunch of inheritance money to throw around."

"It's a fun game." Ember winked. "I won't go too crazy."

"Yeah, I'm not worried about that. Or you, honestly." Cheyenne shook her head in disbelief again and headed toward the front door. "I'll be back before dinner, probably."

"Girl, I don't care *when* you'll be back. I'm not your mom."

When the halfling shot Ember a look of surprise, both magical grad students burst into laughter again. "You *are* on a roll."

"I'm feelin' good today." Ember gave two thumbs-up, then turned the chair around and wheeled herself into the kitchen. "Have fun with the trolls."

"Have fun hiring labor and tipping people."

"Uh-huh."

Chuckling, Cheyenne stepped out of the apartment and paused with the key in her hand. *Nah. She's good.*

The halfling parked the Panamera in the lot in Union Hill and glanced at the time on the dashboard. *One-thirty-two. Cutting it close, Cheyenne.*

She stepped out of the car and locked it. Other people in the parking lot turned to look at the source of that perfect chirp. Two middle-aged women in matching sweaters saw the Goth chick heading toward the parking kiosk and quickly turned around again to fumble with inserting a card to pay for their dashboard tickets.

Yes, I'm still scary and evil. I just have a fancy car. Cheyenne smirked and rolled her eyes as she stepped in line behind them.

"That your Panamera?"

She turned around and peered at a man in his late sixties, maybe early seventies. The man's light-blue eyes glistened with excitement, the tips of his white handlebar mustache fluttering in the autumn breeze. "Yeah. Great car."

The man whistled. "I'll say. I've had my eye on that model since they announced it."

Muttering and shooting Cheyenne wary glances, the matching sweaters finally left the parking kiosk and hurried across the parking lot. The halfling stepped forward for her turn, and the man took the next slot in line behind her.

"You should get yourself one," Cheyenne said with another nod at her car. "Best purchase I've made in a while." The man's eyebrows flickered up in surprise. *He's thinking I barely look old enough to drive the thing.*

Then a soft chuckle escaped him. "Oh, I'm tryin'. But the missus keeps telling me if I put any more cars in our garage, I can move out there with 'em."

Laughing, Cheyenne punched in the numbers of her temporary license plate and pulled out her second debit card. "Tough battle to fight."

"Huh. I tell ya."

"You a collector?"

The man sniffed. "Restoration, actually. Custom stuff. Been doin' it for years."

She pulled her card out of the reader, grabbed the receipt to put on the dash, and turned around. "Really?"

"That's my 1937 Packard 120 over there." The man pointed across the parking lot at the opalescent royal-purple vintage car taking up half of two parking spaces.

He's one of those. Cheyenne laughed. "That's one seriously funky car, man."

"Just the beginning. I like to switch 'em out and take 'em into town now and then. You know, keep 'em running." The guy pulled out his wallet and slipped out a card before handing it over. "If you're looking for custom updates, give me a call."

Cheyenne took the card and studied it. Blast from the Past Auto Restoration by Lee McDurn.

"Updates, huh?" She glanced at her brand-new car and smirked. "You just wanna get your hands on a Panamera, don't you?"

"You got me there." The man stuck out his hand. "Lee McDurn."

The halfling grabbed his hand and grinned. *Oh, what the hell?* "Cheyenne Summerlin."

"Nice to meet you, Cheyenne. Don't lose that card now. I'm serious. Anything you need."

"I know who to call." She raised the card before slipping it into her pocket. *He didn't even blink at my full name. Must spend more time on cars than politics.*

She glanced at him again over her shoulder, but Lee McDurn was busy at the parking kiosk. The halfling unlocked her car, put the receipt on the dash, and locked it again.

Lee turned around at the chirp and waved her off. "All right. We get it."

Chuckling, Cheyenne hurried across the parking lot toward the Fro-Yo place that wasn't really a Fro-Yo place.

The little bell on the door jingled when she stepped inside, and only a few customers looked up when she entered. All of them looked quickly away, except for a family of three standing near the checkout counter, chatting with Tony.

"Cheyenne!" The man with short, spiked blond hair and a button-down flannel a size too big waved at her. The woman beside him, her long blonde hair falling down her back and the bangs cut just above her eyebrows, grabbed his arm and jerked it back down by his side. The little girl in front of them with two thick blonde braids draped over her shoulders grinned and gave the halfling an excited little wave.

They all look exactly the same. Trying not to laugh, Cheyenne approached the troll family and nodded. "Sorry if I kept you guys waiting."

"Don't apologize to *us*, Cheyenne," R'mahr said, his eagerness just as apparent on a human face as it was on a troll's. "We're honored to be invited."

"Well, I need a guide to show me all the best places, right?" The halfling grinned down at Bryl, who bounced up and down. "You're really rockin' the *Little House on the Prairie* look, kid."

The girl's frown squished her whole face. "What's that?"

"Uh, never mind. It's cute. Hey, Tony."

The grumpy man standing behind the counter looked the halfling up and down and shook his head. "You sure have a weird range of friends, doncha?"

"I'm a people person, man." She shrugged and turned toward the door in the back marked Employees Only. Keep Out. "Come on. Let's go."

The troll family nodded at Tony before following the halfling.

"Cheyenne," Yadje whispered, looking mortified, "was he talking about us? Are we your *weird* friends?"

Cheyenne opened the door and gestured for the family to step in first. *All my friends are weird.* "No, Yadje. You're not weird at all."

When she shut the door behind her and leaned against the stainless-steel wall of the elevator down to Peridosh, the troll woman looked like she was on the verge of tears.

"Hey, don't listen to the disgruntled employee behind the counter, okay? He was just as unhappy with my other friends."

Yadje and R'mahr exchanged hurt looks. The troll man rubbed his face and turned pained eyes on the halfling. "You've been here before."

Great. I hurt their feelings. "Uh, yeah. Just once. A spur-of-the-moment thing."

"And they showed you what Peridosh has to offer?" Yadje asked, tossing the blonde bangs away from her cornflower-blue eyes.

"Not really." Cheyenne glanced at Bryl, but the girl was in her own little world, muttering to herself about finally getting her hands on what she needed. "They took me straight through the place to the Empty Barrel, and we didn't go anywhere else."

"Ah." R'mahr's mouth opened with a little pop. "*Those* kinds of friends."

His wife tsked at him and slapped his arm. "She's allowed to have friends, R'mahr. We can't be the only other O'gúleesh she knows."

R'mahr's mouth twitched in an embarrassed smile. "I had hopes."

"Oh, stop it. I already have one child to look after." Her usual rough humor back, Yadje plastered on a smile for Cheyenne and nodded. "We're happy to be here with you now, Cheyenne. And we will *not* be taking you to the Empty Barrel."

"Yeah, not in the middle of the day." The halfling smirked, but the troll couple didn't find it very amusing.

"Not ever." Yadje's lips pressed tightly into a grim line of disapproval. "But what you do on your own time is none of our business. So."

Why does this feel like a scolding a la Bianca Summerlin? Cheyenne dipped her head toward the troll couple, glancing between them. "I'm still glad you guys came with me."

"You're gonna love it." Bryl's high voice cut the tension in the slowly descending elevator. "Really, really love it."

The halfling couldn't keep from chuckling a little. "Can't wait."

"Well. Time to slip out of *these*." Yadje pulled a thin silver ring from her index finger, and her human-illusion mask fell away in an instant. She tossed her long scarlet hair over her shoulder and smiled at her daughter. Her scarlet fingers twisted in a quick spell, and Bryl's illusion fell away.

R'mahr pushed up his shirtsleeve to remove a thin metal band from around his wrist, then he stood there in the elevator with his natural purple skin and scarlet hair and eyes.

All three trolls watched Cheyenne expectantly.

"Oh. Right." The half-drow went to her happy place and found the door locked. *Corian can't be pissed at me for this. Gotta do it if I wanna learn those spells.* She reached up to untie the knot in the thin silver chain supporting the Heart of Midnight pendant. It slithered away from her neck, and she pocketed it before slipping into her drow form.

"Ah." R'mahr's smile widened as the Goth chick's pale skin darkened to purple-gray, the tips of her pointed ears reappearing through stark white hair. "I don't believe I've seen that yet."

Cheyenne stretched her neck from one side to the other. *Locking this up feels like I've been in a cage.* "Well, now you have."

Yadje nodded at the halfling's pocket. "You found yourself an illusion charm."

"Sort of."

Bryl stared shamelessly at the half-drow and slowly nodded. "I like you much better like this."

"*Bryl.*"

"It's *true.*"

"Thanks, kid." Cheyenne gave the troll woman a reassuring smile. "I like it too. Still me, though, right?"

"Yeah, but better."

When the halfling chuckled, the troll couple loosened up a little and offered weak laughs in return. Then the elevator shivered to a stop below the streets of Richmond, Virginia, and the doors opened.

"Yes!" Bryl darted out of the elevator, her mother racing after her.

R'mahr stepped out slowly and waited for the halfling to join him. "You leave it to us, Cheyenne. Your other friends might have thought carousing in an O'gúleesh tavern was the best way to honor you, but they were wrong. Stick with us, huh? We'll show you the true value of what can be found here from back home."

"Thanks, R'mahr." Cheyenne nodded. "That's why I asked you to join me."

"Good." For the first time since she'd met him, the troll man puffed out his chest and strutted down the wide avenue lined with shopfronts and vendor stalls, his confidence buoyed by the drow halfling walking beside him.

Cheyenne caught sight of Yadje tightly clutching her daughter's hand as Bryl tried to jerk away, pointing at something behind a brightly-colored booth. *This'll be interesting.*

CHAPTER SIXTY-ONE

Peridosh was still a busy place, but it had a different ambiance in the middle of the day. *Definitely not like a Tuesday night with off-duty FRoE agents getting into drunken barfights.*

The vendors selling their wares to the hidden magical community scattered through Richmond were a lot happier and much more inviting. Some tried to smile at the half-Drow as she followed R'mahr and his family down the avenue. Most just stared, but it was in curiosity this time instead of wary disapproval.

"So, what do you need to find, Cheyenne?" R'mahr nodded amiably at a skaxen woman in a long-sleeved dress and way too much makeup.

"Ingredients for spells, mostly. Maybe some potions." She rubbed her forearm absently through her black hoody. *These cuts itch like hell when I'm thinking about 'em.* "Some healing salves—"

"Oh! Don't worry about that last one. Yadje keeps everything you could possibly want in that little bag slung over her shoulder. But yes. Spells and potions. You'll find everything you need in Bryl's favorite shop." The troll man chuckled and gestured toward his wife and daughter.

The girl tugged on her mother's sleeve now, still anxiously trying to pull out of Yadje's grip on her wrist so she could step into the potionmaster's shop on this side of the Empty Barrel. Yadje, though, used her other hand to examine more of those glowing blue vegetables they'd tried to feed Cheyenne earlier that week.

"Maji, Maji, Come *on*! There's only one calver fin left. What if someone gets it first?"

"Well, you'd just have to wait until there's more, wouldn't you?" Yadje didn't even look at her daughter, but she replaced the blue vegetable and nodded at the vendor behind the cart. "Settle down. I'm coming."

Chuckling, R'mahr followed them into the shop. Cheyenne paused when she caught a whiff of something cooking farther down the avenue. *Barbequed sausage and...oranges?* Fortunately, the din of customers, window-shoppers, and vendors was loud enough to drown out the grumbling of her stomach. *Too many errands and not enough food.*

"Cheyenne? Are you coming?" R'mahr's head poked back out of the potionmaster's shop, and the halfling nodded.

"Yep. Just smelled something cooking."

"Ah, yes. Nothing like the fare they make down here, is there?" He stopped when Yadje turned around to shoot him a warning look, and the troll man cleared his throat. "Excluding my dear Yadje's homecooked meals, of course."

His wife rolled her eyes, but she couldn't hide a small smile beneath her exasperation.

"Oh, look." Bryl darted toward a shelf of different-sized vials, all of them filled with what looked like sand in every color imaginable. "It's still here."

Yadje nodded in feigned surprise when her daughter picked up the last vial of black sand and thrust it in the air above her head. Then the girl scampered around the shop, touching things here and there, peering into glass cases or open crates of who knew what.

"R'mahr." Cheyenne pulled her gaze away from the girl and leaned toward the troll man. "You remember what I told you the other day about keeping an eye on what Bryl brings home, right?"

"Hmm? Oh, yes, yes." He lowered his voice and dipped his head. "The black magic? Of course, I remember, Cheyenne. And we appreciate the information more than we can say."

"You told Yadje?"

"I did. She's always had an eye trained on what Bryl brings home with her, but I imagine now she'll be going through every little thing twice and three times over." The troll nodded firmly as if that settled the matter.

"Good. That stuff could still be out there. Just be careful."

"Absolutely. Yes."

R'mahr left her to join his daughter in fawning over some kind of bird skull.

Why do I get the feeling he's not paying attention?

A grunt came from behind the counter, and Cheyenne turned to meet the yellow gaze of the wizened orc with the long white beard. His scowl hadn't changed since her last visit to Peridosh. *We meet again.*

"I don't taint my supplies, drow." He said it in defense, yet it sounded like a warning.

"I didn't say you do." The halfling gazed around the shop and stepped closer to the potionmaster's counter. "I'm glad to hear you know what to keep *out* of your shop, at least."

"I know more about the bonds of magical components than any half-cocked O'gúleesh in this cursed realm," the orc spat. "Even you."

Just let him have his moment. Cheyenne slipped her phone out of her pocket and opened her photos. "Also, good to hear. That's why I'm standing in your shop."

The orc's scowl contorted even more when she handed him her phone and made a swiping gesture.

"I need everything on these lists, and I'm guessing you're the orc who can help me out."

The potionmaster's eyes twitched as he scanned the items on one photo after another. When he looked at Cheyenne, the intensity of his gaze made her lean away a little. "Where did you get these pages?"

"They were given to me."

His yellow eyes widened, and he set her phone down on her side of the counter. "Do you know who penned the spells?"

"The same person who gave them to me. I got a copy of the whole book." *Hope we don't have a problem here.*

The orc cleared his throat, then his scowl returned and he reached under the counter and pulled out a basket woven tightly with dark-brown reeds, twigs, and thin leather thongs. He stepped out from behind the counter and muttered, "I don't do this for everyone."

"Hey, I appreciate it. But you could just point those things out to me instead, and I'll grab them. You don't have to—"

"I do, and you know it." The orc's narrow eyes darted around his shop and paused for a minute on the open entrance. "As far as I'm concerned, drow, the old laws still stand. Even in this wretched place."

He searched along the back wall of his shop, peering at the full shelves and the displays of supplies laid out on counters below them.

Cheyenne swallowed and slipped her phone back into her pocket. *People keep assuming I know what the hell they're talking about.* Her curiosity drove her to follow the old, hunched magical, trying to see what he pulled from the shelves.

The potionmaster had only pulled down one bundle of dried herbs to toss into his basket before he turned with surprising speed. "I don't need a guard, drow. I'll abide by the old laws, sure, but not with you breathing down my neck."

"Okay." Cheyenne lifted both hands in surrender and took a step back. "Just trying to watch and learn."

"Then I'd be out of a trade, wouldn't I?" The orc hissed at her, then turned around again and mumbled, "Never part of the agreement, anyway. I'll draw the line on this side."

Not sure the old crazy guy should be selling magical ingredients. The halfling looked up to see all three trolls watching her with wide eyes. She shrugged and shook her head, and R'mahr glanced at the potionmaster making his slow way through his inventory.

"Cheyenne," Yadje called with a last glance at the elderly orc. "Have you seen an O'gúl hornet's web?"

"Nope."

"Come here." The troll woman waved the halfling forward as her husband and daughter turned back toward the wall of shelving they'd been studying.

Clearing her throat, Cheyenne stepped around the crowded display of gemstones and small cups of seeds taking up the center of the shop. The trolls made room for her to join them, and R'mahr leaned in to whisper, "He's one of the best, Cheyenne. Used to serve the Crown, you know."

"Really?" The halfling cast a quick sidelong glance toward the muttering old orc. *Then I need to be careful.*

"Yes. For most of his life."

Cheyenne lowered her voice to just above a whisper. "So, why's he *here*?"

"Cast out," R'mahr muttered. "At the turn of the new cycle. Most of the old masters and advisors were, if not all of them."

"The new cycle is…"

"Ascendance." The troll man's eyes widened, and Cheyenne copied the expression, shaking her head.

Yadje scoffed and leaned toward them. "A new regime, Cheyenne. One steps down, and another steps up as the Crown."

Her husband frowned at her. "You can't sugarcoat it like that, Yadje. No one *stepped down*."

"They used to."

"It's not the same."

"Shh." The troll woman's eyes darted toward the potionmaster, who was slowly making his way along this wall of his shop now. "That's enough."

R'mahr bowed his head and stared blankly at something on the counter.

Cheyenne pressed her lips together. *Trouble in Ambar'ogúl. Sounds like the current Crown started it.* She filed her questions about that for a better time and nodded at the long, gossamer wing displayed beside three others on the counter. "O'gúl hornet?"

Bryl removed her fingers from the wing she'd been gently stroking with a finger and laughed. "You don't know *anything*, do you?"

"Bryl, how many times do I have to tell you to use your *manners?*"

Cheyenne set a hand on Yadje's shoulder and gave it a little pat. "It's okay. I don't get enough of the truth as it is. Your kid's all over it, and I like it."

"Hmm." The troll woman shot her an amused frown and stroked the back of her daughter's long scarlet braids.

"This is an evendrake wing," Bryl added softly. "*That's* the O'gúl hornet's web."

The halfling looked at where the troll girl pointed and cocked her head at the item dangling from the edge of the top shelf by a thin piece of twine—a cross between a dreamcatcher and a spiderweb, the thin threads glinting black and red and silver in the potion shop's low light. "That came from a hornet?"

"*O'gúl* hornet." The kid laughed and shook her head. "Not the same as the little bugs here."

"Little *bugs?*" Yadje bent over to stick her face right up in front of her daughter's. "I don't know where you get these ideas, my love, but that kind of disrespect will get you—"

"That's what they're *called,* Maji," Bryl whispered fiercely. "Over here. Bugs."

"Who told you that, hmm?"

The girl's frown was so intense, it darkened her entire face as a bloom of deep purple rose in her violet cheeks. "One of my library books," she hissed through clenched teeth. "The ones from last week, remember?"

"I *never* would have let you bring home anything about *bugs.*" When Bryl's scarlet eyes flicked toward her father, Yadje straightened and turned slowly to stare at R'mahr in disbelief. "*You* let her bring that sort of blasphemy into our home?"

Her husband chuckled nervously. "It was a library book, Yadje. For children. About Earthside bugs. Two entirely different things."

Cheyenne cleared her throat again. "I don't know what they are on the other side, but here, bugs are insects."

The troll woman blinked at her, oblivious.

"You know. Tiny crawling things. Ants, beetles, worms, caterpillars?" The halfling shrugged. "Not ringing a bell, huh?"

Yadje blinked furiously, glared at her husband, then shot their daughter an uncertain glance. "I never saw this book."

"It only took me a day," Bryl replied, her gaze dropping to the floor. "That's why I brought home five."

"Hmm." When the troll woman met Cheyenne's gaze, the halfling nodded and tried to smile. "If Cheyenne says that's what it was, I must defer to her. But I don't want to hear that word coming out of your mouth ever again. Do you understand?"

"Yes, Maji."

The potionmaster's low mumbles and heavy grunts had drawn closer to them along the wall, and Yadje guided her daughter toward the front of the shop with a hand on the girl's back. "What else did you need from here, my love?"

Cheyenne and R'mahr exchanged glances, caught between the miffed troll woman and the seriously grouchy orc potionmaster behind them. *And I thought* my *mom had weird quirks. That was rough.*

R'mahr leaned toward her and muttered, "The O'gúl hornet's web has powerful uses for wards, by the way. Mesmerizing to look at, no? But *so* expensive."

The halfling muffled a laugh and nodded. "Thanks for the warning."

CHAPTER SIXTY-TWO

Once Bryl and Yadje had plucked everything they wanted from the potionmaster's wares, the troll family gathered at the orc's counter at the back of the store and waited for him to finish his curmudgeonly curation.

"I'll be right back," Cheyenne muttered, then slipped around the huge display in the center of the shop and headed toward the opposite corner again. Leaning against the edge of the narrow counter lining the wall, she had to stand on her tiptoes to reach the twine tying the O'gúl hornet's web to a nail in the edge of the top shelf. A little buzz of energy jolted in her fingertips, and she carefully lowered the entire thing to study it for a second. The web twirled back and forth, the thin, glittering strands winking in red, black, and silver. *Good for wards. I need wards.*

By the time she returned to the orc's counter, the potionmaster was back behind it. He touched each of the items the trolls had set down with a gnarled finger, then rubbed his thumb against that finger and grunted. "Eighteen."

"Yes." Yadje opened her oversized handbag, pulled out a small woven purse that could have been bought here in Peridosh, and handed the orc a twenty-dollar bill.

That's how you know we're on this side of the border.

The orc pulled the change out of his pocket and slapped two ones down on the counter. "Until next time."

"Thank you." The troll woman pocketed the change—and their supplies—before she and her family stepped back to let Cheyenne approach the counter.

"I know this wasn't on the list," the halfling said, lifting the web up over the counter, "but I couldn't help myself."

The troll's eyes all widened, and Bryl let out a little gasp. "Wow!"

"Of course, you couldn't." The orc glowered at her and set the woven basket on the counter with a thud. The thing nearly over-flowed with spell ingredients he'd tossed in there.

Cheyenne nodded. "Thanks for grabbing all that. What do I owe you?"

"Very funny." The potionmaster's crooked fingers reached out to take the twine tied to the O'gúl hornet's web. "I will, however, need payment for *this*."

"Just that? I do want to buy all the stuff in that basket."

He shoved the basket toward her, making two of the vials clink together where they were nestled on top of the pile. "Don't *test* me, drow. I'll not be taken for a fool."

The old laws, huh? Got it. Cheyenne eyed the overflowing basket and nodded. "Point taken. How much for that, then?"

Lifting the web until it spun slowly beside his wrinkled face, the potionmaster sneered. "No coin. Not even here."

"Uh, then what do you want for it?" The halfling glanced at the trolls, who watched the exchange in complete silence and didn't even try to butt in.

"You have it on you, drow. I'll wait."

What the hell? Patting down her pockets, Cheyenne stared at the counter. "I'll…look."

She slipped out both cell phones and placed them on the counter. Then came her wallet and car keys. The old orc grunted. When her fingers closed around the Heart of Midnight pendant, Cheyenne shook her head and slipped that into the front pocket of her hoody. *No way that thing changes hands. No matter how much I hate it.*

"Hold on. I'm still looking..." Smirking, she slipped her hands into her back pockets, then the front, wondering what the old guy could possibly be waiting for. A penny came out of her left pocket, and she set it on the counter to get it out of the way. *Empty pockets are a new problem, literally and figuratively.* That made her laugh at herself, and the potionmaster growled. Next came Lee McDurn's business card, and she glanced at the orc. "No? Okay."

Then the halfling's fingers brushed across a small piece of metal in her right pocket with sharp, cold points. She paused, then pulled out the four-pointed star Mattie Bergmann had made from the half-drow's wayward spell. *Through the washer and everything.*

With a little shrug, Cheyenne set the metal trinket in the center of the counter, then spread her arms. "That's all I got."

"It isn't." The orc leaned down and squinted at the tiny object but didn't touch it. "But this will do."

"Great." *A four-pointed souvenir, huh? Yeah, right.*

The potionmaster jerked something under his counter and pulled out what looked like a thin mailing sleeve sold at the post office, only this one was made of some kind of tanned, hardened leather. He gingerly slid the web into it, then moved the whole thing across the counter beside the giant basket. "Don't get it wet."

"Definitely not." The halfling dipped her head and reached for her free and purchased items. "That's it, right?"

"Until the next time you invoke the old laws, drow."

"I didn't... Never mind. Thanks."

"Oh, Cheyenne!" Bryl's scarlet head popped up beside the halfling's elbow. "I can carry that basket for you."

"Yeah?"

"I won't let anything fall out. I promise."

Cheyenne picked up the handle and lowered the basket into the girl's outstretched arms. "I trust you." Everything went back into her pockets, then she grabbed the weird leather sleeve protecting the strange magical web and turned toward Bryl's parents. "Time to go."

The trolls nodded at the potionmaster, who waved them off and went back to staring at the four-pointed star on his counter. They all slipped out of the shop and back into the medium-sized crowd milling around the Peridosh thoroughfare.

"And I thought we'd be showing *you* something new down here." R'mahr chuckled and shook his head. "You are full of surprises, Cheyenne."

"Tell me about it." *Surprises for me too. What just happened in there?*

"Is there anything else we need to see down here?" Yadje asked her husband, linking her arm through his.

"Cheyenne *did* mention something about food."

"We ate before we came, and what you ate at home is *leagues* better than anything you'll find down here."

The halfling took another sniff of the heavily spiced food, the scent getting stronger as they slowly made their way toward the section of Peridosh lined with taverns and food stalls. Her stomach growled again, and she shot Bryl a quick wink. "Smells pretty good to me."

The girl laughed and hiked the basket higher. "Maji doesn't let us eat anything down here."

"Don't talk to *me* about loyalty, asshole!" A surprisingly skinny orc stumbled out of the tavern beyond the Empty Barrel, his eyes wide as he whirled around to face a gigantic troll with a shock of bright-red hair running down the center of his head like a skunk stripe. "I told you to quit coming in here until you bring what you owe me!"

Two more trolls stepped out of the tavern behind Skunkhead, their arms folded as they glared at the scrawny orc.

"Come on, Majril," the orc whined. "I ain't got none of that yet."

"Then you can piss off."

Most of the crowd walked around the arguing magicals, minding their own business but moving in a fairly wide arc around the terrified orc. Cheyenne saw the thought flash across the skinny greenskin's face a split second before he acted. The terror there flared to rage in an instant, and he threw a shower of bursting green sparks toward Skunkhead and his bouncers.

"Bryl, my love. Over here." Yadje reached for her daughter and pulled the girl toward R'mahr, glancing at the fight and hoping to get away in time.

Skunkhead dodged the sparks that left divots in the front wall of his tavern and hissed. "I'm adding that to your bill, you fell-damn coward!" He unleashed a flaming ball of red fire at the orc, who leaped back and darted aside.

The orc's flailing hand knocked Bryl's shoulder and sent her stumbling against her mother. Both Yadje and the girl cried out, and the orc snarled at them.

"Now you... You..." R'mahr shook a furious finger at the other magical and seemed to run out of ideas.

Another fireball burst on the ground at the orc's feet, and the troll family yelped before struggling to get out of the way.

"All right. Enough of this crap." Cheyenne tucked the hardened leather case under her arm and stalked toward the troublemakers. "Hey!"

"Get lost, bitch!" Skunkhead barked without turning to look at her. He was focused on shooting two columns of sparking yellow energy at the skinny orc. His target yelped and blasted a spray of tiny silver darts. The spell tinkled through the air before thudding against walls and doors and cement like they were bullets.

Cheyenne threw up a shimmering black shield in front of her, and the tiny silver projectiles clinked against it in quick succession. Even that didn't get the fighting magicals' attention. When she lowered the shield and stepped forward, another round of burning drow magic flared up her spine.

The halfling set the leather case down at her feet and didn't give those idiots another warning. Her whipping black tendrils lashed from the fingertips of both hands and curled around first Skunkhead's wrists, then the skinny orc's. They both shouted in surprise, their attack spells momentarily abandoned as they struggled against their new bonds.

"Listen up!" Cheyenne roared. Her voice echoed through Peridosh, and everyone did what she said. *Not what I was going for, but okay.* She tugged sharply on the tendrils writhing around the dumb magicals' wrists. They both jerked toward her, stumbling over their feet and staring at her with wide eyes and gaping mouths. The other magicals who'd stopped at her shout picked up their errands again, giving Cheyenne a wide berth now too. "Whatever issue you guys have with each other, take care of it somewhere else, huh? There are kids here, and people who don't wanna be caught up in your bullshit. Don't make me drag you out of here like a couple of bullies on the playground, all right?"

Skunkhead's mouth opened and closed without any sound. The lanky orc trembled from head to toe, letting out terrified whimpers through his slack jaw. Then the giant troll dropped to his knees right there in the middle of the avenue. "Forgive me."

The orc looked at the now-sniveling troll who'd just tried to burn him to a crisp and slowly bent over until he was kneeling too, arms outstretched with Cheyenne's quivering tendrils tightening around his wrists. "What he said."

The half-drow stared at them and didn't move. *I could get used to this, but what the hell?*

"The people you *should* be apologizing too are those trolls over there. You're screwing up their family outing."

"So sorry."

"Sorry. We're done."

"Uh-huh." Cheyenne glanced at her troll ex-neighbors. R'mahr and Yadje looked horrified that these magicals were even talking to them. Bryl stared at the halfling and seemed ready to start cheering. The halfling gave another sharp tug on the black tendrils holding these guys at bay. "Whenever you're ready to start using your brains, I'm more than ready to forget I had to do this."

Skunkhead and the trembling orc both nodded vigorously, bobbing their heads down between their outstretched arms without a word.

The quivering black tendrils whipped away from their wrists

and retracted into Cheyenne's fingers. The orc fell flat on his face before scrambling back to his feet. Then he darted through the crowd and farther down the avenue, dodging the magicals in his way. Skunkhead stood slowly, looking up at the half-drow with terrified eyes before dropping his head again. Then he slowly backed away toward the front door of his tavern in a never-ending bow.

Cheyenne watched him go until he slipped through the door and slammed it shut behind him. His two cronies whirled to follow but had to fumble with the door before they also disappeared.

When she turned to look at the troll family huddling together on the other side of the avenue, they didn't move an inch. Sighing, the halfling glanced around Peridosh and found everyone else minding their own business like the whole thing had never happened. "Okay."

She picked up the leather sleeve around her super-expensive magical web and went back to her old neighbors. "Even when I'm not looking for it, there's always some kind of mess that needs to be cleaned up. I'm really sorry about that."

"No, no, Cheyenne." R'mahr lifted a hand, his eyes glistening with the start of tears. "I told you not to apologize to us, and I meant every word. I still do."

"Yeah, but you guys shouldn't have to deal with crap like that. You were just trying to get a little shopping done."

Yadje's lips were pressed together so tightly, they'd basically disappeared. "Well, that's why we come on Wednesdays."

Cheyenne and R'mahr both shot her a surprised glance before bursting into laughter. The troll woman's lips quivered a little, then she let out a self-conscious chuckle and patted the top of her daughter's head.

"No more Saturdays, then," the halfling added.

She stumbled sideways when something crashed into her thigh. Bryl craned her neck up from where she'd thrown her arms around the half-drow's waist and beamed up at her. "Thank you."

"Uh, of course." Cheyenne reached down to pat the girl's back, nearly falling over again when Bryl gave her legs another tight squeeze. "I probably shouldn't say that's what I'm here for, but..." She spread her arms and shrugged.

"You're what's missing, I think," the girl muttered.

"Oh, yeah? Missing from what?"

"Come, Bryl." Yadje gently tapped her daughter's back, and the girl released Cheyenne, still staring up at the halfling in awe. Her mother gently grabbed the girl's small violet hand and pulled her back. "I think it's time we head back home, yes?"

"Yes, Maji." The girl bent to pick up the basket of Cheyenne's things and cradled it in her arms.

R'mahr nodded. "Unless there's anything else you wanted while we're here, Cheyenne?"

"Just one more thing, actually." The halfling tapped her fist against her belly and peered down the avenue toward the other end. "I'll be right back, okay? I'm starving."

She brushed past the other magicals moving about through the marketplace. *Follow the trail of anything that smells normal.*

Behind her, R'mahr stuck a finger in the air and took a step after her. "Ah, yes. I could show you—"

Yadje put her hand on his chest and pushed him back. "*You* are staying right here. We have leftovers at home."

CHAPTER SIXTY-THREE

.

Cheyenne returned to the troll family and popped the last bite of that barbeque sausage on a stick into her mouth. R'mahr's hopeful expression fell when he saw her hands were empty.

"So much better," she said around her mouthful and sucked the crust of spices off her fingers. "I tried to be fast."

"Too fast, maybe." R'mahr chuckled when his wife nudged him in the ribs. "Shall we head back?"

"I'm ready when you are."

"Excellent." Tentatively, the troll man steered his family back through the crowd toward the far end of the avenue. "This has been an eye-opening experience for us, Cheyenne. Thank you for letting us tag along."

"You're the ones showing me around, so I should be thanking *you*." The halfling tried to ignore the odd stares coming at her again from the vendors and customers who dared to look at her. A goblin woman veered out of her path and put a good six feet between them. *That's new.*

"Cheyenne, we can't tell you how wonderful it is to have you with us. Our very own *phér móre*, it feels like." Yadje turned around and shot the half-drow a genuine smile. "A *drow*."

"Yeah, friends are pretty great, huh?"

"Oh, yes. But we don't mean just as a friend, Cheyenne." R'mahr reached the closed elevator doors first and waited for the rest of them to catch up. "That's very good for us, of course, but think what this means for the rest of us who made the crossing."

The troll couple gazed at her expectantly.

Pretend like you know what's going on. "Just think." Cheyenne nodded and reached down to take the basket out of Bryl's arms. "Thanks for taking care of my stuff, kid."

The girl grinned.

"We knew you were special the first time you came through our front door," Yadje added wistfully. Cheyenne almost snorted. "But now, seeing you around everyone else down here, the way you dealt with those…those…"

"Scoundrels," her husband finished.

The troll woman sighed. "There's still a chance, Cheyenne, that some of the old prophecies from Ambar'ogúl are finally coming true."

The halfling jerked her head up from where she'd been making faces at Bryl. "Prophecies?"

"Well, they're all muddled and mixed together, aren't they?" R'mahr shook his head. "But the big ones, yes."

The elevator doors let out a groan when they opened, and Cheyenne waited for the troll family to step inside before she followed. "I don't have a lot of experience with prophecies. What do they say? The big ones."

The troll man leaned back against the wall of the elevator as the doors closed again. The shiny metal box started its ascent with a little jerk. "Oh, the usual. We've all heard them from time to time, passed around in gatherings and ceremonies. Ambar'ogúl split in half, rotting from the inside out. An outsider bonded by blood to take their place within the heart."

Cheyenne frowned. "Muddled and mixed together is right."

"It talks about the Crown becoming its own undoing and the savior of a realm all at the same time." R'mahr's eyes narrowed. "For so long, Cheyenne, it seemed like the only parts of any prophecy that came true were the ones nobody really wanted to hear."

"The darkest parts, yes?" Yadje nodded slowly, pulling her daughter closer with an arm around the girl's shoulder. "Drow are not well-known for their altruism, yes? Or heroism. But something about you..." The troll woman's smile bloomed again. "Something about you makes it seem possible. That this might be it. A drow halfling breaking the cycle of her kind to help heal the rift."

"The cycle of my kind?" Cheyenne readjusted the leather case under her arm. *New cycle of ascendance. That's what he said.* "To be honest, I don't know enough about my kind to break any cycle, and there's not a lot of literature floating around for me to brush up on my drow history."

The trolls just gave her thin, sympathetic smiles.

"So, who wears the O'gúl Crown now?"

"I hate her," Bryl mumbled.

"Careful, my love." Her mother pulled her a little closer.

Cheyenne nodded at the girl. "Because she's the reason you guys had to make the crossing, right?"

Bryl nodded slowly. "She doesn't—"

"We left that behind when we chose a life here," R'mahr interrupted, sliding his arm around his wife's shoulders. The hope hadn't left their eyes, but they looked a lot more disturbed than a minute ago. "It's best not to talk about such things. Besides, all this chatter of prophecies is only speculation. Please forget we brought it up."

Glancing at them, the halfling offered a tiny smile and didn't push. *No way am I forgetting that little nugget.*

"Oh." Yadje rummaged in her giant bag for her illusion ring and her husband's bracelet. The moment the jewelry slipped on, two adult trolls became blond, blue-eyed humans with matching smiles. R'mahr muttered a quick word and flicked his fingers toward his daughter. Bryl's illusion shimmered and took over. "I'll hold that for you if you like."

"Thanks." Cheyenne handed over her basket of goodies, then pulled the Heart of Midnight out of her pocket to tie the chain around her neck again. In an instant, the vibrating rush of her drow magic disappeared, snuffed out like a candle under an overturned jar. *Worse than holding back a sneeze.* The pale, black-haired Goth chick shrugged. "Gotta do what you gotta do, right?"

"It's the only way to keep going." Yadje returned the basket and ran a hand over the top of Bryl's blonde head. "Whatever you have to do, Cheyenne, I believe you'll succeed."

"You know, I'm lucky enough to not have had a shortage of that sentiment in my life." Cheyenne wrinkled her nose and smiled at the troll girl. "Still feels good to hear it."

The elevator came to a clunky, thudding halt, and the doors opened. The magicals disguised as humans and the halfling stepped out of the elevator. Tony stood behind his counter and watched them expressionlessly.

"Have a good one, Tony." Cheyenne waved as she passed.

"Not likely." Tony scooped a massive spoonful of bright-pink Fro-Yo up to his mouth and shoveled it all in.

Once they'd stepped outside into the sunny afternoon, R'mahr turned and extended his hand toward the halfling. "An excellent afternoon together, Cheyenne."

"Oh. Yeah." She took his hand and chuckled. "Thanks for all the help."

"We did very little. But you're welcome."

"Oh. I almost forgot." Yadje rummaged in her purse again and pulled out a small brown glass jar with an unrecognizable symbol scratched on the lid in pencil. "R'mahr said you were looking for healing salves and whatnot. Take this."

"Wow. I don't need the whole thing—"

"I just made a new batch at home."

Bryl wrinkled her nose. "She keeps them in my room."

"Well, that's because your room gets the best sunlight, doesn't it?" The troll woman blinked at the halfling and gestured at the jar she'd nestled into Cheyenne's basket. "Don't eat it, but it works very well with most non-life-threatening wounds."

"Anything less than a knife wound, pretty much."

Yadje jabbed her husband in the ribs and glanced quickly at their daughter. "What are you doing talking about knife wounds? When is that a part of daily conversation?"

"It's just an example." R'mahr hunched his shoulders and gestured toward Cheyenne, chuckling. "You don't think a friend like her has seen the wrong end of a knife?"

"What's that supposed to mean?"

Cheyenne laughed. "No knives so far, but it's good advice. I appreciate this too." She nodded at the jar on top of her basket, then turned toward the parking lot. "Can I give you guys a ride?"

"Oh, no. We're not that far, Cheyenne. Just a few more things to do today. Have fun with all your...work." R'mahr pointed at her basket, then wrapped his arm around his wife's shoulders again.

"Okay. Thanks. I'll see you guys later."

"Bye, Cheyenne." Bryl waved, and her parents repeated the gesture.

The halfling crossed the street toward the parking lot, miscellaneous ingredients rattling around in the overflowing basket. She had to set it down to pull out her keyless fob and unlock the car, then everything went into the back seat.

When she got behind the wheel, she flicked the Heart of Darkness pendant resting against her chest. Then she stuffed it down under her sweatshirt and started the car. *It's nonstop today.*

The halfling heard the voices coming from behind her apartment door the second she stepped out of the elevator. Mostly, it was Ember's laughter. *And some dude in there making her laugh.*

When she opened the door, she found Ember sitting beside one of the black leather armchairs. In it was their new neighbor Matthew. They both turned to look at her, and Matthew grinned. "Hey, Cheyenne."

"'Sup?" With a quick nod, the halfling turned left and hurried toward her bedroom at the other end of the apartment. *Right. Like a basket of crazy magical stuff and this leather case under my arm aren't gonna catch the guy's attention.*

Ember and Matthew muttered something to each other, but Cheyenne was too busy jerking open the bedroom door to pay much attention. Then she was too busy staring. "No way."

The basket of supplies went slowly to the polished hardwood floors, followed by the case holding the magical web. Cheyenne took a few more steps into the room and laughed. "She freakin' *did* it."

Black-out curtains hung over the single window on the right. A black chest of drawers sat in the far right corner, with silver skulls on each drawer instead of knobs or handles. In the left corner was a massive Victorian-style wingback chair, the armrests studded with silver buttons and the rest of the upholstery done up with black lace around the edges. Beside that was a tall standing lamp, and the lampshade was an inverted chandelier with sheer purple fabric draped over it. The queen-sized bed hadn't been changed out, but a canopy of black satin and black tulle fell from the ceiling to hang over the side of the bed.

Laughing again, Cheyenne went to the bed first and poked her head inside the canopy. The head of the bed was covered in black and silver pillows of lace, velvet, and satin. One had an intricate dagger printed on the front. Another had a very fancy design of a disembodied hand flipping the bird. With a chuckle, the halfling spread her hands on the comforter. *Christmas came early, didn't it?*

"Purple fucking velvet. Ha." She spun around and headed back to the door, reaching out to flip the light switch on. The intricately curving light switch case with more skulls on it made her pause, then she turned on the light. The purple chandelier only gave off enough of a glow to confirm what she already knew.

"Em. You for real made me a—" Cheyenne stopped when she saw the back of Matthew's head rising over the back of the armchair. *Shit. I really don't like people in my space.*

"You like it?" Ember wheeled away from the armchair so she could get a better view of her friend's reaction.

"That's an understatement, and we can talk about it later." The halfling couldn't hold back a smirk, then she moved farther across the living room to look at Matthew and raise an eyebrow. "Looks like you two are having a lovely chat."

"Just thought I'd stop by and see if I could help."

"He helped hang those paintings." Ember pointed at the wall beside the front door.

"Those are kinda cool." Cheyenne tilted her head to one side and then the other, squinting at the splotches of black, gray, and yellow paint. "What are they?"

"Abstract." Ember shrugged. "I like them."

"That's the only thing that matters when you're the one putting it all together, huh?" The halfling smiled at her friend, glanced at Matthew, then jolted and pulled her phone out of her pocket. "Crap. I have that meeting in like twenty minutes."

"Oh, yeah. Good luck with that one." Ember shot her a thumbs-up.

"Not sure luck's gonna help me with this, but I'll take it anyway." Cheyenne picked her backpack up off the floor beside the couch and double-checked to make sure the copper legacy box was still inside.

"Who has meetings on a Saturday at six o'clock?" Matthew asked.

Slinging the backpack over her shoulder, the halfling spread her arms and walked backward toward the door. "Question I've been asking myself for two days, Matthew. Just can't figure it out. Go ahead and eat dinner without me, Em. Save something if you want. I've been weirdly busy today."

"No problem."

Cheyenne spun around and opened the door, then peered over her shoulder and muttered, "Be good."

Ember's laugh came through the door even after the halfling shut it. Then Cheyenne was off again. *Maybe I should think about building a Goth-box on wheels. This back and forth thing is killing me.*

CHAPTER SIXTY-FOUR

Cheyenne pulled out her phone just as she reached the door to Conference Room A in the Computer Sciences building on the VCU campus. *One minute to spare. That's gotta be good enough for these people.*

When she opened the door, all five of her professors sat around the conference table. Four of them gave the halfling a tight smile; the only one who looked happy to see her was Mattie.

Hersh scowled at his wristwatch. "We appreciate your punctuality."

"So do I." Lowering her backpack to the floor, Cheyenne pulled out the closest chair—which happened to be at the head of the table —and sat. "I'm ready when you are."

"Great." LePlant clapped her hands and interlaced her fingers before leaning forward. "As you read in that email you received on Thursday, Cheyenne, we've all noticed that you've been having a little difficulty making it to your classes on time."

"Or at all." Hersh snorted.

Mattie shot the man a warning glance, but he sat back in his chair and folded his arms.

"Whatever is going on in your personal life is clearly drawing your focus away from your graduate studies."

No shit.

LePlant adjusted the thin silver frames of her glasses and cleared her throat. "Now, this is grad school. You made the decision to apply, you were accepted, and you're obviously an adult who makes her own decisions, just like the rest of us. We don't normally sit down like this with graduate students who find themselves farther over their heads than they expected."

Cheyenne sat back in her chair. "I'm not in over my head."

"Oh, we're well aware. Your startling ability to predict assignments, not to mention the advanced quality of your work, is the reason we even considered having this meeting."

"We want you here," Dawley added. "At this school. In this program. We want you to receive your master's degree, and we're hoping that's what you still want too."

"Of course it is." The halfling gazed around the table at her insanely boring professors before settling her gaze on Mattie. The woman flashed her a brilliant smile, her blazing green eyes widening just a little.

"So, Cheyenne," LePlant continued, "we've put our heads together and come up with a solution we think works well. You'll have a different schedule. Which, I might add, is *imperative* for you to keep if you want to continue with this program. No emails apologizing for not making it. And the five of us can rest easy knowing one of the most talented students to enter the Computer Sciences program at this school is still pursuing a degree she very much deserves."

"What's the schedule?" *I'm not agreeing to anything until I know what it is.*

"You'll be moved to three days a week instead of five. One class a day, Monday, Wednesday, and Friday." LePlant's gaze darted around the table before she took a deep breath and nodded. "And you'll be teaching it."

"I'll be..." Cheyenne snorted and choked on a laugh. "I'll be *what* now?"

"Teaching undergraduate classes."

"Yeah, I don't know if you really want me teaching a bunch of freshmen how to do anything."

"We do, actually." Beckwith drummed his fingers on the armrests of his chair. "It's not a one-hundred-level class, either. Undergraduate Advanced Programming. There's a syllabus, of course, but we're willing to move things around if you feel you can improve the teaching material."

"Oh, I can." The words spilled out of her, and Mattie chuckled before covering her mouth with the tips of her fingers. "But that's not the point."

"Feel free to make your point at any time, then," Hersh grumbled.

"Yeah, thanks. I'm not a teacher. I don't have any qualifications for that. Or experience. You put me up there in front of a room of advanced whatever, and I don't know if anyone else is gonna understand what I'm saying."

"That's part of the reason we came to this decision, Cheyenne." LePlant nodded. "The best way to learn is to *have* to teach. There might not be much left for you to learn at this school, and we've all come to that realization. If you want to keep pursuing your master's here, this is the way you have to do it. There aren't any other options."

The halfling dropped her forearms onto the armrests and swiveled back and forth in the chair. "And you all think it's the best decision to have me"—she gestured at herself from head to toe with both hands—"stand up in front of young, impressionable minds hanging on every word I say?"

Mattie took a sharp breath through her nose—not quite a laugh, but close. "If *you* think you can handle being the center of attention for four and a half hours a week, so do we."

Cheyenne slowly licked her lips. *They're handing me my degree on a silver platter, and I'm hesitant.* "And that's it? Just teach this one class? I'll sail through the rest of my graduate career as a glorified sub?"

"No, it would be your class. Completely autonomous. You decide what to teach and how, as long as it follows curriculum guidelines and adheres to the specified subject matter. Which is quite vague at this point." LePlant shot Mattie an exasperated glance. "But it has to be those days and that ten o'clock class. And you'll write a miniature dissertation at the end of every semester summarizing the course material and certain learning points along the way. For yourself. So, what do you think?"

Plenty of time for breakfast in the morning. "Looks like I don't have a choice."

"You always have a choice, Cheyenne." Mattie raised an eyebrow. "This is just the only *good* one."

"Yeah, okay. I'll do it."

Hersh slapped his hands on the table and pushed out of the chair. "Thank God that went quickly."

Cheyenne and most of her teachers frowned at the man as he sped past the conference table and headed through the door without another word.

"We're very glad to hear it," Beckwith added. "And I, for one, am confident in your ability to switch gears like this. Good luck." He stood too, and Beckwith followed him out with a small nod at the grad student-turned-student teacher.

"Professor Bergmann will fill you in on all the details and help you get set up. You start Monday." LePlant held out her hand, and Cheyenne slowly reached up to take it. "I'm looking forward to seeing what you can do."

"You and me both." Sighing, the halfling turned her chair to watch the woman step out of the room, then spun quickly toward Mattie. "*You're* gonna fill *me* in on the details, huh?"

"Don't I always?" Mattie slung a medium-sized tote over her shoulder. "You can thank me later, kid. Right now, I'm thanking *you.*"

"I mean, it's *my* master's on the line, apparently."

"Well, yeah. And you can do whatever you want with it. Not my place to judge. You also just picked up *my* Advanced Programming class, and *whew*! I feel a million pounds lighter."

"Wait, what?" Cheyenne stood, picked up her backpack, and followed the woman into the hall. "Your class?"

"Yes. I can't *stand* undergrad classes. They bore me to tears."

The halfling scoffed. "How is a class that bores you gonna help me learn anything?"

The Nightstalker college professor turned and wiggled her eyebrows. "Why do you think the specified subject matter is so vague?" She chuckled. "LePlant doesn't appreciate the way I plan my courses. Especially the ones I just… Ugh."

"Wow."

"Oh, come on, kid. Do you know how many grad students get this kind of opportunity?"

"You're gonna tell me, aren't you?"

"*None* of them. This is a one-of-a-kind thing just for you, which is why it fits. Because you don't, and we both know that." Mattie looked quickly away and fought down a laugh. "That's also why I pushed the rest of your professors into accepting my proposal and coming to this meeting."

"This was *your* idea."

"I have a spot of brilliance from time to time."

Cheyenne stopped in the middle of the hall and stared at the back of Mattie's long, wavy black hair. "This is because I stopped coming to your office hours, isn't it?"

"Very funny, kid. Feel free to stop by whenever you like. Door's always open. And look for an email from me coming atcha tomorrow. Now go enjoy your weekend. That's still a thing." Just like that, Professor Mattie Bergmann disappeared around the corner, leaving the drow halfling alone in a closed-up building fifteen minutes after she'd arrived.

Guess I'll pull this off like everything else. Four and a half hours a week, though?

Cheyenne cocked her head and started down the hall toward the front doors of the Computer Sciences building. "Not bad."

CHAPTER SIXTY-FIVE

"Wait, wait, wait. They want *you*—" Ember barked a laugh, then clapped a hand over her mouth and shook her head. "Sorry. They want *you* to teach a class?" The laughter returned as soon as she got the question out.

"Yuck it up, Em. You're looking at VCU's newest and worst student-teacher."

"Oh, you won't be *that* bad." Ember bit her lip and managed to hold back another fit of laughter for maybe five seconds. "No, no. This is good. Take you out of your comfort zone. You just need to brush up a little on your people skills."

"I *have* people skills. I just choose not to use them as frequently as others might want me to."

"Yeah, well, you're gonna have to put on that Summerlin charm in the classroom three days a week."

Cheyenne shook her head. "If I don't, I might get every student to drop out of the class. Then I'm free."

The fae shot her a pointed look and folded her arms.

"Kidding. Just a joke. Doesn't mean I can't wish for a particular outcome."

"Come on, Cheyenne. You were sailing through your classes. It's the showing-up part that got you into this."

"Can you blame me?"

Ember nudged the paper towel holder across the island toward her friend and waited for Cheyenne to wipe the marinara sauce off her chin. "I can't blame you for anything. Kinda self-explanatory at this point. Except for maybe eating that spaghetti like you've never used a fork before."

"I'm starving, okay? One weird orange-flavored thing of O'gúleesh meat on a stick isn't enough to keep me running at full capacity." Cheyenne twirled up another forkful and shoveled it into her mouth. "Thanks for ordering a whole second box of this, by the way."

"I learned not to share meals with you, like, two weeks after we met."

The halfling chuckled and had to wipe more sauce off. "Yeah, I kinda lost it on you, huh?"

"Well, it wasn't full-drow-mode losing it, but a tiny part of me thought you were gonna stab my eye out with those chopsticks."

"See? This is a *way* better conversation."

Ember grabbed the water bottle out of her lap and gulped half of it in one breath. "But I still didn't make my point, which is that you really don't have an excuse *not* to show up for an hour-and-half class three days a week. Are you kidding?"

"But it's not a class. It's *teaching*." Cheyenne swallowed. "A class."

"Yeah, a class you get to build from scratch. Listen, I got shot and still didn't get that kind of offer."

The halfling slowly looked up from her food and smiled when she saw Ember fighting back another laugh. "You're getting good at that. I actually thought you were pissed."

"I will be if you screw this up. You think magical criminals and your FRoE frenemies can work around your particularly open schedule now?"

"I sure hope so." Another bite of spaghetti went in, then Cheyenne dropped the fork into the takeout container and nodded.

"Hit the spot. Have I told you lately that you're kind of the best roommate? Housemate's better, right?'

"Yeah. But I'm starting to feel more like your personal assistant."

They both cracked up at that, and Ember turned around before wheeling herself out into the living room.

"You know, you would be pretty good at that."

"Shut up. I'd never work this hard for someone who paid me to do it."

The halfling joined her friend in the living room and cocked her head. "I don't think your definition of professional incentive matches the actual definition."

"Hey, if I ended up doing all this for someone else, I'd have to figure out what they like first and get the okay on everything and spend all my time doing stuff for someone else before I called it a day and...what? Went to bed? I'm not just doing this for *you*. You don't even like the paintings up there." Ember snorted and pointed toward the abstract pieces of whatever.

Cheyenne wrinkled her nose. "Was it that obvious?"

"Transparent."

"I really don't mind them. Seriously. It's not like I spent a lot of time staring at walls. Or art. Plus, I told you to take the reins, and you did."

Ember wheeled herself back and forth at the edge of the area rug, waiting for the halfling to drop into one of the leather armchairs. "And I can't even tell you how much fun I've had racking up bills on your card the last two days."

Cheyenne waved her off and crossed one foot over the opposite knee. "You didn't make the Goth-box for you, though."

The fae grinned and stopped rolling. "I nailed that one, didn't I?"

"I'll put it this way, Em. If I enjoyed shopping, I couldn't have made that bedroom any better than what you put in there."

"And the pillow, huh?" Ember flipped her friend the middle finger, and they laughed.

"You get me."

"Yeah, well, you're not that hard to read."

They sat there for a moment, then Cheyenne looked over the back of the armchair at her bedroom door. "You didn't...have Matthew Thomas help you with that, did you?"

"Pshh. No. I brought in professionals for *your* room. Matthew was good for hanging two pieces of artwork, then he just sat down and started talking."

"He does like to do that, doesn't he?"

Ember rolled her eyes. "I didn't have the heart to ask him to leave. The dude's really lonely."

"Aw, tell me you didn't fall for that spiel."

"No falling. Just sitting." The fae patted the armrests of the wheelchair. "I don't know. He's not that bad."

"Say that again in a week."

"No."

"Just saying. If he thinks there's even a *tiny* chance of you maybe kinda sorta liking him, he's not gonna give up."

Ember rolled her eyes. "Whatever. New topic."

"I'm drawing a blank." Cheyenne laughed at her friend's frown and spread her arms. "I know. There's always something goin' on in my head. Maybe too much today. Might've fried a few circuits."

"I bet that line would be a hit in front of your new students."

The halfling cleared her throat and slowly shook her head. "New topic."

"New Netflix series?"

"I'm down. *Oh.* I forgot to get your—" A low buzz came from the wall beside the door. The sturdy-looking long black cabinet under the weird artwork wasn't just a cabinet. The top lifted slowly, revealing a massive flat-screen TV inside. Cheyenne turned back toward Ember, who'd pulled a shiny black remote out of her pocket and now wiggled it. "You're unbelievable."

"You're footin' the bill."

"Damn straight. And happy to do it." The halfling turned sideways in the chair and slung both legs over the armrest. "Whatever you wanna watch. I'm going to see Corian in a bit, so I need to zone out until then."

"Yeah, 'cause this might be the last Saturday you have free before you're hunched over your desk grading papers."

"Well, then don't ruin it."

Two and a half hours later, Cheyenne pulled up in front of her Nightstalker mentor's rental unit. With her backpack slung over her shoulder, it took her a little extra maneuvering to pull the basket of magical supplies and the leather case out of her back seat. Then she closed the door and looked across the grass. *At least he's not standing out here this time watching me.*

She moved quickly across the lawn and down the damp concrete steps to Apartment D. The metal door flashed orange and opened swiftly before she could decide on the best way to knock.

"Hurry up." Corian nodded for her to step inside, and he closed the door before putting the wards back up again. Then he glanced down at the basket in her hand and blinked. "What the hell did you bring over?"

"Spell ingredients. Remember?"

"Damn. Remind me never to have you do my shopping for me."

"I'll never do your shopping for you. Moving on."

"Mmhmm." The Nightstalker frowned at her supplies, then nodded toward the shelves. Just set it over there. Trials first. *Remember?"*

"What trials?"

Corian just blinked with zero expression on his feline features.

With a sigh, the halfling gently set everything down beside the overstuffed metal shelves, then opened her backpack and pulled out the puzzle box. "Where to tonight?"

"You know, I kinda like watching you figure it out when we get there." Corian brushed past her and stopped in front of the circle of candles in the middle of the floor. "Hurry up."

"Yeah, okay. You in a time crunch or something?"

"Aren't you? The faster we get you through your trials, the easier this'll be for all of us." He lifted his hands in front of him and waited for the halfling to stop at his side. Several whispered words in O'gúleesh and quickly executed gestures later, a portal opened in the center of the circle.

"I'm so glad it's not an island." Cheyenne stepped over the candles and passed through the dark, glimmering portal toward trees and underbrush and boulders strewn across a hill. Her Vans slid sideways on a carpet of pine needles, throwing her off balance for a second before she caught herself. Then Corian stepped through, the portal disappeared, and the halfling turned back to shoot him a disbelieving glance. "We're training on the side of a mountain?"

"What, you think every piece of terrain you'll have to fight on is gonna be flat?"

"You're right. No problem. If I go flying down that hill, I'll just hope I'm fast enough to catch myself before bashing my brains against one of those boulders down there."

"You're fast enough."

The halfling took a second glance at the steep hill and the large outcropping of moss-covered boulders below. "Speaking of terrain, where are we this time?"

"I don't know. Somewhere in Yellowstone."

"National Park?"

"You know the drill." The Nightstalker crunched across the ground, tilting his body to expertly adjust for the steep incline. "I'll wait."

"Yeah, yeah." *Just what we need. Blasting apart a national park and stirring up more Bigfoot stories.* Cheyenne untied the knot in the chain around her neck for the millionth time and stuck it and the pendant in her pocket. Then she nestled the drow legacy box in the pine needles and leaves beside her and slipped into drow form. "Oh, man!"

"You good?"

"Oh, yeah. Feels like I've been shoved into a box all day and finally broke out again."

"Hmm. Normal side effect. Probably."

The halfling snorted. "Thank you so much for the reassurance. Hey, speaking of said pendant, does that thing have, like, a breaking point?"

"Such as?"

"Such as some part of my magic slipping through in a situation where I *really* wanted to use it?"

Corian stroked his fur-covered chin, his silver eyes fixed intently on his halfling trainee. "That's part of the time crunch."

"Oh, *really*?" Cheyenne tossed her white hair out of her face. "How?"

"More like a countdown with the spell on that pendant. Wearing it while you're actively going through the drow trials messes with the effectiveness."

"You're serious."

"Of course I am. Which is why we need to get you through the rest of your latent abilities and the last few layers of that puzzle box as quickly as possible." He shrugged. "If I timed it right, I'm pretty sure the Heart of Midnight will keep you relatively hidden until that thing opens."

"That thing?" Cheyenne pointed at the puzzle box.

"Yes, Cheyenne."

"And you didn't think it was important to tell me that there's a timer on the one thing keeping me safe?"

"Well, you figured it out anyway."

"Come on, Corian. If I knew it wasn't *completely* hiding me, I wouldn't have been stuffing myself into that magic-dampening box for days."

"Don't even think about it." He pointed at her, his flat cat-like nose wrinkling in a snarl. "I told you at that mansion that I wasn't gonna come after you to save your ass again, and I meant it. This is a lot bigger than just you, Cheyenne. We're all making sacrifices."

"Like whom?"

The Nightstalker dropped his hand and scowled.

"No, seriously? Who else is making sacrifices so I can get

through these trials before that necklace goes boom and throws me out of hiding?"

"We came here to train on a mountain, kid. The bigger picture can wait."

Yeah, just like everything else. "Lemme guess, we'll get there when I'm ready."

Corian stalked across the mountainside.

"These trials better not take much longer. I am so sick of hearing that."

"You're the one who said it."

"Just don't."

The Nightstalker smirked and crouched in his ready stance, fingers twitching a little at his sides. "Let's get to work so we can both stop saying it."

Cheyenne pulled up a crackling sphere of black energy in her palm and lifted it out to the side. "My pleasure."

CHAPTER SIXTY-SIX

"Dammit!" Cheyenne slammed chest-first into a tree, bringing down a rain of pine needles on her head. She pushed herself away from the rough bark and whirled to scan the sloping forest. *He keeps pulling out more tricks, doesn't he? Where are you, you sneaky bastard?*

A swift rustle of leaves came from behind the tree, then a twig snapped farther to the left. The halfling stepped backward on her bare feet, having removed her shoes once she realized Corian was playing a game of "sneak around the woods." Even with the darkness in the woods and the trees blocking out all the starlight, she didn't need her eyes to find the Nightstalker. She could hear him. *And I know he can't hear me.*

Pine needles drifted down to the forest floor about six yards in front of her. Cheyenne stepped around the other side of the tree she'd almost knocked down after Corian's last sneak attack, then glanced at the closest boulder. *Just a stone's throw away. That might have a whole new meaning after this.*

She focused on the buzzing line of enhanced magic flowing through her, her mind quickly settling on the image of the Nimlothar seed. Another shower of pine needles fell from the tree up ahead, and the halfling reached out toward the boulder. An unseen pressure clicked into place around her fingers, and she grabbed it before hurling the entire rock—moss, dirt, roots, and all —halfway up into the tree.

The air exploded with the crack of stone on wood, and the upper half of the tree crashed to the forest floor. A streak of silver light leaped from the falling tree, and all the needles and branches and leaves sprayed into the air. Cheyenne spun and shoved the air. A line of spiked stone erupted from the forest floor and shot after the retreating silver light.

Just before it hit, Corian stepped aside, slipped out of his enhanced speed, and threw a bolt of silver lightning at the halfling.

"How the hell—" She dodged the attack, which left the tree behind her one lightning bolt away from falling over.

"You won't unlock another ability by throwing rocks into trees, kid."

"*Rock*? Did you see—" An earsplitting crack rose from below them, followed by a long, drawn-out echo of the same boulder crashing down the hillside. "You ever hear a rock do that?"

"Stone ogres throw rocks, Cheyenne. You're half-drow. Fight me like you're half-drow."

"I *am!*" She flung another black energy sphere at him, and the Nightstalker all but disappeared in a flash of silver light. With a frustrated roar, the halfling followed the darting light. Then she slipped into drow speed and saw him jogging across the hill above her.

When he saw her, the Nightstalker winked and picked up the pace.

That's it. Cheyenne shoved the ground again, sending another rippling wave of spiked earth up the hill toward him as fast as he ran. Then she slipped back into normal time and reached out with the black tendrils whipping from her hands. Corian darted away from the coiling ropes of drow magic, but she wasn't aiming for him. The tendrils curled around the farthest earthen spear as it erupted from the ground, jerking Cheyenne after it.

The Nightstalker darted to the left again, and Cheyenne swung around the opposite side of the rock spear. Corian dropped out of Nightstalker speed and frowned, exasperated. She reached out and felt the ground reply to her command; a massive crack split across the forest floor, drawing Corian's attention and cutting him off. Then the halfling dove back into hyper-speed, her bare feet skidding on the loose pine needles and leaves a few feet higher than her frozen mentor. Her tendrils retracted and she ran toward Corian, cocking back a fist.

He joined her in the realm of super-speed one more time, turning around to look up at her. He did it just in time to see the purple-gray fist hurtling through the air before it smacked him in the jaw. Cheyenne's blow sent the Nightstalker to his knees and then skidding backward across the loose earth, his deadly silver claws dragging through the dirt to slow him before he reached the massive crevice she'd opened behind him. They both dropped back into normal movement, and Cheyenne took a staggering step to keep from sliding down the mountainside.

For a moment, the only sound in the forest was the cascading rush of more leaves and needles tumbling down the hill, plus the occasional rock thwacking against a tree. Corian's bowed head didn't move as he clung to the mountainside on his hands and knees, breathing heavily.

Oh, shit. I fucking hit him.

Then a low chuckle rose from the hunched Nightstalker. Two seconds later, he threw his head back and roared with laughter.

Cheyenne took another step up the hill. *No way! I socked the sanity right out of this one.*

"Well played, Cheyenne. That was…" Corian nodded and flashed her that predatory grin again, his silver eyes blazing even as he blinked heavily. "Very well played. What the hell made you think of that?"

The halfling shrugged. "Four out of five times, you darted left."

"Ah. If you're saying I've become predictable, I have failed you."

"Not really. I guessed."

He laughed again and pushed to his feet. The corner of his mouth had split open under her fist, and in the darkness of the woods, it was impossible to tell the color of the blood trickling toward his chin.

Silver wouldn't surprise me.

The Nightstalker dabbed the corner of his mouth with two fingers, glanced at the blood, then dropped his hand. "That's not fighting like you're half-drow."

"You're right." The halfling let out a chuckle and spread her arms. "That was me fighting like Cheyenne Summerlin."

"Huh." His silver eyes narrowed for a split second, and his smile widened. "I think you're on to something." Corian sucked in a hissing breath. "It's been a long time since I've been hit like that."

"Yeah, I bet."

He pointed at her. "Your head's the perfect size just the way it is, kid."

When he turned around, they both studied the long, jagged rift that could have cut the mountain in half if Cheyenne had ripped it farther. "Should I do something about that?"

"I'm not gonna stop you. As long as whatever it is doesn't involve your fist in my face."

With a snort, the half-drow centered her focus on the purple Nimlothar seed, let out a long breath, and opened her hands. Almost instantly, she felt that magical pressure in the air, the resistance just waiting for her to reach. Cheyenne hooked her fingers around its edges and curled both hands into fists again.

The ground trembled. Another tree snapped somewhere and toppled to the forest floor before sliding down the mountain. The fissure stretching in front of her slowly shrank, bits of pine needles and twigs shivering over the edge of the crevice and falling into darkness.

The halfling's arms trembled, her hands aching as if she'd been hanging from them for minutes. Finally, the massive crack closed with a muffled thump and a groan of earth and rock somewhere far beneath their feet. The ground rocked, sending Corian and Cheyenne sliding down the loose layer of vegetation.

She stopped herself by falling on her ass and digging her fingers into the ground. *Better than passing out. That was close.* Shaking off the next wave of dizziness, she looked and couldn't find where that huge crack had just been.

"Yeah." Corian wiped the side of his mouth again and nodded. "It's a lot easier to tear things apart than to put them back together, isn't it?"

Cheyenne shrugged. "Guess you gotta really mean it."

"No truer words, kid." He offered her a hand, and she didn't hesitate to take it. "I think we're done for the night."

"Seriously? You've spent hours throwing me around a field and Alcatraz and now Yellowstone, and you can't keep going after one punch to the face?"

"Not *my* drow trials. And as the person guiding you through yours, I'm calling the shots." As the Nightstalker opened another portal on the side of the mountain, Cheyenne found her legacy box in a pile of leaves.

It was cold to the touch, without any of its expected flashing lights or whirring, turning parts. *Really? I finally hit the Nightstalker, and still nothing?* She shook the leaves out of her black Vans and stepped back into them.

Corian watched her return to him and the open portal with a grin, gesturing for the halfling to proceed.

Cheyenne raised an eyebrow, then stepped briskly through the shimmering oval of dark light.

He snorted. "Yeah, you'll be using that look all the time soon enough."

"What?" She stepped over the ring of candles in his unfinished basement apartment, looking at him over her shoulder.

"Nothing." A surprised chuckle escaped him. "You hit me really hard, you know that?"

"Go drow or go home, right?"

"Well, now it's both." Corian gestured around the basement, then his gaze fell on the basket of her magical supplies and the hardened leather case. He nodded toward them and rubbed the corner of his mouth again. "It's probably too much to assume you'll be happy with a raincheck on those spells."

"One point for the Nightstalker." Cheyenne walked toward her supplies and grabbed the basket by the handle.

"Just leave it there. The floor makes a better workspace than anything else."

Frowning, the halfling flicked her gaze toward the only piece of furniture in the basement—that crappy, wobbly folding card table. "Clearly."

"You say that like you've got a better setup at your place."

A sharp laugh burst out of her. "I do."

"Uh-huh. I'll believe it when I see it." Corian hunkered down on the floor, eyed the basket of magical items, then sat all the way. "Not that I plan on seeing where you live."

"What, you're not into coming over for pizza and beer after beating each other up on the training field?"

He smirked. "Not with you."

"You know, somehow, that feels like a compliment."

Shrugging, the Nightstalker didn't clarify one way or another before he got to work emptying the basket and laying out all the materials on the concrete floor. He paused before picking up the brown glass jar Yadje had given the halfling.

"Healing salve." Cheyenne nodded, then her damn forearm started itching again. Grimacing, she rubbed it through her hoody sleeve and crossed her legs beneath her. "It's supposed to be pretty decent."

He unscrewed the lid and took a little sniff. "Woah. Yeah, kid. 'Pretty decent' is a serious understatement. This has darktongue flower in it. Or it's *mostly* darktongue, judging by the smell." The lid went back on, and Corian tilted the jar back and forth. "This isn't easy to come by. Where'd you get it?"

"From a friend." Frowning, Cheyenne took the jar from him and opened it to smell for herself. "Jeeze!" Wrinkling her nose, she screwed the lid on tight and set the jar aside. "Smells like rotting strawberries."

"Well, most O'gúleesh would pay an arm and a leg to get their hands on some of *those* rotting strawberries."

"For real?"

He nodded. "How much did your friend charge for that? Big jar."

"Nothing."

Corian choked and leaned over his lap. The choke became another laugh as he shook his head. "I can't for the life of me figure out how you find yourself in these situations, kid." When he looked at her, his glowing silver eyes narrowed above a smile that was half nostalgic pride and half sadness. "Then I remember who your drow half came from."

"We can skip the part where you tell me I'm so much like L'zar, blah, blah, blah." The halfling waved him off. "I'm not interested."

"Me neither." They stared at each other, then the Nightstalker clapped and turned back toward the supplies. "So. I'm assuming you brought the spellbook that started this hairbrained new venture of yours."

"Dude, you're hairier than me."

His eyes flicked toward her face. "It's fur."

"Uh-huh." She grabbed her backpack from beside the shelf and dragged it across the floor toward her. The loose stack of Mattie Bergmann's handwritten pages was in relatively good shape still when she pulled it out and thumped it on the floor between them. "Here it is."

"Jesus, Cheyenne. I hope you don't expect me to help you with all of this tonight."

"Well, you just gave me more ammunition."

"Don't pretend you have enough energy left for more than one or two of these."

Smirking, the halfling flipped through the first few pages until she found the personal illusion charm. "I wanna start with this one, and maybe get some ward pointers from you before I bail for the night."

"We'll see." Corian took the piece of paper from her, stared at her, then glanced down at the spell. Two seconds later, the paper fluttered to the floor as his fingers shot open like he'd just grabbed a hot poker. The Nightstalker hissed something in O'gúleesh, then his glowing silver eyes widened. "Where the hell did you get this?"

CHAPTER SIXTY-SEVEN

"Why do people keep asking me that?" Cheyenne glanced at the piece of paper resting on the floor in front of Corian. "I told you already. I got that whole book from a friend. I mean, it's not really a *book*, but it's the thought that counts, I guess."

"Cheyenne." The Nightstalker slowly put his finger on the loose paper touching his shin and cleared his throat. "Do you know who wrote these spells?"

"You're sounding an awful lot like the Grinch Who Stole the Potions Shop."

"*What?*"

"Never mind. My friend wrote those down. Then she made me copies, obviously, and gave them to me." Cheyenne tapped her temple. "Said she pulled it out of here and wanted to put it down for posterity or whatever."

"Yeah, I bet she did. You and your friends. Pshh. There something you're not telling me?"

"Probably. Care to be a little more specific?"

Corian studied the illusion charm instructions, then thumbed through the rest of the spellbook, pausing here and there to take a better look at whatever caught his attention. Then he shook his head. "You mentioned the name Maleshi."

"Yeah, and you told me to shut up about it."

"Yes, I remember." Biting his bottom lip, he warily removed his hand from the spell stack and scratched behind one pointed, fur-tufted ear. "And now, obviously, you're ready to have that conversation."

"Because Maleshi gave me her spellbook." The halfling studied every tick in her mentor's face as he took his sweet time to respond. *I knew it. Mattie* was *talking to herself.*

"How the hell did *you* become friends with Maleshi Hi'et?"

"Well, we're not *that* close." Cheyenne raised her eyebrows and shrugged.

"Maleshi. Huh. Earthside, off the grid." He shook his head, blinking furiously as his feline nose wrinkled in confusion. "And she never reached out to any of us."

"Yeah, she's even more hush-hush than you." Cheyenne snorted. "So, you can imagine how much fun it is trying to get her to say anything about anything."

"I don't have to imagine, Cheyenne. I know." Slowly, Corian broke out of his musings and looked at her. "I know Maleshi very well."

"From back home, right?"

"Hmm." A bitter smile spread across his closed lips. "Yes. Everyone back home knows who Maleshi Hi'et is. Even if they never met her, I can promise you they've heard the name."

The halfling squinted. "Let me guess. Escaped convict?"

"Please. Not every role model in your life follows that story."

Just let that one go, Cheyenne. He's obviously wrapped up in the past. "Then why is she here hiding from everyone but me?"

"I can't tell you why she chose to reveal herself to you. My guess is she was tired of being on her own for, oh, the last few hundred years. But she most definitely is not an escaped convict. Or a convict at all." Corian stroked his chin and stared at the spellbook again.

Cheyenne leaned toward him and, in a much softer voice than she expected, said, "You know I won't go anywhere until you tell me who she is."

"I wouldn't expect you to. I just didn't think this would come up as a topic of conversation before you passed the trials. Or ever, to be perfectly honest."

"Okay. Well, it is." She gestured for him to continue. "So, keep being honest."

"Yes." He cleared his throat again and took a deep breath. "Maleshi Hi'et was a decorated, high-ranking general and war veteran. A brilliant strategist. An unstoppable force on the battle-field. Maybe even the Crown's most valuable asset, at one point."

The halfling blinked. "She told me she trained orcs."

"Ha. Yeah, that too," Corian said. "Maleshi was, ah…she was…"

"Don't worry, you painted a clear enough picture." *I'm still struggling to stick Mattie's face on it, though.*

"Well, at any rate, I assume she got fed up with what her position had become under the Crown's command. One day, she was with us. One of us. And the next, she just up and left without a word to anyone. People still say Maleshi was the spark that ignited the O'gúl rebellion."

The halfling swallowed and shook her head. "I just heard you say 'rebellion.'"

"There's nothing wrong with your hearing, kid." The Night-stalker shot her a condescending frown, then caught himself and looked away.

"What rebellion?"

"Now's not the right time."

She scoffed and slapped her knees. "This bullshit again, huh? I'm pretty sure the right time to explain the rebellion is at the end of a conversation about the Nightstalker who *started* that rebellion."

"What happened after she left her post has nothing to do with her."

"I really did punch you too hard."

"Cheyenne."

The gentle, firm command in his voice sounded so much like Bianca Summerlin, it sent a jolt of disbelief through the halfling. She couldn't move.

"If I could predict with one-hundred-percent certainty what's going to happen once you complete the drow trials and inherit what's rightfully yours, I would tell you everything I know in an instant. Trust me. The pieces will fall into place. You *will* get your answers and the bigger picture, but it can't happen all at once. You have to be ready for it, yes. And so many other things have to be ready for it too."

Just another fucked-up scavenger hunt, isn't it? The halfling stared at him, her glowing golden eyes unblinking. "I can keep a secret."

"I know you can. You've proven that over and over. But secrets have a way of turning in on themselves over time." Corian laced his fingers together, palms still spread apart like he couldn't stand to press them together. "I've been keeping certain secrets for centuries. In Ambar'ogúl *and* here on this side. Letting them out now would be like pulling the pin from a grenade glued to my hand. I need you to understand that."

"I don't." Cheyenne shook her head and shrugged. "I still don't know enough to understand much of anything."

"Then please, at the very least, respect a genuine request from a friend. I know I keep asking it of you, but that's as much as I can do. Please just trust me."

Gritting her teeth, the half-drow pressed her lips together and closed her eyes. *I need to pass these trials.* "Yeah, I will respect the request, and I trust you. Just don't drag me around past the due date, okay? I've had way too much of that over the last few weeks."

"I will promise you that much, kid. The old laws have a lot more integrity than a twenty-one-year-old secret Earthside organization pretending they know everything about us."

She laughed. "No. You're not FRoE, that's for sure."

"*So* glad we're on the same page."

Narrowing her eyes, the halfling looked her mentor up and

down and shook her head. "They've got you on the biting sarcasm, though."

"Well, they can have it. Sarcasm's not my priority."

"No argument, there."

"So. I've got a few more minutes of intense concentration left in me." Corian picked up Mattie "Maleshi" Bergmann's spell for a personal illusion charm and flicked it with his other hand. "What about you?"

"Let's give it a shot."

An hour later, Cheyenne moved slowly and deliberately through the hand gestures Corian had helped her decipher from Mattie's drawings. *Focus. This is where you screwed up last time.* She paused, itching to hook her index finger next. Instead, she flicked her right pinky finger out, *then* hooked her finger toward her left palm.

The copper ring Corian had pulled from the equivalent of his junk drawer flashed with white light.

"Holy shit. Did I just…"

Corian tilted his head. One eye drooped mostly closed before he blinked quickly. "That one looked successful."

"Ha! I did it! This drow halfling just bonded an illusion charm. Fuck, yeah!"

The Nightstalker rubbed between his eyebrows with two fingers. "Cheyenne, if you don't quit squealing from two feet away, I will throw you out that door. Or through it."

"All right, party pooper." She took it down a notch and flicked her gaze toward the aggravated magical. "And I don't squeal."

"From where I'm sitting, you might as well be a room full of screaming children wrapped in a drow bow."

"You can try all you want, but *nothing's* gonna make me feel like crap right now." The halfling grinned at the copper ring. "I just opened a whole new world."

"We won't know for sure until you try the damn thing."

"Oh. Right." She snatched the ring off the floor while Corian massaged his temples. The ring slid onto her right ring finger but stopped at the second knuckle. "Damn. I know I have small hands, but this is kinda ridiculous. Where'd you get this anyway?"

"Some fae jeweler just outside the capital."

"Fae, huh?"

"Small hands."

She chuckled. "Whatever." The ring slipped perfectly onto her pinky, and a small buzz raced up her arm. *Now for the real test.* With a deep breath, Cheyenne stared at the ring and shifted back into her human form. She'd grown so used to the heat of her drow magic drawing itself up from the base of her spine that feeling it slip away was like stepping outside buck-naked in the middle of winter. But that was the only change.

Corian looked at her and raised an eyebrow. "Right. See? Sometimes you think it works, but a quick test just shows you it's another dud. We'll have to try again another day, kid. I can't handle any more of this."

"Dude." Smirking at the way he cringed under that address, Cheyenne waited for him to look at her. "Corian…"

"I can't sit through you attempting that spell one more time. It's exhausting, and it makes me want to kill something."

"Good thing you don't have to, then."

That made him look up, just as the halfling slid the copper ring off her pinky. The air shimmered around her, and her drow image fell away into the pale-skinned, black-haired Goth girl. "That looked like an illusion charm."

"Because it is." She wiggled her eyebrows and clenched the ring in her fist. "By the way, have you ever considered getting therapy for that 'wanting to kill something' problem?"

"Silence and solitude are all I need, Cheyenne. No therapist is gonna give me that." He cocked his head and blinked slowly. "But you sure as hell can."

"I get it." The halfling snatched up the three other ingredients they'd used to bind the charm to that ring. Everything went into the front pocket of her backpack, the drow puzzle box slid into the main pocket, and she stuck the brown jar of darktongue salve in behind it. Then she pointed at the spellbook. "Cool with you if I leave that here?"

"If it gets you out faster."

"Damn. Don't hold back or anything." With a wry laugh, she stood and grabbed the hardened leather slip with the O'gúl hornet's web inside. *I'm positive he'll know what this is. I'll bring it back next time.* "Try again tomorrow?"

"Fine."

"Oh, hey. Do you have, like, a cell phone or something? It gets pretty old having to pop onto the Borderlands forum every time I wanna ask to come over."

Corian rubbed his temples again. "I'll call you tomorrow. How's that?"

"You don't have my number."

The Nightstalker's silver eyes flashed with deadly irritation when he looked at her. "Are you sure?"

"Well, not anymore." Shaking her head, the halfling moved toward the door.

"Cheyenne. Pendant."

"Reduced to one-word sentences." He didn't think that was very funny, so she shut up and pulled out the Heart of Midnight on its broken chain. Once she'd tied the knot again, Cheyenne shot him a thumbs-up. Without looking, Corian deactivated the wards around his metal front door, and she nodded. "Thanks for all of it. And you should at least get a mini-fridge with a little freezer drawer."

Corian clenched his eyes shut and whispered, "What the fuck?"

"You know. To ice your jaw. Helps with the swelling."

"Out."

"G'night." Cheyenne jerked open the door and shut it quickly behind her before almost skipping up the damp steps covered in damp leaves. *And I thought I had an issue with personal space. Nightstalker's been spending too much time in a basement by himself.* She slipped her hand into her pocket and felt the copper ring there. That and the chirp of her Panamera when she unlocked it made her grin.

CHAPTER SIXTY-EIGHT

Cheyenne practically stumbled into her apartment. *Good thing I helped Ember to bed before I left. She'd think I showed up wasted.*

The backpack slid off her shoulder and onto the floor beside the gray suede couch. Her black Vans thumped across the floor in the direction of the front door, and she staggered across the apartment toward her bedroom on the other side.

The chandelier lamp was still on, casting a soft purple light over everything. The halfling sighed, her shoulders relaxing as her exhaustion finally caught up with her. She emptied her pockets onto the chest of drawers with the skull handles, making sure not to toss the copper ring behind the furniture in the process. Then her clothes landed in a pile on the floor, and she brushed aside the black canopy around her bed before climbing onto the mattress.

"Oh, yeah." The mattress sank beneath her weight. *I could sleep on top of this purple velvet and be totally fine.* But she forced herself to pull back the comforter and laughed as much as she could for how tired she was. "*And* black satin sheets. Ember Gaderow is officially the patron saint of Goths. I even sound drunk."

She tossed some pillows aside but left the softest ones and had no problem drifting off to sleep, even with the Heart of Darkness pendant pressing uncomfortably into her collarbone.

"Cheyenne."

The harsh whisper made the halfling roll over in her brand-new bed.

"Cheyenne, you need to wake up."

She groaned, grabbed a pillow, and tossed it toward the voice.

"Hey! Get the hell up!" A loud clap echoed through her room.

It jolted Cheyenne the rest of the way out of her sleep, and she pushed up onto her elbows, blinking sleepily. When her eyes adjusted to the low light coming from the lamp she hadn't turned off, she bolted upright and jerked the velvet comforter to her chin. "Shit! What… You…"

"Quit stuttering and listen up." L'zar Verdys glanced at the blackout curtains over her window, then took a step closer to the foot of her bed.

"What the fuck are you doing in my bedroom?"

"I'm not. Technically. It's the Don'adurr Thread. We did it once, and now that we opened the channel…" He clicked his tongue and shot another quick look at her window. "I can only do this so many times, so you need to pay attention."

"Don't tell me what I need—"

"Shut up." The drow's shoulders hunched as he glanced around a room Cheyenne couldn't see. "I need you to get this message to Corian. There's been a breach. Unregulated. My guess is the Crown's behind this, but we need to be sure. Tell him to grab whoever he thinks is up to the job and take them out there ASAP. Today would be good."

"Today?" The halfling gestured around her perfect Goth bedroom, now tainted by L'zar Verdys' astral form or whatever standing in the middle of it. "I just ended yesterday."

"Trust me, Cheyenne. You don't want to wait on this one. It's not

— Shit!" He ducked his head again, golden eyes darting back and forth before he crouched even lower. "We don't... Left... Until the cycle..."

His image flickered in and out of existence with the rest of his words, then he was gone.

Breathing heavily, the halfling searched her room for any sign of her incarcerated father popping back into her personal space uninvited. After about a minute, she dropped back onto the bed and stared at the center of the canopy above her. *Fuck. No more sleep tonight.*

She tossed the covers off and leaped out of bed. Grabbing two of the skull knobs to open the drawers only brought a brief, tense smile. *Didn't even have a chance to enjoy this.* The drawer jerked open, and she found an oversized t-shirt folded neatly on top. An image of some burly guy in the same uniform as the ones who'd stepped out of her apartment flashed through her head—some dude laughing as he folded Cheyenne's clothes, put them in drawers, and went to collect his tip.

"Stop it." She shook out the t-shirt, yanked it over her head, and headed quickly toward the iron staircase up to the mini-loft. Her bare feet were a lot quieter going up those stairs, and she hardly felt the metal mesh digging into her soles.

The office chair up there wasn't nearly as comfortable as hers, but it didn't matter. She turned on her monitor, followed by a quick systems check before setting up the VPN one more time and diving into the dark web. Once she'd reached the Borderlands forum, she scanned quickly through the most recent topic threads and hissed. *Nothing new. Nothing about a breach.*

Cheyenne growled in frustration, then glanced over the side of the loft in the direction of Ember's bedroom. Nothing moved in the apartment. "It's an adjustment period. We're fine."

She pulled up a private message to Corian, her fingers flying across the keyboard.

Shyhand71: Just got an unexpected visit. And a direct message for you straight from his mouth.

Slumping back in the office chair, she drummed her fingers on the armrests and stared at the open chat box. *No way he's still awake. He wouldn't hear the rest of that house fall down around him—*

gu@rdi@an104: Don't say anything else here. Meet me at this address at 8:00 a.m.

And that was it. He sent the address, the chat box closed from his end, and Cheyenne glanced at the clock at the bottom of her screen.

Three o'clock. Great. I get an hour of sleep and have to wait three more.

She logged out of the dark web, killed the VPN, and turned off the monitor. Then she moved quietly down the metal staircase and back into her room. She put on the first thing she pulled out of that chest of drawers without thinking about it—a pair of black skinny jeans and a long-sleeved black shirt with the neckline cut wide to drape over her shoulders. "Whatever. What am I supposed to do for three hours?"

The latest episode of a show she'd never heard of ended and the halfling snatched the remote off the coffee table to find something else. "Well, that was a waste of a whole hour. Just one more to go."

Her personal phone dinged from where she'd wedged it beneath her thigh on the gray couch. Cheyenne pulled it out and read the text from Ember.

Any chance you're up?

Dropping the remote, the halfling texted back. **Yeah. You need some help?**

That would be awesome.

Cheyenne swung her legs off the couch from where she'd stretched out to binge-watch not-so-binge-worthy shows and stood. When she reached Ember's bedroom door, it was second nature to knock first.

"Oh, *do* come in, won't you?" Ember joked.

The halfling slowly opened the door and tried to smile. "Good morning."

"Whoa. Apparently not."

"Yeah, My sleep was interrupted."

Ember cocked her head. "Dreams?"

"More like visions. A visitor from Chateau D'rahl."

"Did he escape again?"

"Nope." Cheyenne approached her friend's bed and held out her arm. Ember reached for the halfling's shoulders, and they worked quickly to transfer her into the wheelchair. "Apparently, that little drow-astral-projection trick made it super easy for him to project himself into my bedroom."

"Oh, creepy."

"Yeah." Cheyenne straightened and waited for Ember to get adjusted. "You good?"

The fae nodded. "Bathroom break. Just gotta go through the morning routine first."

"Okay." Watching Ember wheel herself into the bathroom, the halfling frowned and walked quickly to the kitchen. The fridge had only a few things, the most enticing of which was her leftover spaghetti from the night before.

Just as the microwave beeped and Cheyenne withdrew a steaming container of noodles and marinara, Ember rolled into the room. "Okay, so what the hell was L'zar doing in your bedroom?"

"Giving me a message for Corian."

"Figures."

Cheyenne shot her friend a confused smile. "I've really painted a good picture of both of them for you, haven't I?"

"I have a good imagination. What's the super-important message?"

The halfling slurped up the last of a steaming forkful of spaghetti and leaned over the container. "No offense, Em, but I think it might be a super-secret kinda message."

"None taken. You eating leftover spaghetti at six-fifteen in the morning might be a whole different issue."

"I was hungry, it was in the fridge..."

"You know, sometimes it's really hard to believe that you're Bianca Summerlin's daughter."

Cheyenne almost snorted her next bite through her nose. "Why, thank you."

"Uh-huh." The fae folded her arms. "So, did you deliver the message already?"

"Oh, crap. I gotta go." After shoveling two more heaping forkfuls into her mouth, Cheyenne ripped a paper towel off the roll, wiped her mouth, and flung it into the empty box on the island. "I'm sorry, Em. I gotta drive to DC."

"I see. It's *that* kinda secret message."

"Not the way you might think. Washington's got nothing to do with it."

"As far as you know."

The halfling nodded. "I'm pretty sure I would've found out about it by now, but this isn't a FRoE thing. This is… I don't even know what this is, but I have to go. You gonna be okay?"

"All right, let's recap. I'm good. If I'm not, I'll call you or text you or whatever. If you don't answer, we have a *very* friendly neighbor just across the hall."

"Yeah, okay. Message received."

"Excellent."

Chuckling, Cheyenne grabbed everything she needed off the coffee table, shoved it all into her pockets, then pulled the middle-finger hoodie over her head. "I think that's everything. Wish me luck."

Ember wheeled herself into the living room and wrinkled her nose. "Nah. You don't need that. Just be careful, huh?"

The halfling paused at the front door and glanced at her friend. "I will. Thanks."

She closed the door and headed quickly toward the elevator, the fob already in her hand. *If Corian doesn't know what to do with this message, I have a feeling we're screwed.*

CHAPTER SIXTY-NINE

The address Corian had given her turned out to be an abandoned warehouse on the outskirts of DC. Cheyenne pulled her car into a parking lot overgrown with weeds and frowned at the graffiti plastered all over the building. *This is nuts.*

She got out anyway, locked her car, and glanced quickly up and down the empty street before turning toward the warehouse entrance. A bright-green light shimmered across the metal door, a brief shape flashing once in the center. *Four-pointed star. Definitely not a souvenir.* Before she had a chance to knock, the door swung open.

"I'd recognize that fancy little lock-beep anywhere." Corian stepped aside and nodded for her to enter. "Come in."

The halfling stepped into the not-so-abandoned warehouse and looked around. The place was mostly empty, except for tables set up in a square missing one of its sides. Those tables were covered with computer monitors and mice and keyboards, neatly bundled wires trailing to the various power sources. She saw three main towers through all the dangling mess and figured there were probably more.

Sitting at the center table was a troll, his skin more blue than purple, with a foot-tall neon-orange mohawk jutting from his shaven scalp. He turned slowly in the desk chair, his orange-red eyes widening when he saw the halfling standing there. "By the fell-damn Crown…"

"Cheyenne, this is Persh'al."

She jerked her chin at the odd-looking troll. "Hey."

"Ha. 'Hey,' she says. That's it." Persh'al chuckled and shook his head, leaning back in the chair again. "Yeah, you're L'zar's kid, all right. Corian, is this—"

"Probably." The Nightstalker gestured at the two open chairs on either side of Persh'al. "Let's get to it."

Cheyenne took the closest chair, and the troll wheeled back from the table so all three of them could form a little circle for their chat.

"Heard you got a message," the troll said.

"Yeah. Straight from L'zar." The halfling leaned forward and slid her hands down her thighs. "He said there was an unregulated breach, and he thinks the Crown's behind it. Corian, he wanted you to grab whoever you think can handle it to go check things out. ASAP."

"ASAP, huh?" Persh'al smirked.

"His words. Yeah."

The troll spun again and rolled the chair forward to pull something up on the screen. The monitor flashed to life, and all Cheyenne saw were a bunch of scrolling symbols in blue and green. *That's not any kind of code I know.*

"I had a feeling this was what he meant when you called me, Corian. See this?" Persh'al pointed at a random floating symbol.

The Nightstalker nodded. "The damn breach."

"Yep. I noticed this six months ago. It's popped up every now and then. The most frequently wasn't any more than twice a week. But two days ago…" The troll typed several quick commands, and the scrolling characters moved way too fast for Cheyenne to follow. "Every two hours on the fucking nose."

"Shit."

"You can say that again."

"What is it?" Cheyenne asked.

Both magicals stared at her. Persh'al's head jerked back. "Huh. Still got a lot to learn, doncha?"

"Ignore him." Corian leaned around the back of the troll's chair to meet Cheyenne's gaze. "It's a new Border portal."

The halfling nodded. "Without a rez attached, right?"

"Okay." Persh'al slapped his hands down on his thighs. "I rescind my previous judgment."

"How'd you know about that?" Corian asked.

"I met someone who made the crossing through that portal." *And that's as much as I'm saying. I made a promise.*

"And you didn't think that was an important thing to share at any point in the last week?" Corian folded his arms, his silver eyes blazing.

"As far as I know," the halfling retorted, "it's none of my business. You want me coming to you with every little thing I notice that seems off? Fine. But it's a long list."

"This isn't a little thing, Cheyenne." Corian nodded at the monitor again. "Any sign of how it got there?"

"Not a spore." Persh'al shrugged. "We should go check it out."

"Yeah. You wanna make the calls?"

The troll frowned. "It's just the two, isn't it?"

"That's right."

"On it." Persh'al stood and stalked across the warehouse toward a small room in the far corner. A door closed behind him, and his muffled voice filtered into the warehouse's main room a few seconds later.

"He's calling in backup, huh?"

Corian looked at her and tilted his head. "Something like that."

"So, what now?"

"Now, Cheyenne, we wait. Once our *backup* gets here, we go figure out what the hell has L'zar Verdys so spooked."

Twenty minutes later, the door to the warehouse burst open. Two goblins marched in, grim-faced and ready.

"Corian." A goblin man with huge gages in his turquoise ears stepped forward and held out his hand. "Long time, man."

"Too long."

"Damn." A goblin woman with the shiny scar around her neck glanced around the warehouse and stuck her hands on her hips. "This place hasn't changed a bit in the last fifty years."

"Not true." Persh'al pointed at her. "I added two more tables."

"Sorry. Nice tables." The goblin woman rolled her eyes and froze when she noticed Cheyenne sitting on one of the chairs. "There's a blast from the past."

"Indeed." Corian stepped back and gestured toward the goblins. "Cheyenne, this is Byrd and Lumil."

"Holy shit." Byrd leaned forward and extended his hand toward the halfling. "I can tell who your old man is, even when you look like a human."

Cheyenne gave his hand a quick shake. "Okay."

"You know who your old man is, right?" Lumil stepped forward to shake the halfling's hand next, her smile glistening beneath light-orange eyes.

"Don't we all?"

The magicals had a good laugh at that, then Lumil shot Corian a questioning glance. The Nightstalker shrugged, and the goblin woman turned back toward Cheyenne. "Have you met him yet?"

"Yeah."

Byrd blinked. "In person?"

She nodded. "Mostly."

The goblins shared a look of surprise, then Lumil pushed back her thick, floppy yellow hair, which was cut short but still long enough to fall over her eyes. "Huh. That drow bastard actually did it."

"Well, stick me through and roast me over a battle pit." Byrd shook his head in disbelief. "Corian, you know this was gonna happen?"

"I hoped it would." The Nightstalker nodded at Cheyenne. "We all did."

I'm sick of all this cryptic shit. "Okay." The halfling stood. "Somebody better tell me what the hell's going on and why you're talking about me like I'm not here."

"Oh." Lumil shot Corian a conspiratorial wink. "She doesn't know yet."

"She doesn't know," Byrd repeated, nodding slowly at the halfling. "Well, shit. Took him long enough, didn't it?"

"Good to know we didn't throw ourselves over the fell-damn Border for another failed attempt, huh?"

Cheyenne's eyes grew wide. "What?"

"All right, now," Corian started, but the goblins talked over him.

"At least a dozen, Cheyenne," Lumil said. "So many fucking kids. And still, you're an only child."

"Oh, man. Low blow." Byrd snorted. "The point is, kid, your old man was flailing in the dark trying to overturn the crone's prophecy. Basically, you know, he's trying to find an heir."

"Byrd." Corian scowled.

"She's got a right to know, man. She's it."

Lumil shrugged. "L'zar spent *hundreds* of years trying to find a loophole. Went around in disguise. Abandoned his responsibilities. Had the kids raised in secret to try to keep them safe. But of course, only a drow can train another drow through the trials, isn't it?"

Cheyenne glanced at Corian, who shook his head and dropped his gaze to the dusty warehouse floor.

Lumil waved a hand. "And every time that stupid little dark-elf box changed hands from father to spawn, poof."

Byrd mimed hanging himself from a noose, which got him a glare and a warning growl from Lumil. He glanced down at the scar around her throat and shrugged.

The halfling folded her arms. "The *Cuil Aníl?*"

"Damn, girl." Byrd laughed. "You pick up quick."

"Yeah, and I've picked up that legacy box more times than I can count. No *poof.*"

"That's what we're saying." Lumil grinned. "All of L'zar Verdys' potential heirs dropped like flies the minute he chose to hunt them down so they could complete their trials. The four of us?" The goblin woman gestured toward herself, Byrd, Corian, and then Persh'al, who watched the whole thing with wide eyes. "We came with him when he finally decided the only way to keep you safe was to lock himself up in that fucking joke of a prison."

"Those idiots." Byrd snorted and shook his head.

"Right?" Lumil nodded and folded her arms. "Man, it's like he saw the future and didn't need a prophecy for any of it."

"Future of what?" Cheyenne glanced at the gabbing goblins, gritting her teeth.

"*You*, halfling." Byrd jerked his chin up at her. "He found a fucking way to blast right through the prophecy. You've met him. Spoken to him. Touched the damn drow box. And if you're dead, you're really good at pretending not to be."

"You're an idiot." Lumil punched Byrd's arm.

"And yet, here we are?" The goblin spread his arms and playfully leaped aside when Lumil pulled her fist back even farther for a second blow.

Cheyenne's vision blurred, the rest of her focus turning inward. *That was what I saw in my dream. All those bodies. He tried to get them through the trials, and they all died. Just like the oracle said.* Her gaze flicked toward Corian. The Nightstalker tilted his head in recognition and raised an eyebrow.

"I'm still here because he didn't come to find me," she muttered. The goblins quit screwing around, and all eyes settled on the drow halfling. "He knew I'd come to him."

"He hoped you would," Corian said, his low voice echoing through the warehouse. "There were and still are a lot of moving parts to this, Cheyenne. We all had our roles to play. We still do. Obviously, you blaze your own trail, kid. By the time you and I met, I thought I'd be guiding you through the trials and telling you about L'zar at the same time. You did half the work for me." He chuckled wryly, but no one else did. "And we still have a long way to go."

"Especially with you know who tearing through the whole fell-damn—" Byrd stopped abruptly when he caught the Nightstalker's death stare.

Cheyenne was putting the pieces of this screwed-up puzzle together now. "How many drow are there in Ambar'ogúl?"

"What?" Persh'al suddenly perked up at that. "Oh, thousands. If you can find 'em."

"What about the O'gúl Crown?"

The goblins exchanged another wary glance, then turned toward Corian. No one said a word.

The halfling stepped forward and narrowed her eyes. "That's who's looking for me, isn't it? The drow are running things over there. That's why she's got the last Nimlothar. The Crown is a drow who doesn't want me to open that legacy box. I'm right, aren't I?"

"Cheyenne." Corian shook his head. "Another time—"

"Why won't anyone fucking tell me who she is?" A burst of purple light flared behind Cheyenne Summerlin's human eyes. The three magicals standing before her took a step back. Persh'al rolled away in his chair. The warehouse sounded abandoned now.

A soft ding rose from the center computer monitor. Persh'al shoved his chair over to study the scrolling symbols and nodded. "Yep. There she is again. Trouble at the unmarked Border, kids. Time to do a little digging." The troll rubbed his hands together and spun before storming across the warehouse and out the front door. Bright, morning sunlight spilled into the dark room before the door shut again with a bang.

The goblins followed him out, mumbling to each other until Lumil shoved Byrd against the metal door. It opened under his weight, and he laughed before they went back to bickering again.

The halfling stared at her Nightstalker mentor. "You and L'zar. You're trying to keep the Crown from finding me, aren't you? She doesn't want me to finish the trials."

"We need to go."

"Is it because I'm *his* kid or Bianca Summerlin's?"

"The O'gúl Crown doesn't give a shit about human politics, kid."

Cheyenne scoffed. "I'm talking about the human part. Halflings aren't supposed to start the trials at all, are they?"

Corian met Cheyenne's gaze and took a deep breath. "A lot of moving parts, Cheyenne."

"Just tell me. Please."

"I will." Nodding, the Nightstalker stepped toward her and leaned in closer to whisper, "You know when."

Then he walked away from her toward the door.

"I'm ready now, Corian," she shouted after him, her black fingernails digging into her palms. "You know I am."

"Not for this." He stopped to open the door and nodded toward the overgrown parking lot. "But I know a drow halfling who's ready to take on whatever's sending alerts to Persh'al's system every two hours. If you can sucker-punch a Nightstalker, kid, you can handle just about anything."

CHAPTER SEVENTY

"Are we there yet?"

"Seriously, Byrd? You're over five hundred years old, and you *still* haven't quit being the annoying toddler in the back seat?"

Cheyenne Summerlin turned toward the goblins sitting beside her in the back of Persh'al's SUV, smirking. The goblin woman punched Byrd in the shoulder and rolled her eyes.

Byrd flinched and scowled at Lumil. "I don't know why we have to drive a fell-damn *car* to this new portal. We could've been there in two seconds instead of two hours."

"You think I *like* being stuck next to you for the entire drive? Four hundred years listening to you whine, and I still can't get rid of you—"

"Shut *up*." Persh'al slapped his hands on the steering wheel and grunted. He jerked down the rearview mirror to eye the goblins talking beside Cheyenne, his eyes flicking between the road and the mirror. "Don't make me come back there and carve you both a new victory scar, huh? It'll be *my* mark, not yours."

"She started it. Ow! What's *wrong* with you?" Byrd leaned away from Lumil, his nostrils flaring as he grimaced.

Cheyenne scrunched farther against the door behind Persh'al

and stared out the window. *If I was stuck with someone for four hundred years, I'd probably end up hitting them too.*

"Less than five minutes," Corian muttered from the passenger seat. Persh'al nodded silently and returned the rearview mirror to its regular position.

"Use your brain, man," Lumil whispered, though everyone in the SUV could still hear her. "We're scouting the area, so pay attention."

"I would if I had my own window."

"Shit, use *mine*. You can still see, can't you?"

Cheyenne rubbed her forehead and closed her eyes with a deep breath as the goblins kept bickering beside her. *Just change the conversation.*

She looked quickly toward the front of the car. "What are we scouting for?"

Persh'al replied, "There hasn't been a new Border portal in...huh. I can't even say how long. Longer than I've been watching 'em, that's for sure."

"So, you guys don't know what we'll find." The halfling glanced out the window at the trees passing by on the long dirt road that apparently led to the middle of nowhere.

"Not really." The troll in the driver's seat shrugged, then shot Corian a quick glance. "But it's enough to send up a blaring alarm through my system every two hours, and that's a good enough reason to take precautions."

"What kind of system is that?" Cheyenne sat back in her seat and watched the rearview mirror in case he looked into it again. He didn't.

"The kind I know you can appreciate, kid." Persh'al smiled, his irritation with the goblins momentarily forgotten. "Built it myself."

"Okay, cool." Cheyenne waited for more and kept pressing when he didn't offer anything else. "But unless a new Border portal opens up with its own wi-fi, I don't get how you'd see a blip on any kind of system."

The goblins stopped their fierce whispered spat to turn and look at her. Byrd smirked. Corian stared straight ahead in the passenger seat.

Persh'al's head tilted from side to side as his proud smile widened. "Well, it's pretty damn easy when part of that system's set up to trace high levels of magical activity Earthside. Sends it all back to me."

Cheyenne blinked. "How the hell does that work?"

"You know, kid, if I had my gear from back home, I'd rip the whole thing apart just to show you how it works." Persh'al chuckled. "This stuff we've got Earthside? Rudimentary at best. I nearly pulled my hair out, trying to get human technology to work with magic."

"What's left of your hair," Lumil muttered. She and Byrd shared a snigger.

"Hey, I shave this thing every other day on purpose." The troll pointed at his blue scalp covered in orange dots and the huge, spiked, bright-orange mohawk that almost reached the roof of the SUV. "You might wanna consider checking out a barber, Lumil. Looks like a cat used your head for a permanent bed."

Lumil snorted and waved him off.

The halfling ignored the banter and leaned forward. "I've heard things about O'gúl tech."

"Oh, you have, huh?" Persh'al nodded. "Let me tell ya, kid. Ain't nothin' like what we got over there. Unless it's all been destroyed in the last few hundred years."

Corian turned toward the troll with a small, discerning frown. "It hasn't."

"Yeah? You sure about that?"

"I've had reports."

"Uh-huh. You can have your secrets, Nightstalker. I know you're good for 'em." Persh'al chuckled without taking his eyes off the road.

Cheyenne studied Corian's stoic, expressionless profile. *So I'm not the only one he won't talk to. At least the guy keeps his promises.* Sitting back against the seat, she nodded and looked at the rearview mirror. "I'd still love to see how you built a rig that searches for magic."

Persh'al finally met her gaze in the mirror and held it. Then he chuckled. "I can't get over how much you're like him, kid. Sure. After we figure out what the hell this new portal's been stirring up, I'll give you the grand tour. How's that sound?"

"I'll hold you to it." Cheyenne looked out the window again as the goblins beside her laughed.

"No way you're not L'zar's kid," Byrd said.

"Careful, Persh'al." Lumil pointed at the troll behind the wheel. "You got this halfling holding you to a promise now. You know what happens if you try to back out."

"Not gonna happen." Persh'al's grip tightened on the steering wheel, his irritation returning. "My word's a steel trap, Lumil. Helps that I don't have 'turncoat' on my rap sheet."

Lumil snorted. "Please. If we don't all have a fat black mark on our names by now, we sure as hell will soon enough. Don't tell me I don't know how to keep a promise."

"Nope. Just implying it." The small tablet resting in the cubby below the dashboard let out a series of high-pitched chimes. Persh'al glanced down at it and slowed the SUV to a crawl on the road. "We're close."

"Where is it?" Corian asked, scanning the surrounding trees through his window and the windshield.

"Half a mile west." The troll pulled over and pointed into the thick forest on their left. "I'm not gettin' this thing through the woods. Who's up for a little hike?"

Byrd rolled his eyes. "I'm tellin' ya, portals are the way to go."

"Not unless you wanna get your head blown off the minute you step through," Lumil muttered as she ripped off her seatbelt and shoved the back door open.

"You don't know something's waiting there to blow my head off." Byrd scooted toward the open door as the other goblin's boots crunched across the gravel.

Corian turned in the passenger seat and caught the goblin's gaze. "You don't know something's *not* there waiting for us."

Byrd shrugged and leaped out after Lumil.

When everyone had stepped out of the car and all the doors were shut, Persh'al nodded across the dirt road. "Not too much of a walk. Anyone else think it's weirdly convenient to a road?"

"Convenience or coincidence?" Corian cocked his head. "We're about to find out."

Cheyenne followed the group of L'zar Verdys' long-time magical friends into the thick woods stretching on either side of the dirt road. The five of them moved with practiced silence through the trees, barely making a sound. *They've had a lot more experience with this, and I'm still just as quiet. Byrd should quit breathing through his mouth.*

They'd gone about a quarter of a mile when the halfling felt a foreign prickle of buzzing energy wash over her. The others stopped beside her, feeling the same magical energy, and exchanged glances. Corian pointed at his eyes, then at the goblins. Without a word, Byrd and Lumil nodded and took off to the north and south.

Now they're scouting.

The Nightstalker nodded at Persh'al, then his gaze fell on the drow halfling. He pointed straight ahead, and Cheyenne nodded even as a chill raced down her spine.

Something's not right here. They all feel it too.

For a split second, her body fought the command to move forward. She pushed herself to keep moving after Corian and Persh'al through the thickly wooded forest and the dense under-growth at their feet.

No one made a sound for the next quarter-mile of their little hike. Even the natural sounds of a forest were missing—no bird-calls, no rustling of small animals through the brush. The only thing greeting them was the light shush of a breeze blowing across the treetops.

Cheyenne heard the low hum a full minute before she, Persh'al, and Corian stepped out into the clearing—like a huge motor rumbling from somewhere miles underground. The tingling buzz of a magic she hadn't felt before intensified across her skin.

As soon they cleared the trees, they found themselves standing in front of a hill of jagged black rock jutting up from the forest floor. *Looks more like splintered wood than stone.* Cheyenne gazed at the twenty-foot spires and frowned. *That isn't supposed to be here.*

Beside her, Corian's hands moved quickly, his lips silently muttering another spell. A wave of shimmering light rippled away from him in all directions, washing over Persh'al and the halfling before spreading out toward the black spears of stone that had pushed up from the earth. Then the shimmering air disappeared, and the Nightstalker shook his head. "Nobody here."

"We could've told you that," Byrd said as he stepped around the lowest rise of upturned earth toward them. "This ridge goes on for at least another mile to the west."

Lumil appeared on Corian's right, tossing her shaggy yellow hair out of her eyes. "Nothing around the north side."

Corian turned toward the troll. "Persh'al?"

"With all the magic here, I'm surprised my alarms weren't going off every half-hour instead." Persh'al scratched the shaved side of his head and shrugged. "This clearing's big enough to host decent-sized operations, though. I'm thinking convenience."

"Yeah, me too." Corian folded his arms and turned back toward the spires. "Especially if this ridge runs as far as Byrd says it does. Wouldn't be too hard to reconfigure things into an active tower from here."

"Nope." Persh'al cocked his head. "About a week, with the right gear."

Cheyenne stepped across the clearing to get a better view of the black stone. *Those could be teeth in some giant, messed-up mouth.*

A dark shadow stirred within the rising spires—just a flicker, there one moment and vanished again behind another fist of black stone the next. She cleared her throat. "When you say, 'convenience,' you mean someone might've opened this portal on purpose, right?"

All four magicals turned toward her.

"Yes, Cheyenne." Corian nodded once, his silver eyes narrowed with suspicion. "There's a chance someone on the other side put a lot of work into opening an unregulated Border portal. Still, without any proof, it's hard to say if that's what happened."

The halfling nodded toward the high ridges of jutting stone stretching farther to the west than she could see. "There might be proof in there."

Corian turned to study the stone. Another dark shape rose between the black spires, glistening in the morning light spilling into the clearing. The Nightstalker stepped across the open ground toward Cheyenne, followed quickly by Persh'al and the goblins. Every pair of eyes searched for more movement in the newest Border portal.

"I'd say you're right," Corian muttered. "Only one way to find out."

A bolt of silver light shot from the Nightstalker's hand toward the black stone. It hissed between the two closest spires and struck something. Silver sparks flared as Corian's magic crackled across its target, flashing between the fists of black stone in both directions. A low growl rose from the center of the stone ridge. That growl quickly turned into an ear-splitting roar, and a massive shape as black as the portal stone rose from between the rocky pillars.

"What the hell is that?" Persh'al muttered.

The beast within the stone heaved, rising above the black spires and casting an even longer shadow across the clearing as it reared above them.

Corian sucked a breath through his teeth. "Not what I was expecting."

CHAPTER SEVENTY-ONE

A giant tentacle wider than any of the trees around them lurched into the sky, waving in warning. The creature it belonged to let out another howling roar. The ground shook beneath them.

"That doesn't belong here," Persh'al murmured, his orange eyes traveling up the length of the threatening, glistening appendage.

Byrd scoffed and shot the troll an exasperated glance. "What gave it away, genius?"

"You know what? I have half a mind to shove you through that portal so you can come back with a detailed report—"

"Watch out!" Cheyenne shoved Persh'al to the side as the massive tentacle slammed down with surprising speed. A spray of dirt and brown grass erupted along either side of the tentacle before it withdrew again.

The troll licked his lips and patted the halfling's shoulder. "I owe you for that one, kid."

"Don't worry about owing me anything. Just—"

Another tentacle shot out from between the pillars and wrapped around Persh'al's throat. In a flash of silver light, the clearing filled with the song of metal slicing through the air. Black fluid sprayed, and the now shorter tendril flapped madly in the air before withdrawing. The stump of slick, glistening black tentacle loosened from around the troll's throat.

Corian's hand was still raised after he'd severed the tentacle with one slash of the very metallic-looking claws jutting four inches from the tips of his fingers.

"Damn the Crown and all this bullshit!" Persh'al struggled fiercely to remove the slimy tentacle from around his neck before he chucked it at the ground. It writhed on its own, then fell still.

"Oh, shit." Lumil glanced between the severed limb and Persh'al's throat. Her hand lifted toward the scar around her neck.

"Cheyenne." Corian stepped out to squarely face the jagged stone pillars, his voice steady and firm in the silence of the clearing as the enormous tentacle waved yards above the tallest spire. "For now, I want you to forget everything I said about keeping that pendant on."

"Yep." She struggled with the knot in the thin silver chain around her neck. *I need a better way to secure this thing.* Lifting the pendant out from under her sweatshirt, she gave it a quick jerk and broke the chain. The Heart of Midnight went into her pocket. Her drow magic flared at the base of her spine as if it had been waiting for its moment of freedom.

"Oh-ho *shit.*" Lumil grinned when she saw Cheyenne's transformation from pale Goth human to the purple-gray skin, stark white hair, and pointed ears of the halfling's drow heritage.

Cheyenne ignored her.

"Any pointers on this one?" Byrd asked, his eyes darting between the massive tentacle and the quickening movement between the stone pillars.

"Yeah." Persh'al summoned an orb of spitting, whirring blue magic in his palm. "Don't let those things grab you by the throat."

A spinning circle of blazing red light appeared around Lumil's clenched fist as she raised it. "What's it waiting for?"

"Your guess is as good as mine," Corian replied without turning around. A shock of brilliant silver light flashed from the tips of his tufted ears to his boots. "Just be ready."

Two more thin black tentacles curled around the closest spires of rock, flickering in and out like snake's tongues. Another earth-rattling roar rose from the center of the portal ridge, rocking the ground just before a massive crack split the air. A fast, urgent skitter grew louder behind the black columns of stone.

Sounds like bugs. Cheyenne brought up a sphere of crackling black energy. *Lots of really big bugs.*

The air filled with the crack of heavy stone, and the portal ridge widened. Dark, shimmering light erupted from the gaping chasm growing wider between the spires. It shot straight into the air and hung there like a curtain along the length of black stone stretching to the west.

"Eyes open," Corian shouted.

The first creature to emerge from the crevasse in the center of the ridge looked like a massive black beetle. It darted around the stone pillars and stopped when it noticed the five magicals standing at the ready inside the clearing. Then it rose on what would have been its back legs, and a gaping red mouth opened in its underbelly to let out a piercing shriek.

"Shit." Byrd's hands erupted with green fire. "Not again."

"Not *here* is more like it." Corian didn't move. "We wait."

"For what?" Lumil shot the Nightstalker a wide-eyed glance. "Those fucking things aren't supposed to—"

The beetle screeched again and leaped through the jagged black stone toward them. It scrambled across the clearing toward the goblin woman, flipping sideways and upside-down as a hundred more legs appeared along every surface of its glistening carapace.

Lumil waited until the thing was almost upon her, and sent a crippling uppercut into the not-beetle's underbelly. The red light encircling her fist ripped through the creature, shattering it into hundreds of pieces and raining down thick chunks of black goo on all of them.

"The first attack," Corian said with a nod.

"*What?*" Persh'al scowled at the Nightstalker. "You don't call the fucking tentacle that tried to hang me the first attack?"

"More like a first taste, Persh'al, and you know it."

"Damnit, Corian. We're not equipped to handle the in-between spilling out where it doesn't belong."

"Hold your fucking position, troll." Corian still didn't turn around to face the blue-skinned Persh'al, but Cheyenne could hear the venom in the Nightstalker's command.

Like he's ordered plenty of people around on a battlefield. Is he—

The ground bucked beneath them, sending the five magicals stumbling. The rift in the center of the black ridge opened even wider with a shiver, ripping from some unseen place below them. The skittering of huge, hard legs across stone echoed everywhere, then the newest Border portal unleashed a swarm.

Glistening black carapaces surged up from beneath the ground and from behind the wall of dark shimmering light at the same time. The air filled with screeching cries as the beetle-like creatures rushed into the clearing. One of them launched itself over the top of a shorter black spire, its red mouth stretching wide in its underbelly as it headed for the halfling.

Cheyenne launched her black crackling orb straight at that mouth, choking off the shriek on impact. The beetle exploded in mid-air and rained down hard shell and guts everywhere.

Corian darted through the rushing swarm in a blazing trail of silver light. Huge black bodies the size of ponies flew through the air wherever that silver light erupted. Lumil and Byrd shouted battle cries as the goblin man set green fire to the rushing monstrosities and his partner blasted their mindless attackers to smithereens with the spells swirling around her turquoise fists. Persh'al raised his hand, and when he brought it down, a whip of sizzling green light emerged.

Cheyenne scanned the oncoming rush of creatures and hurled black orbs of energy into them one after another. The black bodies erupted on impact, sending bug parts flying back toward the ridge.

The horrid creatures just kept coming, spilling from the wall of shimmering light. Persh'al's green whip of magic split through the hard shells like a sword, and the other magicals didn't have any trouble fighting back.

Three of the beetles skittered toward the mohawked troll at an abnormal speed. One of them stopped to rear up again and unleashed a vile spray of black goo toward Persh'al. Cheyenne threw up a shield in front of the troll and his whip, then blasted the closest beetle to pieces before reaching out with the black tendrils of her magic. They wrapped around the spitting beetle and squeezed. The creature screeched again before bursting like an overripe berry two seconds later.

This is too easy.

The halfling quickly checked the other magicals, but they were busy handling the surge of the creatures jumping, spitting, hissing, and scrambling across the ground. Then she looked at the massive tentacle waving above the tallest black spires like a banner in the wind.

That's the one to take down.

Without thinking about it, she clapped and summoned black crackling energy in both hands. Her spells converged into a roiling sphere twice the size of her head, casting black and purple light on her face.

"Cheyenne, wait!" Corian's warning came too late.

The halfling's extra-large dose of black energy hurtled toward the tentacle. Her attack rocked it into the wall of shimmering black light, and a quaking bellow rattled through her head.

The rush of disgusting beetle-things stopped, the last few skittering between the rocky spires with undiminished urgency until they were demolished by Lumil's fist and Byrd's green fire.

The ground trembled again, and the huge tentacle pulled itself out of the shimmering wall of light and rose dozens of yards higher into the air. It stopped undulating like a pennant and froze, perfectly straight, above the Border portal.

"Quick thinking, kid." Corian turned toward the halfling and shook his head in a warning jerk. "But wrong."

"That thing's in control, isn't it?" Cheyenne pointed at the stock-still tentacle.

"Probably. But we're not—"

The ground bucked again, and the crevasse that had opened inside the portal ridge shuddered open even wider. The earth groaned, the forest around them creaking with falling trees as the black stone split apart. A dozen more spires shot from the ground, rising taller than the ones that were already there. Then the wall of shimmering black light darkened until it blocked almost all of the sunlight and cast the entire clearing into darkness.

"Yeah, that's what I'd hoped to avoid."

Cheyenne glared at the Nightstalker. "And what's that, exactly?"

"We're standing on the verge of a new portal, kid. And I mean *on the verge.*"

"Like we're about to cross through it?" The halfling glanced around the darkened clearing.

"Not if we can help it."

A grating growl rose from the center of the portal, a lot louder and closer than any of the other cries. The ridge split wider as a massive black shape clawed its way out of the earth and rose to its full height. The tendril reaching into the sky slammed onto the ground between the split group of fighting magicals, morphing into a gnarled claw digging trenches into the dirt as its owner pulled itself out of the crevasse.

Corian snarled at the claw dragging back toward the portal ridge. "Not if we can keep that thing where it belongs."

"Send it right back to Ambar'ogúl." Cheyenne nodded. "Got it."

"No, Cheyenne," Persh'al said behind her. "Whatever that thing is, it doesn't belong on either side of this portal."

"What?"

"That thing lives *in* the portal." Persh'al cracked his green whip and glared at the hulking thing.

"And that's where it's gotta stay," Corian added.

487

CHAPTER SEVENTY-TWO

Cheyenne couldn't comprehend what she was seeing when the enormous creature emerged from the widening split in the portal ridge. Black tentacles waved in all directions like dozens of reaching limbs, clawed hands and barb-tipped legs morphing in and out. The creature's center was a huge, nebulous blob, constantly shifting to show a glaring red eye, a row of razor-sharp teeth in a gaping maw, or a puckered nodule oozing black slime.

One massive claw rose from the crevasse and slammed down onto the ground. The earth shuddered again, and Cheyenne nearly staggered into Persh'al before she righted herself. Then the creature stepped forward with another foot that looked like a giant bird's talons before the shape muddled into some other tenuous form. The thing bellowed so loudly, Cheyenne clapped her hands against her ears and stumbled backward.

"Did I make it do that?" she shouted above the wailing howl rising from the shifting black glob.

"I doubt it," Corian replied. "Just moved up the timeline a bit. Let's go."

Without waiting for anyone to say anything, the Nightstalker disappeared in a blazing streak of silver light and darted toward the shifting, undulating creature crashing across the clearing. Black fluid sprayed in every direction when his lightning-quick attacks sliced through the morphing body. The creature roared again, its mass jiggling like black Jell-O before two tentacles whipped out in quick succession. Corian went flying toward the trees lining the clearing, skidding backward as he landed on both feet with a clawed hand digging into the dirt.

Cheyenne dodged another lashing tendril as the monster sprayed sizzling black goo at Persh'al. The troll ducked and rolled away, letting out a battle cry as he sprinted toward the ever-shifting mass. A pincer the size of a house snaked out from the center of the shapeless horror, the sharp-tipped ends open in anticipation of cutting the troll in half.

The halfling reached out with her tendrils and curled them around the edge of the claw before it reached Persh'al. The pincer cracked when she jerked it aside and half of it thumped to the ground. The troll dodged the other razor-sharp pincer and struck it with his green whip.

On the other side of the clearing, Lumil and Byrd sent their attacks flying into the globulous thing. Red and green sparks flared on contact but didn't do much else. Corian broke into Nightstalker speed again and headed for the center of the beast's looming shape.

The halfling didn't even think about it before slipping into her enhanced speed and joining him. The sight of that undulating black mass slowing to a crawl as she ran toward it almost made her stop in her tracks.

There were faces in that black, shifting flesh. So many faces pressing against the thick, slimy film of the monster's flesh as if they were pounding against a window, trying to get out.

"Ignore it," Corian shouted as he slashed at the creature's center.

"Help me!" a voice shrieked from within the monster's nebulous form.

Cheyenne hesitated only an instant when she saw a female face pressing against the monster's skin. Then the face morphed into a huge mouth with dripping fangs before a tendril materialized where the eyes had been. The halfling sent two bolts of crackling black energy into that transforming visage without a second thought. Black and purple light crackled along the beast's flesh.

More black sludge erupted from the impact site, suspended in mid-air as the half-drow unleashed attack after attack on the changeling creature. Corian did the same beside her, then a shimmering blast of black energy erupted from the surface of the monster's skin and sent them both hurtling backward across the clearing again, smacking them out of enhanced speed.

Cheyenne landed on her ass in the dirt and growled. Beside her, Corian chuckled, his blazing silver eyes locked on the creature. "*Always* on your feet?"

He dipped his head. "Mostly, yeah."

Corian offered her a hand up as Lumil and Byrd kept shouting and screaming and ripping into the creature with their attacks. Persh'al lashed his whip across the next two tentacles that darted out to meet him and severed them both with his slicing magic.

"We're not making a dent in that thing," the halfling snarled.

"I know."

"What the hell do we do?"

"Push it back, Cheyenne. This thing has one foot in this realm and the other where it belongs."

"It doesn't *have* feet!"

"Correct. But if this thing gets loose, we're facing a much bigger problem Earthside than any of us planned for."

The halfling snorted as they took off running toward the creature again. "No shit."

She hurled ball after ball of her crackling black energy and watched the attacks send ripples of force up through the undulating mass, which kept wavering between solidity and a nauseating gooeyness. *How the hell do you send something back when nothing stops it?*

Corian's silver light darted back and forth across the massive creature. Black sludge sprayed in every direction as the Nightstalker hacked and slashed and lit up the monster. When Corian stopped to stave off the black darts headed for the goblin team, the beast let out a quick grunt and nearly doubled in size. Its hulking form rose even higher in the darkened clearing, and five more pillars of black stone burst from the earth, stretching just as high.

"The stone," Cheyenne muttered. She darted away from the creature, which stood as tall as a four-story building now, lashing its claws and pincers and tentacles at its assailants. "Corian! It's the stone—"

A plume of black smoke jetted toward her. Cheyenne lifted a shield, splitting the smoke in two before it raced across the clearing and doubled back toward her again. The closest cloud of black smoke let out a blood-curdling scream as it barreled toward the halfling. She shot a sphere of black energy at its center, but that did nothing. The halfling raised a shield again, and this time, the smoke fragmented and disappeared.

This damn thing's drawing energy from the black stones, just like the Border Reservations.

Cheyenne reached toward the closest black spire and felt around for that resisting pressure in the air. There it was, right at the tips of her fingers.

The monster roared and lashed out at her with half a dozen whipping tentacles. She slipped into enhanced speed and fired round after round of her crackling black energy before the tentacles severed in a suspended spray of oozing black sludge. The torn pieces of monster drifted toward the ground, and Cheyenne dropped into a crouch.

She slammed both palms down into the dirt and pushed.

A wave of moving earth bucked beneath her and headed for the creature. The ground exploded between Corian and the nightmarish thing. It sent the Nightstalker tumbling back across the clearing as the monster heaved and recoiled against the wall of regular earth rising in front of it.

Cheyenne swayed where she crouched, and her drow speed fell

away. The nebulous beast lunged toward her, its entire body drawing up to open in a giant mouth lined with dripping fangs. Another bellow erupted from that mouth and nearly knocked the halfling backward with a fierce gust of air and its nauseatingly reeking breath. *Smells like fear and death. And something else.*

She didn't hesitate before reaching out with both hands toward the black pillars of stone. Her magic found that resistance again instantly, and Cheyenne put all her strength behind it when she tugged.

The closest pillar cracked and moved sideways, but nothing else happened.

"Come *on!*" She reached out again, but the monster sent two more tentacles wider than she was toward her. The halfling darted away from where she'd crouched as one tentacle smashed into the ground. Dirt and chunks of rock hurtled toward her. Cheyenne cried out at the sharp sting of something heavy hitting the base of her skull, and she stumbled toward the edge of the portal ridge.

"Cheyenne!" Corian darted toward her, but even with his enhanced speed, he wasn't quick enough to reach her before another five-foot-wide tentacle smacked the ground and cut him off.

Gritting her teeth, the halfling reached for the feel of the black stone one more time. Only now, instead of trying to break it, she pushed up and forced the stone to rise higher.

The monster screeched and undulated, trying to turn toward her before she darted around the huge pillars. It was a tight squeeze between the first pillar and the closest tree, but she managed to get in there and slap her hands down on the rock jutting from the ground. It was so cold, her hands burned instantly, but she held on.

"Damnit, Cheyenne, get away from that—"

The monster spat a glob of gray ooze toward her and the pillar. Cheyenne darted aside and was vaguely aware of the ground hissing and sizzling behind her. She leaned into the pillar instead and reached out with her magic.

If I can manipulate earth while I'm Earthside, this better fucking work.

Her magic stretched along the entire length of the portal ridge, farther than she realized it could go. All she felt was cold and darkness and something like fear but not quite. An anxious waiting, just below the surface. Then her awareness returned to her, and she whipped her hands off the black spire and out to the sides.

The column of jagged stone burst into thousands of fragments and followed the direction of her hands. The shards of black rock hurtled into the monster trying to squeeze its way around the pillars toward her. Every piece of stone was absorbed in an instant, but Cheyenne still had a hold on each of them.

When the shards of stone had disappeared, the halfling hooked the fingers of her drow magic around the cold energy she felt *inside* the nightmare heading toward her and shoved it all to the side as if she were jerking open a sliding door.

The creature groaned and let out an earth-shattering bellow. Then it slid sideways, jiggling and writhing as the stone shards inside it pulled against the beast's hulking mass.

Cheyenne pulled again, and the creature skidded across the ground toward the massive crevasse it had ripped in the earth to get into the clearing. Snaking tentacles whipped across the ground, writhing and sputtering into claws, barbs, and pincers as they tried to get a grip on anything to stop its descent.

Pushing with all her might, the halfling directed the shattered black stone and the beast around it into the open chasm. She might have screamed at the effort as the ground rocked again beneath her feet. A thin barbed tentacle struck at the ground and found its way around her ankle. Cheyenne hit the ground. *Just send it back. Keep pushing.*

The creature dragged her with it as it morphed and bellowed and squeezed into the rent earth. The halfling couldn't release her hold on the black stone, and she didn't have to.

The air in front of her burst with crackling silver light and Corian's extended claws came down on the tendril around her ankle in a blur. Dark ooze spurted from the severed limb before the creature slid down, down, down into the darkness.

"Damnit! What the hell were you thinking?" Corian grabbed her under the arms and pulled her away from the edge of the crevasse. "This isn't another training session, by the way."

"I know." When she got back to her feet, Cheyenne brushed him off and reached for the glistening black spires of the portal ridge again. "I got it."

"You can't just play around with this until something sticks," he shouted. "We don't even know—"

Black sludge sprayed from the open crevasse like a geyser, and Cheyenne threw up a shield around them both before it rained down from the sky. "You wanna wait around to find out what else is down there?"

Corian's silver eyes darted to her face, then he snarled and stepped back.

The halfling lowered the shield when it was safe and reached out for the black pillars again, searching with her magic. *Might work as a barred door, at least for a little while.*

When her magic found the energy in all that frigid, searing stone, she pulled on it again and roared with the force of her magic coursing through her. The jagged stone spires surrounding the massive crack in the earth shuddered and broke almost as one at the base. Rock crashed against rock, drowning out every other sound in the clearing as the spires toppled against each other, rolling and bouncing and turning into a latticework of fallen stone. Huge plumes of black dust and brown dirt sprayed up in a cloud around them, and after the last smaller pebbles had finished bouncing down on top of the fallen portal ridge, the clearing fell silent.

The wall of pitch-black magic stayed where it was, reaching up into the sky along the length of the jutting ridge of stone. Then it flickered once or twice and let go of the darkness.

Sunshine slowly filtered back into the clearing, and Cheyenne stumbled sideways before dropping into a crouch.

"Hey." Corian bent to put a hand on her shoulder.

"I'm fine," she wheezed. "Just give me a minute."

The Nightstalker removed his hand and stepped back, staring at the destruction across the portal. His lips twitched on his feline face before finally curling into a smirk. "That was definitely not what I expected, either."

CHAPTER SEVENTY-THREE

When the wave of dizziness subsided, Cheyenne rose slowly to her feet and studied the fallen pillars lying over the crevasse of the newest Border portal. A stream of cold air rose from the gaping split in the ground beneath the broken black spires, but nothing else stirred.

"Probably just a temporary thing, huh?"

Corian threw his head back and roared with laughter.

She turned toward him and raised an eyebrow. "It's not *that* funny."

"Not tha…" Another laugh burst out of him before he pulled himself together and cleared his throat. "No, Cheyenne. This issue in front of us isn't a laughing matter, I'll give you that. But *you*? You never cease to amaze me."

"Thanks. I think." The halfling headed toward the open part of the clearing and sucked in a sharp breath. She glanced down at her ankle and the puncture marks through the fabric of her pants. "That's not good."

"We'll take a look at that later, kid." Corian's smile had faded, but his blasé glance at her wounded leg made her feel a little better.

"What the hell did I just watch?" Byrd shouted as he raced toward them.

Lumil flung a glob of black goo off her fist and joined him, cursing in O'gúleesh. "That was much worse than any crossing I've made. I'd make them all again at the same time if it meant I never had to deal with this shit again."

Behind Corian, Persh'al flicked out his hand, and the green whip of his magic disappeared. "I tell you what, halfling. You sure as shit didn't get *that* from L'zar."

"Look at *you* with your massive insights into the obvious." Byrd thumped his palm against his forehead and shook his head.

Cheyenne shook out her hands, the chains clinking against her wrists, and let out a quick, heavy breath. "Didn't get what from him?"

"All that." The troll waved his hand over the broken spires crushed against each other, then nodded at the mound of natural dirt and earth still jutting up toward the portal ridge where she'd raised it. "That's some next-level drow shit."

"And who made you the expert on that?" Lumil asked, folding her arms.

Persh'al blinked at her and gestured toward the destruction across the border ridge. "We've all seen enough drow magic to know that's not usually in the bag of tricks. Unless you've seen *that* before and haven't gotten around to telling us the story fifty million times already."

The goblin woman smirked and tilted her head, her flop of yellow hair spilling down over one eye. "No. That was pretty damn impressive."

When Lumil nodded at Cheyenne, the halfling just nodded back.

"So, now what?" Byrd asked.

Corian scratched the side of his fur-covered face and shook his head. "This thing seems pretty blocked off. For now. And we still don't know if any of this happened on its own or if someone's working double-time to open the portal from Ambar'ogúl."

Persh'al stared at the black rift in the earth, barely showing between the toppled pillars. "You really think she has that kinda firepower over there?"

The clearing fell silent as the O'gúleesh magicals exchanged uncertain glances.

Cheyenne watched their interactions with a small frown. *Nobody wants to come right out and say it. Whatever it is.*

Corian shook his head. "We've been Earthside a long time, Persh'al."

"You said you've had reports."

"I have eyes back home, sure, but not enough to see everything." The Nightstalker's nose twitched into the beginning of a snarl as he glared at the fallen spires. "And I only know one person who'd be able to sniff out the truth behind this."

Lumil scoffed. "Well, good thing we know where she is. Oh, that's right. We *don't*."

"True." Corian turned toward Cheyenne and fixed her with his glowing silver eyes. "But Cheyenne does."

"What?"

"*You* know where to find Maleshi Hi'et?" Lumil folded her arms and grinned despite the dark frown wrinkling her turquoise brow.

The halfling glanced at the goblin woman and the Nightstalker. "Not on a Sunday."

Persh'al chuckled softly.

"Cheyenne, we need to find her." Corian stepped toward the halfling and dipped his chin to look at her beneath the furry tufts of his brows. "She's the only magical I know who has the skill to track the origin of this new portal without us having to make a crossing back to Ambar'ogúl." He glanced quickly over his shoulder at the crumbled stone. "Which I'm even *more* hesitant to do after the last ten minutes."

The halfling swallowed, pursing her lips and trying to keep her composure. "Are you serious?"

"I can't imagine I've given you the impression that I'm overly fond of joking, kid."

"You think—" She laughed sharply before she shook her head. "No way. Mattie won't want to have anything to do with *this*, I know that much. She almost stopped talking to me because I asked questions about the FRoE."

"Ugh." Lumil rolled her eyes.

"Who the fuck is Mattie?" Byrd cocked his head, one giant gauged ear flopping onto his shoulder.

Corian's head turned toward the goblin man, but his gaze didn't leave Cheyenne's. "Maleshi took a new name for herself."

"Say what?"

The Nightstalker ignored him. "Listen, Cheyenne. I don't want to run the risk of letting this portal open again. If I had to take a guess, I'd say whatever comes out of it next time will be a lot worse than what all five of us almost couldn't put back in. You want that kinda weight on your shoulders?"

"Don't talk about it like it's my fault," the halfling snapped.

"It's not your fault, but doing nothing *will* be your fault. I have a feeling you understand that very well."

Cheyenne scowled at him. *He doesn't know about Ember.* "Mattie's my friend, okay? She made it perfectly clear she left all this crazy shit behind her when she crossed over and that she doesn't want anything to do with it anymore."

"She might think that's what she wants." Corian pointed at the border ridge. "But if we tell her what's happening, I know she'll change her mind."

Folding her arms, the halfling tilted her head and frowned at him. "How do you know that?"

The smile he gave her was tight and bitter. "Just a feeling."

Byrd sniggered. "Yeah, you guys had plenty of *feelings* once upon a time, didn't you?"

Lumil slapped him on the back of the head and shot him a disgusted look as she shook her head. "Really?"

The Nightstalker ignored them both. "I'm asking you for a favor, Cheyenne. Please. Tell us where she is."

Cheyenne bit her lip. "I can't. I don't know where she lives."

"But you know how to find out, don't you?"

"Oh, no." She shook her head a little and returned his bitter, humorless smile. "No, I'm not sitting down at a computer to find out where she lives. Especially not so you can knock down her door and force her to help you with this...whatever this portal's doing."

"Ha." Lumil shook her head. "Nobody forces Maleshi Hi'et to do anything, kid. I'm surprised you haven't figured that one out by now. If you really are friends with her."

The halfling spared the goblin woman a quick glance. "I'm *not* gonna spy on her and dig up her personal information so people she wants nothing to do with can find her. She hasn't reached out to any of you, and if you haven't found her on your own, I'd say that's a pretty clear sign she doesn't want *anyone* to find her."

"Except for you."

Cheyenne turned to see Persh'al regarding her with raised eyebrows. "That's different."

"Yeah? She told you who she was. Revealed herself to *you*, L'zar Verdys' only living spawn."

"Mattie doesn't know who my dad is." The halfling shook her head. "We never got that far."

The troll's eyes widened, but he didn't say anything else.

"She might not know he's your old man," Corian added, "but trust me, Cheyenne. Maleshi definitely knows who L'zar Verdys is."

"You all fight for the Crown together or something?"

The four O'gúleesh exchanged another round of knowing glances.

Corian shrugged. "Or something. If you won't help us find her, kid, I'll do it myself."

Persh'al snorted. "You mean, you'll have me do it for you."

The Nightstalker smirked. "Sure. And then we'll pay the general a little visit. It's *long* overdue."

Cheyenne glanced at the group of magicals, all expecting her to give in. *Shit. They're not bluffing, and I can't stop them if they really wanna find her.* "I won't help you find her. I won't give her up like that. But if you figure out where she lives, I'm coming with you."

The Nightstalker dipped his head in concession. "Sounds fair to me."

"Let's get the hell outta here, huh?" Persh'al pounded the heel of his hand against his forehead. "This buzz around here is starting to make me hear voices."

Lumil snorted. "You've been hearing voices since *before* you came Earthside, troll."

"I've heard enough of yours, that's for sure." Persh'al turned to head back into the forest.

Laughing, the goblin woman came up alongside Cheyenne and clapped a hand on the halfling's shoulder. "L'zar would've gotten a kick out of that little show you just put on."

Byrd snorted. "The guy would've made us all bow down and offer ourselves before the next in the Verdys line."

Together, the goblins gave Cheyenne mocking little bows. Byrd's shoulder knocked against Lumil's, and he nearly fell face-first into the dirt when she shoved him away from her.

"That's as good as you're gonna get right now, though," the goblin man muttered, glancing up at Cheyenne to shoot her a quick wink. "Until L'zar decides to show his face again. Then we'll see what half-cocked plan he's cooked up to make us all grovel."

"You're gonna end up eating those words, you idiot." Lumil shoved him as they headed toward the tree line after Persh'al.

The goblin man laughed. "Yeah. *You've* never said anything that came back to bite you in the ass."

"Not about the Cu'ón."

Corian stared after the goblins with a mix of amusement and confusion. Then he turned toward Cheyenne and raised an eyebrow. "I appreciate your attempt to protect her, kid. Maleshi found a good friend in you, even if she doesn't know who you really are."

The halfling shrugged. "Promises must be kept, right?"

"They sure must. We both know how important that is." Gesturing toward the forest, the Nightstalker leaned forward in what could have been a little bow of his own.

Cheyenne headed after the bantering goblins and Persh'al. *He doesn't need to know I didn't officially promise Mattie anything. I won't be the one to force her into this.*

CHAPTER SEVENTY-FOUR

Three hours later, Persh'al slammed a fist on the desk in his warehouse. "Come on, kid. You gotta give me *something*."

"No, I don't." Cheyenne was sprawled on the old, sunken couch behind the troll and his computers, her eyes closed and her arms folded behind her head.

Persh'al spun around in his desk chair and blinked when he saw the drow halfling lying in that position on his couch. "Even in the human get-up, you're giving me serious déjà vu."

"I don't know what you mean."

"Never mind." The troll spun around again and typed some more. "You gotta be kidding me. *Nothing*. Like she just vanished into thin air."

Cheyenne opened one eye to watch the troll's frustration. "I'm pretty sure that's the point."

"Nah." He shook his finger at her without turning around, still typing with one hand. "There's always a trace. Has to be."

"Good luck." The halfling closed her eyes again and took a deep breath. *Doesn't feel like a waste of time. If he gives up trying to find her, I'll know. Then this'll be worth it.*

"Yeah, I had plenty of luck pinging *your* server and playing your entire setup like a marionette. But I can't find one of the most famous Nightstalkers living two hours away."

Cheyenne sat up quickly on the couch and stared at him. "That was *you?*"

"Well, yeah. Surprised you didn't figure that one out already, kid." Persh'al shrugged and still didn't turn around again to face her. "Really nice setup you got, by the way. Grabbing the reins on someone else's rig usually only takes me half as long. So, you put up a good fight, the way you built it." He paused, then let out a knowing chuckle. "Guess my warning wasn't enough to scare L'zar's daughter away from doing whatever the hell she wants, huh?"

The halfling slowly shook her head. "Hey, if you want someone to back off a search you weren't supposed to find, you might wanna consider giving a reason. I don't just drop everything to do what some stranger on the dark web tells me to do."

"Maybe you should." Persh'al typed more commands into his system and let out a frustrated grunt. "Would've stopped you from running blindly into that FRoE raid and getting yourself caught up with those idiots. They have no idea what they're doing."

Cheyenne lay slowly back down on the couch again. *Don't I know it.* "You were spying on *me* to keep me away from the FRoE?"

"Just trying to keep you out of trouble. We all are, kid." The troll smacked the desk beside his keyboard and slumped back so forcefully in his chair that the whole thing rolled back a foot. "You're killing me with this. How 'bout a last name, huh? Maleshi can't hide for very long without one of those. And don't be a smartass and tell me to look up Maleshi Hi'et. I already tried."

"I told you I wouldn't help you find her," Cheyenne muttered. "I made a promise."

"Yeah, yeah. The strongest contract bond. I get it. Doesn't mean I have to like it."

The door to the warehouse burst open and Corian stepped inside, carrying two huge bags of sub sandwiches. "So, where is she?"

"Yeah, question of the day, man." Persh'al rubbed his bald, speckled head beside the jutting mohawk and glared at the symbols on his monitor Cheyenne couldn't read.

The plastic bags thumped down on top of the long center desk. "You haven't found her yet?"

"Okay, maybe we should have a Nightstalker looking for a Nightstalker," the troll muttered. "Isn't there some kinda secret communication thing you guys have with each other? Sniff out her pheromones or whatever?"

Cheyenne snorted. "Is that really a thing?"

Corian ignored them both as he stared at the symbols on the troll's monitor. "Look up the professors at Virginia Commonwealth University. Find a picture or something."

Frowning, Persh'al turned in his desk chair to study Cheyenne's reaction. Apparently, staring back at him was all he needed. "Yeah, I bet that'll work. Don't have to break a promise to give anything away, do ya?"

His fingers flew over the keyboard, and Cheyenne shot Corian an unamused look. The Nightstalker pulled two sandwiches out of the plastic bags and brought them with him when he approached the couch. The halfling begrudgingly sat up and swung her black Vans onto the warehouse floor.

"I know what you're doing and why." He held out a sandwich and waited. The halfling held out her hand, and the thick, heavy bundle thumped into her palm. "Might help you understand a little more why I can't tell you everything right now, Cheyenne. As much as I want to."

"I know the definition of keeping a promise, Corian." She lowered the sandwich into her lap and stared at the white butcher paper wrapped tightly around it. "And I understood why you can't tell me certain things from the very beginning. I also thought I could trust you to keep whatever I've told you to yourself."

"You can." He took a deep breath. "Trying to protect Maleshi is a waste of your time, kid. Especially now, with that new Border portal and everything we don't know about it. And just so you know, she doesn't need protection. Not the Maleshi I know. If anyone needs protection, it's the idiots who stand in her way."

"Or the idiots who dig her up after centuries of hiding. Which she *chose*, right?"

"She'll understand why we're doing this when we tell her what we saw this morning."

Cheyenne shook her head and glanced at the sandwich. "Good luck trying to get her to listen. Never worked for me."

"Well, things have changed since then, haven't they?"

When she looked back up at him, the Nightstalker just raised an eyebrow.

"Yeah. A lot's changed. Just not what people won't tell me." They stared at each other. "What happens if I figure it out on my own before your promise runs its course?"

Smirking, the Nightstalker nodded toward Persh'al and unwrapped his sub. "I'll probably give away the same kinda confirmation you just gave him, and you won't even need a troll hacker to put the rest of the pieces together. If you *do* figure it out before then, I can tell you right now you won't find anything else about it on the dark web."

"Maybe not. But I bet I could hack in Persh'al's system if I gave it enough time."

"Ha! I'd like to see you try." The troll spun and pointed at the halfling. "Please don't try. You'll just hurt yourself."

Smiling, Cheyenne just looked back down at her sandwich and started to unwrap it. *Not a bad idea. I won't hurt myself at all.*

Persh'al slapped his desk again, but this time, it came with a laugh of triumph. "Wow! Take a look at *that*, Corian."

The Nightstalker tore a huge chunk from the top of his sub. His eyes widened at the picture on the screen.

"Professor Mathilda Bergmann, Ph.D." The troll looked at his friend. "Look like anyone we know?"

Corian chewed his bite and swallowed. "Finish up."

"Yeah, I'll find her in less than a minute. Make sure you save me one of those sandwiches, huh? I know how you go through those things."

Turning toward Cheyenne, the Nightstalker shoved another huge bite of fully-loaded sub into his mouth and raised his eyebrows.

Yeah, congratulations. You found your missing general.

She lifted her sandwich toward him in a half-assed salute before taking a massive bite.

"That's what I'm talkin' about!" Persh'al leaped out of his chair and grabbed his phone from his back pocket just as it let off a chirping notification. "We got it."

"Okay." Chewing thoughtfully, Corian glanced around the mostly empty warehouse. "What about the terror twins?"

The troll snorted. "They wouldn't shut up, so I told them to go take their crap out back and pull some weeds."

"Weeds?"

With a dubious grin, Persh'al shrugged. "I'm thinking about bringing them on as full-time gardeners. Nice thought, right?"

Corian took another bite of sandwich and muttered through the mouthful, "Go tell 'em we're on the move."

"Yep." Persh'al rounded the corner of the desk and snatched up a bag of subs before heading for a plain metal door on the other side of the warehouse.

After only three bites of her sandwich, Cheyenne wrapped it back up and stood from the couch. Corian watched her silently until she set the sub down on the corner of the center desk.

"Not hungry?"

"Not a fan of banana peppers." She sucked the bread from between her teeth and wiped her hands on the sides of her pants.

"You're kidding. Who doesn't like banana peppers?" The Nightstalker stuffed his face again with another bite.

"Me, for one."

"Well, just pick 'em out. I'll eat 'em."

She shook her head. "I'm good." *And I'm not hungry. Not before we go shove Mattie's past under her nose and call it asking for a favor.*

The back door of the warehouse squealed open before Persh'al stepped back inside, followed by the goblins.

"We're not driving all the way to *Richmond*, are we?" Byrd whined. "Seriously, four hours in a car with you guys was as much as I need for another century."

"You're unbelievable." Lumil shook her head as she wiped dirt-covered hands on her pants. "We found Maleshi Hi'et, and you're crying about having to ride in a car."

"If I have to ride bitch again, then yeah." Byrd spread his arms and leaped away from the goblin woman's solid swing. "I need my own window."

Corian took one more massive bite of his sandwich before finally setting the thing down on the desk.

"Hey, watch the setup, huh?" Persh'al pointed at his computer. "Last thing I need is Nightstalker crumbs gunking up my keyboard."

Ignoring the troll's half-joke, Corian stepped toward the center of the warehouse and moved his fingers in a quick series of gestures. His lips moved too, silently uttering the words of his spell before a small, dark sphere opened in the air.

Byrd stopped when he saw the Nightstalker's new portal and grinned. "Finally."

"Don't get ahead of yourself." Corian shot the goblin man a warning glance and nodded at the quickly growing portal. "We're going in dark for this."

"Stealth mode. Nice." His comment made Lumil roll her eyes, but she was smiling just like Byrd.

Cheyenne moved around the three long tables and joined the others gathered around the portal. "I'm guessing there's some other kind of spell we need for this."

Byrd let out an uncharacteristic giggle, ending in a snort. "Good one. Just keep 'em coming, halfling." His turquoise fingers moved swiftly and precisely, then the air shimmered around him and he vanished.

Smiling at Cheyenne, Lumil reached out and punched the empty air beside her. Her fist hit home with a thump, followed by the quick scuffle of staggering feet.

"For real?" the invisible Byrd shouted. "I just can't catch a break."

"You would if you got out of the way fast enough." The goblin woman wiggled her eyebrows at the halfling before casting a spell and disappearing like Byrd.

Persh'al went next, and Corian stepped toward Cheyenne before muttering in a low voice, "Keep that pendant on for now. We're going back to our regular precautions."

The halfling nodded and gazed into the dark, shimmering air of the oval portal in front of her. On the other side, a short cement walkway cut through a yard of green grass toward a small white one-story house with navy-blue shutters and a matching door. "No candles for this one?"

He snorted. "This warehouse has enough wards to keep an ogre den out, Cheyenne. Nobody's picking up a portal trail from in here."

When she turned toward him to make a quip about ogre dens, the Nightstalker was gone. "Woah. Okay, I'm adding this to the list of spells you're helping me with."

"Sure."

Byrd chuckled softly on the other side of the portal, his voice growing louder and closer as the other invisible magicals apparently lined up behind the halfling. "You're teaching our girl spells now too, Corian?"

Cheyenne eyed the empty air and turned by instinct when she felt the heat of three more bodies behind her. "Anyone gonna work that invisibility thing on *me*?"

She heard Corian's soft laugh through his nose. "Another time, kid. You're going through this one as you are."

"And that's because…"

"You're gonna be the first thing she sees when she opens the front door. After you."

Never show up at someone's home unannounced, Cheyenne. Mom would be furious if she knew about this. Cocking her head, Cheyenne stepped through the portal and onto the sidewalk in front of Professor Mathilda Bergmann's house.

CHAPTER SEVENTY-FIVE

The soft tingle of the portal's magic flashed across her skin for a brief second before she was out of the low, dusty light inside Persh'al's warehouse. Cheyenne blinked against the sudden brightness of the early afternoon before a harsh whisper came from behind her.

"Make some room, huh?"

She thought it was Byrd, but it didn't matter. The halfling took a quick glance around the neighborhood, but at noon on a Sunday, there wasn't anyone around to see a Goth chick suddenly materialize out of thin air. *That part's luck.*

Moving quickly up the walkway toward Mattie's front porch, Cheyenne almost turned again to double-check that the four O'gúleesh magicals were following her. *Can't hear the goblin's mouth-breathing this time.*

When she made it to the base of the three stairs leading up to the porch, she stopped.

"Can't back out now, kid," Corian whispered in her ear.

The tickle of his breath and what felt like a whisker or two almost made her flinch. "I'm not backing out."

"Just a friendly reminder."

With a deep breath, the halfling forced herself up the stairs onto the porch and toward the navy-blue front door. Her fist rose, and she paused again. *Please just hear them out, Mattie. Then you'll see why I'm doing this. Even if you don't end up forgiving me for it later.*

Cheyenne knocked three times on the front door and waited. None of the magicals behind her made a sound.

Footsteps grew louder on the other side of the door, then two deadbolts slid back, and the doorknob turned slowly. Mattie opened the door with a curious smile, wondering who could possibly be at her door on a Sunday. That smile widened when she saw Cheyenne Summerlin standing on her front porch, and a small laugh escaped her. "You know, I *did* tell you I'd email you before tomorrow. No need to hunt me down at my house. Good to see you're so eager to prepare for your first class, though."

Cheyenne tried to smile back and couldn't quite manage it. "I'm not here about an email."

Brushing a lock of wavy black hair out of her face, Mattie glanced around her front yard. A hint of wary skepticism flashed across her luminous green eyes, and she folded her arms. Then she took a step back into the house and eyed Cheyenne up and down. "You look like you fell into some kinda trouble, kid." The woman briefly closed her eyes. "Well, you're already here, and I can't turn you away. Come on in and tell me all about it, then."

Swallowing thickly, the halfling stepped into her first mentor's house. "I, uh, I'm not in trouble." Cheyenne turned back to glance out the open front door. *Time for these guys to show themselves.* "Sorry, Mattie."

"Come on, Cheyenne, I wasn't born yesterday. Nobody looks over their shoulder like that when they're perfectly comfortable being where they are. Who's following you now?" Mattie stepped forward and reached out for the open door, keeping her gaze on her former student.

The door swung away from her open hand and closed on its own. Mattie's eyes narrowed as Corian's invisibility spell shimmered around him, and the Nightstalker reappeared with his hand on the doorknob. "Hi, Maleshi."

Mattie's green eyes widened. Then Persh'al and the goblins appeared on either side of Corian, and the college professor lifted a finger. "Oh, no. No, no."

"We just need a minute of your time," Corian said softly.

"Get the fuck out." Mattie pointed swiftly at the door, which let off a silver flash before opening again.

Corian pressed firmly on the door until it clicked shut behind him. "Just twenty minutes, Maleshi. Please. Give us that much, and then we'll leave."

"I don't want to give you anything." Mattie's green gaze darted from Corian to Persh'al and she shook her head. "Especially not when you coerced Cheyenne into this. I'm not playing your games, *vae shra'ni.*"

"No games." Corian spread his arms. "And I'm sorry to have to surprise you like this. You've made it very hard to find you."

"That was the *point*, Corian." Mattie's jaw clenched and unclenched as she pressed her lips together. "I came out here to start over, and I've spent way too long on building a life to throw it all away because you want to walk down Memory Lane."

He let out a bitter laugh. "You think I'm here for nostalgia, General—"

"Don't call me that," Mattie hissed and took a lunging step toward him. Corian didn't react beyond holding her green-eyed gaze with his silver one. "I'm a *college professor.* Mathilda Bergmann."

"Yeah, so we heard." Persh'al folded his arms and leaned against the wall beside the door.

"Then you're a lot stupider than I thought possible if you actually believe I'll entertain the notion of sitting down and talking about the old world with you."

Cheyenne stepped toward the staircase just inside the door and bit her lip. *Pretty much what I expected.*

"We need your help." Corian didn't look away from the gaze of the Nightstalker, who looked very much like a human. "Please."

"You've lasted this long without me." One of Mattie's eyes twitched as she leaned toward him and bared her teeth in a feral snarl. "You'll just have to keep it up."

"There's a new Border portal, Maleshi." Corian swallowed and raised his eyebrows when the woman took a small step away from him. "Unregulated. Most people don't know about it. And it's not doing what it's supposed to do."

The woman studied his face before she stepped back. "Not my problem."

"It *will* be. You're the only person I know who can help us figure out why it's there and how we keep it from getting any worse."

"No." Mattie shook her head. "I'm not the same person anymore. Mattie Bergmann's got a pretty good deal going on in this life, and she's here to stay."

"I don't give a shit what Mattie Bergmann does," Corian growled. "I need Maleshi Hi'et."

"Tough shit. You came to the wrong house." Letting out a snarl, the woman whirled and stalked toward the living room. "Now, get out."

Cheyenne sighed when Corian shot her a quick glance. She wanted to say, "I told you so," but settled for a shrug instead.

The Nightstalker avoided the other O'gúleesh gazes as he followed Mattie/Maleshi. Cheyenne could only offer Persh'al and the goblins the same caliber of shrug when they looked at her next.

"It's just twenty minutes, Maleshi," Corian called.

"It's twenty minutes better spent on *anything* else." Mattie spun again and folded her arms. "I'm serious. If you don't take your soldiers and get the fuck out of my house, I won't hesitate to rip your head off your shoulders and make them carry it back to whoever you're reporting to."

"Soldiers?" Byrd whispered to Lumil as everyone else filed into the living room after the arguing Nightstalkers. "Did she forget everything?"

Mattie looked up as Cheyenne entered the room and pointed at

Persh'al and the goblins. "No. What part of no do you not understand?"

"I'm not reporting to anyone, Maleshi." Corian spread his arms. "This was my call."

"It was a very bad call. And I don't believe a single word coming out of your mouth, *vae shra'ni*. I have no reason to."

Corian leaned away from her with a hurt expression. "I didn't think you held my loyalty in such low esteem, General."

Hissing, Mattie turned away from him and waved him off. "Don't talk to me about loyalty."

"That's what brought you here in the first place, isn't it?" Corian gestured toward the rest of her house with a quick toss of his arm. "That's what made you leave. Because your allegiance isn't to the Crown, Maleshi, and it never was. You did this for our *home*. And every O'gúleesh on both sides of the Border speaks your name in the same breath as rebellion."

The Nightstalker woman let out a wry laugh. "Okay. And that's why you forced the halfling to trick me into letting you inside my house, so you could weasel a confession out of me and bring me back across kicking and screaming. What did she offer you, Corian? My old medals? A seat at her wilting fucking feast?"

"The Crown can rip itself apart for all I care, and it's headed that way as we speak. You have the chance to finish what you started when you laid down your banner, Maleshi."

"*Mattie!*"

"General Maleshi Hi'et, Hand of the Night and Circle, Blade of the Untouched Eye," Corian shouted back. "*That* is who you are! The truth runs deeper than flesh, even in the light."

Mattie stiffened where she stood beside the light-brown couch against the wall. She stared at the floor, her hands clenching into fists. "What did you say?"

"You heard me." Corian blinked, his upper lip twitching with the hint of his snarl. "And now I need you to put your rage aside and listen to the rest of what I came to say. I act for Ambar'ogúl, and my loyalty lies with the Cu'ón." When Mattie looked at him, the Night-stalker nodded toward Cheyenne.

Slowly, the Nightstalker who'd spent the last few centuries convincing the world she was human turned toward the other magicals gathered in her living room. Then her gaze fell on Cheyenne standing just inside the doorway, and her eyes widened. "You brought her here with you as a messenger."

"I brought her here so you'd understand what's at stake," Corian muttered. "And hopefully, to help convince you what you're hearing is all there is to say."

Mattie just kept staring at Cheyenne, although the surprise and dawning realization had filtered away from her green eyes. "Do *you* know what this is about?"

The halfling licked her lips and nodded. "Yeah."

Lumil chuckled. "Hell, she might be the only reason we made it out of that—"

"I didn't ask for your opinion." Mattie's sharp gaze cut toward the goblin woman, who pressed her lips together and stared at the floor. "I'll listen to what Cheyenne has to say. Anyone tries to lead her or change her story, I'll rip all four of you apart and drop you into the Atlantic. Got it?"

The woman's gaze roamed across the gathered magicals in her living room, all of whom returned short, firm nods. When she was satisfied, Mattie/Maleshi turned back toward Cheyenne and gestured toward the couch. "Please, Cheyenne. Have a seat."

"Right." Glancing at the other magicals, the halfling moved across the room, feeling Mattie's gaze on her the entire time. She stopped by the couch and waited for everyone else to take seats on the loveseat and armchairs circling the low coffee table.

Persh'al and the goblins approached the furniture and stood in front of their prospective seats without moving. Mattie looked at Corian, and only when she tilted her head did he step in front of the loveseat. Then the woman joined Cheyenne at the couch and gestured for the halfling to sit.

Lowering herself onto the couch, Cheyenne frowned at the

other magicals. They didn't move until Mattie finally sat beside the halfling, then everyone else fell into their seats like puppets with their strings cut.

"I'm ready to listen to whatever you have to tell me." Mattie met the halfling's gaze and nodded slowly. All traces of her usual joking demeanor were gone.

I guess I'm talking to Maleshi now and not Mattie. This is weird.

Cheyenne shrugged and leaned forward with her forearms resting on her thighs. "We went to check out the new Border portal. There's nothing there, not like the others. But then this...I don't know. Corian said the things belonged in the in-between."

Mattie glanced at the other Nightstalker, who dipped his head and raised an eyebrow. "You tried to cross over?"

"No." Cheyenne shook her head. "Those creepy things came *out* of the portal."

"That's impossible."

"Not anymore, I guess."

Mattie/Maleshi licked her lips and took a deep breath through her nose. "I still don't see why you're coming to me with this."

Corian cleared his throat. "We need to know how the portal opened, General. Why it's there."

"Hmm. Convenience or coincidence, is that it?" When he nodded again, Mattie turned back to the halfling. "Go on."

"Uh..." The chains on Cheyenne's wrists clinked when she scratched the side of her head, then she tugged down the sleeves of her baggy hoodie in an attempt to muffle the sound. "I mean, that's pretty much it. Weird creature-things came out of the portal, we fought them, and then Corian said we needed to come and see you."

"A correction, General?" Corian adjusted himself in his chair, knowing he was on thin ice with Maleshi Hi'et even by daring to ask. Those oddly inhuman green eyes flashed at him, and the human-appearing Nightstalker gave him a tiny nod. "I don't think we would have managed to 'fight them back' without Cheyenne, and I have to give her due credit for putting the worst of the in-between back where it belongs before she sealed the portal again. For the time being."

Mattie turned to the halfling one more time and blinked. A slow smile crept across her lips, but she quickly forced it away. "Is that what happened?"

"I mean, pretty much." *Why is this suddenly a halfling interrogation?* "I just did what I had to do. And it worked."

"How'd you hear about the portal?"

Cheyenne adjusted herself on the couch, leaning away from Mattie a little before she sat back against the armrest. *Here we go. This is where I tell her everything she didn't wanna hear in her office.* "I got a...message."

"Cheyenne. Please." The woman dipped her chin and bored holes into the halfling's face with her intense green gaze. "If there was ever a time to put it all out there, now would be it."

"I didn't think we came here so I could talk about myself." Cheyenne cleared her throat. "You're not gonna believe this."

That slow, feral grin she'd seen on Corian's face so many times appeared on Mattie Bergmann's human lips. "You'd be surprised."

"Okay." *Time to spill the drow beans, Cheyenne.* "L'zar Verdys did some kind of astral-projection thing and showed up in my room last night."

Byrd snorted at her description, which turned into a choke when Corian hissed at the goblin man.

Cheyenne couldn't look away from the center of the coffee table. "He told me to tell Corian about the breach, so I did."

Mattie nodded and turned to shoot Corian a mocking stare. One eyebrow lifted, and the smile on her lips was tight and humorless. "Sounds like you finally got to do what you came here to do, Corian. If I'd known one of my students was L'zar Verdys' daughter, I wouldn't have been so disappointed when I realized she didn't need me anymore."

CHAPTER SEVENTY-SIX

Cheyenne straightened on the couch and stared at her professor. "I didn't say anything about being his daughter."

"You didn't have to, Cheyenne. No drow would be as invested in you as L'zar obviously is. And he wouldn't have used the Don'adurr Thread if you hadn't started your drow trials with Corian."

The halfling choked on a surprised laugh. "You got all that from what I just told you?"

"Most of it, yes." Mattie looked away from Corian and fixed her gaze firmly on her former student. "How's that going, by the way?"

"The trials?" Cheyenne shrugged. "I've unlocked two layers of the box. The...*Cuil Ani.*" *That's getting easier to say.*

Corian chuckled. "I'd check it again after what you did at the portal this morning. Might be three now."

She smirked at Corian. "And I punched *him* in the face last night."

The Nightstalker's smug smile disappeared, and he closed his eyes. Persh'al turned to stare at him while the goblins tried to hold back their sniggers.

"Cheyenne, I can't even begin to tell you how much I envy that little victory." Mattie leaned sideways and propped her arm on the

519

couch's other armrest. "If I'm not mistaken, then, everything's already been set in motion."

"You're not mistaken." Corian fought back another smile and shook his head. "Now that Cheyenne's started her trials, L'zar's getting ready to make his move."

"Because he succeeded in blasting a hole right through those fell-damn prophecies." Mattie tapped two fingers against her lips and laughed. "The drow actually did it."

"Well, I'm still alive and kickin', so…" Cheyenne cocked her head.

"You've told her already?" Mattie asked Corian.

"That was all on these clowns." The Nightstalker gestured at Persh'al, Byrd, and Lumil, who responded with sheepish glances.

"Might be the only time a loose tongue comes in handy, huh?" Mattie nodded slowly. "You deserve to know."

"What, you mean that L'zar had a bunch of other kids before me, and they all died when they started their trials because some prophecy said they would? Yeah, that's a pretty important nugget of information. There's a lot *more* I'd like to know on top of it." Cheyenne raised her eyebrows and almost held her breath. *She's known about all this for a long time. No way she's keeping the same promises Corian made.* "Care to tell me the rest of it?"

"Not now, Cheyenne." Corian leaned forward in the loveseat, shook his head, and shot Mattie a quick, warning glance. "Right now, we're here to tell Maleshi what's happening and to ask for her help. We only have twenty minutes."

Mattie flashed him a quick smile, but it disappeared just as fast. "You think the Crown's responsible for opening a new portal that doesn't differentiate between creatures of the middle realm and those of us who belong on either side of the Border?"

"It's possible," he replied. "The Crown's found out about Cheyenne. That she's here, Earthside."

"And no one wants this drow halfling to complete those trials." Mattie dipped her head. "I understand."

"I've done what I could to keep her hidden, but it's temporary."

"The Heart of Midnight was meant to support drow magic."

Mattie glanced at the shape of the pendant protruding beneath Cheyenne's hoodie. "Not to battle it."

"You knew what this was when I asked you about it." The halfling tapped her fingers on the pendant.

"Of course I did. I just wasn't aware of who'd given it to you."

She doesn't want to talk about any of this right now, either. What happened between those two?

"So now you want my help at this new portal." Mattie crossed one bare foot over her knee and glanced at the other magicals in her living room. "Because you think the Crown might have opened it to get at Cheyenne."

Corian nodded. "It's only one possibility of many, Maleshi."

Hearing that name made Mattie close her eyes again, but she seemed to resign herself to the fact that he wouldn't stop using it. "Take me to the portal, then."

"Thank you."

"For Cheyenne." The Nightstalker woman turned to offer her former student a real smile before she nodded. "If the Crown's ripping through two worlds to get to her, it's the least I can do."

Cheyenne's heart sank when she saw the ghost of old pain behind Mattie Bergmann's green eyes. *She really doesn't want this.* "Mattie, you don't owe me anything."

"Of course I don't." The Nightstalker woman chuckled. "If anything's owed to anyone, Cheyenne, the armchairs in my office have yet to be replaced. But I *will* say I've grown pretty fond of you, kid. And the bigger picture is making itself more than apparent." Mattie pushed quickly to her feet and twirled her hand in a gesture to speed things up. Everyone else scrambled up so as not to be sitting while General Hi'et stood before them. "Whatever you have to do to get us there, Corian, I strongly suggest you do it quickly."

Corian forced back a laugh and summoned another portal right there in Mattie/Maleshi's living room.

Mattie leaned toward Cheyenne as the dark, shimmering oval grew in the air. "I always had a feeling you were something special, kid."

"You just wanted to say you trained a drow halfling." Cheyenne looked at her friend and grinned.

"Turns out, I had no idea what I bargained for." The Nightstalker woman smiled at the half-drow, but it lacked her usual mirth. "Hopefully, I can give you guys a better idea of whether the Crown's behind this unaccounted-for portal. That's what we're hoping for, at any rate."

Cheyenne frowned. "I thought we were trying to *keep* the Crown from finding me."

"Oh, fuck the Crown. I can handle that self-absorbed drow with my hands tied behind my back." Mattie snorted. "But if it's not the Crown, there's some other reason this new Border portal appeared without warning. Then both sides of the Border are fucked."

Lumil let out a low whistle at that last statement. Corian pursed his lips. Persh'al tried to hide a chuckle and shook his head.

When Corian's newest portal was fully formed, Mattie frowned at the image of a dark, empty warehouse and a bunch of computers scattered over three tables. "I'm not an idiot, Corian."

"Neither am I." The Nightstalker laughed, his silver eyes shining from across the room. "You didn't have a single ward or bonded alarm around your house, General."

"Because I didn't expect a gang of rogue O'gúleesh to show up at my front door using L'zar's halfling daughter as bait."

Corian shrugged. "I'm sure you've just fallen out of the habit."

She snorted and rolled her eyes.

"And I'm not interested in leaving a trail from the border right back to your living room."

"Aw, man." Byrd grimaced. "Come on!"

"Deal with it, goblin. We're going for another drive." Corian stepped through the portal, which shimmered around him as he disappeared.

Cheyenne watched him reappear in Persh'al's warehouse, walking away from her. The goblins followed, with Persh'al close on their heels.

Mattie winked at the halfling. "Looks like you've had your fair share of portal-hopping too."

"Enough to know I'd really like to learn how to open one on my own."

Chuckling, the Nightstalker woman shook her head. "Good luck."

Frowning, Cheyenne followed her former professor into Persh'al's warehouse. *I could open a portal if someone taught me. And if they won't, I'll teach myself.*

Corian clapped his hands to get everyone's attention, then pointed at Lumil as she headed for his unfinished sandwich on the table. "Don't even think about it."

The goblin woman grunted. "Come on. You can't at least buy enough for all of us?"

When the Nightstalker glanced at Persh'al, the troll turned away and pretended to be intensely interested in the overhead lights hanging above loose metal cages in the warehouse ceiling.

"We'll make it a better trip this time," Corian said through clenched teeth. Then he nodded toward the warehouse door, and everyone headed for it. He stepped up beside Maleshi and lightly touched her elbow. "If you need—"

"Don't." She shot him a warning glance and moved subtly out of his reach. "I don't *need* any of this, *vae shra'ni.*"

They'd stopped just in front of the door, and Cheyenne didn't even have the option of leaving the warehouse so she wouldn't have to watch the private moment. *He seriously screwed something up.*

"And yet here we are." Grinning, Corian looked Mattie/Maleshi up and down, then gestured for her to step outside in front of him. Mattie didn't waste any time, and the Nightstalker glanced over his shoulder at the drow halfling and raised his eyebrows. "I think she's happy to see me."

Cheyenne snorted. "Yeah, that message isn't even a little mixed."

With a smirk, Corian stepped out into the afternoon light and held the door open for the halfling to join him. When it closed, he flicked his fingers toward the warehouse, and the wards illuminated in a soft green glow with a four-pointed star flashing in the center of the door.

"I know that means something," Cheyenne muttered.

Corian glanced at the fading light of the four-pointed star and shrugged. "Call it a family crest, kid. L'zar was the one who built these wards."

"For real?"

"Come on, Cheyenne. I might not be able to tell you everything you want to know, despite how much I'd love for you to finally stop asking. But I have no reason to lie to you."

They headed toward Persh'al's SUV, parked beside Cheyenne's new Panamera in the overgrown parking lot. The other O'gúleesh magicals filed into the SUV, and Cheyenne couldn't help herself. Mattie passed the shiny black Porsche as Persh'al opened the passenger door for her, and the halfling reached into her pocket and pressed the automatic lock on the fob. The Panamera chirped, and Mattie jumped a little before spinning around to glance at the car.

Her gaze settled quickly on Cheyenne, who did everything she could to hold back laughter. "That's *yours?*"

The halfling shrugged, but her grin finally broke through.

"Huh." Mattie took one last glance at the car before climbing into the passenger seat of the SUV.

Cheyenne thought, *Not the response I was looking for. She's still pissed about me blowing her cover.*

That wiped the grin off the drow halfling's face as she climbed into the back seat behind Corian. He shot her a brief, almost apologetic shrug before she pulled the door closed behind her. Then she glanced into the last row of seats and jerked her thumb toward the goblins. "It's a two-hour drive."

"We're good," Byrd muttered, buckling his seatbelt. "I have my own window."

CHAPTER SEVENTY-SEVEN

An hour into the drive, Persh'al pulled off the highway at a truck-stop exit. Corian thumped the back of the troll's seat. "What are you doing?"

"I'm starving, man. And I'm not stepping into that clearing on an empty stomach again. Sorry."

The Nightstalker leaned back in his seat. "I *brought* sandwiches."

"And you're the only one who had the time to eat."

"Here we go," Byrd quipped from the way back. "Somebody who's looking out for the whole team."

"Shut up," Lumil muttered.

"Hey, you can do whatever you want," Persh'al added. "I'm looking out for the only troll here, okay?"

Cheyenne fought back another smile and watched the truck stop grow closer as the SUV turned into a huge parking lot where some semis had stopped to refuel.

Persh'al parked in front of a Subway that shared a wall with a McDonald's and turned off the engine. His illusion charm shimmered around his body, and a short, tanned human with a jet-black mohawk opened the door. "Gotta refuel. Then we'll get right back into all the excitement. I promise." He didn't wait for anyone before walking quickly toward the door of the Subway.

"All right. Come on." Byrd tapped the back of Cheyenne's seat and nodded toward the passenger door. Both he and Lumil had activated their illusion spells and now looked like a couple of grinning Midwesterners back from a week of tanning on Florida beaches. "Pretty please, halfling? I need food."

Cheyenne shucked off her seatbelt and got out, standing beside the open door while Byrd and Lumil squeezed past the seat folded halfway forward.

"You want anything?"

The halfling shook her head. Both goblins shrugged, then Corian finally got out of the car too and followed the others inside. Cheyenne waited for the passenger door to open. *She's not getting out, and I'm not tiptoeing around a Nightstalker. Even General Hi'et.*

Cheyenne climbed back into the seat behind Mattie and closed the door. "Okay, look. I know you're pissed. I did everything I could to keep them from finding you. I mean, short of smashing Persh'al's rig into a million pieces." Just the thought made her shiver. "I just want you to know I didn't just give up your information without thinking about what you wanted. They found you on their own."

"We both know they wouldn't have if you and I didn't know each other."

The halfling's gut twisted into knots, and Cheyenne breathed through the guilt. "Yeah. A lotta things have been happening to a lotta people just because they know me. But this one, Mattie? I mean, I've never made the crossing to either side, but the shit that came out of the portal... It was like fighting some kinda living nightmare."

"Oh, I'm well aware of what exists in the in-between, Cheyenne."

"Then you get why I came with them, right? I'm sorry I tricked you like that. It's not how I would've done things—"

"Maybe not, but it's exactly what I would have done in your situation." Mattie grabbed the side of the passenger seat and turned fully around to meet the halfling's gaze. "You played it out to the end because it was the right thing to do, even if it made you squirm. Don't apologize for it."

Cheyenne swallowed. "Okay."

"I try not to make a habit of tooting my own horn, kid, but I'm pretty sure I'm the only one who can answer the burning question about this portal. And I genuinely hope, for all our sakes, the Crown uncovered even more dark and insanely powerful magic. The kind needed to rip open another Border portal. Otherwise…"

"Yeah, we're all screwed. You mentioned that part already."

Mattie chuckled and turned to peer through the windshield toward the Subway. They both saw Persh'al sitting at a table by the window, and the Nightstalker woman said, "We have a little time. Scoot over."

"What?"

Mattie shoved open the door and got out to open the back passenger-side door and shoot Cheyenne an exasperated look. "Scoot."

"Oh." The halfling moved down the center row of seats, staring at the Nightstalker woman as Mattie closed the door again behind her.

"Now." The woman's green eyes glistened with awareness as she fixed them on her former student. "We have some time to set things straight, at the very least. Let's not waste it."

"I…don't even know where to start."

"I get that a lot. I'll take over from here, then. Feel free to stop me if something comes to mind." Mattie clasped her hands together and set them both primly in her lap. "I'm guessing the very first string tying this all together was when you overheard me talking to myself. You asked who Maleshi was, and I wasn't prepared to answer that question. Now, I suppose, it's a necessity."

Cheyenne couldn't help but chuckle a little. "Yeah, a bit."

"Right." The woman dipped her head and took a deep breath. "I chose the name Mathilda Bergmann when I made the crossing, Cheyenne. That was over four hundred years ago, and at the time, the name had a lot more flavor to it than it does now. Like I said, Mathilda sounds like an old cat lady."

"I mean, you kind of *are*."

Mattie's lips twitched when the double meaning dawned on her, then she shook her head. "I like Mattie so much better. But before I started my life Earthside, as I'm sure you're well aware, I was someone else. General Maleshi Hi'et, insert meaningless titles, et cetera, et cetera. I spent half a century as the Crown's wartime advisor and leading strategist. I trained thousands of legionnaires while I served the Crown. Protected the people of Ambar'ogúl the best I could. Felled armies and quashed rebellions. The list goes on and on."

The halfling's eyes widened. "Sounds like it."

"But none of that's important anymore, you understand? The new cycle began... Well, I despise euphemisms, so I'll just say it was a bloody affair that came about long before its time."

"You mean, someone grabbed the throne."

"In a manner of speaking, yes." Mattie glanced down at her clasped hands and bit her lip. "The new ass to sit upon that prover-bial throne—and I do mean 'ass' in every sense of the word—showed the entire world who she really was when she took things into her own hands. Literally. Things changed, kid. I have no problem getting a little dirty if that's what's required of me, but to say things got messy at the turn of the new cycle is a gross and disgusting understatement. Blood, mud, and black magic. Add a heaping portion of greed and entitlement, and you've splattered an accurate picture of the state of things all over a blank canvas. Make sense?"

"Yeah." Cheyenne studied the pain in her friend's green eyes and frowned. "That's why you left, isn't it?"

The Nightstalker replied, "That's mostly why I left. I've seen things that give *me* nightmares, kid. Still. The things I did by order of the Crown were far, far worse, and no amount of advice or berating on my part made a goddamn bit of difference. So, yes. I laid down my banner, stripped off my badges, and shot the Crown a big 'fuck you' when I hightailed it out of there. It's still home, Cheyenne. It...calls to me from time to time. And for four hundred years, I've been satisfied knowing the Crown no longer has General Hi'et at her side to do the dirty work she was so fond of ordering me to do."

"And you didn't tell anyone."

A wry chuckle escaped Mattie, and she gave a little shrug. "Not a soul. I abandoned everything I believed in because I just couldn't do it anymore, and apparently, that put me down in O'gúl history as the spark of the fucking rebellion!"

The sharp, bitter cackle coming from the Nightstalker's mouth made Cheyenne lean away. *She still hates herself for it.*

"But if that's what it took to keep things from getting as bad as they could have on the other side, kid, I'd do it again in a heartbeat. Every single bit of it."

The halfling nodded.

Mattie caught the hesitation in the halfling's posture and leaned toward her. "What? And don't tell me it's nothing, Cheyenne. I've had enough practice reading you to know a seed of doubt when I see it."

Cheyenne clenched her eyes shut, then turned just enough to meet Mattie's gaze sidelong. "You might've accidentally started a rebellion, but I don't think that kept things from getting worse over there."

"Of course not. They were bound to get worse anyway. Which will always be my shame, and I have to live with it." The woman's eyes narrowed. "Why? What have you heard?"

"Some new friends of mine told me about their village on the other side. The Oronti Valley."

"Oh, *God*. I haven't thought of that place in centuries. Beautiful. Serene. I always wanted to take a few months off and build myself a hut out by one of the lakes. Very happy people. And I mean *genuinely* happy."

"Not anymore." Cheyenne waited for realization to dawn on the Nightstalker woman's face before she said anything else. "The way I heard it, there's nothing left. Even in the valley."

The blissful nostalgia in Mattie's smile disappeared immediately. "I see."

"And it's forcing even more magicals to make the crossing. Whole families. Kids. Christ, after what I saw at the new portal this morning, I can't imagine trying to take a *kid* through even a tenth of that."

"Yes." Mattie interlaced her fingers again. "Sounds like people are forced to do a lot of things they couldn't have imagined beforehand. That's where your trials come into play in all this."

Cheyenne stared at her former mentor and forced herself not to bombard the woman with every question racing through her mind. *Finally we're getting somewhere.* "It's only been about a week, but it feels like I've been waiting forever for someone to spell it out for me."

"Well, today must be your lucky day, kid." Mattie dipped her head in wry acknowledgment. "At least in that regard. Clearly, you know about the prophecies surrounding L'zar Verdys."

"Yeah. All his dead kids." *And my dreams that made me think he killed them.*

"You know, I love that you're just as much a fan of euphemisms as I am." The Nightstalker snorted. "That drow has spent an ungodly amount of time trying to find a loophole through those prophecies, Cheyenne. Honestly, those of us who knew him were ready to toss him across the Border just to get him to shut up about it. Drove us nuts. And he caused more than his fair share of trouble in Ambar'ogúl during his mad search."

"His other kids…" The halfling didn't quite know how to phrase this next part without making it sound like she *wanted* to be his special prophetic-loophole child. "Were they like me?"

"You mean, were they halflings?" Mattie shrugged. "Some of them *had* to be, no doubt. Most of them were not. That's the nature of prophecies, isn't it? They rarely tell you everything you need to know and almost always leave out the most important bits. L'zar Verdys left a trail of mini L'zar's on both sides of the Border. If he thinks you're the one to take up his mantle, kid, I'm damn inclined to agree with him."

"That's why the Crown wants to find me, isn't it? Why they cut down all the Nimlothar trees and only kept the one. So the Crown has to oversee all the drow trials if anyone wants to complete them. Because she's looking for L'zar's kid."

Mattie's eyes blazed in their intensity as she stared at Cheyenne, all traces of her humor gone. "Only *one* Nimlothar?"

"That's what Corian told me."

"Ha! And Corian crosses back and forth to check in on the status of things, does he?"

"I don't think so." Cheyenne shook her head. "He said something about getting messages from the other side. However that works."

"I see." The Nightstalker woman's gaze darted about the inside of the car. "Well, yes. I'd say the soulless hag wearing the Crown has ordered all that just to find you."

"Because L'zar wants me to take up his mantle."

"I see the wheels turning again, kid." Mattie's soft, knowing smile returned. "Keep going."

"With what? I don't even know the guy. As far as I'm concerned, he's a nutjob who broke out of prison to knock up my mom before turning himself in again to serve the rest of his meaningless sentence playing mind games."

Mattie barked out a sharp laugh. "That's an excellent assessment."

"Well, thanks, but I still don't know why the Crown gives a shit about *one* crazy drow's kid."

"Oh, I think you do. Just give it a shot, huh?"

The halfling stared at her former professor with a deadpan expression.

"Come on, Cheyenne. L'zar's best friends are a Nightstalker expat doing who knows what beyond guiding you through the trials, and a discolored troll who built a system to track magical activity on this side as he shoves a foot-long sub in his mouth. And somehow, the way this crazy world works, they all know *me*."

Cheyenne squinted at the former General Maleshi Hi'et and knew she would have felt the heat rising at the base of her spine if she weren't wearing the damn pendant. "L'zar's part of the rebellion."

A Nightstalker's slow, predatory grin bloomed across Mattie's face, her green eyes flashing with pride and excitement and a terrible power even through her illusion charm. "That's one way of putting it."

CHAPTER SEVENTY-EIGHT

"Well, it's either that, or he's leading it." Cheyenne folded her arms. "Or L'zar Verdys did something irreversibly stupid just to piss off the Crown, and now she's coming for his first kid who doesn't drop dead the moment he meets them."

"Hmm." Mattie tapped a finger on her lips. "The fourth option is that it's all three of those put together. I'd go with that one."

"This crazy drow running the entire magical world is hunting me down because she hates L'zar and wants to make this personal." The halfling snorted. "That sounds like a lot to squeeze into one explanation."

"Well, drow are notorious for their ability to complicate things. And it's always personal when someone's trying to overthrow the monarchy, isn't it? At least for the monarch."

"This is insane."

"*Yes*. This is the world you were born into, Cheyenne. Not logistically, of course, but L'zar's Verdys' blood runs through your veins, and there's no way to get it out. You said it yourself. He's a nutjob."

"I'm not."

"Oh, come on." Mattie's teasing had picked back up again to its usual degree of barely tolerable. "There's a little crazy in you. I'll be the first to admit I'm not immune to a bout of insanity from time to time. We are who we are, kid. And *you* are L'zar's kid, who defied some Oracle's omniscient prophecy. Honestly, that might have more to do with *you* than anything your father's done so far."

Cheyenne clenched her fists at her sides and glared at the Nightstalker woman. *Cool it, Cheyenne. She's telling you the truth. That's what you wanted.* "He hasn't done *anything*."

"That's precisely the point." Mattie laughed and shook her head, her long, wavy black hair rustling between her shirt and the back of the seat. "Once you complete the drow trials, which I have no doubt you will, a whole new world will open up in front of you."

"I've heard that one before too. This is what Corian couldn't tell me, isn't it? That L'zar's leading a rebellion against the Crown, and I'm supposed to be the one who helps him take over."

"I can't say what Corian hasn't told you." Mattie shrugged. "But it seems you've already got that figured out. Though I do have to ask, why wouldn't that walking furball tell you any of this? It's not exactly a secret, on either side of the Border."

"Yeah, I gathered that much." Cheyenne shook her head with a wry chuckle. "He told me he'd made a promise not to tell me who L'zar was—or *is*, I guess—in Ambar'ogúl before I completed the trials. And a promise not to go into politics or talk about the Crown, either."

Mattie squinted. "Are those two promises, or just one?"

"Does it matter?"

They smirked at each other. "Not in the slightest."

"It drove me nuts at first." The halfling ran a hand through her black hair and shrugged. "But I know about making promises and what it means to keep them. Or break them. I've been putting together the pieces on my own."

"And let me say, you're doing a damn fine job of it so far."

"Well, I'll be doing a lot better when I pass the trials and figure out how to keep those idiot bull's-head loyalists from popping out at me everywhere I go and blowing up my stuff."

The Nightstalker woman cleared her throat. "I heard 'blowing up your stuff.' Not another euphemism?"

"Nope. That's how I got the Panamera."

Mattie threw her head back for one of her belly laughs. "I'd love a sit-down with your insurance agent."

"My insurance didn't get me a Porsche after my Ford was bombed by an O'gúl loyalist, so…"

"Right. And you have other ways of grabbing yourself a brand new Porsche."

"Sounds about right." Cheyenne playfully rolled her eyes and glanced out the window.

"Look at that." Mattie nodded at Persh'al, Corian, and the goblins —all of them with human illusion charms but unmistakable just the same—stepping out of the convenience store with plastic bags in hand. "Just in time, I guess. I have one more question for you, Cheyenne."

The halfling turned and met her friend's gaze. "Yeah."

"How did Corian react when you told him you knew me?"

Cheyenne couldn't hold back a laugh of surprise. "I asked him if he'd heard the name Maleshi. That's all I had. And he, uh… Well, he might've lost it a little. Told me not to throw that name around, and it had nothing to do with him training me or whatever."

"Fair enough."

"We dropped it until I showed him your spellbook."

Mattie coughed and shot a wary glance out the windshield as the rest of their group approached the SUV. "You *showed* him?"

The halfling grinned. "Believe it or not, Mattie, I found one Nightstalker who was more than happy to tell me about the drow legacy box, train me with it, *and* teach me how to cast new spells. Admittedly, you're a lot easier to get along with."

"Ha. I'm also a lot harder to punch in the face."

"I'm starting to pick up on that."

Mattie shrugged and opened the door so they could get out for the other magicals joining them. "Maybe I got a little sloppy just handing out the spellbook without any warnings. Never occurred to me who else might see it. Just out of practice."

Cheyenne hopped out after Mattie and leaned against the side of the car as Persh'al opened the driver's side door.

The Nightstalker woman leaned toward the drow halfling and muttered, "Wait 'til you see me in action." With a wink, she opened the front passenger side door and slipped into it before Corian rounded the front of the car.

He glanced through the passenger window, then raised an eyebrow at Cheyenne. "You two have a nice chat?"

"Yeah. I think we're all caught up now." She pulled the lever to bend the middle seat forward and stepped aside for the goblins. *He won't ask. As long as he's not the one telling me, he's not breaking his promise.*

"You guys gonna stand there all day while a portal explodes, or you gonna get in the car?" Byrd thumped back against the back seat and chuckled. "Next time I get out of this car, I'm not getting back in."

"Oh, so you're gonna *walk* back, then?" Lumil snorted and strapped on her seatbelt. "'Cause no one's opening a portal for you to jump on home when we're done."

"Shit."

Cheyenne lifted the back of the seat again and slid all the way over to sit behind Persh'al. Watching her with narrowed eyes, Corian got in last and closed the door. "Let's go."

When they pulled off at the same section of dirt road of Green Ridge State Forest in Maryland, Persh'al grunted and peered into the woods on the other side. "Here's to not having a repeat battle, huh?"

"Even if we did, it's a first for me." Mattie opened her door and swiftly got out of the passenger seat. As soon as the others had filed out of the SUV, Corian nodded across the road, and they took off in renewed silence for their half-mile hike through the thick woods.

After about five minutes, Cheyenne paused. "Wait."

The entire party stopped where they were and turned to her, waiting for her to explain the command. *At least I don't have to fight for their attention.* The halfling pushed down a little squirm of discomfort under so many gazes and focused on what had made her stop. "Something's different."

Corian raised his eyebrows and gazed around the forest. "Like what?"

Cheyenne closed her eyes and forced her breath into a calm, slow rhythm. *Heart of Midnight has nothing on drow hearing.* "Voices," she muttered. "Maybe a dozen? Hard to tell from here, but we're not alone."

"Man, I *love* watching drow do their thing." Byrd smirked and eyed the halfling. "Miss having one around, too."

"Go dark," Corian muttered. "If a dozen people are out there making that much noise, they're not watching as closely as they should be."

A round of spells circled the group until only Cheyenne and Mattie were still visible. Cheyenne glanced at the Nightstalker woman, who smirked and gestured with her own invisibility spell. "Maybe we'll work on this one later, huh?"

"I'm down." The minute the words left the halfling's lips, she and the former general disappeared from view.

"Let's move," Corian said directly in front of her. "For now, we're here to watch."

"I'll make that call when we get there, *vae shra'ni.*" Mattie's low voice carried a hint of her former command. The group took off again through the trees toward the clearing and the new Border portal.

Cheyenne listened intently as she stepped through the thick undergrowth without a sound. Looking down and not being able to see herself made her dizzy, so she kept her gaze focused as far ahead of her as she could. She heard light footsteps on her left and her right, though it only sounded like three pairs. *At least half of us know how to be silent.*

The closer they got to the clearing, the louder the dozen or so voices became—shouted commands, grunting quips, a lot of shuffling and sliding and heavy objects clinking together. Every minute or two, a soft pop rose above the growing voices. *Definitely more than a dozen now.*

Then the halfling and her O'gúleesh friends were at the tree line. A faint glimmer of silver light flashed in the air behind the closest tree—a disembodied silver fist lifting, signaling the invisible party to stop.

Cheyenne moved to the right and stopped behind another tree at the edge of the clearing to take a closer look. Most of the black, glinting carapaces from the swarm of beetle-things had been cleared aside, though some parts still lay scattered here and there. A thin tentacle remained where Corian had severed it at the edge of the portal ridge and the jutting fists of black stone. The spires Cheyenne had pulled down still lay over the widest crevasse within the portal ridge, but it seemed the focus of the portal had moved farther down, to where the destruction hadn't touched. The high wall of dark, shimmering light was still there too.

"Little more than a dozen, huh?" Mattie whispered.

"I can't hear *everything*," the halfling whispered back.

At least three dozen magicals milled around the clearing, handling huge crates of black metal. Most of the crates had been arranged into stacks of three or four, differentiated only by the color of their handles—red, white, or silver. All of them had the bull's-head shape stamped on the side in white paint.

Another soft pop filled the clearing, and a huge, roaring ogre staggered out from between the black stone pillars. He waved his arms in front of him, batting at something around his face that wasn't there.

"Got another one," someone shouted.

"Hey, that's Kilresh!"

A hulking magical wearing a black military jacket with a silver bull's head on the back pointed at the disoriented ogre and barked, "Someone better get that ogre in line before he smashes any more supplies."

Cheyenne's eyes grew wide when she saw the gray hand streaked with red extending from the sleeve of the military jacket. The pointed finger ended in a long red claw. *Great. They have a raug giving orders.*

She caught the almost inaudible crunch of dry leaves beside her just before Corian stopped between Mattie and the halfling without bumping into either of them. "Maybe we didn't need you after all, general."

Mattie let out a soft hiss. "The only thing this proves is that someone's taking advantage of the situation."

"Obviously. And the Crown's behind this one."

"Behind the supply shipments and the new legion of peons, yeah. I came here to find out who's behind the new portal."

"Maleshi, wait!"

There was a short scuffle and kicked up leaves before one of the Nightstalkers hissed.

"Get your hand off me," Mattie whispered fiercely. Then she stepped out into the clearing. The air wavered around her figure, and then Maleshi Hi'et the Nightstalker stormed across the open grass toward the unsuspecting magicals sent across the Border by the Crown.

Corian appeared right beside Cheyenne, his fingers working quickly to drop her invisibility charm as Persh'al and the goblins did the same with theirs.

Byrd leaned forward to catch the Nightstalker man's gaze. "What the hell's she doing?"

"Whatever she wants, apparently." Corian grimaced, his feline nose twitching. "Like she always does."

"Aren't you gonna stop her?"

"I'm partial to keeping my head on my shoulders, thanks."

Maleshi's long black hair fluttered in the breeze, the pointed tips of her tufted feline ears the only giveaway that she moved toward the group of O'gúleesh without her human illusion. Cheyenne leaned toward Corian. "Why aren't we going out there with her?"

"Because she wants to do this on her own."

"So, we're just here if she needs backup, huh?"

"She won't."

CHAPTER SEVENTY-NINE

"You know," Maleshi called to the scattered magicals in black uniforms, "I'm a little insulted that no one invited me to the party."

A troll with a huge gap where his front teeth should have been looked up from the stack of crates on this side of the clearing. "By the fucking Crown," he muttered, his eyes wide when he saw the black-haired Nightstalker headed for him.

"Yeah, I figured she's to blame for this."

"Hey. Hey!" The troll nearly fell on his face scrambling away from the stacked crates and the ex-general. "Gu'urs!"

The raug in the black jacket looked over his shoulder and snarled at the scampering troll. "I'm having a fell-damn conversation, soldier. Who told you to take a break?"

"To be fair, that's probably my fault." Maleshi spread her arms and cocked her head. "I'm just trying to talk to the magical in charge here."

The troll stumbled again, unable to look away from the Nightstalker even as he fumbled for the raug's jacket sleeve. "It's her. It's fucking Maleshi—"

Gu'urs snarled and shoved his red-streaked hand into the troll's face to push him aside. Then the raug turned toward the Night-stalker woman and lifted his chin. "I am."

"I figured." Maleshi stopped and glanced around the clearing.

The troll had stumbled around the whole operation, jabbering in a panicked whisper about General Maleshi Hi'et standing right there with them. Whispers of disbelief and fear made their rounds in the clearing, and every magical with the Crown's bull-head seal stopped what they were doing to watch the encounter with their commanding officer.

The Nightstalker cocked her head. "Sounds like I shouldn't bother introducing myself. But *your* face isn't pulling up a name, soldier."

Gu'urs took a step forward, jerking down the lapel of his offi-cer's jacket with a sneer. "I didn't give it. And I don't plan to."

"That's not very diplomatic of you."

"Who the hell *are* you, Nightstalker?"

"Isn't it obvious?" Maleshi shot him a small, bitter smile and nodded toward the frozen magicals around the clearing. Those standing closest to their raug commander stepped back. "If I can hear the whispers from here, it's hard to imagine you haven't picked up on them."

The raug looked her up and down in contempt. "Maleshi Hi'et defected centuries ago. I heard she didn't make it very long after that."

"Really? The general's dead, huh? Look at that." She stuck her hands on her hips and cocked her head. "No invitation to the party, and I *still* haven't heard about my death. These lines of communication have some serious flaws in them, don't you think?"

"I'm done listening to your shit, *nilsch úcat—*"

"And I'm done explaining myself, raug!" The Nightstalker's voice rang across the clearing with terrifying intensity. "If you can't keep your shit together for a friendly chat, I'm more than happy to do this the hard way. For you, of course."

Gu'urs ran his thick gray tongue along the edge of his stained teeth and growled. "Hi'et or not, I'll bring your head back to the Crown on an iron spike."

"See, that's just a waste of everyone's time." Maleshi stepped forward and pointed at the stacks of crates. "I want this explained. Go."

"I don't take orders from you." Gu'urs' empty hand flared with a crackling spell of gray and red light.

"This is the only warning you get," the Nightstalker spat. "Don't waste it."

The terrified magicals watching their commander threaten the greatest O'gúl general to lift a finger for the Crown glanced nervously at the spell in Gu'urs' huge hand. A ripple of tense, uncomfortable foot-shifting passed around the clearing.

A low chuckle rose in the raug's throat. The next second, he hurled the crackling mass of gray and red energy at the Nightstalker intruder.

Silver light exploded in the clearing before the spell left the commander's hand. Maleshi accelerated to Nightstalker speed, growling with her fists clenched at her sides as she stepped around the hurtling ball of slow-motion magic. "It's always the tough lessons, isn't it? Put all the hard work on me. Sure."

She reared back and swung a fist into the underside of the raug's jaw, then slipped back into normal time to watch him fly.

Gu'urs roared. The crackling silver light streaking across his chin and jaw and down the outside of his throat turned that roar into a shriek. The huge gray and red magical slid across the ground when he landed. Thin streams of smoke rose from his gray flesh.

At the tree line, Cheyenne blinked. "Jesus."

Corian shook his head. "Just Maleshi."

The Nightstalker ex-general stomped across the flattened grass toward the raug commander and only stopped when she was almost on top of him. She studied the sharp black jacket with the Crown's military sigil over one shoulder and clicked her tongue. "New getup. I see her style hasn't improved any."

A strangled croak rose from the fallen raug as he struggled to push himself up off the ground. He only managed to sit up, blinking heavily and swaying a little. Spit flew from his obscenely swollen lower lip.

"You're *dead.*"

"So you've told me." Maleshi gave him that grimacing tight-lipped smile again and pointed at another stack of metal crates. "Now tell me what she's ordered you to smuggle Earthside and why, and I'll make sure you don't end up in a hole in the ground. I promise it'll be much harder for you to come back from the dead than it was for me."

"Traitor!" The cry rose from within a group of terror-stricken skaxen and wide-eyed goblins as a streak of orange flame hurtled across the clearing.

Maleshi hissed, stepping deftly out of the line of fire. She dropped into a crouch and sneered at the battered Gu'urs. "You need a better handle on your peons, Commander. Allow me to demonstrate."

Another brilliant flash of silver light exploded around the Nightstalker woman, then she disappeared.

Screams rang out one after the other, silver light flashing everywhere at once while the Crown's soldiers struggled to comprehend what was happening. Spells and shouted commands flew in all directions, most of the magic reaching the source of silver light seconds after the speeding Nightstalker had moved on. Bodies flew or dropped with no apparent rhyme or reason. Two ogres rushed to Gu'urs' side to help their commander to his feet while General Hi'et wrought havoc on their operation.

Cheyenne ripped the pendant off her neck and shifted into her drow form. "We gotta get in there—"

"Wait." Corian grabbed her arm, and the halfling turned to glance down at his fingers clamped around her bicep. She didn't have to say she could break those fingers in an instant if she wanted to. The Nightstalker released her and nodded toward the chaos in the clearing. "Just wait."

After he said it, she still took a step forward toward the fray.

Persh'al, Byrd, and Lumil followed suit, each of them summoning magical attacks to step in if needed.

Two orcs worked at the opposite side of the clearing to pry open one of the crates with red handles. As spells flew, crackling against the black pillars of the portal ridge and throwing up sprays of grass and dirt every few seconds, Maleshi's flashing silver light was one step ahead of everyone.

When the orcs straightened from hunching over the open crate, one of them hiked a massive tube of black metal up onto his shoulder, steadied by his fellow orc.

Cheyenne clenched her fists. "That's a fell launcher."

"No, it's not." Corian took off running into the fight, followed by the other three O'gúleesh. The halfling had no choice but to join them.

One orc slammed a charge into the back end of the black weapon on his fellow orc's shoulder and shouted something unintelligible. The launcher exploded in a flash of red light and thick gray smoke, almost knocking the orc backward into another stack of crates.

A high-pitched whine filled the air as the projectile zipped around the clearing, zoning in on the disappearing, reappearing Maleshi Hi'et in her element.

"Tracker!" Corian shouted.

Maleshi knocked aside two skaxen flying toward her with claws outstretched, then disappeared again. The launched tracker zipped and turned, following her trail of silver light until it finally hit home.

The Nightstalker woman let out a piercing scream as electric red energy shivered up and down her body, rendering her immobile. Corian darted into enhanced speed and made it toward the orcs who'd shot the damn thing before they had a chance to reload. Silver claws flashed in the sunlight and the orcs clutched at their throats and dropped, then the Nightstalker disappeared again.

"Bring her *down!*" the raug commander bellowed.

The ogre on his left saw Lumil coming for him and had enough time to lift a forearm against her first punch. The goblin sent the fist swirling with magical light into his gut and dropped him.

Persh'al's green whip slashed at the loyalist trolls trying to flee the clearing. He snagged first one and then the other by the ankles, dragging them back across the ground before landing a set of knockout punches.

Byrd's orange flames seared loyalist after loyalist, and Cheyenne hit the goblin he'd missed with a crackling sphere of black and purple energy. The goblin went down with a cry, Byrd turned to shoot the halfling a grateful nod, then Cheyenne darted toward Mattie.

The Nightstalker had recovered from the electric attack and spun to shoot a massive bolt of silver lightning at the ogre thundering toward her. It struck him in the shoulder and rocked him backward, but he continued toward her.

A slavering skaxen leaped onto the stack of crates behind her, his boots hitting it with a metallic clang. As he kicked off from his perch, claws outstretched toward Maleshi Hi'et's neck, Cheyenne darted into drow speed and unleashed her whipping black tendrils. They coiled around the suspended skaxen's neck and chest before she slammed him into the stack of crates.

After the top crate toppled, it hung there in slow motion, and Maleshi/Mattie turned toward the drow halfling with a feral grin. "Look who's gettin' the hang of things?"

Cheyenne retracted her lashing tendrils and studied her former professor's feline face, alight with battle fury. "You okay?"

"I appreciate the check-in, Cheyenne." Mattie stepped toward the frozen ogre and whipped her hand out by her side. Flashing silver claws like thin steel blades shot from her fingertips, and she grabbed the ogre by the front of his black uniform shirt. "But I got this. Just another fight on the playground."

She jerked the ogre toward her and sent those vicious, four-inch claws slicing into his side below his thick ribs. Then she released him and turned back toward the halfling. "Fun, right?"

Cheyenne stared at the ogre, who hadn't yet realized what had happened to him. "I don't even wanna know what kinda playground you grew up on."

"A lot rougher than this, I'll tell you that much." The Nightstalker stormed across the grass toward the raug commander, his swollen jaw frozen mid-shout.

Corian joined them and headed for Maleshi, jerking his chin at her. "A little warning would've been nice."

"Oh, is that what *you* do? Give warnings?"

"You know what I mean."

Maleshi pointed at the raug. "I know we're about to get some answers. You ready for this?"

Corian gave her an exasperated glare, and the ex-general laughed.

Then she turned back toward Cheyenne. "We got this, kid. Feel free to step on out of this little bubble. It'll go a lot faster that way, yeah?"

"What will?" The halfling glanced at the Nightstalkers, one with light-brown fur, the other pitch-black and gray. Their glowing eyes were startlingly similar.

"Just a little trick I learned in the Upper Aegúrs. Magical zip-ties and whatnot. And yes, before you ask, it requires an extra spell we don't have the time to teach you right now." Maleshi shot Cheyenne a pert smile and nodded once.

And that's me being dismissed.

"Sure." The halfling nodded and slipped out of drow speed. The clearing flashed every few seconds with blazing silver light, and Cheyenne turned slowly to watch the results in real-time. "Holy shit."

CHAPTER EIGHTY

In under two minutes, Corian and Maleshi had made the rounds of every single O'gúl loyalist in the clearing. When the Night-stalkers fell back into real-time, Maleshi stuck her hands on her hips and surveyed their work. "Four centuries of Earthside hiatus, and I still got it."

Corian eyed her sideways and snorted.

Persh'al slapped a hand to his bald blue head and smacked his lips. "Seeing this never gets old."

He stepped toward the Nightstalkers, joined by Byrd and Lumil. The goblins stared at the Crown's goons, who were sitting or lying in various positions around the clearing, hands bound behind their backs by shimmering magical light.

"Death to traitors!" A troll leaning against a stack of crates beside the part of the portal ridge Cheyenne had destroyed sneered and leaned forward. He spat a fat glob of spit and dark blood toward the Nightstalkers half a dozen yards away.

Lumil sent a swift kick into his side as she passed. "Next time it's your face, asshole. Shut it."

When the group of rogue magicals gathered in the center of the clearing, Maleshi nodded at the raug commander lying on his side, his thick gray wrists also bound behind his back. "Don't worry, Commander. I still have respect for the old laws. We'll start with you in a bit. Excuse me."

Gu'urs grunted and craned his neck to glare at the Nightstalker as she stepped past him toward the portal ridge. Taking a deep breath, Maleshi scanned the spires of black stone jutting twenty feet or taller. She leaned away to follow the long stretch of the ridge moving out to the west, then nodded. "I've still got it."

Corian stepped forward. "I can—"

"No. Thank you." The ex-general didn't turn around to address him before she raised both hands and extended them toward the jutting ridge. "This won't take long."

Cheyenne glanced at Corian and found his jaw working beneath the tufts of brown hair fluttering at the sides of his face. Those silver eyes didn't leave Maleshi.

A soft whisper of an O'gúleesh incantation fluttered from the Nightstalker woman's lips. She closed her eyes and reached out for the energy she hadn't felt in centuries. *Not until it started looking for me several weeks ago. And now I know why.*

Pale, opalescent light tinged with faded pink emerged from her hands. It wavered in front of her, then erupted toward the portal ridge and the wall of dark light. A huge crack split the air, echoing madly against the metal crates. Then the dark wall of the new Border portal took on the same pinkish light.

Maleshi let out a long breath, studied her handiwork, and nodded. "There's our proof."

Cheyenne studied the glimmering wall. "What was that?"

The ex-general turned and dusted off her hands. "Just closed the portal for now."

"You can *do* that?"

The woman grinned at the drow halfling and spread her arms. "Of course I can. But it wears out even faster than that pendant of yours, kid."

Corian glared at the magical wall Maleshi had made and hissed in frustration. "Shit."

"Almost."

Cheyenne looked at her mentor and frowned. "I can't see any way that closing the portal is a bad thing."

He shot her a sidelong glance before gazing at the glistening pink wall again. "It's not. But she wouldn't have been able to seal it—"

"Temporarily, mind you." Maleshi pointed at the other Nightstalker as she turned that feral grin on the raug lying at her feet.

Corian stared at her before continuing, "That wouldn't have been possible with a cast portal."

"Or even a forced rift in the Border." The ex-general folded her arms and wiggled her eyebrows at the disarmed and magically trussed Commander Gu'urs.

"Great." Cheyenne smoothed her drow-white hair back from her forehead with both hands. "The Crown didn't open this one."

"Nope. Just using it to her advantage." Maleshi tilted her head and kept grinning when the raug struggled uselessly against his bonds.

"Then this is the worst-case scenario." The halfling glanced at Corian, and the Nightstalker closed his silver eyes. That was all the confirmation she needed.

"We'll get to the part about all of us being seriously screwed later, kid. Right now, I have questions for our friends. That includes you, Commander." Maleshi lowered herself into a squat beside the raug's head and tapped his red-streaked gray temple with a firm, threatening finger. "I want to know what you're keeping in here."

"Too bad, *nilsch úcat.*" The words were far less threatening through Commander Gu'urs' mashed lower jaw, but he got the point across well enough.

"This is how it's gonna go. I ask you what the Crown's doing sending a whole crew across with all this...gear. You tell me. Then I go through everything you and your peons brought with you, just to double-check that you're being straight with me." Her finger froze on the raug's temple, and her hand slowly lifted away as one devastatingly sharp claw slowly elongated from her nailbed. She pressed hard enough to leave a divot in the commander's thick gray skin, but that was all.

She's about to skewer the guy's brain. Cheyenne opened her mouth to tell her friend to wait, but the back of Corian's hand pressed against her shoulder made her look up at him instead. The Night-stalker averted his gaze and slowly shook his head.

Maleshi twisted her claw in that divot in the commander's gray flesh. "I'm sure even a raug can easily imagine how different the scenarios will be at the end, depending on what you tell me right now."

Gu'urs' glowing orange-brown eyes narrowed as he sneered up at his captor. "I don't know what you've heard, but you've lost all your power. General."

Maleshi removed her bladelike claw from the commander's forehead, retracting it with a soft noise like sheathing a knife and looked around the clearing. "Yes, that's exactly what it looks like to me. All your men tied up like prize radan ready for the spit and a nice, hot, Deaden-Day feast. You got me, Commander. Completely powerless."

Byrd let out a low chuckle but shut up immediately when Lumil shot him a threatening glance.

"All right. What's in the crates?"

"Your fucking doom." The raug glared at his interrogator even as a slow, swollen smirk spread across his bruised lower lip. Then he took a deep breath and roared, "It's the death torch for any of you who tells this *nilsch úcat* a fell-damn—"

The back of Maleshi's hand cracked across the raug's splintered face, cutting him off. "I'm sure we all understand what happens here. And you're out of chances."

When she stood, the group of rebel magicals who'd come to crash this O'gúl smuggling party stepped back from the ex-general's blazing silver gaze, including Cheyenne and Corian.

The halfling watched her former professor stalk across the clearing toward the closest stack of metal crates. *She was right. Two different people.*

When Maleshi reached the crates, those flashing silver claws elongated from her fingertips. In one swift stroke, the Nightstalker woman slashed through the three locks on the crate's lid with a grating squeal of ruptured metal. The locks gave way, and she shoved the lid open to let it fall back on its hinges. "Corian."

It was a command, and Corian went obediently to the ex-general's side. Together, they peered into the open crate. Hissing, Corian reached inside and pulled out a long chain of black metal links. He turned, the link on the end whispering across the grass, and flicked the chain like a whip. The links clicked together and locked into place, unfolding and rearranging until he held what looked more like an extra-long crowbar than a chain.

"Fuck." Persh'al rubbed the side of his mostly shaved head and stared at the bar of metal in the Nightstalker's hand. "How'd they even get that across?"

"Deactivated," Maleshi muttered, scanning the crate's contents.

"More like never activated in the first place." Corian flicked the metal bar again with a twist of his wrist, and the pieces folded back on themselves before the metal links fell loosely toward the ground once more. "Can't bring O'gúl tech across the border, but they can send the parts. And these are old parts."

"How much of this crap did they bring?" Lumil eyed the half-dozen stacks of crates in front of the Nightstalkers before stepping across the clearing to eye the other stacks and the scattered crates that hadn't yet been organized.

"Doesn't matter how much they already sent Earthside." Persh'al joined the Nightstalkers and peered into the open crate, shaking his head. "Only how much more they'll try to push through after this."

Cheyenne took a tentative step toward the Nightstalkers and the troll. *First time I've felt this out of my element.* "What is it?"

"Machine parts." Maleshi stiffened, then stepped quickly back and eyed the black handles on the crates in this stack. "Open the others."

Corian grabbed the handle of the open crate and yanked it onto the ground. Dozens of thick black chains spilled across the grass like metal snakes before he slashed his claws against the locks of the next crate. Sparks flew, the lid rocked back on its hinges, and he pulled out a black metal sphere the size of a basketball.

"You've gotta be kidding me." Persh'al took another metal sphere and ran his hand over it before finding the almost invisible button on the side. He pressed it with a little click, and the sphere opened in his hand. He dropped the thing as the mechanisms whirred and spun and flipped into place. When it was finished, the resulting part looked like a curved black metal shield.

Or the shell of one of those beetle-things.

Persh'al shook his head as he stared at the unfolded part. "What were they thinking? Just throw a bunch of un-activated parts across the border and hope those idiots know how to put it all together?"

Corian stared at the troll. "You're good, Persh'al. But the chances that you're the only O'gúleesh Earthside who figured out how to meld human tech to magic are low."

"This isn't human tech, man."

"Then they've got someone who figured out how to activate this shit with operational magic. Can't be that different."

"It's *completely* different, Corian. Nothing Earthside conducts the same way. If I tried to close a circuit with riverchrome over here, I'd blow my fucking head off."

Cheyenne left them to argue the semantics of magic and other-world tech, her attention captured by Maleshi's march across the clearing toward the crates with the gray handles. She had to pass the raug commander on her way there, and she shot him a scathing glare.

Gu'urs chuckled again through his mashed mouth and widened his orange-brown eyes. "She'll rip this world apart to get to you, *mór úcare.* You know she will. I can see it in your eyes."

The halfling stopped inches from his face and hunkered down. The raug's eyes narrowed, spit dripping in a long string from the corner of his slack mouth, and what little sneer he'd managed faded.

"Obviously, she has no idea who my friends over here are." Cheyenne glanced around the clearing and the incapacitated soldiers of the Crown strewn across the grass. "Her first mistake was underestimating what we can do. If she wants me that badly, asshole, go tell her to make the crossing and find me herself."

The commander chuckled again, but it caught in his throat as his spittle spilled down the back of his mouth. "You're the one who's making the crossing, as a vassal of the Crown or in a box. Your choice."

Angry purple sparks crackled at the tips of the halfling's fingers, and the raug leaned away as far as he could with his wrists bound behind him. "I'm staying right here."

She jerked toward him, and a sputtering hiss of surprise leaped from the commander's swollen mouth as he flinched. Cheyenne stood swiftly and walked toward Maleshi.

The Nightstalker woman had already opened three of the five crates marked with gray handles. The first two had been tossed aside, their contents spilling over the grass as the woman sifted through the third container.

"What's in those?" Cheyenne stopped behind her former mentor and glanced at the tiny black squares littering the ground.

Maleshi poured a handful of the metallic pieces back into the upright crate and shook her head. "Batteries, more or less."

"Batteries." The halfling approached the crate to look inside. She picked up one of the small metal squares the size of a quarter and turned it over in the afternoon sunlight. "These look like circuit boards for the first cell phones ever."

"This is one of those reverse situations where size really doesn't matter, kid. Humans over here think they're smart for cramming the best technology into tiny, fragile pieces. But these? If we were in Ambar'ogúl, one of these could power the state of New York."

Cheyenne dropped the chip back onto the thousands of others filling the crate. "Someone figured out how to make O'gúl tech work over here."

Maleshi let out a quick, mirthless laugh. "This shit was old news when I still wore the crest on my shoulder. The Crown's going old-school for this."

"That's supposed to work over here?"

The Nightstalker woman wrinkled her nose. "Compared to what the Crown had at its disposal when I still served, using this tech is like a structural engineer building a high rise out of Legos. These bastards know something we don't. They wouldn't waste a massive shipment of disassembled parts and power chips on nothing more than a hunch."

"And weapons." The halfling nodded at the single open crate with red handles. The giant launcher the orcs had fired at Maleshi lay on the ground beside it.

"And weapons." The Nightstalker woman grimaced in bitter frustration and went to the red-handled container.

"This crap..." She lifted a smooth metal cylinder half the width of a soup can and tossed it in her hand. "We stopped using these halfway through my prematurely ended term of service."

"But it worked."

"Yes, it did." Maleshi's shoulder blades drew together at the still-fresh memory of the projectile unleashing its attack across her back not half an hour ago. "This is more magic and less tech. Blood magic, but on a race-wide scale."

"Okay." Cheyenne folded her arms and frowned at the canister in the Nightstalker's hand. "Pretend I've never been to Ambar'ogúl and don't know a thing about race-wide blood magic."

The Nightstalker snorted and jiggled the canister. "These things are loaded with potions, kid. Fire one of these, and it's like a heat-seeking missile. Only in this case, it's seeking a magical race and the specific magical signature that goes with it. If Corian had been any closer when they fired this thing, it might've gone for him instead. You never know. This shit is unpredictable at the best of times. Packs a punch, too."

"You look pretty okay to me."

"I've had a lot of practice being shot at, kid. A lot of practice being shot, too." Maleshi's silver gaze dropped to the halfling's right hip for a split second. Then she gazed around the clearing at the dozens of crates and shook her head. "This isn't everything. They'll try to get more across. Maybe not today. Maybe not after my seal breaks over that portal wall. But they *will* try, and we don't have the kind of resources or manpower we need to keep them from succeeding."

Cheyenne frowned at her friend, her fists clenching and unclenching at her sides. "We can't just walk away and let them keep bringing this over."

"We can't stop them either, Cheyenne."

"Bullshit. There have to be thousands of O'gúleesh on this side who would stand up to fight this. I'm pretty sure those born Earthside wouldn't want a foreign monarch shipping weapons and machine parts into our world. That's part of why the FRoE's around, isn't it?"

"Maybe." Maleshi shrugged and stared at Corian and Persh'al, still arguing on the other side of the clearing. Lumil and Byrd stalked back and forth in front of the O'gúl soldiers, their magic at the ready as they kept an eye out for any idiot stupid enough to make a move. "But this portal can't possibly be the only one popping up around the world on its own. And I have a feeling it won't be the only one spilling the in-between out on this side."

"But this one's right here." Cheyenne stared at the Nightstalker as Maleshi made her way toward the arguing O'gúleesh. "We make a stand at *this* one because we know about this one. Hey, don't walk away from me."

Maleshi whirled, her silver eyes glinting fiercely. "I've always loved your spirit, kid. You're a lot like me, and I seriously appreciate your dedication to acting in the moment, based on what you know *right now*. But today, while we're here, I wouldn't repeat the mistake of telling me what to do."

The halfling swallowed. "I'm not one of your soldiers, Mattie."

"But I'm the one calling the shots, so let me take care of it until we know more and can put together another plan." That feral grin spread across the Nightstalker ex-general's face again before she shot Cheyenne a devious wink. "And relax, huh? There's more than one way to skewer a drow."

CHAPTER EIGHTY-ONE

"We need to figure out where they were planning to take this shipment." Maleshi, Corian, Persh'al, and Cheyenne huddled in the center of the clearing while the goblins kept up their patrol over their O'gúleesh prisoners.

"And which asshole figured out how to make all this crap work over here," Persh'al added. "Put me in a room with whoever it is, and I'll have every single piece of information stripped from his brain. Only need half an hour."

Corian shot the troll a warning look. "One step at a time, friend."

"Yeah, but it's the one step ahead that gets me excited."

"Don't get too excited just yet." Maleshi glanced over her shoulder at the tied-up magicals who served the Crown. "I don't think we'll get anything out of them."

"We should try anyway." Corian cocked his head with a dangerously playful smirk when the ex-general raised an eyebrow. "I used to trust your judgment implicitly, General, but we're both four hundred years out of practice with that one."

Maleshi hissed out a laugh. "At the very least, it might be just as fun as tying them all up in the first place."

"Nah. I like this part better." The Nightstalkers exchanged

557

vicious knowing glances before splitting away from the huddle and taking off toward opposite sides of the clearing.

Cheyenne stepped after Maleshi toward the far side of the clearing with the weapons crates, but Persh'al stopped her with a loud clearing of his throat.

"I'd sit this one out if I were you, kid."

"Are you telling me whatever those two are about to do is worse than that shitshow of a fight you and I barely had time to join?"

The troll cocked his head with a one-armed shrug, the tips of his gelled orange mohawk dropping unnervingly close to the halfling's face. "Yeah." He nodded at the closest group of loyalist prisoners. "For them."

"Time for interrogations, huh?" Cheyenne folded her arms and turned to see Corian squat, his fur-tufted fist clutching the front of a sneering goblin's uniform shirt.

"You gonna have a problem with that?"

"Not really. I've seen it before."

Persh'al jerked his chin with a curious smirk. "And you were the one asking the questions, weren't you?"

The halfling shrugged and didn't say anything else. *Durg's the only one who told me something useful.*

A low chuckle rose from the troll as he shook his head. "I shouldn't be surprised at this point."

"Why? 'Cause I'm too cheery to interrogate anyone?"

Persh'al snorted. "'Cause you're too much like him."

She grimaced and glanced across the clearing at Maleshi, who shoved a snarling orc onto his side before looming over him and grabbing his shirt with both hands. "We can stop talking about how much I have in common with a guy I don't even know."

"I'd say it's a pretty good time to get to know him, wouldn't you? Especially after all this." The troll gestured across the clearing, flinching when Corian sent his fist hurtling into the goblin's ribs.

Cheyenne watched the Nightstalkers working their interrogation techniques on either side of the clearing. "They're doing this for him, aren't they?"

"That's part of it." Persh'al sniggered. "Kinda funny, though. L'zar's in that joke of a prison right now to keep *you* safe, and it's the only thing keeping the Crown from coming after him."

The halfling raised an eyebrow. "After everything I've seen in the last few days, I'm not sure Chateau D'rahl could stand up to something like this. Or to magicals like Corian and Maleshi, if they really wanted to get to him."

"Of course not. That's the thing, though, kid. The Crown wants L'zar out of the way, and for now, he's doing all the heavy lifting for her. These forces won't lift a finger to go after him while he's locking *himself* up."

On the far side of the clearing, Maleshi had given up on the orc and now played Nightstalker roulette with two hissing, snarling skaxen. The orange-skinned, rat-faced magicals sneered up at the ex-general without a word, even when she zapped them one at a time with flashing silver darts.

Cheyenne shrugged. "Well, I started the trials, and I'm still alive. If L'zar really wanted to help, now would be the time for him to slip on out of prison and come fight with us."

"Maybe." The troll stroked his hairless chin. His gaze darted toward Corian when the Nightstalker lunged to the next trussed-up loyalist, catching the startled troll by surprise before barking questions into the magical's face. "If I had to guess, Cheyenne, I'd say L'zar's still doesn't know what'll happen when he *does* break out again. He eventually will. He has to. But he won't until he's sure it won't hurt you."

"I'm not worth the entire world on this side of the Border." The halfling shook her head. "If he can stop this from happening, be a part of this rebellion or whatever instead of hiding behind bars, that's what he should be doing."

Persh'al turned to look at her with a sly, crooked smile. "You're the only one who's gotten this far, kid. That's a big deal."

"Well, thanks, but that doesn't do shit for all the monsters spilling out of a new portal and the Crown smuggling weapons Earthside."

"Not yet." The troll folded his arms and returned his attention to the Nightstalkers, who were still making threats and roughing up their O'gúleesh prisoners. "But if we play our cards right, it will."

Byrd and Lumil only had to step in once and bash several of the stupider prisoners back down while Corian and Maleshi interrogated Commander Gu'urs' soldiers. Now, the Nightstalkers had made their way toward each other along the line of tied-up loyalists until they met in the middle in front of the last two.

All this time to watch their friends get beaten up and screamed at. One of them will talk.

Cheyenne watched intently. The final two magicals—a troll woman with a black band tattooed across her face from one temple to the other and an orc missing one ear—looked intimidated, at least, if not terrified.

"Down to the wire now, aren't we?" Maleshi loomed over the tattooed troll and slowly cocked her head. "You have the chance to change the ending for your entire squadron right now."

"The ending's already been written, *nilsch úcat.*" The troll woman spat at Maleshi's feet, her coarse laughter cut off by the Nightstalker's fist connecting with her face.

"The ending is what we make it. Who was supposed to get this shipment?"

A smear of dark, almost purple blood covered the troll's lower jaw. "It came from the Crown, and it goes to the Crown. All of this...this entire world—" The troll coughed and spat again, this time to get the blood out of her mouth. "She takes whatever she wants, General. If anyone knows that, it's you."

Maleshi dropped into a squat, her forearms propped on her bent knees. "That's exactly why I left. But I'm sure you already figured that one out."

"You can't stop her," the one-eared orc growled. "She's seen more of the days to come than you know. Nothing will stand in her way."

The Nightstalker woman glared at him, her upper lip curling into a sneer. "That cursed drow isn't the only one with Oracles in her pocket."

Corian shot her a quick glance of surprise, but she ignored him.

The orc cackled. "Uh-oh. Somebody forgot to slip that little detail into the pillow talk, huh?"

The tied-up troll woman beside him guffawed and leaned back against the metal crate behind her. "That's the trouble with Night-stalkers. Too many furballs, and this one's trying to turn herself into a queen, ain't she?"

Both magicals burst into another round of sneering laughter.

Cheyenne turned toward Persh'al and frowned. "A queen?"

The blue troll grimaced. "A female cat with a new litter. The bad joke's been tossed around for a long time back home."

The halfling's eyes widened before she turned back to watch the Nightstalkers. "Cats in Ambar'ogúl…"

"A whole city of 'em, kid. At least, there were before I crossed over."

One more reason not to cross the Border.

The cackling cut off abruptly when Maleshi sent a hand-sized ball of silver light into the troll-woman's chest. It rocked her backward, her head slamming into the crate with a hollow, metallic bang. Then the ex-general grabbed the troll woman's uniform shirt and jerked her prisoner forward again. "Four hundred years, and no one's come up with anything original. Who's supposed to get this shipment? We know you've got someone Earthside who can make this old junk work, human tech or not."

"It's not you, *nilsch úcat.* That's for damn sure." The orc leaned sideways to leer up at the ex-general. "You're too busy takin' it from this—"

Corian's hand clamped down on the top of the orc's bald head and jerked it back, exposing the magical's green neck. The next second, the Nightstalker's silver claws were pressed to the orc's throat. "If the next word out of your mouth isn't a name, it'll be your last."

The orc licked his lips, glaring at the Nightstalker without fighting to free himself from the grip jerking his head back. "Fuck you."

"General?" Corian stared at the orc and pressed his claws more firmly against the soldier's neck.

Maleshi grimaced in disappointment. "Yeah, we're done here."

Faster than anyone could follow, the blades of Corian's claws sliced through flesh and bone, and the orc fell lifelessly into the troll woman's lap.

The troll jerked forward toward Maleshi, her crimson eyes blazing. "You can't stop the black tide, bitch! And there's no other world for you to run to—"

The snap and crunch of a broken neck cut off the troll's words before Maleshi released the prisoner's head from both hands. Then she stood from her crouch with a low hiss. "Looks like my judgment's still on fucking point."

Corian rose beside her, ignoring the rising shouts and rhythmic growls coming from the other loyalist prisoners scattered around them. "At least we tried. Just give the word, General."

"No. I'll handle it."

With a firm nod, Corian stepped away from the Nightstalker ex-general and the chantlike snarling and hissing coming from the tied-up magicals. He rejoined Cheyenne and Persh'al in the center of the clearing, followed shortly by Byrd and Lumil. Every magical standing beside the halfling firmly set their jaw, watching Maleshi with grim acceptance.

Cheyenne tried to meet Corian's gaze, but he wouldn't look at her. "What's happening?"

Her drow-trial mentor swallowed but said nothing.

Maleshi stopped in front of Commander Gu'urs lying on the ground and didn't bother to squat beside him again. "Still time, if you change your mind. All these soldiers are your responsibility, don't forget."

"I don't forget," the raug spat. "None of us do, traitor. You'll die fighting for the wrong drow, General."

The Nightstalker woman settled her gaze on the shimmering pink wall she'd sealed across the Border portal. "Yeah, so will you."

Cheyenne stepped closer to Corian. "Seriously, what are we gonna do with these assholes?"

He still wouldn't look at her as he muttered, "This is why we're fighting, Cheyenne. When you want something bad enough, you gotta get your hands dirty."

"Corian." She glanced quickly at Maleshi, whose arms were lifted in front of her and spread toward either side of the clearing. "We can't just—"

The burst of silver light erupting from Maleshi's outstretched arms filled the entire clearing, momentarily blinding everyone and drowning out the shape of the Nightstalker standing in its center. A sharp, earsplitting crack rent the air, followed a split second later by dozens of screams. They only lasted a few seconds before cutting out. There was a collective thump in front of Maleshi, then the light faded.

When Cheyenne opened her eyes again, blinking against the burning glare behind her eyelids and waiting for her vision to adjust, her jaw dropped.

Every single bound magical lay still, heads fallen forward or back at impossible angles, bodies slumped sideways or sprawling on the ground. Thin streams of smoke rose from fist-sized black burns on every single prisoner. Cheyenne's nostrils flared at the sickly-sweet stench of uniforms and flesh burning together. Her fists clenched at her sides as she fought to control her rapid breathing.

Maleshi was down on one knee in the middle of all of it, her head bowed as she propped her elbow on her raised thigh. The only sound came from the still-sizzling burns on the bodies and the remaining magicals' expectant breath.

The ex-general pushed to her feet, took a deep breath, and turned toward one of the open crates of black O'gúleesh power chips.

"What?" The searing heat of Cheyenne's drow magic rippled up her spine, and she took off after Maleshi.

"Cheyenne." Corian reached out for her arm again, but this time, the halfling jerked free of his grip and whirled.

"No. We came here to find out how this portal got here, not to kill a bunch of prisoners you guys tied up."

"I told you this was why we're fighting, kid." Corian spread his arms with a tight grimace. "It's done."

"Without even *trying* to find a different solution? Are you *kidding* me?" The halfling spun again and stalked across the grass toward Maleshi. "Hey!"

The Nightstalker woman shoved a handful of black metal chips into her pocket, then bent to retrieve a piece of shattered carapace the O'gúleesh loyalists hadn't bothered to clear away. She tested the weight of the shiny black shell and nodded. Then she headed back across the clearing, brushing past Cheyenne without meeting the halfling's gaze.

"Oh, now you're just gonna ignore me?" Cheyenne followed her former professor toward the group of rebel magicals. All four of them watched her with wary hesitation. "I'm talking to you, Mattie. And you better have an airtight excuse for what you just did, 'cause I can't think of *anything* that makes it okay. Mattie, stop." The halfling pulled up on the grass, the purple sparks flaring at her fingertips beyond her rage and control. "*Maleshi!*"

The ex-general stopped in front of the group and rolled her shoulders back. Corian, Persh'al, and the goblins didn't take their eyes off the drow halfling shouting at the Nightstalker who'd taken down entire armies all on her own.

Slowly, Maleshi turned and fixed Cheyenne with her glowing green eyes. "If you have something to say to me, Cheyenne, say it now. But do *not* raise your voice at me again."

The ferocity behind those flashing eyes made the halfling swallow. The purple sparks snuffed out. "You just killed them all. No warning. No asking what the rest of us thought. Did you even stop to consider that we could do something else with those soldiers?"

Maleshi blinked. "I consider every possible outcome before every decision I make, Cheyenne. You and your new friends came to find me because you wanted General Hi'et to figure out what to do at this Border." She spread her arms. "I've been making these kinds of tough calls for longer than this world has been out of the Dark Ages, and I stand by them."

"You didn't have to kill them."

A bitter smile spread across the Nightstalker's lips. "Is it the killing part that's getting under your skin so much? I find it hard to believe you're a zealous defender of peace."

Cheyenne snorted and folded her arms. "Hey, I've left bodies on the ground behind me. I admit that. But not when they're tied up. Not when they can't *defend* themselves."

Maleshi took a deep breath and let it out slowly. "We're on the brink of another war, kid. This is what war looks like. It's not pretty, and it leaves a bad taste in your mouth, but we have to keep the big picture in mind here."

"I'm all for a rebellion against a monarch destroying magicals' lives on the other side." Cheyenne swallowed again and shook her head. "If there's a way to finish what you started—what L'zar started —fine. But keeping the Crown away from me isn't worth killing a bunch of her soldiers who can't fight back."

The Nightstalker stared at the drow halfling, then her dark eyebrows flickered together in her feline face, and she turned without another word.

"That's it? End of discussion, just like that?"

Maleshi headed swiftly across the clearing toward the tree line and disappeared into the woods.

CHAPTER EIGHTY-TWO

Corian glanced at Persh'al, Lumil, and Byrd, then nodded toward the crates and the O'gúl loyalists scattered around them. The magicals headed toward the crates, gathering as much of the O'gúl contraband as they could to take with them.

When he caught Cheyenne's gaze, the halfling fought down another unintended flare of her drow magic. *I should've done something.*

"How many times do I have to tell you this is bigger than you?" Corian walked toward her, his head low like he was trying to whisper to her from three yards away. "Bigger than Ambar'ogúl, too."

"You've been telling me that since we met, Corian." Cheyenne forced herself to unclench her fists. "I know you made a promise to L'zar, but don't try to tell me that promise included killing a bunch of soldiers with their hands tied behind their backs."

"They would have done the same to us. The fact that the Crown didn't open this new portal doesn't matter anymore. She's using it, and she just sent us a message by moving all this shit across the border." The Nightstalker shook his head and glanced at the shimmering wall of pale pink light rising between the dark stone spires of the ridge. "They're bringing this war Earthside, and the fight won't end with the magicals in hiding over here. The Crown will come for humans too. Maybe even go for them first, given how easy humans are to pick off. And if she doesn't, whatever we fought this morning will end up doing the same kind of damage, if not more."

"The ruler of Ambar'ogúl is gonna send her forces into this world to kill humans." The halfling cocked her head with a dry laugh. "That doesn't make sense. Humans don't even *know* about this."

"It doesn't matter who knows. What matters is how far the Crown's willing to go to get what she wants. Which might not just be you at this point." Corian eyed Persh'al and the goblins as they trudged back across the clearing. The blue troll and Lumil carried one of the crates between them, followed by Byrd with an armful of silver blood-tracker canisters. "Whatever she wants over here, she won't stop until she has it all in her grasp. That's what we're trying to avoid, Cheyenne."

"None of this looks like *avoiding* it to me."

"You have the right to your opinion, kid, but if we wanna make sure a day like today never happens again, we need to hurry it up with your trials. Like yesterday."

"Why?"

"You're gonna help us stop this war. Hopefully, before it really gets bad, and preferably in time for L'zar to put all the other pieces in play to join us."

Cheyenne scoffed, glancing around the Nightstalker to see Persh'al and the goblins vanishing into the woods. "All he has to do is break out of Chateau D'rahl and show up. But he can't even do that."

"He will when—"

"When I'm ready?"

Corian's lips twitched into the ghost of a smile, his brow creasing again in something like concern. "No. When *he's* ready. Time to go."

The halfling scanned the scattered mess across the fresh Border portal. "What about all this?"

"We've got as much as we need for now, and we really don't have time to play cleanup." The Nightstalker headed toward the tree line, knowing the halfling wouldn't be too far behind.

Cheyenne studied the clearing and the portal. *No wonder things went to shit over there. I won't let that happen on this side.*

They made the drive back to Persh'al's warehouse outside DC in complete silence. The goblins had given up bickering with each other, and it didn't pick back up again once the SUV pulled into the warehouse's weed-choked parking lot. While Persh'al and the goblins hefted the O'gúl contraband into the warehouse, Corian stayed outside with Cheyenne and Maleshi.

"Whatever Persh'al can figure out about those machine parts, he'll give us a report in the next few hours."

Maleshi pressed her lips together and glanced at the warehouse's metal door as it clicked shut behind the other magicals. "Have him run whatever searches he can for a different frequency of magical tech."

"At the very least, yeah. I hate to say it, but I hope their expert's been tinkering enough to give off even a minor signal."

"Hope won't get us that name, *vae shra'ni.*"

"No, but it sure does keep that troll motivated." Corian glanced at the halfling and gave her that concerned frown again. "We'll call the whole day another training session, kid. Let me know what happened with the *Cuil Ani* when you get home."

"Checking a copper box doesn't feel like a top priority," she muttered.

"Doesn't matter what it feels like." Corian pulled his phone out of his pocket and typed on it. "Just text me if anything changes."

"I don't have your—" Cheyenne's back pocket vibrated, and the Nightstalker looked at her with a wry smile.

"Now you do."

"Okay." The halfling gave him a curt nod and stepped toward her Panamera. "Mattie—Maleshi... You know what? I don't know what the hell to call you anymore."

"Whatever you like, Cheyenne." Maleshi's gaze was locked on Corian's, even as Cheyenne unlocked her car.

"Right. You want a ride home?"

"Absolutely. Go ahead and start the car. I'll be right there."

After glancing at the Nightstalkers, who were locked in a staring contest, Cheyenne shrugged and walked around the front of her car to slip behind the wheel. Her two mentors didn't say another word until she'd closed the driver's side door and the low hum of the Porsche's engine was audible. The halfling sat back against the seat and closed her eyes. *No way they forgot I can still hear them.*

"Thank you for coming with us," Corian muttered, studying the ex-general's face. "Would've been better to find you under different circumstances, but—"

"But things are the way they are. I get it." Maleshi tilted her head and folded her arms. "I didn't tell that girl to wait in the car so I could get a private thank you."

Corian laughed but didn't sound even remotely amused. "So this is the part where you tell me you never want to see me again. That you disappeared for a reason, and just because I found you, it doesn't mean we'll pick up where we left off. Duty is duty, right?"

Maleshi shook her head. "You said it, not me."

Corian hung his head with another bitter laugh, shoving his hands into his pockets. The ex-general dipped her head, watching him collect himself and waiting until he was finished. When he looked back up at her, his eyes flashed with an intensity she'd missed for four hundred years. "Then why did you tell her to wait in the car?"

"You realize how important it is to get her through those trials."

"Of course I do. Don't insult me."

"And I know you'll do whatever it takes to make that happen." She stepped toward him, forcing him to keep looking at her. He didn't step back or lean away, just lifted his chin enough to meet her gaze. "But if you push her too hard, *vae shra'ni*, if you break that halfling's spirit to get the job done, I'll know. And I will hunt you down just to see the look in your eyes when you remember every word of this conversation."

Corian stared at her, the tufts of light-brown fur down the sides of his face twitching a little when he smirked. "So *that's* what it takes to get you to find me, huh?"

"It's not a threat, Corian."

"I know it's not. I care about what happens to her just as much as you do. It's been a long time, Maleshi, but not long enough for you to forget who I am."

"Hmm." She glanced at nothing behind Corian's shoulder. "Not long enough for either of us to change much, either."

All he could do was shake his head and offer a little shrug.

"Find me when Persh'al has something worth going after." Maleshi spun away from him to head toward Cheyenne's car. Pausing, she glanced over her shoulder. "To be clear, I've wanted to see you again every day since I left. *That's* how much this matters to me."

Corian couldn't think of anything to say as General Maleshi Hi'et opened the passenger side door of the drow halfling's shiny new car and slipped into the seat. He watched the woman cast her illusion charm as Cheyenne retied the broken silver chain that hung the Heart of Midnight pendant around her neck. L'zar Verdys' righthand magical didn't move until the two women in the Panamera drove away.

CHAPTER EIGHTY-THREE

"Wanna tell me what that was all about?" Cheyenne asked as she pulled out of the overgrown parking lot and onto the side street in the nearly empty neighborhood.

"Oh, come on, Cheyenne. We both know you heard every word of that conversation. I'm sure you can put the pieces together for yourself." A slow smile spread across Maleshi's now human-looking face as she glanced at the halfling beside her. "You're getting pretty good at that, aren't you?"

Cheyenne ignored the professor's jest. *Guess we're not talking about those soldiers or Corian. Fine.* She glanced at the scrap of beetle-thing carapace resting in the Nightstalker's lap and snorted. "I'm still having trouble with *that* piece, though."

"Ah. Yeah." Maleshi tapped her fingernails on the curved husk and shrugged. "I have no idea what it is, honestly."

"Why'd you take it?"

"Jealous that I thought to grab a souvenir, are you?"

The halfling rolled her eyes and focused on the road. "You weren't even there for that fight."

"Well, if there's anything left when we're finished, kid, I'm more than happy to hand it over for you to hang on the wall."

"I don't know what to say to that."

"No problem. Just keep driving."

Adjusting her hands on the steering wheel, Cheyenne glanced quickly at the Nightstalker woman beside her. Maleshi just stared out the windshield, her lips moving soundlessly. "Uh, I don't know where you live. Once we get back into town, you'll have to give me directions."

Maleshi finished her muttered spell and turned her head so quickly toward Cheyenne, the halfling flinched sideways. "That won't be necessary."

The half-drow stared at the Nightstalker's feral grin and frowned. "You don't want me to take you home?"

"No. I want you to forget everything you know about avoiding obstacles in the road and just keep driving."

When the ex-general nodded at the road, Cheyenne looked out the windshield in time to see a dark, glimmering oval of another portal hovering in front of them.

"What the—" She jerked the wheel and hit the brakes, but there wasn't enough time. When the Panamera screeched to a stop, they were no longer on a side street outside DC. The back tire bumped against the curb of an entirely different road, and Cheyenne slammed the gearshift into park. "Are you insane?"

"Very much so. I thought we'd covered that already." Maleshi unbuckled her seatbelt and opened the door to leap nimbly onto the sidewalk.

With a frustrated growl, the halfling turned off the engine, nearly ripped her seatbelt from its buckle, and got out to follow her friend. *And I thought she drove me nuts before.* Her irritation didn't keep her from remembering to lock the car, but the chirp and flashing lights didn't bring so much as a smirk this time. "You can't just cast portals in the middle of the road while I'm driving."

"I think it worked out rather well." The Nightstalker stopped at a building Cheyenne only halfway recognized, gesturing toward the banged-up front door of the three-story complex with the beetle shell instead of her hand. "Bet you didn't think you'd be back here, did ya?"

"And you're not even a little worried about someone seeing a dark oval and a Panamera appear out of thin air? It's not exactly low-profile in the first—what?" The halfling finally took in the old industrial neighborhood, the train tracks, and the dirty entrance of the door to the building in front of them. This time the door was closed, but it hit her immediately. "You opened a surprise portal to see the raug Oracle."

"Took you long enough."

Cheyenne shot the Nightstalker a warning glance. "Well, last time, there was a lot of nagging and a bunch of chickens running around. Plus, I wasn't tricked into *driving through a portal*."

"I didn't trick you, kid." Maleshi waved her off and headed down the short cement walkway toward the apartment building's front door. "I just know how attached you are to that car already."

"We could've done that in the parking lot." When Maleshi opened the dented front door, Cheyenne grabbed it and raised an eyebrow.

The Nightstalker chuckled. "You really want to listen to Corian go on about how reckless I am? That one's a stickler for covering his tracks, I'll give him that. I alleviated that headache and got us out of there where he couldn't see."

"What if someone follows us here?" The door shut with a creak and a metallic bang as the women walked down the dusty hallway, which was still littered with leaves and pebbles. Chicken feathers fluttered on the floor when Cheyenne stepped past them.

"Wow. You've known the guy for...what, maybe a week? And you're already starting to sound like him."

Rubbing her forehead and trying not to shout, Cheyenne muttered, "It's not that hard to answer a question directly, you know."

"We're *fine*, kid. If anyone picked up a portal trail in the middle of the road and decided to follow it, they'd have to be looking for trouble."

"Most magicals are when they show up in front of me."

Maleshi gave the halfling a dismissive wave again and stopped at the Oracle's apartment door on the right. "Then we agree that most of those magicals are idiots. If the lack of intent in my portal didn't turn them off, showing up at a raug's front door definitely will. Or they'll step through anyway and get exactly what they deserve. Either way, not a big deal."

The Nightstalker rapped briskly on the apartment door and waited, smacking the edge of the beetle carapace against her palm.

Cheyenne stared at the woman and stuck her hands into her pockets. "It's *amazing* no one found you for four hundred years."

"Not really. But the cat's out of the bag now, isn't it?" Maleshi rolled her eyes. "Ugh. Now *I'm* making cat jokes. I've spent four hundred years casting limited spells and shoving all this brilliant magic into a tiny little box in a dusty corner of a forgotten room, kid. Corian *still* found me, so why not live a little, huh?"

"That's not a good reason to—"

The door jerked open with a creak, and Gúrdu's huge gray head and glowing orange eyes appeared from within the darkness of his apartment. "What do you want?"

"Damn. Has *everyone* forgotten how to greet an old friend these days?" Maleshi glanced quickly up and down the hall before a silver light flashed at her fingertips. Then the black-haired, green-eyed university professor shimmered into the Nightstalker ex-general. "Good to see you too, Gúrdu."

The raug's eyes widened, and he made a grotesque sticky sucking sound with his tongue before fully opening the door. "I don't have all day."

"Well, neither do we. That's why we're here." Maleshi slipped inside the apartment and waited for Cheyenne to join her before Gúrdu shut the door with a massive hand tipped in red claws.

The Oracle blinked vacuously at the Nightstalker, then his gaze drifted toward the halfling and the Heart of Midnight pendant dangling from the neckline of her hoodie.

Cheyenne quickly stuffed the necklace beneath the fabric and raised her eyebrows. *Gotta stop leaving this thing out for every pissed-off magical to see.*

"If you've come about that drow trinket of yours again, feel free to piss off."

The halfling glared at him, and Maleshi laughed. "You haven't changed a bit, have you? We're not here about Cheyenne's legacy. Not directly, at least."

The raug's orange eyes drifted slowly back toward General Hi'et and narrowed. "You're the one who sent her here."

"Who else would send a friend to *you*, Gúrdu?" The Nightstalker grinned.

"Someone who thinks the name 'Mattie' is enough to hide her behind false honor and the lie of claiming exile."

Sensing the building tension, Cheyenne stepped back against the wall of the entryway, her nose wrinkling at the rotting-orange smell she'd caught on the Nightstalker woman just over a week ago. Mixed with the sickly-sweet scent of what the Oracle burned in his pillow-laden living room on the other side of the entryway, the odor made her a little dizzy.

Maleshi's smile vanished. "My honor and my exile are *mine* to claim, Gúrdu. I came here for your sight, not your opinion."

"I don't give opinions. They don't pay nearly as well as prophecies and smoke."

"Well, today, you're not getting paid for any of it." The Nightstalker thrust the beetle-thing shell toward the raug's chest. "You still owe me for Felagtrok."

The Oracle grunted. "I should have paid you in kind that day."

"And I'm sure the thought entered your mind until you reached out into the cosmos and saw how much more I'd end up doing for you. I've spent too much time on the past today, Oracle. I want to see the future. Either let me cash your IOU or quit flinging around insults and calling 'em insights."

Gúrdu glanced at the black shell in her hand, which glistened even in the low light of his apartment and blinked. "Are you done?"

"I don't know. Am I?"

Slowly, those glowing orange eyes drifted toward Cheyenne again. "You were more entertaining."

The halfling lifted her chin and stared right back at him. "You were a pain in the ass."

The Oracle grunted. "Let's get this over with, General."

He turned and stalked down the hall toward the draping curtain of beads separating the entryway from the rest of the apartment. The wood and glass beads clacked as he flung them aside and stooped to get his incredible height through the doorway.

Maleshi looked at the halfling and dropped the beetle shell to her side with a shrug. "Nice guy, right?"

Cheyenne slowly shook her head. "You've got a weird definition of 'friend.'"

"Yeah, you too. Just another reason I like you so much, kid." Maleshi winked, then turned to follow the raug through the beaded curtain. She paused briefly to eye the dangling threads at the end. "Huh."

The halfling waited for the beads to drop back into place behind the Nightstalker. *She almost sounds like Mattie again, but I don't think the Mattie I knew is coming back.*

CHAPTER EIGHTY-FOUR

Both Maleshi and the raug Oracle had taken their seats by the time Cheyenne stepped into the huge, dusty living room. She moved gingerly around the frayed pillows and ornately woven cushions scattered across the floor, trying not to look too closely at the dark shadows that flickered across the room when the hanging lanterns flared to life.

Maleshi scanned the piles of soiled cushions with a grimace. "Business must be booming if you haven't found the time to clean up in here a little."

Gúrdu waved his clawed hand toward the silver tray on one of the low tables, this one with two hookahs. A thin tendril of smoke rose from the dish at the top of one of the devices, and Cheyenne went out of her way to avoid that table and whatever the raug had been smoking there. The silver tray rose from the table and floated across the room toward the Oracle's raised platform of a throne. When it settled beside the raug, who was sitting cross-legged on another pile of soiled cushions, the halfling nudged a pillow beside Maleshi with the toe of her shoe.

"It's fine if you don't think about who sat down before you," the Nightstalker whispered.

"Or breathe through your nose." Cheyenne lowered herself onto the pillow and crossed her legs too.

Gúrdu went through the same weird raug ritual—another bundle of thin twigs dipped into the bowl of water and dragged down the Oracle's face from his forehead to the underside of his chin. The loud crunch of those twigs between his sharp, stained teeth filled the room. Gúrdu closed his eyes and munched away.

Cheyenne leaned toward the Nightstalker. "Does he have to do that every time?"

"No, but I've heard it helps an Oracle see whatever it is they're trying to see. Little power boost to their system, you know?"

Even with her drow hearing, the halfling could barely hear Maleshi's words above the crunch of the raug's messy chewing and the grunting snorts that sounded more like a rooting hog than anything else. "Like the Nimlothar seed."

Maleshi smirked and shot Cheyenne a sidelong glance. "Branches of the same tree, kid."

"He's eating Nimlothar sticks?"

"Not the tastiest treat, probably, but mozzarella cheese sticks don't pack the same punch."

The halfling snorted and choked down the small laugh fighting to escape. She shook her head, staring at the base of the raug's platform. *Doesn't mean I'll forget about what happened at the portal.*

As if the Nightstalker could read her thoughts, Maleshi leaned toward Cheyenne and dipped her chin. "If you have to hold a grudge, kid, I get it. You wouldn't be the first, and I can handle it. Just try to put that aside while we're here because I want you to pay attention."

Cheyenne clenched her jaw. "Is this a lesson you want me to learn?"

"No. Only an idiot commissions an Oracle without a witness."

"What?" The halfling looked into Maleshi's glowing eyes as the raug kept munching.

"Don't get all worked up. He's not gonna attack me. I think."

"Great." Cheyenne turned back toward the platform against the wall and cocked her head. "I'm just here to say I saw the whole thing if he does."

"Don't put words in my mouth, kid. Prophecies get a little...dicey. I didn't have the supplies on me to set up a magical camera, but I had you. Listen to what comes out of the raug's mouth and etch it into your brain. Got it? We'll have to go back through it if we want to make any sense of his blabbering later."

The halfling pressed her lips together and fought the urge to step outside into the fresh autumn air and wait for the Nightstalker there. "Fine. But you're gonna get a bill for personal assistant hours."

"Ha. I might have to transfer this IOU—"

"Offering!" Gúrdu's low, gravelly voice thundered across the room.

Cheyenne and Maleshi both jumped a little on their cushions. The Nightstalker sighed and shot the half-drow a perturbed look, then lifted the fractured beetle carapace in both hands and raised it toward the Oracle. "The offering."

When Gúrdu opened his eyes, they were focused on the shell glinting in the light of the flickering lanterns around them. He flicked his clawed hand toward the Nightstalker, and the black shell rose into the air to drift toward him. Those red claws met around the fragment of the nightmarish in-between creature as he snatched it from the air. Then he gripped the shell with both hands and lowered it into his lap with a low hum. His eyes closed again. "Ask."

Maleshi took a deep breath and stared at the carapace. "How did the offering's source break from the in-between into this world, and how do we stop it?"

The raug's upper lip lifted in a snarl, exposing his stained teeth and the bits of Nimlothar twigs caught between them. "That is more than you are allowed."

"Saving your life allows me to ask as many questions as I want, Gúrdu. Don't fuck with me."

A rumbling laugh escaped the Oracle, but he said nothing more.

The room fell silent. The flames in all the lanterns flickered in a breeze with no source. Cheyenne looked at them just before every flame in every lantern flared to three times its normal height. The low glow of the flames darkened to an eerie, venomous green. Then every ounce of warmth was sucked out of the room.

The halfling hunched over her crossed legs and gritted her teeth to keep from shivering. Maleshi let out a slow breath, staring intently at the beetle-thing carapace. Her breath puffed out of her like smoke, and the thin crackle of quickly formed ice rose from the bowl of water beside the Oracle as it froze over.

Gúrdu's eyelids fluttered, and when he opened his eyes again, they gave off the same eerie green light despite being entirely white. His voice echoed through the room when he spoke, not his voice alone, but in at least half a dozen different others from monstrously low to almost a shriek. "The rot in the center of the heart spreads. There is nothing left within, so it searches now for new flesh to consume. What starts within will end without, and the cycle will turn back before its doom."

The flames roared even higher in the lanterns before falling to a still-abnormal height. When the Oracle drew a long, wheezing breath, Maleshi swayed a little on the cushion beside Cheyenne.

"The one who sees valor in disgrace will fall. The one brought forth in darkness will wield the blade. Cut out the heart, cut out the rot. The shackles of the old laws rise. For the last scion, it is destiny or chains."

Maleshi lurched forward where she sat. Cheyenne turned toward her and saw the Nightstalker's eyes glazed with the vicious green of the flames. Puffs of steam burst in quick succession between the ex-general's parted lips.

If they don't snap out of this in the next minute, I'll climb up on that platform and stop it myself.

"Blood bonds with blood tied to chaos!" The last word barked out of the Oracle's mouth in all those unnerving voices. The green flames in the lanterns roared before snuffing out all at once. Even with the lights on in the hall outside, the room was plunged into darkness. Something cracked and splintered by the platform, then the only sounds came from Maleshi and Gúrdu, both of them breathing slowly and steadily.

Cheyenne lifted a hand toward the Heart of Midnight pendant beneath her hoodie, holding her breath to listen. *What the hell is this?*

The lanterns burst to life again with regular-sized flame and yellow light. The intense cold disappeared, replaced by the apartment's normal temperature, which now felt balmy in comparison. Even so, the halfling shivered and rubbed one arm through her hoodie sleeve.

Maleshi let out a little moan, but before Cheyenne could ask if she was okay, the Nightstalker sat up straight again. Her eyelids fluttered open, and she smacked her lips. "Cranberries. Still."

Gúrdu cleared his throat several times and lifted his massive gray head. His eyes had returned to their normal orange glow too, narrowing as they flicked from one side of the room to the other. Then he glanced down at the shattered fragments of the beetle carapace littering the edge of the platform in front of him. "You failed to mention all the threads tied to this one, General."

Maleshi's nostrils flared as she flicked her tongue against her teeth in distaste. "If I knew of all the threads, *Oracle*, we wouldn't be having this conversation."

"We shouldn't have had it in the first place." Gúrdu leaned sideways to snatch the bowl of water off the silver tray. He flicked the surface with a red claw, shattering the layer of ice, then guzzled the whole thing in under five seconds. Water and bits of twig streamed from the corners of his mouth and off his gray chin. The bowl clattered across the platform when he tossed it aside and wiped his lips with the back of a hand. "You're in over your head."

"Not the first time I've heard that." Maleshi rolled her shoulders and grunted. "And I'm still in one piece. I'll take it with a grain of salt if you don't mind."

"Salt in an open wound." Gúrdu rocked backward as he let out a massive belch. A puff of shimmering green light burst from his mouth and disappeared.

Maleshi leaned toward Cheyenne again. "Did you get all that?"

"Yeah." The halfling stared at her friend with wide eyes. "What happened to *you*?"

"I got my prophecy, kid. That was the easy part."

"And the hard part is…"

"Figuring out what the hell it means." The Nightstalker slapped her hands down on her knees, nodded, and pushed up off the cushions. "It's been real, raug. Now we're even."

Gúrdu slid a clawed finger through the pile of shattered shell in front of him. "Hardly."

"Yeah, well, next time I'll bring payment. What're you charging for your space-case drivel these days, anyway?"

"More than you can afford to give if you pursue this."

"I've heard that one before too. Unless you prophesy something with my name in it and the words 'you will die,' I'll take my chances. A hunch from you isn't another prophecy, Gúrdu. We both know that."

Cheyenne stood and eyed the raug. *He knows something.*

The Oracle looked up from the shattered pile and glanced at the halfling and the Nightstalker. Then his finger lifted and pointed at Cheyenne. "She should have been the one to offer and ask."

"Well, *she's* not the one calling in the favor, is she?" Maleshi dusted off her pants and stepped carefully between the pillows scattered around them. "And if I can't afford another prophecy now, I sure as hell can't pay for the kid."

"You wouldn't have to." The raug lowered his hand again. "This one lies at the center of more than one thread."

"You don't say. Only a complete moron couldn't figure that out. Come on, Cheyenne. I'm feeling creepy-crawly, and the smell in here's gonna make me sick."

As the Nightstalker made her way through the mess of cushions and ash and dust and whatever else was probably growing beneath all of it, Cheyenne found herself unable to move. "What does that mean?"

"Really? I've got a prophecy hangover, and I'm gonna hurl. How much more transparent can it get?" Maleshi reached the end of the sea of pillows and stumbled before catching herself with a hand against the wall. She looked over her shoulder and glanced wildly around the room before finding that Cheyenne hadn't moved. "Oh, for crying out loud!"

"That I'm at the center of more than one thread," the halfling muttered with a shrug. "What is that?"

The Oracle's orange eyes widened. "Is that your ask, then?"

"Yeah, I'm asking you what that means." Cheyenne flexed her fingers by her sides. *And I'd be threatening him with drow magic again if it wasn't for this stupid pendant.* "You said it, and now you need to tell me what you mean by that. What are all the threads?"

A slow, devious smile spread across the raug's thick gray lips. "Make an offering, drow."

CHAPTER EIGHTY-FIVE

"Oh, no. No, no, no. Stop. Cut. Do not pass Go." Maleshi shuffled back across the sea of pillows, reaching out toward the halfling. She almost fell on her face before she got to Cheyenne and brought a hand down firmly on the half-drow's shoulder. "It's time to get outta here, kid. This guy's brain's been fried by at least a dozen trees worth of magic sticks by now."

The halfling scowled at the Nightstalker. "I want to hear—"

"Zip. Zip it. Not another word." Maleshi tugged on Cheyenne's hoodie and nodded toward the door into the hall. "I'm serious. We'll talk outside."

Cheyenne's shoulders ached with the tension of her anger and she had no way to let it out. She glanced at the Oracle, who leaned back against the mass of cushions behind him and chuckled. *He's playing me.*

That only made it worse. Rolling her shoulders, the halfling followed Maleshi through the scattered cushions and the low round tables dotting the huge room. The Nightstalker wagged a finger at the Oracle, gesturing for Cheyenne to go ahead. "You're cutting it close today, Gúrdu. If you spent as much time out there in the real world as you do sitting on your ass pretending to know more than everyone else, you'd be reworking that opinion on false honor. Don't make me remind you again."

Without waiting for a response, the Nightstalker staggered out of the room. The raug Oracle's deep, rumbling laughter followed her like a bad dream. She had to steady herself again on the doorframe, shaking her head and letting out a long, slow breath.

"You good?" Cheyenne watched her from this side of the beaded curtain.

"Almost. Get me outside, and I'll be as good as new. Or something." Maleshi waved the halfling forward before pushing off. The beads clacked as Cheyenne passed through them. The Nightstalker swiped at the dangling strands to move them aside. She missed half of them and got a face full of dangling beads. "Okay, what...why can't he just..."

With a hiss, she grabbed two thick handfuls of the dangling strands and ripped them down from the ceiling. The wooden bar holding them all together at the top tore free from its hook and thumped against her back as she ducked to avoid it. After a mad scramble to get the things off her, the whole beaded curtain and the wooden rod clattered to the floor. Maleshi lashed out with a final irritated kick, missed, and almost fell flat on her ass in the process.

"Need a hand?" Cheyenne frowned in concern as the ex-general reeled and finally steadied herself.

"I need a drink. Two. I need—" Maleshi hunched, her eyes bulging, and pressed a hand against her stomach. "Out."

The halfling didn't wait to see her friend waving her toward the front door. She jogged down the rest of the hall before opening the door and holding it for the magic-sick Nightstalker.

Maleshi stumbled through, smacking her lips again and scowling. "I hate cranberries. I bet he does that just to screw with me."

Cheyenne pulled the door shut behind her and gave the ex-general a wide berth. "Yeah, you two seemed pretty close."

"Ha." With a deep breath, the Nightstalker straightened and held her hands out in front of her. When she didn't puke, she nodded and shot the halfling a thin smile. "Some friends are made by necessity, kid. At the time, my choices were to either let one of maybe a few hundred Oracles go down with the rest of his clan or to sneak the seven-foot POW past my men and kick his ass Earthside. Looks like my momentary lapse in brutality worked out for all of us."

Shoving her hands into her pockets again, the halfling glanced back at the Oracle's closed front door as she and the Nightstalker headed back down the breezy hallway toward the apartment building's front door. "He's been here longer than you."

"You know, a little stretch of the imagination, and you could say that about every Oracle in existence. But technically speaking? Yeah. By several centuries, give or take." A silver light flashed at the Nightstalker's fingertips, and the centuries-old human illusion of Mattie Bergmann replaced the ex-general's feline appearance.

Cheyenne stepped through the battered door and held it open for her friend. "None of that sounds like a friendship of necessity."

"Well, it is for him, I guess." When Maleshi stepped out into the crisp autumn air, she perked up a little more. "Didn't stop him from trying to lure you into his weaselly little claws, did it?"

The halfling looked as dumbfounded as she had the first day she'd stepped into Mattie Bergmann's office for a chat about magic.

Maleshi cocked her head. "You almost got roped into a prophecy back there, kid. Anything you said next could have and would have been used against you in that nasty room."

"Because I wanted him to explain himself?" Cheyenne shook her head as they headed down the short path toward the sidewalk. "I asked him plenty of questions the last time I was here, and hey, not even an accidental prophecy."

"That's the way they are. Oracles." The Nightstalker shook her head, and a little shudder traveled down her spine. "Sounded a lot like he wanted to give you a free reading, kid. Which means if you'd kept pushing him, you would've found yourself using up a free ticket for a prophecy you didn't want. That just muddies the waters, you know?"

"Not really. I'd still have more answers than I got out of him."

"No, you wouldn't." They reached the Panamera, which was

parked a full fifteen inches from the curb, and stopped on the side-walk. "Asking the wrong question with one of those guys is like putting arcade tokens into a vending machine. Only works if you're still in the arcade. I think."

Cheyenne rolled her eyes and stepped around the front of her car toward the driver's side door. "I guess the next time I need a *real* prophecy and have an offering or whatever, I get a freebie."

Maleshi burped and grimaced, smacking her lips again. "If you do, kid, don't let him tell you he doesn't remember saying you don't have to pay. Raug don't forget many things. A raug Oracle holds onto every tiny detail before and after it happens. And speaking of the *next time*, what happened the first time?"

"I brought him the legacy box like you said I should."

"Oh, yeah." The Nightstalker chuckled even as her normally healthy color faded. "Way back when you and I only *thought* we knew each other. How'd he take it?"

The Porsche let out a chirp when Cheyenne unlocked it with the keyless fob and a smile that didn't feel quite so forced. "Nearly pissed himself and said he wouldn't touch that box to save his life. Apparently, it's scarier than a raging half-drow holding an attack spell under his nose."

A weak, distracted laugh rose from Maleshi's throat. "Some-times, it's better not to know—"

The words cut off as the Nightstalker pressed her lips together and hunched forward again.

Cheyenne shot her a sympathetic frown. "You're looking a little green over there. You sure you're okay?"

"Oh, yeah. I'll be fine. I just need—" Maleshi let out a strangled heave and reached for the handle of the passenger-side door. "Let's get goin', kid. I need a six-pack and a whole box of saltines."

The Panamera's locks chirped again just before the Nightstalker tugged on the door handle.

She looked at Cheyenne and shook her head. "What are you doing?"

"You're not getting in my car until you puke or can stand there for two minutes without looking like you're about to."

"Come on, Cheyenne. You're overreacting. I'm fine." Maleshi swallowed thickly and failed to look fine. "It'll pass, okay? It's like reverse car-sickness. I just need to keep moving."

"Not in the Porsche." The halfling eyed her friend and slowly raised her shoulders in a shrug. "I'm *really* into the new-car smell. Not gonna risk it."

"I'm not—" Maleshi blinked, staggered back, then turned away from the car and vomited on the dry brown grass in front of the small apartment building. It was quick and violent, and then it was over. Sighing, the Nightstalker straightened and turned to give Cheyenne an exasperated look. "There. Are you happy now?"

"I'd be happier if you'd held back your hair."

Maleshi grabbed a section of thick, wavy black hair resting over her shoulder and snorted in disgust. "That's what friends are for, isn't it?"

"Not when you didn't give me any warning."

"Okay, you know what? Fine." The ex-general could only keep up the ruse of being insulted for so long. A defeated chuckle escaped her. "No, I'm not gonna make you drive me home like this. Just go. I feel loads better, so we're good."

"You sure?"

"Do I still look green?"

Cheyenne smirked. "Nope."

"There you go." Maleshi glanced up and down the quiet street and lifted her hands. A quickly muttered spell and some hand gestures later, the Nightstalker gestured to a brand-new portal hovering over the sidewalk in front of her. "I'm going home. So should you. Grab some dinner, put up your feet, and as soon as I know what happens next, you'll be the first person to hear about it."

"Okay." Cheyenne let herself smile at the woman who'd started her journey toward controlling a halfling's drow magic. *Even if she's not who I thought she was.* "I guess I'll...see you tomorrow?"

"Nope. I'll be teaching my own class, kid. Just check your email and don't worry too much about standing up in front of a bunch of students who are pretty much your age. You'll be fine."

"Sounds like an hour and a half in paradise."

Shaking her head, Maleshi stepped through the portal into what looked like the inside of her house, then she and the doorway of dark light disappeared with a little pop.

Cheyenne blinked and unlocked her car again before sliding behind the wheel. With the door shut, the engine started, and the seatbelt buckled, she shot one more glance out the window at Gúrdu's ramshackle apartment building and snorted. "And I thought *yesterday* was a lot."

CHAPTER EIGHTY-SIX

The sun had almost set by the time the elevator doors opened on the top floor of the Pellerville Gables Apartments. Cheyenne's footsteps dragged down the hall toward the only apartment on the left at the end of the hall. The keys jingled a little longer than normal as she fought to slide the right one into the lock. She smelled the pizza even before she opened the door but didn't stop to consider what the two chatting voices inside her apartment signified.

"Hey, Cheyenne." Ember wheeled away from the kitchen island, grinning until she saw the look on her friend's face. "Woah. Long day, huh?"

The halfling raised her eyebrows, glancing from the fae to their tall, *dabbling entrepreneur* of a neighbor standing over the island with a pizza cutter in hand. "Something like that."

She headed toward the black leather couch across from the black leather recliners on the other side of the coffee table. Her backpack was right where she'd left it on the floor, and she only paused after she'd slung the strap over her shoulder. "The couch is new, right?"

"Yeah. That came in after you left this morning."

"Nice touch, Em." Nodding, Cheyenne shuffled across the room, now cleared of packing materials and empty boxes, and passed the iron staircase that led to the mini-loft on the way to her bedroom. She looked up at the loft, then shook her head. *I can't even think about computers right now.*

With a quick glance at Matthew, Ember wheeled across the huge living room and muttered, "Just give me a sec, okay? I'll be right back."

"No problem. This pizza's not gonna cut itself."

The door to Cheyenne's room opened swiftly, and the halfling didn't bother to shut it before shrugging her backpack off and dropping it on the floor. Her black Vans thumped across the room, and her eyelids drooped as she stared at the purple velvet bedspread and all the pillows piled beneath the draping canopy of black lace and satin. *I can't think about anything.*

Climbing onto the bed took the rest of her energy. She flopped over onto her back and stared at the peak of the draping curtains where they connected at the hook on the ceiling. Just then, Ember reached her open door and knocked.

Cheyenne gave a humorless laugh. "That's new, you knocking on *my* door this time."

"Yeah, well, no visiting hours in this place." The fae girl smiled softly, her nose wrinkling in concern. "Figured I'd check in really quick. You okay?"

"Yeah, Em. Or at least I will be." The halfling spread her arms across the mattress. "I just need some rest, I think. Rough day."

"I can tell. You hungry?"

"Not now. You guys go ahead and enjoy it. If there's any left, I'll grab it later."

"I'll make sure to save you a piece or two. Or should we get a second pizza?"

They both laughed a little, and Cheyenne pushed herself up onto her elbows to look at her friend. "I'm not in a whole-pizza mood tonight, but thanks."

Ember nodded, her blue eyes taking in the halfling's wild black hair, the dirt smudges on her cheeks, and the punctures in the bottom of her left pantleg. "If you need anything, let me know."

"Thanks. I'll tell you all about it later, Em. I just can't even right now."

"No problem." Ember glanced over her shoulder, then leaned forward and whispered, "I'm kicking Matthew out after we eat, just so you know."

With a snort, Cheyenne nodded. "Does *he* know that?"

"Not yet. But almost a whole day with the guy next door reminded me why I chose to live alone in the first place."

"Let me know if you need someone to muscle him outta here."

"Yeah, okay." Ember wheeled backward out the door, then deftly spun the chair and headed back into the kitchen, laughing. "Who taught you how to cut a pizza?"

"What? You mean it's not an inherent skill?"

"For most people, probably. Oh, come on. You—" The fae laughed again. "How hard is it to cross the lines in the middle?"

"Oh, okay. Next time I'll break out the ruler and find dead-center."

Cheyenne rolled off the bed and lumbered toward the door to gently close out all the noise.

"I don't need dead-center, Matthew, but *that's* halfway between the middle of the pizza and the crust—"

The door shut with a soft click, and the halfling pressed both hands against the wall to hang her head between her arms. *As long as she's having a good time, I can ignore the noise. No problem.*

She slid her hands off the door and turned back toward the bed. Her gaze fell on her backpack, and she paused.

A faint golden light spilled through the seams of her backpack, pulsing every few seconds. Cheyenne bent down with a groan and rummaged until her fingers closed around the cold metal of her drow puzzle box. The second she took it out, the golden light behind the drow runes faded and didn't return.

The halfling turned the box over in her hands, studying the symbols. *That one wasn't there before.*

She tapped the center band of the five that made up the *Cuil Ani's* spinning layers. *One more down. Only two more to go.* "Whoop-de-doo."

Taking the copper box with her, Cheyenne headed back to her bed and fell onto it. The legacy box clinked onto the bedside table, and the drow halfling turned onto her side. With the light still on and the velvet comforter still beneath her, she fell asleep in seconds, too exhausted and numb to think about anything else.

Cheyenne's dreams were eerily like those she'd had of L'zar's prophecy before Corian had given her the magic-dampening pendant, only this time, they were all smashed together. She dreamed of the clearing at the new Border portal instead of the dark, cold room of black stone smeared with blood. The cloaked figure kneeling in the center of all the dead drow bodies wasn't L'zar or his halfling daughter but Maleshi Hi'et, her green eyes glowing above that wickedly predatory grin. The Oracle Gúrdu's voice mixed with a woman's as they laughed together in the same cadence. Black, glistening tentacles rose from the dark spires of the portal ridge. A beetle-thing scurried and scrambled along on its hundreds of legs.

Then the halfling *became* the portal, rising higher than any of the jutting spears of black stone, stretching out like the black wall of shimmering light across the entire clearing. The tentacles waving around and bashing the fallen drow bodies were her black tendrils of magic shooting from unseen hands.

The beetle-thing shrieked and jumped around to face her. When it reared on its back legs and exposed its underbelly, L'zar's distorted face had replaced the nightmarish creature's gaping red mouth, and when he spoke, Bianca Summerlin's voice emerged. *"Blood bonds with blood tied to chaos. Everything has a price!"*

With a startled gasp, Cheyenne jolted up in her bed. "Jesus, these fucking dreams."

She ran the back of her hand across her forehead and the thin layer of sweat coating it. Hissing in frustration, the halfling tugged at the hem of her baggy hoodie. The front of it was soaked through with sweat, making the thing almost impossible to peel off. She finally got it over her head and tossed it onto the floor with a heavy thump.

"Gross." After trying to air out her long-sleeved shirt, she dropped her hands onto the bed. "Like that's gonna work."

Pulling her phone out of her pocket, she woke the screen and blinked at the time. *Seven fifty-two. Is that...yep. Eleven hours of sleep.*

The halfling ran a hand through her sweat-soaked hair and scratched her head a little. Then she slid off the bed and went to the window. The blackout curtains rustled when she swept them aside. Morning sunlight spilled into her room, and she jerked her head away with a groan. *Good thing my class schedule changed.*

Her hand rose to the Heart of Midnight pendant, which was resting a little higher on her breastbone now that she'd tied so many knots in the repeatedly broken silver chain. *Looks like this thing's starting to wear off. Not so great for trying to lay low.*

Cheyenne pulled the blackout curtain over the window again, rolled her shoulders, and nodded. A small, pulsing ache rose from her left ankle, and she stuck out her foot to look down at the puncture marks around the hem of her pantleg. *Should've looked at that sooner.*

Grimacing, the halfling went back to her backpack on the floor, sat beside it, and pulled out the brown glass jar of healing salve Yadje had given her. When she rolled up her pantleg, she sucked in a hissing breath and studied the half-dozen round punctures encircling her ankle. "Ugh. Could be worse, I guess."

She bent her knee to pull her ankle closer as she gave the jar's lid a quick twist. The sharp smell of rotting strawberries blasted her in the face, making her nostrils flare. *Anything less than a knife wound, huh? I'm trusting you, R'mahr.*

The white salve was thick and sticky, stretching like taffy when she scooped out the first bit with her fingers. "Great. Like putting Persh'al's mohawk gel on a magical monster bite." She snorted, got the stringy goo to separate, and dabbed a little onto the first puncture.

An icy jolt shot through her ankle, followed by a searing heat that flared all the way to the tips of her toes. Cheyenne sucked in a sharp breath and thumped her fist on the polished wooden floor beneath her. "Shit."

With watering eyes, she squinted at her ankle and leaned forward for a better look. The agonizing burn subsided a little, and the puncture wound sealed itself from the inside out, closing up muscle and split skin until there was nothing left but flakes of dried blood. A low chuckle of surprise escaped her. "Oh, *shit*."

The halfling stared at the glob of white goo on the tips of her fingers and grinned. "This is gonna suck."

She transferred a bit into her other hand, rubbed her fingers together, then breathed deeply and smeared the salve over the other puncture wounds encircling her ankle. Clenching her teeth, she grunted and threw her head back to grimace at the ceiling while the salve burned through her leg and five more wounds. The halfling beat the floor with the heel of her fist, forcing herself to breathe through it and count. Twenty seconds, then the pain subsided enough for her to lean forward and watch the other five holes seal up around her ankle.

Just to be sure, she ran her fingers along the perfectly smooth healed skin, then dusted off flakes of dried blood. *Just like that. Damn. I'd take a black-magic potion to the shoulder over that any day.*

Cheyenne snorted, then a sharp laugh escaped her. When she imagined herself stuffing those two holes in her shoulder with darktongue salve from a socially confused troll, the halfling doubled over and howled with laughter. *Here I am. Finally lost my mind.*

It took her another minute to calm down, then she wiped the tears from the corners of her eyes with the back of a hand and sniffed. Another chuckle escaped her, and the fully healed drow halfling shook her head before closing the jar. "Hell of a way to start the day. Jesus."

She stood, absently wiped the last of the sticky salve on her pantlegs, then opened her bedroom door and stepped out into the apartment.

"Someone's in a better mood," Ember called from the kitchen. The halfling peered across the apartment, squinting with heavy eyelids until the fae wheeled around the island with a grin.

"Took a lot to get there."

"Bet you slept like a rock, huh?"

"Just until the end." Cheyenne cleared her throat. "Sorry I wasn't up to help you with...whatever."

"Oh. Yeah." Ember spread her arms and glanced around the apartment. "I obviously needed you."

"Ha-ha." Walking toward her friend, the halfling blinked heavily and took a deep sniff. "And you made coffee."

"Best part of waking up, right? This stuff's supposed to be killer." Ember sniggered and lifted the heavy-duty thermal coffee mug from where she'd wedged it in her lap. "Just finished brewing, if you want some."

"Yeah, I do." When Cheyenne reached the kitchen, she smirked as Ember expertly spun her wheelchair to follow the halfling toward the counter. "Man, just the smell is getting me caffeinated."

"That's nothing."

The half-drow glanced at the bag of coffee sitting beside the coffeemaker—black with a white skull and crossbones in the center and the bold-text brand name scrawled across the top. Just to be sure, she picked up the bag and studied it at a closer angle. "Death Wish Coffee, huh?"

"I said it was killer."

Cheyenne chuckled. "This is my kinda coffee. You find this stuff online to match my Goth box?"

"Uh, no, actually." Ember lifted the coffee mug to her lips and took an unusually long slurp from the hole in the lid. "Matthew brought it over."

The coffee bag thumped back onto the counter. "Of course he did."

"His only condition for offering a friendly one-pound bag of neighborly coffee was that I convince you to try it."

Cheyenne squinted at the fae. "He obviously didn't consider that saying it's from him would convince me *not* to try it."

"No, but *I* did. And I call bullshit."

The halfling shot the bag of coffee—perfectly matched to her Goth tastes—a sidelong glance. Then she shrugged and opened the cabinet above the coffee maker to pull down a mug. "Good thing you know me better than he does."

"It would be weird if I didn't." Ember laughed. "There's creamer in the fridge."

"I'm good." Cheyenne filled the mug to the brim and bent over to slurp as much as she could off the top. "Dammit."

"I know."

"Now I'm gonna have to thank the guy for turning me on to..." The halfling picked up the coffee bag again and read over the label. "'World's strongest coffee.' They can actually put that on the packaging and get away with it. Unbelievable."

"Unbelievably *delicious*." Laughing, the fae raised her to-go mug again for another sip. "I think I'm in love."

Cheyenne snorted. "Okay, I'll thank Mr. Matthew Thomas for the coffee, but you're gonna have to tell him that last part yourself."

"What? Shut up. I meant the coffee." Ember wound her arm back with the coffee mug held tightly in her hand and pretended to throw the whole thing at the laughing half-drow.

"Yeah, yeah, yeah." Cheyenne leaned against the counter and brought the mug to her lips with both hands. "I'm with you on the coffee part, at least."

They stayed like that, sipping their beverages. Ember cocked her head and studied her friend's tangled nest of black hair and the sweat stains barely visible on her black shirt. "More bad dreams?"

"Wow. You're takin' pages right outta *Sherlock Holmes*, aren't ya?"

"Seriously, Cheyenne. I don't know why you're *still* surprised when people can see what's going on. It's written all over your face."

"Yeah, people keep saying that."

Ember smirked. "This time it's written in dirt, though."

"Oh." Cheyenne wiped her cheek and smeared a streak of sweat and dirt.

"Aw. That just made it worse."

"Okay. In lieu of wanting to drink the best cup of coffee I've had in a ridiculously long time while it's still hot, are you up for ignoring the way I look right now so I can drink the Death Wish and tell you all about it?"

"Halfling, I thought you'd never ask." Ember wedged the to-go mug between her legs again and wheeled herself across the kitchen and into the massive living room. "And just FYI, I've been ignoring the way you look since we met."

"How very thoughtful of you." Cheyenne pressed her lips together through another smile and followed her friend toward the new black leather couch and the matching recliners. "Next, you're gonna say you never judge a book by its cover, and the only thing that matters is what's on the inside."

The fae pulled her wheelchair up to the edge of the black and silver area rug and shot the halfling a condescending look. "No, next I'm gonna tell you to quit being such a smartass and get to the good stuff already."

"How 'bout one outta two?" Cheyenne lowered herself onto the leather recliner closest to her friend. "I don't think I moved an inch all night."

"You know, I almost came to check on you. Then I figured it was in my best interests not to get my head blown off by a cranky drow halfling needing her beauty rest."

Laughing, the half-drow ruffled her mussed, damp hair, then waved her hand in a circle around her face. "Obviously, that was successful."

"Okay, I know I'm the one who brought it up, but if you can promise me this is the last time we ever say the words 'beauty sleep' again, I'm willing to forget this part of the conversation ever happened."

"Deal." Cheyenne hovered over her steaming mug of coffee and took a long sip. "Okay. Where do you want me to start?"

"How about right after you bounced yesterday morning, rambling about urgent messages and driving to DC?"

"Huh." the halfling nodded slowly and lifted the mug over the side of the armchair so she could pull her legs up off the floor and cross them beneath her. "That feels like three days ago."

"Uh-huh. So does spending all day with our friendly neighbor, who's apparently got an endless supply of ways to 'make himself useful' and excuses to stick around a little longer." Ember smirked over the lid of her mug and took another sip when her friend snorted. "Just a heads-up. 'I've got some time to kill,' is Matthew Thomas code for 'I'll be here all day unless you tell me without smiling that you don't want me here anymore.'"

"That's what you had to tell him, huh?"

"Yeah, and he thought I was joking at first." Ember raised her eyebrows and stared at the coffee table.

"Ouch."

"You know what? It's good practice for me. Forget Sherlock Holmes. I'm taking a page out of the halfling's book. You don't give a shit what anyone else thinks."

Cheyenne licked her lips and tried not to laugh. "Well, don't try to be too much like me, Em. I'm pretty sure that's how I keep getting myself into these screwed-up situations. You're gonna think I'm making this up when I tell you what happened yesterday."

Ember spread her arms and leaned forward in her chair to shout, "So why the hell are we still talking about it? Storytime. Go!"

CHAPTER EIGHTY-SEVEN

When Cheyenne finished rattling off the major points of her messed-up Sunday, Ember blinked and lifted her mug to her lips again. It tilted all the way up before she realized it was empty and jammed it back into her lap. "I'm gonna take a wild guess and go with eighty percent."

The halfling laughed and folded her arms, her right leg slung over one of the recliner's armrests while she leaned back against the other. She'd put her empty mug on the coffee table halfway through the tale. "Eighty percent of what is what?"

"Eighty percent of that story is total bull."

The housemates stared at each other, and Cheyenne almost pushed up out of her chair before Ember barked a laugh. The halfling rolled her eyes and flipped her friend the middle finger. "You gotta cut that out."

"When it puts that look on your face? No way."

"I'm not a gullible person, and you still get me every single time."

Ember shook her hair out of her face and laughed until it ran its course. "I'm just that good. And I'm probably the only person in the world who'd believe everything that just came out of your mouth."

"Maybe." The halfling shrugged. *Except for Bianca Summerlin.*

"Don't call it a lie of omission, Cheyenne. Think of it as a tactful represen-tation of the truth you want to present." She snorted at her mom's voice ringing so clearly through her head.

"What?" Ember's lips curled into a sly smile.

"That's why you're the only person in the world I tell this crap to, Em."

"I'm honored by all your crappy stories. You know that."

"Yeah, whatever."

The fae wheeled herself back and forth, squinting at the abstract paintings hanging on the wall beside the front door. "It sounds like everybody knows about L'zar Verdys' halfling daughter, huh?"

"I guess so. And apparently, all I have to do now is finish the trials to 'claim my legacy,' fight off living nightmares that aren't supposed to exist outside the portal, *and* stop a war between both sides of the Border with L'zar's number-one guy and the greatest O'gúl, General Turncloak, who'd rather kill everyone than be a team player. Did I mention she used to be my Advanced Algorithms professor?"

"You covered it pretty thoroughly, yeah." Neither of them could contain themselves, and they both burst out laughing again. "Just minor requirements for the spawn of a rebellion leader, right?"

"Don't even go there." Cheyenne dropped her head back against the recliner's soft, cool leather cushion. "I'm gonna be pinching myself every ten minutes to make sure this is still real."

Ember shrugged. "No one ever said Cheyenne Summerlin has a boring life."

"Ha. No one ever said anything about anything. Man, if I'd just cornered Maleshi in her office a week ago and shouted that L'zar Verdys is my incarcerated drow dad, I would've been way more prepared for yesterday."

"Maybe. Sounded like you handled it pretty well, though."

The halfling said, "I'm workin' on it. Not sure how I'm gonna keep it together when this stupid necklace shorts out and I'm just wearing a pretty O'gúleesh rock."

"Start a souvenir box."

"You're ridiculous."

Ember threw her head back and let out a full-on belly laugh. "I'm serious. You're over halfway done with the trials. That box is gonna open right up, and bada-bing, you're a super-powerful drow halfling. You'll pull out that pendant just to remind yourself of the good ol' days."

"Right before I smack L'zar across the face with it."

"Or that." Ember stopped rolling and propped one elbow on the opposite arm, stroking her chin. "When's the old man gonna break out again?"

Cheyenne shook her head. "When he's certain it won't kill me, or something stupid like that."

"Oh, of course. What an asshole thing to do, right? *Man*, that's so infuriatingly selfish. This guy inadvertently killed dozens of his kids over who knows how many centuries, and he's finally playing it safe with *you*. You know what? I hope he rots behind those bars."

"Okay, okay. Damn."

Ember raised an eyebrow at her halfling friend with a mischievous smirk. "Don't think I didn't notice how long you let me go on with that before you stopped me."

Cheyenne scoffed and rolled her eyes. "I get it. He doesn't wanna start all over again with some other unconceived kid if anything happens to me. Not like he'd have a lot of time for that at this point anyway."

The fae clicked her tongue. "You realize people *do* still hook up during a war, right?"

"Look at you, throwing around the word 'war' just like Maleshi."

"Equally creepy is that it only took you twenty-four hours to stop calling her Mattie."

The halfling ran her hands down her face and groaned. "I don't think Mattie Bergmann's coming back, at least not anytime soon. That Nightstalker general is one seriously nutso badass."

"It makes perfect sense why you still like her so much." Ember grinned and spread her arms. "If you were a cat-woman, you'd wanna grow up to be just like her."

"Nah, I wanna grow up to be just like me, thanks."

The fae pumped her arm and talked out of the side of her mouth. "That'sh the shpirit."

"Why did we think sharing an apartment was a good idea again?"

Ember's laughter was so contagious, Cheyenne couldn't help but join her. Then the fae settled down and shook her head. "Seriously, though. Have you considered that L'zar does just want to protect you? I mean, serving a hundred-year sentence at Chateau D'rahl just to protect his only kid sounds like an acceptable sacrifice to me."

"He's not sacrificing anything." The halfling swung her leg back over the armrest and sat up straight in the chair. "Corian told me the guy's only interested if there's something in it for him, and at this point, I'm gonna call that one an accurate assessment."

"Huh. You really don't think L'zar would go out on a limb to help anyone but himself?"

"Not if he wasn't also helping himself at the same time, no." Cheyenne shrugged and leaned forward. "So, he's playing it safe until he knows his bargaining chip isn't gonna drop dead like all the others the second he steps out of that prison, which he could totally do whenever he wants. I'm starting to think he's having fun in there."

Ember snorted and pulled her coffee mug out of her lap again before remembering one more time that it was empty. "Any idea what he's waiting for?"

"Just a guess, that I complete the trials and come into my true power with my very own drow legacy, and L'zar says the coast is clear. He comes crawling out of his little vacation hole, then I'm stuck taking orders from Captain Whackjob instead."

"Woah." Ember chuckled. "You've got this all planned out, don't you?"

"Actually, it just came to me." Cheyenne shot her friend a wide grin before she wiped it off her face a second later. "Honestly, if this whole nightmare-leaking-portal and imminent-O'gúl-war thing wasn't happening right now, I'd probably stall the trials just to keep him in Chateau D'rahl as long as possible. For fun."

"You know, I have fun with you, Cheyenne, but beyond that, we have two very different definitions of it."

"Yeah, tell me about it." The halfling pulled her phone out of her back pocket to check the time. "And...I just talked your head off for an hour. Coffee's gone. You look violently confused. Time for me to get cleaned up."

Ember laughed and slapped her hands on the armrests of her wheelchair. "I had no idea violently confused was a thing."

"You're one of a kind, Em." Cheyenne pushed to her feet and clapped her hands together. "It's kinda weird that I have to ask, but where did you—"

"Towels are in the bathroom." Ember nodded toward the second full bathroom below the mini-loft.

The halfling froze and blinked at her friend. "Creepy."

"You are *so* easily impressed by me."

Cheyenne just shook her head and waved the fae off as she turned toward the bathroom.

Ember laughed again and drummed her hands on the armrests. "Go get 'em, Professor Summerlin."

When the half-drow opened the bathroom door, she slipped inside and turned to poke her head back out into the living room with wide eyes. "Kill me now."

Her friend's renewed laughter filtered into the bathroom until it was drowned out by the rush of steaming water.

CHAPTER EIGHTY-EIGHT

Cheyenne parked in the student lot on the Virginia Commonwealth University campus and glanced at the clock on the dash. *Fifteen minutes. No wonder Mattie always looked so rushed.*

The halfling turned off the engine and paused. "Maleshi. Shit, I don't know *what* to call her."

She got out of her car and slung her backpack over her shoulder before locking the Panamera with that brilliant little chirp. A kid in a brown suit with an afro closed the door to his restored Ford Pinto and smirked at the Goth chick. "Nice car."

Cheyenne glanced at him and nodded. "Yeah, you too. Goes with the seventies getup."

"The Pinto's mine. This is just a costume." The kid gestured to the brown suit.

Cocking her head, the halfling gave him a crooked smile. "I'm gonna use that line."

"No, really. Theater Department."

"Okay. Break a leg or whatever." With another nod, the half-drow hurried across the parking lot. The kid's laugh rose behind her, and she shook her head. *I played dress-up today too. We'll see how my new students handle it.*

That made her snort, and she quickened her pace as she stepped onto the sidewalk and took the first path across campus toward the T. Edward Temple building.

She heard the conversation of at least a dozen other students, maybe more, before she reached the medium-sized classroom. Another glance at her phone made her sigh before she reached the door. *Nobody thought twice about Professor Bergmann showing up a minute or two late. I'm fine.*

No one noticed the Goth chick storming into the classroom, even when Cheyenne stopped to pull the door shut behind her with a soft click. Then a girl with half her head shaved who was sitting by herself on the far right side of the front row looked at the half-drow with a raised eyebrow. The halfling returned the gesture as she stepped to the front of the room. *Like looking at myself as an undergrad. Weird.*

The conversation didn't falter at all, even when Cheyenne reached the desk at the front of the room and dropped her backpack on the floor. She counted seventeen students in their seats, most of them laughing and joking, two or three besides the half-shaved-head girl reading textbooks or scrolling through their phones.

For a full two minutes, the halfling waited for more than one girl to notice her standing up there. *I could do this for the entire class. Okay, not if I want my master's.*

"All right." Cheyenne cleared her throat, and the students who weren't talking to someone else looked at her in surprise. A kid with a curly mop of black hair and as much of a mustache as he could grow before he could legally drink folded his arms and frowned. The halfling nodded. "Hey."

That didn't have the desired effect either, and Cheyenne thought, *Okay. Gauging the attention span.*

She glanced at the girl in the front row, who watched her with an eerily familiar deadpan expression, and winked. The girl's eyes narrowed, then Cheyenne swept her arm back and up in a huge arc before her fist cracked on the desk.

All conversation cut off instantly. Some of the kids jumped in their seats, and all eyes turned toward the front of the classroom.

Cheyenne smirked. "That's better."

"Who are you?"

"What, no, 'Good morning,' first?" The halfling raised an eyebrow at the short kid two rows back who apparently thought he could bring back button-up plaid shirts and braided hemp necklaces.

"Uh, good morning?"

"Where's Professor Bergmann?" asked a blonde girl with braided pigtails falling over her shoulders.

There's Bryl's human illusion in twelve years. Cheyenne forced herself not to laugh. "Bergmann's moved on to bigger and better things, so you guys are stuck with me." She spread her arms and scanned the dumbfounded faces staring back at her. "Welcome to my class."

"What do you mean, 'bigger and better things?'" That came from the huge kid sitting halfway back who could've doubled as a football player.

The halfling cocked her head. "Kinda self-explanatory, isn't it?"

"But she's still teaching, right?"

"Did something happen to her?"

"So, you're a sub, then."

Leaning away from her desk and the barrage of questions and ridiculous observations, Cheyenne clapped her hands. The smack cracked through the room, and the voices stopped. She shifted her weight onto one hip, folding her arms. "Okay. Yes. No. Absolutely not." She shot a pointed glance at the students who'd shouted out their questions and figured one-word answers were enough.

Still frowning, the kid trying to rock a nineties look raised his hand. Cheyenne raised an eyebrow at him in reply. "You didn't answer *my* question."

"Uh-huh."

"Who are you?"

The halfling rolled her shoulders back. "Just call me Cheyenne.

That's good enough. And just so we're all on the same page, this is Advanced Programming 4200, not Twenty Questions 101. I get it. It's the fourth week of the semester, and just when you thought you had a handle on things, your whole world's crumbling apart because Professor Bergmann shucked this class onto someone else. Yeah?"

Thankfully, no one said anything to that one.

"Awesome. So here's the deal. I'm now teaching this class, and there's a *really* low probability that it's gonna be anything like what you've been doing in here for the last three weeks." Cheyenne tried to hold back a snort and failed. "I'm not gonna take attendance, because I don't give a shit if you're here. That's *your* job. If you show up, you wanna be here, so we have that in common." *I just called myself out on that one, didn't I?* She shook her head and shrugged. "And if you're not in class, you better be able to prove you have a handle on what we're going over and can do the work."

She blinked and glanced from face to face. *Either way I spin that, I sound like a hypocrite. They don't know that.*

"Any other questions? 'Cause this is the only day I'm answering stuff that has nothing to do with Advanced Programming."

"How old are you?" Two guys sitting in the back row smirked. When Cheyenne's gaze darted toward them, the kid on the left leaned over the long desk stretching across the seats and rubbed his forehead to hide his face. The other one stared right back at the halfling and raised his eyebrows once.

"That's cute. You'd pass with flying colors if I was your How to Be an Asshole instructor. Obviously, I'm qualified to teach that one too, but I hope for your sake you can handle *this* class even half as well. We'll see."

Some of the students laughed and looked at each other with wide eyes. The kid rubbing his forehead glanced at his friend and couldn't help a laugh, either. "Oh, shit, dude."

The kid who thought he was funny smirked again, but it looked pissed-off this time. "You're totally a sub."

Cheyenne pressed her fingertips on the desk and leaned forward. *Wow. Channeling Bergmann.* "You sound really sure of that."

"It's obvious." The kid gestured toward her with a flippant wave. "I mean, the school's not gonna bring on Evanescence full time."

The guy's friend stared at him and shook his head.

"Oh. And I even got dressed up for the day." *The black lipstick always seals the deal, doesn't it?* The halfling pursed her lips, the corners of her mouth drawing down as she dipped her head. "Guess I missed the memo about discriminatory hiring based on personal fashion choices. But it doesn't apply to students, right? 'Cause, I mean, *you're* here."

The laughter this time was a little less amused and a lot more nervous. Cheyenne stared at the kid glowering at her and trying not to show it, waiting for him to throw another dud her way. He didn't. *Time to tone it down a notch, Cheyenne. You made your point.*

With a deep breath, she closed her eyes briefly and tapped the desk with her fingertips. "Look, you're all here to learn. I don't care what you look like or how you spend your time outside this class. None of my business. And since we're all legal adults, I'm assuming you guys can handle the fact this goes both ways. If you don't like the way I dress or how I teach, you can suck it up and push through one semester, or you can get out and do something else. Your call, and trust me, I won't lose any sleep over it. But while you're here, I think I've made it perfectly clear that I *will* call you out for screwing around, even if I have to be an asshole about it. Which, by the way, isn't my priority. Showing you guys how to write anything and everything your brains come up with is the only thing I'm here to do. We good?"

The students nodded, glanced at each other, and shifted around in their chairs. The kid who thought he was hot stuff folded his arms, pressed his lips together, and stared at her. *At least he's paying attention.*

"Okay. So." Cheyenne clapped again and didn't know what else to do with her hands, so she shoved them into her pockets. "Professor Bergmann gave me a laughably vague rundown of what's been going on in here so far. What was the last thing she went over with you?"

The girl with the half-shaved head, her feet stretched out in front of her and one ankle crossed over the other, lifted a finger.

The halfling blinked at her and tried not to smile. "Yeah."

"Hacking into high-security data mainframes."

The class burst out laughing. Cheyenne let herself break into a crooked smile and pointed at the girl, who had to be only a year or two younger than the half-drow. "Nice try. This school would throw me out on my ass if I stood up here teaching that."

"But you *could* teach it, right?" The girl shot her new instructor a sidelong glance.

Cheyenne wiggled her jaw, then huffed out a laugh. "Let's start with where you guys are in your infinite undergrad wisdom, huh? We'll build from there. And any questions about stuff beyond what's covered in an advanced programming class, which is honestly where the fun starts, should be sent in encrypted emails."

The girl sitting in her seat, just like Cheyenne had been sitting in hers for the last four years of college, was the only student in the room who seemed to get the joke. "Do you keep office hours?"

"Ha. No." The half-drow forced herself to drop the conversation right there and instead heaved her mostly empty backpack onto the desk to pull out her laptop. "I'm assuming everybody brought their own. Otherwise, you're probably in the wrong class."

Slightly more amused chuckles rose in reply as Cheyenne Summerlin's new undergrad students pulled out their laptops and charging cords. The room filled with rustling and the click of plastic and fingers on keys. The halfling pulled the chair up behind her, sat, and watched kids who had no idea who she really was as they got ready to learn more than they bargained for.

Serious déjà vu, and a whole new appreciation for Bergmann. Even if she's not real.

CHAPTER EIGHTY-NINE

C heyenne nearly skipped out of the elevator and down the hall to her apartment. She didn't even think to pull out her keys before trying the doorknob, which was unlocked. Matthew's laugh echoed through the apartment as she opened the door, and she smashed the skippy feeling down into a tiny box. *Gotta keep up appearances, right?*

"Hey," Ember called and wheeled herself around the kitchen island. "How'd it go?"

"Meh. I called a kid an asshole and found a non-Goth version of myself from two years ago." The halfling shrugged and slung her backpack over the back of the leather couch. "I didn't have any expectations anyway, so I guess it's not so bad."

"You...called a kid an asshole." The fae bit her bottom lip and frowned. "For real?"

"He asked me how old I was."

"Huh."

"Yeah, which isn't automatic grounds for assholery, but he said it just to piss me off. Or maybe flirt with me, I don't know. Then he made it personal about how colleges don't hire Goths, so I felt justified."

Ember snorted and shot her friend a sidelong glance as Cheyenne leaned against the back of the couch and folded her arms. "But they *didn't* hire you."

The halfling slowly shook her head and leaned toward the fae. "But *they* don't know that."

"What didn't you get hired for?" Matthew wiped his hands with a paper towel and chucked it into the new trash can against the side of the island.

Cheyenne stared at the trashcan, then caught their new neighbor's gaze. "What's up, *neighbor?*"

The guy chuckled as he stepped around the island, either oblivious to the halfling's sarcasm meter on low or really good at ignoring it.

"She taught her first class today," Ember answered for her.

Cheyenne shot her friend a warning glance. Ember's gaze darted to the side, but Matthew was still behind her, so she mouthed, "Be nice."

The halfling rolled her eyes.

"Hey, cool." Matthew stopped beside Ember and stuck his hands in his jeans pockets. "Don't grad students normally get paid at least a little for teaching?"

"For a full course load, probably." Cheyenne shrugged.

"But they're not paying *you.*" Their tall neighbor smirked and narrowed his eyes.

"Didn't know you were interested in my academic pursuits, man."

He laughed, shrugging with his hands still in his pockets. "I'm just curious."

Yeah, but he won't add the part where it's none of his business, will he?

Raising an eyebrow, Cheyenne spread her arms. "Yep. I'm teaching one class for free. VCU's gonna hand over my master's in Computer Sciences just for teaching one class, so not technically for nothing, but it's not an internship or volunteer work."

"No kidding." Matthew's eyebrows drew together in curiosity. "That's all you have to do for your degree?"

So many questions. "I gave you the full rundown, man. Four and a half hours a week for three semesters after this, and I'm walking down that aisle in one of those ridiculous gowns." The halfling clicked her tongue and waited for the barrage of more questions prying into her personal life.

"Huh. That's awesome."

"It's a compromise."

Matthew chuckled. "What class are you teaching?"

"Advanced Programming 4200."

"Really?"

"You sound surprised, Matthew. You heard the part about me calling someone an asshole for thinking a Goth chick can't teach an upper-level undergrad course, right?"

"Yeah, I heard you." The man shot Ember a quick glance. The fae stared at the floor in front of her, her eyes wide and her lips pressed together so tightly they almost disappeared as she tried not to laugh. "And I *am* a little surprised."

"Uh-huh."

"Has nothing to do with you being Goth, though. I just didn't peg you as a computer nerd."

The halfling smirked and jerked her head toward the mini-loft. "The giant rig up there with all the high-tech gear didn't give me away?"

Matthew raised his eyebrows and glanced at the loft over the bathroom. "Ember told me not to go up there."

"Oh." Cheyenne chuckled. "Well, Ember was right. And now you know what I do."

"I just…" He let out a sheepish laugh and shrugged again. "I had this image in my head of you getting a Masters in Women's Studies or something."

Cheyenne and Ember let out sharp snorts of surprise.

Their neighbor glanced slowly between them, his smile widening. "And now I have to start all over and replace it with computers and software and…honestly, I don't know what else is included in all that."

The halfling's nose wrinkled when she tried to smile at him. "I'm not sure how I feel about an image of *me* being in your head."

"You know what I mean." He rolled his eyes and shook his head. "Cheyenne handling...all the stuff that goes with your various expertise."

"We don't have to get into it right now. Or ever, really. It goes right over most people's heads."

"Yeah, I don't think I'm an exception." Matthew chuckled. "I mean, I do some stuff with cybersecurity—"

"You *what?*" Cheyenne lifted her chin and stared at him sidelong. *Don't laugh and point. Might be crossing a line.*

"Not like that. I'm on the sales side of things. Networking, handling accounts. That kinda thing."

Ember let out an exasperated snort and shot her friend a pointed look. "Or he could just go with the actual title and say he owns two cybersecurity firms."

"Hey, nothing I said was technically wrong." Matthew grinned down at the fae and shook his head.

The halfling set her hands behind her on the back of the couch. "Just dabbling, huh?"

"I don't go around telling people unless I'm handing them my business card."

"I don't need one of those." Cheyenne snorted. "If I'm trying to find you, all I gotta do is walk in my front door."

"Woah!" Ember looked down.

The halfling glanced at her friend and their overly friendly neighbor, then rolled her eyes. "Sorry. I think I'm in 'stun undergrad students into silence with barbed sarcasm' mode."

Which is kinda my go-to mode anyway.

The fae looked at Cheyenne with a resigned expression that said the same thing.

"I can only imagine. And I *know* I wouldn't be able to stand up in front of a room of students and try to get anything through their heads, so no offense taken." Matthew smiled at the halfling and looked genuinely okay about the whole thing.

"All right." Cheyenne nodded and pulled her cell phone from her back pocket. "Hey, what time was your PT?"

"Oh. Two o'clock."

"It's a little after one. Should we get outta here?"

Ember nodded. "Yeah. Yeah, I'm ready to rock the hell out of PT."

"Anything I can do to help?" Matthew was only asking Ember. He seemed to have forgotten about the bitingly sarcastic Goth chick standing across from him.

"I don't think so."

"We got it, Matthew. Thanks for the offer."

"I'm more than happy to tag along. Help with the chair. Go grab food or whatever while you guys are there. We were just talking about lunch."

"That's really awesome of you." Cheyenne pushed herself away from the back of the couch. Then she clapped her hand on their neighbor's upper back—hitting his shoulder would've been ridiculous with at least a foot between them in height—and guided him toward the front door. "Right now, this is a housemates kinda deal, you know? And we gotta get ready, so thanks for coming over. We'll see ya later, huh?"

"Yeah. If you need anything, really, guys, I'm right across the hall."

"Oh, we know. Much appreciated, neighbor." Cheyenne opened the door and finally removed her hand from his back. "Have an awesome Monday."

Matthew chuckled and stepped into the hall. "Yeah, you too. Oh, hey. How'd you like the coffee?"

The halfling blinked. "It's to *die* for."

"Ha. Good one. I thought you'd like it."

"Good taste in coffee, man." She started to close the door, but Matthew spun and pushed it open again. "Seriously?"

"Sorry." He stuck his head through the partially open door and grinned at the fae girl watching the whole thing. "Bye, Ember."

"Yeah, see ya."

"Yeah. Okay." Matthew pulled back, nodded quickly at Cheyenne, then stepped all of five feet across the hall and into his apartment.

Cheyenne shut the door all the way and twisted the deadbolt with a jerk. "Are you *kidding* me with that guy?"

Ember threw her head back and laughed. "He's a lot."

"*So* a lot." The halfling scrunched her face and closed her eyes. "I can't believe you spent all day with him yesterday and still let him come back this morning."

"Come on, Cheyenne. Do you know how hard it is to tell someone, 'Hey, sorry, I know we live right across the hallway from each other, but I need you to not come over for a full twenty-four hours?'"

"Didn't sound like that was very hard."

Ember rolled her eyes. "Yeah, well, I don't have a problem with you."

"You have a problem with Matthew? 'Cause I can take care of that."

The fae stared at her friend. "Please don't."

They burst out laughing. "Then what? You're just gonna let him drive you crazy? And that's exactly what'll happen, by the way. He's the kind of guy who won't back down until someone gives him a flat-out no. Even then, it probably takes three or four times to get through his head."

Ember folded her arms and blinked. "You haven't spent more than ten minutes in the same room with him."

"I don't have to, Em. He's a carbon copy of half the people who used to show up at my mom's house asking her for advice, endorsements, or a good word put in with whoever. They're still knocking down her door, and I spent most of my life watching them do it. If Matthew Thomas dabbles in politics, I bet you he at least knows someone who's been out to see my mom."

"That's crazy."

"Yeah. But hey, if you need someone to be upfront with the guy, let me know. I also spent most of my life watching Bianca

Summerlin gracefully put her foot down with no room for argument, so I'm sure I'll be able to handle it for you."

"You did a pretty good job two minutes ago."

"That was nothing." Cheyenne wiggled her eyebrows, and her fae friend rolled her eyes.

"I feel really sorry for anyone who gets on your bad side, halfling."

"My bad side is like ninety-nine-percent of the whole thing."

They laughed, and Ember ran a hand through her hair. "I'm in the Cheyenne Summerlin one percent. Go, me. And on that note, we really should get going."

"No problem. What do you need?"

"I got it." Ember wheeled quickly through the kitchen and into her bedroom.

Cheyenne went to the fridge and pulled out the two leftover pieces of pizza wrapped in tinfoil. She'd eaten one of them by the time Ember came back out with her purse in her lap.

"Wow. My whole worldview of how fast a person can cram pizza into their face has officially been shattered."

"I have a lot of talents," the halfling muttered around a mouthful.

"Clearly." The fae eyed her friend and the cold pizza dangling from Cheyenne's hand. Then she nodded at the front door. "Let's go."

"Right behind you." Tossing the crumpled foil into the trashcan, the halfling skirted around the kitchen island and raced to the door first. She leaned against it to peer through the peephole, then unlocked the deadbolt. "Okay, the coast is clear."

"Come on. Give him a break, huh?"

"What, like he's giving *you* a break." Cheyenne laughed. "We'll be late if he opens his door and sees us for even a second."

Ember shook her head. "Then we better be fast."

"I got you, Em." As she pulled open the door, the half-drow turned the lock on the handle and held the door open for her housemate to wheel into the hall. Then she pulled the door closed and grabbed the handles on the back of her friend's wheelchair. "Hold on."

"What are you—"

It wasn't drow speed, but it was as close as Cheyenne could get without yanking off the pendant again and maybe giving Ember a heart attack. Ember shrieked and laughed as they raced down the hall, then the halfling punched at the elevator call button over and over, staring at Matthew Thomas' apartment door at the other end of the hall. "Come on, come on!"

"Oh, my God. He's not the boogeyman."

"Really? 'Cause he keeps showing up at the worst times."

Finally, the doors opened, and Cheyenne spun the chair around and pulled her friend backward into the elevator. Ember punched the button for the first floor. Just before the doors closed in front of them, the halfling heard their dabbling neighbor's front door swing open and cracked up all over again.

CHAPTER NINETY

As Cheyenne wheeled Ember toward the front doors of the physical therapy clinic in Midlothian, the fae pulled out her phone and checked the time. "Hey, look at that. I didn't think we'd have enough time, but we're ten minutes early."

"I told you I was fast."

"You're definitely getting better at helping me transfer in and out of this chair."

The automatic doors slid open, and the halfling pushed her inside. "Speaking of transferring..."

"Uh-huh."

"I couldn't help but notice you were already up and out of bed when I fell out of my room. You're not asking Matthew to—"

"Okay, stop right there. First of all, no. No. Absolutely not. Just —" Ember laughed and shook her head.

Patients sitting in the lobby looked at her before slowly returning to their magazines and cell phones. *And they're not even staring at the Goth chick. Huh.*

"Check-in's over there." Ember pointed toward one of the many windows sectioned off along the counter in the back, and they headed that way.

"And second of all?" The halfling prompted.

"What? Oh. Second of all, I got something that helps me do that on my own. You're off the hook."

"Oh." Cheyenne slowed them down to fall in line behind a woman leaning on crutches with her foot in a cast. "I didn't see it as being *on* the hook in the first place."

"Sorry to disappoint."

"Please. I'm not disappointed. I just didn't know how that was working out. And honestly, Em, I feel bad for leaving you hanging. You know, if you needed me—"

"Hey, I told you I'd call you if I needed help, okay? There's a lotta stuff I can still do, including figuring out how to do things with fewer people around."

The halfling nodded. "Fair enough. Consider me guilt-free." She grinned when Ember snorted and brushed the hair out of her eyes. "So, what did you get?"

"I'll show you later. We're up." Ember nodded toward the next check-in window, and Cheyenne pushed her forward to get the ball rolling.

"Ember Gaderow. I have a physical therapy appointment with Dr. Boseley at two o'clock."

"Ember. Yes." The middle-aged woman behind the counter with a massive bun of thick brown hair on the top of her head grinned. "We're so glad to have you here." She typed on her keyboard and nodded. "It looks like Dr. Andrews sent over all your records and...every single piece of information we need for your files here. Huh. He must've wanted to get you in as soon as possible."

Ember turned over her shoulder to shoot Cheyenne a questioning look. The halfling raised her eyebrows and shrugged. *Busted.*

The fae turned back toward the woman behind the counter. "Is that not normal?"

"Oh, uh, the process usually takes a little longer for new patients at this clinic. But unless your personal info has changed in the last few days, we're good to go."

"I moved on Friday, actually."

"Really?" The woman glanced at Cheyenne and immediately back at the new patient. "You're taking on a lot, aren't you?"

"Not by myself. Trust me."

"Hmm." With a tense smile, the woman pulled up Ember's file and nodded. "I'll put that in right now. Go ahead."

As Ember relayed the new apartment address and verified everything else, Cheyenne turned to take a sweeping glance around the clinic. *Clean. Quiet. Low key. So why is the back of my neck tingling?*

"Cheyenne?"

"What?"

Ember smiled in confusion and waved behind her at the chairs set up on the other side of the lobby. "We can go now."

"Right. Sorry." She wheeled her friend away from the counter and headed toward the waiting room area.

"Okay, let go." The fae reached up to brush her friend's hands off the handles, and Cheyenne released them with a chuckle. Ember wheeled herself toward the mostly empty waiting room and stopped beside the closest chair. "Are you okay?"

Cheyenne glanced around the lobby again and narrowed her eyes. "I'm great."

"Right. 'Cause you zoned out back there, and now you're looking for something in a PT clinic. Wanna fill me in?"

Spinning to face her friend, the halfling offered a closed-lipped smile with innocent eyes. "Can't a friend just check out another friend's medical facility?"

Ember snorted. "Not when it looks like you think you're being watched."

She's reading that *too?* "It's all good, Em. I just wanna make sure you're in the right place, you know?" Cheyenne stepped toward the chair on the other side of her friend and sat.

The fae frowned and studied the half-drow with a scrutinizing intensity. "Okay, the only reason I'm *not* telling you to leave that decision up to me is that you—" Ember leaned toward Cheyenne and lowered her voice. "That you're paying for all this. And don't even try to deny it to my face. We both know what's going on."

Smirking, the halfling crossed one black Van over her knee and slung her arm across the backs of the chairs lined up against the wall.

"If you're trying to scout this place because you don't think it's the best place for me to be, that's cool, and I seriously appreciate it. I'm not gonna bite the hand that pays my PT bills."

Cheyenne laughed and didn't say anything.

"But seriously." Ember sat back in her chair and tilted her head. "If there's something else going on, something that's *not* related to me getting out of this chair at some point in my life, you better tell me."

"*Nothing's* going on, Em. I promise." The tingling prickle rose again on the half-drow's neck, moving slowly across her shoulders. *Not my drow magic. No one is standing behind me. What the hell?*

"You promise?" Ember raised an eyebrow, and Cheyenne met her friend's gaze and held it.

Don't look away. "I promise. And I'll get it out of the way now and also promise that I'll tell you about anything else that comes up, whether you're with me when it happens or not. Like I've been doing."

"Yeah, okay." A skeptical smile bloomed on the fae's lips. "Then stop looking like an amateur PI undercover for the first time, huh?"

"You know what? I've been sneaking around places without anybody seeing me for, like, as long as I can remember. No amateur sleuthing here, okay?" The halfling laughed and tried to ignore the constant tingling on her neck and shoulders. "Honestly, Ms. Gaderow, I'm a little insulted by your assumptions."

"Uh-huh. Save the Bianca Summerlin act for your students, Professor."

"You're getting way ahead of yourself."

"Maybe."

They sat like that for a moment, and the halfling found her gaze drifting back toward the lobby and the patients milling around among nurses and assistants passing in and out of doors.

"Ember?"

Both magicals turned toward the open door on their left, and Ember raised her hand. "Yep." Then she wheeled toward the nurse standing with a clipboard in hand and looked over her shoulder at Cheyenne. "Come on."

"What?" The halfling sat upright in the chair. "No, it's okay, Em. I don't need to go with you."

"I know that. Get your ass out of that chair and come with me."

Cheyenne gripped the edge of the chair and looked at the woman. "Is that okay?"

The woman shrugged and glanced at Ember. "If that's what she wants, no problem."

"So get over here." The fae jerked her head toward the door.

Leaping to her feet, the halfling rubbed her hands down her pantlegs and made her way through the door while the woman held it for her. "Thanks."

"Of course. Right this way, Ember. My name's Sarah. I'm Dr. Boseley's assistant."

"Hi. This is my friend Cheyenne."

The halfling nodded with a thin smile. "Moral support."

Sarah chuckled. "That's great. Everybody needs someone in their corner now and then, right? That's what we're here for too. Dr. Boseley already has an excellent treatment plan written up for you. She'll go over all that with you first. Talk about how you're doing now, what you'd like to see happen in the next six, twelve, eighteen months. Then she'll explain the different phases of your personalized physical therapy plan, and you guys can start today if you're ready."

"I was ready before I left the hospital."

Sarah opened a glass door into what looked like a weight room at a gym, only with machines Cheyenne didn't recognize and a bunch of other unknown equipment. "This is the 'gym' where you'll be doing all the hard work with Dr. Boseley. You'll also have a list of exercises you can do at home between sessions. Feel free to take a look around. She should be in here in just a couple of minutes."

"Great. Thank you." Ember smiled sweetly at the assistant, and

Sarah returned the gesture to both magicals before opening the door again.

Cheyenne peered through the glass wall of the gym, watching the woman walk down the hall toward another office or exam room. "Seems like a decent place, right?"

"It looks like a gym."

The halfling chuckled. "Yeah, I had the same thought. But look, you have this whole giant PT playground all to yourself!"

"Ha-ha." Ember pulled a hair tie off her wrist and twisted her hair into a high ponytail. "Is it weird that I'm only slightly nervous?"

"Not even a little." Cheyenne gave the room and all the equipment another sweeping glance. "Three days a week in here, and you'll be back on your feet in no time."

"That's the plan. I don't care how low the full recovery rate is."

"You got this, Em." Looking down, the halfling saw her friend's hands clench around the edges of the chair's armrest. "Oh, my God. It just hit me."

"What?"

"These are *your* trials."

Ember leaned sideways in her chair and barked a laugh. "This isn't anything like that."

"Okay, yeah, you're not a—" Cheyenne glanced through the glass walls and lowered her voice. "You're not a drow, and you don't have a stupid box that spins and flies and throws spells at you." The fae girl scoffed. "*But* this is your big thing, right? You come in here, you have Dr. Boseley to help you through it. I haven't even met the woman, and I'm pretty sure I'd take her over Corian any day."

"Oh, jeeze."

"I'm serious." The halfling chuckled. "You do the work, you have an endgame, you level up, and when you complete your trials, you get a badass cane from your best friend."

Ember groaned and dipped her head. "If I were anyone else, Cheyenne, I might be insulted by the comparison."

"Hey, if you were anyone else, you'd think I was insane, talking about flying boxes and spells and drow trials."

They shared a laugh. "I appreciate your attempt to make me feel less weirded out by all this."

"Is it working?"

"By a marginal percentage, maybe."

"You're telling me it's working." The halfling pointed at her friend and grinned. "I'll keep it up."

"Totally not necessary."

"But it's working!"

Ember smacked the half-drow's wrist with the back of her hand. "Cut it out."

"Oh, one more point for Ember's trials. *You* don't have to run around dodging lightning bolts. That's a good one."

"Make it *stop*."

The door opened, and a woman with tight, bright-red curls falling just below her chin stepped in to join them. "Hi, Ember. I'm Dr. Boseley."

"Hey." The fae reached out to shake the smiling woman's hand.

"Nice to meet you. How you doin' today?"

"Ready to get started." Ember let out a nervous chuckle.

"Good. We have some things to go over first, and then we will start."

Cheyenne didn't realize she was frowning at the doctor's yoga pants and long-sleeved thermal shirt until Dr. Boseley thrust her hand under the halfling's nose.

"Dr. Boseley."

Blinking quickly, Cheyenne took Boseley's hand and gave it a firm shake. "Cheyenne."

"Nice to meet you too. I love to meet my patients' friends and family. Puts us all on the same team, you know?"

"Yeah, she's been ridiculously helpful." Ember shot the halfling a quick glance and shrugged.

"Good. So, if you're ready, let's talk about what's going on with you right now. You were discharged from VCU Medical Center just this last Thursday, correct?"

Ember nodded. "Yep."

"I'm sorry. Excuse me." Cheyenne jerked her thumb toward the windows and the hallway beyond. "Where's your restroom?"

"Oh, yeah. Down the hall to your left, then you'll pass the other hall on the far end of this room, and it's the first door on the left."

"Great. Thanks. You good?"

Ember looked at the half-drow and slowly nodded. "Totally. Are *you?*"

"Yeah, once I find the bathroom. Sorry."

The fae gave her a dismissive shrug, and Cheyenne opened the glass door to step into the hall.

"Just come right on in when you get back," Dr. Boseley called after her.

The halfling shot them both a thumbs-up and let the door fall quietly shut behind her.

CHAPTER NINETY-ONE

She headed down the hall toward wherever the bathroom was supposed to be and tried not to peer conspicuously into every open door or window she passed. *What the hell is this tingling crap?*

She rubbed the back of her neck and along her shoulder, but of course, that didn't do anything. *Can't just stand out here staring at people. Make it look real, at least.*

When she passed the hall running along the far end of the gym, she slowed to gaze at as much of it as she could. Only one other nurse walked quickly down it toward her, smiled, and opened a door before disappearing into the next room. *Something's up.*

Cheyenne stepped into the bathroom and turned on the light before locking the door. She hiked up the bottom of her black corduroys and bent over to study her ankle. "All good there. They would've told me about darktongue side effects, right?"

The halfling turned and searched her reflection in the mirror. With a deep breath, she stared into her eyes and tried to will away the tingle across her back. The sensation flared, and she slapped at the top of her shoulder in reflex. "Ugh. Feels like...bugs all over me."

Something flashed in the mirror, and she glanced back up to see the reflection of the Heart of Midnight pendant letting off another soft silver pulse. "Oh, come on."

Rolling her eyes, Cheyenne grabbed the pendant and dipped her head to look at it. The Heart hadn't changed, but if she focused hard, those little streaks of silver within the sparkling black stone looked like they were moving. *Can't take it off. Might not even be the stupid pendant.*

She looked back up at her reflection and shook her head. "Snap out of it, Cheyenne. Pay attention to everything. Don't assume what's happening. Okay. Good talk."

Opening the door again, she smacked off the light and stepped into the hallway again. This time, she paid attention to the tension in her face and forced herself to relax. The halfling stuck her hands in her pockets and moved down the hall at a leisurely pace. *Just checking things out, right? Nobody's gonna care.*

When she got halfway toward the other side of the gym, she stopped and leaned against the wall between two closed doors. On the other side of the glass walls, Dr. Boseley knelt in front of Ember. She lifted one of the fae's feet in both hands and slowly lowered it again before looking up to ask her patient a question. Whatever Ember said, it made the redheaded doctor laugh and nod.

Okay. Good clinic. Good doctor. At least Ember's being taken care of right now.

One of the doors beside her opened, and a man a little taller than Cheyenne's five feet three inches stepped into the hall beside her. He wore sweatpants and a short-sleeved thermal, his biceps bulging out from beneath the thin material like they were at a real gym.

"Hello." His gaze fell to the Heart of Darkness pendant, but he didn't react in any other way. The halfling forced herself not to cover the necklace. "Can I help you with anything?"

"Oh, no. I'm good. I just came with my friend." She nodded toward the gym.

The bodybuilder guy nodded and folded his arms. "Her first time in?"

"Yeah, actually." Cheyenne turned toward him and raised her eyebrows. "Good guess."

"Well, I've been watching people come in and out of here long enough. Plus, Dr. Boseley *really* puts on the charm with new patients."

"Uh-oh. Are we looking at Dr. Boseley and Ms. Hyde here, then?"

He chuckled. "Definitely not. She's really good. And admittedly, I was working through the schedule before I stepped out here and saw she had a new patient appointment right now."

"Right. Got me."

"Wasn't sure *you'd* come, though."

Cheyenne froze and stared through the clear glass into the gym. "What was that?"

"Well, it's usually just really close friends and family who come in with new patients for the first few sessions."

The knot of hyper-awareness in the half-drow's mind loosened a little. *He's just talking about normal medical stuff.* "Well, it's kinda both with Ember and me. We're not related, but I think I'm the closest thing she has to family right now. It's just been her and me since...well, since she was put in that wheelchair in the first place."

"I get it." The guy beside her nodded, then leaned toward the halfling.

Cheyenne glanced at him and leaned away. "What are you doing?"

"You don't have to explain it, *phér móre*. You've chosen. We'll take good care of her here. Don't worry about that."

The halfling stared at him. "Chosen what?"

"Like family, right?" He nodded toward Ember and Dr. Boseley on the other side of the glass. "It's a good thing fae have such a strong smell. I wouldn't have been sure about that one, otherwise. A human's not gonna cut it, but your friend's full-blooded fae all the way through. Just without her magic, huh?"

Blinking slowly, Cheyenne nodded and tried not to act clueless. *If he was a loyalist, he'd be trying to kidnap me right now.*

"Three." The man smirked and bounced on the balls of his feet before sinking back down.

"I'm sorry?"

"Three of us in this clinic, *phér móre*. Just a coincidence that you brought your *Nós Aní* in here over anywhere else, but I'm glad you did. If you were worried about leaving her alone until she's strong enough, you have my word we'll keep her safe while she's here."

"I appreciate that. Gotta admit, though, it sounds like you're telling me Ember's in some kinda danger."

He shrugged again. "You never know, right? Especially in times like these. Hey, I gotta get back to work, but send a word to the Cu'ón for House Keldryk, huh? We're ready. Guess that's kinda meant for you too, huh?"

"I guess." The halfling frowned and took the risk anyway when she stuck out her hand. "What's your name?"

"Marsil." He took her hand and gave it a firm squeeze. When he dipped his head, it looked like a little bow. "Mark around here, but that's just on Earthside paper, you know what I mean?"

"Yeah. Cheyenne."

Marsil grinned, then they released each other's hands, and he brought a fist quickly to his chest before dropping it again. "Of course, I already know who you are. Wasn't expecting to get your name, though. Thank you."

"Well, it's the only one I have, so you won't run the risk of getting them confused."

"Funny." The magical, who was wearing a human illusion charm as a medical professional at Ember's PT clinic, dipped his head again and headed slowly down the hall toward the front of the building. "For as long as you need, *phér móre*. We'll take care of her."

He spun again and disappeared around another corner before she had the chance to thank him again.

Cheyenne cleared her throat and glanced down at the gently pulsing Heart of Midnight resting against her chest. *Apparently, I've chosen Ember as my* Nós Aní, *whatever that means. Magicals popping out of the woodwork.*

Shaking her head, she tucked the pendant beneath her loose black shirt. The pendant looked ridiculous, pushing against her shirt, but she wasn't taking any more chances by leaving it out. *Good thing Corian finally gave me his number.*

With a glance up and down the hall, the halfling pushed off and headed back toward the door into the gym. It opened quietly enough, but Ember was focused on what Dr. Boseley was showing her on a chart of the human spine in full color and she didn't hear her friend step inside. Cheyenne went to the metal chairs with black plastic seats and backs against the glass wall and sat. Then she pulled out her phone and opened the text from Corian, which was the letter C.

"Good enough," she muttered and opened a new text.

P find what he was looking for yet?

She tried not to stare at her phone while she waited for a reply. It took him about forty-five seconds.

Not yet.

Guess that's pretty obvious by now. The guy does go the extra mile to keep his promises. She wrinkled her nose at her phone, then shrugged and wrote the text she actually wanted to send.

What's a Nós Aní?

The little dots at the bottom of her screen blinked on and off.

Second in command. Race-specific for you. Could be anyone. Can talk more in person but scrub these messages. Stupid to send on an open line. You know that.

"*Sorry,*" the halfling whispered with a little sneer at her phone. She deleted all but the first text straight from him. *I'll scrub harder when I get home.*

Cheyenne leaned back in the chair and crossed one leg over the other, folding her arms. She offered Ember a smile and a thumbs-up when the fae glanced over her shoulder and saw the halfling sitting in the room. Ember shrugged and turned back when Dr. Boseley asked if she was ready to try again.

For the rest of the two-hour session, Cheyenne zoned out, turning everything from yesterday over in her mind. *Ember's gotta have a choice in taking this Nós Aní gig. I promised her I'd tell her everything, but how the hell am I gonna explain that one?*

She didn't even notice that the tingle along the back of her neck had disappeared.

CHAPTER NINETY-TWO

"Hey. *Cheyenne!*" Ember leaned forward and waved the papers Dr. Boseley had given her in the halfling's face.

Cheyenne started, her foot sliding off her knee to thump onto the floor, and she blinked quickly. "Sorry. Got caught up in a whole bunch of thoughts."

Frowning, Ember tipped her head back and squinted. "Thoughts. You sure you're okay?"

"Yeah, yeah. I'm good. Are you guys done?"

"Yep. I'm ready to get outta here and stuff my face with something delicious because I was an idiot and didn't eat anything before we got here."

Chuckling, the halfling stood. "Then let's go get something. You could've had another piece of pizza."

"I wasn't nearly hungry enough to eat that when we left."

"Okay. I get it." Cheyenne headed toward the door and held it open from the hallway. "After you."

Ember cocked her head. "How kind."

They moved more slowly down the hall on their way out, and the halfling shot a quick glance at the fae. Ember's arms trembled a little every time she pushed down the wheels, but she didn't stop, and she didn't look like she was all that bothered by it.

"You want me to take the wheel, so to speak?"

The fae girl shook her head and stared intently at the door leading out into the waiting room and the lobby. "I'm good until we get to the car. After that, I might be Jell-O for a while."

"Okay. How'd it go in there?"

"You know what? I like that doctor."

The halfling opened the next door and held that open too. "It seems like you really lucked out with the awesome docs, huh?"

"And I can only blame you for one of them." Ember grinned and didn't stop on her way into the lobby and toward the exit. "You picked a good one, though, Cheyenne. Seriously. Thank you."

"Thank *her*. I just drove you here."

The fae snorted and paused just long enough for the automatic doors to open in front of her. "I'm not quite sure where your modesty ends and some kind of weird Cheyenne embarrassment begins."

"What? I'm not embarrassed."

"Okay. Then admit that the only reason I'm getting such good treatment right now is because of you."

Cheyenne's nose wrinkled automatically. "I'm just helping my friend."

"Honestly, would you be helping me like this if I hadn't asked you to come with me that night? If I just showed up at the hospital with a bullet hole through my spine and you had no clue what happened?"

If she hadn't asked me to come with her, she wouldn't have made it to the hospital. The halfling unlocked her Panamera as Ember wheeled down the ramp off the sidewalk and into the parking lot. "Yeah, Em. I'm pretty sure I'd still be doing exactly what I'm doing, even if you hadn't asked me to come and I threw a fit about it."

"So this isn't because you feel like it's your fault I have to come here three times a week?"

Cheyenne opened the passenger side door, and Ember bent over to lock the wheels in place. "You said it before, Em. I'm not the one who shot you."

"You're right. You're the one saved my life." Ember stared at her, then looked away and waved the half-drow toward her. "Let's do this."

The halfling bent and half-lifted, half-supported her friend into the passenger seat of the Panamera. Ember shot her a thumbs-up, then Cheyenne wheeled the chair behind the car, folded it up, and hauled it into the trunk. When she got behind the wheel and started the engine, Ember finished buckling her seatbelt and stared straight ahead at the entrance to the clinic.

"You okay?"

The fae squinted and turned slowly toward the halfling. Her gaze took a little longer to pull away from the front doors. "This is gonna sound crazy."

Cheyenne bit her lip to keep from laughing. "Try me."

"I think I...felt something weird in there. And before you make a smartass remark about it, yes, I'm sure it's not just the effects of PT."

"It's really creepy how well you know me, Em."

The fae replied with a distracted chuckle and turned toward the clinic again. "It's not very hard. But this was...okay, I don't even know what it was." Ember's hand rose absently to the back of her neck beneath her swinging ponytail.

"Like someone holding a vibrating cellphone and an Icy-Hot patch on your neck at the same time?"

Ember's eyes grew incredibly wide before darting toward Cheyenne. "And bugs."

"Yeah. And bugs." The halfling forced back another laugh. "Uh, so this is pretty cool."

"It doesn't make sense."

"But it's cool."

"Cheyenne, I don't know what the hell to do with this! I'm already up to my neck in figuring out how to do life all over again in that stupid chair. Which is really great, by the way. Thanks for that too."

The halfling pursed her lips and didn't say a word.

"But that's all I can handle right now. I can't... I mean, no. No, no." Ember shook her head vigorously, her ponytail slapping the headrest. "This is crazy."

"Hmm, not really."

"Don't start." The fae pointed a finger in Cheyenne's face and tried to keep looking as stern as possible. A confused laugh burst out of her anyway. "No way this is happening."

"It *never* occurred to you that this was a possibility?"

"You know what? You don't get to be the voice of reason right now. You didn't even know I was fae, and your brain almost exploded when I told you I don't have any magic."

The halfling sat back and folded her arms. "And now *your* brain's exploding."

"Of *course,* my brain's exploding! I gave up wishing for magic when I found out Santa Claus and the Tooth Fairy aren't real."

"That's a perfect comparison, Em. Holiday mascots for kids and actual magic. Makes perfect sense."

"Thank you."

"To an eight-year-old."

Ember rolled her eyes. "I was five, by the way. My idiot cousin spilled the beans on that one right before bed on Christmas Eve."

"Ouch."

"Yeah."

"Well, my mom didn't even entertain the idea of letting me believe in stuff like that, so I don't have anything to compare to that letdown."

The fae lurched forward with a surprised laugh. "Are you serious? No Santa? No Easter Bunny, leprechauns, Tooth Fairy? Nothing?"

Shaking her head, Cheyenne shrugged. "Nothing."

"That's one of the saddest things I've ever heard. Why wouldn't your mom play along?"

"Because I have magic, Em." The words burst out of Cheyenne a lot louder than she'd intended, and Ember leaned away from her a little. "And probably also because Bianca Summerlin's not the kind of person to indulge in fairytales and make-believe. You know, childish games and all that."

"But you *were* a child."

The halfling shrugged. "Meh. I grew up a lot faster than anyone expected, and that wasn't because of who my mom is. I've got the drow side to thank for that."

"Unbelievable. Explains a lot, though, if you think about it."

Cheyenne laughed and slammed her hands on the steering wheel, gripping it tightly and shaking herself back and forth. "But we're not talking about *me*! We're talking about you and the best discovery of your life!"

"Oh, God." Ember rubbed the back of her neck again and stared at the entrance to the clinic. "I have magic."

"The magicless fae has magic! What's *happening*?" Cheyenne slammed her hand on the horn. A woman walking toward the clinic jumped and spun around with a glare.

"No, not you. Sorry!" Ember shook her head and waved the woman off as the halfling burst out laughing. "Seriously, cut that out. You're gonna give somebody a heart attack."

"I'm freaking out!" Cheyenne whipped her head toward her friend and grinned. "And we have no idea what's gonna happen. It's great."

"Ugh. Only you would be excited by that idea. I'm screwed."

"No way, Em. You're just getting started."

"Shit."

Tilting her head, the halfling strapped on her seatbelt and shifted into reverse. "You still hungry?"

"If I say no, I'm gonna regret it later."

"Excellent. Where do you want to go, hypothetically speaking?"

Ember shoved her friend's shoulder and shook her head, unsuccessful in her attempt to look irritated. "Anywhere that's not this parking lot, halfling. I need to stop looking at that building."

With a curt nod, Cheyenne pulled out of the handicap parking spot and headed toward the street. She tapped on the horn and bobbed her head from side to side. "Fae just got her magic back. And I get to drive her around."

"Stop with the horn. Jesus." Ember covered her face with her hands and laughed. "Don't turn this into something it's not, okay? I can't 'get my magic back' if I never had in the first place."

"Or *did* you?"

Ember took a deep breath, clenched her fists, and closed her eyes. "Just drive."

CHAPTER NINETY-THREE

The Chesterfield Towne Center was only about a five-minute drive from the clinic, and when Cheyenne pulled into the parking lot, Ember laughed and covered her mouth with both hands. "Are you serious right now?"

"Hey, you didn't give me anything to go on, so I went with the closest selection." Shifting into park, the halfling turned and raised an eyebrow. "Or did you want me to stop at the McDonald's back there?"

"No. That's not what I'm saying." The fae glanced around the parking lot. "But a shopping mall full of high school kids on a Monday afternoon wouldn't have made the list, if there was a list."

"You know what? I think all that magic's short-circuiting your brain right now."

Ember unbuckled her seatbelt and raised her hands in surrender. "You're one of the most infuriating people I know."

"I get that a lot. Fortunately for you, you're kind of joking." The half-drow flashed her friend a brilliant grin that disappeared a second later. Ember clenched her eyes shut with another disbelieving laugh, and Cheyenne opened the trunk to get the chair.

They got Ember into it in record time, then the halfling grabbed the handles and pushed her friend toward the department store entrance. People turned to look at the shiny black Panamera when Cheyenne stuck her hand in her pocket to lock it.

"You're never gonna get tired of that, are you?" Ember looked over her shoulder. "Watching how many people wish they had your car."

"Would you?"

"I don't know anything right now."

"Just roll with it, Em. Besides, it's better for people to be staring at my car than at either of us, right?"

"I know why people would stare at you," Ember said, smirking and readjusting her purse in her lap, "but why *me?*"

"Oh, you know. Just in case your magic starts leaking out all over the place."

"Seriously?"

"Hey, I'm in the perfect position to have serious empathy for you here, okay?" Cheyenne choked down another laugh and spoke in her best impersonation of Bianca Summerlin. "I've had the rare opportunity to gain personal experience in these types of situations, Ms. Gaderow. I would be more than happy to provide you with some insight if you agree to my conditions."

"All right, Bianca," the fae muttered through clenched teeth. "Name your price."

"Oh, very good." They laughed. "You got that immediately, huh?"

"Your mom's the only person I've heard you impersonate like that, so it wasn't that hard."

Cheyenne cut a straight line through the department store and out into the center walkway of the mall. Groups of teenagers either swerved out of the way at the last second or split down the middle to walk around the Goth chick and her friend. "I guess I need to diversify, huh?"

"You know, Matthew mentioned something about dabbling in trading too."

"Why am I not surprised?" The halfling peered down the line of shops, searching for the food court she thought was right there.

"New rule. I won't keep taking cracks at the whole fae magic thing if you don't talk about Matthew Thomas the dabbler unless it's immediately before or after we have to deal with him for some reason."

"Done. Oh, my God. What am I supposed to do about him now?"

Cheyenne snorted and nodded with raised eyebrows at a pair of women in their seventies, arms linked together, who passed the magical friends and couldn't stop staring at the Goth chick's getup. "Same thing you were planning to do with him before, I hope. Which is not letting him weasel his way into everything, right?"

Ember leaned over the side of her chair just enough to catch a final glimpse of the gray-haired women scowling at Cheyenne's back and shaking their heads. "Those ladies have serious judgment issues."

"That's nothing. Some guy once told me I was going to hell for worshipping the devil."

"How insightful of him."

"I know, right? I tried to ask him what he suggested I do to fix that oversight on my part, and he ran away."

Ember burst out laughing and turned toward the storefront coming up on their right. "Oh, boy."

Cheyenne glanced at the Hot Topic sign above the door in thick black letters and leaned down to mutter in her friend's ear, "Watch this."

She slowed their pace a little and stared into the store as they passed. Four teenagers stood around one of the clothes racks in the center, all of them decked out in punkier versions of the Goth clothes the halfling had been wearing since 2012. The three girls and one guy looked up from the clothes rack and saw Cheyenne slowly pushing Ember past the storefront. The halfling wiped every ounce of expression off her face and met each of their gazes. Only one of the kids had any piercings—two studs on either side of his bottom lip—and two of the girls had added rainbow glitter to their eye makeup. The third didn't wear any makeup at all, and she was the only one who didn't join the others in making faces at the drow halfling staring them down.

Yeah, okay. Cheyenne stopped at the very end of the storefront's window and stared at the teenagers trying to make the wrong person uncomfortable. The three joking around and making faces caught on pretty quickly that the Goth chick glaring through the window wasn't going anywhere. Their smirks fell away in seconds, then Cheyenne glanced at the girl without any makeup. A slow, admiring smile lifted the corner of the girl's mouth, and that was it.

The halfling turned slowly away from the window and pushed Ember down the mall once again. "Amateurs."

Ember looked over her shoulder and shot the halfling an incredulous smile. "Maybe you should be a high school teacher instead."

"What, and teach computer lab? No fucking way." She grinned when Ember threw her head back and cackled. "That one on the end wasn't so bad, though."

"The one who smiled at you?"

"Yeah. I think she appreciated the gesture."

Ember pointed over her shoulder at her friend. "I think she wanted to *be* you."

"Oh, to be young and naïve!" They laughed again, and Cheyenne's gaze settled on a man and his two sons under ten walking toward them. The boys stared with wide eyes, and their dad didn't set a much better example. The halfling jerked her chin at the man and kept walking. "How's it goin'?"

The guy tried to return the gesture, but his head twitched away from her instead before he put a hand on each of his kids' shoulders and hurried them away from the scary lady who said hello.

"Wow. Is this a regular thing for you?" Ember glanced back at the boys and gave them a little wave. They hurried to put their dad between them and the much more normal-looking woman in the wheelchair.

"Absolutely." Cheyenne winked at the woman in the tailored power suit walking briskly toward them, her heels clacking on the shiny floor. The woman stumbled away from the Goth chick, did a double-take, and hurried toward the opposite side of the mall's center walkway to avoid passing within arm's reach.

Ember cracked up again. *"People."*

"I know. It's pretty revealing. Some people don't care what anyone looks like, and then I get decent conversations in. Like this old guy at Union Hill the other day. Dude was drooling all over my car and gave me his business card."

"For your car?"

"Yeah, like custom work or whatever. Regular-looking guy, giant white handlebar mustache."

"What?" Ember stretched her mouth open wide and wiggled her jaw around, trying to get her cheeks to stop hurting after laughing for so long at all the people here.

"Who knows? Maybe I'll go check out what he can do."

"You're gonna Goth out the Porsche?"

"Why not?" Shrugging, the halfling caught sight of the Red Robin at the end of the shops before the next mall exit. *"There* it is. You good with burgers?"

"I don't care at this point."

"Sweet." They pushed on, and Cheyenne paused when her phone buzzed in her back pocket. "Oh. Hold on a sec."

"What's up?"

"Phone call." The halfling pulled out her cell phone and frowned. "From my mom."

"The way you said that makes me think that's not a normal thing." Ember turned in the chair and glanced at the cell phone and then the halfling's confused expression. "Everything okay?"

"Who knows? You mind?"

"You don't need my permission to answer the phone." Ember scoffed and turned back around.

Cheyenne accepted the call and brought the phone to her ear. "Hey, Mom."

"Hi, Cheyenne. I just got off the phone with your finance manager. He called to notify me of a suspiciously high level of activity on your card over the weekend. His words, not mine. It's none of my business what you do with your finances, but all parties involved wanted to be sure that the activity was authorized. You understand."

The halfling grinned and forced down the laugh threatening to bubble up. *Nobody laughs at Bianca Summerlin during a courtesy call.* "It's all authorized, Mom. Thanks."

"Good. I'll give the man another call, and then I'm going to put in a request for him to remove my contact information from your account. You'll probably have to go in and confirm, but I'd prefer not to be bothered by someone else's suspicion when you clearly have everything under control."

"Yeah, no problem. Sorry for the inconvenience."

Ember turned again to shoot her friend a confused frown, and Cheyenne just shook her head.

"I've already forgotten about it," Bianca replied. "Where are you? It's a little hard to hear you over all the background noise."

Cheyenne bit her lip to pull herself back under control. *Ember's face is gonna get me yelled at.* "At the mall with Ember, actually."

"Oh. Interesting choice for a Monday night."

"Just to grab dinner."

"Is this the same Ember you met your first year at VCU?"

The halfling made a surprised face at Ember. *A question about my friends. Whole day of surprises.* "Yeah, that's her. My housemate now, actually."

"Really?"

"Yep. It's working out pretty well so far."

"Well, that explains all the charges. Since I can hear voices but no kitchen, Cheyenne, I'm assuming you two haven't ordered dinner yet."

Cheyenne shrugged at Ember's questioning glance as the fae spread her arms and raised her eyebrows. "No, not yet."

"Well, why don't you come on up to the house? It's still early. I'll tell Eleanor to set two extra places, and then I will finally have a chance to meet your friend. Dinner's at seven. You'll get here in time for a cocktail or two before we eat."

"Tempting. Let me run it by her."

"Sure."

Cheyenne pressed the phone against her thigh and wiggled her eyebrows at Ember. "We've been invited to dinner at my mom's. What do you think?"

"I...think I really can't say no to that."

Grinning, the halfling lifted the phone to her ear again. "We'll get back in the car and head on up."

"Wonderful. See you soon." Bianca hung up in her usual perfunctory manner, and Cheyenne sniggered.

"Did that just happen?"

The halfling shrugged and stuck her phone into her pocket. "Looks like it."

"Wow. I'm about to go have dinner with Bianca Summerlin." The surprised smile faded from Ember's lips, replaced by a wide-eyed stare.

"Okay, Em. You look like a mouse staring at a chunk of cheese in a mousetrap."

The fae swallowed. "It's creepy how well you just nailed the feeling."

"Look who can read someone like an open book *now*." Cheyenne laughed and turned the wheelchair around to head back toward the car. "Relax. It'll be you, me, my mom, and Eleanor. Nothing fancy. Nothing super-special, just a casual dinner at chez Summerlin. You'll be fine."

"Honestly, that was the most surreal thing I've heard you say all day. I don't... I mean, I don't have a clue how to be around someone like your mom."

The halfling shook her head and didn't even bother to glance inside the Hot Topic again as they moved much more quickly past it this time. "Just be yourself."

"That's the worst advice you could possibly give me right now, and totally cliché."

"Okay, okay. How's this? Don't try to impress her. Don't lie to her. Don't try to filter yourself. Bianca Summerlin's bullshit detector is worth millions."

Ember dropped her head back onto the thin edge of the back of the chair. "You're making it worse."

Cheyenne pulled a face at her upside-down fae friend. "We'll make it in time for a cocktail or two before dinner. Those were her words, Em."

"Oh, now we're *drinking* with Bianca Summerlin."

"Hey, keep your voice down, huh?"

"Sorry."

Cheyenne glanced quickly at the other pedestrians walking past the storefronts of the shopping center and shook her head. "It's a good thing. As long as she doesn't break out the good scotch, everything's peachy."

"I don't know anything about scotch."

"No problem. She's got a fully stocked bar *all* the time. Gin and tonics for Ms. Gaderow. As many as you want."

Ember finally lifted her head and ran her hands down the sides of her face. "I feel slightly better."

"We don't have to go—"

"Are you kidding me? Yeah, I'm a little freaked out, but the thought of turning down a dinner invitation from Bianca Summerlin is, like, terrifying."

Cheyenne burst out laughing and unlocked the Panamera as they drew closer. "Yeah. She's gonna love you."

CHAPTER NINETY-FOUR

"You've gotta be shitting me right now." Ember's mouth dropped open a little less than two hours later when they made it up the shallow incline of the gravel drive and Bianca Summerlin's valley lodge came into view. "You grew up here?"

"I grew up here." Cheyenne eyed the estate house and wrinkled her nose. "So, full disclosure here, Em. You're the first person I've brought out here. Like, ever."

"What?"

"I know it might be surprising, but I'm not a big people person. Like, intrinsically."

Ember just blinked and slowly shook her head. "I don't even have words."

"All right, at least close your mouth before we get to the front door. She's a stickler for first impressions."

"Like anyone could leave a better first impression than *this*." The fae gestured at the house and leaned forward in the passenger seat. "This is unreal."

"Yeah, until you get used to being here. Then it's very, very real." The Panamera came to a smooth, rolling stop on the gravel yards away from the wide stone steps leading up to the front door.

Cheyenne turned off the car, unbuckled her seatbelt, and froze. "Shit."

"What?"

"I didn't think about the gravel or the stairs."

When the reality of that inconvenience dawned on the fae, Ember groaned and thumped her head against the headrest. "First impressions. Off to a *great* start."

"Okay, hold on. We're here, and we'll figure it out, okay? You mind waiting for a minute?"

Ember shrugged. "I could stay here the whole time and have a much better chance of not humiliating myself."

"Whoa. Em."

"What?"

"Come on. Look at me."

The fae slowly turned her head, one eyebrow raised. "What?"

"Everybody wants you here. Nobody cares about anything else, got it?"

"*I* care."

Cheyenne laughed. "Well, cut it out already, okay?"

"Yeah, easy for *you*. You don't give a damn what other people think of you."

"A skill honed by years of practice, just to be clear." The halfling nodded and popped the trunk. "You got this. And I'll help."

When she got out of the car, the crisp, fresh scent of pine trees and earth and the flowers in the front garden settled the halfling into a calm she'd forgotten she knew how to reach. *There are still benefits to coming "home."* She grabbed the chair from the trunk, opened it up, and brought it around toward the passenger side door.

Ember stared at her when the halfling opened the door. "What are you doing?"

"I'm gonna help you into this baby." Cheyenne patted the back of the chair. "And then I'm gonna figure out the best way to get you inside the house *before* you meet my mom."

Ember steeled herself to just go with it. "Okay. Let's do it."

"That's more like it." Cheyenne bent down and helped her friend out of the car. Ember barely had enough energy in her arms to steady herself on the armrests, then she was in, and the halfling closed the door. "That's gotta be a record."

"Really? Felt like hours."

Shooting her friend a knowing glance, Cheyenne swiveled the chair around on the gravel until Ember sat a foot in front of the Panamera, directly in front of the door. "Lookin' good. I'll be right back, okay?"

"Yep."

The halfling hurried toward the wide stone steps and almost laughed. *So much better than the last time I was here. Zero FRoE agents.* She skipped up the steps and smoothed down the front of her shirt before knocking quickly on the front door.

It opened, and Eleanor's perpetually flushed, smiling face greeted her on the other side. "Well, look at you!"

The woman opened the door all the way and spread her arms. Cheyenne stepped into the crushing embrace Bianca Summerlin's housekeeper and close friend never failed to deliver, grunting a little at the pressure. "Hi, Eleanor."

The woman released Cheyenne and stepped back, squeezing the halfling's shoulders before releasing her. "Don't tell her I said anything." Eleanor glanced briefly over her shoulder and lowered her voice. "But she almost danced across the house when you didn't think twice about accepting her invitation."

Cheyenne smirked. "She doesn't dance across anything."

"I said, *almost.*" Eleanor batted her employer's daughter with a playful hand, then glanced out the door onto the front stoop. "I thought you had a friend coming?"

"Yeah, she's here." Stepping back out the onto curved landing at the top of the stairs, Cheyenne turned and swept her arm out toward Ember. "And there she is."

Eleanor grinned. "Hello. So glad you could make it."

When the housekeeper gave the fae an enthusiastic wave, Ember's anxiety eased enough to make her chuckle sound genuine. She waved back and called, "Thanks for having me."

"Oh, she's lovely. I can tell already." Still smiling at the fae in the wheelchair, Eleanor clasped her hands in front of her and muttered to Cheyenne from the side of her mouth, "You need a little help getting inside, don't you?"

"Yep. Hey, I won't say anything about the dancing part if you don't say anything about what we're about to do."

The housekeeper cleared her throat and cocked her head. "You drive a hard bargain, Cheyenne."

"I learned from the best."

"I'm going to pretend you're referring to me and take that as a compliment."

The halfling smirked. "Of course."

"Let's get to it, then." Eleanor stepped quickly down the stairs, a new grin spreading across her face as she and the half-drow approached their guest for the evening. "So nice to meet you, Ember. I'm Eleanor."

"Nice to meet you too." Ember shook the woman's hand and shot Cheyenne a curious glance. "Everything okay?"

"Totally. Ready to go?"

"Uh, yeah. How are we—"

"Why don't you just let us handle that part, Ember?" Eleanor nodded with her hospitable smile as Cheyenne stepped around the back of the chair and spun her friend around. She tipped the chair back just enough to lift the smaller front wheels and pulled Ember backward toward the stairs.

Ember's eyes widened, and she glanced at the halfling over her shoulder. "Cheyenne—"

"We got it, Em. No problem. Another two minutes, and you'll be getting the grand tour." They reached the bottom of the stairs, and Cheyenne positioned the back wheels squarely before stepping up. "Just a few bumps. Probably."

Eleanor caught the fae's gaze and let out a little giggle as she reached down for the frame of the chair below the seat. "You know, Ember, Cheyenne failed to mention she'd be driving up in a new Porsche tonight." The housekeeper grunted as she and Bianca's daughter lifted the chair's huge back wheels over the first step. "Honestly, I'm more inclined to believe the story of how she got that car if it comes from her friend."

"Wow." Cheyenne laughed as she stepped onto the next step and got ready to pull. "After all this time, you don't trust me enough to brag about my car, huh?"

The housekeeper lifted again as the halfling pulled back, then she puffed out the breath she'd been holding and glanced briefly up at the girl she'd helped raise on the estate. "That's precisely what I'm trying to avoid, my dear. Your bragging."

With another grunt from the housekeeper, they made it up another step and were over halfway there.

"I don't brag, Eleanor." Cheyenne lifted up one more time and glanced over her shoulder. "I just save the best stories for *you*. And I haven't said a word about the car."

"But you *want* to." Lift, grunt, drag. "Don't forget, I've been anticipating your every move since you were two."

The halfling barked a laugh and moved onto the last stair. "And I'm *still* a step ahead of you."

"No, you're — Oh. You meant literally." Eleanor chuckled, her face flushing even deeper as she and the half-drow lifted Ember's chair one final time up the last wide stone step. "Don't underestimate these gray hairs, Cheyenne. We both know most people can't keep up with you, but I am certainly not one of them."

The housekeeper dusted off her hands as Cheyenne pulled Ember's chair up over the threshold of the front door and into the grand foyer of Bianca Summerlin's secluded estate in Henry County.

"So many things make so much more sense now," Ember muttered.

"Ha! I like her."

Cheyenne smirked at her mom's closest confident and shrugged, brushing loose strands of hair away from her face. "Yeah, she's okay."

"Thanks, Eleanor. I like you too." The fae's grin made the other woman burst into quick, sharp laughter that echoed around them in the massive house.

"Aren't *we* in for a night!" Eleanor pressed a hand to her cheek and shook her head. "This is all—"

"Oh, good. You made it." Bianca Summerlin stepped into the foyer from the north end of the house, presumably her study, and offered the other three a calm, appraising smile. Her discerning gaze fell on Eleanor, and the woman's eyebrows twitched into a brief frown. "Are you all right?"

"Absolutely." The housekeeper was still trying to catch her breath as she nodded quickly.

"Eleanor, you're much more flushed than usual."

"Oh, it's just the heat from the stove and scurrying here as fast I could to let these two inside." When Bianca raised an eyebrow, Eleanor nodded and glanced at Cheyenne, then gave another quick burst of laughter before cutting it off entirely. "I'll go check on dinner."

The woman bustled toward the other end of the house and the kitchen, and Bianca Summerlin's smile bloomed again when she looked at Ember. "Welcome. Drinks first, I think, yeah?"

"Definitely." Ember nodded, and Cheyenne bit her lip to force down her laugh.

Yeah, she'll be just fine.

CHAPTER NINETY-FIVE

"Ember, I hear you and Cheyenne are housemates now. Is that right?" Bianca Summerlin stood at the bar behind the dining room table and mixed Ember Gaderow a cocktail.

The fae stared out the wide swath of floor-to-ceiling windows stretching across the back end of the Summerlin house. Sunset lit the sky with brilliant orange and pink, all of it spilling across the valley behind the estate, over the veranda, and into what served as the living room. Cheyenne glanced at Ember and cleared her throat.

"Oh." The fae blinked quickly and nodded. "Yeah, we just moved in on Friday. I thought *our* view was amazing, but this…"

"It's breathtaking, isn't it?" Bianca offered her guest the first cocktail of the evening in a highball glass. "I hope you don't mind Nolet's, Ember."

The fae's eyes almost bulged as she reached for the glass and nodded. "Uh, Nolet's is perfect. Thank you so much."

"My pleasure." The woman's smile widened as she watched Ember take the first sip of her gin and tonic a la Bianca.

Cheyenne's friend closed her eyes and sighed. "Damn, that's good." The Summerlin women chuckled, and Ember's eyes flew open. "I'm sorry. I need to watch my mouth."

"Trust me, I've heard much worse. I'm happy to hear you enjoy the gin so much."

Ember's cheeks reddened, but she pushed through it gracefully and stared at the drink in her hand. "I haven't had a drink since...well, since Gnarly's."

The halfling offered a small, reassuring smile when Ember looked at her. *At least she's not saying, "Since the night I got shot."* "So, like three weeks."

"Yeah." Ember gave a little chuckle. "Feels like forever."

Bianca ignored the glance the young women shared and turned back to the bar beneath the grand, sweeping staircase. "You two met your freshman year in college, correct?"

Ember swallowed the much larger sip of gin and tonic and nodded. "That's right. Haven't been able to get rid of Cheyenne since."

"Ha!" Bianca didn't turn around, but the young magicals looked at each other again in surprise.

The halfling shot her friend a discrete thumbs-up and raised an eyebrow. *Get Mom to laugh, and that's like a thousand extra points.*

"Well, I'd love to hear how you two came to the decision about the apartment. Your usual, Cheyenne?" The woman lifted a bottle of Elijah Craig toward her daughter and raised her eyebrows when the halfling nodded once. She set to making her daughter the next drink, playing the perfect hostess, as always. "I have to admit I never expected Cheyenne to live with anyone since she's rather like me in that way."

"Hmm. Well, you have a housemate too, don't you?"

The small freezer door set in the top of the bar clicked shut, and Bianca paused. "I suppose you could say that." One large, square ice cube clinked into the rocks glass, and the woman turned to glance at the fae again, her lips pursing in amusement. "And I'm starting to understand why *you're* the friend with whom my daughter decided to share an apartment."

Cheyenne almost laughed when her mom shot her another quick glance of approval before returning to the halfling's drink.

"Beyond the fact that we get along pretty well," Ember started swirling her cocktail, "Cheyenne's been helping me out."

"Really? It goes without saying, but I hope it's all legal."

Ember choked on her drink, and Cheyenne snorted a laugh before covering it by rubbing her mouth.

"All legal, Mom. Promise." When the halfling caught her friend's mortified expression, she shook her head and mouthed at Ember, "She's joking." *That never happens.*

"Uh, as far as I know, yeah," the fae replied. "I just needed a little extra help, you know?" Then, realizing how much it sounded like she was using Bianca Summerlin's daughter for her money, Ember quickly added, "The wheelchair's new. Lots of adjusting."

"I can only imagine." A splash of purified water topped off the bourbon on the rocks, then Bianca handed the drink to her daughter and got to work mixing her own.

"Yeah, what Ember's not saying is that she decorated the entire apartment by herself over the weekend. Better than I would have, honestly."

The fae laughed. "Easy as point and click, pretty much. And it wasn't by myself. Who knew you could pay people to come in and unpack all your new stuff for you, huh?"

Bianca pressed her lips together and dipped her head. "A lovely convenience. Where were you over the weekend, Cheyenne?"

"Oh. Uh, errands."

Ember snorted and covered it with another long sip.

"While your new housemate took care of setting up the entire apartment, hiring movers, and putting things together the way they need to be?"

"Yeah, it's a pretty good deal for both of us." Cheyenne took a sip of her bourbon. Then she stopped and glanced at Ember with wide eyes. "Oh, *man.*"

"What?" Ember frowned above a confused smile.

"It just hit me, Em. You're my Eleanor."

Ember and Bianca burst out laughing at the same time. The sound surprised all three of them, and when the fae and

Cheyenne's mom looked at each other, they fell into another round.

"Don't let Eleanor hear you say that," Bianca muttered as she poured a large amount of vodka over a very small amount of ice.

"I'm flattered, really." Ember grinned at her halfling friend and pointed with a warning finger. "Don't expect me to cook your meals, though."

"I'm good with leftover pizza, Em."

"Despite how much that makes me want to cringe, Cheyenne, I'm glad the apartment's working out, at least. Which apartments?"

"Pellerville Gables."

"Oh, yes. Senator Berkley's son has the second floor of one of the buildings there, I think. I heard it's nice."

Ember's mouth popped open. Cheyenne hummed in agreement and raised a mocking eyebrow at her friend. "Very nice."

"Now." Bianca turned to face the young magicals beside the dining table and lifted her vodka soda with lemon toward the glass double doors. "Shall we move out onto the veranda?"

Ember stared at the wide stone terrace in front of them and took another sip of her gin before handing the glass to Cheyenne. "Best idea I've heard all day."

"Excellent." Bianca approached the double doors and pulled them open one at a time, then stepped outside into the cool evening air.

Gripping the wheels, the fae looked at her halfling friend with a crooked smile. "How am I doing?"

"You got her to laugh *and* make a joke. She might want to adopt you."

"I might let her." Ember nodded matter-of-factly and wheeled herself across the dining room toward the double doors.

Grinning, Cheyenne followed and balanced both their glasses in one hand so she could grip one of the handles with the other. "Go for it. I got you."

Ember gave the wheels a quick shove to get her over the lintel and onto the veranda. The chair lurched forward, and a pale violet light flashed around the small front wheels beside the fae's feet. The bump and jolt both young magicals had expected never came. Instead, Ember's chair hovered above the veranda, and a second later, she lowered it gently to the stone.

The fae's hands jerked away from the wheels, and she and Cheyenne stared at the chair. "Did you do that?"

The halfling stepped around the chair and handed Ember the tall glass of gin and tonic. "Pendant, Em. That was all you."

"My face feels funny."

Cheyenne bit her lip. "Maybe it's the gin."

Ember looked at her with wide eyes and slowly shook her head. "I can't believe this."

"Believe it or not, it just happened." The halfling wiggled her eyebrows, then glanced at her mom.

Bianca stood a foot away from the balcony surrounding the curved veranda, her vodka soda lifted to her lips and her face turned slightly toward the young magicals just outside the double doors.

Yeah, she's listening.

"Come take a look at this." Cheyenne nodded toward the balcony and headed that way. "The view's even better when you're right over it."

Ember cleared her throat and nestled the glass in her lap before wheeling across the smooth stone toward the Summerlin women. She stopped beside Cheyenne and ignored the thin, intricately carved stone posts supporting the railing every few feet. After a moment, having to look through those columns didn't matter as she gazed at the acre of well-kept lawn behind the estate house before everything opened into the wide valley beyond. "This is incredible."

"Thank you." Bianca took another sip of her drink. "I can't tell you how often I find myself out here. There's nothing quite like being able to see as far as one can imagine."

The fae lifted her glass to her lips again. "I always thought I liked the city. This just changed my mind."

Bianca let out another thoughtful hum. "I remember the feeling."

All three women soaked up the rare moment of peace in silence. Then Ember found herself full of questions. "Do you do all your work from here, Ms. Summerlin?"

"Bianca, please." The woman stepped back to meet the fae's gaze behind her daughter. "Unless you're here on business too."

Ember laughed and shook her head. "I wouldn't know where to start."

"That's fine. Visits from close friends are necessarily infrequent, living all the way up here, though I'd rather host friends than associates and colleagues. And to answer your question, Ember, yes. I have everything I need up here to keep up with my work, and I accomplish more than I expected when I first moved onto the property."

"Do you miss the city?"

Cheyenne turned and leaned against the balcony railing, smirking as her mom and her friend made polite small talk that sounded much more like genuine interest than the type of pleasantries she had grown up hearing. *I knew they'd like each other. We all need a good distraction.*

Bianca nodded and glanced back out over the valley. "Sometimes. After over two decades of running things out here in my domain, it's difficult to imagine leaving this for so much…"

"Noise."

The halfling's mom blinked and caught Ember's gaze again. "You and Cheyenne are remarkably well-matched as friends, aren't you?"

"Pretty much."

"It's good to see." Bianca smiled at the fae, then glanced at her daughter and raised an eyebrow. "You're really enjoying this, aren't you?"

Cheyenne grinned and offered her mom a blasé shrug. "Nice to switch things up a little, right?"

"As long as you're certain all the *switching* can be balanced." The look Bianca shot her daughter carried a warning and a challenge at the same time.

Thanks, Mom. I'm being careful. "I've got a pretty good handle on things so far."

"I'm sure you do." Bianca nodded, then rolled her shoulders and took another sip of her drink. "It's getting a little chilly for me."

"I don't even feel it," Ember said dreamily, gazing out across the sweeping valley below them.

Glancing at her wristwatch, Bianca nodded. "Dinner will be ready soon. Ember, can I make you another drink?"

"Uh, yeah. That would be great. Thank you."

"I'm more than happy to do it. And please don't feel obligated to thank me for every individual thing tonight. Once before you leave will suffice." The woman headed toward the open double doors without another word.

Ember blushed again and stared up at Cheyenne. "Did I say the wrong thing?"

"No, Em. That had nothing to do with you."

"I'm gonna take your word for that one. She just kinda flipped a switch, didn't she?"

"Yeah. Never a dull moment with Bianca." Looking away from the outline of her mom standing at the bar again, the halfling glanced at her fae friend and grinned. "She likes you."

"Seemed like it until she told me to stop thanking her."

"Nah. That's just her version of hospitality. She's trying to..." Cheyenne scrunched her face.

"Trying to what?"

"Well, level the playing field, I guess."

Ember laughed. "I don't know what that means."

"Honestly, I think you're the first person in a long time who's made her think about who she was and what she was doing with her life before all this happened." The halfling gestured at her face with a flick of her wrist. "She was a little older than we are, but I know she wasn't ready to give everything up and steal away to the countryside to raise a half-drow on her own."

"And *I* remind her of that." Ember frowned and wrinkled her nose. "That's a little weird."

"Not really. I mean, you and I weren't *ready* for what's going on with either of us right now either. Different situation, same feeling, I think."

The fae blinked up at her friend and opened her mouth with a sharp breath. It took her another try before she could get out what she wanted to say. "You've spent a long time analyzing your mom, haven't you?"

"Well, there weren't a whole lot of options up here." Cheyenne laughed. "Run through the woods, sneak onto the dark web and learn to hack into pretty much anything, and spy on Bianca Summerlin so I could maybe one day figure her out."

"Sounds like you got there."

"Possibly." The halfling lifted her glass toward Ember in a toast and dipped her head. "Just wait. If she doesn't give you an open invitation to the Summerlin estate before we leave tonight, I'll bake Matthew Thomas a cake."

Ember barked out a laugh. "That's on *you*. I don't know what I'd do with an open invitation."

"Whatever you want, really." Cheyenne took a long drink of bourbon and nodded toward the open double doors. "We can—"

A huge crash split the air from the other side of the valley. The halfling turned and scanned the tree line at the edge of the manicured lawn below them. "You heard that, right?"

"Sounds like a tree fell over, yeah." Ember peered through the stone pillars beneath the rail and frowned. "I don't see anything."

"Me, neither." Cheyenne squinted and studied the trees a little longer. "Must've just been a dead one finally breaking free or something."

That tingling buzz passed across the halfling's shoulders and the back of her neck again. She glanced quickly at Ember and found that her fae friend had lifted one hand to the back of her neck. "Cheyenne?"

"Yeah, I know." With a final glance out over the balcony, the halfdrow nodded toward the doors again. "We'll just keep paying attention, right?"

"Kinda hard not to when it feels like my back just turned into an anthill."

"Nothing we can do about it until something happens."

Ember blinked and slowly turned her head to meet her friend's gaze. "You spend half your time feeling like this, don't you?"

"You mean, feeling like something's about to happen and not knowing what the hell it is or when? Pretty much, yeah. At least the other half of the time, I get to fight asshole magicals and train toward completing the trials. Still working on the balance."

"I don't know how you do it."

"Me, neither, Em. Come on, I think your next cocktail's ready."

They headed back inside. "Your mom's gonna get me wasted."

"It's actually an honor."

CHAPTER NINETY-SIX

"Eleanor, this looks amazing."

"Oh, it's not all that." The housekeeper waved off Ember's compliment as she passed the salad bowl to Bianca. Even so, she couldn't hide a proud smile flickering at the corners of her mouth. "But thank you. I hope you enjoy it."

"I know I will." The fae scooped another helping of the braised vegetables—Brussels sprouts, mushrooms, onion, chunks of fennel, carrots, and cauliflower.

"There's a warm beet salad too," the housekeeper added. "Goat cheese, candied pecans, and a balsamic reduction. Where did that one go?"

Bianca offered the smaller bowl of bright-red beets with a small smile without turning to look at her friend the housekeeper.

"Thank you."

Cheyenne loaded her plate and smirked as the dishes were passed around. "Whose idea was it to have dinner without any meat or bread?"

Eleanor looked at the halfling with a deadpan expression and dipped her chin. "Take a wild guess."

The halfling chuckled, and beside her, Ember grinned.

"You know perfectly well why I made the decision," Bianca added, pointing toward Eleanor with the tines of her fork turned down. "We've always been healthy, keeping good food in mind. But there's a lot of evidence to support wheat and gluten adding to joint inflammation and, of course, putting more carbs in our bodies than we need."

"We've been having this conversation for months now," Eleanor added, waving her hand toward her employer and shooting the young magicals an exasperated glance. "I told her I'd restock that kitchen and change the entire menu if she finally admitted that time might be catching up with her a *little*."

Cheyenne laughed. "You mean, she's trying to deny it?"

Bianca reached for her second vodka soda and took a demure sip. "Denial is one thing, Cheyenne. Lack of proof is something else entirely."

"Ha!" Eleanor shook her head and scooped a heaping spoonful of beet salad onto her plate before passing it along. "Maybe lack of proof on the outside. I mean, look at the woman. Ember, can you honestly tell me these two couldn't pass as sisters if you saw them walking down the street?"

"I would never tell you that," Ember replied, forcing herself not to look at the mistress of the house as she said it.

"Stop it. Both of you." Bianca's voice was flat and dismissive, but her small smile betrayed that she appreciated the compliment.

"Oh, sure. Pretend it's not true. That's what she's been doing for years. Not all of us were blessed with the ability to only age five years in twenty."

"Well, she must've said *something*." Cheyenne made a show of studying the dishes on the table. "Because I only see three out of five food groups."

"Congratulations. You've solved the mystery." Bianca lifted her chin toward her daughter in that haughty way she'd mastered. "Whatever I said is between Eleanor and me. We both got what we wanted, so let's leave it at that."

Eleanor looked at Ember and pulled a surprised face, the corners of her mouth turning down as her eyes widened. The fae laughed and opted for a glass of mineral water instead of a third cocktail. Cheyenne did the same.

"Are you also pursuing a master's degree, Ember?" Bianca lifted a bright-red beet slice to her mouth, her forked turned upside-down as she plucked it off with her teeth.

"I was." Ember shrugged. "But accidents happen, and plans get postponed."

"I understand." Bianca nodded and dabbed the corner of her mouth with a cloth napkin. "I can't speak for your experiences, of course, but I *will* say that from what I can see, you're handling the entire thing with more grace than most people who don't go through half as much in a lifetime."

Ember's swallow was so loud, they all heard it. She quickly took another sip of mineral water and nodded. "Thank you."

"Hmm." Bianca smiled and pointed her fork at the fae. "That one had nothing to do with my hospitality, so I'll let it slide."

"Oh." When the fae understood the joke, she laughed. Eleanor shook her head and picked more goat cheese out of the beet salad to add to her plate. Cheyenne rolled her eyes and dug into the braised vegetables.

"Will you be picking up your studies again in the future, do you think?"

"I have no idea right now. The school's given me a temporary leave, I guess." Ember stabbed more than a huge mouthful's worth of salad onto her fork. "I have some time. Right now, I'm just focusing on myself."

"That's important. Necessary for everyone. You can discover quite a lot about yourself with that kind of focus to your time."

Ember and Cheyenne exchanged glances and almost laughed. "It's already happening."

"Oh, I have no doubt. Especially if you're spending a good bit more time with Cheyenne."

"What's that supposed to mean?" The halfling looked at her mom with an expectant smile.

"I'm wondering the same thing," Eleanor added.

Bianca raised her glass and dipped her head. "My daughter has mastered the ability to carve her own path by stirring pots no one's touched in years while opening her home to a friend in need. And she still makes time for her mother. If anyone spending any amount of time with Cheyenne doesn't pick up a thing or two about authenticity and perseverance, I'd say they need to reevaluate their priorities."

The table fell into a stunned silence.

"Wow." Cheyenne licked salad dressing from her lips and raised her eyebrows. "Mom's dishing out the flattery tonight."

"It's not flattery if it's well-deserved. You know that."

"I feel like making a toast," Eleanor added quickly. "To Cheyenne."

"Oh, come on." The halfling chuckled but grabbed her glass of bourbon.

"To Cheyenne *and* Ember." The mistress of the estate raised her glass higher.

"Well, of course. And to blazing new trails." Eleanor was almost shouting now, grinning from ear to ear.

The halfling smirked at her friend. "Can't say no to a toast like *that*, right?"

"Even if I wanted to, I'd be too afraid of what would happen."

That made everyone laugh, and then all the glasses were raised toward the center of the table.

Eleanor laughed. "I can't even remember what I said."

"That's what happens when people keep adding to a toast." Cheyenne grinned. "What Eleanor said."

"What Eleanor said."

Grinning, the four women clinked glasses and drank to whatever they wanted. Bianca lifted her glass to her lips and met her daughter's gaze over the fine crystal rim. She took an incredibly long sip, then looked away and lowered her glass. "Tell me about the car."

"Oh, boy. Here we go." The halfling playfully rolled her eyes.

"I saw it when you pulled up, Cheyenne. If you wanted to hide, you should have bought something else."

Eleanor guffawed and almost slammed her glass back down on the table.

"Mom, if you want me to take you for a ride in my Porsche, all you have to do is ask."

"I'd rather drive it myself."

"Of course, you would."

Ember nodded toward the front of the house. "You should at least show her your favorite part."

The halfling frowned and looked down at her plate. "Nah, we don't need to go there."

"Right." Ember looked at Eleanor and Bianca earnestly. "I almost expected her to roll up that driveway and start honking at the house."

"The horn is your favorite part of that Panamera?" Bianca clicked her tongue as she lifted another bite to her mouth.

"No." Cheyenne shot Ember a warning glance but couldn't help another laugh. "You don't have to say anything else, Em."

"Oh, well *now*." Bianca's small smile widened. "What is it?"

"It's the other sound," Ember answered for the halfling. "You know, the little beep on the automatic lock."

Eleanor stared at the halfling, her lips pressed together as she laughed silently through her nose. Bianca choked, lurched forward, and grabbed her glass of mineral water. "Excuse me." She took a long drink, then set it slowly back down and blinked. "I certainly hope you didn't buy that car just for the *little beep*."

"Oh, yeah. That's the only thing I look for in a car." Cheyenne shrugged and glanced around the table. "I really like the way it sounds, okay? And it's a great car."

"It's certainly better than the rusting shell you've been driving for years."

"Yes, Mom. I'm well aware of the difference."

Bianca smirked. "What'd you do with the Ford?"

Cheyenne and Ember shared a brief glance before the halfling looked quickly away. *No way Mom didn't see that.* "It was time."

Ember snorted.

"I see." Bianca eyed her daughter for a little longer, then returned her attention to her plate. "I admire your decision to make so many large changes all at once. It wipes the slate clean in most regards, doesn't it?"

"Yeah, things are clean." Cheyenne laughed when she caught the flutter of her mom's eyelids, the closest Bianca Summerlin came to rolling her eyes.

"At least you're still keeping up with your schedule at school."

The halfling sat up a little straighter in her chair, and Eleanor let out a little hum of intrigue.

When Bianca looked at her daughter again, the amusement had vanished from her features. "Cheyenne, please tell me you're still in school."

"Of course, I'm still in school. That's the same."

"But?"

Cheyenne glanced at the ceiling and tilted her head from side to side. "My schedule has changed a little."

"Mmhmm."

Ember pointed at her halfling friend. "She went from advanced grad student to—"

Without warning, the floor, table, chairs, and their dinnerware trembled. Ice clinked in glasses, and from somewhere on the other side of the house came the tinkle of crystal rattling against other crystal. Bianca set her palms firmly on the table, staring at the polished wooden surface in front of her. Ember snatched up her tall gin glass before it fell over, and Eleanor let out a little squeak of surprise, gripping the edges of her chair with both hands.

Cheyenne glanced around the dining room and gritted her teeth.

Almost as quickly as it had started, the earthquake stopped.

The table fell silent again as everything in the Summerlin house stopped rattling and shaking. Bianca lifted her napkin to the corner of her mouth again. "Eleanor, remind me to thank you for talking me out of installing that chandelier in the dining room."

"I stand by my decision." Eleanor nodded slowly, her eyes wide. "That was…"

"Unexpected, yes. I'll look into it after dinner. Just one more benefit of living all the way out here away from the city, Ember." Bianca smiled curtly at the fae and returned her napkin to her lap. "Even the natural surprises feel a lot more isolated than—"

The second wave rocked the house with surprising force. The metal salad bowl jolted off the end of the table and clattered to the floor, followed by the bottle of mineral water.

"All right. Everyone out from under the staircase." Bianca lurched to her feet and stumbled away from the table, helping Eleanor out of her chair with a firm grip on the other woman's hand.

Cheyenne leaped up and grabbed the handles of Ember's wheelchair before whisking her friend away from the table.

"Cheyenne?" Ember rubbed the back of her neck and looked at the halfling with wide eyes.

"I don't know." The half-drow pulled Ember away from the table and out from beneath the staircase, then turned to look out the wall of windows and past the veranda. A flash of dark light bloomed from within the trees at the edge of the small meadow. A wide swath of oak trees and loblolly pines rustled violently before crashing down against each other. The shaking house settled down a little, a slow rumble still rising from beneath the floors. The halfling barely noticed, her attention split between the almost painful tingle across the tops of her shoulders and the second flash of dark light between the trees. "Shit."

CHAPTER NINETY-SEVEN

"Cheyenne." It wasn't a question the way Ember said it. Not from Bianca Summerlin.

"I don't know, Mom." The halfling wheeled Ember toward Bianca and Eleanor, then set a hand lightly on her friend's shoulder and nodded at her mom. "I'll be back."

"If you don't know, Cheyenne, I doubt it's a good idea to go chasing after it."

"Yeah, but at least it won't come chasing after *me* into this house." The halfling shot her mom a warning look, and the fiery determination Bianca saw in her daughter's eyes sucked the breath out of her. "Just stay here."

"What's happening?" Eleanor squeaked.

No one had the time to answer her before the house rocked again. Cheyenne staggered toward the double doors and threw them open. The calm air outside on the veranda was at odds with the shaking stone beneath her feet and the echo of groaning trees and earth before both snapped and split open. Black and purple light bloomed in long flashes within the trees.

The halfling stopped halfway to the balcony and ripped the

Heart of Midnight pendant off her neck for what felt like the thousandth time. *This is really getting old.*

As soon as the chain broke, Cheyenne's magic flared with an overwhelming intensity up her spine and through her entire body. The force of it sent purple sparks shooting from her fingertips as her hair went from black to white and her pale skin darkened. For a second, everything went violet in her vision as purple light flashed behind her glowing gold eyes, then she stepped back before sprinting toward the railing at the edge of the veranda.

She vaulted over it and dropped nearly two stories.

"Oh, my God, *Cheyenne!*" Ember fumbled to get a grip on the chair's wheels, but Bianca stepped toward her and just barely touched her fingertips to the fae's upper arm.

"It's all right. She's been doing that since she was nine."

"What?"

Eleanor clasped her hands together and raised them toward her trembling lips as all three women stared at the edge of the veranda. "We asked her why she would ever need to put that skill to use."

"Apparently, Eleanor, we were wrong."

Cheyenne landed on the grass and dropped into a roll. The next second, she was back on her feet and racing across the manicured lawn toward the flashing lights and the huge patch of felled trees and snapped branches. *I don't care what it is as long as it stays away from the house.*

Slipping into drow speed, she sprinted toward the tree line and almost staggered backward when she saw what was behind the dark flash of light suspended in front of her.

A frozen black tentacle rose halfway behind the light, two more crossing behind it, blurred by the frozen shimmer of the light. "You've gotta be kidding me."

She dropped out of drow speed to study the flashing lights in real-time. The ground bucked again beneath her, and more trees splintered and crashed into their neighbors. A huge, thick oak shrieked before the entire thing fell sideways. Dirt and grass, leaves and twigs erupted when the massive trunk crashed to the ground at the edge of the field, the entire base ripped out of the earth. A shower of dirt and shredded roots rained down on the forest floor.

Cheyenne stretched out her fingers, gritting her teeth and breathing heavily as she scanned the woods. *They can't get through if there's not an actual portal.*

As if the earth read her mind, another earsplitting crack rose from the ground, and a jagged black line ripped across the earth from where the giant tree had been uprooted. It zig-zagged toward the halfling and through her feet before she leaped aside. Then the ground shuttered and roared. The black and purple lights strobed faster between the trees.

The halfling's eyes darted across the tree line until the magical flashes were too much for her to follow. A muffled bellow like some beast roaring through a pillow rose at Cheyenne's feet. Her drow hearing was more than enough to tell her it came from below. *From the Border. The in-between.*

"Fuck this." She steeled herself and waited because that was all she could do. *Maybe not.*

She reached out with her magic, focusing on the jagged crack in the earth that hadn't opened much more than a foot or two. Stretching her power, she felt for that bit of resistance in and around the earth and found it.

Her arms and shoulders ached as she hooked her fingers over that magical ledge and used her ability to manipulate earth and stone to pull everything back together before the mess got any worse. The ground shivered and groaned again, and the edges of the jagged crack jerked together. *Yes.*

The ground erupted at her feet, and a black spear of stone burst from the ground right where the halfling stood. It knocked Cheyenne backward and sent her skidding across the ground. The air roared as spire after glistening spire punched through from that non-world of the in-between into this very real one.

The halfling leaped to her feet again and raced down the line of erupting stone columns. She reached out with both hands and tried to find the pull on her magic so she could stop the rest of the portal ridge. Two more spires punched through just beyond the tree line, launching half a dozen trees into the air. Then the portal ridge stopped, only stretching about ten yards.

Cheyenne dropped her hands and hissed, catching her breath. The woods fell silent as the last bits of broken earth tumbled from the tops of the black spires. Then there was nothing.

"Okay." The halfling bobbed her head, scanning the line of rocky spikes through the middle of her backyard. *Just a little one, then. Maybe it won't—*

A piercing whistle like a teakettle made her stagger away from the portal ridge just before a wall of shimmering dark light shot from between the black spires and straight into the sky. It didn't rise nearly as tall as the portal that morning, but it didn't matter. From within the realm that wasn't supposed to be here, dark, slithering shapes moved back and forth.

"Dammit!" Cheyenne summoned spheres of crackling black energy in both hands and waited.

Back at the house, Bianca stood behind Ember's chair at the edge of the open double doors. Beside her, Eleanor covered her mouth with both hands and stared at the huge, jagged ridge of black stone jutting in a straight line from the edge of the woods and across the lawn. Ember gripped the armrests of her chair and bit her lip.

Bianca lifted her chin and raised an eyebrow. "I don't think even George will be able to repair the landscaping after this."

Eleanor clicked her tongue. "Oh, yes. Of course. That is the most pressing issue right now."

"If you're waiting for me to be concerned about my daughter, Eleanor, you'll be waiting a very long time. Cheyenne can handle this."

"I can't fathom how you can be so sure of that."

"I just know." Bianca glanced down at the young woman in front of her. "I'm sure Ember will agree with me. You've seen her fight."

The fae swallowed thickly. "Actually, no. I haven't."

"Hmm. Well, I have." The drow halfling's mother sighed. *I should have grabbed the vodka.*

She almost turned to do just that, but the sight of two long, snakelike tentacles shooting from the thin line of dark light she could barely see made her stop.

The tentacles whipped at Cheyenne, bashing the ground as the halfling darted from side to side, launching attack spells.

Eleanor shot her employer a sidelong glance. "You've seen her fight something like this?"

Bianca pressed her lips together. "Stop talking."

CHAPTER NINETY-EIGHT

Cheyenne launched crackling black spheres at the two tentacles whipping through the split in the portal. One of them lashed at her head. The halfling ducked and lunged to the side, launching another attack just as a tiny mouth opened in the underside of the tentacle and spat. A thick, smoking glob hit the shimmering surface of the halfling's well-timed shield, burning a hole in the grass the second it fell.

With a grunt, Cheyenne faced the portal rift head-on. *Just another training session, halfling. That's all this is.* She shook out her hands and bounced a little on the balls of her feet. *Let's go, Nimlothar.*

When she thought of the glowing purple seed, a sharper burst of tingling magic spread from her core. She took a deep breath and watched the tentacles waving above her. *Here we go.*

A third tentacle shot from between the two and headed toward the halfling's chest. Cheyenne shouted and moved without thinking, throwing her hand out like she meant to swipe away a thick cobweb. A screech burst from the portal as the third tendril jerked in the same direction as the halfling's arm. The thing ripped apart at the center, spraying black fluid everywhere as the end of the severed tentacle flew into the forest.

"Okay…" Cheyenne paced slowly in front of the other tentacles, which were whipping back and forth madly. "Bring it."

The tentacles stopped their wild flapping, stiffened, and bent at an angle before slamming down to spear the earth with pointed tips. She took a few steps back and caught a glimpse of glowing red eyes from within the shimmering wall of black portal light. Two more crackling spheres hurtled from her hands into the center of those blurry red eyes, and the tentacles that were barbed legs now rose to slam back into the ground again. Then the thing emerging from the in-between pulled itself across the grass.

Leg after spike-tipped leg slammed into the dirt. The blurred red eyes solidified as a roiling, shifting face broke free from the portal. Two gaping mouths opened one right after the other, displaying two rows of fangs each and dripping with a slime Cheyenne couldn't bring herself to look at.

She blasted the nightmarish creature again and again with her energy spheres, stepping slowly backward across the grass. A shadow loomed over her from behind the portal wall, then a thick, snaking tail with a curved bulb and a sharp, glistening tip sailed through the air toward her.

Cheyenne darted aside again and sent more attacks crashing into the huge tip of that hard-shelled tail. *Great, now there are scorpions.*

The tail tugged itself free from where the stinger had lodged in the ground, spraying dirt and grass in every direction. Then it struck out toward her, and the halfling shoved it aside with both hands this time. The creature's body lurched sideways. One of the legs still speared into the soil broke free with a crunch, and the thing screeched again.

Next trial ability. Use it.

She thought of the Nimlothar seed again and used that fresh burst of magical energy to pull her hands away from each other. The nightmare-scorpion shivered and split down the middle, one gaping red mouth tearing in half, but the two thicker tentacles bursting through the portal wall from either side of the thing's twitching body wiped the halfling's smirk off her face.

Cheyenne blasted one with a black sphere as the other wrapped around both her thighs. No barbs this time, but it squeezed tightly enough to make her cry out. She clamped her hands around the tentacle and summoned up more black energy, but the second tentacle cracked against her hands like a metal rod.

"Ah!" The halfling jerked her hands away, her legs and hips aching from the growing pressure. The second tentacle whipped around her torso and both arms, pinning them to her sides.

"Fuck you!" Cheyenne struggled against the tightening grip as the pulsing black tentacles squeezed, sliding farther around her. She pressed her palms against the underside of the nasty appendage pinning her arms down and almost managed to summon more spheres. Barbs shot from the tentacles beneath her hands, slicing through her palms, and all she could do was roar and jerk her hands away.

The nightmarish creature rose on newly sprouted legs, lurching and dragging itself out of the newest Border portal in Bianca Summerlin's backyard. Two more pairs of glowing red eyes shimmered behind the wall, blinking slowly at her as the tentacles lifted Cheyenne slowly from the ground.

She grunted, gritting her teeth, and tensed every muscle against the increasing pressure. Her breath came in short gasps and she clenched her hands into fists, ignoring the searing sting of her pierced palms. *I'm not going out like this. No fucking way.*

The ground trembled again as the rest of the tentacled scorpion-beast shoved itself through the portal opening. Then the thing lifted itself onto thick, squat back legs and opened the split Cheyenne had ripped in its body into another red mouth. Pulling its tentacles back toward itself, the thing squeezed the halfling even tighter and started to pull her toward the rows of razor-sharp teeth in that gaping mouth.

The halfling couldn't breathe. She could barely move. She closed her eyes and focused on the image of the glowing Nimlothar seed as she remembered it. *I'm not done.*

Black tongues of flame burst to life across the half-drow's skin. The creature shrieked and lifted her back into the air, but it was too late. When L'zar Verdys' daughter opened her eyes, their golden glow was replaced by a black light even stronger than that coming from the ripped portal. Black fire burned around her eyes, and as her lungs screamed for air, Cheyenne gave herself over to the drow magic coursing through her.

The flames covering her erupted into one massive, churning ball of dark light. They consumed the tentacles squeezing the life out of Cheyenne, racing down the undulating flesh of the in-between nightmare until there was nothing left. The tentacles crumbled into ash, and still the halfling was suspended in the air at the center of drow fire.

Cheyenne pulled a searing gasp of breath into her empty lungs and screamed.

The flames burst away from her, streaming toward the screeching beast and blowing it away in glittering fragments of black shell and charred remains. Every piece of the thing that had entered this world from beyond the portal disintegrated, cutting off the last piercing screech before there was nothing left.

The halfling dropped to the ground and crumpled when her legs wouldn't hold her up. The fire was gone, and when she opened her eyes with another gasping breath and a groan, the golden glow behind them had returned.

"Cheyenne!" Bianca's shout echoed across the swath of green lawn between them.

Growling, the halfling pushed to her feet and fought to catch her breath. She had to bend over and prop herself up with both hands on her knees, but she lifted one of those hands toward the house.

"I'm fine." The words croaked out of her. "I'm fine!"

The shallow echo barely made it back up to Bianca Summerlin, who stood at the edge of the veranda, gripping the railing with both hands. She swallowed and pulled herself together, but she didn't move until she saw her daughter straighten and head back toward the house.

The woman's eye twitched as she walked toward the open French doors into the house. Eleanor stood beside Ember just inside, their mouths hanging open as they stared at the dark ridge of stone and the drow halfling walking away from it. Bianca gave them a perfunctory glance before slipping inside. "She's fine."

Eleanor shut her mouth and cleared her throat. "I'll just…" She patted Ember's shoulder and turned in a daze to head toward the front of the house.

The fae watched Cheyenne until the halfling disappeared beneath the wide edge of the veranda, then she slowly wheeled the chair around. One of her sweaty hands slipped on the wheel, but she caught herself and tried again.

At the bar, Bianca filled her glass with vodka and didn't bother with the soda water or the lemon. Not even ice. She knocked back a huge gulp and sucked in a breath through her teeth. "That was certainly entertaining."

Ember's mouth opened and closed quickly before she found her voice. "That's one way to put it."

"Mmhmm." Bianca took another long swig and set the half-empty glass back down on the bar. "That's enough." She looked at Ember and took a deep breath through her nose. "In case you're wondering, Ember, I'm still very glad you two decided to join us tonight."

An unintended chuckle burst from the fae's mouth, which she clamped shut immediately. "Me too."

The woman nodded and gestured toward the other side of the staircase. "Shall we?"

"After you." Ember dipped her head, her eyes burning because she couldn't seem to blink.

Bianca quickly headed past the fae, and Ember forced herself through the shock so she could wheel across the shiny floors of the Summerlin mansion.

When they reached the foyer, Eleanor had already opened the

front door. The Goth version of Cheyenne appeared around the right side of the house. She brushed carelessly past the bushes in the front garden, snapping off branches. No one said anything about it.

The half-drow climbed the wide stone steps and paused when she looked up to see all three women in the doorway. "Well, at least we know what caused the earthquake."

Then she stepped into the house and past everyone to give herself a little space. Eleanor closed the door firmly and stayed there with her hand on the doorknob.

"Perhaps you'd care to enlighten us as to what that thing was?" Bianca murmured.

Pulling her cell phone from her back pocket, Cheyenne unlocked the home screen and looked at her mom. "Something that's not supposed to be here."

"Yes, that's more than obvious, Cheyenne. But that's not what I asked."

"Well, you didn't actually ask me anything," the halfling spat. Immediately, she dropped the phone by her side and looked at Bianca. "I'm sorry, Mom."

"I appreciate your apology, Cheyenne, but would not have held it against you if you hadn't given it." Bianca raised her eyebrows and nodded. "I would still very much like to know what's happening in my backyard."

"Even if it's magic stuff?"

The foyer filled with a tense silence. Bianca stepped back and turned to meet Ember's gaze. "Which, by your lack of reaction, I assume you already know plenty about?"

The fae dipped her head with a little shrug. "I might be a part of that whole world, yeah."

"All right." Bianca nodded and glanced at Eleanor. "As illuminating as that information might be, it doesn't change anything about what just happened outside."

"I know." Cheyenne lifted her phone and caught her mom's gaze again. "I need to make a call. After that, hopefully, I'll know more too. Then I can tell you what that was if you still want to hear it."

Bianca studied her daughter and pursed her lips. "We'll give you some privacy."

Eleanor jumped when her employer took off around the side of the huge house toward her study in the back. The housekeeper followed quickly, stopping to throw her arms around Cheyenne and kiss the halfling's cheek with as much force as her crushing hug. The halfling winced, and Eleanor instantly released her. "Sorry. I'm sorry. What hurts?"

Cheyenne grimaced and shook her head. "Everything."

"Hmm." The housekeeper raised a hand to the halfling's cheek, nodded, and stepped around her to hurry after Bianca.

CHAPTER NINETY-NINE

Ember stared at Cheyenne after both women disappeared behind the curve of the grand staircase in the center of the foyer. "Does *anything* scare her?"

"Not much, no." The halfling pulled up Corian's number and pressed the phone against her ear.

He answered on the third ring. "I know you're smart enough not to call me about the same thing after your little slip up with that text earlier."

"Yeah, I'm fine. Thanks for asking. Almost died, though."

"Where's the pendant?"

"It's here. I'll put it on when we're done."

"Cheyenne, I'll wait."

Rolling her eyes, she stuffed the phone into her back pocket and pulled out the broken silver chain with way too many knots in it, tying a new one. The Heart of Midnight flashed pale, silver light, and she took out her phone again. "There. I think it's starting to wear off pretty quickly now, by the way."

"That was bound to happen. We'll address it when we have to. What happened?"

"Okay. Uh, that little issue we ran into on our drive out to Maryland yesterday? The first time."

"Yes?"

Cheyenne glanced at the vaulted ceiling of the foyer. "Well, I just found another one. Or it found me. I have no idea." The line was silent, and the halfling pulled the phone away to double-check that they were still connected. "Corian?"

"Where?"

"At my mom's house."

A long hiss came over the line. "Has it opened yet?"

"Oh, yeah. Definitely. I think I took care of it for now, but I have no idea how long that's gonna last."

"By yourself."

Cheyenne nodded and shot Ember an exasperated glance. "Yeah, by myself. I'm the only one here who could do anything about it."

"Is it as big a threat as the last one?"

"Corian, I have no idea. That's why I'm calling you. It's not nearly as big as the last one, but it's right behind my mom's house. *On* her property. It could've brought the whole place down on top of us if it was any closer to the house."

"Hmm. Well, it's a good sign that you managed to take care of it on your own."

The halfling snorted. "Not really. I wasn't joking about the almost-dying part. Black fire. That's as much as I can say on the phone—"

"Cheyenne, stop. You *used* that one just now?"

"I mean, maybe ten minutes ago, but yeah. That's the only reason I'm still here, making a phone call to such a cheery guy."

"Check the box."

She gritted her teeth. "I can't. I left it at home."

"I'll see if I can work around that one. But we need to see—"

"Hey, I don't care about that right now. The only thing I need to do is make sure that thing doesn't open again and start tearing the place apart. What are we supposed to do now? That's why I called you."

Corian paused again, and the halfling didn't bother checking her phone this time. "The best thing is for everyone in that house to vacate the property. Go somewhere safe. Get away from the threat. Which I'm sure you already know."

"Yeah, and I'm also sure that's not gonna happen. I'll ask, but in case she refuses, what do I do?"

"The next best thing is to call in your F-force friends."

Cheyenne rolled her eyes. "Nice touch with the forum code over the phone, by the way."

"Call them, Cheyenne. Have them send up a team to stand guard for a while, at the very least. If anything else tries to come through, they'll handle it."

"None of those magicals have made the crossing. They won't know what the hell to do."

"That doesn't matter. They're soldiers. Sort of. And their weapons are almost as powerful as m—as our weapons. Understand? Have them stand guard, and she'll be fine."

"Fine. What about you?"

"What about me?"

"Can you get out here?"

"No. I'm neck-deep in trying to put together those parts we brought back yesterday, and we're about to follow up with a lead on that name."

"Oh, great. Thanks for telling me you found something."

Corian cleared his throat. "It just happened, kid. I almost didn't answer my phone. Make your other call, sit tight, and text me your address."

"Really?"

"If I have time, I'll stop by to pick up some things. Where'd you leave the box?"

"Nightstand. And hey, if you do end up sneaking into my apartment, grab the darktongue salve too. Please. I need to start keeping that stuff on me."

"Have you used it yet?"

"Uh-huh."

A low chuckle escaped the Nightstalker, then Persh'al's voice came from somewhere else in the room. "I gotta go, kid. I'll let you know if you need to expect me. Anything else comes up, send me another text. *Clean.* My phone'll be on silent for a while tonight."

"Okay. Thanks."

"Cheyenne? If you took care of it the way you say you did, we're close. Understand?"

"Yeah."

"I'm proud of you."

A wry laugh escaped the drow halfling. "Have fun following your lead."

She hung up and took a deep breath. "Shit."

"What's up?" Ember sat rigid in her chair, staring at her friend with wide eyes.

"I can't believe I'm upset that I don't have that burner phone on me."

The fae frowned. "I didn't think all this stuff had much to do with the FRoE anymore."

"Normally, it wouldn't, but Corian seems to think they can handle it. At least better than not doing anything. And I'm out of options."

"Hey, I'd offer to drive back home and grab it if that was even remotely possible."

Cheyenne looked up and gave her friend a wan smile. "Thanks, Em. I don't *need* the phone. I was just *really* trying not to taint this one by calling them with it." The halfling tapped her temple. "I've seen that number come up so many times, it's stuck in here."

"That's lucky, I guess."

"Yeah. Hey, feel free to go hang out with them. They're probably getting lit right now, so at least it'll be laid back."

Ember laughed. "You could just say you want some privacy, you know."

"Stay if you want to. I don't mind. It's gonna be a...rough conversation."

The fae blinked and smacked her lips. "I think there's still some gin left in my glass. I'll go find out."

Cheyenne snorted and watched her friend wheel out of the foyer toward the broad hall leading down the side of the house. "Uh, just please don't tell her who I'm calling right now, okay?"

"I seriously doubt any of us wanna talk about that." The fae winked at her friend and paused. "That was a close one out there, wasn't it?"

The halfling chewed the inside of her bottom lip and nodded. "Close, but no dice."

Laughing, Ember shook her head and left the half-drow alone in the foyer to make one more call.

Cheyenne stared at the keypad on her phone and grimaced. "He owes me one, and he'll owe me another one after this."

She dialed Major Sir Carson's FRoE number from memory and slowly lifted the phone to her ear. She thought he wasn't going to answer when the call made it through five rings, but he picked up on the sixth.

"Where's the goddamn phone I gave you, halfling?"

She frowned. *Of course, he looked up my number.* "Unavailable."

"Well, make it available. That's part of the deal."

"Doesn't matter now, does it? You've had my personal number for a while, and you can give up trying to explain that one. Right now, I don't give a shit."

Sir cleared his throat. "So, what happened?"

Here goes nothing. "I need a team at my mom's house, like, ten minutes ago."

He snorted. "Are you wasted right now or something? Maybe too much LSD, or you smoked too many magic mushrooms?"

"Uh, I don't think that's how—"

"'Cause I can't think of another goddamn reason why you'd call me from your *personal number* to make demands, halfling. And I don't appreciate being drunk-dialed."

Cheyenne paused and slowly closed her eyes. "You done?"

"Are *you*?"

"No, and you really wanna hear what I have to say right now."

"I'll be the judge of that. Go."

Jesus, he's insane. "Just so you don't accuse me of being on drugs again, I'm saying this the way it is because we're on an open line."

"Are you trying to tell me you haven't done some fancy little trick with your phone to keep it extra-private?"

"No, I have. But I'm also pretty sure people you don't know about might be able to tap it anyway, so just hear me out. There's another opening."

"A what?"

"Another place to cross."

"Get your head out of your ass and say something intelligent."

Cheyenne let out a little growl of frustration and forced herself not to chuck her phone across the house. "The whole reason you people started doing what you're doing, man. Come on! The damn *openings* you guys regulate all over the world. Ring any bells?"

Sir paused for an unnervingly long time. "Are you telling me there's one on your mom's fancy ranch right now?"

Finally. "Yes."

"Are you—"

"Yes, I'm sure."

"Goddammit!" Sir roared.

The halfling jerked the phone away from her ear and could still hear every curse and made-up half-curse the FRoE director bellowed. When it died down, Cheyenne slowly pressed the phone to her ear again and heard his heavy breathing.

"I already checked it out," she told him. "And it's not...normal. That's why I need some people up here. My mom's not leaving her house, as I'm sure you already know, and I can't keep watch on it by myself."

"What do you mean, 'not normal?'"

"Stuff coming out that shouldn't be able to come out. Again, I can't *tell* you over the *phone*. But I'm all for telling your guys in person once you send them."

"*If* I send them."

"We don't have time to fuck around with your superiority complex, *Sir*. I didn't have to call you and tell you about this."

"And I don't have to send you shit."

Cheyenne nodded slowly. "Okay, fine. You're right. We'll call it a fair trade, then, huh? Your guys get full control of this thing for as long as you need to."

"We already have full control over all of them anyway. That's our goddamn job."

"Not the ones you don't know about."

Sir growled. "Watch it, halfling. You're *this* close to being cut off."

"No, I'm not. You need me, and I'm pretty sure you need to get this new *opening* under control if you don't want the whole secret world to know you guys screwed up and can't keep a handle on every single one of them anymore."

"You're a goddamn Venus Flytrap, Cheyenne. You know that?"

"Actually, you're the first person to say it quite like that, but thanks anyway."

"What about your mother? She made it pretty damn clear she doesn't want me anywhere near that property."

"She's not leaving. I know she won't. But she saw what happened with that thing, and she won't try to stop you, either."

Sir sighed, and the clink of ice against glass came over the line. "You better give these guys every single scrap of info you have. Got it?"

"Yeah. No problem."

"One hour. And do me a favor, huh? Don't ever call this number again, telling me what to do with my organization. I call the shots. You're expendable."

"Get back to your drink." Cheyenne hung up and felt quite a bit lighter because of it. *Asshole.*

CHAPTER ONE HUNDRED

"I most certainly will not leave my home, Cheyenne." Bianca sat back in the armchair on the south side of the house, one leg crossed elegantly over the other as she held her daughter's gaze. Eleanor glanced quickly between them and grabbed a pillow from the settee beside her before squeezing it tightly in her lap.

Sitting on the sofa with Ember beside her, the halfling took a small sip of her watered-down bourbon and nodded. "That's what I figured, but I had to ask."

"I hope your foresight led you to consider an alternative."

"Yeah, and I went ahead and put it in motion."

A small smile crept across Bianca Summerlin's tightly pressed lips. "I knew you would."

"They'll be here in an hour."

When her daughter didn't offer any more than that, Bianca uncrossed her legs and leaned forward in the armchair. "If I'm to be entertaining guests, I expect to know who they are ahead of time."

"You won't be entertaining anyone. They're coming for that thing outside. To keep it from doing anything worse than what you guys saw earlier."

"It was very impressive," Eleanor added, nodding at the halfling until her employer shot her a quick, expressionless glance. The housekeeper lowered her gaze and squeezed the pillow even tighter. "Mmhmm."

"Cheyenne." Bianca raised an eyebrow.

"FRoE agents, Mom. They're the only ones who have the ability to handle something like that. I'll have to fill them in, but they'll keep you safe until we're sure that thing outside isn't a danger to you or anyone else in this house. I promise."

"Will that obnoxious man who insists on withholding his name be joining them?"

"I doubt it. At least not tonight."

"Good. I really don't like him."

Eleanor laughed and changed it into a fake cough.

"I don't like him either, Mom, but this is all I can do right now. I'm sorry."

"Cheyenne, I don't want to hear another apology from you tonight. You handled a messy situation beautifully, and I'm prepared to put all the decisions about this issue into your hands so you can continue to do so."

The halfling froze, staring sidelong at her mother. *All the decisions. She's scared.* "I'll take care of it."

"I know. I'm still very interested to hear what else you can tell me about that eyesore cutting down the center of my view." Bianca gave her daughter a tight, bitter smile and took another sip of her latest drink, whatever it was.

"Sure." Cheyenne glanced at Ember, who now held a glass of red wine and had already downed half of it. "That's not the only one. I don't know how many there are. Hundreds, maybe thousands all over the world. Most of them are regulated."

"By that organization."

"Yeah. For the most part. Those things aren't supposed to be popping up out of nowhere, though. That's new. Pretty much like an earthquake or a tornado or any other natural disaster."

"It's quite unnatural, in all honesty. But I understand. What *is* it?"

Oh, she's really gonna hate this. "It's a portal."

Bianca Summerlin blinked twice, lowered her glass to her lap, and looked over her daughter's head to stare at something down the south hallway. "I'm listening."

"To the other side."

"I'm familiar with science fiction, Cheyenne. That would be how a portal works." The halfling's mother swallowed, her nostrils flaring as if saying a word related to any kind of magic put a rotten taste in her mouth.

"A different world, Mom."

"That's—"

"*His* world."

"Quite enough, thank you." Bianca downed the rest of her drink and stood. "I'll be in my study. Do let me know when your friends arrive. I don't enjoy being caught off-guard at any time in my own home, but twice in one night would be more than I could handle."

With that, the woman turned and headed past the dining table and the bar toward her study on the other side of the house. Cheyenne and Eleanor exchanged glances, then the housekeeper neatly fluffed and replaced the pillow she'd squashed and stood as well. "If you need anything, sweetheart—"

"I'll know who to find. Thanks."

With a tight smile, Eleanor set a firm, gentle hand on the halfling's shoulder, gave it a little pat, and headed down the south hall closest to the circle of armchairs and the sofa. A door opened and clicked softly shut somewhere, and Cheyenne turned toward Ember.

"You okay?"

"Uh-huh." The fae buried her face in the large wineglass, gulped, and nodded. "This is amazing."

"Yeah, she's got a pretty impressive collection."

"And I'm drinking it." Ember chuckled. "You know, I think I like it better when you go through all the crazy stuff and come tell me about it later."

"Oh, it's much more entertaining for you that way, huh?"

"Entertaining, period." Turning her head slowly, the fae girl met her friend's gaze with a frown of concern. "You make it sound like some awesome adventure with some assholes along the way. I had no idea there was all this other scary crap."

Cheyenne smirked. "Are you talking about the giant scorpion that almost squeezed me to death or the weird way I have to tiptoe around my mom about the whole thing?"

Ember chuckled softly and shook her head. "All of the above. I had no idea, and I still can't figure out how you manage to make jokes right after something like that."

"Meh. It's much easier to get caught up in all the dark and terrible deadly shit. I guess I just like a challenge."

"You're unbelievable."

"Yep. We've been over that too." With a tiny smile, Cheyenne took another sip of her bourbon and set it down on the glass coffee table. "We still have, like, an hour before anyone shows up. You want a tour?"

Ember's eyes widened. "A *what?*"

"A tour, Em. Of Chez Summerlin. Trust me, all this looks like a lot right now, but what you've seen so far isn't even half of it."

"I am *not* letting you and Eleanor drag me up that giant staircase."

With a snort, Cheyenne stood from the sofa and walked around the wheelchair. "Not a problem. Want me to take the wheel?"

"Please don't let me drink and drive."

"Ha." Cheyenne grabbed the handles and spun the fae around to push her down the south hall toward the other side of the house. "So, Bianca's study is on the other side, obviously. That's pretty much the only room over there, and I don't get to go in there very much. We'll skip that part."

"Yeah, I bet it's bland and boring as hell, anyway."

They both laughed.

"Okay. Giant half-bath for guests." Cheyenne opened the first door on their left.

"Jesus, that's bigger than my closet."

"Yep." The halfling shut the door again and continued. "I can't believe I just showed you a bathroom."

"Hey, it's an important thing to know."

"All right. There's a giant mudroom and coat closet down by the door. Also bigger than your closet. And over here…" The halfling gestured to the swinging double doors with round windows up top used by high-end restaurant kitchens. "Eleanor's not *just* an amazing chef, all right? She does a whole bunch of other stuff I don't even pretend to know about, but this is pretty much her domain. Besides her room, obviously."

Cheyenne turned and pulled her friend backward through the swinging doors.

"She lives here?"

"Yeah, didn't I tell you that?"

"I can barely remember my name right now, halfling. Don't make me take a pop quiz."

Laughing softly, Cheyenne spun her friend around again. "Behold. My childhood kitchen."

"My brain's gonna explode."

"If it hasn't by now, Em, I think you're good." They moved through the industrial kitchen toward the very back. "I'm pretty sure my mom had this modeled after one of her favorite chef's restaurants. I can't remember the guy's name."

"Seriously?"

"Yeah. I'm into a lotta different things, but food's just food, honestly. You eat it, it's gone, not that big a deal."

"You're gonna get struck by lightning for saying that in here."

"Nah. Eleanor's busy doing something else." The halfling pulled up beside a plain white door in the far corner of the kitchen and flipped the light switch on the wall beside it. "You're gonna love this."

"The pantry's bigger than my closet too, isn't it?"

Cheyenne laughed. "Definitely. That's on the other side next to the walk-in fridge."

"Of course, it is." Ember rolled her eyes and gazed at all the stainless steel appliances in the massive kitchen that could run a five-star restaurant. "So why are we waiting here?"

The halfling didn't say anything.

"Cheyenne?"

The door in front of them slid sideways into the wall, and the half-drow pulled her friend backward into a small square room the size of a normal closet.

"No way."

"Yes, way." The halfling pressed one of four buttons on the panel, and the door slid shut again. The elevator lurched a little when it left the ground floor and headed up. "Uh-oh. That wasn't a problem last time."

"Which was when?"

"Oh, I don't know. Ten years ago, maybe."

"There's an elevator in your mom's house."

Cheyenne laughed. "Much easier for Eleanor to bring up a tray of breakfast, isn't it?"

"And she gets breakfast in bed. I'm... I don't even know what I am."

"No breakfast in bed. And usually, it's both of them. At least, it was when I still lived here. I can't imagine they'd change things up after I moved out."

The elevator rumbled again when it came to a stop, but the door opened as smoothly as ever. Cheyenne pushed her friend out into the hall and paused for effect.

"Okay. Another hallway. Something normal."

"Yeah, a normal hallway in the upstairs living quarters."

Ember looked at the halfling over her shoulder. "What the fuck did you just say to me?"

"You'll see."

CHAPTER ONE HUNDRED ONE

"You know how many kids dream of living in a house like this?"

"I hope not *exactly* like this." Cheyenne left the door to her old bedroom open and pushed Ember toward the last room at the back of the house on the second floor. "If anyone else gets their hands on the plans to this house, I'm pretty sure someone's getting sued."

"She really takes her privacy seriously, doesn't she?"

For a second, Cheyenne didn't say anything. *How do I answer that kind of question?* "Yeah, she does. That's been priority number one my entire life, Em. Don't give anything away. Don't let people see the real person behind the image the rest of the world sees. Everything's a secret, and every secret has a price tag."

"People pay her for secrets?"

"Sometimes. It's not always money, though. Among all the other things she does, Bianca Summerlin barters and trades in secrets. That might be the only thing about her that people *do* know. And that she's the person to go to if you want to get the job done right. Politically, at least."

"Crazy. That was your whole childhood here too, wasn't it?"

"Yep. I mean, sure, there were certain perks." Cheyenne tried to wipe the smile off her face when Ember laughed. "I'm not sure I'd change any of it, honestly. But it wasn't all quality family time and happy days making lifelong memories in the Summerlin house."

"I know what *that's* like."

"But I turned out pretty okay." They both laughed, then Cheyenne left her friend in front of the set of French doors in front of them, these of lightly stained, polished wood. "Before I figured out how to basically plug my brain into computers, this was my favorite room in the whole house."

"I can't fathom how anything could be better than your room, but okay. Show me."

The halfling grabbed both handles and twisted down, then shoved the doors open. The room beyond was cut in a half-circle, the wide, curving wall at the back made entirely of windows. A different set of furniture occupied either side of the room—sofas, loveseats, rocking chairs, and end-tables. In the center of the room in front of the sweeping windows were two cream armchairs and matching ottomans, both of them facing out toward the huge expanse of forest and the gently sloping hillside behind the house.

Grinning, Cheyenne grabbed the handles again and wheeled Ember across the room toward the window, stopping to the right of center. "Best seat in the house."

"No shit." The fae's mouth fell open as she scanned the valley in front of them. The sun had almost set, but the pale light and a faint orange glow still flooded the valley with enough light to see twice as much as from the veranda jutting out below them. "This is the most beautiful thing I've ever seen."

"Yeah, it's something."

"Okay, so everything else in this place has a name. What's this one?"

Cheyenne chuckled and folded her arms. "The breakfast room."

"Kill me now."

With nothing more to say to that, the halfling swept her gaze across the lawn and the valley. The scar of the new portal ridge ripped toward the house from the edge of the tree line like an open wound. *Sure changes the overall look of things.*

"I'd lock myself in here and never leave if I had the option." Ember took another sip of her wine but couldn't bring herself to look away.

"I did that once."

"Ha. I can see them trying to break down the door."

"Pretty much." Cheyenne studied the portal ridge below. *No lights. No monsters. So far, so good.*

The sound of tires crunching slowly across gravel made her turn around. "That was fast."

"What?"

"Couple vans hauling FRoE agents up the hill."

Ember squinted at the half-drow above a smile of disbelief. "I *know* you can hear all the crazy things all the time, but I'm still amazed."

"Well, thanks." Cheyenne leaned around the side of her friend's chair and nodded. "I gotta go get things sorted out down there. I can bring you down with me if you want."

"No way. Leave me right here. Lock the door behind you. I'm good."

Smirking, the halfling patted the back of Ember's chair. "I can manage the first one. Not gonna lock the doors, though. A Summerlin doesn't make the same mistake twice."

"Okay, get outta here."

Cheyenne spun and hurried across the few feet of hall between the breakfast room and the massive staircase. She ran down the center two steps at a time, grabbing the banister on the bottom to swing herself around before heading back toward her mom's study.

"Mom?" She slowed in front of the open French doors and peered into Bianca Summerlin's wood-and-leather-decorated private room. The chair behind the heavy executive desk at the back was empty, but her mom had left the bottle of Glenmorangie single malt out on the tray. *And now she's into the good scotch. Careful.*

The halfling moved quickly down the house as the crunching of the tires grew steadily louder out front. The French doors onto the veranda were closed, but Bianca Summerlin stood at her place in front of the railing, gazing out over the steadily darkening valley. The glass of scotch in her hand was half-empty.

Cheyenne opened one door and took a tentative step outside. "They're here."

"Thank you, Cheyenne." The woman raised the glass to her lips, her elbow propped on the opposite arm crossed over her midsection. "Do make it perfectly clear that no one sets foot inside this house."

"I will." The halfling waited in case her mom decided to turn around. It became clear that Bianca wasn't moving from that position for a while, so her daughter withdrew into the house and quietly pulled the door shut again.

Eleanor stepped into the room from the other side of the dining table before Cheyenne made it into the opposite hall.

"Hey, Ember's upstairs in the breakfast room, just so you know," the halfling said, glancing at the bottom of the staircase.

"That's fine, Cheyenne." Eleanor nodded, focused now on how she could help Bianca through the rest of this crazy night. "I'll go up in a bit and see if she needs anything."

"Thanks, Eleanor. Those people just pulled up out front, so I'm gonna..."

"Whatever you need to do, sweetheart." The woman smiled at the half-drow until Cheyenne finally turned to head toward the front door. With a slow shake of her head, Eleanor stepped out onto the veranda to weather the unexpected storm with her closest friend.

When Cheyenne slipped out the front door, the FRoE agents were just getting out of the three black SUVs that had pulled up in front of the wide stone steps. She pulled the door firmly shut behind her and moved quickly down the stairs toward them.

Rhynehart emerged from the passenger seat of the closest SUV, already wearing a dampening vest. He wedged the helmet under one arm and shut the door before heading toward the stairs. "What the hell's going on up here?"

"Not that way. Come on." Cheyenne brushed past him and headed around the side of the house, noticing the bushes she'd damaged and grimacing.

With a sharp whistle and a wave, Rhynehart nodded after the halfling, and his team of agents followed with their vests and helmets and fell pistols and rifles and grenades.

The halfling didn't slow down or stop to wait for them as she headed down the flagstone steps cut into the hillside between the house and the tree line of the thick woods. Rhynehart quickly caught up with her, and they jogged down the stairs together. "Seriously, kid. I get my door busted down at seven-thirty and have to listen to Sir's drunken rampage about a halfling know-it-all and however many heads are gonna fly because she's trying to do our job for us."

"That's seriously all he told you?"

"Yeah, before he said to load up a containment team. Said I'd hear the rest straight from the drow's mouth."

"New portal, Rhynehart."

"Very funny. Try again."

"Right. Sure. New portal."

They reached the bottom of the stairs and walked swiftly across the grass toward the other end of the field. The other agents' boots clomped down in quick succession behind them.

"Are you shitting me right now?"

"As much as I'd love to bring three cars of your guys all the way out here for a practical joke, no. No bullshit. This is real."

"That's not possible."

Cheyenne shot him a scathing glare before she couldn't look at him anymore. "Tell me that again when you see this thing."

Almost all the light had disappeared from the clear sky overhead, but it was more than enough to see the dark spears of black rock jutting twenty feet in the air in front of them. The halfling clenched her fists as they approached, and she moved to the right around the first stone spire to give Rhynehart the whole view.

The agent's eyes widened when he looked at the wall of shimmering black light shooting from between the black pillars. "This doesn't look anything like—"

"The Border portals you know? Yeah, that's the point. It doesn't act like one, either."

"How the hell did this get here?"

"Ripped a giant crack in the ground, and everything else just shot up. That's not the most important question right now."

Rhynehart set his helmet on the ground as the other agents fanned out behind them. Some of them whispered to each other about what the hell they were looking at, but Cheyenne ignored them. "I'm guessing you know what the most important question is, then."

"Yeah. Can your guys handle it until I figure out how to shut it down?"

The man shot her a sidelong glance. "We can handle it. That's what we do."

"Okay. Minor detail. This portal isn't just different on the outside."

"Is that some kind of Goth code for something?"

Not gonna touch that one right now. Cheyenne closed her eyes. "You're not keeping magicals from crossing over. Honestly, I doubt you'll even *see* any other magicals come through here."

"Then I don't know why the fuck we made this drive."

The halfling lifted both hands to show him her palms. "I didn't stab *myself*, in case you're still confused. You ever hear the O'gúleesh who made the crossing talk about the in-between?"

"Once or twice."

"Yeah, that's what makes the Border crossing so awful."

Rhynehart glanced at the shimmering wall of light and shook his head. "Please don't tell me you tried to go through that thing."

"No. But the asshole *things* that are only supposed to exist between either side of the Border tried to come through. Right here on this little patch of grass where we're standing."

"You can't be serious."

The halfling pointed at her head. "This is my serious face, Rhynehart."

"Like I can tell the difference between any of your faces. Do you know how crazy you sound right now?"

"Oh, yeah. I know. You're just gonna have to believe me on this one, or we're all seriously fucked."

The man sniffed and pinched his nose, then gazed down the length of the portal ridge and nodded. "Fine. I'll take your word for it, but if I find out you're just blowing smoke up my ass—"

"You won't. Just make sure anything that tries to break through stays on the other side of that black wall. Got it?"

"Yeah." He started pulling on his dampening gloves and didn't look at Cheyenne when he muttered flatly, "Anything else?"

"Uh, shooting the biggest tentacle is a great way to make the main thing angry enough to try coming through. But if you take that one down first, you might catch a little break for, like, a snack or something."

"What the fuck are you smoking?"

Cheyenne clapped a hand on the agent's shoulder and gave it a little shake. "Oh. They're shapeshifters, too. So, whatever it looks like you're fighting, don't expect it to stay the same thing for very long. And don't hold back."

Rhynehart's head wobbled on his shoulders when she gave him another shake of mock reassurance, but all he could do was stare at the black wall rising from all the black spears of stone. "Shapeshifters."

"Thanks for making the drive. You guys can do whatever you need to do out here, but the house is off-limits."

"Uh-huh." He turned away from her without another word and headed toward his agents, who had gathered in a loose group behind him.

The halfling scanned their faces and didn't recognize a single one of them. *'Cause Sir doesn't want the halfling making friends with his operatives. Message received.*

She spun again and headed back toward the house as the last of the light faded to black. When she looked at the veranda, her mother's silhouette was stark against the house lights spilling through the wall of windows. Bianca Summerlin didn't look down at the drow halfling making her way across the lawn, focusing instead on the team of agents in black fatigues milling around the edge of the woods on her property. The woman lifted the glass of the good scotch to her lips and barely tasted it.

CHAPTER ONE HUNDRED TWO

Cheyenne had offered to drive Ember back to their apartment, but her fae friend had refused without a second thought. "I'm not gonna make you drive me home so you can come all the way back out here and miss three and a half hours of whatever might happen. I'll just take one of the guest rooms, and we'll head back in the morning."

The halfling didn't have enough energy to argue, so she'd set Ember up in the guest suite next to her childhood bedroom and didn't leave until Ember shouted to quit smothering her so they could both get some sleep.

Now, lying in a queen-sized bed in a room that was at least the size of her old crappy apartment, Cheyenne found herself unable to get to sleep. *Big surprise. FRoE agents out back, a broken portal about to spit out monsters at any minute, and everyone's pissed about it.*

She rolled onto her other side and stared into the darkness. The outline of her massive bookshelf in the moonlight spilling through the window made her frown. *Showing up for dinner's one thing. I hate this room.*

The halfling closed her eyes and willed herself to sleep, focusing on slowing her breathing until it fell into one long inhale and exhale after another.

Just as she felt herself slipping off, a jolt of buzzing energy flared across her body. She opened her eyes to bright white light and L'zar's glowing gold eyes staring at her. "What the fuck!"

She tried to sit up in her bed but couldn't move. There wasn't a bed beneath her anyway, and she glanced down to see her bare feet standing on white nothingness. *Good thing I put on pajamas.*

"What happened?" L'zar stood in front of her, dressed in his Chateau D'rahl prison uniform.

"Okay, why are we standing in the middle of nothing?"

"Don'adurr Thread, Cheyenne. I initiated it. Are you okay?"

"There's gotta be some kinda warning signal before you pop into my head right before I fall asleep."

"It doesn't work that way. I'm sorry if you don't like it, but I had to make sure you're all right."

Frowning, the halfling stopped her spinning mind and focused on L'zar's face in the white light. His gold eyes were wide, his shoulders hunched as he studied her in concern beneath disheveled white hair spilling over his shoulders. *If I didn't know better, I'd say he's worried about something.*

"I'm fine," she said slowly. "Are *you* all right?"

"Knowing the Thread worked and I could still find you, I'll be fine. Tell me what happened."

"Lots of things happen to me. You're gonna have to be a little more specific."

"I can't." The drow pressed his lips together and took a sharp, anxious breath through his nose. "But I felt—" He sniffed and looked away from her, blinking quickly. "I felt you *fade*, Cheyenne. And don't try to tell me I'm imagining it. I've felt the same far too many times before, and none of them were there when I—" L'zar hissed out a breath and bit his bottom lip in irritation.

He's scared, and it pisses him off. Cheyenne stared at her wild-eyed father. "I faded, all right, and then I came back and took care of it. A new portal burst out of nowhere on Bianca's estate. Right behind her house."

"A new—" The drow growled. "If it just opened, Cheyenne, it can't possibly be as strong as the others. Not yet. How did you almost die at a brand-new portal?"

"A lot easier than I expected, actually. I went down to check it out; you know, to keep it away from *my mom*, and I might have overestimated my abilities a little. But I took care of it."

"Alone?"

She glanced around the white nothingness and nodded.

"Where was Corian?"

"I don't know. Out on one of his weird errands. You wanted him at that first portal, so that's what he was taking care of."

"But he's with you now. And you're okay."

Cheyenne shook her head. *L'zar Verdys, too panicked to put two and two together.* "I'm okay. He's not here."

"What?" A sharp, furious snarl escaped the drow, and he closed his eyes to try pulling himself back together. "He *knows* how important it is to make sure you stay on track. You can't be left unprotected!"

"Hey, I did a pretty damn good job of protecting myself, thank you." She wanted to step toward him but still couldn't move. "And I had tricks up my sleeve that came in pretty handy. I'm fine."

L'zar's eyes flew open. "What tricks?"

"The other two abilities I have left, I guess. Whatever telekinetic thing I can do and the black fire."

"Black fire. Black—" A sharp laugh escaped him. "Fire. You used black fire." L'zar took a deep, shuddering breath, and that wild, feral grin split his face. "Where's the *Cuil Ani*?"

"Not with me. I told Corian that part too."

"You need to get it, Cheyenne. Find that box and tell Corian if anything's changed. That's crucial, do you understand?"

"Yeah, I get it."

"Is that how you finished it, then? The black fire?"

Am I the only sane person I know? Cheyenne shrugged. "Yeah.

That's how I did it. Finished the thing off and got the hell outta there."

"Excellent." Chuckling like a cartoon villain, L'zar wrinkled his nose above his predatory grin and nodded. "That's good, but we have to be sure. Check the *Cuil Ani*, Cheyenne. Have Corian bring it to you, wherever you are. Tonight. Use the Don'adurr again as soon as you know what's happened. I'll be waiting for you."

"Come on, I don't even—"

The world spun madly around her, then she felt like she was falling through the sky before her eyes flew open. Cheyenne gasped and doubled over, her head jutting over the side of the bed as she heaved. Nothing came up, but she gave herself a moment just in case. Once her breathing had slowed and the dizziness had faded, she rolled onto her back and stared at the ceiling of her old room.

"I should've dumped that stupid potion on the ground."

She snatched her phone from the bedside table and texted Corian.

Had another visit. Anytime you wanna bring that box over would be great. Call first if you're gonna show up.

Double-checking to make sure the phone wasn't on silent, she turned the volume up all the way and put the phone back down on the nightstand. Then she turned over again with her back to the bookshelf and closed her eyes. *He'll call or he won't. I'll check that stupid puzzle box tomorrow, but I'm not gonna lose sleep over it tonight.*

L'zar paced back and forth in his cell at Chateau D'rahl, whispering to himself in the darkness of Alpha Block. "It's been three goddamn hours. What's taking them so long?"

Some asshole several cells over let out a massive fart. The orc in the cell next door turned over in his sleep with a grunt, the cot squeaking and as his hand and forearm thumped against the stone wall.

The drow glanced up at the red light keeping watch beside the guard tower, then spun around again and paced back across his cell. *Something's not right. Another portal, right there in front of her. If she told him about the fire, he'd know we're close. He'd get her that fucking box already.*

Another frustrated growl escaped him, but he squashed it back down again before it grew any louder. *I have to be sure. This whole thing's a waste of time unless I'm sure.*

An inmate fell into a fit of dry, hacking coughs, and L'zar shook his head. "I can't. She'll reach out."

His other neighbor smacked the wall, either in sleep or to get the muttering drow to quit talking to himself.

For two more hours, L'zar paced back and forth across his tiny, useless cell, turning the old crone's prophecy over and over in his mind. *I can't risk it, not after I've gotten this far. Not after twenty-one years of breaking through the veil.*

He felt the tug at his core again; had been feeling it since before lights out, when he thought he'd lost another young magical he'd been so sure would make it this time. *Not just another one. She's different. She found* me. *That's worth something.*

The door to the guard tower creaked open and shut with a bang as the night guard on duty stepped out to relieve himself. The drow heard the man muttering about drinking too much coffee.

But she's not safe. L'zar spun again and paced back toward the bars. *That's what this is. If Corian can't find her tonight, it's over. And I can't do anything from this fell-damn joke of a hellhole.*

When he reached the bars at the front of his cell, the drow slowly reached out and curled his fingers around two of them. Gripping the bars, he pressed his face against the cold iron and glanced at the empty guard tower. He took a deep breath and tried to dampen the urgency overwhelming him, stronger than it had been almost twenty-two years ago.

By the time he opened his eyes again, his rapid breathing had calmed, and he'd made up his mind.

I can't let her face this alone. There's still a chance she'll make it, but not if no one's with her when the Crown makes her move.

He released the bars and slowly withdrew, his gold eyes glowing in the darkness. Then the drow who'd spent the last seventy years in Chateau D'rahl by choice turned toward the back of his cell and glared at the stone wall. *Fuck this. I'm getting out early.*

The End

The adventure continues in *The Drow There and Nothing More*. Dark magic is seeping into this realm from the other side of the portal. Cheyenne Summerlin is mastering her abilities, completing the Drow trials to unlock that puzzle box. Now, to claim her true legacy and the only power strong enough to stop the coming threat. The Goth Drow halfling must cross the border herself to face the enemy in her father's world.

Get sneak peeks, exclusive giveaways, behind the scenes content, and more.
PLUS you'll be notified of special **one day only fan pricing** on new releases.

Sign up today to get free stories.

or visit: https://marthacarr.com/read-free-stories/

AUTHOR NOTES - MARTHA CARR
MARCH 31, 2020

Afternoon everyone. Notes from the dream house where I'm sheltering in place with the good dog, Lois Lane and the sweet pittie, Leela. I think this is week three but frankly when I get the day right, I'm a little excited. It could be week 4, I've kind of lost count.

I spent last weekend testing the elasticity of my brain. An ER nurse in my neighborhood put out a request for as many headbands as we could make with buttons sewn on just above the ears. The elastic from face masks was wearing out their skin. Well, of course we all answered the call.

For some of us, like me, that meant brushing off very old skills and looking up the directions online for that sewing machine we haven't looked at it in years. Or decades.

Let me just add in here, big shout out to the Girl Scouts. They're the only reason I have these skills and they must have done a pretty good job because before long I had successfully threaded a bobbin again. I felt like a rock star. Things got a little rocky from there. Stitch tension turned out to be a bugaboo for a while. But a few YouTube videos and FaceTime with a crafty friend and I figured out most of it.

It took an entire weekend to almost complete four of them, but I'm picking up speed.

Every time my back ached, and I wanted to give up, I thought of how selflessly nurses and doctors around the entire world were performing against overwhelming odds and thought, I'm making headbands from the safety of my house. Try again.

It's a unique moment in time where for once we all feel how connected we are around the globe in a very real and necessary way. We've always been this connected, but it's so easy to lose sight in the pursuit of ambition or family or a million other things. The choices we make reverberate out and affect others, but that's easy to forget when I can't see everyone else.

Now, we all see the world as a collective and as each day creeps by and the news get harder to look at, we are digging deeper to let each other know a few very important things. We are all connected, we all matter, we are willing to take care of each other, we all have unique gifts that benefit others, and the smallest kind gesture has an echo that can be heard around the world.

One day, all of this will be solved, and we will get the chance to go back out into the world and hug each other and gather together around tables and hold hands. When that happens, I will remember how the world became one crazy large family for just a little while and we laughed and cried and grieved and rejoiced as one. Love you all, stay safe, find a little joy in the day.

More adventures to follow.

Note: I'm out here reading a chapter a day from Guardians of Magic, Book 08 in the Leira Chronicles right now from my Facebook author page every day at 1 pm. The completed Adult Story Times can be found on my YouTube channel so you can catch up or play them again.

AUTHOR NOTES - MICHAEL ANDERLE

APRIL 13, 2020

THANK YOU for reading our story!

We have a few of these planned, but we don't know if we should continue writing and publishing without your input.

Options include leaving a review, reaching out on Facebook to let us know, and smoke signals.

Frankly, smoke signals might get misconstrued as low-hanging clouds, so you might want to nix that idea.

I don't sew

Last week, I went by the amazing BBQ place Jessie Rae's and supported their effort to make sandwiches for the hospitals around Las Vegas during this pandemic.

I have to admit I didn't even KNOW about it until after it was over.

Like, this event was mentioned on their Facebook Page, complete with pictures type of over. So, I did what anyone who has shamelessly plugged Jessie Rae's and used my sources (read Mike Ross, the owners, phone number) and called him, asking about helping.

Seems Jessie Rae's just did this for the hospital folks. Then, I asked him how we help pay for the efforts, and the conversation went something like this:

Author: So, how can I contribute some money for the effort?

Mike Ross: Actually, we didn't ask for any. I don't feel comfortable asking.

Author: You didn't ask, I did. So, how do I do that?

Mike Ross: I don't know. We aren't set up to do that. We aren't a non-profit.

Author: Mike, it's pretty easy. I come in and you charge me $100 for some French fries, and I buy five of them. I'm not expecting a non-profit receipt here, buddy.

<pause while Mike R. thinks this over.>

Mike Ross: Well, my mom is taking orders and she knows you, so if you want to do that, thank you.

Author: You are welcome. Plus, you know, I'm going to order a pound of meat. But that's just because I want to support you guys, too. It has nothing to do with the fact I need some <redacted> BBQ in my life.

Mike's mom allowed me to order the meat, then gave it to me free. That's the type of people Mike and his folks are. I made a non-tax-deductible donation, and we all feel a little better in life during these annoying times.

If you want to buy some "James Brownstone French Fries for the Medical Professionals" (That's a mouthful) number is below – but do NOT feel any obligation. You will count under the donations I push on him.

Jessie Rae's Phone number is: +1 (702) 541-5546

You might have to explain this to whoever picks up the phone. I haven't told Mike Ross about it yet.

Hehehehe.

Here is how I suspect a call would go:

"Hello, Jessie Rae's."

"I would like to buy Brownstone Fries."

"What? We don't sell Brownstone Fries."

"You know Brownstone, the signed books you have in the restaurant to give to fans of Michael Anderle?"

"Yesssss? (maybe no?)"

"Well, I want to buy some Brownstone Fries for <donation amount.>"

"So, you want <donation amount> of French fries?"

"Sort of. Except, I'll never pick them up as I don't live in <your city>, so I hope you don't actually make any Brownstone fries. It's just a donation to help you guys pay for the effort and food to help medical professionals. Take my credit card, charge me <donation amount>, use the money for providing food for the medical professionals, and we all do a little better during these times, man."

I'm going to have to try this phone call on them this week. BWAHAHAHAHAHA.

Mike's Diary: "Sometimes life just *is*."

So, my company is testing new software to allow us a virtual experience while we work. As of now (4/13/2020), it is performing better than I could have hoped in bringing those who collaborate with LMBPN together, no matter the location or time of day (or night.)

This same software, I hope, will allow us to create virtual meetings with fans, and (I'm trying, but I'm not sure the company behind the software will make it affordable) I want to create a place for fans to get together and create all sorts of fun stuff with LMBPN.

And frankly just have a place to hang a while.

If you would like to know more (and are on Facebook) join us on the Kurtherian Gambit Facebook Group For Fans and Authors

Link: https://www.facebook.com/profile.php?id=127989844503323&ref=br_rs

I hope to have something up to start testing this in the next week or two. We will start with small groups, and possibly move up from there.

Clean is the New Dream

My office isn't messy... exactly. It is lived-in *chic.*

Honestly, a whole *lot* of the lived-in part. (If you add chic to the end of any descriptor, you immediately sound artsy. No, really, try it.

"That's ugly."

"No, that's ugly-*chic*."

"That man-cave crap has got to go."

"No, that's man-cave *chic*. It stays."

"That's hideous."

"No, that's hideous—"

"If you end that with 'chic,' I will shove my cottony house slippers so far up your ass you will be burping tiny clouds."

"Right. So, what now? I lost my train of thought with that visual."

(You thought 'Hideous *chic,* and that would have worked, #AmIRight?)

I will have to take another set of boxes to the storage room tomorrow after our meetings, and maybe then I'll have a bit of "clean" in my office. Judith cleaned the living room and Kitchen (both places she works from) yesterday, and believe it or not, I am a bit #Jealous of her clean areas.

(Don't worry, I'm having trouble believing it too.)

I'm So Going to Regret This.

So, I have the new 2020 iPad (#SupportApple and #ItsGoodTo-HaveAppleEmployeesWithDiscountsAsFriends along with #Sup-portFriendsByBuyingApple), but I don't like using it just as it is.

I want either a Smart Keyboard Folio or the new More Magic Keyboard for the iPad, or maybe something clamshell (but won't that effectively make it a Mac?).

Have I mentioned I'm seriously impatient? I work six often seven days a week (#ThankGodILoveWhatIDo), and when it comes to my technology, I splurge on myself. It's the one thing I can point to my wife and say 'it's a write-off' and 'Don't harsh my (writing) buzz, woman.'

(Actually, only one of those responses works on Judith. #Thank-GodAppleDoesn'tRefreshOften and #IReallyDoWait2YearsBe-tweeniPhonesNow.)

I swear Apple better not upgrade their keyboard on the larger MacBooks in 2021, or I might have to try therapy to hold-back on an upgrade (yes, I have the 2016 MacBook 16".) If therapy is more expensive than my purchase, doesn't that make it smarter just to purchase the product?

I think it does.

Are you paying attention, Steve? (#StephenCampbellNeedsaNew-Macbook13Pro)

Anyway. My iPad is sitting in its box unopened because I don't have a keyboard for it. I can't get the Magic Keyboard until May at this point, or maybe later. Since I suffer from #ImpatienceIsAThing, I am looking to see if anything cool is out for my iPad that includes a touchpad for mousing around.

You know, if—and this is for the benefit of my fans who might wish to know—I buy a clamshell with touchpad and report that information back here in a future *Author Note*, that's research and something I can write off on taxes, right?

So, I might sacrifice a larger credit card bill on the altar of #DoingItForTheFans.

If you happen to write a review for any of our books, maybe drop a line in the review "I Support Mike and his Magic Keyboard!" (Or, if you hate Apple products, feel free to suggest I buy other technology. Especially really *REALLY* expensive hardware that I can point to and show my wife how frugal' I was with the purchases I have already made or might <snicker> make soon.

Ad Aeternitatem,

Michael Anderle

CONNECT WITH THE AUTHORS

Martha Carr Social

Website:
http://www.marthacarr.com

Facebook:
https://www.facebook.com/groups/MarthaCarrFans/
Michael Anderle Social

Website:
http://www.lmbpn.com

Email List:
http://lmbpn.com/email/

Facebook
https://www.facebook.com/TheKurtherianGambitBooks/

OTHER BOOKS BY MARTHA CARR

Series in the Oriceran Universe:

THE LEIRA CHRONICLES
I FEAR NO EVIL
REWRITING JUSTICE
SCHOOL OF NECESSARY MAGIC
SCHOOL OF NECESSARY MAGIC: RAINE CAMPBELL
ALISON BROWNSTONE
THE DANIEL CODEX SERIES
FEDERAL AGENTS OF MAGIC
SCIONS OF MAGIC
THE UNBELIEVABLE MR. BROWNSTONE
THE KACY CHRONICLES
MIDWEST MAGIC CHRONICLES
SOUL STONE MAGE
THE FAIRHAVEN CHRONICLES

The Terranavis Universe

THE WITCHES OF PRESSLER STREET

THE ADVENTURES OF FINNEGAN DRAGONBENDER
THE ADVENTURES OF MAGGIE PARKER
THE LONE VALKYRIE

Other series:

THE LAST VAMPIRE
THE WITCH NEXT DOOR

OTHER BOOKS BY JUDITH BERENS

OTHER BOOKS BY MARTHA CARR

JOIN THE ORICERAN UNIVERSE FAN GROUP ON FACEBOOK!

BOOKS BY MICHAEL ANDERLE

For a complete list of books by Michael Anderle, please visit:

www.lmbpn.com/ma-books/

All LMBPN Audiobooks are Available at Audible.com and iTunes

To see all LMBPN audiobooks, including those written by Michael Anderle
please visit:

www.lmbpn.com/audible